Colin Brook was born in England to parents who could trace their family line back to the time of the Norman Conquest.

He has travelled extensively throughout Western Europe, North America, Australasia, Southern Africa and parts of Asia, and has spent ample time in Russia and the Czech Republic.

Apart from travel, for which he has a passion, he enjoys downhill skiing, motor sports, an eclectic range of music, most sports on or in the water, Rugby union, the company of attractive women and a decent pint of English real ale.

First signed copy
to Toby Richmond

THE ALMETI AGENDA

For your encouragement, help
and general assistance in the
writing of this book, and for your
continuing friendship

Thank you

Colin A. Brook

THE ALMETI AGENDA

Colin Brook

THE ALMETI AGENDA

Olympia Publishers
London

www.olympiapublishers.com
OLYMPIA PAPERBACK EDITION

A CIP catalogue record for this title is
available from the British Library.

ISBN: 978-1-84897-087-8

This is a work of fiction.
Names, characters, places and incidents originate from the writer's
imagination. Any resemblance to actual persons, living or dead, or to
places is purely coincidental.

First Published in 2010

Olympia Publishers
60 Cannon Street
London
EC4N 6NP

Printed in Great Britain

Acknowledgments

I wish to express my heartfelt thanks and deep appreciation to those men and women of Her Majesty's Armed Forces whose daily acts of selfless heroism, bravery and willingness to stand in harm's way allows me, my family, friends and the loyal peoples of our fair isles to rest easy in our beds at night. I salute you all.

Author's Note

This work is woven around historical events, including the so-called 7/7 tube bombings, which provided the trigger for the story. Regrettably, here in Britain, due to an ongoing policy of overprotection of minority interests, we have lost much in recent years. Whilst I believe any society can be judged in how it treats its minorities those minorities should never be allowed to overwhelm majority interests, as the very essence of democracy is then lost, as are freedoms of speech and expression, most commonly through censorship.

In technical terms censorship is the suppression of speech, or deletion of communicative material, which may be considered objectionable, harmful, sensitive, or inconvenient to a government or others as determined by a censor. Quite apart from the justifications of pornography, language and violence, books are censored due to changing racial attitudes, fears of causing religious offence, or simple political correctness gone mad. It is claimed this then avoids ethnic or cultural offense, wholly irrespective of any lost artistic value, presumably because the reading public are considered too stupid to be discerning, and can therefore only be exposed to that deemed beneficial by self appointed wiser beings. Such censorship, if then applied, would not have allowed many of the greater works of man, let alone either Bible or Quran as each would be tagged inflammatory and seditious.

Fundamentally censorship means prior restraint, screening the content of the written word before publication. This is used in conjunction with punitive penalties, punishing those who publish 'offending' material. Either way, in the current climate, British publishers are cowed, reluctant to take any risk with legislation that appears ever more repressive.

The work you are about to read is censored. Neither original title nor cover design could be used as it was considered the city name may in itself cause offence to some, as may its reproduced image. Passages were removed and key words such as religion and faith replaced with culture and ideology. In references throughout, including the final attack, the city name has been replaced with Bakkah, its ancient name. Hopefully this should not now inflame certain readers, cause severe offence, or be construed as intent to do so.

Whilst freedom to read, and therefore freedom to write, is intrinsic to our democracy, it remains under continuous attack. Public authorities and private pressure groups across the nation constantly endeavour to remove books from sale, censor and alter children's history books, label literary works as controversial and list authors and their scripts as offensive. Legislation surrounding hate crimes, race and religion has exacerbated this already troubling trend, but has nothing to do with national security 'loose lips sinking ships', or to protect an individual as with certain kidnappings, but everything to do with political expedience. I firmly believe public interest is best served by publishers, retailers and library's making available the widest diversity of views and expressions, even those which are unorthodox or unpopular. It should be their responsibility, as guardians of the people's freedom to read, to contest encroachments upon that freedom by all those seeking to impose their own standards or tastes upon the greater community. They don't.

Introduction

Mary Bryant didn't know the man who killed her. She never so much as saw his face.

She was enjoying a beautiful mid spring morning. The sky was a perfect eggshell blue and crystal clear, the air as a result was cool and clean. Fresh the English call it, warm enough for breath not to hang upon it, but only just. The trees were finished with their budding and now new growth abounded and could be seen all around. Everywhere nature had reawakened from its winter slumber. This time of the year Mary loved beyond all others. Like most she enjoyed the warmth of the sun in summer and was keenly looking forward to her coming summer holiday on the Greek island of Rhodes with her husband Tom, but this typical English mid spring morning was her all time favourite, and the reason she had elected to walk to work that morning.

Mary was an attractive thirty-nine year-old who, despite giving birth to two sons at the beginning of her twenties, had kept a very pleasing figure. In doing so she was most fortunate as she didn't diet or workout at any gym but just ate healthy food and walked to work on the mornings the weather permitted, and at weekends when Tom was free they would take their bicycles and cycle around the New Forest. Previously it had always been with the kids, but the kids hadn't accompanied them for a while since both had started to developed interests of their own.

The holiday loomed large in Mary's mind as she walked the three quarters of a mile pathway from her home to her office in Lymington. It was to be her fortieth birthday present from Tom, and they would leave for it just two days after her party. Two weeks in the sun. Two weeks of Greek food and drinking sweet red Greek wine. Two weeks of splashing about in the sea and driving around the island in a little hire car. A ride on the Russian built hydrofoils to visit the Turkish bazaars at Marmaris, and warm steamy sensual nights of making love to the only man she had ever known and loved beyond measure since the time they had first met, four days before her fourteenth birthday. It was to be the first trip since the birth of their sons they would take without them, but both were sensible lads and well able to look after themselves at home.

At nineteen, Danny was their eldest. He had finished his 'A' levels the previous summer and left school to take a job at the oil facility at Fawley. She and Tom were somewhat disappointed at the time as they hoped he would choose to go on to university as he attained all the grades required. However Danny was adamant – he had had enough of education and wanted to get himself a decent job and earn some money, and Dan was the determined sort who usually, as in this case, got his way. As it happened he had landed well and truly on his feet.

Danny was big, and Danny was bright but Jack, their younger son, was a long way brighter, and he would go to university. Jack was to finish his 'A' levels a full year early and was expected to pass with A's in all five subjects he was to take, all of which were languages. It would be the best academic results the entire local area had ever experienced. He was a gifted child, always incredibly quick on the uptake, and was born with an ear for languages.

Although her office opened at nine o'clock Mary had always made a point of arriving at least five minutes early, especially when, as with this morning, it was her turn to open up. It was a walk of about twelve minutes, so she had left her home at eight forty. She was one of four at the office, a real estate business which was part of a national chain, and although she had worked there off and on since leaving school she had never sought promotion, twice declining an offer of the manager's job.

From the beginning she had loved the work, always thrilled when a property came on the market which then gave her a chance to take prospective buyers to for a viewing. So much so that over the years it was often remarked she was more interested in the homes than the potential buyers themselves. This she would shrug off with a smile, explaining she was just interested to see the changes which occurred to the buildings, most of which she knew well and usually had had a hand in selling several times before. In fact it was her place of work which was responsible for finding their home nearly twenty years earlier, a property they had both instantly loved but which then remained well outside their price range. Somehow they had managed to scrape together the deposit and bought it and both worked hard in the first few years to keep it, especially whilst Mary was pregnant and the boys were young, but it had proved to be so well worth doing.

Another smile flitted across her face as she thought of their home, a stone built eighteenth century cottage which had been perfect when they first bought it and remained perfect now. Certainly she and Tom had felt the need to extensively extended and modernise twelve years earlier as the boys grew, with the additional costs of completing the works back then once again stretching them financially. But that was then. Now the twenty year mortgage they had taken out to buy the property, and the additional loan for the extension, had but eight more payments to go. Then every brick, stick and blade of grass would be theirs, totally, completely and utterly beyond question, and the prospect of that felt great.

She hadn't fully discussed things with Tom yet, but her plan for the following year, after the mortgage ended, was to cut back to a three day week where she worked. She felt Mondays, Wednesdays and Fridays would suit her perfectly, and would in no way harm the agency. She could of course give up work, but she valued her independence, enjoyed the variety it brought to her life and had always believed relationships were healthier if people didn't have to live out of one another's pockets. No, she would keep her job. After all, it would pay for the big solid fuel Aga cooker she had always promised herself, which in turn would allow her to do the baking she had wanted to do all her married life. She smiled again as she thought of the additional disposable income the agency would then generate, and how it could be used for more holidays away with Tom.

"Oh Tom, we're going to have such fun!" she said out loud to herself still smiling.

Her smile broadened when she thought of all the little things she and Tom could get up to away from the boys. She may be a mother of two, and just about to enter her forties, but there was still an eighteen year old girl locked away inside her somewhere, and she looked forward to being able to let her out. For her and Tom life could not have been better. Her smile broadened to almost a grin, which remained on her still pretty face as it slammed into the concrete slabs of the pavement.

She was already dead.

Peter Parfitt was on final approach. It had been a long yet uneventful flight into London's Heathrow from Cape Town International, but the South African Airways Airbus A340-600 made easy work of it, with the four Rolls Royce Trent 500 engines whispering through the skies far above the continents of Africa and then Europe. The Airbus was one of nine operated by SAA as the backbone of its Ultra Long Haul fleet and, as usual, flight SA0220 non stop from Cape Town would arrive on time. The Cape to London was Parfitt's favourite flight, and Frankfurt his second, because Parfitt felt at home in Europe, preferably the south east of England, but really anywhere in Europe.

This was not unreasonable as Parfitt started life in the tiny but pretty village of Broomfield, Near Maidstone in Kent, within spitting distance of the must-see tourist attraction, Leeds Castle. The sixties had just begun when Parfitt was born into services life. The Royal Air Force to be precise. His father was a fly-boy and young Peter simply followed him into the service. Throughout his childhood his father, and consequently his family, was posted to various far flung places, but Peter's special memories, apart from England, were of the sun on Cyprus and life in Germany.

He had grown up not just amongst officers but amongst RAF pilot officers, and it costs Her Majesty's Exchequer a great deal of money to train a pilot. During the First World War the Royal Flying Corp pilots of the early biplanes were not issued with parachutes. The reasoning behind this was in those days aircraft production was time consuming and very costly and if the pilots were issued with parachutes they would jump out at the first sign of trouble in order to save their own skins, but at the cost of the aircraft. As little as seven hours flight training was considered perfectly adequate for these pilots, whose life expectancy once they arrived at their allocated squadron was a matter of minutes, which consequently usually cost the nation the aircraft anyway. Things had moved on since those days, and moved on a lot.

The modern day pilot is highly trained, usually highly regarded, and looked after by government and the institution which is the RAF accordingly. Not exactly cosseted in every way, but not far short. They are sometimes revered and sometimes derided by members of the other armed forces but, be that as it may, their training and the cost of their training is second to none and, as assets, as a group, those costs are reflected in their value. Such value can be seen in the standard of living they tend to enjoy when compared with those of the other services both at home and in other lands, even when on active service.

Pilot Officer Parfitt endured the mild rigours of flying school training, did not fall by the wayside, and passed out with his wings. Flight Lieutenant Parfitt then progressed through the big RAF machine until he reached his personal high point, flying Jaguars, which he was lucky to have never flown in anger. His military career proved flawless if somewhat unexciting. He was never posted to a hot spot and completely missed the 1982 armed conflict between Britain and Argentina which history has labelled as the Falklands War, despite the fact neither side ever actually declared war.

Outside the regular and the occasional intense training missions he was never called upon to respond to any form of emergency. He had however patrolled the skies of the free world, and in his time helped to keep it a safer place than might otherwise have been the case were there not such a highly visual deterrent. The Cold War quietly raged, and he had flown eyeball to eyeball with Russian pilots in their various Tupolevs as they approached the line in the sky which suddenly became NATO airspace but he, like most of the other pilots of his time, regarded such things as a game rather than a mission. A dangerous game perhaps – but a game nevertheless. The Russian pilots were there to probe the airspace, to prove they too still existed in their most visible way, but not to mount an attack. Should an attack have come it would have come from above, with ICBM's raining down from the stratosphere. The Russian attack never came and economics took over, the Cold War ended, and man's most potent symbol of the division of ideology, the Berlin Wall, fell on the ninth of November 1989.

Two and a half years later, and at the end of his twenties, Parfitt became too old to continue passing altitude tests and, despite the benefits of pressure suits, G forces were better handled by younger bodies. Parfitt moved sideways to low level operations, and from there moved again into flight school, this time as an instructor, and as an instructor he excelled. With his background and easy manner he was a natural teacher who could easily explain complex concepts to the fine young people who were destined to become the next generation of guardians of free world airspace. In the late nineties he left the Air Force with both a reasonable pension and better than fair job prospects.

He clearly remembered when British Overseas Airways Corporation and British European Airways were amalgamated in 1972 under the then newly formed British Airways Board, with the separate airlines coming together as British Airways (BA) in 1974. Since the days of BOAC and BEA the RAF has been popularly regarded as a natural provider of pilots for the British flag carrier and, as was to be expected from the Old Boy's network, an invitation to apply for a vacancy was not slow in coming. Interviews would follow, which would be a sham, a mere formality, for the job was there if he wanted it.

He wanted to do something, but did not want to carry on in England, much as he loved his homeland. He didn't like the politics anymore, strongly disapproved of the way Britain seemed to be aping American culture with its violence, lack of compassion and even litter, and hated the weather, which seemed to be getting progressively worse. He was also somewhat conscious a move to BA may be a move backwards. By many industries standards BA pays its staff well, but not necessarily by airline standards. BA also looks after its staff, but this they tend to do in an overbearing, dictatorial and often autocratic manner. A number of their staff, including many pilots, loathed their jobs, and were only hanging in there to pick up what had once been a good pension, although it too was sliding down the scale.

He knew his way around the block, knew what he liked and disliked, and opted to leave. As a child he had once spent time in South Africa and loved the place, the people, the foods, the smells and the exquisite seemingly endless sunshine. He fully realised a child's view may well be very one sided, at the very least clouded, but took himself off to Cape Town just the same with a plan to travel around the country and find a spot he liked and felt comfortable enough to settle in, if any. The plan failed, causing him to wait a while to see the rest of the country, because twenty three days after stepping off the plane at Cape Town he was still there. He had fallen in love with the city hook, line and sinker.

Day twenty three was important because that was the day he had found it. Camps Bay boasts quite literally one of the most beautiful beaches in the world. With the Twelve Apostles of Table Mountain as the backdrop, and evening sunsets which leave all who witnesses them spellbound, there are certainly worse places in the world to set up home. The place he found was a large three bedroom apartment on the third floor of a purpose built development which faced and overlooked the sea. It was beautiful and a mere fraction of the cost it would have been back at home. Built just off Victoria Road, with a view along it, the property was protected by a private security company staffed with ex-police officers who took their work seriously and, just four weeks later, it was his.

The city centre was a few minutes drive away, as was the spectacular, bustling and cosmopolitan centre which is the Victoria and Alfred Waterfront. There it was too easily possible to while away an hour or ten nursing an ice cold glass of Castle Lager whilst Cape Fur Seals cavorted about in front of all comers in the warm and busy waters of the harbour. Unlike Johannesburg or Durban, Cape Town's crime is of a lower level. It is undeniably there, but homes can be protected and, unless a person is stupid enough to leave valuable items on display in a car, street crime was no more of an issue than it was at home in London, Manchester and Nottingham. The biggest downside he could come up with was the sea could sometimes be cold and on occasions the wind blew. Balanced against which the area boasted some of the best tanned and heavenly female bodies he had ever seen. Here they walked their dogs, did their shopping and jogged – jogged – in bikinis. Let the wind howl and the sea freeze, thought Parfitt. He loved the place!

Parfitt was still in his late thirties and knew he was too young to retire, even had the funds been there to make it possible. He toyed with the idea of starting a business of his own, but his only trade and specialist knowledge was in the air. He looked into setting up a small flying school, reasoning that South Africa is a large country and many a property inland had room for a landing strip, but he judged it to be the wrong time for the country which had undergone so much recent change and it was therefore too big an economic gamble. Maybe he would revisit the subject at some time in the future, maybe ten years, maybe more, who knew? For decades good pilots have been in constant demand and with world demand for their skills increasing, and with his RAF background, Parfitt quite literally walked into a job at SAA. From there to flying the big bus seemed to have taken no time at all.

Although all ex-fighter pilots turned airline pilots regret handing in the keys of the super-car to be given those to the bus Parfitt, unlike his BA counterparts, enjoyed his job, especially when he worked out of Cape Town's international airport. Jo'burg was alright, just, but when he flew from there he sometimes got the Perth flight, and Australia was a country he had little regard for. That was Perth, and that was Australia, but now he was flying into England, to London, and he liked London, enjoying the West End shows, the pageantry and the deep rich vibrant culture of the place.

He also liked Tammy Wild, who owned a property just outside London. Actually her house was just outside Maidenhead in the exclusive upmarket village of Cookham Dean. Tammy Wild was thirty five, five foot nine tall, with a perfect thirty-six, twenty-four, thirty-six figure, and long flawless legs. She had once married well, then divorced better, resided in a splendid five bedroom property, enjoyed a tidy stock portfolio and a highly desirable large figure bank account, not that any of it meant a thing to Parfitt. He liked Tammy a lot, in fact he had loved her to bits since the time they met, and in four days time she would be Mrs Tammy Parfitt. At last!

Tammy would be there to pick him up from the airport. She had just taken delivery of her new Porsche Cayman Coupe 3.4S, and wanted to show off. He knew what that meant. Doubtless she would be waiting for him as he left the arrivals building, wearing a plain silk blouse which left nobody with any doubts as to her curves, calf length hand sewn leather cowboy boots and a short black leather mini skirt which in many cultures would be regarded as a belt. The mini skirt would ride up as she eased herself into the leather seats of the car, leaving his mind empty of all other thoughts and considerations. Within twenty-five minutes they would be inside her house, and within thirty minutes they would be in her spacious bed. It was always a long flight through the night, and he was suitably tired, but the sleep would have to wait a while. She was without question the most obliging woman in bed he had ever known, and he had the rest of his life with her. He felt himself starting to swell at the thought of it and consciously changed his thoughts. The sky was clear and visibility good. Ten minutes to landing.

"Cabin crew; take your seats for landing." Peter said over the aircrafts communication system.

Part One

One

Chris Spencer was born in December 1962 at Scarborough General Hospital. Scarborough in summer is a seasonal tourist destination, but in winter it is bleak and cold, facing as it does onto the North Sea, the next piece of land being the German / Denmark border over three hundred miles to the east. His mother would have much preferred to give birth at the little hospital at Malton, which was nearer to her home, or to have a homebirth. She was talked out of both those options for her first delivery by the midwife, who advised Scarborough in case of complications, especially as roads could be impassable at that time of year. "You'll have to go to Scarborough at that time of year to have your baby, love," she said. "You never know what the weather will do then," There were no complications, and two days later both mother and baby were once again at home in their little cottage in Thornton-le-Dale near Pickering, then in the North Riding of Yorkshire.

The county system of England at the time of his birth had remained unchanged for centuries, many counties having their foundations in older land divisions such as the Anglo-Saxon kingdoms. Originally there were thirty-nine ancient, traditional and historic counties, but on the first of April (a suitable date) 1974, when Chris was still only eleven years of age, the Local Government Act 1972 came into force and the old map of England was overwritten with forty-six counties. Where boundaries changed and new counties came into being public dislike of the change was to continue for generations, and some were eventually destined to change back or change once again.

Before the redrawing of the county boundaries Yorkshire was the largest county in England and contained about one eighth of the country's area and a tenth of its population. It was considered too big and politically unwieldy to control so it was quite literally chopped to pieces. A new county of Humberside was created which swallowed the former East Riding, including the Wolds. The newly created counties of Cumbria and Cleveland took healthy slices of the hitherto mammoth county, as did Durham. A drastically reduced Yorkshire was then divided into three administrative zones: West Yorkshire which still embodied the former West Riding; North Yorkshire, comprising most of the old North Riding; and South Yorkshire. The super-county of Yorkshire and its Ridings was gone forever. But not for Yorkshiremen!

Chris Spencer was born a Yorkshireman, grew up as a Yorkshireman and, no matter where he lived in the world, would remain a Yorkshireman until the day he died.

He had grown up a very determined and fit young lad, excelling at anything physical, and was a must have first choice player in every team sport throughout his school days. Academically he was always marked as 'Could do better' in his school reports and he could easily have done better, but at the cost of being shut away inside, and that was never going to happen. Young Chris lived for the open air and for any activity which took him there.

Until shortly after the birth of his son Chris's father enjoyed a 'job for life' working out of Pickering railway station for British Rail. The Beeching report of the 1960's had however put pay to that and he was forced to move to a job in the postal service. His mornings started early, but he usually finished work and was home by lunchtime. This then enabled his wife to continue to hold down a local part time clerical job for a small light engineering workshop. Two and a half years after the birth of Chris the family were blessed with another child, this time a girl, Jennifer. As far back as Chris's memories went both his parents had constantly enjoyed the same jobs, and always lived in the same little cottage. Their entire lives were built around enduring stability and permanence. Unusually, and unlike those children who rebel against the parental status quo, part of their stability and need for security rubbed off on Chris as he developed and throughout his young life he knew he wanted a job which would last.

"The railways were the arteries of the nation, especially this region." Chris's father had explained. "Then a fat faced little southerner named Richard Beeching wormed his way up through a committee chaired by a decent chap called Sir Ivan Stedeford. Beeching published a report ahead of Stedeford which was seized upon by a government hungry for change, and one third of Britain's railways were totally destroyed as a result, along with the jobs those railways supported and, in some cases, the communities they serviced. Do yourself a favour, son. When you're old enough get yourself a job you both like and one which will last!"

The lesson had gone home – Chris wanted the surety of long term employment – but he also had a highly developed thirst for adventure, especially for the more robust, devil may care, rough and tumble outdoor kind.

Unlike most boys his age he had throughout his school days known exactly what he wanted to do when he left. He fully understood academic subjects and roles had their place, but they were not for him, and nor was school. He was going to join the British Army, he was going to join as a regular soldier, and he was going to join just as soon as he possibly could. Unfortunately for Chris by law he could not leave school until completing five years of secondary education, which meant he was sixteen and a half before he escaped.

At the end of June 1979, Chris Spencer boarded a bus alone and made the journey to Scarborough so he might visit the Army Careers Information Office in person. There he was able to talk face to face with men who had done the job, ask his questions and learn as much as he could.

"Good morning," Chris had said to the Sergeant behind the desk.

"Good morning. How can I help you?" the Sergeant asked.

"I would like to join the army, and I would like to join as soon as possible. What do I have to do and what paperwork do I have to fill in?" Chris had asked, and it would have proved an incredible feat for those he met there to have then been able to talk him out of his chosen career – and that is most definitely not what an Army recruitment office is about.

Given a completely free hand army life would not have been Chris's parents first choice for their son, but from the time he started senior school it was the only pursuit he had shown any interest in, and one way or another he was going to join. There was little to be gained by any attempt to delay him, so Chris's father returned with Chris to the ACIO and gave his permission for his son to join.

Chris took and passed aptitude and literacy tests, successfully completed his GP questionnaire and flew through the full army medical, including the one and a half mile run which he did in near record time without breaking into a proper sweat, despite the temperature. He suffered no medical conditions, no allergies and was pronounced fit and well in every way. At a touch over six feet, with wide shoulders and narrow waist, he was every inch a strapping young man. He could run, jump, throw, catch, cycle and swim with the best. He was a great team player, could see off most on the athletics track and almost all at cross country, where he had twice been short listed for the county, and at sixteen he had not yet come anywhere close to reaching his physical peak.

Tammy Wild was born Tammy Hunter in February 1970, and was born to parents living in the small town of Woodingdean, which is to the east of Brighton on the South Coast of England. Her father worked for an insurance brokerage in Brighton and her mother held down a part time job at a ladies outfitter in Woodingdean itself. The family home was a small three bedroom detached property set slightly to the north of the town, and just a little south of the South Downs Way in what was a peaceful and tranquil spot so typical of middle class South East England.

Terry and Theresa Hunter had decided to name any children they may have with the letter T and accordingly named their son Timothy. He was two years Tammy's senior and throughout school always looked out for his little sister, whose own childhood was easy and relaxed. Her parents were never going to be so much as comfortably off, but they were not destined to be poor either, not that anything of the kind was ever a worry for young Tammy as she grew up in what was, for a child, an idyllic setting. With the walks, views and fresh air the South Downs had to offer on her doorstep, the coast only two miles to the south, and the liberal, bustling, cosmopolitan town which was Brighton only three miles to the west, Tammy had everything on hand a growing child could wish for.

Tammy was born a natural blue eyed blonde, with symmetrical balanced features. Due to the climate of the area in which she lived her skin had long been exposed to the effects of the sun and she always tanned easily and naturally. Plenty of exercise and a good diet had done her no harm, and her physical development had been a joy for her parents to behold. Whilst her friends had grown through love affairs with their ponies Tammy's interests were more to do with the beach and the sea. She learned to windsurf and to sail, and spent a large amount of her spare time either on, in, or next to the water and she became a strong swimmer, with the shoulders and physique which go with the sport.

At the age of fifteen she had been 'discovered' on Brighton Beach. Tammy had always tended to prefer the eastern end of the beach, nearer to Black Rock and what was once the Brighton Lido until its demolition in 1978. She loved to watch the boats and craft coming and going from the marina, which had developed into one of the biggest in Europe. Having finished using a friend's sailboard she pulled it up on shore on a fine warm early summer day. Her wetsuit was tight on her and was always a struggle to remove. At fifteen she looked physically older than her true age and had filled out much more than most of her still coltish looking friends. During the previous summer she had grown used to the stares of other people on the beach, and what may have developed into insecurities in other girls had grow as confidence in her. She actually welcomed and enjoyed the attention, the poorly masked lust of the men and the open admiration or ill concealed jealousies of the women.

Many times she had been aware of strangers taking pictures of her as she peeled off her second skin and stripped down to the bikini beneath. Seldom however were people as direct as the man that day. He had stood close by and used a very expensive looking camera with a large lens, and he was taking a lot of pictures as well she had thought as she heard the motor speeding the next frame forward again and again.

"Do you want any particular pose?" Tammy asked the man who laughed.

"No thanks, you are doing just fine!" the man had answered before walking over to where she stood and introducing himself. "My name is James Martin, and I'm a photographer. Have you ever considered a future in modelling?"

Tammy dried herself, pulled a loose fitting dress over her head, slipped into a pair of beach sandals, and went for a coffee and a chat with the man. James Martin was an agent and freelance talent scout with dozens of contacts in the fashion and glamour business. The two talked and Tammy walked away with his card. During dinner that evening with her parents and brother she mentioned what had happened, and things very nearly stopped there. Her father was deeply suspicious as to Martin's motives and even her big bro looked most uncomfortable with the story she had told. Had it not been for the intervention of Tammy's mother Terry may even have called the police and complained. However Theresa took charge and phoned the man. She was aware her daughter was a good looking girl, but then most mothers probably thought the same of their daughters she constantly reasoned.

Nathan Jefferies was born with a face which only a mother could possibly love, although his never had. Standing at five foot nine inches he wasn't tall, and his frame was not the type which would ever excel in any type of sport. Without any form of academic drive he had never done well at school, with the sole exception of computer sciences, a subject which, unfortunately for him, had only been introduced to his school the year before he left.

Nathan's father was a boozer and a loser, and his family suffered badly because of it. Nathan was a September baby, conceived after a drunken Christmas party, and never really wanted, let alone planned. His education was at best poor and it hadn't helped that neither parent showed any interest whatsoever in his development, physical or intellectual. His home life was such that social services really should have become involved, but they never received a report from his woefully sub-standard inner city school, or any other body, and anyway they were far to busy covering their own shortcomings and inadequacies to concern themselves with extra work.

Nathan was never abused or hurt in any way – just neglected – and social services had plenty to do with other cases without getting involved with minor neglect, especially concerning a child from the indigenous population. He was fed – poorly, and he was clad – poorly, but both were done. He didn't have a record for truancy and no official body had any reason to offer him help or care. His parents didn't care, his grandparents didn't care, his school didn't care and the society in which he lived didn't care. He was just another little unloved person trying to survive in a world which really didn't give a damn. On his thirteenth birthday, after years of rowing over money, their home, food, drink, how to make a bed, how to wash a dish, how to brush their hair, his parents finally split up and his father disappeared. His mother then took up with one man after the other, none of whom ever made any time for him, effectively isolating him ever more. Nathan never again saw his father, and knew he never would.

Brought up in East London in a poor neighbourhood he was lucky to avoid problems with gangs, drugs, violence and crime generally. This was mostly because he kept himself to himself, didn't go looking for trouble, had a very low level of desires, and absolutely no ambition. His upbringing had knocked all thoughts of betterment out of him. The only thing he knew was one day he would break the mould and somehow he would get out. Unfortunately, although rightly so, he was tagged as an underachiever despite never being given any sort of chance or opportunity from the moment he was born and, as a direct result, had shown no promise of any kind. Apart from being somewhat ugly he was particularly unremarkable in every way. Except one. Yet neither his school nor his family had ever taken the time to notice that Nathan was incredibly gifted at computer sciences, so even Nathan knew nothing of this.

Growing up proved difficult for him. His looks certainly contributed to his inability to attract friends, and in reality caused him many problems with a lot of teasing throughout his formative years, utterly destroying any confidence he may have otherwise developed. He had a high forehead with coarse untrainable dark mousy hair above it, thick eyebrows which met in the middle, ears which stuck out at ninety degrees to his head, a round nose which looked as if it had been fashioned from putty, and bad gappy teeth in a mouth with thin lips set above a rather sharp and prominent chin. Not a pretty sight at all. Partly as a consequence of his looks, and partly because his upbringing forced him to become a loner he enjoyed few friends, and none which were close. At sixteen he left school and went out into the world of work. He had no career plan, and nothing like it was ever provided or discussed at his school. He didn't know what he wanted to do or where he wanted to go, and would have had no ideas of how to get there should he have known. He just instinctively knew he had to work to pay the bills and to get away from the dreadful place where he lived and the terrible life it provided

Unfortunately for Nathan at the time Britain was in the grips of a recession which had seen the collapse of many companies across industry, and in turn the loss of huge numbers of jobs. Those companies which still survived were looking to shed jobs, not to add to their liabilities, and for those few jobs which were available there was always a long and hungry queue. Nathan's quiet, shy and retiring nature often came across as a sullen attitude at the few interviews he was fortunate enough to be offered, and therefore did not last long. He knew he was not born lucky, and understood the odds were stacked against him, just as they had always been. Despite trying desperately hard to find employment in order to change his life, failure followed him like a cloud, but to him failure and rejection were as normal as relentless and remorseless bad luck, and bad luck was what his life had always been about. Most people from better off backgrounds would have wallowed in despair and self pity, but Nathan knew nothing of being better off.

However, Lady Luck, who had been an utter bitch to him from the moment of his birth, was about to smile kindly upon her unfortunate and unloved son.

Two

At sixteen and a half Chris Spencer entered the British Army as a junior entry recruit and as such underwent the standard two phase training scheme. Those who joined between the ages of sixteen and seventeen and one month were sent to the Army Apprentices College (AAC), now known as the Army Foundation College, which is located four miles to the west of the centre of Harrogate. Terms start in January and September, so Chris had to wait for eight long weeks to pass until he could take his place. The AAC gave junior recruits a head start and, in some cases crucially, allows those recruits the chance to earn money whilst learning. Senior entry recruits, those older than seventeen years one month, go to one of three Army Training Regiments for a fourteen week course before passing out and moving on to Phase 2. Junior entry recruits at the AAC attend a forty-two week course, plus holidays, three times the length of the seniors, before they too pass out and move on to Phase 2.

Training at the AAC for the juniors consists of twenty-three weeks of military training, five weeks leadership and initiative training and the remaining fourteen weeks acquiring vocational skills. The military training element falls under five basic categories which are physical fitness, first aid, fieldcraft, skill at arms, and NBC (which is nuclear, biological and chemical defence). Skill at arms above all else teaches the recruits how to be at one with the British Army's chosen weapon which, at the time, was the L1A1 SLR (self loading rifle).

Nature itself designed Chris Spencer for the life the Army now offered him. Some with him found the first weeks terribly rough, but not young Chris. He simply breezed through them and loved every minute. Of course it was nothing like school, and when things were done either badly or wrong voices were raised and there was a price to pay. The price he would happily have paid all day long and more. There was discipline – but there were rewards beyond his dreams, and the weeks simply sped by. He thoroughly enjoyed the physical fitness and was continually at the front of his class. He excelled at fieldcraft and field exercises, learnt everything there was to know about his weapon, could use it extremely effectively and, for the first time in his life, actually enjoyed the classroom for lessons on military tactics and history.

He found leadership and initiative training interesting, demanding and thought provoking. First aid was something which in civilian life he would never have considered, but the need to understand it in the military was immediately obvious to him, so he learned all he could as it was clear it may well save a life or lives one day. The NBC training he was not at all keen on. To be suited and booted in a hot sweaty and uncomfortable outfit which hampered movement was not his idea of fun, but then pictures of the alternatives looked like a lot less fun – so again he learnt everything he possibly could.

In fact the only thing young Spencer didn't like was the thing most of the other recruits looked forward to. Time off. Chris loved his family and his home, but he had found a new home and a new family, and he passionately loved them too. He took the view six weeks on and one week off was for kids. Yeah it was great to go home, but a long weekend every three months would have been more than enough – it was just so boring!

For Private Chris Spencer, his classmates, and those who went before and after him, approximately half way through the Phase 1 training course the students made their final choice of the regiment or corps they wished to join. Most recruits knew which they wanted, although some wavered, and a very few even then had not fully decided. Chris had known what he wanted before he was ten years old, and throughout the years since never once changed his mind. He was going to join the Green Howards and had been waiting to join them since he first saw the Regiment marching through the streets of Pickering with bayonets fixed, drums beating and colours flying when he was still a little boy in short trousers. Pickering is one of eight towns and cities which accorded the Regiment the honour of Honorary Freeman as a mark of appreciation for service to their county and country throughout the previous three hundred years.

This was the Regiment the young Chris Spencer had always craved being a part of, and this was the regiment to which he would proudly go. He was a Yorkshireman, and The Green Howards were THE Yorkshire regiment. For a young man from the North Riding intent on serving his country it could not possibly get better than that.

Completing Phase 1 at the AAC does give those who join as junior entry recruits several advantages over those who join as seniors. The forty-two weeks of training packs much more into the younger and more receptive minds than any fourteen weeks at Army Training Regiments. The weeks off between training cycles, although hated by Chris Spencer, also gives the knowledge gained a chance to bed down in those absorbent young heads and when moving on to Phase 2 most juniors arrive with much greater and clearer knowledge. The leadership and initiative training the formerly younger soldiers received, in what is effectively a full years training, allows them to take charge of situations which those who have gone in as seniors may well shy away from.

Leadership qualities are rarely missed in the modern day army. Gone are the days when social position equalled rank, and today senior time-served non commissioned officers (NCOs') command every bit as much respect as some lower ranked officers, if not more. Young Spencer was not on an officer training program, nor would he want to be, but he did show natural leadership qualities, certainly did not lack courage and showed complete loyalty to his squad – right or wrong – when he was a team leader. His performance report was marked forward accordingly.

Chris Spencer completed his Phase 1, took his allocated leave and moved on to his Phase 2 training. For those moving on from the AAC with the intention of joining the infantry another fourteen weeks of training, similar to Phase 1, is required to take infantry skills to a much higher level. It also gives recruits essential preparation in readiness for their first posting. This takes place at Catterick which, fortunately for young Spencer, is in North Yorkshire. The town of Catterick, known locally as Catterick Village, nestles alongside the A1, with Catterick Garrison lying some three miles to the west. Catterick's military heritage goes all the way back to 80AD and the Roman camp at Cataratonium. It has grown since those days, and has grown a great deal, to become the largest army base in Europe, the largest British Army garrison in the world, and therefore quite obviously the largest of the three Infantry Training Centres in the United Kingdom.

Phase 2 was completed by Private Spencer with the same ease with which he passed through the training of Phase 1. It was hard demanding physical work designed to push and stretch individuals, yet at the same time teaching them to consider others within their squad and help if and when required. This was team building and group bonding at its very best, taught by experts at the highest of levels. The British Army has time and again proven to be amongst the most professional and highly regarded military organisations in the world. For three hundred years the reason for this has been simple. The quality of its people and the training they receive has seldom been equalled. It has never been bettered.

At the beginning of 1981 Chris Spencer joined 1 Battalion of his chosen regiment, which at the time was conveniently deployed and garrisoned at Catterick. For a full year he continued to train and hone his skills as part of 5 Field Force. Throughout 1982 he remained in Catterick deployed as part of 24 Infantry Brigade which was reformed to become part of 2 Infantry Division which, in January 1983, led to his deployment to Osnabruck, Germany, to 12 Armoured Brigade, and the seemingly constantly changing composition of the men at arms stationed there.

The 1 Armoured Division then consisted of 7, 12 and 22 Armoured Brigades. The unfortunate 12 Brigade, in its varying guises and homes, had been disbanded four times, and re-named five times. Despite a somewhat turbulent recent history for the various divisions and brigades Chris Spencer enjoyed his time in Germany, and the warmth demonstrated by many of the German people. No longer were the British an invading army or force of occupation. They were there to defend and protect, and the West German people clearly understood the horrors of Soviet occupation, something they were not particularly keen to experience first hand, as their countrymen to the east were forced to endure day after day.

Chris arrived in Germany having just turned nineteen years of age, and he was to stay for three and a half years. Whilst there he learnt to speak conversational German, earned his first stripe, chased several very pretty pigtailed Frauleins with varied levels of success, and had his eyes opened to a people and culture he had previously always been taught to regard with more than a little suspicion. He found Osnabruck wonderfully central with easy access to Hanover, Hamburg and Amsterdam, all of which had an excess of delights to a very fit young man from the somewhat sheltered if not staid background of West Yorkshire. He also improved his working knowledge of armoured vehicles and the support they required and, as did every other member of the armed forces stationed there, waited for the attack from the east which never came.

In June 1965 Jennifer Spencer was born into the same family, the same home and the same living conditions as her older brother Chris, and had then followed him through the same school. From her days as a toddler she had endlessly looked up to her big brother. There was no sibling rivalry and no vying for attention. She didn't want to copy him or in any way compete with him. To her Chris really was everything any girl could ever want, need or desire in an older brother, and she completely idolised him. The fact Chris was totally oblivious to her feelings could not have mattered less to her. He was her big brother. He looked out for her, was always there when he was needed, was adored by all of her girl friends and was a real man long before she hit puberty, even though he was only two and a half years older. As she grew through her teenage years she came to realise her big bro's boots would be very difficult to fill by any other man in her life. As an attractive girl with a neat figure she had a few interested parties, but none she was particularly impressed with, certainly none who even part way measured up to Chris, and she had always known she would never be satisfied with some skinny little office boy or slippery handed salesman. She wanted someone big and strong, as hard as nails, but soft as a kitten. Just like her big brother.

Three

At the beginning of June 1985 the relatively easy life which went with being stationed in Germany ended when Chris Spencer and his comrades were ordered to West Belfast for an operational tour.

Training for army personnel generally tends to cover a multitude of activities, professions and careers as, quite apart from the needs of any large body of people, soldiers can be called upon in times of emergency to cover such weird and wonderful things as destroying diseased cattle all the way through to the putting out of fires. Unquestionably one of the most difficult roles any army faces is the policing of its own people, which is precisely why most democratic countries endeavour to constantly keep the duties of their police and of their armies well separated.

However, on the fifteenth of August 1969 the British Army, in the form of The Queens Regiment, was sent into West Belfast. Operation BANNER had begun and it was to prove to be the longest continuous deployment in British Army history, lasting for thirty eight years. The intention was for the troops to act as an interface, which was political speech for a buffer or barrier, between the Protestants of the Shankill area and the Catholics to their immediate south in Lower Falls. By the time Lance Corporal Chris Spencer arrived the army had been in occupation in the troubled land for almost sixteen years. An entire generation had grown up knowing nothing but armed soldiers on their streets.

The original intention was to protect the Catholics from the majority Protestant population. The notorious and hated (by the Catholics) 'B' Specials, responsible themselves for various atrocities, were disbanded and later replaced by the Ulster Defence Regiment (UDR). This move so angered the working class Shankill Road area Protestants that serious rioting followed leading to shooting in which twenty-two soldiers were injured before permission was given to open fire in self defence. Within six months of the original deployment youths in the close packed ghettos which formed the Catholic estates began to resent the presence of those troops who were sent in ostensibly to keep both communities apart.

The Green Howards had previously carried out seven operational tours of the province, and Chris was left in little doubt as to what to expect. The reality however proved much worse. The young troops sent in were there to protect their fellow British nationals from one another. The soldiers spoke the same language as the indigenous population, watched the same television programmes, played the same sports, voted for the same parliament and most prayed to the same god. None of which counted. Ultimately the troops were hated, spat upon, injured and killed by elements of both sides. During the five month tour those present, whilst on foot patrol, had to face petrol bombs, mortars and blast bomb attacks. The anniversary of Internment brought on a week long series of violent street disorders, all of which led to soldiers requiring hospital treatment. It was a matter of fortune the tour yielded up no serious casualties. For the young lance corporal from Thornton le Dale in North Yorkshire, Belfast was as far from home ideologically as he had ever been. His only respite was his one week of leave, which fell at the end of September and the beginning of October, when he went home with his friend Jimmy.

Autumn had arrived in 1985, and Jenny was twenty years old when Chris came home for a spot of leave. He brought a friend from the regiment with him, a big rangy guy called James Andrews, who really was on the wrong side of the country for a Lancastrian. But what's the colour of a rose between friends? Jenny saw the two of them walking up the pathway together and she was in love before the key slid into the lock of the front door. Quite apart from the effect his looks had on her, and he was perfect, Jimmy Andrews was a friend of her big bro, which told her more about the man's character than anything else in the world could possibly do.

On bonfire night, the fifth of November 1985, The Green Howards were pulled out of Northern Ireland, and a wiser Chris Spencer returned with his comrades to the better life by far which Osnabruck and 12 Armoured Brigade offered. For the following seventeen months he continued to train, take part in various exercises, acquire new skills and improve his German. The previous year a landslide victory had re-elected Ronald Reagan as US President and the Iron Lady, Margaret Thatcher, was the enduring Prime Minister of Britain. The cold war had earlier heated up somewhat with the two hawks in power, especially since Mrs. Thatcher encouraged British financial institutions to make mortgages available to those wishing to build nuclear fall-out shelters. NATO exercises were stepped up as were those of the Warsaw Pact, but a major change had occurred within the secret rooms of the Kremlin which was set to transform the world.

On the eleventh of March 1985, upon the death of Konstantin Chernenko, Mikhail Gorbachev, at the age of 54, was elected General Secretary of Russia's Communist Party. Chernenko only held office for thirteen months, having succeeded Yuri Andropov who himself had only seen fifteen months in office when he succeeded Leonid Brezhnev. Brezhnev, by comparison, had held power for eighteen years and was always a hard liner. Andropov as the former head of the KGB would have most certainly followed Breznev's lead, but it would never be known what Chernenko may or may not have changed. His period in office was dogged by ill health, and much of his short term was served in hospital, but it is probable he too would have followed the conservative old school train of thought.

In 1984 Gorbachev visited Britain and met with Margaret Thatcher. The PM appeared most impressed and later said he was a man she could do business with. The wind of change which was to blow across Europe did not come howling in as a great gale, but slowly built from a light breeze, gathering force as it went, until it became an irresistible hurricane. Perestroika with all its accompanying radical reforms was spelt out at the XXVIIth Party Congress between February and March, 1986. Slowly the big freeze which had for many years been the Cold War started to see a thaw.

Those serving in the forests, amongst the hills and on the plains of Germany, where it was long assumed the first shots of World War III would be fired, could let their trigger fingers relax a little. In January 1986 Gorbachev made his boldest international move so far in his new position when he announced his proposal for the elimination of intermediate-range nuclear weapons in Europe and his strategy for eliminating all nuclear weapons by the year 2000. Three months later, on the eighth of April, he announced the suspension of the deployment of SS-20s in Europe as a move towards resolving issues related to intermediate-range nuclear weapons. The Cold War suddenly became a lot less chilly. Although moves of this kind by the Soviets had never previously occurred, it could be seen Gorbachev was meeting resistance from conservative elements, and what had changed could change back. So despite a great deal of hope on the part of the greater population of Europe in general, and Germany in particular, the military machine took an understandably somewhat more cautious approach.

For Chris Spencer, and those of the Green Howards based in Osnabruck, life and training went on as usual, with only one notable exception. During 1985 the British Army had accepted into service a new rifle, which was designated the SA80 – the SA stood for small arms and the 80 referred to the 1980's. The family of SA weaponry consisted of the L85A1 IW, an individual weapon, and the L86A1 LSW, a light support weapon. These new weapons were so accurate they ushered in a new era of target practice as they made the old systems utterly obsolete. Training with the new weapons, for a short period, overrode other exercises. Chris Spencer, who had been deadly with his old rifle, passed out at the top of his group, and then went on to win every rifle range competition into which he was entered. The new rifle was, at the time, an outstanding success story for all who used it.

On the sixteenth of January 1987 The Green Howards returned to Northern Ireland, specifically Londonderry, to begin what was to be their second residential tour. This did not mean all Green Howards were immediately transferred to the province, as there was a degree of rotation with the various companies, and previous schedules and commitments were first completed. It was to be the end of March by the time Lance Corporal Spencer was redeployed to Ulster.

At twenty four years of age Chris had grown in every way possible. He had always been a big, fit, strapping lad and the constant exercise and training he had undergone increased the width of his shoulders and size of his chest. The contrasts between his life at home, Catterick, being stationed in Germany, and the operational tour he had already completed in Northern Ireland developed his character, personality and opinions, and started to forge him into the man he was to become. A man with deeply held convictions on rights and wrongs, with strong leadership qualities, enormous devotion to his country and seemingly limitless determination. It was more than seven years since he had signed up, and over six years since he had passed out of Phase II training. He was by then an experienced soldier already noted and rewarded for some of his qualities. Four weeks after arriving in Londonderry a second stripe followed the first.

Corporal Spencer returned to England in June for his sister's combined birthday and wedding to his closest friend Jimmy Andrews, and three days of family love, celebrations and peace. Bliss.

The two married on Jenny's twenty-second birthday, and then enjoyed a brief honeymoon in Paris. When they returned to England Jenny moved across to the other side of the country, to the pretty village of Slyne, just north of Lancaster, where Jimmy Andrews's family lived. Jimmy's kin had resided in and around the village for generations, and along the way many acquired property. Jimmy had an older sister who was already married, settled, and started her own family. So when a maiden aunt died her property was left to Jimmy and money to his sister. The property was a reasonably narrow but deceptively deep three bedroom terraced cottage on the main road through Slyne, with a large back garden, an outbuilding with toilet, and wonderful panoramic views across Morecambe Bay. For Jenny the cottage was a blank canvas and she loved it, even when she was alone. Jimmy's family, his friends, and the local village people were all most helpful and very friendly, which allowed her to rapidly and easily settle into her new life.

Corporal Chris Spencer of The Green Howards was a busy man during the summer of 1987, but this certainly did not mean he did not have time to think. Opinions he already held were reinforced over the next year and a half. He led his men out onto the streets undertaking foot patrols where they faced random shootings, sometimes from mixed and multiple weapon attacks, and more sophisticated explosive devices ranging from mortars to rockets were now being used against the peacekeepers. Kneecappings, murders and days of total civil unrest were commonplace, and a fellow corporal was killed when the unmarked van in which he was travelling, along with six other soldiers, exploded on the way back from a charity run. Despite all such episodes it was said the Royal Ulster Constabulary was continuing to take control of the security situation, and it was a truism that the level of violence had dropped dramatically since the early seventies, where in 1973 alone there were over five thousand shooting incidents.

Chris tried to understand the intricacies of the problem which was Ireland, but failed as the issues were far too complex. With most historical problems historians can usually look back and find an individual cause or event which set wheels in motion. Even this could not be done in Ireland. The animosity between the Catholics and Protestants led to a tortured history and ravaged land, which even time itself had never been able to heal. Although set over sixty years earlier Chris could see a lot of the problems he and his men were facing stemmed from the line set by the Boundary Commission in 1924, when the new Province of Ulster was set to the north and the Republic of Eire to the south. The voting system until 1969 had not helped, based as it was on property rather than people, and left non-ratepayers disenfranchised whereas those with more than one property had more than one vote.

As the Protestants were not only greater in number but also in general wealth, and therefore property, Protestant Unionist majorities were maintained, with housing allocation and constituency boundaries gerrymandered in order to ensure perpetuity. Under these conditions polarisation occurred and widespread discrimination against Catholics in all forms of public employment and even state education exacerbated the situation. The Protestants enjoyed overall control, not just of politics but also of wealth and education, and Catholics adopted a virtual siege mentality. This had eventually, and understandably, spilled over into violence. However, understanding even such simple things did not help Chris Spencer, his men, The Green Howards, or even the British Army as a whole. Their job was simply this, to continue to maintain peace – of a sort.

In early November of 1988, when Jimmy Andrews was home on leave, the young couple enjoyed a few days to themselves, and some good nights out at the local pub. Nature took its course, and to the joy of both the Spencer and Andrews families Jenny was left pregnant, also giving Chris the opportunity to endlessly tease the couple about their bonfire night baby. To his greater amusement young Charles Christopher (named after him) Andrews was born the following year, a week or two prematurely, on American Independence Day, the forth of July.

"Fireworks at conception and birth!" Chris would laugh good-naturedly as he ragged Jimmy Andrews whenever the two had a chance to enjoy a pint together, "I guess the poor little devil will have to get used to the sound of explosions around him. He'll have it to the day he dies, and then he'll probably go out with a bang!" Riotous laughter would usually follow, but Chris's light-hearted banter fooled nobody. Little Charlie really was the apple of his eye, the product of the union of his closest friend and his kid sister, and named after him. He would have cheerfully gone to the depths of hell and dragged the devil himself out by his beard for the little lad, and well beyond if ever he were called to do so. Woe betide anyone who ever messed with his little nephew – ever!

The Londonderry tour had ended on the nineteenth of March 1989, and Corporal Spencer was once more returned to Catterick. Apart from short periods of leave he had been away from his beloved Yorkshire for more than six years, and a great deal had changed in that time. In February of the previous year Gorbachev had announced the full withdrawal of all Soviet forces from Afghanistan. America and Russia met and enjoyed far ranging talks, eventually culminating with a treaty signed the previous November in Geneva, eliminating intermediate range nuclear weapons. The most dangerous weapons man had ever devised were to be completely withdrawn from mainland Europe.

Chris Spencer was deployed to 24 Airmobile Brigade at Catterick, which after its reformation in 1983 became part of 2 Infantry Division. It had the war role of putting an airmobile anti-tank barrier in the face of any Soviet breakthrough of I (BR) Corps defences in Germany. Nuclear weapons may well be in the process of being removed from the European mainland, but a perceived threat still existed in the land forces. All that too was set to change.

In his speech of the sixth of July 1989, arguing for a 'common European home' before the Council of Europe in Strasbourg, Gorbachev declared: "The social and political order in some countries changed in the past, and it can change in the future too, but this is entirely a matter for each people to decide. Any interference in the internal affairs, or any attempt to limit the sovereignty of another state, friend, ally, or another, would be inadmissible." This policy of non-intervention in the affairs of the other Warsaw Pact states would go on and prove to be the most momentous of all Gorbachev's foreign policy reforms. With Moscow's abandonment of the Brezhnev Doctrine a string of revolutions occurred in Eastern Europe throughout 1989, and Communism, the evil and frightening monster which had terrified those of Western Europe for generations, simply collapsed and died.

Unfortunately the world was set to change again.

Four

It is said bad luck normally comes in threes, but for Nathan Jefferies, who had never known anything but bad luck, when good luck came it too came as three. His woefully inadequate school had not prepared him or his classmates for life, nor had it succeeded in putting across even basic educational standards. Almost without exception the pupils left the school no better off than when they had entered it five years earlier. The exceptions either left worse off having been shown there was absolutely no point in trying, or were already detained at Her Majesty's pleasure serving custodial sentences. Indeed the only thing Nathan and his school mates left school with was the knowledge of how to claim benefits from the state, and it was to the benefits office Nathan eventually went in order to claim some money so he might put bread in his mouth.

After waiting for three and a half hours for his number to flash up on the overhead screen, Nathan sat down in front of a plate glass window behind which sat an overweight middle-aged woman with a plainly bored and contemptuous look on her fat and mean mouthed sour face.

"So you expect the country to support you, do you?" she asked.

Uneducated Nathan may well have been but he did know his rights and what his entitlements should be, and he was certainly not the type to be marked down as a victim of pride.

"I've tried really hard to find a job but there just isn't anything out there," Nathan replied. He explained his position and what he had attempted to do, but there was not the slightest flicker of understanding from the woman's piggy eyes, and the look of complete disdain never left her lips throughout the interview. However Nathan did come away with enough money on which to frugally exist so long as he regularly visited the Job Centre and continued to actively search for work.

It was the Job Centre which inadvertently provided him with two slices of what would turn out to be good luck. He was interviewed by a Mrs Shirley James, who was, in complete contrast to the woman at the benefits office, a friendly, outgoing and positive, dark haired young woman in her early thirties. She was somewhat unusual in that she both believed in what she was doing and really felt she could sometimes help to make the difference. She had been in the job long enough to understand the problems, but not yet anything like reached the age when people in her profession start to turn cynical. She smiled at him and encouraged him and, almost beyond belief, talked to him as if he mattered and was an equal. In his entire life to that moment nobody had ever shown him even the remotest kindness and certainly nobody had ever let him believe he mattered. Not in any way. Not ever. At that moment he would have done anything for Mrs James.

She in turn felt truly sorry for this ugly young lad in front of her. She had seen many types in her job and in ever increasing numbers since the recession hit home.

Time and experience had taught her to be quick to accurately judge the character of those before her, and this young man, like so many others in this area, had nothing behind him, but unlike others he was still trying. Above all she admired those who tried, probably because she was of the type herself, and she liked the attitude of this quiet, shy and ugly, but polite young man. Wholly because of this she decided she would both probe a little deeper into his character and would take a personal interest in his case. She would help, and she would try and find him something. No, she would find him something!

Although it went well beyond the requirements of her job description Shirley James did probe into Nathan's past.

"Tell me about your family, friends and education," she prompted, and Nathan did. She was beyond being shocked at the stories she heard about how dreadful some peoples lives and upbringings were, but it certainly did not mean she lacked compassion.

"Was there any subject you particularly enjoyed at school? Shirley had questioned.

"I wasn't really any good at anything." Nathan responded, looking at his hands. "The only thing I liked was working with computers, but we only got them two terms before I left. If I'd had a chance to use them a bit more I think I would have got on well with them, but it's too late now."

It was with interest she discovered Nathan had enjoyed working with computers at school, even if his association with them was so short lived. She would look into things on his behalf to see what she could find, and asked him to return to see her two weeks later.

Nathan could not wait to get back to see her. Although he continued to try to find work on his own he failed dismally, finding nothing. This came as unsurprising news to Shirley who had access to the government's own figures and realised over a quarter of a million others who had recently lost their jobs were also unable to find anything. Interestingly nor had any of the long term unemployed, but then they wouldn't, would they?

Back at the beginning of her twenties, long before she met her husband, Shirley had enjoyed a two year fling with Jake Ferris, twelve years her senior and a local car dealer. Jake the Lad as he was known locally. She was an attractive girl with a good figure, and Jake Ferris had a love of fast cars, fast money and attractive young ladies, which he had a tendency to change as often as he did his cars. She had done remarkably well to retain most of his attention for two years, during which he taught her a great deal about life, and love, and sex, and about how to make things happen. He was a big man with a character to match and seemed bestowed with boundless energy. His clear blue eyes always twinkled with mischief, merriment and mirth, the smile never seemed to slip from his face, and in the two years with him she had not once see him frown. Jake always seemed to take the view every day everything in every way was an opportunity just waiting to be exploited, and his contacts, which seemed to number in the thousands, were always there to help make the latest project work. Their relationship eventually ended, but on particularly good terms as it would have been completely impossible not to have done so with Jake, and they had remained good friends ever since.

Black Monday, the nineteenth of October 1987, had come and gone. City traders had lost their shirts, their bonuses and their homes. They had also lost their Porsches and Ferraris, and at bargain basement prices Jake Ferris had bought them by the dozen, later selling them on at frightening profits. In the decade which had passed since their split Jake made millions and owned several small companies as well as the car business he started with, which he had also substantially expanded. During those years Shirley had many a time helped him with his employment needs, and helped her clients by placing them in what she knew would be an ever growing business which should provide them with many future opportunities. However the economic times were dreadful and even Jake had not been in the market to hire more staff for several months. Away from work, and in her own time, Shirley rang Jake Ferris.

"Hi Jake, it's Shirley, and I'm after a favour," she started by saying. "I've had a young lad come in to me who I believe would be good for you. I know you are not looking to increase your payroll, but this young lad will not cost a lot and I believe he would be utterly loyal and never let you down. His background is dreadful beyond belief but he has never been in any sort of trouble. He desperately needs a leg up, a start in life, and I would consider it a huge favour to me if you will consider it."

"Shirley, as you know and have said, times are hard, but if you are personally recommending the lad he must have something about him," Jake Ferris responded.

"The problem is Jake he has absolutely zero confidence in himself, and he will not come across at all well at an interview, but he has got something about him. I don't know what it is and can't put my finger on it, but there is something there for sure!" Shirley James assured him.

"In which case let's arrange an interview," Jake suggested. "He'll have the job anyway unless I discover something badly wrong, but we'll keep that information between ourselves."

Although he was never to know anything of it, the call was the reason Nathan Jefferies secured his first job, during what was at the time an employment wilderness.

Keen to see her again Nathan arrived five minutes early at the Job Centre and was surprised to find himself immediately asked in to see her in a private room. Shirley told him nothing of the arrangement she had made with Jake Ferris, except she had arranged an interview for a job working from the car site. The job was not much, mostly the cleaning of cars and preparing them for sale, but it was employment and it may provide him with a start. She explained she had also taken it upon herself to look into computer courses run by the local authorities and found starter courses which, if he enrolled whilst still unemployed, were free. She had explained to Jake Ferris this young lad would have to have time off work to attend the classes, and Jake went along with her suggestions. Having already spoken to the right people at the learning centre she had received the course enrolment forms and filled them out for Nathan. All that was needed was his signature. A shocked Nathan signed and Shirley took the papers and placed them in a Job Centre envelope which was already addressed to the person she had spoken to. Finally she enclosed a compliment slip on which she added a personal handwritten note and consigned the envelope to her out tray.

It was late August and Nathan was approaching seventeen. For the first time in his life, as he walked home, he felt tears well up in his eyes and spill down his cheeks. Tears of gratitude for what was little more than an act of common human decency. Something never previously experienced by the boy.

Two days later Nathan Jefferies walked the mile and a half to Jake Ferris's pitch, the garage his car business operated from, on the Barking Road. Again arriving early he waited around outside on the pavement until it was almost the appointed time then walked in and was ushered through to Jake's office. He was terribly nervous, but Shirley had told him to just be himself and this he tried to do. It was probably a good thing he didn't know he already had the job, or that the job was being created for him as a favour to Shirley James. Had he been aware of the situation the pressure it would have placed him under, to impress and do the right thing, could very easily have led to his undoing.

He started the job the following Monday, rising at six o'clock in order to be there on time. Over the weekend a letter for him from the learning centre arrived at his home confirming an allocated place and asking him to start the course two and a half weeks later. As he walked in on his first day a car pulled over next to him three hundred yards short of the garage. The young lad behind the wheel was the same person who had shown him to Jake's office, and he wanted to know why Nathan was walking.

"Haven't you got your own car?" the young lad asked Nathan.

"No, I can't drive and anyway I can't get a licence until I'm seventeen," Nathan replied.

"Haven't you got a bike either then?" the lad questioned him.

"No, we couldn't ever afford anything like that!" Nathan answered.

"Ah well, don't worry about it mate," the young lad said. "Hop in now and I'll give you a lift. Can you ride a bike?"

"Oh yes, I can ride, it's just the cost," Nathan explained as he climbed into the car.

The following morning when he arrived at work there was a clean and tidy used mountain bike waiting for him. Jake Ferris liked to look after his people, and they understood it. The mountain bike was the first meaningful present young Nathan had ever received and he was frankly both astounded and hugely grateful, realising it would save him an hour a day in getting to and from work.

The work in the garage itself Nathan found undemanding. His duties included the cleaning of cars, stacking shelves in the forecourt shop and to run simple errands, many on the mountain bike. He worked hard at every job he was given and was noted for it. From his first wage packet he took the time and trouble to buy Mrs James a bottle each of red and white wine, and a large bunch of flowers. These, along with a written note of explanation, he had delivered to her by taxi as he didn't want to ask for time off work for any reason whatsoever. She in turn was quite moved by the young man's gesture and discreetly let Jake Ferris know. Ferris knew Nathan was completely unaware of any relationship he had with Shirley James, and had therefore bought the wine and flowers out of a genuine sense of gratitude for what Shirley had done and not in some form of attempt to gain favour with him. The act told Ferris much about the depth of character and spirit of young Jefferies, and he liked what it showed him about the lad. He liked it very much indeed!

Ferris himself drove Nathan to the learning centre the day his computer course started, and on the way suggested to Nathan he should apply for his provisional driving licence.

"You seem to be working out alright Nathan," Jake told him. "Get your licence sorted. It really is pretty much essential all staff can drive!"

Nathan agreed without having a clue about how he would go about learning, the costs involved with lessons, or even how to apply for a provisional licence.

The computer course he started was CLAIT-1, a basic computer literacy course, and the computer room fascinated him immediately. It was nothing like school. Here there were actually more computers than pupils, not the other way around, and all the computers were the latest highest speed 386 models. The teaching process was very much based on showing pupils what they had to do and letting them get on with it, with the tutor returning to anyone who struggled or could not grasp what was required. To the tutor's amazement Nathan instantly understood everything he was shown, and she never once had to go over the same thing with him a second time, as the concepts of working a computer came as naturally to him as crying does to a baby. His only problem was the one most common to all males, and most young females, which was the lack of keyboard skills.

Speed on a keyboard comes with time and training. An instinctive grasp and understanding of computers on a binary level is a gift of nature, and Nathan Jefferies had the gift in spades, and then some. It was usual to complete the CLAIT-1 course at the pupil's own pace. The course however was generally based on one two hour session once a week spread over twelve weeks, with extra time put in for those who could not keep up. Despite his lack of keyboard skills Nathan completed the course half way through his third session. The tutor had never heard of anything like it, and could see that had Nathan already possessed keyboard skills he would have taken in everything the course entailed in less than two hours, a phenomenon beyond her comprehension.

CLAIT-2 Nathan completed in two sessions. The tutor took him to one side to ask about his background, what computer he used at home and how much practise he got on it. She found it almost impossible to accept his answer that he didn't own a computer and, apart from about eight to ten hours use at school a year earlier, he had had no knowledge of computers before he started his first course. The tutor, a bright young woman named Sally Brown, realised this pupil was different to the rest. She had taught some smart people in her time, and some not so smart, but she had never seen or heard of anyone like this. This unattractive and funny looking lad would be teaching her in under a month if he were given the chance, so why not give him a chance?

She had. The 386's the class was using had replaced the older 286 models, most of which had already been passed on to a local school. Three however were still sat in a cupboard gathering dust and would shortly be disposed of, so she had a word with administration.

"We have three obsolete 286 computers in the store room taking up valuable space." Sally told them. "I have a student from a deprived background and with no formal education. He has no chance of being able to afford anything, but he's different, he's got some sort of gift I've never seen or heard of before. His abilities go way beyond incredible but he doesn't know it. I want to help him. How much will you charge me for the computers so I can give them to him?"

"Oh hell, Sally, take them. They're of no commercial value, and you're right, they're in the way," she was told, so when Nathan was collected, all three went into the car with him.

Ferris was a hands-on opportunist who had done extremely well for himself and others following trends. For some time he had been interested in getting things on computer, and liked the possibilities the machines had the potential to offer, but knowledge of how to do such things was beyond him and he had a certain reluctance to take on something he knew he would never be able to master. He was practical, sharp and shrewd, had an excellent working knowledge of mechanical concepts and could spot an opportunity where most could not. The problem was for him the workings of a computer would always remain beyond him and in very real terms he found them quite scary.

So what the hell was this weird looking little bugger doing with three of them on his forecourt? Jake had to find out, and went outside to ask Nathan what he was doing and did he understand the things. Nathan's answer was as strange to Ferris as his looks.

"I believe I understand how they think, but not how they work. I will though!"

In August 1988, a ceasefire was signed ending a war between Iran and Iraq. It had raged for eight years, leaving Iraq virtually bankrupt and heavily indebted to both Kuwait and Saudi Arabia. The following year, in flagrant defiance of agreed OPEC quotas, Kuwait increased its oil production by forty percent. This caused a general collapse of oil prices and the knock-on effect to the Iraqi economy was nothing short of catastrophic. Iraq then claimed Kuwait was slant drilling cross border into the Iraqi Rumaila oil field, and described the entire scenario as a form of economic warfare. This was followed by much sabre rattling on the part of the Iraqis, accompanied by meaningless negotiations.

Kuwait had historically been part of the Ottoman province of Basra. Its ruling dynasty, the family al-Sabah, concluded a protectorate agreement in 1899 assigning full responsibility for its foreign affairs to Britain. However no attempt was ever made to secede from the Ottoman Empire and subsequent Iraqi governments, for this reason, steadfastly refused to accept Kuwait's separation. The British High Commissioner of the day had drawn lines which deliberately constricted Iraq's access to the ocean in order to ensure that Britain's domination of the Gulf would then never be threatened by any future Iraqi government. Unfortunately these borders were never clearly defined. Nor mutually agreed.

Towards the end of July 1990, negotiations stalled and Iraq massed troops on the Kuwait border. Saddam Hussein summoned April Glaspie, the US ambassador, to a meeting in order to outline his grievances regarding Kuwait. In response to Glaspie's expressed concerns with regard to the troop build up, it was promised Iraq would not invade before attempting to resolve matters with a further round of negotiations.

On the second of August, without any attempt at further talks or negotiations, Iraq crossed the Kuwaiti border under force of arms and carried out a full scale invasion. Within hours the UN Security Council, sitting at a meeting called by US and Kuwaiti delegates, passed Resolution 660. This condemned the invasion and demanded the withdrawal of all Iraqi troops from Kuwaiti territory. The following day the Arab League also called for a solution to the conflict, but warned against foreign intervention. On the sixth of August UN Resolution 661 imposed economic sanctions on Iraq, and the following day US troops were moved into Saudi Arabia to defend the kingdom from attack by Iraq. Operation Desert Shield had begun.

Iraq had manufactured a number of grievances with regard to Saudi Arabia. The Saudis had lent Saddam Hussein something in the region of twenty six billion dollars to assist his invasion of Iran because, following Iran's Islamic Revolution, the Saudi's feared the influence of Iran's mainly Shia population on its own Shia minority. The majority of Saudi oil fields remained in territory populated by Shias and, as with Kuwait, the long desert border was also ill-defined.

In theory the United Nations is a wonderful organisation, set up to protect and promote the better character traits of man. Under its auspices big nations can no longer threaten and bully smaller nations, natural disasters can be coped with much more smoothly by the brotherhood of man, world hunger should cease to exist, and world poverty and disease eradicated forever! Theory is a wonderful thing.

So it was with the Kuwait invasion. Had the United States, the world's only remaining superpower, not continued to beat upon the doors of the UN, Kuwait would have been consigned to the history books. After many discussions, debates and eventual resolutions the UN, working at a whirlwind pace when compared with its usual performance, finally set a date for Iraq to withdraw. The date was the fifteenth of January 1991, five and a half months after the invasion occurred. Iraq failed to comply.

Eventually a coalition of thirty-four nations was put together by the United States. Some joined reluctantly at best, cajoled, bought and bribed, coaxed with offers of economic aid and the forgiveness of outstanding debt. Iraq's ongoing belligerence towards other Arab states persuaded some, and others joined from a sense of duty. America supplied more than forty-five percent of the troops and Britain, with approximately a fifth of the US population, almost twenty percent, the highest percentage in terms of population of any contributing nation. The remainder consisted of representative troops from the other thirty-two nations. For constitutional reasons, their constitutions having been written for them after World War II by those who won, neither Japan nor Germany could contribute any forces, however they did make financial contributions of ten billion and six point six billion dollars respectively.

Operation Granby, the British operational name for Operations Desert Shield and Storm, got under way with the deployment of some forty-three thousand troops and two thousand five hundred armoured vehicles. Corporal Chris Spencer, as part of a Green Howard contingent, was shipped out to Saudi Arabia in late September 1990 under the command of 7 Armoured Brigade which, along with 4 Armoured Brigade were then under the command of the 1 Armoured division. During the war the entire British operation came under the command of US VII Corps. The British contingent, with Falkland Islands and Northern Ireland experience, were the only experienced battle hardened troops available, and were also the most highly trained within the entire theatre of operation, with the single possible exception of certain minor elements of the French Foreign Legion. It therefore fell upon the two brigades of the British division to spearhead the advance.

On the seventeenth of January 1991 Operation Dessert Storm commenced. As the main air attack got under way it became obvious to those on the ground the art of warfare had changed. Many troops finished the tour calling it the computer war, mainly because General 'Storming Norman' Schwarzkopf originally firmly believed it was a war to be waged solely from the air. Using over the horizon targeting (OTH-T) systems Iraqi boats were taken out as they attempted to flee into Iranian waters. US Navy BGM-109 Tomahawk Cruise Missiles struck targets in Baghdad. EA-6Bs, EF-111 radar jammers and F-117A stealth planes were heavily used in order to elude Iraq's extensive surface to air missile (SAM) systems and anti-aircraft weapons. Coalition forces flew over one hundred thousand sorties and dropped eighty-eight thousand five hundred tonnes of bombs at a cost of seventy-five aircraft losses.

Whilst the coalition forces air power was overwhelmingly superior the ground force situation was more balanced. However coalition ground forces had the significant advantage of being able to operate under the protection of their air superiority. Coalition forces also had two key technological advantages. Firstly the main battle tanks of the coalition, such as the American M1 Abrams, the British Challenger 1 and the Kuwaiti (Yugoslav manufactured) M-84AB were vastly superior to the Iraqis Soviet-built T-72's. Secondly with the extensive use of GPS it was possible for coalition forces to navigate without reference to roads or other fixed landmarks, allowing them to fight a battle of manoeuvre rather than a battle of encounter. Crews knew where they were, and knew where their enemy was, which enabled them to attack a specific target. In addition to technological advantages it was notable the coalition crews were also significantly better trained, and their understanding of the concepts and principles of armoured warfare was far better developed.

The coalition swept the Iraqis from Kuwait, stopping temporarily at the border. After leading a small squad on mopping up duties from the relative comfort of two Warriors, Corporal Chris Spencer received a battlefield promotion to sergeant. Using two desert proofed Warrior Tracked Armoured FV510 Infantry Section Vehicles, he and his squad had come upon a detachment of Iraqi Regulars defending the main road home to Bagdad. They had four trucks and two Armoured Personnel Carriers (APC's) at their command, and had set up two machine gun posts with crossing fields of fire. They were supported by a small infantry unit of some fifty troops who were lightly dug in and, to their rear, it could be seen through binoculars, there appeared to be another group of troops relaxing amongst a further six trucks. Corporal Spencer was faced with the obvious choice of calling in air support, then either falling back or maintaining position and reporting.

The Warriors were equipped with two-man turrets, to each of which were fitted L21A1 thirty millimetre RARDEN cannon and L94A1 EX-34 7.62 millimetre Hughes Helicopter coaxial chain gun. The cannon was capable of destroying most modern APCs at a maximum range of almost a mile. The chain gun could cut a sturdy oak tree in half at closer range. The vehicles were also NBC proof, and fitted with passive night vision and defensive grenade launchers which were usually used with Visual and Infrared Screening Smoke (VIRSS), not that any such equipment was needed during the encounter.

Standard operating procedure was to call in air support, but Corporal Spencer's squad were deep in bandit country, and aircraft losses were beginning to tell with the low level daylight missions the various air forces pilots were called upon to fly. The Iraqis had proved to be quite adept at using hand held and shoulder launched SAMs. In the situation in which they found themselves training and morale was everything. Chris had two APC's at his disposal with driver, gunner and six troops in each including himself. The opposition had an estimated force in excess of one hundred and twenty men, set up with machine guns, two APC's of their own, and partially dug in. Chris had grinned at his crew and said the unthinkable, "We'll attack. They don't stand a bloody chance!"

To the jeers of the Iraqis they had 'run away'. Circling out to the left Chris had dropped two men at a time equipped with both their Individual Weapons and a Light Support Weapon between them. This was done under the cover of the dust kicked up by the tracks of the Warriors. One Warrior, when empty of troops, he sited just off the road to the rear of the Iraqis. With the other he crossed the road and completed the circle, again dropping troops as he went. Finally he ordered the second Warrior back to the road where they had first caught sight of the Iraqis. After checking everyone's personal radios he ordered the Warrior in the rear to advance and to open up with the chain gun as targets came to sight. The Iraqi's had suspected something was going on as they watched the dust cloud circle out around them, but assumed the Warriors were circling out of trouble whilst they called in air support and had only taken the precaution of mounting a light defence to their rear. They were clearly far more concerned with aircraft than two APC's, whose crews they would vastly outnumber.

The chain gun cut their rear to pieces. Troops relaxing amongst the vehicles ran out in every direction, heading out but slightly forward, away from the rattling chain gun which was spitting death and destruction in their direction. Chris had the troops at three and nine o'clock open up with their LSW's. Iraqi's fell and some tried to run back. With little cover, apart from the odd small boulder, those caught in the open immediately thrust their hands towards the sky. He ordered the Warrior on the road to his left to move in and take out the Iraqi APC's. As the Iraqi machine guns opened fire on his advancing Warrior Chris ordered the one to the rear to also continue advancing, and to take out the trucks with the chain gun. The first Iraqi APC erupted as the cannon came to bear, and an entire line of the 'dug in' Iraqi's broke cover and ran – straight into the LSW's. As the second Iraqi APC burst into flames the rattling of the chain gun could be heard from behind their positions. More Iraqi's broke cover and ran, all with arms as high as they could possibly go. Those who remained in position faltered then started to break.

The last resistance came from the two machine gun posts, both of which were manned with three men each rather than the customary two. Perhaps they were brave, or possibly they felt safe with numbers and a machine gun. Either way it was stupid and their stupidity cost all of them their lives. Both chain guns opened up and the six men were quite literally chopped into pieces. Every surviving Iraqi seemed to be reaching for the sky. Chris Spencer stood up, ordered his men to stay where they were and went forward carrying his individual weapon. This was dangerous practice, as a habit of playing dead had evolved amongst the Iraqi's, who would shoot those they had lost to in the back as they passed. Those standing he was safe with. The wounded appeared obvious. As he went he put a single round into the heads of the dead. Two dead leapt into the air in front of him as he approached, their arms too thrusting upwards. One foolishly still held a pistol in his hand. Chris gestured for him to drop it, but the Iraqi started to lower it in his direction. "Silly man", Chris said as two bullets slammed into the Iraqi's forehead and took the top of his head off.

Silence descended across the battlefield, broken only by the sobbing of several Iraqi's, some of whom had also lost control of their bladders. Chris ordered his men forward in standard defensive posture, one of each pair constantly covering the ground behind them. The surviving Iraqi's were herded forward into a group. None now played dead. It was indicated they should collect their dead and wounded as they went, which they did. One hundred and forty-two Iraqi's had stood in their way. Eighty three survived, two of whom would not for long. Sixty-one remained uninjured, and the injured varied from minor flesh wounds to the two who would never make it. The two Iraqi APC's were history, as were seven of the ten trucks. The remaining three were badly beaten about, but serviceable – just. Battlefield dressings were applied to the wounded, the worst of which were loaded into the Warriors with one of Corporal Spencer's troops guarding each vehicle. The dead were loaded onto the wrecked trucks, for burning, burial or removal at another time. The prisoners were then loaded into the three still mobile trucks and, with one Warrior at the front and one at the rear, the little convoy returned to barracks and debrief, with the prisoners handed over to intelligence.

The skirmish proved a resounding success. None of Chris's men were injured. Three of his positions had not even needed to use their weapons. High cost and highly prized assets were not risked. Munitions costs were very low. Human casualties were lower than may have been the case with an air strike. There was a one hundred percent clear-up, and those taken prisoner may well pass on valuable information. All in all a good job executed and delivered in a thorough and professional manner.

Sergeant Spencer was involved in several skirmishes as the coalition continued to mop up Kuwait, but by that time many of the Iraqi's who remained were so demoralised they willingly gave themselves up at the fist sign of coalition forces. As far as Chris was concerned the war had gone exceptionally well for him, with only one minor problem rearing its ugly head, the reliability of his standard issue personal weapon. On several occasions it was the cause of some concern. It appeared not to perform well in the harsh desert conditions, and when compared with the US M16A2 assault rifle it seemed to leave a lot to be desired. From choice Chris would have gone with the M16, but such a choice was restricted to the Special Forces only.

The first troops into Iraq were a squadron of Britain's elite Special Air Service. The squadron was split into two half squadrons which was again divided into two sub-units, each with the four troop disciplines – Air, Boat, Mobility and Mountain – split and divided up between the main two units. By midnight on the twentieth of January four of the SAS units were crossing the border into Iraq. Their call signs were Alpha One Zero and Two Zero, and Alpha Three Zero and Four Zero. These highly trained gentlemen were tasked with tracking down Scud missile launchers, calling in attack aircraft to deal with them, and the destruction of fibre optic communications arrays which lay across the country in pipelines. This was done to prevent Israel from being provoked and drawn into the war, which would have led to an inevitable split with Arab and Muslim contributors within the coalition forces.

Early on Sunday the twenty-fourth of February 1991 the U.S. VII Corps, who had assembled in full strength, launched an armoured attack into Iraq, just to the west of Kuwait, taking Iraqi forces by surprise. A simultaneous assault carried out by the U.S. XVIII Airborne Corps launched a sweeping attack across the largely undefended desert of southern Iraq. This was led by the 3rd Armoured Cavalry Regiment and the 24th Infantry Division (Mechanised). The movement was protected on the left flank by French 6th Light Armoured Division. This included units of the French Foreign Legion and was a fast-moving force which quickly overcame the Iraqi 45th Infantry Division. Suffering no more than a handful of casualties they took up blocking positions to prevent any Iraqi force from attacking the coalition flank. The right flank was protected by the British 1st Armoured Division. Having penetrated deep into Iraqi territory, they then turned to the east, launching a flank attack against the Republican Guard.

The coalition advanced far more quickly than U.S. generals expected. On the twenty-sixth of February, Iraqi troops began retreating from Kuwait en masse, setting fire to the Kuwaiti oil fields as they left. The retreating troops formed an extended convoy along the main Iraq-Kuwait highway, the one defended and so effectively defeated by Chris Spencer and his squad. This convoy was bombed extensively by coalition forces, and later became known somewhat melodramatically as the Highway of Death. Forces from the United States, the United Kingdom and France continued to pursue retreating Iraqi forces over the border and back into Iraq, moving to within 150 miles of Baghdad before withdrawing.

One hundred hours after the Iraqi ground campaign started, President Bush declared a cease-fire. On the twenty-seventh of February politics took over and Bush declared Kuwait liberated. A peace conference was held in Iraqi occupied territory and the war was over. The Americans wanted to avoid further American losses, and worried about fragmenting a fragile coalition by pushing home the advantage and removing Saddam Hussein. A wise, sage, worldly and battle hardened twenty-eight-year-old Sergeant of the Green Howards summed up the feelings of many of the troops on the ground, and many more people around the world. "That is going to prove to be a mistake." Chris Spencer was heard to say, "Now we will have to come back one day!"

Sergeant Spencer was once again returned to Catterick, was given a spell of leave, then continued where he had left off with 24 Airmobile Brigade. At the time the British Army employed a process generally known as 'arms plot'. This involved infantry battalions performing one particular role for a certain period of time, which generally consisted of between two to six years, following which they would be re-trained to take up another role. This usually meant a re-posting elsewhere, although not always as Catterick could be used for more than one role.

Within the British Army, there are four main types of infantry. These consist of Air Assault, Armoured, Light, and Mechanised. Air assault infantry are trained to be deployed using aircraft, helicopters or parachute. Armoured infantry are equipped with the Warrior APC which Chris Spencer had learned to master in Germany, and had used so effectively in Kuwait and Iraq. Light infantry are trained to hold an area without the use of armoured vehicles, and certain units are trained to specialise in such things as artic or jungle warfare. The mechanised infantry were equipped with Saxon APC's. As a wheeled vehicle the Saxon was primarily a road vehicle with the ability to be deployed over rough terrain.

Chris Spencer enjoyed all aspects of working with the Airmobile Brigade. Back in his early training days he was fascinated by the Normandy Landings of WWII, especially the glider and parachute landings. As a boy he loved climbing trees, spires and rooftops, anything which gave him clear and unrestricted views. As a junior entry recruit he was taught just how important it was in the past for forces to command the high ground. Such an advantage in part disappeared with modern day warfare's use of air cover, but even with air cover it was basically a question of the advantage of height.

The war in Kuwait/Iraq upset training schedules for many of those involved, and some patterns were changed. To the great joy of both men the upset threw Chris back into the same training schedule as Jimmy Andrews. Wonderfully, for the two friends, they were at times set against one another in training, and the competitive elements of both Sergeant Spencer and Corporal Andrews characters burst to the fore, both pushing their squads just that little bit more in a deeply satisfying friendly rivalry. Jimmy had missed Iraq, but instead brought stories from home which no amount of letter writing could ever have covered. Chris heard a great deal about how his sister and his deeply loved little nephew were doing, how little Charlie was talking, and how much the young lad seemed to love the animals which were to be seen all around them in their little cottage at Slyne.

Chris and Jimmy trained together for three months, and both thoroughly enjoyed the experience, but change was always going to come and in June 1991 Chris Spencer, although remaining at Catterick, transferred to the Saxons of the 19 Mechanised Brigade. He and Jimmy could still socialise, but the training together element was removed. Of all the training Sergeant Spencer received at the hands of the British Army the Mechanised Brigade was to prove to be the area he enjoyed the least, and was mainly due to what he considered the inadequacies of the vehicle involved.

He had seen Saxons before, indeed he had been transported in them during his tours of Northern Ireland, but never liked them. Perhaps, he reasoned, it was because of all the thoughts and emotions they conjured up which related to the sorry state of affairs in that land, but it was also for their lack of flexibility. The Warrior he thought of as a much more flexible tool with its all terrain capabilities, heavier armour, and far better armament when compared with the Saxon's single machine gun for local air defence.

He could understand there were advantages to the Saxon. It was far easier to maintain, with the cost of operation therefore reduced, and it was undeniably much faster when used on roads. As a re-supply vehicle, urban action ambulance or higher speed long distance troop carrier it was fine. If it were kept for the use for which it was originally designed, the longish journeys from Britain to reinforce BAOR, then it would have proved perfect, as it shared many parts and characteristics with commercial trucks. As it was only armoured against shell splinter and small arms fire it would not stand up to any form of anti vehicle weaponry, and Chris could easily remember how the Iraqi APC's disintegrated when hit by cannon fire and could imagine the carnage within if a Saxon was hit whilst carrying its design load of ten men.

As a sergeant he was responsible for the well being of those men, hated to see his men killed and wounded needlessly, and loathed the pain it put their families through. He firmly believed cost cutting in armed conflict did not work, as the proportional cost of additional lives lost was much too high. He had a well defined sense of duty, to his country, family and most definitely for those for whom he was personally responsible – those under his care, command and control – and for those no sacrifice was too great.

Five

The months passed, computer courses followed computer courses, ever more demanding, but never so to Nathan. He broke down one of the computers Sally Brown had given and studied the parts to a level whereby he knew every component piece, where it went and what it did, and could strip and rebuild it blindfolded. He borrowed and bought books and magazines, keenly devouring all the information they possessed. He purchased various component parts and experimented with all he had, increasing the memory and speed of his two working units, one of which he kept at home and one at the garage, and started to experiment, successfully, with programming.

Jake Ferris had instructed him to apply for his provisional driving licence, and this he did as soon as he was seventeen, almost a year earlier. He quickly mastered the basics of moving cars around the forecourt as part of the job, was relaxed around vehicles, and confident in them. However he had not taken any lessons as he didn't see the need. He had the bike with which to get to and from work, could still run the little errands on it, and needed no licence to move the cars whilst on company property. Besides driving lessons cost a lot of money, and that would have seriously detracted from what he had available to spend on computers – and Nathan spent every penny of his disposable income on the machines he had come to love.

In order for the lad to do his work, Jake had allocated him a small room at the rear of the garage in which to keep all of the required shampoos, tools, buffing mops, steam cleaner and of course his bicycle. The room was not very big, smelt strongly of polish and detergent, but was dry with a large fluorescent light and plenty of electrical sockets, into which Nathan plugged his computer and monitor, and then built a very small desk to sit at. He also purchased a second hand printer and set it up on a shelf immediately above the cramped desk. Whilst looking for him one Tuesday morning Jake Ferris stumbled across him in his utility room working on his computer.

"Ah," Jake said, "so this is where you are hiding! What's that you are playing with?"

"I'm sorry," Nathan stammered in reply, "I wasn't playing Jake. I'm waiting for a car to come back, and whilst I was waiting I thought I could update the stock sheets."

"Stock sheets? What stock sheets?" Jake asked.

"I've made up my own programme to cover every item in the shop, and everything to do with all the cars from the moment they arrived at the garage until the time they're sold, then a note of the buyer, the Ministry of Transport test certificate date, when any road fund licence runs out and any suggested maintenance requirements. The shop programme takes into account the stock rotation requirements of products and advised shelf life of anything which has one, purchase prices and sale takings. I've also written a sub program for fuel sales, servicing costs, and another one for my cleaning costs. I've added in staff holidays, what sales were made by whom and a complete sickness record," Nathan had explained slowly and very nervously.

Jake was quite simply flabbergasted. He had never seen anything so comprehensive in his entire life. He had an office full of filling cabinets, record boxes and several stacks of trays, yet all of which combined would still only give him a mere fraction of the information available on this strange looking young lad's computer. There was also the fact it would take him or someone else time to go through his current files to find what he wanted, and time to put them away. From this lad's amazing box he would be able to get all he ever needed, and more, right there and then. It really was incredible.

Never slow on the uptake, Jake Ferris instantly realised it would give him the ability to follow trends, cut waste, reduce duplication of work, and manage the whole business far more efficiently, which meant saving money, and a pound saved was several earned.

"Find someone to cover your work for the rest of the day, and as soon as that is done, come to my office," Jake said before walking off.

Nervously Nathan made his way to Jakes office. He didn't feel he had done anything badly wrong, but he was worried Jake might think he had over-stepped the mark, and pried into things which were not his business. Above all he hoped he wouldn't get fired as he thought the world of Jake and looked up to him almost as the father he had never properly had. He should not have worried. Although Jake was blissfully unaware as to how the younger man viewed him, he could clearly see Nathan had a very great deal to offer, and it would have proved hugely uncharacteristic for him to let any gift get away from him. When Nathan walked into Jakes office he was asked, "Have you sorted out a replacement for yourself for the day?"

"Yes, everything is covered for as long as you need me," Nathan replied shyly, looking at the floor.

"Okay. Then come with me please Nathan. I wish to talk to you," Jake Ferris requested.

Unexpectedly Jake walked from his office to his car and both climbed into his large Mercedes. They dropped down onto Newham Way eastbound, following it out along the Barking Bypass, Ripple Road and on to Thames Gateway. Nathan came from a poor background and his family had never owned a car. In fact he had rarely travelled in one, and certainly never travelled so far before. He sat in silence, wondering where on earth they were going and how long it would take them to get back. Jake merely made small talk as they passed South Ockendon, Stanford le-Hope and Basildon, then skirted the north of Southend-on-Sea. Eventually, nearly an hour later, they pulled into a pub car park at the edge of Great Wakering, overlooking a part of Foulness Island and out over the North Sea. It was the first time the previously sheltered Nathan had ever seen the sea and he felt as if he were almost at the edge of the world.

Jake led Nathan into the pretty lawned beer garden where he found an empty table. He told the lad to sit there whilst he went and ordered and, without asking what he wanted, Jake bought a simple pie and a pint of Courage Best for Nathan. It was early August and Nathan was a month shy of eighteen. He had never before touched alcohol, but he was certainly not about to tell Jake, not that Jake didn't know his age, or suspect it would probably be the poor little devil's first pint. Pies and pints on the table Jake came to the point. On the way out he had subtly probed Nathan, trying to find out more about the younger man without being too obvious, or asking anything directly. He knew about his driving licence, a little about his family background and enough about the way he was forced to live to feel genuinely sorry for the strange looking youngster.

"Alright Nathan", Jake began, "I have two possible proposals for you. Firstly I want you to tell me all you can about computers, and explain to me what you are capable of doing on them. Later I want you to show me what you have told me and, where possible, teach me a little of it. In return, if you agree, I'll pay for all of your driving lessons, pay for your test, and provide you with a car. If I like and understand what you tell me I'll then have something else for you."

Nathan could not believe what he heard. This smart, shrewd and clever man had just offered him hundreds if not thousands of pounds in very real terms just to be told about something which was as easy to him as breathing.

"I couldn't take it from you!" Nathan blurted out. "You've been really good to me, you gave me a job and you bought me a bike, and you've taught me so much. I just couldn't take it. It's much too much! I'll tell you and show you anything I can, but I don't want anything for it, it just wouldn't be right!"

"Nathan – please – let me be the judge of that," Jake Ferris responded. "You tell me what you can, and we'll consider what it's worth afterwards. Okay?"

So Nathan started. He explained what he had done with all the information he had acquired, how he applied it, processed it, what it showed him, how it could be used, how it could be expanded, and how he had done everything in his own time at home, working the problems out on his own home computer and transferring all data on floppies to the computer at work. Jake had caught him uploading his latest figures from a floppy when he entered the store room that morning.

"And you can show me all these things?" Jake asked.

"Oh yes!" Nathan replied, "But that's not anywhere close to the really interesting stuff! The really, really interesting stuff is going to come with the World Wide Web, and what will happen on there will change the world as we know it forever!"

Nathan had been born in 1974, and the year was now 1992.

Jake Ferris knew nothing of the web then, which was hardly surprising as the first successful test had only been carried out a year and a half earlier, on Christmas Day 1990, and very few people in the world knew about it. However, Jake did know enough about people to realise this strange little guy was extremely excited about it, obviously had a passion about computers, and had already shown him something that morning he would not have believed had he not seen it with his own eyes. He asked Nathan to continue, and to tell him what he knew.

This was Nathan's subject and he was in his element, so he started to explain about his hero.

"Timothy Berners-Lee has been working at CERN, that's the European High-

Energy Particle Physics Laboratory in Geneva. Berners-Lee is the English developer who invented the World Wide Web back in March 1989 with the help of a guy born in Belgium, called Robert Cailliau, and the young student staff at CERN. He implemented his invention sending the first successful communication between a client and server via the "Internet" Christmas Day, 1990."

Nathan continued, explaining about media-rich documents known as web pages, and how they could contain formatted text and images. How each web page had a unique address known as a Uniform Resource Locater or 'URL', which allowed a page to link to any other page on the web via hyperlinks, and about the first Web server called HyperText Transfer Protocol 'http'. He explained the first Web site built was at CERN and was first put 'online' on the sixth of August 1991, not quite one year earlier, and how it provided an explanation about what the World Wide Web was, how anyone could own a browser and how to set up a Web server. It was also the world's first Web directory, since Berners-Lee maintained a list of other Web sites apart from his own.

When Nathan came up for air Jake bought them both another pint then asked Nathan to explain where he thought this new communications form would take everyone. He was interested as he could see potential in what Nathan was outlining, just as he had in the fax machine and mobile phone, both of which he owned and used daily, and both of which had rapidly become more sophisticated, particularly his mobile phone. He now had a Motorola which not only no longer needed to be attached to a car, or even a huge battery, but would now fit into a large pocket, and he was sure would eventually get smaller still. He could see how telephone technology had moved on a lot, and understood electronic impulses could carry a lot of information. He still marvelled at how someone could put a printed piece of paper into a fax machine in another part of the country and how it would almost instantaneously print out on another piece of paper on the machine in his office. It would seem if what this young man was enthusing about was actually true, then he would be able to do all sorts of things by using its web.

"So you understand all these things, and can work with such weird and wonderful systems can you?" Jake asked, knowing it would probably always remain well beyond his ability to understand.

"Oh yeah!" Nathan exclaimed. "They're simple, anyone can do it. There's no magic to it. Computers are easy and they do all the work for you so long as you program them properly and ask the right questions! I really don't understand what all the fuss is about that you hear from people with them. There is no need to be scared of them. It would be like being scared of a spanner. They just do what you tell them. Easy!"

"So if I were to put in an extra telephone line to an office at the garage, and bought the latest, highest spec computer, could you make it all work?" Jake asked.

"Of course I could!" Nathan replied. "But you could too. Anyone could. All you have to do is plug everything in! It really is incredibly simple. Anyone can do it Literally anyone at all! There is one other thing though which is worth remembering. All computers are technically obsolete by the time you buy them, something which will continue for years. They are advancing so rapidly with memory size, speed and general spec, as well as ever better programs, that you must be prepared to constantly update if you want to get the best out of what you have. It doesn't mean you constantly have to change the computer itself, but it does mean you have to be prepared to buy the best of the latest technology."

Jake listened with interest. It was clear this young lad loved computers, to the degree he almost seemed to live for them. The flash of inspiration he had had back at the garage was beginning to take on a tangible shape and form. Would it be possible he wondered. The costs were negligible, and if this funny looking, intense and passionate little guy was correct in what he was saying, and there was little reason to doubt it, then this world wide web was going to be something big, and if it was going to be big then the sooner he got involved in it the better. The chances of engaging with a wider audience and the ability to advertise on a much grander level would appear to be almost limitless. In time, with his products, he would be able to reach into the very homes of everyone with a personal computer, and from the comfort of their own living rooms they would be able to view what he had to offer. Never in the history of the world had anyone ever been able to extend so far, and for such a paltry investment.

"Then Nathan," Jake said, "That takes me to my second proposal. Would you be interested in a change of work? Frankly just about anyone can clean a car, but I kind of think no matter how easy you find it, or what you say about it, there are few people out there in the world who will ever know their way around a computer the way you seem to! And if you do, as I suspect, know your way around them as well as it would seem, then you are totally wasted cleaning cars. What I propose is as of tomorrow you come in to work, see me, and we both sit down and thrash out the feasibility and practicalities of what is needed. I will give you both a pay rise and a free hand. Are you interested?"

For Nathan's part he was astounded. Was Jake really offering him a job working with computers? He loved what he did with computers. For him time spent on a computer was a form of escapism. He understood them, they were logical, they were his friends, they were both intellectually stimulating and rewarding, they were never nasty to him and none had ever let him down. He couldn't work with computers. It was just too strange a concept. Work was tedious and boring but had to be done for the money it produced. Computers weren't tedious or boring. Computers were uplifting and enlightening. Was Jake really, seriously, offering him a chance to be paid to do the one thing in the word he loved?

"Jake you wouldn't have to pay me any more!" Nathan spluttered. "The entire thing with the garage – everything – wouldn't take me more than a couple of hours a day and that would be doing much more than I have ever done at home. I could do it and still have plenty of time left over to carry on with other jobs for you!"

"Then it's settled." Jake said. "Tomorrow come to work an hour later, you'll be starting at nine from now on unless I need you earlier, and come directly to my office. We'll sort things out from there! As for now, drink up and let's be going. I better get you back, and I have things to get on with myself."

They drove back in relative silence as both had much on their minds. Jake was going over the possibilities of what Nathan had said regarding how long it would take him each day to sort out everything at the garage. If that was all the time it would take then he may be able to put the young man to use doing the same sort of thing with some of his other business interests, and if such were the case it would save him a small fortune. He had long been conscious of the horrendous duplication of work which went on with his various businesses. If he could reduce it then he would be quids in! Well worth looking at!

Nathan's mind was whirring all the way home. He could not let this man down! He would spend his entire evening researching everything which was currently available, and by the morning, when he went in, he would have all the information about everything which was out there, what it did, how fast it worked and any limitations. He would be ready, and he would have all the facts and figures at his finger tips!

Nathan went into work the following day armed with all the information he would need. Although he had been told to come in for nine o'clock he did in fact arrive at eight as usual. He immediately went to his store room, stripped out his computer, monitor and printer, and generally tidied the room, putting everything in order before he left it. He then took his equipment around to the front office and put it in a corner out of the way.

Bow Creek Garage sold cars, fuel, associated oils and parts, some light refreshments and carried out the odd running repair. Accordingly Jake had never required such a thing as a secretary, let alone a personal assistant. There were two car salesmen, Pete and Dave, who were usually on the premises or working from it, a girl named Sally who controlled the fuel and shop sales, and a guy everyone called Bodger who did small repairs and ran the cars around. Then there was the other young lad, Simon, who had originally shown Nathan to Jake's office and picked him up on his first day. He did the same sort of work as Nathan, but also ran the cars around, and finally Nathan himself. That was the entire complement of full time staff who worked from the Bow Creek pitch. To Nathan's knowledge Jake Ferris owned two other car sales pitches, both with slightly larger forecourts, but neither had the shop or fuel sales. Consequently only two salesmen worked at the smaller of the two premises, and three at the larger. All the cleaning, repairs and paintwork was completed or arranged at Bow Creek, as was all administration with the sole exception of the actual car sales themselves which were undertaken at the other sites.

Jake's second, although largest site, was Great Fields Garage, at Barking. It was set behind fairly imposing railings and consisted of little more than a large flat strip of tarmac with a small office at one end with an outside tap to wash the dust from the cars. Within the office block there was a partitioned off toilet, a small sink, microwave and kettle in one small room, and a slightly larger room containing a desk, four chairs and an electric heater. This was where the car sales took place. The entire site was situated almost directly beneath the Barking Bypass at the junction of River Road. The Great Fields Park, from which the garage derived its name, was directly opposite the pitch on the other side of the roundabout

River Road is the main artery providing access to the areas countless large and small business parks and industrial estates, and the throughput of daily traffic was huge. All vehicles had to slow as they negotiated the roundabout and, as they did so, the full stock of the garage was displayed to every motorist and vehicle occupant. As a consequence the garage thrived. It didn't hurt that the Volunteer At Arms public house was also situated on the roundabout and much business was either completely carried out or at least concluded there. For all types of trade the amount of business done in British pubs is nothing short of astronomical. For some car traders and small dealers pubs provide their very life blood, and the Volley had helped Great Fields Garage for years.

There was no formal arrangement as such for the picking up of paperwork from Great Fields. Anyone dropping a car off there or picking up a 'chopper', a traded in vehicle, would collect any available files and return them to Bow Creek. The only regular collections were made on a Wednesday morning when Jake's part time bookkeeper would pick anything available up on her way into the office at Bow Creek.

Jake Ferris arrived at work thirty minutes earlier than he had indicated to Nathan. It was his intention to get in and clear the main desk and to put away all the files which were lying around before Nathan arrived. This was not because he wanted to hide anything from Nathan, but because he intended the office to appear somewhat more businesslike and to give himself a clear space to work from. Unfortunately, with much on his mind, he had forgotten his bookkeeper would be in, although it would not have changed anything should it have been remembered. During the previous evening and overnight he had given a great deal of consideration as to what was to happen this day, even making several notes, something he very rarely did. However there were questions to ask which were well outside his area of expertise and he did not want to forget things.

He was slightly surprised, although not shocked, to see young Nathan standing in front of his desk as he entered, and noted the lad had brought his own computer and printer into the office already – one thing to tick off his notes. Nathan was holding a folder which seemed to be bulging with brochures and Jake chuckled inwardly to himself thinking the lad must have been busy overnight too. Telling Nathan to pull another chair around to his side of the desk and to take a seat, Jake piled up all the files and paperwork which were strewn across his desk and unceremoniously dumped everything onto a smaller desk, which was the one Dawney always worked from.

Mrs Richardson, Dawney, as she was known to all, lived in a small terraced house backing on to the sports ground at Becontree near Dagenham and, had she not stopped at Great Fields on the way in to work, would have driven directly over the top of it whilst on the flyover. Dawney was an indeterminable late forties divorcee with looks well past their sell by date. She was struggling to pay for her house and, although not a man hater, was fiercely independent and really did not need the problems in her life associated with relationships. She was happy to spend time in the company of men, to chat, to laugh and to joke, sometimes even to have the odd drink with them – but that was definitely where it stopped!

She plodded through her work and could not be hurried, but she was absolutely dependable and one hundred percent reliable. She was there every single Wednesday of the year without fail at nine thirty, and worked without a break until she finished, usually just before five. She had never missed a day since she started the job eight years earlier, unless it fell on Christmas Day, Boxing Day or New Years Day, in which case she worked the Tuesday or Thursday instead. She could not afford holidays, nor did she want them. She worked for Jake one day a week, and for four other people, three of whom had come through Jake, on the other days of the week. Every three years she replaced her car with the best of the 'choppers' Jake had available, and paid him every penny he allowed on the trade in. She did not steal, did not take, and wanted no favours or special treatment. She would pay as she went and that was all there was to it!

Nathan had met Dawney several times during the eleven months he had then been at the garage. Both treated one another politely and courteously, and there it ended. Nathan lacked the skills needed to attract friends, and Dawney would not have responded had he tried.

Dawney was very much a creature of habit, doing things her way and at her pace. She worked to her own timetable and worked to it exactingly, hating any form of change or anything which could upset her established patterns. This particular July morning was bright, warm and sunny. School had broken up for the summer and the traffic coming in was as a consequence particularly light. Britain at its best! She stopped for the paperwork at Great Fields, enjoyed a cup of tea with the sales team, spent ten minutes chatting about their past week, picked up the sales paperwork and documents, and then drove in to work at Bow Creek. The unusually low volume of commuter traffic allowed her to arrive an uncustomary three minutes early, which slightly upset the little clock ticking inside her head. Entering the office she was further confused by what she saw before her. It was not going to be a good day for her timetable or work patterns.

As Dawney walked through the door carrying the files from Great Fields she was staggered to see the amount of work on her desk. Not realising it was not for her, but had just been piled there, she immediately knew she would not be able to clear it all in her allotted time. In a fluster she turned to Jake and said, "Jake, I won't be able to clear all of this on my own today, I'll have to bring my niece in to help next week when I come in. I'll get as much done as I can, but there's simply just too much!"

Jake's mind was on other things. Nathan had long since opened his folder and removed all the brochures, which were spread across the desk in front of the two of them. He had also finished discussing his reasoning about the requirements of a modem and why he preferred a separate external model as opposed to internal, and moved on. He was in the process of explaining why any computer they were to buy should have the new Windows system and how he knew the system would completely overtake MS DOS. Jake was still struggling to understand what a modem was and, without looking up just answered, "Okay Dawney. Just do whatever you need to, it's never a problem – you know that!"

Somewhat comforted Dawney straightened up the pile which had been unceremoniously dumped on her desk and continued with her usual weekly work. Secretly she was somewhat relieved at Jake's easy response. Her niece was due to arrive the following Sunday and would be staying with her for at least the next few weeks, and was coming to London in the hope of finding work. The recession was easing and, as is always the case with a boom and bust economy, what had gone down was now coming back up again. Things were starting to change for the better, and the change was gathering speed.

Dawney's niece was a pleasant girl from a good background. Shortly after Mr. Richardson had swept her off her feet – damn the man to hell – Jane, Dawney's younger sister of two years, met and then married a reasonably prosperous East Midlands based property developing builder. They had gone on to have three kids. The eldest, a daughter they named Sheila, was now married and pregnant. The son, Clive, was at Manchester University on a degree course, and the youngest, Susie, had just finished her 'A' levels and left school. Susie didn't know what she wanted to do, but decided to take a gap year before making any decision and had asked to come and stay with her aunt as a jumping off ground for London and the world.

Susie's father, Phil Gatting, had done well by his family. Through hard work and long hours over time he had successfully built up a small three man jobbing building business into a property developing company which employed some one hundred and forty people directly, and countless sub contracting small builders and tradesmen indirectly. An astute and far-sighted man, he had foreseen what the dramatic effects Chancellor Nigel Lawson's interventions in the housing market and removal of multiple applications for a mortgage on a single property were likely to have. On gut instinct he had sold his entire portfolio of properties only slightly below full market value just before the crash. Six months later he was able to buy back a very similar portfolio for only three fifths of the price. Margaret Thatcher's retirement convinced him to get out of the housing market and into commercial properties in early 1991. The move successfully enabled him to avoid Chancellor Norman Lamont restricting mortgage interest tax relief to the basic rate of income tax later in the year, and that too seemed to have been a sound move.

He acquired what was to become the family home some twenty years earlier, and his son and Susie were both born there. The property was in the quintessential English village of Foxton, on the outskirts of Market Harborough in Leicestershire. Foxton, famous for its set of locks forming a staircase on the Grand Union Canal, is a beautiful village, and had provided a wonderful setting in which to raise their children. All would have lifelong memories of the village and then small town schools, bee keeping in the garden, playing endlessly in the surrounding fields and watching boats slowly climb the picturesque locks. Then of course there was Clive's unstinting attempts to build a homemade go-cart for the annual down hill race on the road closed to all other traffic and of the caring sharing camaraderie of village life, village locals and the patrons of the villages only two pubs. It was a wonderful and idyllic life for the children, in a location which somehow remained untouched by Britain's changing fortunes, bizarre open-door immigration policies and horrendous lowering of educational standards. All three children turned out to be courteous, well adjusted, polite, and well educated young people. A testament indeed to their background and family.

Delightful though the village could be, and as enviable as their upbringing was, the children had grown up and, as with the young of all species, they had wanted to spread their wings and express their independence. Market Harborough offered no escape and had very little by way of industry, so unskilled short term or holiday work did not exist. Nearby Leicester had long since been overrun by the Asian community which swallowed up every non-skilled job going, and was fast devouring the skilled market. Over the county border in Northamptonshire Corby boasted a huge industrial area which continued to grow, but was a singularly unpleasant place to be. Birmingham, further away but still accessible, was similarly blighted – but Aunty Dawn lived to the east of London – and Aunty Dawn had a spare room. Pity she didn't live in Mayfair. That would have been fun!

Whilst Dawney got on with her work Nathan and Jake remained huddled over brochures, discussing the various options and abilities of the various machines available. It did seem to Dawney, who could not help but overhear, the conversation the two were having was a bit one sided, and she was quite surprised to hear Jake, who she secretly always considered to be the most able person she had ever met, so completely out of his depth. It would seem the ugly little cleaner knew his stuff when it came to computers. Well maybe Susie would have someone of her age to talk to if Jake did have the lad in the office, and it certainly sounded as if he meant to.

Nathan and Jake read the brochures, then Nathan switched on his own computer and showed Jake the basics of how it worked, what was loaded onto it and how to get the information out which was stored there. Jake listened and did the things Nathan told him to do. He was fascinated at how much was there, and at how easy it seemed to be to look at the data, but he realised he really didn't have a clue about what he was doing. Certainly he could follow the instructions as Nathan spoke, and he could see this magic box was definitely the way ahead, but as to being able to work it when he was on his own – fat chance! That however was not going to put him off getting one of these fascinating machines. Indeed if anything it was actually encouraging him to buy one. In time he would be able to do the simple things he had just been shown, and in time he would be able to use it himself – a little, but he would never become at one with them as Nathan was.

"Enough of these brochures" Jake said, "Let's go and buy one!"

In November of the previous year a company, called Vision Technology Group Limited, opened a store in Croydon to the south of London which was set up specifically to sell computers and their associated products. There were already smaller shops which specialised in computers, and there was an availability of parts for enthusiasts, especially those who were keen amateur builders, but nothing on the scale of the new PC World had ever been seen in Britain before. Croydon was an hour drive away, but well worth the effort. With Nathan giving advice to Jake which flabbergasted the salesman they eventually came away with an expensive but comprehensive working computer. Nathan suggested the latest technology for everything, and Jake bought an IBM 486SLC, a model which had fortunately been introduced just two weeks earlier. He also insisted it came fitted with the very latest Compact Disc Read Only Memory, a device which was an option but such a new one very few people knew what they were. Additionally Nathan chose twin memory cards, a sound card and a network card, all set up to run through the state of the art software operating system, Microsoft Windows 3.1, which had also only just come on to the market that month but had already totally eclipsed the 3.0 version.

They returned to Bow Creek Garage in the late afternoon, and immediately went about setting up all the equipment which they had purchased. At the time the garage boasted three telephone lines, one of which was dedicated to the fax machine. Neither wished to wait for British Telecom to deign to give them an appointment date, then wait for the linesman to eventually do his job, so Jake decided to sacrifice one of his main lines so he might take a look at this World Wide Web which had Nathan so excited. Both were so focused on their work neither noticed the time passing. When Dawney called out, "Well I'm finished here for the day. I've done some of the work on my desk, but the rest will have to wait until next week. I'll see you then and I'll bring Susie with me", Jake, without looking up or even fully taking in what she had said, merely grunted "Okay Dawney, see you then."

Completely unbeknown to all, for Nathan, life changing piece of luck number three had just dropped into place.

It was late when they left, but neither cared about the time as what they had accomplished during the afternoon and evening proved deeply rewarding to both albeit for different reasons. Jake had watched as the whole computer system came together before his eyes, and it was now set up and functioning on his desk. Nathan networked in his massively upgraded but still vastly outdated 286, and transferred raw data across to the new IBM, which he then was to configure to Windows and set up little icons so Jake could access everything off screen at the click of the mouse. This Jake could follow and do. MS DOS had frightened him, but clicking on a little picture – well he knew he could do that!

The World Wide Web, which people seemed to be calling the Internet, had interested him greatly the day before when the two of them discussed it. He thought he saw great potential for it then, but was completely unprepared for what he found on there, what was available, and just how unbelievably huge it was. It really did span the entire world linking people with computers just like him in places like Watford and Scotland and America and Australia. Australia! The other side of the world! This thing was going to be huge! Huge!

For Nathan it was every bit as exciting, if not more so. He really did feel like the proverbial kid in a sweet shop. He had some experience of the Internet from his training courses, but time had always been limited, he had had tasks to perform, and surfing was not exactly a part of the curriculum. Here he was free to show Jake anything he wished and he thoroughly enjoyed doing so. He too was mightily impressed with the speed of the new setup, which seemed so fast when compared with the machines he was originally given, despite the many little updates he had since carried out on them. Whilst surfing with Jake he checked for sites for their main suppliers, particularly the fuel suppliers, and found what he was looking for as he suspected he probably would. He didn't mention it to Jake at the time as he was only ninety nine point nine percent certain, and he wanted to be the full one hundred percent, but he knew the fuel pumps signalled the till as to the amount of fuel customers drew, and he was positive he could get the same information to record to the computer as well. If he could do so, and he was sure he could, then he would be able to compile the sales into a sub program, and he could then get the program to order fuel as required automatically over the Internet without any human input. To do so would save time, but far more importantly it would save costly mistakes. He would have to look into it, but if it worked with fuel, and there was no logical reason why it should not, then it may well be possible to make it work with almost all the other things they bought in.

The two of them worked together for most of the next week and, as they did so, an understanding started to grow between them. Jake was highly impressed by this ugly little guy's ability, and tried to keep up with and take in what he was being shown, but it was a battle he was rapidly losing. It was not that Nathan was a bad teacher so much as Jake had no head for the concepts involved. If Nathan were working with someone with more natural ability he should have been able to teach them rapidly, but Jake did not have it, and the more he struggled to understand the more he bogged himself down. Nathan on the other hand was impressed by the older man's determination, his willingness to continue with something he was clearly struggling with, but most of all with his overwhelming enthusiasm for the project. He also learned to greatly respect Jake's integrity, which screamed out at him with every completed transaction Nathan saw.

Jake had told Nathan he would pay for his driving lessons, and Nathan knew he would do so. What Nathan had not expected was Jake would also arrange those lessons, and arrange for them during his working time. So not only were his lessons paid for, but he was being paid to learn. Jake had taken the lad under his wing, and Nathan both understood that, and was immensely grateful for it.

The lessons were arranged in two hour blocks twice a week, once on Tuesday mornings and once on Thursday afternoons. Nathan had not received any road experience before the first lesson despite moving a lot of cars around on the pitch, although this in itself was of great help to begin with, as the instructor did not have to go through the basics of clutch, brake and throttle control. The first lesson moved along swiftly around the quieter streets of Upton Park, the lesson ending with Nathan driving all the way back to Bow Creek Garage. Nathan however, despite his confidence on the forecourt, was not a natural born driver. He would learn to drive up to test standard, and he would pass his test, but he would never be able to drive a vehicle in the same cool, relaxed and confident manner Jake did. Jake could hold a proper in depth conversation whilst driving a car at reasonably high speed, in heavily congested traffic, and not miss a thing. Not a single thing! Jake made it look ridiculously easy, and now Nathan realised just how aware a driver had to be behind the wheel, how many things they sometimes had to do at once, and just some of the problems they had to look out for – constantly.

The driving lesson also taught him one other hugely important thing. Throughout his life he had found practical skills difficult to learn, whereas the computer courses he attended had never been about learning at all to him. They were just fun. Jake however seemed to be able to pick up practical skills without the slightest effort, but had difficulty following even the basics of computer skills. The driving lesson taught Nathan how very different people could be.

Apart from the driving lesson, and a couple of appointments Jake attended, the two were almost inseparable for the entire week. They sat and surfed the net together, and Nathan managed to teach Jake a few things which he could now do on his own. They completed the setting up of various programmes which Nathan tailored to their specific needs, and Nathan started to slowly load past information onto the computer in order they would eventually have a full record stretching back over several years. The only thing which slowed the process up was the lack of speed on the keyboard, which meant the job would be stretched out over several months, rather than completing it within just two to three.

The two were sat at the desk together on the Wednesday morning when, at nine thirty precisely, Dawney walked in followed by another much younger woman. The younger woman wasn't particularly tall at about five foot four, but was slim and had a fresh, wholesome look about her. She was dressed casually but neatly in clothes which were obviously chosen to suit her, but with disregard to cost. There was nothing which screamed of affluence about them and no showy designer labels, they just looked good and were obviously not cheap. She was not an outstanding beauty but was on the pretty side of plain with an air of quiet confidence about her. Her hair was very dark and her eyes blue, quick and intelligent. She was not the type to instantly turn heads in a crowd, but then none would recoil from her in horror. All in all a reasonable looking young woman built on a good chassis. But what was she doing here with Dawney? Was she a customer?

"Good morning," said Dawney entering the office, "this is my niece Susie. Susie, this is Jake who we have spoken about, and this is Nathan." Susie stepped forward and shook hands with each of the men in turn as she was introduced. Her hand was warm and dry, and her handshake firm for a girl, especially one of her age and build. "Hello, and pleased to meet you", she said to each as she shook their hands, looking both in the eye as she did so.

A short embarrassed silence followed, which was broken quickly by Dawney. "Susie is here to help me with all the extra work which was piled on my desk last week." she said by way of explanation.

Unusually for him Jake was completely taken aback. "Sorry Dawney, we've been rather tied up with all this," he said, sweeping his arm across the table to indicate the computer and piles of paperwork and files. "Remind me of what was said, would you? I'm afraid I've lost track over the past week and forgotten."

"Well, when I came in last week there was a large pile of files, notes and papers on one side of my desk. I realised there was too much for me to do and told you so, saying I'd need help and would bring my niece in. I did all my normal work, and some of the extra filing, but couldn't finish it all. When I left I reminded you and, well – here's Susie to help." Dawney told him.

Somewhere at the edge of his memory things fell into place as he vaguely began to remember the disjointed conversations of the week before.

"Ah! Yes, of course!" Jake said. "I afraid I didn't listen or understand Dawney. I was concentrating on the new computer and didn't really take in what was being said. The paperwork on your desk was mine. I'd just wanted to make a bit of room so we could both work together at my desk. I've sorted all of that out now myself." He turned to Susie. "I'm sorry Susie. I don't mean to mess you around, and I'll happily pay for your day and any expenses, but I don't know what you can do here."

While this short conversation was going on Nathan had returned to inputting data and information into the computer, at his usual rate.

"Well," said Susie, breaking the awkward silence, "whilst I'm here I could help you with the work you're loading onto that computer."

"Can you type then?" asked Jake.

"Well, I'm not brilliant, just around seventy words a minute or so, but I know my way around computers, and can input a whole lot faster than Nathan is doing." Susie said looking in Nathan's direction. "Sorry I don't mean to offend. It's just we were taught all that at school from about twelve years old on, and my father always had me help him with his letters and anything he didn't want anyone else at work to see. So I've typed quite a lot since I was a kid, worked spread sheets, and we have Microsoft Works and Word on the computer at home. I did an awful lot of my 'A' level work on it, so if you want some typing done, I can do it!"

"That's fine with me." Jake said, then called across to Nathan "Nathan, do you mind having some help with the typing?"

"No, not at all," replied Nathan, who understood his own limitations with a keyboard.

So it was settled. Dawney got on with her normal weekly work, Jake left the office to a prearranged appointment, and Nathan and Susie sat down at the desk to continue loading past files into the various sub systems. Nathan was forced to sit close beside Susie, which he found very testing. It had always been difficult for him around girls. He was fully aware of his own looks and knew he was no towering intellect. He had never once been able to make any of the girls he had ever met laugh, knew no one liners which he had any chance of delivering, and chat up lines were as alien to him as the surface of Venus. From his school days he remembered the girls would rather sit on a wall topped with broken glass in the rain than sit within twenty feet of him in class. At the best of times he enjoyed very little self confidence, with girls it was an absolute zero.

Susie however came to his aid. "This computer is amazing!" she said. "The one Dad has at home is really good, and has some neat programmes, but this one is ace! I've never seen some of these programmes before. Whoever wrote these for you really knows their stuff. You must have paid out an absolute fortune for them. I started with MS-DOS, and Dad upgraded to Windows as soon as it hit the market. Cutting and pasting can save so much time, but you have shortcuts within these programmes which are simply brilliant. I really haven't seen anything like it! Working with this will be a breeze! You'll have to tell me who did these programmes and I'll tell Dad. He would have all of this on every computer he has tomorrow if he could – this is unreal!"

Nathan didn't know how to react. Everybody likes a compliment about their work, and this girl was obviously genuine in her regard for his, especially so as she didn't know it was his. Furthermore she hadn't flinched away from him or called him names. On top of which she smelt good and spoke well, just like the ladies on the television news, and none of these things was Nathan used to.

"Well I made them up myself." Nathan mumbled, looking down at his hands.

"You're joking!" Susie said. "These things are wizard. These are the sort of thing Bill Gate's team turn out and make hundreds of millions of dollars with! You didn't really do them yourself did you? You're kidding me – right?"

By now Nathan was really flustered. "Well some of the programmes are basic off the shelf products, but they were too general and didn't fit our application properly. I just altered them to make them fit. It's easy. You just have to get inside the program itself and chop, alter and add bits. It doesn't take any time at all if you think about it right," he stammered out quietly.

Susie found this fascinating. Was this poor ugly little guy for real? Had he really done this himself? Had he, in a few days, managed to get into programmes that teams of highly trained, enormously well paid professional engineers had spent months and years developing? And had he really done it from this desk in an East London garage? If he had he was a man of incredible talent, gifted beyond belief. No! No, it just wasn't possible! She was the new girl and he was setting her up. Still, two could play at that game. She would wait for the opportunity and she would test him. Something would come up as they sat there inputting information.

The morning passed quickly and the amount being stored on the computer grew rapidly. There was no doubt about her typing skills, or her working knowledge of a computer. By midday Nathan could see the pair of them had loaded more information than he had expected to get done in two days and they had been at it for less than two and a half hours. In addition everything was fully backed up on floppies and labelled in Suzie's neat clearly legible handwriting. So far it was a good job well done, and Nathan knew Jake would be very happy with what they have accomplished in so short a period.

At twelve-thirty they decided to take thirty minutes off to give their eyes a rest and to get a bite to eat. Susie asked what Nathan usually did, and was horrified by his reply that he usually just bought a pasty from the garage shop and heated it in the microwave.

"What, don't you have any shops or supermarkets near here?" she asked.

"Well yes, there's a supermarket about five minutes walk away." Nathan replied. "But what do you want to get there?"

Susie didn't answer directly. "Do you have clean plates, knives and forks here, and does the supermarket have a deli counter?"

"We've got plates, knives and forks, and I can make sure they are clean. There is a deli counter, but I wouldn't know what they sell there. I've never eaten any of that sort of stuff before. I don't know what it is." Nathan replied.

"Well that's about to change then Buster!" Susie stated. "You cannot live off pasties. They are full of fat and yucky muck. They'll kill you if you have too many of them! I'll go and get some proper food whilst you get the cutlery and crockery cleaned. Clean for the three of us because I'll get Aunty Dawney something too!"

Nathan cleaned everything as he was told but Susie had still not returned by the time he finished so he went back to the computer. He had previously written up a little program for the fuel in line with what he felt was needed. It seemed to be working as the first on-line order had gone through on Monday and a fuel load arrived the previous afternoon. The talk of pasties had made him think about the program. He wanted to use it to include other products within the shop, and had searched around on the net to see which suppliers he could actually work with. He was happy to have found several and intended to see what could be done to include them in a separate but similar program.

Well he had time on his hands, so he started. He took the fuel program he had created across to the other computer and copied it there, then stripped away all of the fuel content and broke it down until it was void of all records. From there he started to rebuild it with the program set to look for till activity. All till takings would then be monitored from the computer through the network lead which was already set up. The buttons on the till were generally single product specific. There were general buttons which covered more than one item, but these were under sub headings on the till and priced differently to one another, so could be picked up upon with the program. All the information the program then gleaned could be amalgamated into an order for the relevant supplier and, if they too were on-line, could be ordered directly as with the fuel. The system would work and was foolproof at the garage end as long as the till was operated correctly, and the program would soon show if it wasn't. Those suppliers who were not on-line could be ordered from directly using the information from the same program, which he set to print out all requirements at four every afternoon Monday to Friday. It was a simple thing for him to do and he had it almost finished by the time Susie returned from the shops.

Susie came in with a bag full of groceries, and started to pile them up on the edge of the desk. First out of the bag were a number of clear plastic tubs, full of items Nathan didn't recognise. Then there were plastic wrapped packages of what could only be sliced meats and wedges of cheese, followed by fresh salad produce, two white plastic containers and a container of cranberry juice.

"It's a pity we're so short of time." Susie said. "There are some really lovely scrummy things around there, and it's particularly well stocked. How on Earth can you eat pasties when you have that on your doorstep Nathan?" she asked as she set about spooning things out of the various containers. "Is there anything there you don't like? The meats I have are pastrami, green pepper salami and honey roast ham. The cheeses are Blue Brie, Havarti and some Mild Cheddar. I've got prawn coleslaw and three cheese coleslaw, mushrooms a la Grec, stuffed olives, cherry tomatoes, little gem lettuce and watercress. There is also a tub of cottage cheese with pineapple and another of taramosalata. I thought to get a bottle of wine – but we are working and Aunty Dawney has to drive, so I got cranberry juice instead. So, tell me – what are your favourites and what do you hate?"

Nathan didn't know what to say. With the sole exception of the mild cheddar he had not the faintest idea of what anything was, but now was really not the time to let anyone know such a thing. He would eat what he was given and swallow it no matter what it was, how badly it tasted or what it looked like!

"Oh, not at all! All of it looks great to me! I'll eat whatever you would like to dish up. There is nothing I can think of I don't like." the poor lad managed to stutter.

"That's great then." said Susie "I'll just dish out a bit of everything onto each plate. If you are hungry there is plenty of it, so help yourself to more if you like."

Nathan knew he wasn't going to enjoy this, but there was little he could do but eat what was there. It didn't look anything like food to him. It certainly didn't look like the mince pie chips and peas or sausage chips and beans he got at home, or the really exotic curry stuff which came out of a can his mother had once served up because her boyfriend at the time liked it. That had been nice, but he had never seen it again. It was far too expensive his mother had explained, and she couldn't afford it since cigarettes had gone up in the budget. This was going to be dreadful – he just hoped it didn't make him sick. It didn't even smell right, and there was no salt and vinegar. He would have to leave the cheddar to last, even though he wanted to gobble it up straight away. That way at least he would have something to take the dreadful tastes out of his mouth.

Susie plated the food for the three of them. She washed the lettuce and cherry tomatoes off under the tap and shook them dry into the sink. She served the leaves with the stalks towards the centre of the plate, placed the cherry tomatoes on top and then and dolloped taramosalata over both. All the other items she put onto the plates she kept separated. "I'm sorry," she said, "I'm afraid I've served it the way I like it. I love taramosalata as a salad dressing! There's nothing better."

At least Dawney knew what she was eating. In the summer such salads were common at the lunch table of her sister's home. What she had before her was a far reach from her normal diet, but it was a most welcome and pleasant change, even more so to have it bought, plated and presented to her. She liked her young niece. Nathan liked her too, but he really did not want to embarrass himself in front of her or Dawney, and Dawney seemed most pleased with what was in front of her. He would try so hard to eat it and not be sick.

The worst things seemed to be those funny looking mushrooms. They were very small and round and looked completely out of place in that weird sauce with no fried egg or bacon next to them or baked beans over the top. Next to the mushrooms were round green things with red stuff in the middle. They couldn't be right. They looked the size and shape of the gravel a man down the road had on his driveway, and he wondered if they were there as some form of decoration like the plastic things on a fancy cake. He decided to take a huge risk and, preparing himself as best he could, he lifted a mushroom to his mouth.

His first taste was tentative and cautious. His second far less so. By the time he had finish his plate the last thing he wanted was the small slice of cheddar. What he wanted, and helped himself to, was more of all these wonderful tastes and textures which hitherto he had never known. The food was exquisite, the tastes delicious and the smells divine. In all his life he had never even dreamt foods like this existed – and all he had eaten was a simple salad.

The thirty minutes they intended to stop for drifted past the hour. Guiltily they all realised they were neglecting their work, despite the fact Nathan and Dawney had continued working until Susie returned with the shopping. Within five minutes of being back at the desk Susie realised something was wrong. Something had changed. Something was not as it was earlier. The program had altered! Something was affecting the way the information from the shop was being stored, and that something had not been there before she went to the shops. So what on Earth could have done such a thing she asked herself?

"Nathan, this program is not responding the same way as it was earlier. There seems to be a wholly separate shop sub program in place which wasn't there before, but I know that's not possible. So what is it? What can be causing it?" she asked.

"Sorry Susie, I didn't mean to cause you problems!" Nathan replied "It's just I rewrote a sub program for the shop whilst you were at the supermarket. It was something I had meant to do some time later, but with your help here today I had plenty of time to do it now."

"Nathan, I was gone for under forty minutes. It simply is not possible for anyone to do something like that in the time." Susie argued.

“Well I didn’t have to start from scratch Susie.” Nathan retorted. “I already had a model to work from with the fuel routine. That took me a little longer when I originally did it, but once it was done I can just piggyback anything else along with it. That’s what I did, but I also stripped out the whole of the fuel input so if there are teething problems it will not affect the fuel reordering. It’s quite simple really. Nothing to get excited about”

Jake returned a little after four in the afternoon. There were a total of sixteen filing cabinets spread throughout the office space, although two contained the various bits and pieces, parts and paraphernalia associated with running the garage. That left fourteen four drawer cabinets which held all the paper records of Jake’s mini garage empire, along with many files and folders relating to his various other interests. Although Dawney knew everything he was involved in she never spoke of it. Nor did Jake. This was not because of any wish for secrecy on his part, but more to do with the way he compartmentalised his mind. When he was at Bow Creek he had Bow Creek problems at the forefront of his thoughts. When at Great Fields he considered their needs and concerns, and so on throughout his various business interests. It was just the way he worked and it gave him a chance to concentrate and put all of his energies into the task at hand.

Nathan previously had no idea how much Jake was into. He knew of a couple of shops, and of a house and flat or two, but working in Jakes office with not just permission, but with full encouragement to get actively involved with the files, opened his eyes to just what a successful man Jake Ferris really was. Dawney looked after the paperwork for the three garages which virtually filled her one day a week with Jake. If she had time left over, or if the car sales were slow, then she would fall back on other things from other enterprises, although she never got involved in the books of Jake’s other business interests. Other people did those, after which an independent accounts partnership took all his books from his various companies and prepared a full set of accounts for each business.

The cabinets were filled with cash analysis books, spreadsheets, VAT returns, end of year accounts, letters, receipts, all manner of historical files, active files, motor vehicle records, company car and van records, shop records and, it seemed to Nathan, just about every piece of paper Jake had collected in years of business. It was also clearly evident he must have many other caches of filing cabinets such as this in other buildings. With Susie’s help the two managed to clear an awful lot more than he could possibly have done on his own. Nathan thought his earlier estimate regarding the amount of work they were clearing was about right. The two of them working together were clearing what to him would have been a day’s work in under an hour. They had got into a pattern in the afternoon and the pace at which they were working had actually increased.

When Jake returned to the office he was immediately impressed with the amount of work they had cleared. It was obvious from the stack of files on the floor they had waded through at least two full drawers, recording and cataloguing as they went. This was much more than he’d expected. Whilst appearing to look at something on Dawney’s desk he secretly studied the two young people and was pleasantly surprised by how well they seemed to be able to work with one another in less than a day. He was already aware of what he had found with Nathan, but had previously never even heard of Susie, let alone met her. He had been out of the office almost since the time she arrived and had intended to return, pay her handsomely for messing her about, mainly so as not to offend Dawney, but to let her down lightly by explaining about the earlier misunderstanding with her aunt, and let her go.

As he watched the couple he was struck by her quiet confidence and her undoubted ability. Not a stunning looker he thought to himself, but she's a bright little thing. If she were interested I could pair the two of them up and put them to work all over town if they work that well together.

"Susie," he said, "I need to talk to you about the misunderstanding with Dawney."

"Oh, don't worry, I understand," Susie said, looking up from the screen. "I'll find something, I know. It's a shame though because I can see you need loads doing here, and it would have been fun to work with this computer genius you have!" She smiled and nodded in Nathan's direction.

Nathan didn't know what to make of that and instantly coloured up.

"No, that's not exactly what I meant," Jake said grinning. "What I wanted to do was talk to you about a job. The only thing is I don't know what it is you want to do, what time you have available or what sort of money you would ask for your time. To be perfectly honest with you I haven't even thought it through yet myself, but seeing the way you work I would be foolish to lose you if you are available!"

"Oh I see. Well that's a shock." Susie chuckled. "Now it's my turn to be honest I guess. I don't really know what I want. I would like to travel a bit and to see a bit more of this old world of ours. I think in time I might like to go to Uni, but I'm not sure on that one yet. The jury is still out. For the here and now I would like to find a job to give myself experience in the world of work which isn't tied to my family. Not that I don't love my family, it's just I want to do something I've done on my own. So I guess what would be really cool would be to find a full time job which will last several months at least, if my aunt will put up with me, which pays me enough to live on and still have a bit of fun, whilst also giving me enough extra to save so I can travel. Simple really, but where am I going to find one of those?" She laughed again.

"Well in that case, and to be perfectly frank, I think you just have!" Jake said. "There is work here which will keep you and Nathan going for weeks, if not longer. Then, if Nathan gets to pass his test, the pair of you can take one of the cars and go and do the same thing with some of my other interests. There ought to be plenty to keep you going for as long as you wish to stay. The only problem may be for you to get to and from work here without Dawney."

"Hey brilliant!" Susie exclaimed. "I'll take it. That'll be wicked! And you don't have to worry about me getting to and from work, or about Nathan and me getting around because I have my own car. Dad gave it to me for my seventeenth birthday and I passed my test three weeks later. A year ago now. You must remember I come from a little village. You have to drive to survive there! So no probs!"

Jake and Susie negotiated over payment, although it was a bit of a bizarre negotiation. Jake had a figure he would have liked to pay in mind, and Susie asked for considerably less. Jake insisted on fifty pounds a week more than she indicated she wanted which was still less than he was prepared pay. Both remained very happy with the outcome. Jake had earned a lot of money in his time. He understood the need for good people, and understood you kept good people by rewarding them. Besides he had a gut feeling this little girl was going to save him an enormous amount of money in time and it had been a very long time since his gut had let him down.

Nathan's second driving lesson was the following day, and Susie had only arrived at Dawney's the previous Monday afternoon. It was therefore agreed she would start properly at nine o'clock the following Monday, which would give her enough time to settle in at her aunts, who was thrilled at the prospect of several months of her favourite niece's company, and give her a chance to get accustomed to the area in which she would be living.

Susie arrived thirty-five minutes early on the Monday, mainly because she was nervous of the London traffic, and could not yet calculate how long it would take her to get to places. She was a reasonably accomplished driver for her tender years, had frequently negotiated her way around the centre of Leicester, and twice driven up to Manchester from Market Harborough to see her brother. Driving itself did not bother her, nor did the congestion, but she had been brought up to be punctual so started earlier than she needed, despite her aunts advice, just to make sure she wasn't late.

Nathan cycled in for eight-thirty. He was always early, as there was nothing at all to keep him at home, and lots of reasons to be at work. The two of them were working away quite happily, with files already beginning to pile up around them, when Jake walked in.

The days went by, the driving lessons came and went, the files were entered, catalogued and piled up. Two weeks had passed when Susie found out it was Nathan's eighteenth birthday the following week, and that nothing at all was planned for him. She was exactly seven weeks older than him, but a gulf of education, upbringing and financial backgrounds separated them. Her eighteenth had been simply marvellous. She had had a massive house party with a stage built within a marquee in an adjoining field, a live band, hog roast, barbeque and fireworks. The local village had turned out and friends and family arrived from all over the country. There were childhood friends, past teachers, and people from her father's company she knew or had worked with. All in all, it was calculated over five hundred people attended for what turned into thirty plus hours of celebrations and revelry. Phil Gatting proved unstinting in his planning of his youngest daughters coming of age party, and his pockets were deep. He wanted all his guests to have a good time, which all did, but most of all he wanted his daughter to have a time of celebrations she would never forget for the rest of her days, and in that he overwhelmingly succeeded.

Susie fully realised no two people were ever born equal, and she had certainly enjoyed a privileged upbringing. Disregarding his corporate wealth, her father's personal fortune stood at well over fifty million pounds, yet he had never lost his common touch. Despite his prosperity he had brought his children up to care about others and, wherever possible, never to hurt anyone either physically or financially. It spoke volumes of the man's convictions that he had always steadfastly refused to put any of his children into private schools. It was true they had gone to good state schools, and for them the system had not failed them because her parents had chosen an area of the country which offered a standard above the norm, but they were still state schools none the less.

Her father still remained in business rather than retiring because he wanted to steer the company he'd created his way. He'd done exceptionally well by reading the market and then reacting both rapidly and appropriately. Certainly he had profited by problems in the market, but they were never problems he created, just ones he had foreseen and reacted to. He had always bought at the market rate and often sold beneath it, reasoning it was always good policy to leave something in it for others as they would always want to come back and do business again. He had a good board of directors and an experienced, hand-picked management team of very capable people. All worked well both with him and beneath him. However his refusal to stand down was based on the fear that once he was out of the driving seat those in charge may well become consumed by greed.

Throughout the rise of his company Phil Gatting had seen others in the same line who successfully grew their businesses repeatedly make what he considered to be the same mistake. They got greedy – and their greed always squeezed and eventually hurt the little man. He had never forgotten his youth, his time on the tools, when most things were done manually. Long hard hours of manual labour, sometimes working in driving rain and many times working in the bitter cold. Always hard. Unrelenting and unforgiving. Day after day. Over time he worked his way up out of it, considering himself one of the lucky ones, but for every one of him there were thousands of others who never made it. Those who didn't still had the need to feed their families, pay their rent or mortgage, fuel their vehicles, cloth their kids, even buy the tools they required to do their job – the very tools of their trade. Others were the small jobbing builders as his own father once was, employing just one or two men.

His father had always remained sensible and kept his own work, a porch here, a small extension there, always doing a good job which kept the work coming in through personal recommendation. It had worked for him, although he never made real money, and died at sixty-one literally worked to death. Others had taken what seemed to be the easier option and worked for the bigger companies, those growing their businesses. They were always the first to suffer the consequences of a downturn in any market, or if a greedy developer overreached himself and went bust, as so many had along the way. It was always the subbies who got hurt, and they passed the pain down to any staff they may have.

Gatting was never able to understand the greed factor. His father's greatest legacy had not been the passing on of the tiny family business, but much more that which he had instilled into his son over the years. Honesty, reliability and a sense of fair play were what old Dave Gatting had always been about. A deeply honourable man he passed his ideals on to his son and, in turn, he then passed them on to his children. His children learnt the lessons well. He had been lucky with them. They were all bright kids, all with a sense of independence, and none of them expected anything from life they could not get for themselves. Sheila had married well. With luck Clive would come back from Manchester and take up the reins of the company, although the decision must be his choice, but until it happened he would continue to run the company himself. Never in his lifetime would he allow his board or managers the chance to become greedy wolves and turn on all those little people who had helped to make his company what it was.

Susie loved and admired her father beyond measure. As she had grown she had been a daddy's girl, growing through adolescence into a girl who saw her father as some kind of hero. She was past such a stage now but as a young woman she could see him for the hard working fair minded idealist he was. She was the youngest and knew in many ways she was the favourite, not that her father would ever show it, and probably didn't even realise himself. It had always been the joke of her siblings as they all grew up, if any had wanted something done, really, really wanted it – get Susie to ask Dad. It had never been resented, and never would be, it was just she was the youngest – and the darling of the family.

So Susie's coming of age party proved to be a wonderful event, and she had loved every minute of it, but Nathan was going to experience precisely nothing. His eighteenth was going to slip by unannounced and unmarked, forgotten by even his mother. He was not going to go anywhere, do anything, or see anyone, and he hadn't even mentioned it at work. If she had not been inputting personal data relating to the staff she would have been completely unaware of it herself. But she had found it, she had seen it, she had noted it, and by God she was going to make sure he was going to get a party to remember – or her name was not Susie Gatting!

Those of Susie's generation and educational background usually saw the world in terms of black and white. Everything was crystal clear. There were no greys, no if's, but's or maybe's. It was right or it was wrong, it was up or it was down, it was wet or it was dry. Their sense of justice reigned supreme. Most of those she knew were passionate defenders of the very essence of the spirit of mankind, and Susie Gatting had her passions honed to a knife edge by her age, hormones and family background. Old Dave Gatting would have been immensely proud of his young granddaughter had he had the chance to know her.

To Susie there was no question as to whether Nathan's background made the situation different in any way. He was a fellow human being on the journey through life, and fate had determined the two of them should tread the same path at the same time. Therefore as fellow travellers they had a duty one to the other. Susie cared about everyone and everything, and hated to see any form of suffering, real or perceived. The situation with Nathan was clearly, blatantly and horrendously wrong – and she was not going to let it happen!

The first person she approached was Jake Ferris. She explained the situation as she saw it, and asked for his help. Nathan had no friends. He had workmates, but his quiet, shy, retiring one tracked nature had never attracted friends. Susie was probably the first true friend he had ever had, and he had only known her for three weeks. Susie was adamant – they had to do something for Nathan's birthday, and they had to do it without his knowledge. Jake liked this girl. He had liked her the first day he met her. He liked her still more the first day she started work properly for him when he had come into the office and found her already at work with Nathan, and his liking for her had grown as the days went by. She worked hard, was incredibly accurate in her work, possessed an outgoing caring sharing almost cheeky character and real fire in her belly. His only regret in taking her on was he had not found her and Nathan years earlier, but then they would have been far too young he thought with a wry smile. The two worked wonderfully well and tirelessly together, and at an amazing rate. He firmly believed in the old adage 'Good staff make you, bad staff break you', and these two were by far and away the very best staff of their kind he had ever known.

He also liked young Nathan very much indeed. Nathan would not have known it but Jake had watched him grow as a person over the last year. Shirley James really was an excellent judge of a person he had thought on many occasions since the boy who had been Nathan started for him. Nathan worked hard in every job he was given, and the fact had not gone unnoticed. Nathan himself did not see it but he was growing as a person. He'd accumulated a working knowledge of the way things were done along the way, kept his head down and not caused any problems. He always responded well to others when asked for help, and this was something which was appreciated by all.

Slowly, unrecognised by him, the first green shoots of confidence started to show through in the boy, and he was gradually becoming more outgoing. Without question Susie was the catalyst of much greater change. In the past three weeks the lad had become immensely more outgoing. In fact his very appearance had changed. His sallow almost grey skin was taking on some colour, and the flesh around his cheeks was filling out, which helped to improve his ill-favoured looks. This, without doubt, was as a direct result of his diet which Susie had successfully altered. Apparently one salad lunch had changed his diet forever. On the day Susie started she had taken Nathan to the shops at lunchtime and gone through a list of foods for him, and the lad certainly looked healthier and better for it.

Jake heard Susie out and, without a moment's hesitation, not only agreed to help but insisted on financing the whole event. It could never be as lavish as Susie's but Nathan would have a birthday to remember. Jake organised the event to be held in a nightclub all could get to. It was easy for him to do so as he owned the club. He also arranged taxis both to and from the venue for everyone, all at his cost, but then he owned the taxi company too. Secretly every member of staff from all three garages was invited with their families. None were exactly coerced into going, in fact almost all agreed immediately, but none were left in any doubt as to the fact Jake would very much like to see them there, and to keep the secret from getting back to Nathan.

Fortuitously Nathan's birthday fell on a Friday, just as Susie's had seven weeks earlier. The day passed without incident or mention of the party. Using her womanly wiles, and diet and foodstuffs as the subject, Susie had managed to get Nathan to reveal his measurements to her. She used the information to do what girls do best, and had gone shopping for him. At five minutes to five on the afternoon she went out to her car and returned with his present. The shirt, tie, socks, boxer shorts, shoes and suit cost her every spare penny she had earned since she coming to London and she would happily have spent ten times the amount. Nathan was told to change into the new clothes and she would wait outside whilst he did so. He was to come out and show her how he looked when he was done.

Nathan was shocked to the quick by the present. He had not mentioned his birthday. His birthdays were non events and had never been celebrated or marked in any way. He didn't know how she could have possible found out about it, but was far too tongue tied to argue with her, so just nodded dumbly and watched her walk out the door. He changed, more than a little self consciously in the office, and as he did so he realised both how well the clothes he had been given fitted, and the quality of the materials. The pale grey tie and navy boxers were silk, and he had never worn silk before. He had never even actually touched silk before, let alone worn it! The white cotton shirt had a button down collar and the socks were black as were the classic brogues. The dark grey pinstriped woollen suit fitted him like a glove. Clothes such as these were completely outside his life experience. Not only had he never owned such things but he had never so much as tried them on. What would have been the point? Things like this were not designed or made for people like him! They were made for important people. For people who mattered.

He finished dressing. He made a mess of the tie the first few times as it was many years since he had been show how to tie one and it was never a requirement of his school. Eventually he mastered it, to a degree, straightened himself up and walked out the door to find Susie. Somewhat ill at ease he opened the door and stepped out of the office into the bright light of the forecourt. Blinking in the sunlight he did not notice them at first. In fact it wasn't until many voices started with "Happy Birthday to you" that he clearly saw how many people were assembled on the forecourt. Susie and Jake stood at the middle and slightly to the front of the group. Besides and behind them were Sally and her boyfriend, Pete, Dave, and Bodger, their wives and Simon and his girlfriend. Dawney was there, as were the salesmen from both other pitches, and their respective wives or girlfriends. Collectively over twenty people stood there, singing to him, smiling and clapping.

He stood frozen to the spot, caught like a rabbit in a car's headlights. His jaw dropped and his eyes widened. What on earth were these people doing? Susie sensed his discomfort, stepped forward and taking both his hands in hers, leaned forward and kissed him on the cheek.

"Happy birthday Nathan!" she whispered in his ear, and Nathan flushed. "We are all of us off to your party now. The taxis are ready, so come along."

Nathan followed her like an obedient puppy. He didn't know what else to do. He certainly didn't have the first idea of what to say.

The night was a terrific success. Jake had invited along several people from his other enterprises which he though both Nathan and Susie ought to meet in an informal manner before they went to work at their respective businesses. Work at the garage was running down. During the previous three weeks Nathan and Susie had gone through most of the filing cabinets and greatly reduced the amount of paperwork held. A great number of the records were now on the computer and backed up with non relevant paper copies destroyed. The exercise also provided a great opportunity to get rid of everything which was out of date or no longer needed, and the once bulging filing cabinets were reduced in number to three, the third a long way from full. All the empty cabinets were removed from the office to the back of the garage under a tarpaulin, and the two which were filled with general paraphernalia were placed in the store Nathan previously occupied. As each cabinet left the office the room seemed to grow in size, and what once seemed reasonably cramped now felt quite large, certainly large enough for another desk. Jake was mightily impressed with the job, and wanted it repeated in every business he controlled, and therefore used the opportunity of the party to both swell numbers and to successfully introduce people.

The night wore on. Susie had personally delivered an envelope contaning an invitation and twenty five pounds for her taxi money that morning to Nathan's mother after he left for work. She failed to turn up, as expected, and Nathan was never told. The drink flowed, and food was provided. Everyone present made sure Nathan had a drink, which ultimately proved more than his system could handle. He got drunk. As he did the inhibitions and barriers which had so long been around him started to slide away, and so he was in a far less reserved frame of mind than usual when Susie approached him and asked him to dance with her.

In a sober state he would have turned her down instantly, but in his intoxicated and jubilant mood he was more than willing to try yet something else new. He was a dreadful dancer! He had no ear for music and no sense of rhythm, and his moves resembled the mating dance of a one legged kangaroo. Had he not known everyone there and had they not wished to avoid offending him he would have brought the house down, as to most it was one of the most bizarre and amusing things they had ever seen on a dance floor. Somewhat embarrassed Susie took his hand, led him off the floor and found a seat at a quiet table.

A few weeks previously, when Nathan and Jake had driven off for a quiet conversation, Nathan had enjoyed his first pint. The second one had left him feeling very slightly tipsy. He had long since lost count of how many he had drunk at the party. The alcohol surging around his system gave him a sense of courage which was not normally his own. Still holding her hand he leant over and kissed Susie on the cheek. She didn't resist or try to pull away, but just turned her head to him and asked, "Well, what was that for?"

"Oh Susie", he slurred, "you're such a great person. You are so smart and pretty, and you're so, so kind. Nobody has ever been as kind to me as you have with this party tonight!" Then he dropped the bombshell which would eventually change both of their lives. "And nobody has ever kissed me before, or let me kiss them!"

"You silly thing," Susie said, "of course people have kissed you before. Your mum and dad, your grandparents, and you must have kissed a few girls at school."

"No," replied Nathan looking at the floor, "in all my life no one ever has. You were the first one this afternoon at the garage, and you were the first person I ever kissed just now."

He had a look of such overwhelming sincerity Susie just knew he was speaking the truth. Her heart went out to this poor, wretched, pitiful boy, and the tragedy his life had been. She too had been drinking, but it was her nature not the alcohol which made her react. She flung her arms around his neck and, burying her head on his shoulder sobbed her heart out for him, and a very special connection was forged between them as her tears fell.

Their work at the garage drew to a close. Although Jake wanted them to carry on with all the other business interests he had, and there were some fourteen of them, he realised it would be impractical for them to try and load everything onto the computer at Bow Creek Garage, so he asked Nathan's advice. The obvious answer, he was told, would be to set up a smaller cheaper computer at each company, teach someone there to use it as they went, and link up for downloads over the internet, but it would depend greatly on how much money he wished to spend on the project. Jake followed Nathan's advice, and Nathan and Susie moved swiftly through the various businesses.

Ten months had passed since Susie had come to work at Bow Creek, and almost all of the work was by then completed. Nathan finally passed his driving test at the third attempt and Jake presented him with a small Volkswagen Polo 1300 hatchback. During the previous nine months Nathan and Susie had seen much of one another socially, and they got along together very well as their friendship grew. However Susie had always harboured the wish to travel and it was a bug within her which could not be suppressed. She saved as much as she reasonably could whilst working until finally there was enough to do what she wanted.

It was with heavy hearts for both that they parted. Each was genuinely deeply fond of the other, but neither was yet nineteen, far too young to even think of commitment let alone talk of it. So it was in late August 1993 Susie Gatting along with an old school friend, Jenny Palmer, left the greying skies of southern England for the much bluer skies of New South Wales, Australia, not to return until September 1994.

Six

Jim Martin was not a pervert – he was exactly what he said he was. It had taken five weeks for Tammy Hunter to progress from the chance meeting to having her picture in the first magazine. The magazine was to most a small circulation rag, but it didn't matter, she was featured and had something to show by way of a portfolio. Life did not change for her overnight as it is said to do for some. For her it was more of a natural progression, a small photo shoot here, then a slightly larger one there, always gathering a degree of momentum. At seventeen, with school behind her, the pace increased, as did her popularity. She was never going to be a catwalk model, and had no dreams of being a supermodel, as she realised her breasts and bum were too big, and she had no intention of following the constant diarrhoea route of some of the silly girls she met along the way with their half a bottle a day constipation tablet habit.

She was offered glamour model work, but always turned it down. Not because she was in any way ashamed of her body, or because she could not handle the idea of her own public nudity, but because she loved her family and knew such a thing would create problems at home and embarrassment for them, and that she did not want.

Despite the fact she wouldn't get naked on film she remained in much demand, especially for swimwear and lingerie shoots. It was whilst on location outside Takamaka in the Seychelles, the January before her eighteenth birthday, that she finally had a full on sexual experience. Her life had been a bit of a whirl since the time she met Jim Martin, and she had not found the time, or in fact the inclination, to find a boyfriend. She had already met Sean Hall on a couple of shoots and appreciated he knew his stuff about photography, and she trusted his judgment the other side of the camera. He was an easy going open sort of a guy with a wide smile, and an obvious interest in girls, something many of the cameramen in the industry seemed to lack. Tammy had always been a physical girl, had thoroughly enjoyed the sex, and wondered why she had never tried it before.

Several short term relationships followed as she made up for lost time. Along the way she learned what men liked, and even dabbled with a passing interest in what some of the girls liked. However she recognised that although she was prepared to have sexual fun with some of the girls she had essentially a heterosexual nature. Some of the shoots were for goods of a more erotic nature, and some were fantasy wear. Through these she began to understand something of the desires of men and what drove them, and learnt to dress both accordingly and, at times, just for the sheer fun of the effect it had.

Her big break came at a swimwear collection shoot for an American company which was set to launch a new range internationally. The chosen location was the palm fringed beaches of Cape Verde in the Bahamas and, unusually, one of the client's executive directors decided to oversee the event from beginning to end. Cy Blundell had instantly liked the look of the beautiful curvy British girl with the classy accent and made his interest obvious. Tammy was no fool and, although she was both drawn and somewhat flattered, decided that to jump straight into bed with this man would not necessarily be to her long term benefit. It took Blundell three days of persistent chasing before she caught him. Tammy had played the game well and won his respect out of bed. In bed she just blew him away.

Men are simple uncomplicated creatures. For most a full belly and mind-blowing filthy sex with a beautiful girl is all they really want and, once they have had it, they want to keep it coming. Cy Blundell, executive giant or not, was no different to his universal brothers in this regard. Unfortunately for Cy he was married, so he had to find another way to keep this girl close. A two year contract followed where she would be the face, more correctly the body, of the company. The collection was a great success and Tammy's became a household name. For two years which became three, as did the contract, Tammy remained Blundell's mistress, something Blundell never once regretted.

Tammy made very good money throughout the three year period but never forgot how fickle and short lived a career in the industry could be. At twenty-five she had to start thinking hard about her future. She would never become, nor did she want to be, Mrs Cy Blundell. Her life as a mistress had been wonderful. She was paid well for what she did, loved the work, was deeply satisfied with the decisions she had made, went to many of the world's most stunning places and was always on the 'A' list for the best parties. Sexually she was not committed to Blundell, but she was always available to him when he desired her. In fact her only commitment was to her contract, which she knew would not be renewed again at the end of the third year. It was time for her to seriously consider her options.

For three years, Chris Spencer remained at Catterick training in the use of a 'truck'. Between July 1992 and January 1993 half the battalion, including Jimmy Andrews, were deployed first to South Armagh and then to North Belfast. Chris remained with the 19 Mechanised Brigade, but in July 1994 he was once again deployed to Germany, and to Osnabruck, this time to 7 Armoured Brigade. In 1940 7 Armoured Brigade had a red jerboa as its emblem, the red jerboa being a nocturnal rodent which is indigenous to North Africa. 7 Armoured Brigade is better known around the world as the 'Desert Rats'.

Following the dissolution of the Soviet Union in December 1991 the Cold War had ended. BAOR was disbanded and in 1995 British Forces Germany (BFG) took the place both of BAOR and the Royal Air Force Germany, and personnel strength was reduced by almost thirty thousand. However for Sergeant Chris Spencer serving in Germany, September 1995 had brought some very welcome news of a personal nature. Jimmy Andrews had been granted home leave during the previous Christmas period. As a direct result of an obviously warm homecoming Chris's sister, Jenny, had given birth to twins Michelle and Juliette. The entire family including little Charlie, now six and at school, were delighted. None more so than big old Uncle Softie, privately sitting reading the letters and looking at the pictures of his new nieces being cuddled by their big brother, little Charlie, Uncle Chris's favourite person in all the world. His entire squad would have been completely dumbfounded had they seen the small tear trickle down the cheek of the toughest man any would ever know as he looked at those pictures.

Seven

The year dragged by slowly for Nathan although he and Susie kept in touch via the internet almost daily. Susie had not much liked Australia, hating the seemingly non stop bombardment of flies, so she and Jenny had moved on to New Zealand a lot earlier than they had planned, and wholly rejoiced in the fact they had, as both girls passionately loved New Zealand, especially the South Island. She told Nathan of people who were the friendliest she had ever come across, in a land which was as green and pleasant as anything she could previously have imagined. The fruit, even in the supermarkets, was always local and picked fresh the same day. Some of the lakes were a shimmering azure and turquoise in colour, and the mountains never lost their snow all year round. There were deserted roads and heavenly views, and she thought the land was heaven on earth. She told him of the adventure wonderland and world playground which was Queenstown and of the sports all comers could indulge in day in day out for weeks on end without ever repeating the same thing twice. She wrote of countryside almost devoid of human habitation, and of beaches in little coves, accessed only from the sea, where she had left footprints in the sand. Footprints which some said were quite possibly the first ever to have been left by a human being.

For him work was slow, painfully slow, with days dragging gradually into weeks, and weeks passing into months at the pace of an old and very sick snail. He and Susie had completed so much it appeared there was barely a thing to keep him occupied. He understood he was of use to Jake because he did keep on top of the needs of the various computers and sort out any minor glitches, but the systems he and Susie had installed were pretty good, and very little needed to be done to maintain them. Therefore most days were spent in various offices tweaking this and refining that. There was nothing to stretch his growing intellect or to present him with the challenge which would have increased the speed of the passage of the days which separated them.

And then she returned.

One day she was half a world away, the next she was less than two hours drive. She was back at her parent's home in Market Harborough and she rang him at work to see how he was, and to invite him to come up and stay for a few days if he wished to.

Since Nathan started work for him Jake often suggested the lad should take a holiday, but Nathan never had anywhere he wished to go, and nobody to go with. So for well over two years he took no time off at all except enforced public holidays, all of which he thoroughly loathed. Since he started driving, and had a car, he came in earlier and stayed later. He learnt many of the jobs Jake did just by watching him, and had taken it upon himself to sort many of them out in order to relieve the boredom. Jake was becoming ever more dependent upon the younger man, and was beginning to deeply respect his abilities. Nathan's confidence had grown greatly whilst Susie was there, and continued to grow after she left. His improved diet helped his skin tone a great deal, and his face filled out, as had his shoulders. He now had his hair cut by a proper hairdresser and grew it slightly longer, which again improved his look. He underwent dental treatment where his teeth were repaired, polished and whitened and, although still gappy, at least now when he smiled his teeth looked good. He would never be handsome, but he had moved forward a long way from the scrawny ugly little gnome who first turned up to work at Bow Creek.

Jake paid Nathan well, in fact very well, but the more he seemed to pay the more hours Nathan appeared to work. Jake knew Nathan's home life was deplorable, and that was a lot of the reason he spent so much time at the garage, but it could not be healthy for him to work so many hours week after week without a break of any kind. So when Nathan approached him to ask him if he could have a few days off, and explained the reason why, Jake grinned widely at him and said, "Go, and go now. Full pay and all expenses, and stay as long as they'll have you!"

Nathan rang Susie on the new mobile Jake had provided for his right hand man, and Jake had been right, the size of the units had decreased to an easy pocket fit. The drive north to Susie's family's home though necessary seemed tedious to him. At Lutterworth the boredom of the motorway disappeared, and his general dislike of driving was forgotten as he headed east through pretty little villages, where natural stone and odd red brick cottages abounded, set behind discreet hedges, so typically English in character. After some ten miles of beautiful countryside he reached Lubenham and turned left at the far side of the village. The small country road started to climb a slight hill and, as it did so, the sky in front of him lit up and seemed to glow, just as Susie had said it would, from the lights of Gartree Maximum Security Prison, built on an old airfield. He followed the narrow road around the bends and up a long shallow rise to the start of the village of Foxton where he crested the brow of the hill and drove down past the church and a pub on the left, over a hump back canal bridge into the centre of the village, and to her home.

The property was set well back from the road, with a tarmac driveway leading to a large open gravelled courtyard and turning area. It stood in about four acres of partially wooded ground on the side of a gently slopping hill which in daylight would promise wonderful views of rural English countryside. The building was a large natural stone structure which looked perfect in its setting, in no way formidable or imposing, as it almost appeared to have sprung from the very land it was surrounded by. Automatic sensors on the driveway triggered lights as he approached and as he swung into the courtyard the whole area lit up for him. He was not even fully out of the car when he heard running footsteps on the gravel behind him. As he turned she literally threw herself at him.

"Oh Nathan, I'm so glad you came, and came so quickly!" she gasped, hugging him and kissing his cheek "I've just so missed you! But come, bring your bag. You don't need to lock the car here. Leave the keys in it in case anyone needs to move it. Now come and meet my family."

Inside the hallway they both stopped and regarded the other. She looked fit and toned; her hair bleached by the sun and much lighter than it had been, and her skin had browned under the southern nation's sun. Without a hint of makeup her blue eyes shone out of her tanned face like a pair of sapphires, twinkling with merriment in the light. She liked this man a lot, one hell of a lot, for his kind, polite and caring nature. He had never looked good, but it had never mattered to her. She had seen through his physical side to the warm giving gentle person he really was. But this man who stood before her looked so much better than she remembered. He had filled out all over – much better. His face was rounder and the pointy chin almost disappeared. His hair was cut much more in keeping with his features, swept forward slightly covering the high forehead, and longer so his ears did not seem to protrude as they had but, she smiled, he was never going to be an oil painting.

"Come here you." she said wrapping her arms around a physically larger chest.

Nathan had been nervous about his coming meeting with Susie's parents and was acutely conscious of the social gulf which separated them. Within minutes of meeting them he realised he should never have been so. They were both almost exactly as he had visualised them, precisely as Susie described them, and neither wanted, liked or expected formalities, certainly within the walls of their home. Susie was the spitting image of her mother, just a younger version, and they really did look as if they had come out of the same mould, just at different times. The similarities were almost uncanny. The same face, hair, build and stance, even the mannerisms and ease of movement were the same. It was almost impossible to see her as Dawney's sister. He knew only two years separated them, but Jane Gatting could easily have passed as Dawney's daughter, never her sister.

Phil Gatting commanded respect. Despite the fact he was dressed casually and smiling warmly there was something about the man. He was taller than Nathan, probably about six foot Nathan guessed, with what had once obviously been dark hair but which was now noticeably greying, especially around the temples. He had quite obviously been fit in his day and still stood squarely, but it was his eyes which held Nathan. They were grey, literally grey, level and unflinching, and gave the impression they saw everything, which they probably did. They were not cold eyes, and the laughter lines around them indicated this man had enjoyed his life, but they certainly were not warm. It was his eyes which did it Nathan realised. It was not his confidence, personality or even known wealth which commanded respect, it was those eyes! They were lasers which looked into you and through you. Nathan knew he was a good and kind family man who did well by others wherever he could, but he could also see Phil Gatting was probably not a man to intentionally cross.

It was the early hours when Susie showed Nathan to the bedroom he was to have. The house was split in two by the main staircase with what were effectively wings with three bedrooms either side of the landing. Her parents had the master bedroom at one end of the house, and Nathan was to stay in the room which stood at the top of the stairs in their wing. Susie muttered something about being sorry the room wasn't the biggest, kissed him on the cheek and went off to her room at the far end of the other wing. His room was slightly larger than the whole of the downstairs of his mothers house, had an en suite and a very comfortable double bed, in which he enjoyed the best night's sleep he had had since a baby.

Nathan stayed for just over a week. He was shown all around the area and greatly enjoyed himself. He loved the little ironstone buildings in the quaint picture postcard villages, enjoyed the lunches in the various low ceilinged and beamed village pubs, and delighted in the very feel of Uppingham and the country's smallest county, Rutland. He spent a full two days with Phil Gatting at his corporate headquarters to the south of Lutterworth and, whilst there, performed some minor miracles on the company's main computer which left Phil Gatting extremely impressed, something which was not usually an easy thing to do. The entire trip exceeded his wildest expectations and gave him the chance to view life from an entirely different perspective. Jake telephoned only once to see how things were going and told him to stay as long as he wished. It was the only call he received.

There was nothing to spoil the time at all until Susie broke the news to him she had made up her mind to go on to university. It was now two years since she left school, which was a big gap, but following an application put in on her behalf earlier in the year she had been accepted at Durham University, and was supposed to start the following Wednesday.

Nathan was at first stunned and then devastated. He had neither made plans nor considered the future, as was his way, but just been inordinately happy to be back in Susie's company again after a year of enforced separation. She was his only true friend in the world of his age, and now she was going away again. True she was not returning to the other side of the world once more, but she might as well have been, going as she was to the other end of the country. He looked so dejected and crestfallen she put her arm around him, held him, and promised him they would stay in touch all the time, and she would see him during holidays without fail.

The following day Nathan returned to work. Jake could see he was down and understood why when he heard the reason. Although Jake had never taken up with a woman for a long committed relationship it did not mean he could not understand others who felt the need to do so. He liked this lad, and had liked him for a long time. He didn't have and would never have children of his own, and this young lad was the closest he would ever come to having one. From the moment he had taken young Nathan under his wing Jake had watched him develop. He wasn't a lad any more; he was a young man, with all the needs, loves and desires which go with it. It seemed obvious to Jake there were three major problems in Nathan's life. One he could do nothing about, that was down to time and time alone. Not only were these two young people made for one another, but they both deeply loved each other. The problem was they didn't know it yet. It was amazing how unbelievably stupid bright young things can be. The other two things he ought to be able to do something about in order to help.

The weeks passed and became months. Christmas and New Year had come and gone, and the two young people met up once again at Susie's parents, but it was over all too quickly for Nathan and, if anything, he came back to work even more down as a result of it. One of Nathan's problems was that he was bored. He did his work, and he did it well, but he sped through it in no time at all, and was soon back looking for extra jobs. The difficulty there was he had done such a good job in the first place there rarely was anything of a supplementary nature. Over time Jake introduced him increasingly to the businesses, and now Nathan probably knew more about the day to day running and general functions of the various companies than Jake himself. Jake trusted Nathan absolutely, and the trust had never been misplaced, nor would it ever be betrayed.

Nathan was completely capable of administering the various businesses, and even running them for short periods when Jake was not around. Nathan's only real shortcomings in business were his lack of ambition and any form of drive. He was hard working, diligent and as honest as the day was long, but he exhibited no form of entrepreneurial flair and Jake knew without it Nathan would never be able to move any business forward. Jake had always held true to the belief there were three types of individuals involved in business, just as there were three types of drivers. There were those who were naturals, those who worked hard at it and learnt, and those who would never be able to do it as long as they drew breath. Well Nathan sure as heck was not a natural car driver, nor was he a natural businessman. He had worked hard at his driving and eventually mastered it, the big question was could he do the same in the world of business?

The answer, if it existed, was to find the key, and Jake spent many a long hour pondering over that one. When it hit him it seemed such an obvious thing he could not for a moment understand why he had not thought of it before. Now how was he going to put it to Nathan? The next day Jake walked into the office carrying a small bag and emptied the contents onto Nathan's desk. It was four boxed CD computer games.

"I have a proposition for you Nathan," Jake started, "and I would like you to hear me out."

Jake's idea and proposition worked, and it worked well. In fact it set the pair of them on a path to riches which even Jake Ferris would previously have been hard pressed to have dreamt of.

A man very good at identifying problems, and with a natural disposition towards finding solutions, Jake Ferris accurately assessed the difficulties in young Nathan's life. He knew of Nathan's background and his home circumstances, and realised Nathan would have to leave and get away from all which was represented by his home, past and community if he was ever going to gain a decent future for himself. However he also knew Nathan would not accept it, or perhaps better put, would not fully appreciate it, if what he had in mind was seen as an act of charity. The lads housing needs were obvious, and the solution, to a man with Jake's assets, was an easy one, but the complication was how to put it to Nathan in order that Nathan would not view it as a gift. With the money Jake paid him, Nathan could easily have bought himself a property, but Nathan did not come from a home owning background, and the concept of ownership was completely alien to him. To Nathan's mind owning property could only be done by wealthy people and, despite watching as Jake had gone on to buy property after property, Nathan felt it was not something he would ever be able to do himself.

Real estate was something Jake understood. His philosophy was he sold cars, but he bought property, of which he now owned dozens, from residential to commercial to light industrial. He had recently acquired a small terrace of six shops in close proximity to the Upton Park tube station, and within walking distance of the West Ham United Football Club grounds. He purchased the block because he considered it to be in a prime location and, although they were fairly run down he should be able to move them on at a reasonable profit to a developer or, depending on time and planning issues, may develop them himself. Either way he would have them for some time. The mix was an odd one in that some of the shops had residential use over them, one had a separate office upstairs, but one had a self contained one bedroom apartment above it, with a wholly separate entrance, and that particular apartment was empty.

"Nathan, as you know, a few weeks ago, back at the beginning of January, I bought some shops out at Upton Park." Jake started. "Eventually they'll be redeveloped, but that'll be at some time in the future. I don't yet know if I'll want to do the work or have someone else do so. Either way the best thing to do is to work out the possible trade and general footfall in the area, and the best way to do that is to have someone watch it throughout the day and at night, weekdays and weekends."

"Well I could help with that!" Nathan said. "I seem to have spare time at the moment, so I could go and watch for a few hours at a time, and I'm sure you could do the same with others."

"Yes, I did think about it," Jake retorted, "but what I really need is someone to live there for a while. That way they could see patterns evolving and get a proper feel for the area. There is an empty apartment there which has its own parking space to the rear, but it only has one bedroom. It would suit a single person or a young couple. I thought if I let someone have it free of rent and they just paid for the water, gas and electricity they used, and then let me know what went on locally, we would both benefit. The only problem is I don't know anyone to ask and wondered if you might?"

Nathan looked thoughtful. "Well, there's a new lad out at "Fields" that seems to be good and quite bright. He may be interested."

Jake shook his head. "No, I know who you mean, and I've heard he shows quite a bit of promise, but he's too new and, although I said young couple, he's too young. I need someone I both know well and can trust completely. It is a bit of a challenge, and I admit it's got me beaten!"

An immediate answer had not come to mind to Nathan, and he wandered off to carry on with some other tasks, but the question kept circling around inside his head. Eventually he thought he may have the solution, so went back to see Jake with his thoughts and found him where he had left him, still in his office.

"I have an idea about the question you asked me earlier." Nathan said. "I've thought it through and must admit I can see the problem. I think I may have an answer, but I really don't want you to think I'm trying to take advantage."

The penny has dropped Jake thought, grinning inwardly. "Okay, so what might that be?" he asked.

"Well," Nathan paused, "I think the only sensible solution given the circumstances is that I move into it and do it myself. The work you are asking to be done is easy, and just about anyone could do it, but the problem is the people I feel you could best trust are married with kids. There are a couple of others, like the lad out at "Fields", but they too are not old or responsible enough, so there really is only me left."

"I wonder?" mused Jake, "I'll be honest, I did think of you, but thought you wouldn't be interested, so didn't want to ask you. The thing is Nathan; I don't want you to feel you have to do it out of duty. I know you are one hundred percent loyal and completely trustworthy. I also know if I were to ask you to do it I know you would, but I don't want to do that, and now I feel that is precisely what you are doing because we cannot think of anyone else. Don't worry about it, something, or better, someone, will eventually come to mind."

"I'm not putting myself forward out of loyalty Jake," Nathan replied. "I'm suggesting myself because there is no better solution, and believe me we would be helping one another. You know little of my home life, but it is utterly, utterly shit! There is no quality of life there at all. My room at home has always been small. The house has always been squalid and, no matter what I do to try and improve it, it is immediately trashed. I can keep nothing there. If I do my mother or one of her 'boyfriends' steals it. I cannot work, think or even sleep comfortably there, let alone ever take a friend or, heaven forbid, should I ever get one, a girlfriend back. I am now twenty and have never 'lived' anywhere, with the sole exception of ten days at Susie's parent's home. As for the rest of my life, the best which can be said is that I have existed. This to me could well be my big chance to get out. Hell, it could be the only chance I ever get! I don't want to squander it, and I'm not prepared to. I can do what you are asking standing on my head – and you of all people know it! I will respect the fact it is your property, and will look after it and treat it accordingly. I can note improvements which need doing, make suggestions as to the direction developments could take, will provide a very real on site sounding board for problem tenants, and would be there overnight which would undoubtedly help with security issues. Just let me do it and I will prove my worth time after time!"

Jake Ferris was amazed. He had never heard the lad being so forceful before, and had certainly not expected him to come back with such a well reasoned argument as to why he should do it. Nathan even included aspects to his reasoning which he himself had overlooked and there was no faulting his logic, even had Jake wanted to.

"Well if it's what you would like Nathan, then of course it's yours. I have to say I am relieved as there is nobody better I could possibly think of, and you have given me food for thought, I must say!" Jake answered. "So, let's consider it settled then. All you have to do is let me know when you want to move in and I'll get things sorted. Now there is another issue you can help me with, and that's to do with these games I brought in this morning."

The four boxed computer games Jake had brought into work that morning were, according to the young man working the sales counter of the shop from which he had purchased them, the very latest ones on the market. Not that Jake would have had the first idea about such things. They were four very different games according to the salesman. One was of a battle which included troop movements with big guns and tanks, another was of some sort of war between humans and creatures from the centre of the Earth, the third was a two plus player game of nation building over the millennia, and the last seemed to be about a rocket attack which was hell bent on the destruction of the planet. With the salesman's assurance that the kids all loved them still ringing in his ear, Jake had paid for the games and beaten a hasty retreat, rejoicing in the fact if such were the case he was glad he had no kids.

After sorting out the apartment for Nathan the next thing on Jake's agenda was to attempt to tackle the issue of Nathan's boredom, and his pining for Susie. He wanted to find something Nathan could get involved in which would keep him occupied, which should in turn rectify the boredom, and something in which he could immerse himself which would keep his brain focused. Jake knew whatever happened time would resolve the matter, and what Nathan needed now was a major distraction. He had high hopes for them as a couple, and was sure their relationship would eventually happen but, in the meanwhile, Nathan needed something now. From Jake's perspective, although his motives were in essence wholly altruistic, if what he was about to propose worked, well – then it should also bring in some return.

Jake Ferris was a shrewd and canny businessman who had pulled himself up in life by his own bootstraps. His parents had been poor, living in privately rented accommodation, and he had had but one sibling, an older sister who died of rubella as a child. His parents were now also both dead, and he had inherited nothing, not that he would have wanted or needed anything from his parents or for that matter any other being. When he wanted something in life he always found a way of getting it. He was by anybody's standard of measurement now a very wealthy man, with vast investments in property, and a hoard of business interests. He could easily have retired years earlier and lived the good life, but he craved the need to get up in the morning, and the craving led him to business. He needed to 'have a deal' in the same way alcoholics need a drink or smokers need one more cigarette. It was his reason for being, something, along with the common touch, he had never lost. Even with his net worth getting close to a nine figure amount he would still take joy out of personally selling a can of oil in one of his auto-parts shops, knowing he was earning a few pennies profit. His vast wealth was an abstract to him, wonderful to see on paper, but still nothing like shaking a man's hand when he had just sold him a car or a light truck. He had a marvellous understanding of what money can do, coupled to an almost unique imagination. Where business was concerned he was a human divining rod, and could almost smell oncoming trends and business opportunities on the wind.

However, despite his prodigious wealth, extensive experience and wonderful imagination, nothing in his past, or his wildest dreaming could possibly have prepared him for what was to follow his suggestion to Nathan Jefferies that day.

"What I would like you to do Nathan," Jake started by saying, "is to play those games. I have seen them being played, and know they are popular with young people these days, heavens knows why, but frankly I think they are pretty crap! What I feel they need are much better backgrounds and more realistic looking characters. Basically a huge upgrade of what I believe they call the graphics. Also the noise they make is dreadful and totally unrealistic, so that needs major improvement too. Firstly I want you to mess about with the things and see what you can do. Don't bust a gut on it at this stage, and if it can't be done, well then it can't be done, but knowing you as I do I don't expect you to fail. If you succeed I would like you to invent your own game or games. If and when you get to that stage I will invest heavily in the new venture and set it up as a separate company with you as a full partner with a fifty percent stake. How does any of that sound to you?"

"Okay," said Nathan grinning, "you've got me beat. I can't see where this is going. Where are the cameras? Or what's the punch line? What is this? Candid camera?"

"I'm being serious!" Jake said.

Nathan looked uncertain. "So what you are telling me is you want me to come in to work, play games on the computer, and you'll pay me for it?" he asked.

Jake nodded. "Yep, that's about it to begin with, but I hope you do more."

"And if I can improve them and then make my own you will set up a company with me in full partnership?" Nathan questioned.

"I see you were listening." Jake said, and then went on, "I realise this sort of thing cannot be done overnight, that you have other work to do, and you have to move home, so please don't think I want anything dropped and this made a priority, because that's not the case. However you seem to be on top of things, have spare time and refuse to take a break, so I thought I would find you something to do which I believe you will enjoy and, if successful, will earn us both an honest shilling or two."

Nathan had done just what had been asked of him. Three years or so earlier he had been amazed when Jake asked him to work for him with computers, as he hadn't considered anything to be done with computers to be work. Three years on he still thought it was incredible he had been so lucky as to have found someone who was willing to pay him the money he received for what he did. He could easily see the benefits to Jake's operations, the way most were then able to expand using the technology and systems which were put in place, but he still didn't really look upon it as proper work. It was still fun and he had never stopped thoroughly enjoying it.

Although wholly unrelated to the task Jake had now put before him, and unknown to Jake, Nathan had already played around with simple games between computers, and in doing so had become interested in communications. As a result he had carried out experiments of his own with computers at Jake's businesses based in various locations around the East End of London, starting by experimenting with sending signals between those under his control using mobile phones. He thought it was a given this would work because the current system worked through land-lines, and it had worked, because the difference in the signals they received were indistinguishable to the computers.

There was however a huge difference in the way the signals were sent, and this was the area in which Nathan had been experimenting. The standard way of connecting with the Internet was through dial-up, but this was a slow and inefficient way of both connecting and then in sending raw data. The problem was the whole system relied on copper wires, the speed with which they could carry data, and their very limited capacity. Each non networked computer needed its own dedicated telephone line which, to connect to a potential recipient, had to first go through a switching station and find an available line, then to transmit at what was a relatively slow pace, only to go through another switching station before eventually being delivered. He knew the system was destined for the technological scrap heap, but the question was – what would take its place? The two main contenders were broadband or satellite transmission, both of which had certain inherent advantages and both certainly had the potential to leave dial-up standing.

The experiments had not gone very far. His interest was in sending data by radio waves, realising it would have to be encrypted, and he set about sending a couple of test signals, which worked successfully. His best results came through satellite dishes set up on two of Jakes buildings, but this was literally a line of sight operation which Nathan realised was the twentieth century equivalent to the semaphore lines of the eighteenth century. He abandoned the experiments because he could see to continue would certainly contravene the Wireless Telegraphy Act 1949 and, although the act was in need of a major overhaul to take account of technological advances, it was not his place to try and usher in change. That was for the big boys in the industry. However the results of the experiments proved interesting and he thought he may be able to make practical use of what he had learnt one day. The experiments had provided a distraction of sorts, and had eaten up some of his spare time.

The computer games conundrum was vastly different to the problems surrounding computer communications and was destined to eat up a great deal more time, and without contravening any archaic acts or Neanderthal laws. The games were all played, and then played again many times over as Nathan worked his way up through the various levels. He quickly understood Jake's comments about sound and graphics, and set about seeing what he could do to improve things. The sound he thought would be the easier of the two main problems to tackle, and the first thing to do was run all sound through higher quality speakers. With that done he could play around with the various aspects of the programming controlling the sound, then work on the sound itself, which really meant starting with the sound card.

A sound card is a piece of hardware which facilitates the input and output of audio signals going to and coming from a computer, and its use includes providing the audio component for multimedia applications such as music composition and the editing of video or audio. Nathan's interest in it was for entertainment, specifically games. In order to use a sound card the operating system usually requires a specific device driver which is a low-tech program handling the data connections for the operating system.

Following Nathan's advice, and at the early part of the New Year, Jake had purchased an IBM Aptivas 2168 which came in tower unit form. It had been introduced in September 1994 and provided Nathan with a chance to go for a major upgrade. Almost a year earlier, in March 1993, Intel had introduced the Pentium as the fifth generation micro architecture, succeeding the Intel 486 in which the number 4 signified the fourth-generation, following on from its previous numbering system. Intel had chosen the Pentium name after courts had disallowed the trade marking of names containing numbers such as 286, i386, i486. The Pentium fitted IBM Nathan chose was designed to run at over 100 million instructions per second (MIPS). It came loaded with Microsoft Windows NT 3.5 which was also released in September 1994, and had sound capabilities built into the machine. However what he had been tasked with led Nathan to have serious concerns about those capabilities and he believed he would need to upgrade the expansion card to provide the required audio output.

Nathan had not specified the machine they purchased with gaming in mind, and may well have gone for a totally different computer had he known. Based on what had been achieved with computers Jake would happily have spent huge amounts of money on them if asked, but that was not Nathan's way. However this mindset did force him to make certain changes to the one they now had which, in the long run, probably contributed to his success. Nathan knew it wasn't a case of adding just any sound card if he wished to upgrade, he had to the get best available, and that meant making sure the card had the right chip. The Philips SAA1099 showed promise, but instead he went for the Sound Blaster 1.5 with the OPL2 chip as it produced square waves and noise at three different frequencies. Also important was its main feature, it could output in stereo, which therefore meant it was possible to set the left and right channel volume independently. Additionally it had a nine voice mode where each voice could be fully programmed. With this additional piece of hardware he felt he should be able to start playing around with the sound.

If sound proved to be a bit of a problem, then graphics were going to generate much greater ones as computer graphics are concerned with digitally synthesising and manipulating visual content. The term often refers to three-dimensional computer graphics, but also encompasses two-dimensional graphics and image processing, and is a complete sub-field of computer science. It was not until 1993 that anyone even seriously considered three dimensional graphics, but for Nathan it had to be the way ahead.

The easiest way for Nathan to create a complex image from scratch was to start with a blank canvas, known as a raster map. He decided at a later stage he may well return to 2D for programming more advanced card games and the like, but the job in hand had to be done in 3D if anything like the desired result was to be obtained. Fortunately, manufacturing technology had again progressed, and video, 2D GUI acceleration, and 3D functionality had now all been integrated into one chip, and the one Nathan went for was Rendition's Verite.

He was not about to consider anything which could not later be upgraded, mindful as he was of the rate of technological advancement. He found multiple cards could draw together a single image, doubling the number of pixels and enabling anti-aliasing to be set to higher quality. 3D graphics, as opposed to 2D, called upon three dimensional representations of geometric data but, although a 3D model was the mathematical representation of any three dimensional object whether inanimate or living, the model was not a graphic until it was visually displayed.

As time passed Nathan found the process of creating 3D computer graphics could most easily be considered when divided into three separate processes, modelling, animation and rendering. Modelling formed the shape of an object and its layout, with the two most common sources being real world objects scanned onto the computer or created by an engineer or artist using a 3D modelling tool. Animation covers the motion aspects of all objects including their placement within any scene, defining spatial relationships, location and relative size, which in turn alter according to distance, perspective and time. Rendering converts the model into photorealistic images in two main operations. The first is light, and how much travels from one place to another, and the second is how the affected surfaces interact with that light, colour changes and shadows being the most obvious considerations. Finally all scenes then had to be altered so they may be viewed in the two dimensions available on any screen, and for viewing all scenes are converted from digital signals to analogue.

It took Nathan weeks to understand the basic principles of creating 3D games, and to gather together the hardware and software which would be needed for what he was about to attempt. His first experiments were with the games Jake supplied and he had played. He radically rebuilt the computer in order that it should be capable of carrying out the task Jake suggested, and in the process it was changed beyond recognition. Unfortunately his initial attempts consistently ran into problems with image blurring and hold, which was rapidly followed by breakdown. This he eventually traced back to overheating, so he had to set about curing the problem before he could resume his experiments.

The cooling devices available were not very sophisticated, and his tests showed the greatest contributor to the heat build up was due to the working of the video card, so not something he could ignore or bypass. He felt a simple heat sink based on copper or aluminium would not be sufficient, nor would the inclusion of a small internal fan be enough to overcome the problem when the equipment was used intensively, as his was bound to be. Besides they created noise, required maintenance and were prone to breakdown. After further thought and research he opted to build his own water cooled device which had the advantages of silence, with a small pump remotely located, consistency of operating temperature and, apart from the pump, was completely free of maintenance. The only real disadvantage was one of portability, but fortunately that was not an important consideration.

With the cooling problem resolved he got to work in earnest. He rapidly reviewed the games he had and found he could make improvements across the board with all of them. He did however realise by working on and with games which had already been produced and marketed would never be of advantage to him or Jake, and he liked the idea of being a fifty percent shareholder in a company he worked for which operated in an area of the greater computer industry.

In many ways the move into the flat at Upton Park had a life changing effect on Nathan. Although by many standards it was not a very big apartment it did at least give him a place he could look upon as his own and, large or not, it gave him much more room than he had ever enjoyed at his mother's. She was only too glad to see the back of him, and Nathan had not seen her since, despite calling in and attempting to see her on several occasions, and leaving messages. Jake had asked if help or a van was needed to facilitate the move, but Nathan's possessions were minimal and he moved everything in one trip with nothing more than his little hatchback.

The apartment though clean was only partially furnished, so for the first time Nathan went shopping for furniture, curtains and the items which make any property a home and, deprived as he had been throughout his entire life, he rather enjoyed the experience. He embarked upon the task in such a fastidious manner that he would have put even a hospital matron of a bygone age to shame. Everything he did about the place and cleaned or purchased was given consideration to even the smallest detail. When he eventually finished cleaning, decorating and furnishing, the little place was utterly transformed. His visits to Susie's parent's home were the only times he had ever slept in a double bed, and he enjoyed the lack of physical restriction the extra room gave him. A double bed now sat squarely in his bedroom and, to him the height of luxury, a remote control television sat on top of the tallboy chest of drawers beyond the foot of his bed. Never again would his mother or her boyfriends steal his possessions, so now he was free to equip himself as he would always have wished.

He stayed in daily touch with Susie, mainly over the internet, but also often by telephone, and she was thrilled to learn of his move. The time simply sped by after Jake charged him with the computer game project, and he was deeply shocked to discover her first year of university had passed. He hoped in some ways he might get another invitation to her parents home for a part of the nine weeks she was about to have off, but had not received anything. Although disappointed he did understand she would want to spend some time with her parents, but still hoped he would be allowed the chance to see her and enjoy time in her company. She had hinted in her e-mails and on the phone that they would see one another, but he still had no idea of any firm plans.

Although Jake could easily have afforded to move from the Bow Creek garage to some purpose built plush offices he had never done so, explaining to those who became involved with him in a discussion on the subject that Bow Creek was where his roots were and where he felt he belonged. However expanding company growth had at least forced him to compromise, and shortly after Susie left for Australia he had the site completely redeveloped, with a sizable car showroom built on the ground floor and a suite of offices built above, a large one of which he shared with Nathan.

Since she left for her gap year tour Jake had not seen Susie, despite having heard a great deal about her and, on several occasions, talking to her on the phone. He liked the girl a lot, and in several key ways she reminded him of Shirley James, the only one he ever regretted letting get away. He liked her easy relaxed manner, her bubbly personality and above all her sharp intelligence and genuine compassion. Technically she was already a young woman when he had last seen her, but he had only ever really viewed her as a girl, skinny and a little plain looking. The same definitely could not be said of the very attractive and somewhat familiar looking young lady who had just walked into his office completely unannounced late one afternoon at the end of June, and who then proceeded to walk around his desk and kiss him on the cheek. Who the hell was she?

"Hello Jake." Susie said straightening up, in a voice he would have instantly recognised anywhere.

"Susie!" Jake responded, with a look of shock on his face which was comical to behold. "What on Earth happened to you? I mean – umm – you were a girl!" He realised how stupid the remarks sounded even to him and decided it would be better to keep his mouth shut for a few minutes.

“Ah, we all grow up!” Susie said, laughing out loud as she walked over to where Nathan had until that moment been working, and where he still sat, mouth open, looking if anything more shocked than Jake. He stood as she approached, and she walked straight up to him, threw her arms around his shoulders and kissed him full on the lips. He had kissed her many times before, usually on the cheek as she had just done to Jake, occasionally on the lips as a son might his mother, but she had never kissed him like that before, and never, never, had anyone ever stuck their tongue in his mouth. He was totally numbed.

“What? What are you doing?” he managed to blurt out.

“I’m kissing you silly.” Susie chuckled.

“No! I mean what are doing here?” Nathan managed to get out, swallowing hard.

“Now Nathan, is that any way to talk to a girl? I’ve come to stay for a couple of months.” Susie replied, still smiling.

Nathan was astounded. “Dawney didn’t say a word.”

“Aunty Dawney doesn’t know, so she couldn’t have told you.” Susie explained.

Still shaken he asked, “Well, how do you know it will be alright to stay with her then?”

“I’m not staying with Aunty Dawney, so it doesn’t matter.” Susie told him.

“So where are you staying?” Nathan asked, with a hint of concern in his voice.

Susie looked him straight in the eye and said, “I’m staying with you Nathan!”

Neither heard the door behind them close as Jake left the office.

“Yes!” he said as he walked down the stairs. “Yes, yes, yes!” he shouted across the forecourt, startling customers and staff alike, a huge smile radiating across his face.

Nothing in Nathans life experience to that point had in any way prepared him for what the visit by Susie would bring to his life. At almost twenty one he was still a virgin, mostly due to his home circumstances, previous gawky looks and his own lack of confidence. Girls had never been interested in him, and he had gone out of his way to avoid them, always feeling inadequate and painfully shy in their presence. Susie remained the only female he had even so much as kissed.

The same could not be said for Susie. She was a bubbly and outgoing character born to enlightened parents who had themselves been teenagers in the swinging sixties. She had never been encouraged to be sexually promiscuous by her parents, or even sexually active, but they courted no hypocritical Victorian values, and had never frowned upon or discouraged her earlier relationships. As loving and responsible parents they pointed out the risks and advised emotional involvement in a stable relationship, if she were to choose to follow a path which led to intercourse. She was not a stupid girl, and also had the benefit of guidance from an older and sexually active sister. Susie had lost her virginity some four and a half years earlier, during the Christmas holidays following her sixteenth birthday. It had been to a then long term boyfriend of well over a year, a long time indeed for a sixteen year old. Since then she had only experienced any form of sexual relations with two other males, one of which had proved to be a major mistake, and a contributory reason as to why she wished to put distance between herself and her home when she originally moved to stay with Dawney.

In the three years since she met Nathan she had gone without sex. Not because she was waiting for him, or saving herself for him as such, but mostly because she had not found anyone else she felt any desire to go to bed with, and because she really did like Nathan a great deal. Whilst working with him she never once considered him as a potential bed-mate, and her touring kept her mind busy on other things, but university had given her plenty to consider, both academically and personally. The time allowed her space to think, and the more she thought the more she came to understand just how much Nathan meant to her, and how very much she obviously meant to him. Since starting university she had heard from him every day without fail, and she began to realise she would be mortified if their contact missed on so much as one single occasion. He had never asked or expected anything from her, made no demands of any kind at any time, and had always been there for her, always would be, and would never fail her. She came to understand just how deeply he must love her, even though Nathan himself was probably unaware of it.

She was immensely pleased to hear the news he had moved into the flat, as she knew much about his diabolical home life. She was also aware of the gulf in social circumstances which Nathan felt separated them, much of it reinforced because of the huge differences in their family homes and backgrounds. For her part she knew he was gifted, and if he could properly channel the gift he should do extremely well in life. He had mightily impressed her father, whom she considered to be an excellent judge of character, and she had never heard him speak so approvingly of any of the people she or her siblings had previously brought home. After much thought and a great deal of careful consideration she felt she would be best able to help Nathan by doing for him what he had long done for her, which was just to be there for him. He would succeed, that she could see, but he would get there a lot faster if he had her encouragement but, and to her most importantly, whether he succeeded or not, whether he became wealthy or not, it was the quality of his heart and the depth of his love for her she cherished.

Her studies certainly occupied her a great deal, but not to the exclusion of all else. Sex was something she had not really thought about a great deal for a long time. Of course it cropped up in conversation with some of her friends, but they mostly accepted she was not in a meaningful relationship, and the subject usually moved on. However it started to occur to her there was a void in her life which needed filling and, as she tried to rationalise objectively, she was a young woman in the prime of life to whom sex was a perfectly natural physical requirement. Therefore who could she have a worthwhile and fulfilling sexual relationship with? She had absolutely no interest in going out 'on the pull', or in having any other form of meaningless relationship. She knew if she and Nathan had continued working together it would almost definitely have happened between them by now. He was the only one she was at all interested in, but he was so remote geographically. To start a sexual relationship with him, especially given he was so sexually unaware, in fact he was probably still a virgin, bless him, may well be upsetting for him with her so far away, and she would not wish to hurt him for the world!

The reality remained that she was terribly drawn to him in many ways. In fact if she were honest with herself it was true to say she loved him, but had fought admitting it to herself for a long time, mainly due to his perceived hopelessness of the situation. The silly man! The situation was only hopeless if he allowed it to remain that way. She had seen how troubled and nervous he was around women generally, particularly so around younger ones, so could see the approach was never going to come from him. Well holidays were coming, and if he was not going to make the first move then she would, and if he didn't like it, or couldn't accept it, at least she would leave him the wiser for the experience – not that he wouldn't accept it, the silly darling.

No, there was no other alternative she could possibly see, she would have to take the initiative and would have to guide him, and cement the relationship as she knew only she could. She would turn up unannounced and give him no alternative but to take her to bed, and she knew that once she did so Nathan would never let her go, which would suit them both perfectly!

She planned everything without so much as a hint to anyone as to her intentions. After driving down from Durham to Market Harborough three days earlier, she completed her family duties, prepared herself, and then driven down to London and to Bow Creek garage. Jake looked so shocked when she walked in she knew she had succeeded with her surprise, although she failed to understand it was her physical appearance as much as her presence which contributed so much to his astonishment. Jake, she knew, was a man of the world, and although she had not heard him leave the office she heard his shout from below, immediately understanding he at least could comprehend what she had in mind. Nathan however had not the slightest grasp of the situation.

"Susie, that would be wonderful, but I don't have anywhere for you to stay! It's only a one bedroom apartment, and I have only the one bed. You can have it for tonight, and I'll sleep on the settee. Tomorrow we can sort something out." Nathan told her hopefully.

"Well we can worry about the details later." Susie assured him, "As for now you can take me out for a meal and a drink, as I'm only a poor and lowly student. Now, when do you stop playing computer games and get off?"

Nathan closed down his computer, left Susie in the office, and went to fine Jake in order to let him know he wanted to get away. He found Jake in the shop still grinning to himself. When he asked Jake if he might get off a little early Jake had replied.

"Go! Go now, and I don't want you in tomorrow. I've got a big meeting with lots of people in the office and I think we would all get in your way. In fact it may go on to the following day, so don't come back to work until after the weekend, and I would like Susie to phone me on Monday morning before you come in! I'll send Susie down to you." With that he walked back to his office still grinning. When he got there he walked up to Susie, kissed her on the cheek and said, "It's great to see you again, you wonderful girl. I've told Nathan I don't want to see him until Monday, and even then I want you to call me before he comes in. I hope it gives the two of you enough time to – catch up!" He winked at her, grinned, and added, "Now go on, get going before he gets cold feet."

She grinned back at him. "Thanks Jake, I'll do all that I can!" Susie said as she left.

Susie had a plan, and it was working. She suggested there was no point in taking both their cars back to Nathan's apartment. The most sensible thing was to leave hers at the garage and pick it up as and when they needed it. Nathan could then drive back to his apartment with her, drop his car off and show her the apartment. They could then change and head back into South Kensington to eat, where she knew there would be plenty of romantic French restaurants where they could eat, drink and converse.

She loved the apartment, and all that he had accomplished with it. There they freshened up, changed and caught the tube across London where they found just the right restaurant to suit her needs, and spent a wonderful four hours on three courses of simply delicious food and two very good bottles of wine, before catching the tube back across the city. Susie really did like what he had done with his apartment. It was typical of Nathan to such a degree it almost seemed to her to reflect his very essence. It was a long way from beautiful in a girly sense, but it didn't seem to have the typical Teutonic functionality to be found in many male apartments. Thought had obviously gone into what he had done, and everything fitted together smoothly, whilst at the same time functionality and purpose had taken priority. It also appeared all the various parts could be effectively removed and replaced without damaging the effect as a whole. Basically things can be changed as upgrades become available she though, smiling as she did so. She particularly approved of his bathroom when they had stopped to change, or perhaps it should be called a shower room rather than bathroom. It had not been a big room and Nathan had apparently taken the view there was not enough space for both shower and bath, so the bath had gone, to make room for a mini wet room with power shower.

After they removed their shoes, Susie opened a bottle of wine she had dropped off earlier and poured a glass for each of them.

"I suggest you take a shower first Nathan, and I go in after you. You know what we girls are like in bathrooms," she said.

"That's okay, I don't need a shower," Nathan replied. "You just go straight on in."

"Nathan Jefferies, just go and take a shower right now!" Susie instructed, to which Nathan wandered off to do as he was told. Susie walked into the bedroom and folded the duvet back to the end of the bed, switched on two lamps and turned the main light off. She stood back and surveyed the scene, and was satisfied with what she saw. Hearing the shower start up she removed all her clothes and hung what she could in the wardrobe then, with a last contented look at the room, turned and walked naked into the shower.

Nathan was in the process of shampooing his hair, and was massaging the soap into his scalp with his eyes closed as Susie walked in and he knew nothing of her presence until he felt an extra set of fingers on his head. His eyes flew open, immediately filled with shampoo which stung them and forced him to close them tight, but not before he had glimpsed her naked body before him.

"Susie! What are you doing?" he coughed out nervously.

"Calm down Nathan." Susie replied soothingly. "I'm just helping you wash your hair, then I'll help with your back, and then you can help me."

"But you're a girl!" Nathan blurted out, instantly understanding how silly it sounded.

"Yes. It works so much better that way." Susie said as she continued washing the shampoo out off his hair. Nathan was stunned, and had no idea as to what he should do or how to react. He was thoroughly enjoying the sensation, and the smell of her scent was intoxicating – but this he had certainly not expected.

"Now turn around and I'll do your back!" Susie instructed, lathering up the soap as he did. She worked her way down his back, over his buttocks and down his legs. She then worked her way back up, reaching around to the front of his legs, feeling his leg muscles tensing as her hands rose.

"Okay, you can turn around now Nathan. It's my turn." Susie said, standing provocatively in front of him with her hands on hips and her legs slightly apart.

Not only had Nathan never been with a woman before, he had never seen a naked female in the flesh either. There had been pictures on the walls at the garage, and some of the lads had brought magazines in which showed naked women in all sorts of poses, so he knew how they looked, where the bits went and what they did, but this was something else. Susie was beautiful, and even inexperienced Nathan could see that. Her breast had filled out over the last year and thrust out firmly in front of her, tipped with hardened dark rosy pink nipples. Her waist was nipped in at the bottom of her ribcage, swelling out again over her hips, and from beneath the ribcage her belly was almost flat, broken only by a small naval. The base of her belly was totally devoid of hair, something Susie had spent much time on that morning before leaving her parents home, and her sex resembled a perfectly formed but smooth skinned peach. Dragging his eyes away Nathan continued down, marvelling at the look of her faultless legs.

"Are you just going to look, or are you going to clean me?" she asked him huskily.

Nathan could not believe the touch of her. The skin had such a different texture to his own. It felt – wonderful, but he did not know how to touch it, frightened to rub it in case he damaged it, because if felt so soft and fragile under his hands.

"Rub harder please." Susie purred. "Soap me down like you would yourself, and don't worry, I'm not made of glass!"

Nathan did. She turned away from him so that he may follow her lead, and he had been a quick learner. Her bottom was not at all what he expected, again so very different to his own. The skin on top was so soft with a surface texture akin to fresh dough, yet with a surprising firmness beneath which stopped his fingers squeezing into the flesh. The tops of her legs were almost the same in texture, firming significantly as he ran his hands down to her calves. He turned her around and continued up her body, soaping her breasts and feeling the nipples harden under his fingers. He had not known what to expect, but he had never expected another's body to feel so good. She put her arms around his neck, crushing him to her, kissing him full on the lips, again pushing her tongue into his mouth. This time it felt good and he used the tip of his tongue to dance with hers, whilst his erection stuck out awkwardly into her lower belly. At least that would not be a problem area later she thought mischievously.

They rinsed and dried, each helping the other as they did so then, holding him by the hand, Susie gently led him to the bedroom and had him lie on the bed. She knelt on the bed next to him gently kissing him and then ran the tip of her tongue over his lips, slowly moving down over his chin and neck to his chest, licking and kissing as she went. Shortly after she straddled him, and lovingly ended his virginity. That hadn't taken long Susie thought happily afterwards, laying a finger on his lips to quieten him. It may not have been the best sexual experience she had ever had, but it was definitely the best lovemaking, with every single movement meant and enjoyed. She reached down and pulled the duvet up over the pair of them. "Now hold me through the night my darling," she murmured in his ear, "and I want to practice that again in the morning, perhaps twice!"

Eight

The fickle moves of fate are often difficult to follow, and so it appeared quite ironic that Tammy Hunter, international swimwear model, should find herself at a party following a re-launch in her home town of Brighton. Jeffery Wild, recently divorced, was a merchant banker eighteen years her senior. Wild came from an old moneyed background and lived on a large country estate in Surrey, from where his family had been taking care of business in the City for generations. Tammy was not immediately attracted to Wild, which was something Wild was not at all used to. He was immensely rich, considered himself extremely good looking, had travelled the world – and knew he could have any woman on the planet he wanted. So who the hell did this girl think she was to ignore him, beautiful though she was or not?

Cy Blundell had proved attractive to Tammy. He was big, he was outgoing, he was direct and he was married. There was no commitment and no complications. Jeffery Wild was not really her sort of man. He appeared lofty, patronising and most definitely snobbish. Although on the tall side he was small framed and round shouldered, overly well dressed and had an unfortunate superior manner about him. It was also obvious he expected her pants to hit the floor with a splash just because he allowed her to be presented to him. The toffee-nosed little prig she thought making no attempt to hide her own disdain, and Wild was most definitely not used to that sort of treatment. A couple of centuries earlier he would have had the filly whipped for her disrespectful attitude. Unfortunately nowadays one had to endure such insolent and insulting behaviour from these lower class creatures. How much would it cost him to bed the wretched beast?

It had taken Wild several months to do so. Tammy had not liked him, and did not like him, but she was well aware of his influence, and instinctively understood he may well prove to be a useful contact in times to come. Three months later her contract ended and she returned to Britain properly for the first time in years. Along the way she had used some of her earnings to purchase a detached family home overlooking the beach at Kemp Town, two miles from her former family home. It was a large property with a small two bedroom cottage within the grounds. Her parents now lived in the main house but, since her brother had married and moved out, the cottage was empty and usually used only for guests. It was into the cottage she decided to move whilst she took stock of where she was in life before jumping into anything else.

Jeffery Wild had perused her relentlessly. The more she resisted his advances the more inflamed his desires became. Eventually, more due to the war of attrition than any finer reason, he succeeded in taking her to bed and in bed Tammy was what every son's mother hopes her little boy will never meet.

Nine

Without a doubt of any kind the next eight weeks of Nathan's life were the happiest he had known from the moment he first drew breath. Just two months on, looking back to those first few days and nights together, he could not believe how ignorant he then was of love and sex, nor just how wonderfully understanding Susie had been taking the boy he then still was on his journey to manhood. Never in his wildest dreams had he before thought of sex as anything more than a necessary reproductive process couples went through in order to create a new life and, therefore for him, not something to waste time on. The shenanigans he had seen going on with other males as they spend time, money and undue effort in chasing females had, in the past, always seemed both bizarre and somewhat stupid to him. That outlook had now gone forever.

Computers had previously completely filled and fulfilled his life. He had been born with a special gift, he basically thought in algorithms, and his upbringing, with all of its neglect and lack of social interaction, had honed the gift. Sex, sexuality and sexual desire had had no logical place in his brain, in essence they did not compute, so effectively had always been deleted. In very real terms Susie had added another massive programme overwriting many of the varied minor programmes which had previously been the workings of his brain. To all intents and purposes a dormant section of his head was lit up and he finally grasped just what it is to be human, with a full range of previously non experienced emotions and desires, from love to lust, enjoyment, satisfaction, and core level happiness. He learnt the benefits of consideration, mutual cooperation and even of sheer physical appreciation. There was no doubt in his mind now he both loved and was in love with Susie, and the love was fully reciprocated.

Susie phoned Jake on the Monday morning as requested, and Jake knew, just knew, from the very sound of her voice, the two stupid bright young things had finally worked out that which had remained blindingly obvious to him for nearly two years. If he held back any doubt it was blasted away the moment he saw Nathan. In those few short days Nathan had changed. Changed didn't actually come close, Jake thought. Nathan had become a completely different person, and looked much the better for it. His head was up, his shoulders were set, his entire face looked more relaxed and there was a fluidity to his movement which was never there before. At first glance Jakes overwhelming thought was – the puppy is gone!

If the puppy was gone in those first few days, then the following two months saw it banished forever. Work could not and would not stop just because of Susie's unexpected visit, nor would she have had it that way if she could. Indeed instead she set about helping where she could, shamelessly encouraged by Jake, and the effect of her help was to totally release Nathan from any and all day to day administration work. She literally took over the lot and, to Jake's surprise and overwhelming joy, demonstrated the sort of entrepreneurial spirit he had always hoped to foster in Nathan. She needed no help, advice or suggestions, but just took over as if she were born to it, with a flair and natural poise which took his breath away. If Nathan was the son he had never had, then Susie would have been the daughter or daughter-in-law he would have longed for. Not only in Jake's eyes, but also in the view of all she came into contact with, Susie could not put a foot wrong.

Those eight weeks seemed to have disappeared in a flash, and once again, all too soon, it was time for Susie to return to Durham. Her earlier concerns regarding Nathan's ability to deal with her going proved both right and wrong. She had been correct in thinking he would be upset at her leaving, he was, and so was she, but she realised her earlier concerns about the possibility of his being hurt were groundless. He understood and accepted the fact she was leaving, but this time both knew she would be back, and would be back as often and for as long as any period would allow. To both themselves and to the world they had become a couple, and the relationship they had cemented was now unbreakable.

Without the restrictions of administration Nathan's progress with the games he was working on had been rapid, and all were much improved. Before Susie departed he showed the enhanced versions to her and Jake, and both were suitably impressed. What he did not show either was a pair of games he was then working on, which he'd started from scratch, keeping the information back because he had not then perfected either game and had no wish to show off, especially with something as yet unfinished and unproven. However it was suggested to Jake it may be a sensible idea to start looking into the production and marketing of games, and Jake promised he would take care of that side of the operation.

Susie's covering of the administration work left Nathan with a clear mind each day, with no distractions save what the two of them would again get up to each evening. With the quality time then available to him he managed to work wonders. Susie's departure did once more leave him with other tasks to perform, but also once again left him with a lot of spare time on his hands, and he threw himself into the work, generally working seven days a week, never less than fourteen hours a day and sometimes more than eighteen. Jake repeatedly tried to slow him down, but without success.

It was nothing short of miraculous the project bore fruit as quickly as it did, but by the end of October Nathan had completed two separate games, and no matter how hard he tested them they withstood any form of breakdown or crash problem. Trade magazines somehow obtained the news and took copies away to play with, then featured Nathan and his products in unbounded glowing prose. The clarity of the sound quality was said to be on a completely separate level to even the very finest of anything else available on the market, and the 3D graphics were later said to have ushered in a new era of gaming. Jake, having known something was in the offing after Nathan's suggestion he should source production and marketing companies had done just that, and the two games from the newly formed NJF Industries Limited swung into production in early November, with product rolling off the belts ready for dispatch by the end of the second week.

The trade magazines were unstinting in their singing of the praises for the new games, the abilities of the new geek on the block, and the openness of the new company. The popular press became involved as did television news, and the effects were staggering. Products for the Christmas market had long since been sourced and ordered by the large chain stores, and a November release would normally be months too late to get Christmas shelf space for a new product. However, such was the interest in the new games, many of the buyers of these large chains changed their purchasing patterns in order to take advantage of the phenomenon and not to lose out on sales to competitors, or concede any competitive market edge. Unfortunately the sudden demand vastly outstripped supply in the first week of production, which was then stepped up to a twenty four hour a day operation. During the same week NJF Industries was approached by a large US games retailer for what amounted to a piece of the action and when they were told of the problems with supply they suggested a manufacturer in the United States who would manufacture under license.

At the end of the third week of November Nathan and Jake flew out of Heathrow to San Francisco, where they were picked up from the airport in a super-stretch limo, the longest car Nathan had ever seen, and taken to a meeting in silicone valley. Before leaving Britain Jake arranged to have specialist lawyers present at the meeting, and three very well paid legal gentlemen were already there. The pace of the meeting was much faster, and the content more businesslike and far more to the point than Jake expected. The entire proceedings completely eluded Nathan on every level possible, but the size, scope and speed of the US operation deeply impressed Jake. Costs, margins, quantities and intellectual rights were all discussed and hammered out. Provisional documents were drawn up and signed. Two days after the first meeting full mutually binding contracts were also signed, and US production swung into action. Three days later production in the US, which had already exceeded that of Britain despite the British two week head start, also ran into problems satisfying demand. The two games were the biggest selling gaming products in history at that point, outselling their closest rivals by more than three to one.

If Jake struggled to understand the financial implications, Nathan had no chance. He could work out it was good, even very good, but the true reality of the developing situation completely escaped him. Certainly he understood figures, and could see the zeros, but then he was used to dealing with long figures with many of those in a chain. If anything Nathan was a little bored with all the talk, and regretted the fact Susie was not there with him. This was the first time he had ever left the country and was fascinated with everything he saw around him, and the American way of life as a whole. The sun was so warm for what should be winter, and everywhere things seemed bigger and the pace faster than back home. There was so much to see and to do, but he and Jake were stuck away in an office talking about figures. Admittedly it was a large and comfortable office, and the hotel rooms reserved for them were incredible, but still he would much rather have been there with Susie, who just seemed so very far away. One day he would return he decided, and when he did it would be with her!

They flew home via New York, where there were more papers to sign, and yet more interviews to contend with because, as with the home market, Nathan's games had taken America by storm, and he was fast becoming a celebrity, much to his apparent concern. That aside, he liked New York. Despite the huge buildings it reminded him much more of home than California had. It was dirty, it smelt, and the people were abrupt and often rude, but it had a good feel about it, and it was cold, and in December the cold felt right. They were not pushed by meetings and lawyers and big offices, but instead had time between the few meetings they attended to do to see things, and Nathan thoroughly enjoyed the little luxuries of the common man. He visited the twin towers of the World Trade Centre, dining in the Windows on the World restaurant at almost the very top, and took a helicopter flight around Manhattan Island. Leaving Jake at a meeting he went alone to the Liberty Island ferry and out to the Statue, where he lined up in the freezing cold for the dubious pleasure of climbing dozens of stairs in a humid crush to try and get an appalling view from a tiny window running with condensation – but he loved every minute of it! Back on the ground he and Jake lunched in Little Italy and then visited China town, where Jake laughed until tears rolled down his face as Nathan tried to haggle over the purchase of a five dollar imitation Rolex watch, which he eventually walked away with for the princely sum of three dollars.

"Why on Earth don't you buy a real one?" Jake had enquired.

"Because they cost a lot of money!" Nathan retorted to Jakes utter disbelief.

They returned to Britain less than two weeks after leaving, aboard a Virgin flight on which Jake absolutely insisted on travelling Upper Class, much to the shock and consternation of Nathan, who knew he could easily buy a not so cheap car for the cost of the two seats. London was cold and wet, but they were home, and Susie did not now seem so very far away.

Susie had just over two weeks off university for Christmas, and Nathan was looking forward to seeing her. He hoped she would take the train straight down to London, where he could meet her, but felt a little disappointed when she said she would have to go home to Foxton and spend her Christmas there with her family. She promised she would try to come down to London just as soon as she could, but that Christmas time really was, and for her family had always been, a time for families.

Feeling a little dejected Nathan returned to drawing up ideas for the next game and got more than a little involved with a project Jake was looking into, namely the possible purchase of their own production facilities. Jake remained most concerned about the supply and demand aspects of both games sales, and felt although there may be certain advantages in controlling supply in order to keep potential buyers keen, failure to meet demand once created was in no way beneficial. He also considered it worthwhile to market only one product at a time in future. That way production could be concentrated, and the products would not effectively compete. Salutary lessons had been learned, and it should not be forgotten the European market, the largest consumer market on the planet, had so far been completely neglected, something which would have to be addressed and resolved in the New Year.

This was an area into which Nathan had already done extensive research, arranging for recordings in German, French, Spanish, Dutch and Italian, which were all completed whilst he and Jake were visiting the United States, and would soon be ready to launch. Regrettably it could not possibly happen until after Christmas, when the domestic market should stabilise, and should then allow production variations. He was also considering the possibility of translating into Japanese, the emerging former Eastern European nations, particularly Polish and Czech and, in view of the size of the potential future market, Russian.

Honestly believing he was not going to see Susie until after her family Christmas, Nathan was bewildered to receive a rather expensive looking card cordially inviting him to spent Christmas and New Year at the Gatting's home, written by the hand of Phil Gatting himself. No RSVP was required, but he was expected on Friday the twenty second of December staying for fifteen nights. Susie had done it again, and once again the surprise for him was complete, although not for Jake, who had been an informed party to the little charade.

Correctly expecting the roads to be busy, and wishing this time to arrive whilst it was still light, Nathan set off at lunch time, eventually pulling onto the gravel courtyard at four in the afternoon. The weather from the M1 across to Foxton had become murky, with ground mist starting to build up as the temperature dropped, and he was glad to have started out at the time he did, but no misty murky weather could possibly dampen his spirits. There were several cars parked on the gravel, at least two more than on his last visit and he guessed they must belong to Susie's brother and sister, neither of whom had he met before. Again Susie was awaiting his arrival, and again she ran to him as he got out of the car, wrapping her arms around his neck and giving him a long deep passionate kiss, which he now knew how to handle.

Her parents were the only ones to be seen as he entered the house. Susie's mother came towards him, kissed his cheek, and said, "It's wonderful to see you again Nathan! I hope you enjoy your stay. Please, please, whilst here feel free to help yourself to anything you like at any time. Now, as to your room. We have put you in with Susie. We hope that is alright with you?"

Nathan was totally taken aback at both her directness and the content of what she had said. "Of course Mrs. Gatting, whatever you think is best." he managed to mumble back, blushing bright red with embarrassment.

"You had better get used to calling us by our Christian names Nathan, especially if you are going to be sleeping with our baby daughter." Phil Gatting chuckled as he stepped forward to shake Nathan's hand. The words did absolutely nothing to relieve Nathan's embarrassment.

If the Christmas period had in the past been a time Nathan enjoyed not at all, Christmas 1995 was unlike the twenty he had previously experienced in each and every conceivable way – and then some! The greater Gatting family, he had now met Susie's sister and brother-in-law, and her brother and brother's fiancée, were perfect hosts, and certainly knew how to make guests feel comfortable and relaxed. The quality of Susie's mother's cooking was exemplary, wine flowed freely and conversation could be stimulating, humorous, interesting, informative or relaxed, or a combination of all. Eating and drinking, talking and laughing by day, and making love to Susie by night, was the thing which dreams were made of. Despite Nathan's humble background and lack of any form of proper education the entire family went out of their way to engage with him whenever they met.

Dawney arrived on Christmas Eve, and was shocked at the change in Nathan, whom she had not seen for nearly eight months because of the work he was doing with the computer games. There was a confidence about his manner and a certain set to his bearing which had never been there before, and her younger sister laughed at the observation when it was mentioned to her, pointing out he was a man now, and he had been a boy before. Christmas dinner was prepared by the women whilst Phil and Clive Gatting, along with their two male guests, were banished from the property, and it was to the local pub they went where Nathan was interested to see the genuine warmth exhibited by the locals for the Gatting family. All four tripped home some two hours later, merry from the ale, relaxed and comfortable in the company of one another.

Dinner was served when they returned, the table laden with food, groaning under the weight. Never had Nathan seen so much food on any family table before and, belly full of good beer or not, he made such an impressive inroad even the Gatting males, not unused to good food in large quantities, found it difficult to match. After dinner they all withdrew to the generous open living room. A wide log fire was burning brightly, throwing heat around the room, and a beautifully decorated Christmas tree stood in a corner, surrounded by presents, each with a little name tag carefully attached. Nathan felt his heart skip a beat, he hadn't considered presents and these people had given so much. He hadn't so much as written out a card! What on Earth was he going to say?

He need not have worried. Susie had assumed he would not think of such things and had bought and labelled accordingly. The presents were pulled out and opened completely at random, with whoever opened the last present selecting the next one to pass on, which sometimes meant they could select another for themselves to the good natured joshing of the rest of the family. Susie had bought a leather bound pewter hip flask each for her brother, father and brother-in-law, with love from her and Nathan, a pair of leather gloves and matching handbag for her mother and similar for Dawney, and Janet Reger lingerie for her sister and brothers fiancée, telling both the items were hand picked by Nathan, much to his consternation.

It was Sheila who picked out Nathan's small present and handed it to him. The label read 'To Nathan with love – The Gatting Family'. Nathan opened the present with care, acutely aware the eyes of the whole family were upon him. The present was beautifully wrapped and tied off with a ribbon, so he pulled the bow and removed the paper gently. There was a small plain cardboard box inside, inside of which was a presentation box. Clearly seen inside that was the timeless beauty and seeming simplicity of what is indisputably one of the world's foremost watches, the Rolex Oyster Perpetual, infinitely more attractive than his Chinatown copy.

The day after Boxing Day, that year a Wednesday, was a day which by tradition the Gatting males would get themselves dropped into Leicester, to Welford Road Stadium, home of Leicester Tigers Rugby Club. Each year, on the twenty-seventh of December, the mighty Tigers took on the Barbarians, a side for whom players could only play by invitation, and the invitation only came to the best of the best, based wholly on merit and ability. The Baa-Baa's were a scratch side, with players who had not trained together – it was theoretically possible some hadn't before met one another – but played a few games together in the same black and white hooped strip, apart from their socks which denoted their home team, and were considered by seasoned selectors to be the best available player for the chosen position. It was invariably a day of the finest rugby to be seen anywhere in the world, easily rivalling that of the New Zealand, South African or any British club sides.

Whether Bath or Leicester were the countries superior rugby team was usually a question of home geography, but 1995 saw the Tigers returned as champions. There was never any doubt about the Baa-Baa's – they were the world's most prestigious rugby club and were held in the highest esteem by all. It has long been argued by many who love the sport that to be selected for the Baa-Baa's was the sports supreme accolade, and put those so selected into a group of the finest, perhaps eclipsing national sides and the British Lions. The club motto is 'Rugby football is a game for gentlemen of all classes, but never for a bad sportsman in any class'. The belief of the club was the game of rugby should be an attacking game, and those selected as Barbarians must always exhibit a style which demonstrated a commitment to hard, clean, attacking rugby. Winning at a game of any sport is generally the desired result, but to the true Barbarian it is the quality of the play and of the game in general which is of primary importance, with winning or losing very much a secondary consideration.

Nathan had not attended a rugby match before; in fact he had not been to any sort of match, so he was in for a rare treat. Phil Gatting was a lifelong member of Leicester, just as his father before him, as was Clive. Rugby – Tigers Rugby – ran in their veins, and Phil had four tickets in his pocket for front row seats in the recently completed Welford Road end Alliance and Leicester stand. Raised in the East End of London, Nathan had lived through a period of highly publicised soccer violence, with marauding gangs of knuckle dragging 'supporters' destroying everything and everyone in their path, and had always assumed all sports attracted that type of moronic psychopath. He was therefore quite astounded at the spirit of good natured camaraderie and open friendship demonstrated en masse at the Tigers ground, and was simply staggered at the number of different coloured team shirts present passing hip flasks backwards and forwards. He had endured years of news reports picturing police officers with linked arms, covered in spit, attempting to control lunatic crowds, yet here, with a near seventeen thousand capacity crowd, there were four policemen on duty, and they were all watching the match, never the crowd!

Arriving an hour before kick-off they immediately headed to the club house and the large Captains Bar on the ground floor, where they enjoyed a couple of pints before taking their seats. After the game they returned once more to the club house, but this time to the Tiger Bar on the first floor, where they were to join the ladies before the post match entertainment began. During the match they all indulged in a gently warming nip or ten of the Rusty Nails with which Phil, Clive and Tony, Shelia's husband, had chosen to christen their new hip flasks. They each bought a round of drinks apiece by the time the ladies arrived, and were all beginning to feel the effects of the alcohol they had consumed. Phil Gatting was struggling to keep up with the three younger men, not because of the quantity of drink, but because of the number of times he had to break off to shake hands and exchange pleasantries with passing Tiger supporters. Jane Gatting arrived with her two daughters, her sister Dawney, and Helen, Clive's fiancée, turning the heads of many of the men present as they tracked the women across the floor. Nathan politely asked the ladies what it was they wished to drink, and then turned to Susie and asked in a slightly slurred voice, "Would you look after my phone for a few minutes? It's noisy at the bar and I won't be able to answer if it rings. Not that I'm expecting any calls!"

Nathan had not received a call on his phone in days, but those words to Susie were heard by the Gods, and they mischievously chose the time to ring. On his way back from the bar, negotiating the press of people, he watched as she raised his phone to her ear. The colour drained from her face as she cast around for a seat and sat down. Nathan reached her side at the same time as Jane Gatting. Both heard Susie say, "I'm sorry, it's very loud here. Could you repeat that slowly please?"

"Thank you. I will tell him," Susie said as she ended the call, looking at Nathan open mouthed and white faced.

"Susie, darling, what on Earth is the matter?" Jane Gatting asked, concerned for her daughter. Susie continued to stare open mouthed at Nathan, not uttering so much as a whisper.

"Susie. Susie!" Jane Gatting was mildly worried and the rest of the family picked up on her concern, congregating around a still open mouthed Susie, who hadn't taken her eyes off Nathan.

"Who was it Susie?" Phil Gatting asked, and the question went home.

"It was Jake," Susie answered in a murmur they all struggled to hear.

"Is there a problem darling?" Phil Gatting asked, squatting in front of her and trying to make eye contact.

"No. Well no! It's Nathan! He's rich! Jesus Daddy, he's fucking loaded!" Susie managed to say in a dazed whisper, uncharacteristically swearing in front of her family, tears welling up in her eyes and spilling down her cheeks completely out of control.

Phil Gatting was a man used to taking charge of situations and comfortable in doing so. He reached out and took the mobile telephone from his daughter's fingers and pressed the buttons to return the call.

Jake answered on the third ring and, thinking it was Nathan, launched into speech. "Hi Nathan, did Susie give you the news already? What do you think of that then?" Jake managed between laughter.

"I'm sorry Mr. Ferris; this is Phil Gatting, Susie's father. I'm sorry to call you back without being introduced, but Susie cannot speak. I think she is in some kind of shock. Could you tell me what it was you told her, and I'll try and sort things out this end?"

"Not a problem at all, and it's Jake Phil, no need for formalities between us I'm sure." Jake replied, and then proceeded to tell Phil Gatting the same news he had just imparted to Susie. Reaching for a chair Phil Gatting sat down next to his daughter, put an arm around her, and he too looked at Nathan with a curious expression on his face.

Eventually he ended the call and he too sat gazing at Nathan almost as Susie had, but without the open mouth or loss of colour.

"Are either of you going to tell the rest of us what is going on?" Jane asked after a few moments silence. It was more curiosity than concerned this time, as she could see from her husband's expression it wasn't exactly bad news – but what was it?

"Well, I don't think this is going to be private, mainly because all the nationals are running with it tomorrow apparently, but it would seem young Nathan here can afford to award himself a pay rise!" Phil Gatting relied.

"Dad, please, stop the cryptic stuff. What has happened?" Clive Gatting now asked.

"Well if Nathan doesn't mind, I'll tell you all." Phil Gatting answered.

Nathan was finding it hard to contain himself. Susie reached out for his hand as he asked her father to tell them what he knew.

"As you no doubt have all gathered, that was Jake Ferris." There were nods from all. "Jake has been contacted by several people in the past hour or so. The provisional figures are out for Christmas sales here in Britain for Nathan's two games. The manufacturing and shipping figures were already known, and all three are very much in accordance with one another. The figures for the States will not be out until tomorrow because of the time difference, but manufacturing figures and shipping figures are known, and sales figures are expected to follow as they did here in the UK due to the popularity. A large, make that very large, American corporation has approached Jake indirectly with an offer for NJF Industries, wishing to buy all intellectual rights and keep Nathan for five years." Phil Gatting explained to them.

Susie spoke for the first time, "But you haven't mentioned figures Dad."

"No, I didn't." Phil replied. "Now the thing is the figures are only provisional, and the true ones will not be known for ten days to two weeks because of the holidays, but as far as the United Kingdom is concerned you, Nathan, as NJF, are thought to have netted a little over eighteen million pounds so far, and I have no idea what was grossed. The American market is set to bring you in at least three times that, and you have an offer, although not a firm one, and it has not yet been offered formally, for NJF, for one hundred and twenty million dollars or ninety million pounds, with five years contracted employment at twelve million dollars a year. As of today that puts your company worth a little over one hundred and sixty million pounds, half of which is yours, and a contract worth sixty million dollars over five years for you. Any which way you look at it, you are worth over one hundred million, and that is before the European, Asian and Australasian markets have even sniffed your product. Personally I thing congratulations are in order," Gatting held out his hand, and as Nathan took it he added, "And the drinks are now most definitely on you!"

Ten

The public face some men put on is not the same as the one they wear in private, and Jeffrey Wild was certainly a man with more than one face. For all his outward arrogant contempt of those lesser beings around and about him, Wild craved complete sexual submission in the privacy of his bedroom. Tammy Hunter had learnt enough about men's sexual preferences to know to give them exactly what they want, and then to go the extra distance and give a bit more. She was quite happy to be put across a man's knee and given a mild spanking or light caning, and had on occasions played around with light bondage. Her philosophy was – What the hell, if both sides enjoy it, it cannot do any harm. That said she did have limits. Anything to do with children, animals and body wastes were completely out, as was any form of permanent marking or severe pain. She may have been a girl ready for a good time and fun, up for most things and just a little kinkier than many, but by accepted normal standards in no way was she a sexual deviant. Jeffrey Wild most definitely was.

Wild's home was his castle, and within his castle he had his very own well equipped dungeon, where his cravings for personal pain, suffering and degradation could be met and meted out in full. In there his public persona and haughty façade crumbled before his masked and leather clad dominatrix. Tammy found some of the costumes he insisted she should wear quite erotic, but everything else most distasteful. Whilst she had no problem with a bit of fun in handcuffs she found nothing attractive about the clamps, cages, benches and chains she found there. Whilst a mild spanking could be sensually arousing the whips, knotted ropes and other flogging devices belonged to the dark ages, and not really even there. She utterly despised this contemptible and pathetic creature. He could see that – and could not get enough of it.

Despite huge reservations on her part they were married inside a year. To the world he had his trophy wife, and she had made a marriage second only to royalty. Married at twenty-six she divorced at twenty-nine. Tammy had never been a greedy grasping gold-digger. She had done well for herself financially in her time, had had the sense to put much of it by for the proverbial rainy day, had looked after her parents and helped her brother. She accepted a reasonable settlement from Jeffery Wild of ten million pounds lump sum, and two hundred thousand a year for life to ensure her silence, which he would have had from her anyway. Both divorce lawyers advised their clients not to settle for the amount agreed between the two of them privately, but to fight. Neither of the lawyers had the background explained to them and Tammy's lips were sealed for life. To the tabloid press she became even hotter property during her divorce, and they raised her profile to celebrity status after the settlement, not at all what the girl from Brighton had ever really desired.

Eleven

The formal offer for NJF came in by the middle of January, by which time Jake and Nathan had discussed things and sought advice. The offer was rejected, as was a revised offer. Another large player got involved and a bidding war followed, by which time production had started to catch up with demand. The European market had taken off and the figures were, as Jake so accurately described them, simply astronomical. Susie had returned to Durham in a still somewhat shell shocked state. Nathan had enjoyed two weeks during Easter with her, both flying down to Athens to take in some early summer sun whilst sight seeing and shopping.

Nathan remained extremely busy and time passed more rapidly than he could ever remember. Each day was filled with work of one kind or another, and he found himself suddenly catapulted into a world of high finance, for which he was singularly ill equipped. The press constantly dogged both him and Jake, but the spotlight fell well and truly on Nathan. He was featured in trade magazines repeatedly, then newspapers and finally had pieces and articles written about him in major international magazines.

His lack of ease with his new found wealth both helped and hindered him. Throughout his life he had wanted to earn sufficient money to break the mould and escape from the life to which he was born. However in many ways he had already accomplished such when he moved into his little apartment which so adequately provided for all his needs. The money which then suddenly became available to him was not 'real', and he found it impossible to use for everyday life. With tens of millions at hand for immediate disposal, many would have followed the seventies pools winner Viv Nicholson's spend, spend, spend philosophy, but not Nathan. One of the interesting things about his character was he had never forgotten those who had helped him.

He employed a financial investigator to track all financial records of Shirley James from the Job Centre and Sally Brown from his early computer course. He had the administration staff, those who had allowed him to have the three old 286's, at the computer centre traced, and then made secret provision for them all. Shirley James had a mortgage and a loan for a car. Nathan paid them off. Sally Brown lived alone in rented accommodation and had little outstanding in the world. Nathan matched the money he had given Shirley James, and had then added fifty thousand pounds to each of their accounts. For Simon, the young lad he had worked with, who had picked him up on his first day of work, and who was responsible for the present of the mountain bike, Nathan bought a three year old model of the car Simon had always talked about – the three litre inline six Mercedes 300SL. For the computer school admin staff and all the staff of Bow Creek garage he had bought a number of cruises which varied in terms of geography and duration, and reflected how he had in the past been treated.

It is said that no good deed should go unpunished. His self appointed role of secret benefactor failed. The press got hold of the story and once again he became front page news and, as an unfortunate consequence, he was temporarily forced to move from the flat in order to avoid the throngs of reporters and cameramen, and seemingly endless irritating and time wasting callers. He also found it necessary to employ a secretary, specifically to deal with the bags of begging letters which came as a result, each of which was replied to politely, but firmly rejected without Nathan viewing a single one of them.

Days passed in a blur, becoming weeks which rapidly turned to months. Whenever possible he devoted himself to the next game, and by the time Susie arrived at the beginning of July game three was finished. By then he was back in his little flat, the place where he felt most comfortable, and life almost returned to that which was regarded as normal before the previous Christmas. European and US sales had peaked and were now subsiding, whilst Asian and Australasian were growing, but the demand could now be managed. Susie easily stepped into a managerial role working alongside Jake whilst Nathan started organising early production of his latest creation. A factory had been purchased in Plaistow, a few hundred yards from the West Ham tube station, two stops from Upton Park and three quarters of a mile from Bow Creek garage. The building was completely refurbished and fitted with all the latest technological and manufacturing equipment required to cater for the growing needs of NJF Industries, and the tail end of some orders were completed on site, successfully testing both equipment and staff.

Once again Susie excelled in her role. Jake came to understand what Nathan may lack in entrepreneurial flair he certainly made up for with creativity, whilst without a doubt Susie was incredibly bright and perceptive. She worked well with her people, understood their needs, and had an intuitive grasp of business and business principles. As a team the two young people would go a long, long way, and in less than a year Susie would have taken her degree and university would be behind her. All the indications were she would want to pick up the reins at NJF, and Jake could not think of another person who could match her capabilities. By the turn of the millennium he could take more of a back seat and allow these two talented and gifted young people the chance to take a very prosperous and successful company forward into the twenty-first century.

The third game hit the streets running. Lessons had certainly been learnt from the first release, and a substantial production run was stockpiled in advance, ready for immediate distribution. The press were superbly handled by Susie, with favourable and well versed articles appearing in a managed time frame prior to the planned release date. Interviews, when held, were arranged and all but stage managed, with those reporters which had previously been regarded as the most helpful given both greater access to the product and more time for evaluation.

A launch date was set. On the twenty-third of June the Nintendo 64 video game system was released. NJF liked the idea of a Saturday launch date, but wanted the market to settle a little from the Nintendo impact first, and to give themselves time to let the press do their thing, so a six week window was decided upon, with the UK and this time also European launch to be held simultaneously on Saturday the third of August. The US launch was planned for one week later, Saturday the tenth, to allow for the closing of the Atlanta Olympics on Sunday the forth of August. Susie's birthday was on the thirtieth of July, with Nathan's seven weeks later on the seventeenth of September, the day after Susie had to be back at university. They had both missed their twenty-first birthdays the previous year mostly because they were so wrapped up in one another and enjoying themselves so much the birthdays just seemed to have slipped by, although they had gone out on the town for Susie's.

Many things were coming together, this time in a planned way. It was decided the full European launch should be left to Jake, with Nathan and this time Susie flying out to the US to oversee the American launch. Nathan wanted to spend time in the States with Susie without undue pressure of work, and it was therefore decided they should fly out to Los Angeles on Sunday the twenty-first of July, which would give them almost three weeks in California before the big day, and plenty of time to recover from any jet lag before Susie's birthday.

This time Nathan had a chance to relax, to travel and to enjoy, and enjoy they both did, hiring a car and touring, staying in cheap motels and ordinary hotels. Although Susie was to do most of the driving even Nathan enjoyed the odd spell behind the wheel, something he usually hated and avoided at home. They landed at LAX and took the Lincoln Boulevard north west to Santa Monica as soon as they picked up the car. There they found a hotel and went to their room and slept, trying to adjust as rapidly as possible to the nine hour time difference. The next day they took the Santa Monica Boulevard into West Hollywood and toured around the homes of the stars in Bellaire and Beverley Hills, marvelling at the buildings and architecture, without it once occurring to Nathan he could buy anything he chose. That night they stopped in Malibu and the following morning headed north west, sticking where they could to the old Route 1, travelling through places with the familiar sounding names of Ventura, Santa Barbara and Guadalupe, until they got to the fishing town of Morro Bay where they again stopped for the night in a Travelodge. That evening they dined on the pier, eating fish landed by the trawlers and handed up through the hatches to the restaurants above straight off the boats.

The morning saw them visiting the Hearst 'Castle', a conglomeration of buildings with varied historical and architectural backgrounds, a Teutonic hunting lodge next to a Grecian pool and a Gothic library with surface mounted wiring and gilded plastic light switches. A seedy, tasteless mishmash to Susie and Nathan's eyes, but the height of sophistication, poise and elegance to many of the other tourists. On up Route 1 to Monterey. Then across to San Francisco for three nights on Fisherman's Wharf. Visits to the Golden Gate and Alcatraz, and a brief meeting with lawyers, and then off again to the spectacular beauty of Lake Tahoe's mountains, with a desert on one side, snow covered peaks above and a huge bright cobalt blue lake at their feet. A night staying at a casino in Heavenly on the Nevada side of the state line, then south to the simply incredible sights of Yosemite National Park with its narrow passes, Giant Sequoia trees, sheer buffs and craggy peaks. A night in a log cabin, then east out of the park and south on the interstate to Lone Pine, turning east once again through Death Valley, stopping at the Visitor Centre at Furnace Creek, then on again for three nights in Las Vegas, and time to enjoy Susie's birthday. They visited the Hoover Dam and took an extended flight through the Grand Canyon, landing for a lunch of rattlesnake and crow pie. Leaving Vegas they headed south to Lake Havasu City, the new home of London Bridge, moved there in the sixties and rebuilt, spanning a lake in an area which to both offered little but poor planning regulations, and tasteless tourist traps.

Crossing the Arizona California border the following morning, which had the appearance of an international frontier, they headed west passing the Mojave Desert to Barstow where they picked up the road to Bakersfield and then north to Fresno where again they stopped for the night so they might be fresh the next day. On the second of August they cut across to San Jose and the Silicon Valley. The main part of their tour was over and from then on they had to mix business with pleasure, but the production unit was working well and everything was well in hand for the US launch. They had asked the advice of their lawyers, whilst staying on Fisherman's Wharf, and had been provided with recommendations to several real estate companies who specialised in industrial premises, with particular emphasis on technology.

The term Silicon Valley refers to the north western end of the Santa Clara Valley, which in turn is located at the southern end of the San Francisco Bay. The silicon part comes from the high concentration of technology related companies in the area. Where once there had been orchards there were now semiconductor and computer related industries and electricity companies.

Before leaving Britain, Jake, Nathan and Susie engaged in a conversation about the possible way forward for NJF Industries. They had taken an enormous amount of money on the sales of the first two games, and would continue to do so as they advanced into other markets. However there were major costs associated with what they had done which, had they had knowledge and understanding of what was involved, they may have arranged and handled differently. One of their early decisions was to furnish themselves with their own production premises in the UK, and this had been accomplished. Production costs for the new game would be considerably less per unit because of that decision, and the same thing would probably hold true in the US, if they could find suitable premises in the best possible location. The State had to be California and, if it was to happen, the San Francisco Bay area would have to be the location of whatever site they chose. Having been there twice, and after three days of looking at and researching into the various possibilities, Susie and Nathan narrowed the area down to a comparatively small triangle which was made up of Menlo Park to the west, Palo Alto Airport to the east and Stamford University to the south.

The geological background to Susie's geography degree course suggested any venture should be located much further east, as far away from the San Andreas Fault as possible, but practicalities suggested the centre of the triangle would probably provide the ideal location, somewhere near the Stamford Shopping Centre. This was the very heart of Silicon Valley, and consequently prices were extremely high, and still rising fast. Computer sales worldwide were growing exponentially, and manufacturers of hardware, component parts, games, software and those involved with all associated supplies were rapidly growing alongside. Many of the companies whose names were familiar to Nathan already had headquarters in the area, and venture capital companies had followed them. One particular area, West Menlo Park, drew the attention of both. Susie had been brought up with property, property deals and market demands. She could see that although the area was horrifically expensive the value was going to keep increasing because of the location, despite the Fault.

They spoke to Jake mid morning on Monday the fifth of September, which was early evening for him back in the UK. Sales of Armageddon – Final Conflict, the third of Nathan's games, launched on the Saturday, had gone as ballistic as the name of the game itself implied and, despite having stockpiles in advance, and the factory churning out the product, they were once again struggling to meet demand. The game had then been available for only three days, and Nathan was a phenomenon at home, with the press clamouring for interviews a constant. As far as Jake was concerned they were both sensible people. Susie possessed wonderful knowledge of property and Nathan was responsible for creating the wealth in the first place. If they wanted to go for anything then they could, and were assured of his full and unconditional backing.

That afternoon they met agents at four possible sites, discussed purchase prices, building costs, purchase complications and all manner of things relating to the acquisition of the plots. Overnight they discussed the various possibilities and rejected two. The following morning they revisited the sites, drew out rough plans, contacted the respective agents and offered full asking price on both pieces of land, either of which would suit them and both were in the same area, almost touching one another, just off Sand Hill Road. Nathan could not fully come to terms with what he was doing and, had Susie not been there he felt he would probably have run away. The millions he had available to him were still not real, and since arriving in America they had driven themselves in a hired compact car, staying overnight in cheapish mid range hotels and motels. The only extravagance of the trip so far was the flight over the Grand Canyon – yet here he was suddenly doing property deals worth millions of dollars – dollars – what the hell were they?

As if still in a dream the following morning the offers for both plots were accepted. The same afternoon they visited their lawyers, and Susie made the decision to proceed with both purchases, reasoning they had the money, they wanted a property and if they had both and put in for plans on both they were more likely to get one passed. Besides the values were increasing almost daily and if they wished to dispose of land later they would probably do so at a substantial profit. Nathan just nodded his head and went along with it. Whilst sitting in the meeting he had not really been listening as this sort of thing was beyond him. He had however worked out, when one of the lawyers stopped to blow his nose, that the real cost of the man wiping his nose was more than two hours pay back at Bow Creek Garage. He wished he had tried to listen, and not work that out.

Armageddon – Final Conflict launched in the US to much fanfare and media interest. Due to the unprecedented runaway success of his previous games most sections of the media seemed to cover the launch. Advance orders had been met in full, and major quantities were also shipped on a sale or return basis. By 11.00 a.m. it was clear there was unlikely to be any returns, and by midday that was a confirmed certainty. Armageddon – Final Conflict tore across the United States and Canada almost as rapidly as the real falling missiles may have done had the Cold War turned hot. Nathan's concerns about the cost of the lawyer wiping his nose were pushed to one side when the news came in that for one short stage sales were breaching the one hundred thousand dollars a minute barrier. NJF Industries could afford the land at West Menlo Park.

With the deal for the land progressing Susie felt they could leave the remainder of the purchase in the hands of their lawyers, and turned her attention to architects, who she knew would have their own contacts and favoured construction companies whom they would have worked with before. She and Nathan set about sorting out some of the fine details of what they would eventually want, and asked for plans to be drawn up and sent on to them for approval or suggestions of amendments. The wheels were in motion with regard land purchase, design and building, but the big problem was always going to be staff, and running a remote operation. In the mid nineties Silicon Valley was arguably the best place in the world for growing corporate entities to lay their hands on fresh, keen techno-weenies, and there were no shortage of recruitment consultants. The only possible problem Susie foresaw was how to properly recruit a decent recruitment consultant. The obvious answer was to pay the money, which they now had in abundance, and go for the bigger agencies with a long term proven track record.

Leaving everything in the hands of lawyers, architects and recruitment consultants, and having spent almost a month in and around California, the pair could see there was little more they could do themselves to progress anything, so they made the decision to return to England. Once more Nathan stopped off in New York, but this time he was with Susie and, much as he got on with Jake, almost like father and son, there were many things he could do with Susie he could never have done with Jake and he was looking forward to seeing the town with her and winding down after their trip. Here there would be no need to drive, to hurry to meetings or to work out the costs of anything more than their food or a couple of drinks. They watched The Phantom of the Opera on Broadway, had a delightfully romantic candlelit meal whilst cruising around Manhattan Island by night, watched the girls rollerblading in Central Park as they took a buggy ride, dinned in the revolving restaurant above Times Square and viewed New York from atop the Empire State Building and the Twin Towers. Again Nathan took the helicopter flight around the island, this time far more happily with Susie, and once again climbed the this time baking steps of France's most visible gift to the people of the United States of America, the Statue of Liberty.

This time when returning to Britain Nathan had fewer qualms about flying Upper Class with Virgin, and this time the weather when they stepped off the plane at Heathrow was wonderful, a warm sunny day and a cloudless sky. Jake had had them met at the arrivals hall and they were whisked away from the airport and out onto the M4, to then sit in the traffic as it slowly inched across London. It took over an hour and a half of fatigue, frustration and fumes to cross from Heathrow to Upton Park. They had flown through the night and, comfortable as the flight was, it remained a flight through the night. Their bodies were still endeavouring to adjust from Pacific Time to Eastern Time whilst in New York, and now they were another five hours removed from that, leaving their body clocks confused as to whether they should tick or tock. Pleased though they were to be home the first thing they needed was sleep, which was just what they did.

A little over a month had elapsed since they had flown out to the States, a month in which Jake had worked wonders with many of the functions at Plaistow. The offices over the production floor now seemed to be filled with competent staff, and the people on the factory floor were working well, with games making their way down the line from component parts to finished goods, which were then dispatched by day and night.

Nathan went straight back to work on design. Two months before leaving for the States another young designer was employed to help Nathan with background, and had done a lot of work whilst left on his own. Mike Hall was older than Nathan, had gone through a school which taught their pupils, and then progressed through college and university on a graphic design course. He was good at what he did, and was thorough to the point of being exacting. Unfortunately he lacked a little imagination where new projects were concerned, which had meant, good as he was at what he did, he could not be left with a complicated project of his own. However due to the quality of his design work and his painstaking nature Nathan had left him with a card game and a game of Chinese checkers to work on, and was extremely happy with the results.

There had been another development whilst they were away in that another young lad was recommended to Jake by a very grateful Shirley James. Nathan invited him in for a hands-on interview, and the youngster demonstrated lots of raw talent, though no formal training. He was taken on for an extended trial, and Nathan made time available to help steer and guide him. By the time Susie returned to Durham young Iain McGregor was starting to show a great deal of promise.

Iain was from Highland stock, born in the village of North Ballachulish, south of Fort William, on the banks of Loch Leven, beneath the iron bridge where the fresh run off waters of the Ben Nevis and Glen Coe mountain range meet the salt waters of Loch Linnhe. It could well be argued that the West Highlands sheer rugged beauty is the most spectacular on offer anywhere in the British Isles. With the single exception of the notorious and persistent Scottish midges the area is a joy to visit in the summer months, with tourism understandably increasing year on year. In winter there is skiing at Aonach Mor and Glencoe, but the industry there has never grow as the French, Austrian and Swiss resorts have, due mostly to its remoteness, short daylight hours, lack of range of skiing and overwhelming cold. Beautiful though the region is, without industry or guaranteed continuity of long term employment the long dark winters and hard lives drive people from the area in search of easier and more comfortable lifestyles.

So it was with Iain's family. His father had worked in the kitchens of one of the two hotels set facing one another across the mouth of the loch, and had never seriously considered change. Iain, two years older than his brother Hamish, grew up without ever considering future change. An unexpected and unplanned pregnancy changed all their lives and, at the ages of fifteen and thirteen, Iain and Hamish were presented with a baby sister, Morag. The cost of another mouth to feed and back to clothe proved too much for the family budget, and they were forced to move south in search of work. The Lowlands and North of England were bypassed. The money was in the south, primarily the south east, in and around London, but London was expensive, especially so to a West Highlander. Eventually work for his father was found in a hotel at the new Custom House development off Royal Victoria Dock which paid enough to rent a modest home, and continue to raise a small family.

Iain completed his education whilst struggling to adapt to the major change which had overtaken his life. He had been around computers before puberty and grew up with them, finding them a release throughout the long winter nights of his early teens. The move south, lack of friends and 'funny' accent meant he spent more time on them since relocating than his parents thought healthy. He was not born with a gift as Nathan was, but he enjoyed a particular natural talent and flair for the concepts involved which went well beyond the grasp of the average person, and Nathan saw his lack of formal training as an enormous plus point. Iain possessed undisputed talent, and possessed it by the bucket full. This young person, only four years Nathan's junior, was a person Nathan could not only work with, but someone he could teach and train in a way which would not have been possible with anyone who had already gone through a methodical or rigid training processes.

The differences between young Iain McGregor and the older Mike Hall, both working in the same sector of the same industry, could not have been more apparent. Mike was somewhat staid and unimaginative, but a dedicated slogger, whilst Iain had a wild and vivid imagination, but lacked discipline, flitting from task to task and never properly completing anything. Individually they would be an aid to any graphic design organisation, but would never excel. Put in harness together the whole became much greater than the sum of the parts, and by the time Christmas came around again even Nathan was impressed with the quality of the work they were jointly turning out.

Twelve

In October 1996 The Green Howards deployed to Bosnia, taking over from The Worcester and Sherwood Foresters. The Battalion was part of 20 Brigade. B Company were co-located with the Battalion and Battle Group HQ in Gornji Vakuf. C Company were originally garrisoned at Previa but moved to Jajce taking over from a Dutch Armoured Infantry Unit in the early part of December. Thousands of UK personnel were there serving as part of a vital peacekeeping force in support of the UN, who had pulled out in 1995, NATO and the EU. For every single person involved without exception it was a thankless, deeply frustrating and a monumentally confusing deployment.

If Chris Spencer found the problems with Northern Ireland difficult to follow they now seemed like a walk in the park by comparison with the conflict which occurred in Bosnia-Herzegovina, and was still bubbling beneath the surface. The war between the multi-ethnic population which broke out in Bosnia during 1992 was brought to an end with the Dayton Peace agreement signed at the end of 1995. At least that was the official version for the world press. Certainly relative peace and stability in Central Bosnia was restored and further Bosnian Serb bombardment of Sarajevo deterred, which helped keep open the main supply route into the beleaguered city. Fighting was at an effective standstill. All of which was to the good.

However what NATO troops from all nations found sickening, and which sickened them to their very core, was what had happened, and would happen again if they pulled out. For any who were drafted in or visited the area through those times it was impossible to explain to sane people elsewhere the depravities which had occurred when people who lived side by side for generations turned upon one another. The term ethnic cleansing was first used and established by the free press around the world as an acceptable, almost sanitised, even hygienic, term. Mutilation, gang rape, assassination, mass killings, butchering of entire families, and genocide were all covered by – ethnic cleansing. To Chris the term itself was unacceptable, should never have been used, and certainly never been popularised. Those on the ground bore witness to acts of untold cruelty, barbarism and extreme examples of man's inhumanity to man. There was nothing sterile in that.

In the early 1990's, aware of some of what was occurring on its south eastern border, the mainland European Unions various delegates discussed the matter amongst its members and, unwilling to act alone and without UN approval, merely condemned the activities. Unsurprisingly this changed nothing and the killings continued. Despite the fact Britain, with John Major as Prime Minister, and the US, with George Bush as President, wished to sit on their hands and look the other way, the EU, pushed by Germany, eventually involved the United Nations. As always happens when anything is put before the UN, delegates debated the issues in depth, condemning the atrocities, and calling on all sides to desist. Despite a great deal of talk, little thought seemed to have been given to the root causes based on the history of the disintegrating Yugoslavia, or of the then current practicalities.

In 1929 the Kingdom of Yugoslavia came into being, replacing the Kingdom of Serbs, Croats and Slovenes. In 1941 it was invaded by the Axis powers and, due to the events which followed, was officially abolished in 1945. During World War II, in 1943, the Democratic Federal Yugoslavia was proclaimed by the communist resistance movement, only to be renamed the Federal People's Republic of Yugoslavia in 1946 when a communist government was established. In 1963 it was once more renamed, changing to the Socialist Federal Republic of Yugoslavia, and was made up of six socialist republics and two autonomous provinces. From north to south these were Slovenia, Croatia, Bosnia and Herzegovina, Montenegro, Serbia (including the autonomous provinces of Vojvodina and Kosovo & Metohija, which later became simply Kosovo) and Macedonia. Starting in 1991 this amalgamation of states disintegrated in the Yugoslav Wars which followed.

They were characterised by bitter ethnic conflicts between the peoples of the former Yugoslavia, mostly between Serbs on the one side and Croats, Bosniaks or Albanians on the other. However, the Bosniaks and Croats in Bosnia, and Macedonians and Albanians in the Republic of Macedonia, also more than played their part. The conflict had its roots in various underlying political, economic and cultural problems, as well as long-standing ethnic and religious tensions, but that was not the full story. Unmasked, open aggression released the floodgates to bloodletting which had not been seen in Europe since WWII. The chance to settle old scores was rarely missed, and any bearing personal grudges used the opportunity to remove those who troubled them under the guise of ethnic or religious cleansing.

Eventually continued EU pressure, still led by Germany, now with help from others, including the US, by then under the Clinton administration, forced the issue and in December 1995 NATO was given a one year mandate to implement the military Annexes of The General Framework Agreement for Peace in Bosnia and Herzegovina. Strengthened for the first time by American troops, Operation Joint Endeavour with a NATO led multinational force assembled as The Implementation Force (IFOR). The Joint Force Commander for the operation was Admiral Leighton Smith, who became Commander in Chief Allied Forces Southern Europe (CINCSOUTH). On the nineteenth of December 1996 IFOR disbanded and the NATO led Stabilisation Force (SFOR) took over with seventeen non-NATO nations also involved. SFOR had a deployed strength of over thirty thousand men for what had then become Operation Joint Guard, part of which was a five thousand strong British force which began an eighteen month tour in Bosnia-Herzegovina as Operation Lodestar.

The British forces in Northern Ireland had experienced severe problems at times in keeping warring factions apart, and in protecting communities from one another, but generally those communities were at least reasonably clearly defined over generations. Throughout the Balkans this was not the case with peoples from different ethnic, cultural, and religious backgrounds mixing and mingling far more freely. By the time Chris Spencer arrived with the Green Howards that had ended. Ethnic cleansing had made sure communities were 'pure'. Those who did not belong were gone. The lucky ones fled, mostly empty handed, leaving all their worldly possessions in the hands of their oppressors. The not so lucky were also gone, butchered and exterminated, some buried in shallow communal graves, some piled high and their bodies burnt, and others left where they fell, swelling and putrefying as a poignant reminder to all who saw them. Properties had also been burnt, blown up or bulldozed, often with the occupants still sealed inside. Dwellings which still stood were occupied by those who had disposed of the original owners and land redistributed as seen fit. Serbs had conducted a strategy of sexual abuse on Bosnian Muslim girls and women, herding them into rape camps where they were forced to live in intolerably unhygienic conditions whilst being systematically raped and sodomised.

Historical suspicion and mistrust had helped fuel the tensions in Northern Ireland and extremists on both sides were able to exploit the situation, sometimes for no other reason than personal advantage or betterment. Chris and his men soon came to understand the situation they were faced with in Bosnia was infinitely worse. It was not just religious factions in conflict, but mainstream cultures, complicated by major cultural differences and diverse ethnic backgrounds. Suspicion and mistrust were replaced with deeply rooted jealousies and compulsively motivated hatred for all who did not conform to the ideology of the greater community. Years of grinding poverty, oppression and suppression had inflamed the passions of the various communities. When communism which successfully held all in check for decades finally failed, the pent up pressure exploded into rampant genocide.

Sergeant Chris Spencer led his men through streets where extreme personal danger was the order of the day, and could be so every day. Saxon and Warrior APC's were used on occasions, but the greatest requirement was for the deterrent effect produced by conspicuous foot patrols. Under Sergeant Spencer's direction and guidance his men carried out stop and search operations, armed arrests, underwent fire-fights and provided protection services for visiting dignitaries, big brass and high profile prisoners. All he and his squad completed was done without loss or injury. Wherever possible the use of firearms was restricted, prisoners were taken unharmed, and none were ever abused by those on his watch. In demonstrating fairness of recommendation in both punishment and reward he earned the respect and confidence of his officers as well as that of his men. His tactical and technical proficiency and the exercising of initiative by taking appropriate action in the absence of orders, coupled with outstanding leadership qualities earned him a crown above his stripes. To some a staff sergeant but by convention in infantry regiments, a Colour Sergeant.

Thirteen

Mike Latham and John Cartwright had remained close friends since their early childhood. They grew up a few streets from one another, and went to school together for eleven years in the small Hampshire town of Hamble-le-Rice. Hamble nestles alongside Southampton Water, which leads to The Solent, on a relatively small triangular peninsular to the south east of Southampton, and is therefore obviously surrounded on two sides by water. Hamble is boat country, pure and simple.

Both boys grew up with a love of boats and the water, something which had never left either of them. Mike Latham remained in Hamble and eventually bought himself a decent waterside property with its own small jetty from which he could make the daily twelve minute journey to and from work on the opposite side of The Solent, saving himself a couple of hours a day in the car. John Cartwright's parents moved when John was sixteen to Thatcham, east of Newbury in Berkshire, some forty-five miles away, in order that John's father may take advantage of a promotion working from his company's head office at Theale, just outside Reading.

John and Mike continued with their education, although now separately, passing through college into university. From the time of his family's move John desperately missed the sea, sailing and boats in general. As soon as he passed his driving test every holiday and long weekend he repeatedly drove back down to Hamble to stay with Mike and his parents. The habit remained, continued through college and university into his early working career, and even after he married.

John Cartwright met Sandra Marlow at a work function. She was a Home Counties girl from Virginia Water in Surrey, was tall and slim with long wavy brown hair and indeterminate coloured eyes which seemed to change with the light. She was bright and well spoken with an obvious rounded education. They had fallen for one another and married quickly. Sandy also loved the pilgrimage to Hamble almost as much as John, and fitted in perfectly with the local boating set where she cut a fine figure in a bikini or T shirt and shorts, and looked as good as she sounded in heels or deck shoes.

Throughout their lives Latham and John Cartwright had remained the closest of friends and Latham automatically extended the friendship to include John's wife. The three of them, along with various passing lady friends of Mike's, spent many a splendid time on or around Southampton Water, The Solent and the waters around and about the Isle of Wight. Long weekends and summer holidays continued as they always had for the two friends, the only real changes in their lives being ever larger salary cheques and, as a consequence, ever larger motor cruisers. Both could sail, and sail well, and the purist in both enjoyed wind in sails, but both had a passion for the internal combustion engine, the power generated, and the deep sense of satisfaction produced when properly manoeuvring a large craft in difficult water.

Sandy came to love life near the water. After marrying she and John bought a cosy three bedroomed detached thatch cottage just outside Hungerford, to the west of Newbury. It was a costly move because properties in the area commanded a high price, but both enjoyed well paid jobs, the cottage was exactly what they wanted, and each could easily commute to work from their new home, John on the motorway to Reading, and Sandy with an easy drive to Newbury. Their next move they both promised one another would be to a property next to the sea, preferably to Hamble, certainly near The Solent.

John Cartwright's drive to work was usually an easy one with the trip normally taking about half an hour. The morning showed all the promise of a beautiful day to come. There was a trace of ground mist in the low lying areas as John left home, but he knew it would burnt off by mid morning to be followed by a clear and beautiful sunny day. The traffic was of the usual mid week kind and John thought nothing of the patch of low lying mist in a hollow on a stretch of motorway between Newbury and Reading. He eased off the throttle slightly as he drove into the mist and entered at just over sixty miles an hour. There was no outward sign of the density of the fog within, or of the tangled twisted wreckage of vehicles already smashed and destroyed beneath its covering. His car ploughed into the back of an articulated vehicle laden with steel from the Port Talbot steelworks. He had no chance to even hit the brakes but just slammed straight into rear of the truck.

His right leg snapped on impact, his left foot was trapped under the pedals and he dislocated his right shoulder as the inertia reel seatbelt wrenched his bones apart, but he survived the initial crash. Two seconds later an eight wheeler bulk grain carrier weighing just over thirty tonnes and travelling at fifty one miles an hour tail-ended him, crushing his car down to less than half its original length and John was impaled on his steering column. His life ended three seconds later. Both trucks, very little damaged, were later driven clear of the pile-up and taken to a Ministry of Transport pound for checks.

John Cartwright's death devastated Sandy and deeply shook Mike Latham. For Latham his lifelong friend was dead, and the boating, sailing, diving and water skiing the two boys then men had endlessly enjoyed together were gone forever. In many ways it was a coming of age event for Latham, after which he got his head down and concentrated far more on his work. Fleeting relationships with passing women occurred, but nothing and nobody held his attention as much as his work. None of the women were prepared to sit around and play second fiddle to bitumen, not that Latham ever considered asking one to. His relationship with Sandy continued, but she was his best friend's wife, in death as in life, and neither ever tried to bridge the gulf.

For Sandy Cartwright, Mike Latham remained a solid unmoving rock to which she could cling during a period of total desolation. Her life was turned upside down by the sudden and unexpected death of her husband. Before his death she and John were young aspiring professionals who earned well, and both made suitable provisions for the other in case of an accident neither ever expected to happen. Due to this Sandy was left well provided for financially, but she cared not a jot about the money. A large part of the very centre of her life was gone. In some ways it was partly to do with keeping the memory of John alive that she continued to make the journey down to Hamble. It was also because she had enjoyed the life which went with it, and very much still did, along with the friendships she had developed amongst John and Mike's friends and acquaintances.

Nine months after John's death she made the decision to change her life and lifestyle. She had passed her mid thirties and had had enough of chasing the tiger. Her job paid well but put her under pressure, and stress at work was one thing she really did not need, so she put the house on the market and as soon as she found a buyer who could complete quickly she handed in her notice. She dropped ten thousand pounds on the price of the house to avoid buyers involved in chains, sold the property four months later, banked the proceeds and headed for Hamble where she bought herself a charming little cottage in the village of Bursledon, and took a job as the manager of a store in the new Hedge End shopping mall. It was a break with the past, and a complete lifestyle change, with less money to be sure, but with a much improved quality of life. Slowly, with the help of the new job, the new friends which came with it and the friendships she already had established in the area, the joy of life crept back into her shattered world.

Despite the feeling of helplessness which bordered almost on inadequacy in the face of such abject horror, Chris Spencer's nine month tour of Bosnia fortunately passed without incident and in July 1997 he was returned to Osnabruck and 7 Armoured Brigade. The deployment was akin to a holiday after Bosnia. With the Soviet threat now seemingly removed forever and a significantly smaller deployment in Germany, life was comfortable, and it remained comfortable for the next twenty months. He was extremely well suited to the needs of the Armoured Infantry, and in all simulated battlefield confrontations used Warrior APC's with great proficiency.

With the time and training facilities available which smaller active personnel numbers made possible Chris underwent an intensive course in close quarter combat, including hand to hand fighting and unarmed combat. The unarmed combat instructor was superb, and had, when younger, been short listed to represent the country at the Olympics with his chosen discipline, Judo. During his very early training at Catterick Chris had gone through a similar course and he, as with others, was put through refresher courses periodically, but never before had he gained so much from an instructor. For the duration of the deployment Chris made it his business to learn and to train in the arts of unarmed combat whenever time permitted. By the time he left Germany he was arguably as deadly with his bare hands as he was with his individual weapon or a Warrior APC.

Fourteen

Eventually Susie's studies at Durham came to an end. She left university, stopped off at Foxton for a week, then in July 1997 finally moved in with Nathan full time. She, along with Nathan and her family, returned to Durham for her graduation ceremony. Registers were signed, scrolls changed hands, caps were flung in the air and Susie left with her Geography first.

For Jake, who was invited to attend the ceremony but was forced to decline due to pressure of work, the day was the best he could remember for more than five years. Susie would finally be coming back, and Susie possessed the brains required to head NJF Industries better than anyone else he had ever known, including himself. He could certainly help her with contacts but understood his own limitations. He had lucked out big time in life and done very well for himself thank you very much, and made millions with good sense, good luck and the ability to understand and foresee market movements. Over many years his little empire grew from nothing into a reasonable sized conglomerate and, apart from the rewards, it had been fun building it all up. Unlike Nathan he had not been born into abject poverty, but his upbringing was a long way from the silver spoon. He was a self-made man who throughout his life operated legitimately and was able to hold his head high in the circles in which he operated. Finding Nathan proved to be the greatest gain of his financial life, and the rewards which had since flooded in were not just beyond his experience, but quite literally vastly exceeded his comprehension.

Building his business empire, which was now worth millions, had started even before he left school at fifteen. He was now turned fifty. Thirty-five years work saw him grow his interests from buying and selling bicycles at school to doing the same with entire companies. At times it had proved to be hard work with many hours devoted to chasing very little reward. To onlookers it probably seemed easy – Jake the Lad, as he was once called – but those others were not up before four in the morning sorting out problems, nor were they still working at well past midnight. No, it had not always been so easy! Thirty-five years to acquire seventy plus million. Never the time for education, or to learn the niceties and nuances of big business, and now he owned half of NJF Industries. In less than two years it had grown so far and so fast it scared him. To be precise, it terrified him. He was a 'little man' who over time, because of hard work, long hours and dedication, had grown big. NJF Industries were new, but they were not big, they were already huge, with an annual turnover which exceeded that of many nations, and he was not comfortable with it – not comfortable at all. This was something much bigger than he had been born to, but not so Susie.

This was something Susie could handle in her stride. She was born into money in very much the same way a child of his would have been, should he ever have had one. He had not. The closest he would ever come to having paternal feelings was for young Nathan, and he still hoped Nathan would want to take charge of some of his business interests, although Jake knew in his heart Nathan never would. To Nathan money was an abstract. How many people worth countless millions would want to live in a tiny one bedroom flat – and a flat they didn't even own? He could buy the block with one weeks interest on the money available to him, the road if he wished, in fact much of the town. But no. He wasn't interested. There were but two loves in Nathan's world, Susie and computers. Wealth, power and social position meant less than nothing to him, and Jake could see they never would.

In almost every way possible he saw Susie as his salvation. The first day he met her he saw something of a spark inside her. She demonstrated a certain poise and confidence which was rare in people generally, and almost unheard of in a child of just turned eighteen, as she had then been. He still could not help but see her as a child looking back, but child she most certainly was not now. He watched and studied her at any and every opportunity available to him, and goodness how she had she grown. Had he doubted any of his conclusions, although he had not, then the visit to the US the previous year would have dismissed them forever. For some time before the trip he had pushed her slightly into working environments and situations which would easily have fazed a great number of people with vastly more experience than she possessed. She never once faltered or hesitated or, even more importantly, put a foot wrong. She repeatedly demonstrated an uncanny knack of leaving every person in each meeting she attended feeling they had come away well ahead, despite the fact it was she Susie who always carried the day.

Property purchase was an area of business Jake understood well, and it had made him millions. The deal Nathan and Susie managed to put together at West Menlo Park had seemed horrendously expensive at the time to Jake, but he would have been the first to admit he knew nothing of US property prices generally, let alone any specific geographical area. He had given them their heads. Susie had lived around the property market all of her life, and he already knew she was no fool, but still he privately regarded the purchase as both excessive and expensive, especially as she, and he knew it was Susie not Nathan, decided to continue with the purchase of two sites rather than just one. However they were awash with money, and he trusted her, so he had given the project his approval.

That said he too was no fool, and had not acquired his small fortune by throwing money around like confetti, so as a precaution decided to make a few checks on what she had done, quietly and secretly. In time the reports came back, and a large smile spread wide across his face when he opened them and read the contents, particularly one line – Sand Hill Road was growing rapidly in value, with per square foot prices exceeding central Manhattan and London's West End to make it the highest priced commercial property on the planet. So Susie hadn't done well, she had done magnificently. At just turned twenty-two years of age she had sat down and negotiated figures which were simply staggering to normal people. It was time to hand over the reins of NJF Industries and concentrate on his other projects.

Susie's return to London brought change with it. The flat had served its purpose, and served it well. As a property for Nathan to set up on his own, which was both convenient and easily affordable, it had excelled. It provided a place for her to visit, sometimes for weeks at a time to be with the man she loved, and for that she would never forget it. As a primary residence for a multi millionaire couple to live a full time life, it was woefully inadequate. She was fresh out of university and the small rooms which went hand in hand with student life, yet had enjoyed a wonderful childhood in a large and very comfortable family home where there was seemingly always room to expand. She wanted to put down roots in a property she could call home. Her home! Their home! The flat offered two wardrobes, one of which was overflowing before her arrival. A move was certainly called for.

Susie knew Nathan had no illusions of grandeur, and all he had ever desired was a comfortable life, away from the neglect, poverty and squalor in which he grew up. Well he had her now and was never going to be neglected again as long as she lived. The way the market had taken to the games he offered already guaranteed neither of them would ever again experience the poverty of his early life. The little flat was neat and tidy, certainly not squalid, but it was not capable of meeting their current needs. In time she knew they would marry and a while after which she knew she would want kids. Those kids would be born into a loving caring family where their every need would be met, just as hers had, but for that to work they would need a property which was a substantial family home. The problem was – where?

Despite the almost limitless funds available, to properly suit their requirements any property would have to meet many criteria, one of which was to avoid at all costs anything flamboyant or ostentatious as Nathan would never settle. It had to be in the Greater London area, certainly within the M25, but with easy access to the motorway, and preferably to the north of London so travel to and from friends and family would not be difficult. She wanted a large family home, not necessarily matching the one in which she had spent her childhood, but also not so different from it either. It would be wonderful to find something backing onto open countryside yet still be capable of fully securing from intruders, a problem their wealth may create. It was a basic requirement that it had to be within easy access of the tube system, because neither ever again wished to contend with driving across London, and it would have to be relatively close to a decent primary school.

Six months passed as she searched for property, viewing many, discarding most without viewing. She didn't stop, didn't give up and would not compromise as it was just not in her nature. She knew her home was out there somewhere, and she was going to find it no matter how long it took. Towards the end of the year, with the build up for Christmas, the property market can go a little flat, generally reviving with the coming of early spring, so she was not surprised at the reduction of property details which arrived with the post.

The details she had long waited for arrived at the end of the first week of December. With some kind of sixth sense she instinctively knew this was going to be the one as she drew the pages from the envelope.

She went to view alone the same day. The house was substantially built with six large double bedrooms, four with en suite facilities, a wonderful open kitchen diner, separate dining room, study, library and two spacious reception rooms with a sizable conservatory across the rear. There was a four car garage and a generous courtyard to the front, with a long and wide rear garden which stretched down to farmland to the right and woodland to left. Junction 24 of the M25 was a mile and a half away. Cockfosters Station, which was the final northern station of the Piccadilly Line, was less than two miles easy drive straight down Cockfosters Road, and there was a perfectly positioned primary school within walking distance. Access to the property could not have been better from a road where the traffic was remarkably light. It was everything she could have wished for. The vendors had already purchased a retirement property in Provence, and would be most happy to sell to a buyer not involved in any chain, which Susie was not.

Title searches at the Land Registry Office, general checks and the transfer of deeds can take solicitors months to perform. A well motivated solicitor, which in legal speech means well paid, who is prepared to personally travel between all relevant offices can cut the time considerably. Susie had found what she wanted, had agreed full asking price with two very happy vendors, and wanted to be in the property by Christmas. Her solicitor was very well motivated, and performed the minor miracle as instructed. Ten days later the property was hers. She used some of the intervening week to do what women the world over do best – shop. The Monday morning on which the property changed hands saw a small fleet of delivery vehicles arrive with a mass of furniture and furnishings. A professional workforce carried, laid and assembled as Susie instructed, and by late afternoon the property had become a home. Susie travelled back across London by tube, met Nathan and returned to the flat with him. There she told him to pack an overnight bag as she had a surprise for him. He drove her to their new home and entered before she broke the news to him he was then standing in the house they were going to spend many years in.

Whilst property hunting, Susie also took the reigns of NJF Industries from Jake. She settled easily into the role, exactly as Jake knew she would, and everything about the company was moving forward seamlessly. She and Jake left Nathan behind working on his next game whilst they flew out to San Francisco for three days to check on progress. Fifty year old business entrepreneur and property tycoon Jake Ferris was astonished at what this girl at his side had managed to put together. Some fifteen months earlier she had flown over in many ways unprepared, bought land, discussed building requirements, engaged architects, who in turn, at her direction, involved construction companies and crews who had now almost finished the remarkable structure he saw in front of him. By the early part of the New Year not only would the building work be finished, but it would soon afterwards be fitted out and ready to start up production.

It was time to seriously consider engaging staff. Nathan would have to be involved further down the line if it was thought necessary to employ graphic designers, but until such a point Susie could manage things herself. The agents she contacted the previous year had been at work, and notification of her and Jake's intended visit allowed them time to set up interviews with potential candidates. There would eventually be many positions to fill, but at this stage they wanted to engage a project manager to oversee the last of the building work and all the fitting out. They would need a Chief Executive Officer, Finance Director, Sales Director,

Marketing Director and a Technical Director who would head up research and development. They would also later need to interview someone to fill the chair of the personnel manager, or Human Resources as it was increasingly becoming called, and someone to take charge of security. In all eight positions, five executive and three non executive, but their most important immediate concern was the pressing need for the project manager.

Jake viewed the pile of CV's for the various positions, and realised the decision he had taken to encourage Susie to head NJF was certainly the correct one. Most of the potential candidates had a string of letters after their names, and Jake did not have the first idea what any of them stood for. He knew he would have been completely out of his depth had he attempted to arrange interviews for any of the prospective executive officers. In fact he very much doubted he would even be able to hold a conversation with some of them. Susie on the other hand had no such qualms or uncertainties. They short listed three potential project managers, and interviewed them all. Each of the three seemed eminently well qualified but were very different personalities, and ranged in age from twenty three to thirty nine.

Susie conducted the interviews personally, with Jake sitting in to add or inquire as he wished, something he could do with this part of the project as he was used to and comfortable with dealing with project managers, many of whom he had previously required for his various projects. The first to be interviewed was the oldest of the applicants. He was rejected at the interview by a very blunt Susie. Throughout the interview, despite being asked questions by Susie, who sat directly in front of him, he directed his answers to Jake, and on two occasions when he did respond to Susie his answers verged on the patronising or condescending. She told him quite matter-of-factly he need not wait for any form of written confirmation; he would not be further considered. The next interviewee was in his late twenties. He was tall, bright and handsome, and he knew it. Susie fully appreciated the people of the United States were somewhat more forthright and brasher than the majority of those in the United Kingdom, but she wished to engage someone she knew she would be able to work with for a long time to come. This guy was well qualified for the job in hand, that was certain, but she did not like his braggart attitude, and knew she would struggle to deal with him. He too was rejected at the interview.

The final person was the twenty-three-year-old, whose CV was quite impressive despite their lack of age, but whose photograph did not do them justice. Chi Lu Herepath was Eurasian, and a product of the union between a USAF father and a South Vietnamese mother. Colonel Herepath had rushed through a marriage with his heavily pregnant girlfriend just before the collapse of Saigon in 1975, and succeeded in bringing her out. He and his wife returned to the States, where Chi Lu was born. Chi Lu had passed through school with an exemplary report, eventually winning a two year MBA course at what Susie knew was one of the most selective graduate programs in the world, Harvard Business School.

Brought up to speak both Vietnamese and Mandarin Chinese Chi Lu was fluent in both and, partly as a result, had chosen Doing Business in China as the Elective Curriculum whilst at Harvard. If the CV and resume were impressive, then Chi Lu in person was much more so, and Susie very nearly said you have the job when Jake stood as the door opened. Some people are unimpressive and only ever gain respect through rank, position or power, whilst some appear to be respected from birth. Others can be missed and overlooked even if standing on an empty railway platform, whilst others stand out in a crowd. Jake and Susie already knew Chi Lu was very, very bright, and had the best of the best CV's they were presented with. What did not come across on paper, or indeed the photograph, was Chi Lu's presence, or her outstanding stunning beauty.

Chi Lu at just turned twenty-three had inherited everything which was physically the best from both racial backgrounds. At five feet ten inches she was tall, exceptionally tall when considering her mother's background, with a straight slender frame, long finely tapered legs and skin which had a natural lustrous 'well tanned' appearance. Her face, framed with long silky black hair, was a picture, with fine eyebrows above slightly almond eyes and a hint of cheekbones. Her nose was straight and relatively narrow, and sat above plump full lips. She could easily have stepped off the cover of Vogue or Cosmopolitan but strangely it was not her beauty, bearing or carriage that shone through so much as the aura of quiet, calm, self-assurance.

She spoke and broke the spell. "Good afternoon. My name is Chi Lu Herepath. I would like to thank you both for seeing me." She smiled slightly, displaying a line of perfect small white teeth. The words, slightly drawn out, were spoken quietly but her voice carried well, in a soft North American accent.

"Please, do sit down Chi Lu." Susie said.

The interview began and Susie ran through a number of questions, listening closely to the answers and probing a little into some of them. Finally they got to the end of the formal questions when Susie threw in an extra one. Something which revealed to Jake she had been paying a lot of attention and held the same concern he did.

"Chi Lu, you seem perfect in every way for us, if anything a little too perfect. You are by far the most highly qualified person we have had for this job, and frankly you could do a lot better. Why have you applied for this position?" Susie asked, expressing genuine concern.

"Susie – if I may?" Chi Lu arched one beautiful eyebrow, and Susie nodded. "I have chosen to work for you because you are going places, and I will go places with you. Sure, I can get a much better job, and much better money than the one you are currently offering working for some of the more established players, and slowly work my way up. With you I come now as your project manager, but the job I want is CEO, and in six months time you will give it to me."

Susie was a little shocked at Chi Lu's openness, and said, "Well that's a very straight answer, and much more than I expected, but I'm not sure what the future will bring, and certainly would not be prepared to make a commitment of that sort."

"I'm not looking for it," Chi Lu replied with a slight smile. "What I am looking for is a chance to start with you as your first employee on this continent. I am well qualified, and I am a very competent person. You are already aware of that or I would not be here. What you cannot be aware of is what I can do, as that has yet to be tested. I'm not looking for any form of promise from you as to what the future will bring, but I am here to promise you I will do my best by you, and my best is very good. I will be loyal, always look after your best interests and will never let you down. The rest will be up to you, based wholly on my performance. That takes all the pressure off you and puts it all on me. I know I am safe with that, but I am also aware I have to prove it to you. That I will do."

"That's quite a persuasive line, but I would like to take you back to something you started with, if I may? You said you have chosen to work for us. That's an interesting concept. Should it not be us which choose you? Susie asked.

Chi Lu laughed out loud, completely disarming Susie, and answered, "Sorry for laughing. Let me explain. I've been following markets and trends. Most large and wealthy companies have got there by following a certain set of standards. Rules, for want of a better term. That's always taken time. Until now. The computer age has changed all that. Apple, Microsoft, Yahoo, Intel and several others have changed the rules. You don't have to be male and old to run high flying big companies any more. You just have to be smart! You're smart. That's not a compliment. I've read about you. You are a very smart young woman. So am I! You are one year older than me, and you are the partner of the genius who is Nathan Jefferies. That has given you a huge advantage, but you haven't lost your common touch, and if our roles were reversed you would want to be given the chance to at least prove yourself. That's all I'm asking. All the companies I mentioned are American companies. I am an American. Yours is the only company which bucks the trend. You are both young, and your company can go a long, long way, but you will need good people to get there. So – let me ask you the question. Would you want to be given the chance?"

Susie looked at the slightly younger woman without speaking for a few moments. Their eyes were locked with neither blinking nor flinching. Slowly an understanding passed between them, and very slowly the tissue at the corners of all four eyes started to crinkle slightly as smiles grew on both faces.

"You will have your chance Miss Herepath," said Susie, "and I think we are going to like one another."

"Why thank you Miss Gatting," Chi Lu responded, "and I am equally sure you are right!

Chi Lu proved a simply incredible find, exceeding both Jake and Susie's expectations, if not her own. She single-handedly oversaw the finishing of the building work, and then controlled the fitting out. By early March of 1998 the four and a half thousand miles of multi-core cabling needed in the building was installed and fully tested, and the site was due for completion by the end of the month, ready for trials before going active immediately after Easter on Tuesday the fourteenth of April.

Jake, Nathan and Susie flew to California once again as soon as the installation was complete. Susie, Jake and Chi Lu then held interviews whilst Nathan inspected the site. Chi Lu had had her chance and passed all tests with flying colours. The press were all over the official announcement, and all four were dogged by reporters and camera crews. The media generally was somewhat interested in NJF Industries, and having two very attractive and highly intelligent young ladies at the head of the corporation, one each side of the Atlantic, did nothing to drive reporters away.

Nathan fascinated Chi Lu. She had read much about him, and knew he lacked a formal education, but had still managed to create a huge corporation almost overnight with the help of little more than a contacts man, as she saw Jake, and a particularly bright and personable girlfriend. There was no doubting his talent and she had long looked forward to meeting him. However, when she finally did so, she was a little shocked. She had seen many photographs of him in magazine and newspaper articles, so held a fair knowledge of his general appearance, and knew plenty about his background, as she had made it her business to find out long before approaching the agents who sent on her CV for the original interview. What shocked her was his obvious complete devotion to Susie and, more importantly, his utter lack of reaction to her and her general appearance. Chi Lu was a highly intelligent and extremely attractive female, and knew both those things about herself. She was used to people admiring her, generally for both her intelligence and her looks. As an attractive female she was comfortable with the way men looked at her, sometimes appreciatively, sometimes lecherously.

What she was not used to, and was not at all comfortable with, was being ignored, and to her mind Nathan totally ignored her. Not in an intentional way, not as a slight, that she would have been curious about and could have handled, but he just responded to her as he did the chairs in the office, as a functional object. She had subtly power dressed ready for the meeting, artfully applied her makeup to give the appearance there was none and used a delicate perfume, everything a girl could do to create a great first impression. Nathan was polite and shook her hand, thanking her for what she had accomplished, then wandered off to look at the machinery for which the building was designed without so much as a sideways glance at her. Apart from one or two homosexual males she had met in the past, and she knew Nathan was not one of those, no man had ever ignored her in such a way – and she found it fascinating. Aside from Susie this man appeared uninterested in any other female. Her respect and admiration for Susie Gatting greatly increased. The lucky girl.

During the following two weeks all four remaining directors were found, as was HR and security. It was a young company, and with only one exception all the positions were filled with people under the age of thirty, with the emphasis based solely on the individual's ability and proven track record. The exception was that of security, and at forty four years of age, ex-marine Mike Johannson, although the oldest was quite obviously by far and away the fittest. With those who would steer the US end of the business found Jake flew home. Susie stayed for another week and spent the time getting to know what she could of their new people, and familiarising herself with the local area. Chi Lu appeared to be always on hand, ready willing and able to do anything required of her and, as a result of the time she and Susie spent together, a friendship grew from a mutually respectful working relationship.

The London end of the business could not be forgotten just because of the opening of the US project, so Susie followed Jake back to London, leaving Chi Lu with instructions to sell the second plot of land, as land prices had risen so much it was pointless to just sit on it. The card game and Chinese checkers Nathan had originally tasked Mike Hall with creating, was completed months earlier but had never gone on sale as such in retail outlets. Instead Susie oversaw a deal whereby the games came preloaded on several manufacturers' new computers as part of the package. NJF Industries had done well out of the commission and from further ongoing royalties, as they had with their Christmas release, Box Canyon Breakout. A game for the younger end of the market was due to be released at Easter, and Susie had to manage the launch of Bun Fight at the OJ Corral, a slapstick courtroom farce game with overly dramatic stereo typical characters for pre-teens which had been created by Mike Hall and Iain McGregor, without any input from Nathan.

This time Nathan stayed behind in the States to watch over the start up, and to assist with any problems. Chi Lu decided that with Susie gone she would once again see if she could create a reaction, not because she actually wanted to form a relationship of any kind with Nathan, apart from the one they already had, but because she was deeply curious. To her amusement and interest the attempt completely failed. She came to see that if she turned up naked Nathan would probably not notice her. Another mark of respect to Miss Gatting.

The US start up went off without a hitch, with the low cost Bun Fight at the OJ Corral leaving the shelves ten days behind the European launch. Considering the age of the target market the game did extremely well, proving that as a team the Hall-McGregor partnership worked well, which would be most helpful to the long term health of NJF Industries, and would leave Nathan under less pressure, with the possibilities of taking the odd holiday. It would also leave him with time to start experimenting with another area on which he had been keeping a close eye, mobile games, played on telephones rather than dedicated hand held devices.

Fifteen

Danny Bryant was a big lad who stood six foot six tall bare footed and weighed around a hundred and six kilos, probably twenty grams or less of which was fat. Starting as a mini playing at Fawley throughout his school days he excelled at rugby, and had played for the county for three years. If they as a family lived closer to the cities of Bath or Bristol, or to the clubs of London, Dan would undoubtedly have played for one of them, and from there he would have most certainly gone on to be capped for England. However his home region had never been renowned for its rugby and none of his family ever once expressed so much as a wish to move from the home his parents had struggled so hard to make their own in their early years.

On leaving school Dan had taken up a position at the huge Exxon owned Esso site at Fawley, and six weeks later was moved sideways into a department run by hands-on go-getter Mike Latham. Latham was in his early forties and never been married, but was passionate about his work which was at the bitumen end of crude oil refinement. Outside of work, to which Latham seemed to devote about seventy-five percent of his waking life, he had but two interests, rugby and boating, and possessed his own power cruiser. Latham had liked the look of the big, fit, straight talking, somewhat rugged young man who came into his department and took him under his wing. Within six months Dan received a minor promotion and Latham had watched him play rugby. Latham instantly realised there was never going to be a thing he would be able to tell or teach the younger man about rugby, as Dan's talents there already vastly exceeded his own knowledge of the game. He could however teach him something of boats, which he did, and Danny aquired the new skills easily, instinctively understanding how to balance the power of the big inboards against tides and swell.

Dan's younger brother, Jack, possessed a special gift for languages. Many a time it was said 'If Jack heard it once he would never forgot it'. This he clearly demonstrated five years earlier at the age of twelve when he went, as part of the school exchange programme, on an early exchange to France for three weeks. Living with his exchange partner's family he returned, to everyone's amazement, with the ability to speak French at simple conversational standard fluency.

He continued with French, and German, but fell in love with Spanish because of its wide geographic spread. Russian he had taken up, at his own request, because he was told it was the most difficult language in the world to master, owing to its huge number of irregular verbs. Well he had mastered it, and mastered it well. He would not pass in Russia for a native Russian speaker as incredibly few non Russians ever can, but he would never be marked down on grammar, spelling or punctuation. The school had found it impossible to provide him with a Russian language course so he made the journey by bus twice a week, every week, on the ten mile trip from his home to a language school in Bournemouth. As with his older brother, Jack did not lack dedication or determination.

Where his incredible brain came from neither Mary nor Tom Bryant had ever been able to work out. Danny's height came from Tom, and his build from Mary's father. Jack, at six foot one, was not as tall as either Tom or Danny, and his build was slimmer, most likely from her mother's side of the family, but his brain could only be accounted for as genetic serendipity. In his early years Jack proved to be slightly hampered by his intelligence and found things difficult when trying to interact with other children. Danny on the other hand had never suffered so, and was almost universally popular, especially, throughout his teens, with girls. At four Jack had learnt to play chess. At seven he had beaten his headmaster and everyone at the local chess club. He had never once been beaten since, but rarely played as he failed to find the game stimulating, and other player's slow ponderous moves either bored or irritated him. With his Grandmother's and mother's flaxen hair, blue eyes and fresh looking face Jack was a good looking lad but, unlike his brother, who didn't have Jack's looks, he was not so widely liked, as others felt threatened by his seemingly boundless intellect.

Unfortunately the vagaries of the English infant school intake system had caused Jack to miss a full year by a few days, a tragic blow for such an inquiring and absorbent mind. During his first school year this was corrected by the school, and the junior school later helped again by moving him up yet another year. Living in a small community where everybody knew one another also helped in that although some were slightly apprehensive no one saw him as a freak, but Oxford, where he was destined to go, would certainly have the ability to stretch, channel and expand his mind.

Sandy Cartwright spent some of her weekend time with Mike Latham, doing the things she had shared with John, and still enjoyed. She had developed a love of the area, which was why she had moved there, its people and the slower easier pace of life. Latham, red blooded male as he was with the ladies, was a man who also enjoyed the company of males. He liked a beer with the lads and the easy going joshing camaraderie which went with the territory. It came as little surprise to Sandy when, on a summer weekend when they were spending time together messing around on the water, she was introduced to a big fit rugged looking young man who worked in Mike's department. Danny Bryant was a perfect gentle giant, and easily the biggest person she had ever met. He was, she thought, quite simply huge.

Over the months which followed she met Danny many times, and got on particularly well with the polite, well mannered and courteous young man. She was impressed by his strength and his intellect, not something which usually goes together with athletic prowess, and could easily see why he had such a following of fawning young beauties constantly vying for his attention, not that he ever seemed to notice. He picked up everything to do with the water as if he had been born in it, and very quickly learned to manage all manner of craft, much to Mike's unconcealed approval. In addition Mike encouraged Danny into trying out diving, and taught him what he could about such basics as mask clearing, some of the complexities of buoyancy, and buddy breathing skills. Danny loved it and, of his own volition, joined the British Sub Aqua Club (BSAC), then went on and separately studied to get his Professional Association of Diving Instructors (PADI) qualifications, all of which he easily mastered. His only problem was one of finding equipment which was big enough for his giant frame, especially wet suits.

In many ways Danny partially filled the void left by John's death during the months which followed, in that there was another man with a strong pair of hands and arms to help with the manual tasks boats of all kinds require. Later in the year his skill and courage on the rugby field, which Mike often took her to watch, helped to add another sport to her list of interests. Sandy first met Danny's parents after one such rugby match, as all five stopped for lunch together in a little country pub on the fringe of Burley, in the New Forest, near Ringwood. Sandy found Tom and Mary Bryant a friendly easy going couple, and she deeply admired their obvious unwavering love for one another.

The five enjoyed lunch together on several occasions after that, sometimes joined by Danny's younger brother Jack, although it seemed Jack spent most of his time studying. A very real friendship gradually developed between Sandy and Danny over many months, and each had a great deal of genuine respect for the other which, as it matured, in time turned to genuine fondness.

Sixteen

To the Western World, especially Britain, obsessed as it is with racial profiling, Abdul Ahmad Khaled was a Pakistani. In reality he was a Pashtun, born and raised in the rocky and mountainous land lying to the north west of the province of Balochistan, which itself occupies a part of the world which is the south western corner of Pakistan, and in turn forms a large section of the border with Afghanistan. This border is sometimes called the Durand Line, named as it was after Sir Mortimer Durand, the foreign secretary of the British Indian government during the ten year period between 1884 and 1894. It was then intended to form one of many lines in the sand drawn up as part of the 'Great Game'. The 'Great Game' being the attempted expansionism of the Russian Empire, and The British Empires' endeavours to thwart, stop or otherwise contain Russia's colonial desires. No account of tribal regions was taken into consideration when drawing the line, which effectively left the Pashtun people living on either side. The free movement of the regions native tribes has ever since contributed to the highly porous and 'leaky' nature of the border.

Abdul Ahmad Khaled was born in a small tribal clan hamlet near Pishin, which gives its name to the areas county style region. The town of Pishin is to the north of Quetta, the regional capital. He did not know exactly when he was born as no proper records were then kept, but he knew the year and knew it had been early winter. None from his village could then write and none afterwards accurately remembered, not that it would have meant anything to him if they had. He grew up as those from his region did within a greater extended family, and with a full understanding of severe climatic conditions, a punishing work regime and an overwhelming distrust of everything perceived to be Western.

He knew nothing of history and the West to him was an abstract. It was both the Great Provider and the Great Satan. It was either something to aspire to and become a part of, or something which must be brought to its knees, vilified, humiliated and destroyed. The background to his culture was wholly contradictory. Passing Imams, the all knowing and learned wise men, taught him fleetingly in the ways of the Koran. His peoples culture with its entrenched avarice, greed and aspirational values taught him to covert worldly goods. He therefore grew up in a world of contradiction, disliking those perceived to be the haves for their opulence, power and possessions, yet not wanting to be a member of the poor, one of which he fully realised he was.

He was not a deep thinking person and had no form of what would to the vast majority of the world's population be regarded as an education, had scant knowledge of the happenings outside of his village, and none at all of the world outside his small part of his province. He was the second born son of his parents. A female child born between him and his brother had died within hours of birth, as so many girl children did. His older brother and three of his older cousins left Pakistan for a strange land peopled by peculiar men with pale skin. He had never seen a white man but knew from the Imams teachings they were non-believers, and they were to be despised, feared and ultimately either crushed or subjugated.

A cousin of supposed considerable wealth once returned to his village with wild and impossible stories of the far away land and, despite the fact his stories could not be true, took the wife which both families' parents had long since agreed upon and returned with her to that land. When Zulfikar Khan, another cousin, returned and again spoke to him of this strange land Abdul knew he should join his cousins to claim his share of the riches, no matter how many devils lived there.

The small community which formed his home had as a consequence a relatively shallow gene pool which resulted in striking family resemblances. Karim Ali Khan was a cousin two years older than Abdul, yet to most they could have been twins. Karim, now twenty one, went to England as a dependant at fifteen, had nationalised, taken British citizenship and held a British passport. He was living in England in a place called Heston, which was outside the big city of London, a city said to be even bigger than Quetta, as if such a thing were possible. Zulfikar explained that England was a difficult place to enter if the proper rules were followed. However the English were a deeply stupid people. If you carried the correct paperwork and said the things they wanted to hear they would always believe you. So long as you paid some of your taxes no one ever checked up on you, which meant once you were in you could stay as long as you wished. The fools of the country didn't even have an exit policy for aliens, and he was not going in as an alien.

Eight weeks later, in early October, Abdul Ahmad Khaled entered Britain at Heathrow Airport as Karim Ali Khan accompanied by Zulfikar. His passport was in order, he was well briefed, and he literally walked straight in with no questions asked. The great British security machine was powerless to act. Another triumph for enlightened humanitarians.

The closed shop which in Britain is the Asian working community immediately provided Abdul with gainful employment. British employment legislation relies on honesty from both employer and employee. For those who are prepared to work and exist wholly outside the established framework of rules, regulations and statutes there is very little the state can do or, more accurately, is prepared to do. Coupled with the fact anyone in Britain with so much as a decent suntan can toss down the racist card and the relevant authority's hands become well and truly tied. Over time many of the bodies responsible for checking and policing have been infiltrated to the extent many are overrun with former 'foreigners', both legals and, more worryingly, increasingly, illegals. This is graphically underlined to those unfortunate people who have had cause to visit Lunar House in Croyden, the Home Office site charged with the application of the tests of immigration legislation, and almost exclusively staffed by people with skin colours and accents which are about as indigenous to Britain as the kangaroo. That illegals have been found working even there does clearly point to the fact the system has irrevocably broken down and all checks and balances either destroyed or removed, although presumably the relevant authorities will continue to repudiate the point.

Abdul Ahmad Khaled shared both his cousin's identity and his squalid home. A job as a warehouseman was quickly found for him in a 'family' run business on the Green Lane industrial site in Hounslow, within walking distance of Staines Road mosque. A clever, educated and intelligent man he was not, but he had the ability to quickly absorb new practical skills. Within a few days he was driving a forklift truck and shortly afterwards he could be found shunting all manner of trucks around the yard and onto the loading bays. One of his 'family' took him out in the evenings and taught him to drive properly and, using his cousins name and driving licence, Abdul obtained a job as a local delivery driver driving a large Iveco panel van.

Most of his work was of a local nature and within a triangle which was made up of Staines, Bracknell and High Wycombe, and he rapidly acquired a good working knowledge of the area. His starting time was 06.00 hours, when he would collect his run sheet and delivery notes and, with help, put the notes into drop order and then supervise the loading of the van. Many of the deliveries were regular drops so he knew where to go on delivery and who to see, which saved a lot of time after the first few weeks. The job was easy and, to him, well paid. However he had come to England to gain riches from the non-believers. He usually finished his work by two in the afternoon so found himself with time to spare. He filled this time by taking on a second job, part time in nature, again loading heavy trucks after they finished their day runs so they would be ready for early despatch the following day. This work started at four each afternoon and finished when all the vehicles were properly loaded, sometimes by seven, sometimes as late as ten.

One early April morning when arriving at his day job Abdul was informed his normal days work had been changed because a driver had failed to show up for a run with time critical deliveries. Abdul's was the easiest run to cover, the other vehicle was loaded ready to go, there was a map and the delivery notes in the cab – and he better get going. Abdul was not properly prepared. He had then been in Britain for just over six months and worked hard without any time off to rest or relax, with the sole exception of the Christmas – New Year break. Recently he had worked over seventy hours a week, and the previous night was a bad one, with hard physical work through to past ten in the evening, handballing goods from one vehicle to another because a forklift had broken down. In addition he was to drive a seven and a half tonne truck and had never driven a vehicle of such size on the road before, despite assuring his employer he had at interview in order to get the job. He also did not have the faintest idea about tachograph regulations or indeed even what the tachograph did. This he thought best not to bring to anyone's attention, so left the yard tired, in a wholly unfamiliar vehicle, bound for a destination he had never before heard of.

He did however know his way onto the M3. At quarter past six the traffic was still relatively light and he was travelling against the flow which headed into London. By the time he passed the familiar Bracknell junction he found himself adapting to the feel of the truck. On reaching Eastleigh he pulled off the motorway at the motorway junction, followed the slip-road down to the unusual 'T' junction at the bottom, and crossed the road straight into the bakery which was his first and time critical drop. The bakery ran a twenty-four hour operation and his two pallet delivery was speedily offloaded within minutes. Just past eight o'clock he eased his vehicle back onto the motorway which was beginning to get somewhat congested, as was the M27. The traffic cleared noticeably when he passed the M271 as commuter vehicles streamed into Southampton, and he could again increase his speed.

At the end of the M27 Abdul turned onto the A337 following signs for Lyndhurst, which is where he got lost. Lyndhurst has an interesting one way system around the town. It is reasonably well marked and not particularly difficult to follow when the volume of traffic is low, but following it does much depend on being in the correct lane when approaching any form of junction or turn off. As many of the markings are on the road itself this can be difficult to do at peak times as the congested traffic obscures the very road markings a driver is to follow. For the locals this does not present a problem as they do not need the markings. However for drivers who are not familiar with the area, especially drivers of larger vehicles, rush hour can be problematic and lead to confusion over which route to follow.

The New Forest dates back to the days of William the Conqueror, yet still offers an attractive and appealing face to visitors at any time of the year. Throughout spring this is particularly so. Parts of the forest were cleared centuries ago but still nearly one hundred and fifty square miles of virtually undisturbed deciduous and coniferous forest remains in an area of rugged beauty. Gorse bushes abound, surrounding wooded enclaves which provide a natural habitat to multitudinous species of flora and fauna. Commoners – the local people – maintain traditional practices which include the pasturing of cattle and pigs. Hardy surefooted New Forest ponies wander freely and appear wild, but are in fact privately owned. A sight like this Abdul had never before seen. How was it that these non-believers were so well blessed?

His mistake at Lyndhurst inadvertently put him on the road to Beaulieu. He had intended to stay on the A337 and follow it to his next delivery point, a small yacht builder at New Milton. Having realised his mistake he pulled over to check his map, and could see it was now quicker for him to go on to Beaulieu then cut down through Lymington than it would be to go back, and decided to do so.

With that decision Mary Bryant's fate was sealed.

The minor 'B' roads he followed were virtually devoid of vehicles but were reasonably signposted. He easily found the road to Lymington where he would once again get back onto his chosen route. As he entered Lymington he spread the map across the steering wheel. He was certainly not going to make the same mistake twice. Apart from a pedestrian on the pavement and one oncoming car the road ahead was empty. He took the opportunity to have another glance at the map. Looking up he saw he had strayed slightly to the right and automatically pulled the wheel to the left. Disorientated, tired and in a strange vehicle he misjudged the width of his truck and clipped the kerb. The sudden drag on his nearside front wheel pulled the steering hard to the left and he mounted the kerb.

The Mercedes Atego 818 seven and a half tonne curtainsided truck he drove that day was fitted with at least one piece of non standard equipment. Having broken several mirror lenses the usual driver, after sitting through an ear-bashing on the subject from the transport manager, had fitted a piece of steel tread-plate to the mirror arm to protect the mirror glass from protruding branches. Travelling at close to thirty miles an hour, with an all up weight of a little over six tonnes, the steel plate smashed into the back of Mary Bryant's head killing her instantly. The force of the impact physically threw her face first onto the pavement where the momentum ripped her face away to the bone.

The steel tread-plate worked perfectly in protecting the mirror glass. After hitting the back of Mary Bryant's head the sprung loaded arm swung the mirror back to its proper position. Abdul Khaled panicked. He realised he had hit the woman pedestrian and could see her on the floor in the mirror as it sprang back into place. Suddenly and almost instantly he understood what he had done and, more importantly, what these white skinned devils would do to him if they caught him. They were non-believers and would not accept it was only a woman and was obviously God's Will. If they caught him they would question him and they would fine him. They could take away the money he had worked and saved hard for. Then he would not be able to buy the tribal land he wanted and had been working for. If they found out he was an illegal they may even send him home, and without the money. He could not allow that! He must get away!

The car Abdul had seen coming towards him was driven by a man who lived on the outskirts of the town. Gary Barker worked for his father's timber business in the forest, and had worked around trucks all his life. He was a part-time fireman and a well known local. He recognised Mary as she walked towards him. She had recently sold him and his lady friend a property in a perfect spot for them, and his younger brother had also been in her eldest boy's class at school. He was about to give her a friendly toot on the horn and wave as he noticed the truck drifting onto his side of the road. He could see the driver had a map spread across his steering wheel and was looking at the map rather than the road. "Stupid sod," he said out loud as he hit the brakes and pulled a little further to the left, "and all the way down from Hounslow!" he continued as he read the signage on the front.

Gary watched as the drivers head came up, realised he was drifting, and pulled the steering wheel to the left, overcorrecting. The truck's near side front wheel touched the curb stone and Gary could see what was about to happen, but was numbingly powerless to do anything about it. He watched in slow motion horror as the mirror hit the back of Mary's head and she went down. The wheels of the truck missed her body but he saw she had been hit hard. As the truck slowed Gary reacted rapidly and slewed his car across the road behind it, switching on his hazard warning lights as he did so and jumping out before his car had quite stopped moving. As his feet hit the ground the truck's engine raced and the vehicle started to accelerate away. Hit and run. The bastard! He must remember the name on the back and what he could of the registration number. Harris of Hounslow. R registration 1997. A one or two year old white Mercedes Atego 818. Navy blue sign-writing.

Mary twitched twice. She was dead. Gary Barker pulled his mobile telephone from the breast pocket of his shirt, keyed in 999, and asked for the police and ambulance services. He was a perfect witness, unshakable, unbreakable. Just what the prosecution case was going to need.

Abdul Khaled had panicked. He hadn't really known where he was, or where he was supposed to be going. All he knew was he must get away and he must give himself a chance to think. He had hit some stupid female – what was she doing there? It was not his fault. God had willed it, but that would not be seen or understood by these non-believers. He must get away, he must get rid of the truck and he must hide. He knew he had been quick to think and to leave the scene, and he was grateful he was so clever. The person in the car would not have seen anything because he, Abdul Khaled, was too quick for them. Besides the woman would be alright, and even if she wasn't it was only a woman. God had willed it! Everything would be alright. He just had to get clear.

He drove fast to get as far away as possible as quickly as he could. He heard a bang and felt an impact in the cab as the goods in the back crashed to the floor. They did not matter. Nothing mattered. He must get clear and get rid of the vehicle then he could make his way back to Hounslow where he knew he would be hidden. He would not go back to his job just in case. He would lose a few days money, but better that than chance losing a lot more. Another job would be found for him. In a few months he would have enough money to leave this place and its stupid people behind him and buy the land he wanted. He picked up the A337 and followed it up through Brockenhurst back towards Lyndhurst. He would get back up the M3 towards London. He had seen some services on the way down between junctions 4A and 5. Fleet Services, that was it, not far from Bracknell. He would dump the truck there. He could get home from there. He would make it. He was smart.

The cans of paint which crashed to the floor in the back of the truck lost their lids on impact. The paint covered the bed dripping through the cracks in the boards, splattering against the windscreens of following cars and leaving a trail.

Gary Barker did not move once he made his phone call to the police. He understood it was a crime scene and any further unnecessary movement on his part may make it more difficult for the Scene of Crime officers and for forensics. He waved away several passing motorists who stopped, and waited the five and a half minutes it took for an officer to arrive. Gary knew the young police constable who was first on the scene, as he did the police constable and sergeant who followed. The constables cleared the onlookers and closed the road whilst the sergeant questioned him. All the information Gary gave was written down and radioed through to the area control at Lyndhurst. All three of the police officers attending had known Mary. This was a callous and cowardly hit and run accident to a very popular local woman. This was a small community. This was personal to all those at the scene.

Samantha Madison waited until after 09.00 to leave the family home to the south of Brockenhurst. Earlier she had driven her husband to the local station so he might catch the train to work, and then returned to her home to pick up their daughter Catherine, before the two of them headed into Southampton on a girly shopping expedition. It was a beautiful morning and she dropped the roof on their BMW 3 series convertible. Cat loved it with the top down – the little show off.

The road was empty behind the white truck as it sped past their sweeping driveway, and Samantha followed it out onto the road. Approaching Brockenhurst they gained on the truck in front of them and, as they did so, Samantha noticed there were dots and spots appearing on her windscreen. They were not flies, and certainly not rain. She flicked the wiper on for one sweep of the screen. The marks instantly became red and blue lines which became purple smears as they ran together. It took about three seconds for Samantha to put it together, and then she was outraged. She loved this car and it was getting covered in paint. She glanced at her face in the rear view mirror and could see dots on that too, and on Cat's face. It would be in their hair and all over the leather work of the upholstery. What on earth did the imbecile in front think he was doing?

Samantha knew Catherine had her mobile phone with her – she would rather go out without makeup than without her phone, neither of which was ever going to happen – and told her to phone the police on 999. Cat did as she was told, reported the details of the vehicle in front, explained what was happening and gave her mobile number. The police asked her to stay on the line which she did. Samantha dropped back so as to minimise contact with the spilling paint, but she was not going to let this idiot out of her sight until she knew what was going to happen about an insurance claim. The police asked Catherine if she would let them know which road the truck took out of Lyndhurst and then drive directly to Lyndhurst Police Station and make a statement. A police car would follow the truck and someone would most definitely be waiting at the police station to take a statement from both her and her mother.

The truck stayed on the A337 towards the M27 motorway. A police car followed.

Lyndhurst is a small provincial town wholly surrounded by the natural splendour which is the New Forest. The area is affluent and crime levels are very low. The local police can justifiably boast the area is one of the safest places to live, work and visit. Hampshire Constabularies Western Operational Command Unit is based in Lyndhurst, and retains approximately five hundred police officers and one hundred and twenty police support staff. They work out of thirteen operational police stations in eight sectors covering a population of some four hundred and forty thousand people spread over an area of five hundred and sixty square miles. Their main crime areas involve beauty spot vehicle crimes, thefts from caravans, road traffic accidents involving roaming animals, antisocial behaviour and graffiti.

Whilst road traffic accidents did happen in the area they were not as frequent as in most other parts of the country because of the very nature of the forest. Hit and run accidents were in themselves rare and such accidents involving people almost unheard of. None of the officers involved could remember a human hit and run fatality in the forest, so this one they would pursue immediately and with the utmost vigour.

Abdul Ahmad Khaled had made many mistakes along the way in life, just as everyone does. That particular day saw a series of previous mistakes deceits and falsehoods on his part culminate in the death of an innocent family woman. However his judgemental errors were not finished for the day. His reckless and panicked attempt to flee the scene of the accident virtually took him past the front of the local areas police headquarters. It therefore became a simple matter for them to apprehend him. With a police car following and radioing ahead another police vehicle had only to pull across the front of his truck at the roundabout where the A31, A336 and A337 all meet the M27 and Abdul Khaled was arrested without further trouble and taken into custody.

The truck was taken to a secure compound where it was exactingly examined by Ministry of Transport engineers. They found the vehicle to be road worthy with no mechanical defects. There was however an issue of driving without a tachograph, and an insecure load offence. The near side mirror assembly was examined and tissue and hair samples taken from it later confirmed the vehicle was responsible for the death of Mary Bryant.

Examiners from the Ministry of Transport and the police called upon the vehicles operators in Hounslow. The company was an old and well established road haulage operation which had previously enjoyed a good name. Their records were complete and up-to-date. Drivers driving licence details were kept and regularly revised, tachographs were retained for eighteen months, exceeding the Ministry's one year requirement, and completed run sheets and delivery records were kept for charging and analysis purposes. Neither the Ministry examiners nor the police could sensibly fault the company's operation and it was given a clean bill of health. Karim Ali Khan, although a reasonably recent employee had until then done his job without causing problems. The company held a photocopy of his driving licence and supplied the police with his home address.

As part of their ongoing enquiries the police called upon the address given, and were surprised to be met by the occupant, who claimed to be Karim Ali Khan. Five minutes later he was taken to a local police station for further questioning and, as a result of which, the police obtained a search warrant and the property was thoroughly inspected. A small but significant amount of paperwork, passports and visa's were recovered during the search which eventually led to the detention and recommended expulsion of a further nineteen illegals, although eventually none ever were forced to leave the country. It also uncovered the fact the person they had in custody in Lyndhurst was not Karim Ali Khan, but was in fact Abdul Ahmad Khaled, an illegal immigrant with no visa, work permit or driving licence. The case against him was growing.

Seventeen

In February 1999, Chris Spencer, along with other senior NCOs, was called to a briefing given by an army intelligence officer and two NATO colleagues. The intelligence officer started his address with an explanation that the briefing would be a departure from the norm in that it was felt essential those about to embark on a planned deployment should have an adequate working knowledge of the background to the situation they were to face.

"Although still a part of the Balkans," the officer had started, "and previously a state within the formed Yugoslavia, the problems facing Macedonia are not an exact copy of those which previously occurred in Bosnia, for those of you who saw action there. With Skopje as its capital Macedonia claimed independence in 1991, and was supported in doing so by many nations, particularly European Union nations, with the exception of Greece, and by the UN. In 1993 it gained UN membership under the unfortunate name Former Yugoslav Republic of Macedonia (FYROM). The United Nations Preventive Deployment Force (UNPREDEP) came into existence in March 1995 when the Security Council set up the successor missions to the United Nations Protection Force in the territories of what was formerly Yugoslavia. Greece, although having no desire for the territory involved, objected to the use of the name Macedonia by the new state, as Macedonia was once part of Greece and, in February 1994, imposed an economic blockade on the country. This severely damaged the economy of the 'Republic of Macedonia' by closing its access to the sea through Thessaloniki. The blockade was lifted in 1995 following an agreement between the two governments on the name issue, which was by then accepted by the other EU nations."

There was a slight pause as the officer took a sip of water from a glass placed on a planning table and consulted the notes next to it. He replaced the glass, picked up a pointer, and turned to a large map projected onto a screen behind him.

"By the end of 1995, UNPREDEP troops operated twenty-four permanent and thirty three temporary observation posts along the two hundred and sixty mile stretch to the Macedonian side of the border with the Federal Republic of Yugoslavia and Albania," he said, indicating the border with the pointer. "It ran approximately forty border and community patrols daily, and UN military observers complemented the work of the hard pressed battalions. In July last year the Security Council extended UNPREDEP for a further period of six months, until the twenty-eighth of this month, and increased troop levels by three hundred and fifty. In October the Security Council demanded full compliance by Belgrade on Kosovo agreements. They failed to get it!"

There was silence in the room. Many had been following events in the Balkans, especially those who, like Chris, were involved in the Bosnia conflict, and most had long expected trouble to once again flare up out of control in the region.

The question was not so much 'Will it happen?' as 'Will we become involved?' It appeared they were about to receive an answer.

"Concerns regarding possible overspill of the Kosovo conflict into Macedonia," continued the intelligence officer, "due to its shared border, directly concern UNPREDEP. A further increase in UNPREDEPs military component by three hundred all ranks was authorised by Security Council resolution 1186/1998. This was completed by the beginning of last month, bringing the strength up to one thousand and fifty troops. In line with resolution 1160/1998 UNPREDEP took up the new tasks of monitoring and reporting on illicit arms flows and other activities prohibited by that Council decision. Newly set up UNPREDEP mobile reaction teams now respond to sighted smuggling activities by moving quickly to continue observation and provide more accurate information on whether arms, ammunition or explosives are involved. On average, UNPREDEP military personnel conduct some four hundred patrols per week, including three hundred border and community patrols, have established eighty temporary observation posts, and conduct helicopter patrols. Additionally civilian police monitors carry out approximately one hundred weekly patrols."

"With all that said the reason this briefing cannot be regarded as routine is that currently there is no mandate for NATO to operate within this theatre as it falls wholly under the UN jurisdiction. However should any Security Council member block UNPREDEP renewal that situation could rapidly alter."

On the twenty-fifth of February 1999, China used its veto in the Security Council to prevent a renewal of UNPREDEP in Macedonia. By a vote of thirteen in favour, to one against (China), and with one abstention (the Russian Federation), the Council failed to adopt the eight nation draft resolution. As far as Macedonia was concerned their UN protection had just been removed leaving them terribly vulnerable to the Serbs as the UN pulled out.

NATO could not stand back and watch. Mobilisation was immediate.

Almost within the hours that followed B Company the Green Howards, and Colour Sergeant Chris Spencer, saw a return to the Balkans. They had to initially supplement 1 Battalion Irish Guards, who were the main infantry component of Britain's lead battle group, but were so understaffed because of military cuts they had to be augmented from other regiments.

By March the Royal Fleet Auxiliary ships Sea Centurion and Sea Crusader had arrived and unloaded their cargos whilst eight thousand British troops deployed in Albania. The Challenger tanks, Warrior armoured vehicles, and artillery previously stationed in Germany and most familiar to Chris and those who served with him were on hand. Despite the forces rallied against his, Milosevic refused to sign an international peace plan for Kosovo which called for the withdrawal of Yugoslav security forces and, on the twenty-fourth of March, NATO began a bombing campaign against Yugoslavia due to its treatment of Kosovo Albanians. Within days of the first air strikes reports of atrocities and forced evictions by Serb forces on Kosovo Albanians sent the number of refugees soaring, and the mass expulsion and killings led to an exodus into neighbouring countries, including Macedonia.

On the thirteenth of April Robin Cook, the British Foreign Secretary announced, "Last night Alliance forces pursued our vigorous air campaign against Milosevic's war machine. The new intensity of our air campaign represents a step change in our action against the Serb forces in the killing fields of Kosovo."

Two months of intense NATO bombing was to follow. In early June, Chris Spencer, along with thousands of NATO troops were moved forward, close to the Kosovo border, under the command of Lieutenant General Sir Michael Jackson.

On the tenth of June 1999 NATO called off its eleven week air war against Kosovo following the beginning of the withdrawal of Serb troops. Secretary General Javier Solana announced the halt to the seventy-nine day bombing campaign three hours after the first Serb convoys were seen leaving the province. The Serb leader, Slobodan Milosevic, had finally agreed to the pull out after winning a concession for extra time to complete the withdrawal. Belgrade then had eleven days to move its forty thousand security forces out of Kosovo, and under the terms of the ceasefire agreement the Yugoslav forces were instructed to suspend hostilities immediately. A detailed plan was drawn up for their withdrawal, which included the removal of mines and unexploded bombs on their way out.

Colour Sergeant Chris Spencer led his men over the border and into Kosovo on the twelfth of June, two days after the air campaign ceased. Evidence of the brutal systematic effort, as outlined by US President Bill Clinton, to remove the ethnic Albanians from the land was plain for all to see. Despite all possible precautions to the contrary within two hours of stepping on to the soil which was Kosovo the unthinkable happened, and Chris lost one of his men to a mine. One of the very same mines the Serbs had sown and been charged with removing. All were aware of the dangers, but Chris was not prepared for the anger he felt at the unnecessary loss of one of HIS men – after the hostilities had ended.

Since passing out in January 1981, more than eighteen years earlier, Chris had observed and dealt with a great deal of death and destruction. As a young private on the streets of Northern Ireland he witnessed many injuries and the occasional death, amongst security services, the local population, and so called armed combatants. During the Gulf War he dispatched many who bore arms against him and all he represented, and witnessed first hand the effects of armed conflict on those which wore his uniform, unfortunately due to 'friendly fire'. Bosnia had shown him the depravities of man, and he was sure it would be reinforced with what he was to face in Kosovo, but never, not since his first stripe, had he lost a man. It was his first and a hard lesson, but it would not be his last whilst in uniform, nor would he escape Kosovo without his own blood spilling.

After the incident Chris adopted the unprofessional and dangerous job of repeatedly taking point. Unprofessional because he was experienced and needed – by his men and, as a senior NCO, by his officers. Dangerous because constant intense concentration cannot be maintained, yet any diminution could prove lethal. Tiredness and fatigue could quite literally kill. Hostilities were officially suspended on the tenth of June, and the Serbs were withdrawing. Despite heavy bombing by the Allied forces representing NATO a huge number of tanks remained intact, hidden in farm buildings, woodlands and damaged properties. In many cases the Serbs protected their tanks whilst trucks and troop carriers were sacrificed. With forty thousand troops and supporting equipment to remove over damaged roads without troop carriers the withdrawal went slowly, with looting a constant problem as the Serbs tried to remove anything of value as they left.

Motor vehicles of all kinds were highly prized, both for their value and due to their ability to carry men, armaments and, most importantly, the spoils of war. The duty of the NATO protection force was to support and defend the indigenous population and prevent further looting. Whilst leading a small patrol Chris heard the unmistakable sound of small arms fire, and was duty bound to follow up. He and his small squad advanced in the direction of the sound and came upon a small hamlet of three somewhat dilapidated houses. There were trees which afforded cover as they approached, but as they did so they could hear other sounds, the crying of a child and the sobbing pleas of a woman. Less than a hundred yards out a dog started to bark. The burst of gunfire which silenced it was followed by the sound of riotous laughter.

Taking point Chris mover closer, surveying the ground as he did so. Tired or not adrenalin cut in and his senses were all on heightened alert. A young boy emerged from a gap between the buildings. He instantly reminded Chris of his young nephew, Charlie. The boy too was about ten years of age and a very similar height and build. One eye was swelling up from a large bruise, blood was running from cuts to his mouth and nose, and tears streamed down his cheeks. A man followed him out and, swinging the barrel of his rifle into the side of the boys head, ordered him back. From fifty yards out Chris heard the blow clearly and could have happily killed the man with a single shot to his head, but there were others present and he didn't know how many, or what armaments they controlled. He moved sideways glancing amongst the trees as he did, and signalled his men to move up once he determined the ground was clear.

Moving in closer he reached the remains of a small wall, most of which had long since collapsed and was overgrown, twenty yards from the gap where the boy appeared. There were more sounds now. Chris could hear another quite sobbing as well as the pleas of the older woman. The child was still crying and Chris guessed it must be the boy. Having first beckoned two men forward to cover him from the wall he signalled behind him for his men to fan out and circle around either side of the dwellings. A track which passed as a road lay the other side of the fallen wall, and he surveyed it carefully as his men moved into position. There was nobody in sight, and no sign of previously disturbed groundwork or anything else which may indicate a booby trap. Stepping out with rifle at the ready he crossed the road and flattened his back to the wall, looking back from where he had come. His men were in place, apart from those moving around to the rear, and there was no sign of any other life. The sounds were louder now, although the woman's screams had stopped to be replaced by heart rending sobs.

He glanced at the ground around his feet and to his right. He didn't want to step on a twig or anything which could break underfoot thereby announcing his approach. There was only grass. Inching along the wall Chris reached the corner, and very slowly moved his head to take in an ever increasing view into the gap. An outreached bloody hand came into view, followed by an arm and then a head. It was an old man's head, weathered sun browned creased skin with almost white hair. The eyes looked into infinity, but would never see again. His chest and neck had taken several bullets and the old man was past any help. A young girl came into view. She was naked, slumped against a wall to the left where she had been thrown. Her face was badly beaten and her immature breasts had been slashed with a knife or broken glass. Her hands covered the area between her legs almost in an act of modesty, but blood oozed and dripped between her fingers as she lay semi-conscious, whimpering in pain and terror.

A man's boots appeared next, then naked buttocks, and legs with knees between a woman's feet. She too was naked. The man, covered in body hair, had his trousers around his knees, and was roughly taking her from behind, fingers digging deeply into the flesh of her hips, rhythmically thrusting her backwards and forwards. They were sideways on to Chris, and could not see him without turning. At the woman's head another man knelt in a similar position, fingers curled tightly into her hair. He too was rocking her backwards and forwards in the same rhythm as he forced himself deep into her mouth, choking her as he went. Neither man was interested in anything but their victim. The back of the man with the gun appeared next. He was laughing as he watched his comrades. He held an old Kalashnikov, the ubiquitous armament of the Balkans, in his right hand, and a bottle of cheap red wine in his left. Not a good combination.

The two men raping the woman had no weapons in sight. As he moved further forward Chris caught sight of another pair of boots. A sturdy looking man was sitting on the front bumper of an old truck with another Kalashnikov partially resting across his knees. If anyone were in charge of the little group it would be him Chris thought. Suddenly the action got out of hand. The man with his back to Chris finished the bottle of wine. Angrily he hurled it at the wall and shouted at the boy. Obviously he wanted more. The small boy cowered and answered. It was plain the family had none. Not the answer the man wanted. The Kalashnikov started to rise. Intervention was required.

Chris stepped from the cover of the wall gun raised. It was unlikely any present spoke English but he needed their attention if they were to live.

"Stand down!" He spoke loudly and firmly. Five heads snapped in his direction including the boy's. The man sitting on the bumper of the truck started to move his gun.

"Don't do it!" Chris ordered looking at him. In any language the message was plain. The Serb with the boy continued to bring his gun to bear on the child. His finger was already on the trigger. The top of his head changed shape before anyone heard the shots, and his lifeless body catapulted forward.

Chris sensed rather than saw it. It might have been the click of the safety being released, or a slight movement caught out of the corner of his eye, but either way he reacted instinctively, diving back and to his right, fractionally too late. The high ground, he hadn't looked up at the roof. He had focused on saving the boy because of his likeness to Charlie. There was another gunman upstairs presumably alerted by his voice, who reacted to his shots by returning fire. As he went down he felt two bullets pluck at him and knew he was hit. He also instinctively knew they were flesh wounds only and there were still two people with guns in front of him who would want him dead, and two more who could well have other guns.

The Serb sitting on the front of the truck was raising his gun, was an obvious immediate threat, and was a clear shot. From the ground Chris fired into him, two shots to the chest and one to the head. All went home and the man went down. Chris rolled clear and again raised his gun. The two men raping the woman had reacted quickly, thrusting her away and reaching for weapons which were out of sight. Too late to consider prisoners Chris thought as he put three bullets into each of them, and both men died with their pants still down. There was a crashing noise as the Serb inside and above kicked the window out trying to get a bearing on his target. A silly mistake. His actions announced exactly where he was and his intention to fire. He could not see Chris without leaning forward, and Chris already had his weapon levelled. The Serb's body became visible at the smashed window as he looked for his target. As his head moved into a viewing angle he saw it, and in doing so he looked into the business end of one of the world's most accurate weapons. He watched as two bullets slammed into his chest, but was already dead as a further two destroyed his head. All five men were down. All were dead. Every shot fired from Chris Spencer's weapon found its target. From the moment Chris dived to his right the fire fight lasted twelve seconds.

His men arrived on the scene moving forward to give covering fire but there was nothing left to fire at. They then carried out a standard search operation and threat assessment. All the bodies were checked and all confirmed dead. Those of his men coming in from the side and rear reported there were no more Serbs hiding anywhere near the properties, nor were there any more inside any of the buildings. However there was another young female in the upstairs room and she too was badly beaten and raped. Chris called it in and requested transportation with medics for the woman and children. Whilst waiting he attempted to do what he could to help the three females. The woman had come through her ordeal better than the girls, the worst of which was the youngest, who remained totally traumatised and had possible internal injuries which neither Chris nor any of his men were qualified to help with. Their collective cuts were cleaned and dressed, and clothes were found for all three, though they still looked a sad and sorry sight.

Having seen to the needs of the women Chris turned his attention to himself. He had been lucky. Both bullets had only lightly winged him, one to the left arm, and one to his left leg. The shot to the arm had only just touched the flesh leaving a two inch gash just below the shoulder. It would be sore for a week or so, but it was nothing a field dressing wouldn't sort out. His leg was a similar story. The bullet had scoured a line across the outside of his upper thigh. It was a little deeper than the wound to his arm, but not anywhere near any major arteries and looked worse than it was. He cleaned it and again applied a field dressing. It would stiffen up his leg a little later, but that aside he could see there would be no lasting damage apart from slight scarring, and he could live with that. He realised he had been very lucky, and a valuable lesson was learned.

The medics insisted Chris travel back with them and the four civilians. He was checked over, the wounds cleaned again, the dressings changed, and he was given the obligatory injection. It transpired the Serbs were attempting to steal the family's aged truck when the old man tried to stop them. They shot him then discovered the females. The old man was the woman's father-in-law, her husband had already been killed during the fighting months earlier, and all three children were hers. The mother, eldest daughter and son, though all battered and bruised were released the following day. The younger daughter remained in hospital. She had received internal injuries, and would probably never be able to bear children. It was a sad and unfortunate story and all too common, but all owed their lives to the intervention of the Green Howards.

The Serbs were eventually removed from Kosovo. War crimes investigators then headed into the country hunting for evidence of massacres, ethnic cleansing and torture. Chris Spencer's wounds healed quickly and he was returned to active service. Another promotion had come his way, and he was now a Warrant Officer Class 2. By the time he and his men were pulled out, in September 1999, the rebuilding of Kosovo was already underway and the country was able to slowly move forward with international help and, most importantly, international recognition.

Nineteen

All three Bryant males were utterly devastated by Mary's sudden and violent death, and the event was destined to radically change all. Tom became almost suicidal. Since boyhood Mary was the very centre of his life. Not only was she his wife, lover and mother of his children, she was infinitely more, she was his friend, and she was the closest, dearest, kindest friend he had ever known. Everything about his life from the age of fourteen onwards revolved around her. Togetherness! Since their childhood they had at times gone without together, even gone hungry together, and together built a house and a family to love and be immensely proud of. It was not so much Tom viewed Mary as his 'other half', as she was something far deeper and more profound to him. In reality she was truly a fundamental and intrinsic part of his being, and when she died so too did a large part of Tom.

Tom Bryant had throughout his life been hard working, dedicated and devoted, yet easy going. He was a person who put his family and their needs far beyond any needs of his own, and remained a relaxed and likeable family man from a small community which tended to look after and take care of its own. He was in every way possible a decent man who had never once done wrong by anyone, and nobody would be able to remember him having had so much as a cross word, as such a thing just never happened. Whenever he was in a position to help any living soul he consistently went out of his way to do so, and was never heard to say a bad word about another living creature, least of all another person. In fact, if pressed on the subject, none would be able to say they had heard him so much as swear.

Mary's death changed all that, and the change would be with him for life. Friends and workmates sympathised, rallied around and tried to help. Some extended invitations to dinner parties, most of which were turned down flat. Others tried to encourage him to join them at various local pubs for a pint but, apart from an odd glass of wine with a meal, Tom had never been a drinking man. The only crutch he had ever needed was his family life, particularly life with Mary. Those whose offers Tom accepted learned not to repeat the offer too many times. Tom Bryant had changed a lot and was still evolving. The kind, thoughtful, mild mannered, loving husband he had once been was gone, replaced by a sullen, smouldering man consumed by hatred, constantly appearing to be on the very verge of exploding in an uncontrolled destructive fury.

His sons, already depressed by the loss of their mother, lay in their beds listening to their once strong father sobbing himself to sleep night after night, endlessly lamenting the loss of his deeply beloved Mary. Their nights were long and their sleep short as they were awakened repeatedly by his nightmares. For many weeks which stretched into months they worried about his mental state, and were justifiably concerned he might take his own life. Time passed, the weeping, at least out loud, subsided and eventually stopped, but their father was not the man they had grown up with. Something about him was gone, the kindness, the compassion, the very love of life around him – it had all disappeared. He was not the same man at all.

Every day Tom visited Mary's grave, cleaned it, placed a small spray of flowers upon it and sat with her as he told her of his day, rain or shine, day in day out. Every day on parting he made her the same chilling promise, "I will avenge you my darling. One day, in some way, I will avenge you, I swear to you!"

His grief was all consuming but lacked direction. It could well have been his mental undoing, but over the weeks and months it started to change, forced out of his head by a stronger far more focused emotion. Hatred! An underlying all consuming raw hatred for everything that brown skinned bastard who had killed his Mary was. Everything about Abdul Ahmad Khaled's lying, cheating, underhanded, deceitful people, and their shortage of any form of tolerance or kindness, and terrible absence of accepted human values. He even learned to loathe the very land from which they sprang. If he were able he would have destroyed them all, and one day he would find a way to at least make a start. As the months passed his loneliness and feeling of isolation deepened, and his detesting of them increased.

Jack Bryant took his 'A' levels at arguably the very worst period of his still young life. The school offered to put his exams back a year and explained to both him and his older brother Danny that if his marks did not come close to expected grades he could re-sit the exams the following year. It had to be Danny who took charge of things at that stage because he was the only one who could. With their father still an emotional wreck Danny was superb, a veritable rock in an ocean of misery. It was Danny who worked unstintingly, pushing his younger brother forward in order he might still achieve much of what was expected of him, and Danny who encouraged Jack to put thoughts of their mother to one side and so concentrate on his exams. After all, was it not what their mother would have desperately wanted?

The difficulty Jack had had as a younger child interacting with others helped him during that terrible time. He simply shut down the part of his brain which dealt with pain and grief and locked it away until there was time to deal with it. Jack's was a probing, deeply analytical mind, with the inborn ability to concentrate solely on one thing at a time, pushing all else well beyond the periphery of his thoughts. His single minded, single subject concentration could be total, completely excluding any and all distractions. Despite his family's horrific loss, with his brother's encouragement, and his own concentration, Jack obtained the grades which were expected of him. Oxford beckoned.

Oxford University, more accurately, The University of Oxford, can be found in the centre of the city of Oxford and is the oldest university in the English-speaking world. Consistently ranked in the world's top ten universities it is also regarded as one of the world's leading academic institutions. The university can trace its roots back to at least the end of the eleventh century, although the exact date of inauguration remains unclear and will probably never be known. Interestingly it was after an altercation between people of the town and students which erupted in 1209 that some of the Oxford academics fled north-east to the town of Cambridge, where the University of Cambridge was founded, and the two universities have since enjoyed a long history of mutual competition.

Oxford is a collegiate university which essentially acts as a federation. There are thirty-nine colleges and seven Permanent Private Halls, each with its own internal structure and activities. All students, and most academic staff, are affiliated with a particular college, but are subject to a central administration headed by the Vice-Chancellor, who is the de facto head of the University. The colleges join together as the Conference of Colleges to discuss policy and to deal with the central University administration. In addition to residential and dining facilities, the colleges provide social, cultural, and recreational activities for their members, and are responsible for admission and organising undergraduate's tuition.

Jack Bryant, despite his inability to connect and bond with his fellow man, was without doubt a highly intelligent and intellectually gifted pupil. IQ readings are based on that of the average human adult with the benchmark set at one hundred. Those with a reading below ninety are considered to have below average intelligence, as average is ninety to one hundred and ten. Both Albert Einstein and Stephen Hawking have been attributed with varying scores around the one hundred and sixty mark, and both belong to the category of undisputed geniuses. Jack was also to prove to be a member of this exclusive group.

Most students take three 'A's, although some take four, with the results marked from A to F. To enter Oxford the minimum requirement is three straight A's. Jack was a language student. One year early he took four 'A' levels at school – English, French, Spanish and German receiving straight A's in all four. In addition he took a separate 'A' level at the language school in Bournemouth in his chosen second language, Russian, where he once again received an A. He had flown through all five of his 'A' levels, an outstanding achievement in itself, but all the more incredible when taking into account the distracting effects caused by the loss of his mother. His place at New College Oxford reading Russian was assured.

New College's official name is the College of St Mary which is the same as that of an older college. Therefore it was and has continued to be referred to as the New College of St Mary, or simply New College. It is one of the most famous of the Oxford colleges and stands along Holywell Street and New College Lane, known for its Bridge of Sighs. At the time of its founding, New College had the grandest collection of college buildings in Oxford. Despite its name, New College is one of the oldest of the Oxford colleges, having originally been founded in 1379, and centres on a main quadrangle with student rooms, study rooms, a dining hall and library all within the square ring of buildings and gates which form the college.

Within that ring of buildings many of the decisions of Empire have, if not been made, then certainly first taken root, something which has not changed in over six hundred years. It was within those buildings, and the extremely well connected and influential young people who attended, that Jack found himself. Many of those studying there have continued to be the offspring of presidents, captains of industry, the upper echelons of the legal world, international bankers and senior politicians. Those not originally from a similar background, but are there because of their intellect, often find themselves gravitating upwards into that world, and filling those positions themselves later in life.

It provides an unrivalled forum for those with the ears of the most powerful, wealthy and influential people of the planet, and those destined to become such. It was a place where Jack at last made meaningful friendships with equally talented and intellectually superior young people. Friendships and relationships forged and formed within those hallowed walls have in the past changed both the course of history and the world as we know it, and can, does and will continue to do so.

'Manners Makyth Man' is the College's motto and was for its time in many respects fairly radical. Firstly, written in English rather than Latin makes it most unusual in Oxford, and bordering on revolutionary when considering the College's age. Secondly, the motto is of itself a social statement. Whilst suggesting it is advantageous to demonstrate good manners this really does not capture the depth of the motto's full meaning.

What it really means is it is not by parentage, wealth, property or social position that an individual is defined, but in how he or she behaves and reacts towards other people and the world around them.

Twenty

The trial had not helped Tom Bryant. It took place at Winchester Crown Court, after seven months of police investigations, and was suddenly over in a week. To the Bryant males the wait seemed to be an ongoing nightmare with no end in sight. Each day of the trial Tom made his way to the court, sometimes with his sons, but usually alone, and listened as layer after layer of duplicity and subterfuge were stripped away from the prisoner's stories. Abdul Khaled was not an intelligent man. Consequently his fabrications, inventions and untruths, which ran throughout the length of his trial, were easy to see through by judge, jury and all those present at court as a whole.

The press showed intense interest because of the complexities and ramifications of the case, and all three Bryants were pursued relentlessly from the time of the accident, which was the last thing any of them needed. Instead of being given the chance to grieve properly, and the time to themselves which was required to completely revise the structure of their lives, particularly that of Tom's, they were instead questioned endlessly by the British tabloid press, constantly reminded of their loss and the circumstances surrounding it.

Some from the police did at least keep the Bryant's partially informed, but for others of those investigating the case was the mother-lode on which careers are either made or destroyed, so the family's complete involvement with developments was discouraged from on high, leaving them guessing, uninformed or even misinformed. This did nothing to help Tom's feelings of isolation or anything to help the recovery process. A quick investigation and a short clean trial may have done wonders for the three's acceptance of what had happened, and their ability to come to terms with the realities of their new lives, but between press and police it was not something they were destined to get.

The complete lack of morals, scruples or any form of remorse demonstrated by Abdul Khaled throughout his trial shocked the jury and the press as he constantly sought to blame anyone but himself for both the accident and the circumstances leading up to it. He never once apologised or expressed regret for taking the life of Mary Bryant, nor did he so much as look at Tom, who sat for days staring at Khaled with unmasked loathing and hatred written large across his face. It came across loud and clear the only true regret Abdul Khaled had was that the incident had cost him money, and the fact that his attitude to the court was likely to cause him an increase in his custodial sentence clearly never occurred to him.

Under British law the presumption at the start of any criminal trial is one of innocence. The fundamental safeguard in this system of justice has always been the premise that defendants are innocent until they are proved guilty, of the crime or crimes with which they have been charged, beyond all reasonable doubt. The onus is therefore on the state prosecution to put a case before the court which outlines the facts in the hope of a successful prosecution which is seen to be in the public interest. In Britain this is work carried out by lawyers or barristers representing the Crown Prosecution Service (CPS), which in turn works in partnership with all manner of agencies in the hope of reducing crime and the fear of crime. Amongst others the main agencies and bodies involved are the police, courts, Home Office and now the Department for Constitutional Affairs (DCA).

These collectively form the Criminal Justice System whose duty it is to dispense justice both fairly and efficiently whilst simultaneously promoting confidence in the rule of law and reducing the economic and social costs of crime. The head of the CPS is the Director of Public Prosecutions (DPP) who, in England and Wales, is ultimately responsible for determining any charges and prosecuting criminal cases investigated by the police within these two countries. The DPP makes decisions concerning the most complex and sensitive cases and advises the police on criminal matters accordingly. He in turn reports to the Attorney General who is the government minister who answers for the CPS before a democratically elected parliament.

Hair and tissue samples taken from the mirror guard of the truck Abdul Khaled was driving proved to be an exact DNA match with samples taken from the body of Mary Bryant. Irrespective as to this, and the weight of irrefutable evidence ranged against him, under British law he remained innocent until tried and found guilty.

Despite his wrongful entering of the country Abdul Khaled enjoyed the right to legal representation and a lawyer was provided for him at the cost of the public purse, as none of his family or countrymen came forward to assist him financially. His lawyer's advice was to plead guilty, apologise humbly to all concerned, and accept a much reduced custodial sentence. However it was his duty to point out to his client he could plead not guilty and fight the case, although he would get a longer sentence if found guilty. Abdul Khaled could see these people were idiots. Not only had he killed the stupid woman, but he was seen doing it and later caught by the police. Now they were giving him a chance to get away with it and were paying the man who had to do all the talking for him. The man's advice was stupid too. Did he really think he, Abdul Ahmad Khaled, would be crazy enough to plead guilty when others were prepared to pay for the silly man to tell everyone he didn't do it? Madness!

The criminal justice system was therefore forced to waste a ridiculous amount of time and public money proving the guilt of the prisoner. Much needed to be established, and slowly but surely it was. He was an illegal immigrant having falsely entered the country using another person's identity. He had not possessed a driving licence of any sort either in Pakistan or in Britain and therefore never taken any form of driving test. He had operated a goods vehicle fitted with a tachograph without a tacho-chart, contrary to Construction and Use Regulations, operated a vehicle with an insecure load, and left the scene of the accident. There were also additional issues to do with various acts of misrepresentation, but all of these were insignificant alongside the charges of causing death by dangerous driving, and attempting to pervert the course of justice.

The police and CPS built the case up carefully, checking and double checking all aspects and procedures as they went. The DPP himself became personally involved, mindful not so much of the legal complexities of the case, but of the possible political ramifications because of Abdul Khaled's nationality and ethnic background. If anything was at all wrong with the structure of the case the liberal pressure groups, along with an assortment of misguided bleeding hearts, and of course the tabloids, would start baying for blood. Something which was certainly best avoided.

The police and criminal evidence act requires interviews to be recorded on tape. Because Abdul Khaled's native language was not English, a translator had to be present throughout all interviews, and at trial. The charges which were to be brought had to be carefully considered, and the surrounding circumstance taken into account. Those charges which were finally drawn up took account of all relevant factors. A possible charge of Causing Death by Reckless Driving was upgraded to Causing Death by Dangerous Driving because of the lack of control Khaled maintained over the vehicle whilst having a map spread across the steering wheel. As he continued to assert he was Karim Ali Khan after his arrest a charge of Attempting to Pervert the Course of Justice was brought. These two were by far the worst of the charges but there were others to face which included Driving Whilst Disqualified, by virtue of not having a driving licence, a charge to do with failure to keep records because of the tachograph and a charge of insecure load. There were no charges surrounding his illegal entry status because it was widely thought a guilty verdict to either of the two main charges would take it into account as an aggravating circumstance by the judge. All of this took time, and it proved to take more than seven months before the case was brought before the court.

The prosecution had cause to call many witnesses and several experts. The defence could call none, save Abdul Khaled himself. All others Khaled suggested and attempted to blame or involve, in order to muddy the water, either could not be found or their evidence, such as it was, could not stand up to any form of scrutiny. It did not help his cause when during cross examination he was asked if he was sorry or regretted what had happened he blurted out, "Of course not. What was the stupid woman doing there anyway? Obviously it was God's will, and it was only a woman!"

This was delivered in a manner which could only at best be described as contemptuous, to a packed court which included Tom Bryant and both sons. The tabloid press lapped it up, but the outburst undoubtedly extended Khaled's term at Her Majesty's pleasure.

To the Bryants the investigation and trial had dragged on, but finally it was over. The jury retired for less than ninety minutes and came back with a finding of guilty on all counts. The judge nodded and summed up the case. Abdul Ahmad Khaled was found guilty of causing the death of Mary Bryant by dangerous driving. The fact that he originally entered the country illegally, possessed no licence, hit her on the pavement, left the scene of the accident and provided the police with a false identity were all considered aggravating circumstances. The complete lack of remorse he demonstrated throughout the length of the trial coupled with his outburst under cross examination encouraged the judge to exercise his discretion and give Khaled the maximum term as laid down, which is seven years. For attempting to pervert the course of justice he was given three years, to run concurrently. For leaving the scene of the accident a six months sentence was handed down, again to run concurrently, and the motoring offences attracted fines totalling nine hundred pounds. A deportation order was attached to the sentence to be implemented at the time of his release from jail. Khaled was taken down, and the trial was finished.

To Tom the sentence seemed paltry and insignificant when compared with what it had cost him, and left him feeling even more bitter when it was explained to him the concurrent sentences meant the maximum sentence was seven years not ten and a half, and Khaled would only serve two thirds of that, less the seven months he had already spent on remand, so he would be out in just over four years, certainly before 2005.

Nathan and Susie's daily commute from their home at Hadley Wood was far more time consuming than the two stop journey from Upton Park had ever been, but it was a relatively easy journey, taking the Piccadilly Line from Cockfosters to King's Cross St Pancras, changing there onto the eastbound Hammersmith & City Line and then out to East Ham. For Susie their home made it well worthwhile and even Nathan, who really didn't care where he was as long as he was with Susie, grudgingly admitted it was a lot more comfortable. In the two years since purchasing it the house had well and truly become their home, with dozens of additions and improvements made along the way to get it just as they both liked it.

During those two years things had gone well in every area of their lives. In the United States the land had sold virtually as soon as it was put on the market, making a huge profit which covered the cost of the purchase of both strips. Unfortunately since then the dot-com bubble had burst, and land in the area dropped back in price somewhat, but the US interest was working well, with vast profits still flooding in from both sides of the Atlantic. This was helped and augmented by another diversification for NJF, which had started relatively slowly, but rapidly gathered pace, and profits.

Nathan, who disliked shopping every bit as much as most normal males, devised and constructed an on-line shopping mall, selling advertising space and connected sites to national retailers. The virtual mall offered all which could be found in a real mall or average high street shopping centre, in fact much more, where virtual shoppers could browse and window shop without being jostled, contending with traffic, or braving adverse weathers. Those interested could wander the site in virtual world or consult comprehensive directories of products or stores they were interested in from the comfort of their own homes or offices. Everything seen could be purchased directly on-line through the NJF site, with a mere ten pence per item purchased paid to NJF for hosting sales within the virtual site, and where all transactions irrespective of supplier could be undertaken with a single sale. Initial take up of the new and innovative idea was slow, but within a year retailers had to be turned down, so great were the sales through the site to a truly global market. Shortly after the start of the second year he was forced by demand to open virtual shopping malls on each continent except Antarctica, all of which rapidly reached capacity.

In addition to the malls Nathan created three more games and the Hall

McGregor partnership another four, all of their more funky kind. NJF games were continuing to sell extremely well around the world. Nathan's first tentative step into the mobile phone game market had worked remarkably well with a game designed to be embedded into the handset which was quickly bought up by an international mobile phone manufacturer. With the extra time at his disposal Jake managed to grow his own empire which was rumoured to be worth well in excess of one hundred million pounds, without the inclusion of any part of the now fabulously wealthy NJF Industries.

For the year 2000, with both their twenty fifth birthdays behind them, Nathan and Susie once again returned to California. The intention was to once more be there at the launch of yet another game, The Millennium Bugs, and to enjoy an extended holiday. Whilst there they intended to purchase a property to serve them both as a base whilst in California on business, and as another home, just in case the times they were forced by business demands to spend in the region became extended. A few years earlier they had thoroughly enjoyed their journey north on the Pacific Coast Road, following Route 1 all the way to San Francisco, passing through some delightfully interesting areas boasting simply gorgeous properties. This time they headed north, past Fort Bragg, until they picked up the 101 which they followed as far as Eureka.

The north of The Bay demonstrated beautiful scenery, but proved too remote for their needs, so they turned once again for the south, back in the direction from which they had come, re-crossing the Golden Gate and heading for Pacifica. Ideally, for maximum convenience, they would have preferred to find something between Pacifica and Pillar Point, on or very near to the coast and overlooking the ocean, outside of a town, but not isolated. There were properties for sale along the stretch of coast they liked, but none came close to the mental picture either had. Having allocated themselves a month to find something three weeks passed fruitlessly, leaving both all but resigned to giving up on the trip when, five days before they were due to return to England, the perfect property was suddenly placed on the market.

Half Moon Bay sweeps south of Pillar Point, and gives its name to a town approximately one mile to the south east. A large marina lies within the bay backing on to the little town of El Granada, and to the north is the modest Half Moon Bay airfield. North of the airfield is the town of Moss Beach, and the property was located to the southern extreme of Moss Beach, one hundred and twenty paces from the sea, sheltered by a large sand dune and a row of wind bent trees. It was a large five bedroom house set at the end of a small service road which was itself a spur leading directly to Route 1. There were six other properties on the road, all sizable, and all private, none overlooking its neighbour, and all were segregated by rows of well established hardy looking trees. It was comfortable. It was in no way flashy or pretentious. It was everything they had both wanted, and ideally situated with regard access to West Menlo Park. Before they left for England a deal was agreed and lawyers completed the transaction in their absence.

The appalling tragedy which was Mary Bryant's untimely death had a shocking effect on the males who were formerly her family. Young people by nature are generally reasonably resilient and can deal with, and get over, the death of a loved one at a faster rate than those who are older. From Sandy Cartwright's viewpoint Jack seemed to turn even more to the safety of his studies, aided and supported by Danny. Danny, of the three, seemed to deal with the awful situation the best, and almost took on the mantel of man of the house. Tom completely went to pieces. Knowing the man she could relate to him to a degree, understanding the closeness of the relationship he had enjoyed with Mary. Sandy was less than two years away from her own loss and still at times looked back on things with profound regret as to what might have been yet now never would. Fortunately the gap between such times was growing, and as each month passed she strengthened a little more.

Danny continued to live the life he did and enjoy the things he had before his mother's death. The loss of his brother to Oxford University and the ongoing rigours of the build-up to the trial of the man who had taken his mothers life seemed to sap a little of his energy but, for the most part, he remained generally unchanged. The thing which did change noticeably about him was his tolerance and attitude to those who were and claimed to be Muslims. That was mostly as a result of the time delay between Mary's death and the trial, the ongoing lies of the defendant, and the overall effect the entire ghastly episode was having on his father. It seemed the man in the dock was not content with killing a woman he had never known, but he now appeared to wish to destroy the mental well being of the woman's former husband as well. Sandy was enormously grateful as news from the trial emerged that she had not had to endure a similar burden following John's death.

Twenty One

Somewhat bored with her now humdrum life Tammy took herself off to experience the change of millennium at Cape Town, a venue second only in global popularity to Sydney, but without the jet lag. At a huge party on the V & A waterfront, with the laser clock counting down on Table Mountain, she reached out and grabbed the hand of the man next to her at the stroke of midnight. As one of the world's greatest firework displays burst in the skies over their heads they held hands and sung Auld Lang Syne to one another. Peter Parfitt could not believe his good fortune. This vaguely familiar stunning vision before him was the very embodiment of Aphrodite, Freya and Venus all rolled into one. They sang together, they drank together, they danced together and eventually they went home together. They knew nothing of each other's backgrounds and neither of them cared. Parfitt had found a goddess, and Tammy the first real, natural and unaffected single man she had met since leaving school.

To Tammy Wild, Peter Parfitt was absolutely perfect, and everything she had ever really wanted. She never wished for the celebrity status which was continually foisted upon her, and in her heart she never wanted to be more than the girl next door type who eventually found her man, married, had kids and lived a normal life. She was 'discovered'. It was not something she had consciously gone looking for, but then one thing followed another until it took on a life of its own. She had made mistakes to be sure, but then she was human and was young and very naïve at the start of her 'career'. However the year had now just changed, the century had just changed, the millennium had just changed and, by God, she was going to make absolutely sure her life now changed.

She could see Parfitt had no real idea as to who she was despite her face, and more often than not, body, having been splashed over many magazines and papers for years. He obviously moved in such very different circles to her, wasn't at all interested in tabloid papers, and the only magazines she could see in his apartment related to cars and model aircraft. He was all male, had done well for himself in his own way, was seven years older than her and, not only was he a pilot but an ex-fighter pilot who had in his time been prepared to defend his country, her country, with his life.

He was in ever way possible and imaginable much more than she would ever have secretly dreamt of and, what was more, he seemed as interested in her as she was in him.

Parfitt most definitely was every bit as interested in her. She was without any question whatsoever by far and away the most beautiful woman he had ever seen, let alone taken to bed, and in bed she was unbelievable. That in itself would have been enough to keep him interested for a long time, but he found so much more depth to the gorgeous girl once they had both satisfied themselves in bed and taken the time to get to know one another properly. He had some leave due and he took it. Tammy's visa was valid for up to six months so she encountered no problem with cancelling her flight home, which she did, in order to remain for the full period of his leave.

South Africa was a country Tammy had visited twice before when working, but on both occasions was unable to tour or view the country, apart from a very limited area around where the photo shoots took place. Parfitt opened her eyes to the sheer majesty of the country. In a whistle stop tour they took Peter's car and followed the N1 north east out of Cape Town. The countryside changed around them as they headed up into the foothills, and the road which had for the most part remained a straight one started to meander as they gained height. The scenery was spectacular with craggy peaks and plunging drops into the valleys. Still in the Western Cape they crossed the Hex River Mountain and dropped slightly the other side as they headed out into the Great Karoo.

Although Tammy had heard of the Karoo she was unprepared for the haunting beauty of the place. The simplicity of almost featureless countryside stretched endlessly in all directions to distant horizons. An empty road seemed to unfold forever in front of them, in air which was bone-dry and land seemingly arid in the intense sunshine. Parfitt explained here the rainfall was at best minimal, and in the height of summer the ground was so hot it had been recorded for rain to fall for fifteen minutes from a storm cloud before any raindrops hit the ground, so great was the evaporation above the heated ground. The few isolated farmsteads and the flocks of sheep were sustained by underground waters, drawn to the surface by the odd distant windmills.

They drove without stopping for more than two hundred and fifty miles, and it was late lunchtime when they eventually pulled into the pear tree lined streets of Beaufort West, birthplace of heart surgeon Christian Barnard. Here they needed to refuel the car as the next fuel station was approximately one hundred and fifty miles further on. They stopped at a roadhouse, left the car with the windows down under the shade of a spreading tree in order to keep the interior relatively cool, and ate huge juicy burgers washed down with ice cold orange juice. Afterwards, leaving the town behind them, they headed east on the R61 for Aberdeen and Graaff-Reinet, their destination for the next two nights.

Peter had already booked them into the Drostdy Hotel, and the place was simply outstanding. In all her travels as a model Tammy had usually been very well looked after and catered for. She was accustomed to luxury hotels, wonderful food and excellent service, but she had never experienced anything like the Drostdy. As Peter explained to her whilst en route a Drostdy is unique to South Africa, and was basically the residence of a 'landdrost', an official whose duties combined those of tax collector, magistrate and local administrator in his area or region. However a Drostdy is much more than just a residence, as it includes the landdrost's office and a courtroom, along with the living quarters of his family. After Cape Town and Stellenbosch, Graaff-Reinet is the third oldest town in the Cape Province, and the fourth in the country. Its landdrost therefore controlled a large area and held in his time a very important position, with a residence to match his standing.

The Drostdy was originally built in 1806 and in the mid nineteenth century cottages were built for freed slaves. Both could see everything had since been beautifully restored then turned into a hotel. The cottages almost seemed to form a small town of their own, with walkways and passageways between each big enough for cars to pass through freely. The old courthouse was now a restaurant steeped in character, with a huge crystal chandelier in the centre. Reception was also located within the original court buildings, and the old cells were used for those hotel guests who wished to pay a premium for their accommodation. The restaurant served some of the best food Tammy had ever eaten, with courses which appeared to constantly keep arriving.

"What do you think of the food and wine?" Peter asked her towards the end of their meal.

"Peter, I can't believe it. The Karoo lamb was incredibly lean yet exquisitely tasty. I will admit I was a bit apprehensive having seen them in the wild, the poor scrawny looking things with ugly tails, but it was divine! Also, you do realise we are on our seventh course, don't you?" Tammy replied.

Parfitt chuckled. "I take it you approve of the place then? It was recommended but I've never been before. Actually I was told it was comfortable with good food and service, and it certainly lives up to that!"

The service was at least as good as the best she had ever known, with a waiter permanently hovering over each of them and a third replenishing their glasses of the beautiful fruity Cape wines after almost every sip.

The following day they explored the town, which seemed to be fully contained within a bend on the Sundays River, tripped along the boardwalks, browsed some of the local shops and admired the architecture of the old Cape Dutch houses, many of which were registered as national monuments. They took their lunch in The Coral Tree on Church Street, and both opted for kudu steaks served very rare. They wandered all day, and returned to the Drostdy in the early evening to enjoy a carbon copy of the previous evening in the restaurant, then headed to bed for an early night.

The following morning saw them away early, heading south towards Port Elizabeth, some one hundred and fifty miles away, then splitting off to the east towards Kirkwood and on to the Addo Elephant National Park. Here Peter drove Tammy around the reserve, looking everywhere for elephant without seeing a single one until, suddenly, a large bull walked straight into the road in front of them. It had remained invisible just twenty feet from them until it wandered into the open then crossed the road and walked into the bush with branches cracking and groaning as he passed. In seconds the massive creature once again disappeared, but never to be forgotten by either of them.

They left Addo and drove down into PE and to their hotel in Summerstrand, where again they planned to stay just two nights. In the morning, after Peter stopped at a butcher come grocers, they drove along the motorway to Van Stadens river mouth, where Peter had a simple treat in store for Tammy. South Africa is arguably the very best place in the world to enjoy a barbecue, which they call a braaivleis, now shortened to braai, and it is taken very seriously. Parfitt loved braai's, and was convinced Tammy would. He had taken his time in the butchers and bought exactly what he wanted. He knew of Van Stadens by reputation as an area where some of the workforce of PE still congregated at weekends as they had done for decades, and knew it would have the facilities he needed. When they reached the relevant exit they left the motorway and followed the road at the side of the river which continued as a dirt road after the tarmac ended. Eventually Parfitt pulled the car over into a parking place only a couple of hundred yards short of the sea. The area was completely deserted, devoid of any form of human life, and was strangely, wildly beautiful.

On the eastern side of the river where they were parked there was scrubland with small bushes near the water, and trees a little further back disappearing into the distance. On the other bank were steep golden yellow sand dunes running down to the water which to Tammy's mind looked as if they had just been moved there from the Sahara Desert, so incongruous did they look in this setting. The crystal clear waters of the river next to them sat low on the banks, and a sand bar completely blocked its exit to the ocean.

"So, what do you think of it?" Peter asked.

"It's incredible!" Tammy replied. "I've never seen anything like it. It's almost surreal. If you look in any one compass direction it is an utterly different landscape. To the west there are desert sand dunes, to the north a typical African river scene, off to the east is – well semi tropical forest and to the south a beautiful azure seascape. It is – it really is – incredible!"

"Well I'm glad you approve," Parfitt said grinning. "I just hope you enjoy lunch as much!"

"Oh Peter, can't we just stay here for a while?" Tammy asked. "It really is just so incredibly beautiful."

"We are staying here." Pete answered. "In fact we are going to stay here all day."

"So what did you mean about enjoying lunch? I'm sure there is no restaurant tucked away behind one of those trees." Tammy said, nodding in an easterly direction.

"Nothing so crass," Peter laughed, "I'll be cooking lunch today, my lady, and there is my state of the art kitchen." He pointed at an old forty-five gallon oil drum cut through the middle end to end. "And I had better get to work if lunch is to be served on time!"

Tammy merely raised her eyebrows and watched as Peter scurried about collecting dry grass and twigs which he loaded into the half drum. She noticed there were other half drums placed along the riverside as Peter headed to them collecting any charcoal and small branches which remained within them. These he brought back, loaded on top of the dry grass and twigs and then set light to it. As it caught and started to burn he collected more dry wood and placed it on top. Eventually there was enough in the barrel to almost fill it. When it reached that level Peter pulled a grating from the grass Tammy had not previously observed and placed it on top.

"Well that's the cooker heating," said Parfitt. "Fancy a swim before lunch to build up an appetite?"

"That would have been great, but I haven't brought a bikini or a costume, or a towel for that matter." Tammy replied.

Parfitt laughed. "Here?" he asked incredulously. "Nor have I! Come on, lets go."

They walked a few hundred yards along the coast, then threw off their clothes and ran naked into the sea. The water seemed cold after the warmth of the sun, but in seconds their bodies adjusted to it and both swam easily, ducking under the waves as they rolled gently in to end their long distance journey on the golden sandy shore. They swam together for about twenty minutes, each marvelling at the beauty of the other's body, as parts emerged shinning from the water. Both swam well with powerful strokes but neither tried to race, both content to swim with slow relaxed strokes, each thoroughly enjoying the company of the other. Finally they emerged from the water, collected their clothes and, still naked, walked back towards the car.

Although it was only a short stroll back to where they had parked, and where the braai was burning, most of the sea water dried on them by the time they returned, leaving a crystallised salt patchwork on their skin. The braai looked ready, with just a slight shimmering of heat haze rising above it, so Peter went to the back of the car and returned with the two grocery bags he had picked up at the butchers, and a little wicker basket Tammy had seen in the boot of the car several times before. He opened one of the bags, removed a number of items, and placed them across the extreme edge of the grating on top of the braai.

"Come on. Into the lagoon with you. Let's get that salt off you," Peter said and ran down the bank and dived head first into the water. Tammy followed laughing all the way. The fresh water of the lagoon was significantly warmer than the waters of the ocean, but was only a few feet deep so both could stand easily, with the water up as far as Tammy's shoulders. She swam straight up to Parfitt, threw her arms around his neck and kissed him deeply.

"Oh Peter, this is just so perfect!" Tammy said, and kissed him again.

Parfitt grinned back at her, "Good" was all he said and started rubbing her body to clear the salt. Tammy stepped closer to do the same to him with her arms around his back, which began to arouse Parfitt, and she felt him start to stiffen.

"Oh yes please." Tammy said huskily, and wrapped her legs around him. He guided himself into her, holding her around the shoulders and using the buoyancy of the water to help support her weight.

Afterwards they swam to the side, climbed the bank, and Parfitt checked the food.

"I bet it will be burnt to a crisp by now." he chuckled, but fortunately because of the way he had loaded the grill the meat was still all good, if a little bit well done on one side.

"That's a relief." Tammy laughed, then continued seriously, "You'll have to tell me what all those things are. I can see those are sausages and that's a chicken kebab, but I suspect there is much more to it than that."

Parfitt struggled, still a little wet, into a pair of shorts. "Well yes there is, but you don't have to remember it all. Most self respecting butchers will always help you here in South Africa because braai's really are what the country is all about. It's far more of a cultural thing here than a common barbecue could ever be anywhere else. It may sound a little overstated or even pretentious, but braai's have helped unite the peoples of this land for generations. You must remember the country was settled by those from often diverse backgrounds and different nations with a variety of tongues, and times in the past were hard for many of those settlers. One of the things which brought those people together, and arguably the main thing which brought them together in their leisure time, was the braai. This is a meat eating culture, with big, strong men and hardy women. The protein was necessary because of the temperature and because work was hard for these people, and braais provided a source of food which could be eaten communally, which in turn strengthened the bonds between those who participated. They literarily brought communities together and welded them into a people."

Tammy, now reasonably dry, put on her shorts, and pulled a T shirt over her head.

"But sorry, you didn't want a speech you just wanted to know what these things were." He chuckled, a little self consciously, before continuing, "These are Boerewors, which basically means farmer's sausage, and are an inheritance from the early German settlers. They are spiced mainly with coriander but sometimes using more fancy ingredients, such as sun-dried tomatoes, but I kind of prefer the non fancy version.

"Here we have Skilpadjies. That literally translates as little tortoises and are so called because of their shape. They are real traditional farm food. Liver is minced and spiced and then wrapped in caul fat before grilling. The dryness of the liver is offset perfectly by the fattiness of the caul and with a good sprinkling of cracked black pepper it becomes a delight. Butcher shops often make these up and keep them ready for keen braai lovers. Fortunately the shop I went into did just that."

"Sorry to interrupt, and do please pardon my ignorance, but what exactly is caul fat?" Tammy asked. "And what are those kebabs, just out of interest?"

"Caul fat is the fatty membrane which surrounds the internal organs of some animals, such as cows, sheep, and pigs. They often use it as a natural sausage casing and to encase things like faggots or even pâté. These kebabs are Sosaties. They are cubes of chicken, skewered with a combination of dried fruit, such as pears and apricots, quartered onions and, as with these, sometimes bacon is added. They are usually marinated overnight in a light curry sauce. They are lean and very tasty, and for best results they should be barbecued slowly. In essence these three things represent South Africa on a plate."

Parfitt turned the meats over with a metal spatula he had removed from a roll of cooking tools he had taken from the wicker basket. Tammy could see there were plates and plastic mugs inside along with a small cooking pan and other assorted outdoor eating implements.

"I see you come well equipped." Tammy said looking at the basket, and the bag of salad ingredients.

"Why thank you!" Parfitt said making a suggestive face and squeezing the crotch of his shorts, "You're not so bad yourself." Tammy laughed out loud and stuck out her tongue as Parfitt continued, "Again it is a part of the culture here. I guess over half the cars you see on the roads here will have their own equipment either with them or close to hand, and no one would dream of leaving home for a holiday without their own gear."

"You seem to really love this land." Tammy said, looking at him seriously, and taking the plate of food held out to her.

"Oh hell yeah! How could anyone not?" Parfitt replied, "It really is God's own country, but there is much more to it than that. I love its people too. Black or white, brown or yellow, they all have a place here. I particularly hated that ridiculous balls up which is multiculturalism in Britain, mainly because it's social experimentation and engineering, and is doomed to be a very unpleasant failure. Here it works, maybe not perfectly every time, but infinitely better than our own forced home grown version. Here it is vastly more complicated than it is at home, not that you would ever hear such there, but here it works." He took a big bite of one of the Boerewors on his plate.

"In what way is it more complicated here then?" Tammy asked. "Surely it's just a black white thing?"

"No, not at all," Parfitt replied smiling, "but I think I would bore you to death if I went on."

"Honestly Peter, I can see you have a passion for the place, and I would love to learn more. So do please tell me. I'll let you know if you start to bore me," she said, grinning cheekily. "Ooh, these are wonderful!" she said, biting into a Skilpadjie.

"Well okay, but the black white thing doesn't even come close. Let's first take the whites. Back home anything to do with 'White' South Africa all comes under the same banner. White. But it really is not so simple. There is more than one white. You have the Boer whites and Afrikaner whites, which at home we all regard as Dutch, which is in itself miles from the truth as their background includes Germans, French and a whole bunch of other disaffected and dispossessed European peoples from the seventeenth, eighteenth and even nineteenth centuries. Then you have the white South Africans. Those who can trace their background back to good old Blighty perhaps centuries ago, but have always maintained a British passport and have remained in essence British. Add to that the white migrants who made their way to South Africa in the decades after the Second World War, and were mostly British working class. Then factor in the Portuguese who migrated south as Portuguese East Africa and West Africa became independent, and again add those British Rhodesians, from North and South, who also migrated south after independence. Add them all together and you then have the very basics of a working understanding of the 'Whites', although none of which will explain the pecking order."

"The 'Blacks' at home include all non 'Whites'. Bullshit – utter bullshit! This is Africa. Africa is made up of many tribes, and those tribes are tribal, many fiercely so. The Zulu and the Causa loath one another. An offshoot of the Zulu, the Matabele, took over the land of the Shona, in what is now Zimbabwe, and their territory spreads down into the north of this country. Offshoot or not they and the Zulu do not get along, nor do the Bushmen, who don't even look like other African tribes and are in some ways ideologically in tune with the North American Indians, in that they have no concept of ownership. They belong to the land, rather than the other way around, as does everything else on it to them. This brings them into major conflict with all the cattle owning tribes because the Bushmen believe the cattle are there for everyone and take them for their meat as they will. There are also the Hottentots down in the Cape. They were on the verge of extinction with a depleted gene pool when white man landed. White man gave them a new lease on life by making their womenfolk pregnant, but which then gave rise to the Cape Coloureds, and that just scrapes the surface of the 'blacks'."

"There are then the peoples of Asian extraction. In the days of the Raj we Brit's had a highly trained workforce in India, especially as far as railway construction was concerned. We found it difficult to train and motivate an African workforce, so we shipped in tens of thousands of Indians, whose families later followed. They were an industrious and motivated workforce, who remained in various countries and multiplied long after the work on the railways had finished, and are still here today. The Chinese, seeking trade, followed and set up not only their own businesses, but their own areas, much as they have done with various Chinatowns around the world. They too are still here. There is a lot of friction between the 'blacks' of most tribes and the Indians, partly for historical reasons, partly both ethnically and culturally, and partly due to jealousies of position and wealth. Historically the Indians provided a buffer between the whites and the 'Bantu', the black people, and are still hated for it. Ethnically, and certainly culturally, they are seen as different, and many of the blacks would still quite happily see them swept into the ocean because of it. Interestingly the blacks can far more readily accept white rule than share power with the Indians. The jealousies spring from the perceived advantages the Indians have enjoyed in all manner of things from education to social position. To generalise sweepingly the Indians worked harder, tried more and were brighter, so they were rewarded in terms of payment and promotion at their places of work, taking on the tasks of foremen and the lowly management positions. They were then the ones who controlled and commanded the blacks, and were not liked for it. This is not just a problem of South Africa so much as one of Africa itself. You will doubtless remember what happened in Uganda with the Ugandan Asians under Idi Amin back in the seventies. That was just an extreme version of what is the general outlook towards Asians here in Africa. In many very real ways they represent in Africa what the Jews did to the peoples of Europe before, during and in some cases even after the Second World War."

"So there you go – not as easy as it would seem to those sitting in their armchairs in middle class British suburbia," Parfitt ended.

Tammy had listened with interest throughout. "You were right, I really didn't have the faintest idea about any of that, and I very much if doubt many people outside of this country do either. The one thing I don't understand with what you have told me is, if as you say there are so many warring factions and unsettling elements, how on earth does it work as well as it currently seems to?" she asked.

"That is an interesting question." Parfitt answered. "Frankly I don't really know the answer, and don't think anyone else truly does either. I surmise much of it has to do with mutual dependency. Recently the system has gone through a huge transition, something all sides are still trying and learning to come to terms with. It must be remembered the vast majority of the people here have got nowhere else to go, and this is their home and homeland. Back in Britain we hear strident voices shouting all too often the whites should leave Africa, without any thought given to the consequences. Interestingly it is more often than not the same silly mouths shouting all immigrants should be made welcome to Britain, and generally comes from the misguided and ill informed bleeding heart liberal halfwits. How they square the hypocrisy of that circle is anybodies guess.

"I honestly believe the whites here are the white tribe of Africa, and consequently have as much right to be here as anybody. One of the things which definitely makes this country work is it has retained a democracy. Now think on that – a working democracy in Africa. Generally once given the vote, a free and fair election – what a joke – a totalitarian one party Marxist government is voted in and immediately bans all other political parties, and executes any who would try to oppose. South Africa has so far avoided that. They are the continent's wealthiest country and all here benefit from it. Without doubt they have the best health system in Africa. They have massive mineral deposits from gold to diamonds to uranium to chromium to name but a few. They manage huge forests, South Africa Paper Pulp Industries, SAPPI, is one of the worlds biggest players, and they harvest cash crops which are sold around the world, despite which agriculture forms only three percent of GDP.

"Now restrictions have been lifted which were imposed because of apartheid, something we the British in essence brought here, their wine industry is the fastest growing in the world, and will probably in time threaten the Australian and America vineyards at the rate it is expanding. South African Breweries is the largest brewer in Africa and the second largest in the world. There are major European and American automobile assembly plants, the worlds fifth largest armaments industry, built up again because of sanctions, and South Africa Airways, the chaps I work for, is by far Africa's biggest airline. All of that, and I repeat all, is to do with what whites have brought to this country, and for the most part still manage and run. All of her neighbours are failed nations. Many had the same, or at least similar, advantages, and all here have seen how those nations have squandered all they had, whilst at the same time everyone here, black, white and brown, have prospered. The people here, of all colours, are by a long way the best educated in Africa, and most can see it. So mutual wealth helps bind all together and allows them to overlook some of their differences."

"I have to say they also seem to have another big thing going for them," said Tammy mischievously, "and that is this food. I'm loving this! It's the best barbecue I've ever had!"

Parfitt laughed. "Yeah, I'm sorry." he said. "Enough of the speeches. It's just I tend to get a little carried away on the subject. I absolutely love this land, and all its peoples. I don't care a toss about the colour of any man's skin, or what culture any choose to follow, it is the quality of the man which is the only important thing to me."

"Oh Peter," Tammy chuckled, "I'm only teasing you. I can see the passion you have, and in all honesty, from what I've seen so far, I can completely understand it! This truly is a beautiful land,"

The two finished their braai, and Peter cleaned the plates and all the cooking utensils in the sand, an old beach braai practice he explained. He loaded everything into the car, pulled out a travel rug and the two wandered along the shore for about a mile until they found a spot they liked. There they laid out the rug stripped off their tops and shorts and lay together soaking up the sun and chatting amiably for almost two hours. Eventually they returned to the car and drove slowly back to PE, cutting down to the old coast road, and coming into town via Summerstrand where the African market, which stretched along the beach road, was still in full swing. Parfitt parked so they could wander along past the stalls, browsing as they went. Many sold beautifully intricate hand made African artefacts, from wood carvings to beadwork and cotton goods, and Tammy bought several, whilst Peter teased her about her baggage allowance.

The following day they left early once again, this time heading west, picking up the Garden Route at Storms River, driving along to Knysna, where Parfitt planned for them to spend two nights, and had booked a self catering log cabin right on the beautiful Knysna Lagoon, with quite simply breathtaking views. They snacked on local fresh oysters sprinkled with lemon juice or fiery chilli sauce for lunch, and washed them down with a locally brewed Marshall's draught ale, afterwards wandering along the road at the side of the lagoon to The Heads. Knysna's Heads are two imposing sandstone cliffs which stand guard over the entrance to Knysna Lagoon, and provide an excellent vantage point for views over the natural splendour of the surrounding area. That evening they wandered down to Crab's Creek restaurant and sat under an umbrella on the very edge of the water, eating locally produced food, and drinking a couple more Marshall's. The following morning they took the John Benn, a twenty ton pleasure boat, from the local jetty for a day of sightseeing, wining and dining.

They took things easy, leaving Knysna in the early afternoon, and continued along the Garden Route, through George, then left it as they headed up to Oudtshoorn, where they again stopped for the night. They found a highly recommended local restaurant and dined out on crocodile and locally produced ostrich steaks. In the morning they visited Cango Caves, a complex of huge caves, once partially inhabited, which rank amongst the most remarkable of Africa's many natural wonders. After the tour they left the caves and headed for one of the local ostrich farms, where Tammy was thrilled to watch ostriches being ridden, and where they learnt much about the huge birds, their meat, leather, eggs and feathers, and of the history of the feather trade and the feather millionaires it produced. Leaving once more in the afternoon they drove back to George, again picking up the Garden Route as they headed down to Mossel Bay.

Before leaving PE, Parfitt explained to Tammy a little about the Garden Route, and what he told her she found fascinating. He had certainly not exaggerated. They followed an enchanting shoreline of lovely bays and deserted coves, high cliffs and wide estuaries full of colourful birdlife. The lagoons and lakes around Wilderness, and where they had stayed at Knysna, were simply magical stretches of water, with good hotels and restaurants, pleasant little villages and peaceful looking resorts, all set with the backdrop of the warm waters of the Indian Ocean. In the hinterland she had seen mountains and rivers with waterfalls, and spectacular passes with wooded ravines. All in all the area boasted a vast expanse of gorgeous natural beauty, quite literally Mother Nature at her most dazzling and impressive.

The morning found the couple swimming on an excellent beach at Mossel Bay, but they finished early, dried off, and Peter drove them down to Cape Agulhas which, geographically, is the southern tip of the continent of Africa, and the place which is officially accepted as being where the Indian and Atlantic oceans meet. A marker indicated the official dividing line, and each took their turn to stand on the rocks behind with their feet in the waters whilst the other took pictures. However, although the waters near the coast are quite shallow and are renowned as one of the best fishing grounds in South Africa, Cape Agulhas was relatively unspectacular, and there was little reason for them to stay. They found somewhere for a late lunch, then made the drive back to Cape Town and Peter's apartment.

The next few days passed in a whirl as they visited the wine growing regions, starting in the incredibly picturesque area surrounding Stellenbosch, the town itself with its historic buildings and oak lined streets, then east to Franschhoek, founded by French Huguenots at the tail end of the seventeenth century, and then north to Paarl. The Cape-Dutch homes in the area were stately and the vineyards immaculately kept with mown lawns in front and white picket fences or painstakingly whitewashed stones following the roads. The well established vines grew well in the fertile soil of the region and the mountain backdrop was endlessly impressive.

They visited Robben Island, the Castle and took the cable car up Table Mountain, and on another day drove south to Cape Point via Simon's Town, headquarters of the South African Navy. The drive along Victoria Road heading south to Hout Bay, and then via Chapmans Peak, as they made their way south, was without doubt the most spectacular drive of Tammy's life, and Peter had saved it to last as it was one of his favourites.

"What do you think?" he asked.

"I can't answer that Peter. I just don't have the words for it. I have seen, stayed in and experienced many a beautiful location, but I've never seen anything to better this. It's simply stunning!" Tammy replied in a hushed yet emotional voice.

All too soon it was time to leave and Tammy, who had never before in life demonstrated excessive emotion, cried without restraint for nearly three hours. Nothing Parfitt said or did would console her, she just did not want to leave him, or the wonderful country he had shown her. Never in her life had she felt anything like the emotional bond she now felt for this man, and she would rather stop breathing than be out of his company. She cried again, and again, but eventually with red rimmed eyes she made her way with Parfitt to the airport. Parfitt had made arrangements, and it was on his flight she was to return to England.

After they cleared immigration at Heathrow, Parfitt accompanied Tammy by train down to her little cottage in the grounds of her family's home in Kemp Town, on what was a grey, wet and cold winter day. It was many years since Parfitt had last visited Brighton. It was a town he had previously liked, and he found he still did, but it didn't come close to Cape Town. It obviously didn't for Tammy either. She had telephoned her parents after landing at Heathrow so they were expecting the two of them and made Peter more than welcome during the lunch they laid on. They were friendly open people, and Parfitt believed they would be easy people to like, something they obviously also felt about him. Tammy and Parfitt retired to the cottage after lunch, for a couple of hour's sleep, as Parfitt had flown through the night, returning to eat with the family again in the early evening. That night they retired to bed and made love passionately before falling asleep in one another's arms. Neither wanted to let the other go, although both knew they had to. In the morning they made love again, slowly and tenderly, then spent a lazy day in Brighton, freezing as they wandered the Lanes in the depth of an English winter, made all the colder having just left Africa's summer. They walked hand in hand and talked earnestly and incessantly. It had proved to be a whirlwind romance for both, and neither were kids any more. They had been together for less than three weeks, yet not spent more than a few minutes apart during that time. It had all been very intense and, for Tammy, a holiday romance. Passions may well cool a little when they parted they each tried to convince the other, and themselves, both secretly knowing for them it was a lie.

The next morning arrived all too soon. Tammy had arranged to borrow her mother's car and drove Parfitt to Heathrow very early so he may make the flight. For Tammy it was another tearful parting. What they had said to one another the day before, the logic, the reasoning and the sensible plans, were all forgotten. She just didn't want him to go. Parfitt had to wrench himself away in the end as it would have been just too easy for him to stay. He too felt as she did, but what they had said and agreed was sensible, and he was responsible to his employers, passengers and crew, and duty had to come first. No matter how it was viewed, how it was dressed up, or even what he personally wanted, duty would always have to come first.

Parfitt made the long flight home in relative silence. His co-pilot tried hard to make conversation, but eventually gave up thinking, rightly, that the old boy seemed to be completely loved up. Parfitt didn't care about all the well reasoned conversation he and Tammy had exchanged the day before, he just knew he wanted to be with her. He hadn't exactly been short of women in his time, but they had come and gone more regularly than buses, and he had never once previously regretted in. This time it felt like his entire guts had been ripped from his body. Training took over and he could fly the plane, but he wasn't interested in the food the stewardess brought to the guys up front, didn't want to talk and just could not for a moment keep his mind off her, irrespective as to how hard he tried to concentrate on other things. By the time he landed at Cape Town, after a great deal of thought along the way, he had come to one overwhelming conclusion. Despite the scorn and ridicule he had heaped upon others in the past, when they had said the same sort of thing to him, he realised he had met the woman he could not live without. In his entire life he had never felt or had to deal with this idiotic and debilitating emotion, but could see it for exactly what it was – he was head over heels in love, and one day, if he could, he would marry Tammy Wild and spend the rest of his days with her!

Tammy watched as Peter Parfitt walked away. She knew he had to go, and understood as best she could, but the knowledge and understanding did nothing to help. She just wanted to be with him – it was that simple. She understood the concept of duty, and knew he had a job to do, but it mattered for nothing in comparison to her need for him. She had experienced her share of relationships along the way, some she would have been better off not having, and some she regretted, but in all her travels she had never before met a man to whom she felt so attracted and such an uncontrollable need to be with. Apart from her father, when she was chastised as a small child, no man had ever once made her cry. Now she though, sitting in a lay-by because she could not see to drive through her tears, she just could not stop crying. By the time she eventually got back to the little cottage at Kemp Town she had come to one towering conclusion. Despite the long held view that to lose control of emotions and to 'fall in love' was only for silly young girls, she had in fact done just that and, that said, no matter how long it took, or what she had to endure to get there, one day she would marry Peter Parfitt and spend the rest of her life with him!

Twenty Two

A further six months in Osnabruck followed, again with 7 Armoured Brigade. In March 2000 WO2 Chris Spencer returned to England, to the Warminster Infantry Demo Unit. The 1st Battalion of the Green Howards were based at Warminster, in the county of Wiltshire, where it formed the Land Warfare Battle Group. They were to assist in the testing and trials of future weaponry and infantry equipment, and were to provide a permanent 'enemy' to all forces training or undertaking battle simulations on Salisbury Plain. With B Company as the Battalion's Armoured Infantry Company its troops had the opportunity to frequently exercise with Warriors, this time as Armoured Fighting Vehicles. Dismounted infantry also spent time engaged in operations on the Plain.

On his return the personal weapons, the SA80's and their various derivatives, of all who carried them were recalled and withdrawn for modification. What Chris earlier noticed as a problem during desert operations in 1991 continued to dog the weapon and, under certain conditions, had caused some serious problems. In all he was given to understand some three hundred thousand weapons were recalled for modification. At last the Army had taken the complaints of the men in the field seriously.

The School of Infantry had long been based at Warminster and occupied a large area to the north of the town. It was almost two hundred miles from either his parent's home or his sister's on the other side of the country, but it was England, and it was home. Leave, when taken, could be enjoyed with his family and it gave him a chance to catch up with Jimmy Andrews, who was now a sergeant. By the time Chris got to see his sister, his favourite person in the world had just passed his eleventh birthday. It was the middle of the school summer holidays and Charlie was excitedly looking forward to senior school. He had developed a real passion for animals, and the family's small cottage looked, sounded and smelt like a menagerie, with small furry creatures everywhere.

Although he lived amongst several other relatives, and with his father also in the army, Chris had remained Charlie's hero throughout his young life, and the young lad was overjoyed to again be able to spend time with the uncle he always thought of as his country's greatest hero of all time. In return Chris loved the little guy beyond measure and was thrilled to see how well he was developing physically, academically and emotionally. Charlie was doing very well at school and completely vindicated his parent's choice to establish a permanent base from which the children could grow up, as opposed to following Jimmy's postings. His twin nieces Michelle and Juliette were lovely little girls and were approaching their fifth birthdays. They too were looking forward to following their big brother into school, which they were due to start around the time of their birthdays.

To Chris the whole ensemble epitomised a sight of complete domestic bliss, and was everything he wished to protect and preserve, but for the first time in his life he realised the depth of personal loss his life decisions had cost him. His feelings about the well being, safety and security of his country were deeply held, and he fully understood the job he did must be done. He knew he was good at his chosen profession, and his experience had without doubt saved lives in the past, and undoubtedly would again in the future. He had certainly not been a monk over the years, and harboured no complaints about missing out on the joys which only a woman's body can bring, but long term meaningful relationships were never a serious option, and he still believed, certainly in his case, marriage and family would never have worked. One would have suffered, and he understood himself well enough to realise duty would always have come first, and it takes an incredibly strong woman to understand that. Jimmy Andrews was a lucky man because Jen was one of those women, but even if he had found a similar one marriage would not have followed, as he would not have wished to put any woman through the uncertainty which went hand in hand with a professional soldier's life.

It was an unfortunate consequence, but the reality of life was such that it was probable he would never have a family as Jimmy had. It was perhaps regrettable, and not a consequence he would have ever considered until recently, but that was life. At least he was close to Jim and Jen's kids. With a deployment in Britain he would get the chance to see quite a bit of them, and Charlie did fill the space in his life he believed a son would have done. It was therefore his job to make sure they were safe, protected from the bad guys, and comfortable in their beds at night. Without a family of his own he would make absolutely sure he would do that – for all the little Charlies, Michelles and Juliettes of his country.

It was many months before Sandy Cartwright once again saw Tom Bryant and she was astonished at the changes to the man in both his physical state and character. The once tall, straight backed and commanding figure had not only lost weight, but seemed to have physically shrunk since last she saw him. He appeared to have less hair and there was now a definite appearance of grey to it. His stature was changed and he was now slightly stooped, as a man might be if trying to carry far too much weight. His previous outgoing, relaxed, friendly and sociable way of meeting and greeting the world was gone. He now seemed terse, somewhat testy and almost robotic. It was instantly apparent he was having difficulty dealing with his loss, and equally apparent this was not a new state of affairs. He was obviously not eating well and was probably getting very little sleep judging from the deep black lines below his eyes. He appeared to have aged twenty years. His place of work had at first given him compassionate leave which was extended by a doctor's note, and he was clearly still unfit for any form of work.

Sandy Cartwright's heart went out to the man. Whether it was something to do with the similarities they shared in having a loved one's life ripped away suddenly and dramatically, some form of suppressed maternal instincts coming to the fore, or just the desire to assist another human being in their time of need would never be known. She didn't even know why herself, but one day she found herself knocking on his front door and insisting she took him out for a drink and a meal, and had not left his door until he agreed to a date.

It was the much needed turning point for Tom Bryant. Friends had tried repeatedly and failed, as had workmates, but he would have none of it. Sandy's approach was very different, and she would not take no for an answer. Their initial outing proved difficult for the pair of them. Sandy at first tried to be light and friendly, virtually trying to follow on from where they had left off when they all met up for lunches, but it didn't work. Next she tried to draw him out of himself a little but if anything that was worse. Eventually, mostly because she was getting so little back from him, and because he was more playing with his food than eating it, she fell back on the subject on which she alone in all the world was the expert, Sandy Cartwright.

The death of her husband must have got through to some dark place buried deep in his soul, but get through it did, and he started to ask her questions about what happened, how she felt and what followed. As a result what actually happened was another date, and another, followed by many more. Tom Bryant slowly began to enjoy this woman's company and it showed. She wasn't his Mary, and never tried to be, but she was a kind and warm hearted woman who had also suffered badly.

The trial and the build up to it had taken a seemingly long time, and the toll it took on Tom was undeniable. The eventual guilty verdict to all charges lifted him, despite the apparent woefully inadequate sentence, and at last he could move forward as it did at least offer partial closure to an absolutely dreadful chapter of his life. Although the event touched him so deeply he would never again be the same person, colour progressively returned to his features and Sandy's meal dates helped to put some weight back on his frame. Gradually he began to sleep slightly better and the deep dark shadows under his eyes slowly faded and almost disappeared, as did most of the stoop. He would never again return to exactly what he had once been but, with Sandy's constant help if not supervision, bit by bit he lost fifteen years of the twenty he had put on.

For Chris Spencer spring and summer of 2001 was arguably the most relaxing time he had enjoyed in his adult life. He had risen through the ranks to a position where he was respected by both officers and men, and was a senior NCO in an army which was regarded by most around the world, both friend and enemy alike, as the best trained, disciplined and professional there is. He was as physically fit as he could possibly ask for as he approached his forties, and was as experienced at his chosen profession as any man ever could be. Training manoeuvres were simplicity itself to him, yet he could still grasp new concepts almost instantly, and experimented with new equipment with great interest. He had managed to see more of his family during the previous year than in the ten years or so before, and life for him at the time was the best he had ever known, without so much as a cloud of any kind on his horizon.

For millions of people around the world that was about to change and the change would usher in a new era. Many people would be affected by the coming changes. Some would be uprooted and have their lives turned upside down. Some would die.

Another year sped by in a flurry of corporate activity. Chi Lu had visited China, which was fast becoming a prominent world economy, and a subsidiary was created in the land of the dragon. Somehow a simple conversation between Susie and Nathan about the future of the company, and the direction it should take over the next decade, spilled over into a general conversation about far more wide ranging subjects, one of which was about their personal relationship, and it inevitably led to talk of marriage. Neither knew which one actually asked the question, or how it came about, but once the subject was discussed events seemed to take on a life of their own, and a date was set for August of the same year.

They were to be married in the church at Foxton, and the reception was to be held in a marquee to the rear of her parent's home, very much as Susie's eighteenth birthday had been arranged nine years earlier. Jake Ferris was delighted to be asked to be best man, and Phil Gatting was, if possible, even more excited about the prospect of giving his baby daughter away than his wife was about helping to organise the event.

Susie was an outstanding organiser as had many times been observed by those who followed her accomplishments at NJF Industries. It became apparent to many where some of her talent came from, as Jane Gatting swung into action planning, organising and tying up every loose end. Her attention to detail was absolute. She had quite obviously organised events for her husband and family in the past, so could draw upon experience, but it was a major credit to her that nothing escaped her. It was Susie's wedding, and Jane in no way interfered, but if she was asked to help with anything it could be considered not only done, but done perfectly, something which may have been made slightly easier for her as no account of cost was ever considered.

It was the biggest private event any of the guests had ever attended, but the church was comparatively small, with only a fraction of those invited able to attend the ceremony inside the building. This was considered a problem which had to be resolved. The marquee was gigantic, set to seat fourteen hundred people. In the centre four giant roll down screens were suspended and a live feed from the church was instantaneously projected so all could follow the proceedings. All present in the church could hear the roar from the giant tent three hundred yards away as the 'I do's' were repeated. Despite living with Nathan for several years Susie wore a beautifully cut and fitted raw silk white wedding dress. She was supported by four bridesmaids in pale yellow, and Chi Lu, who looked breathtakingly beautiful as her maid of honour. Every man in the church except the vicar wore top hats and tails, which most could not wait to shed.

The wedding reception was a sensational, extravagant affair with a staff well in excess of one hundred taking care of the needs of guests, from valet parking to table service. The bar inside the marquee was one hundred and twenty feet long and serviced by twenty bar staff. In addition both local pubs were 'open', with drinks provided to all throughout the celebrations from the deep pockets of Phil Gatting. A firework display which could be seen from three counties lit the night sky for more than an hour, and rivalled the millennium celebrations of many cities. Almost every member of the village attended, with those who had suggested there may be a noise problem sent on an all expenses paid four day holiday of their choice. A separate disco tent played a mix of music until the early hours of the morning, whilst a live jazz band rotated with a string quartet in the main tent. From mid afternoon until past midnight a well stocked barbeque fed all comers, while hogs sizzled as they slowly roasted over open pits.

Provision was made for press and two crews from local TV stations, all of whom expressed an interest in covering the wedding. A small fleet of minibuses was organised to collect partygoers and return them to their homes and hotels. Mr. and Mrs. Nathan Jefferies greeted as many of their guests as was possible before being picked up by helicopter and taken to East Midlands Airport. There Jake had an executive jet standing by to fly the newly-weds to Paris, where they planned to spend a quiet week in an anonymous three star tourist hotel, just the way Nathan liked it, before returning to the daily grind. Jake, who had spoken to Phil Gatting by telephone on only the one occasion, remained as a guest of the Gatting family, as did Chi Lu, getting along famously with the couple who were their hosts. The four, despite their varied backgrounds, found they had much in common, and held many similar opinions on a wide range of diverse subjects. The seeds of friendship were sown which in normal circumstances would remain for the duration of their lives.

The connection and friendship would remain. The events which were to overtake all were to be anything but normal.

Twenty Three

On the twenty-first of August 1959 the islands officially known as Hawai'i Territory were admitted to the Union of the United States, making them the fiftieth state. They had become a United States territory less than two years after the signing of the Newlands Resolution on the seventh of July 1898 by President William McKinley, officially becoming Hawai'i Territory, a United States territory, on the twenty-second of February 1900. For over forty years most Americans never even knew Hawai'i existed. All that changed on the morning of Sunday the seventh of December 1941 when the Japanese navy mounted a surprise attack against the United States' naval base at Pearl Harbour in an attempt to remove the US Pacific Fleet and thereby preventing America from intervening in Japan's planned Pacific operations. The attack on the base took the lives of two thousand three hundred and fifty people, including sixty-eight civilians. According to President Roosevelt it was "... a date which will live in infamy."

Although not then a state Hawai'i was a recognised American territory. The plan to exclude America from the war which was to follow badly backfired on the Japanese, and immediately brought America into a war they had for some time been trying to avoid. Although the Hawaiian Islands are a long way from the American mainland the sleeping giant was rudely awakened. It was not since the British signed The Treaty of Paris in 1783, ending the American Revolutionary War, also known as the American War of Independence, that the Americans had been attacked at home, and even with the losses inflicted at Pearl Harbour continental USA had still not then been attacked.

On the morning of the eleventh of September 2001 (often referred to as 9/11) that again changed with a series of coordinated suicide attacks by an organised and well funded terrorist group known as al-Qaeda. Four commercial passenger jet aircraft were hijacked, two of which were intentionally and deliberately crashed into New York City's World Trade Centre, the third was crashed into the Pentagon, the headquarters of the United States Department of Defence. The forth crashed into a field in rural Pennsylvania, near the town of Shanksville in Somerset County after, it is believed, passengers and crew attempted to retake control of the aircraft. With the exclusion of the hijackers two thousand nine hundred and seventy-four people were known to have lost their lives as an immediate result, which included nationals from more than ninety countries, with a further twenty-four people missing and presumed dead. The twin towers of the World Trade Centre collapsed, removing a vast area of New York office space and causing the economy of Lower Manhattan to grind to a halt. The stock exchanges closed for almost a week and, upon reopening, posted enormous losses.

A declaration of war had been delivered, which was heard clearly and resounded around the world.

As with the Japanese attack on Pearl Harbour no warning was given, but there any similarities ended. The World Trade Centre was not a military target but a civilian one, staffed and filled with workers, visitors and tourists from around the world. The attack in the heart of New York, and Arlington, Virginia, was most definitely an attack at mainland America. The acts and the action were not carried out by any form of state, but rather by a self appointed illegal organisation abhorred globally. Although indefensible the lack of warning from the Japanese was unintentional, and occurred because of time zone differences and inadequate typing skills. There was never any intention to warn on the part of al-Qaeda, nor a claim or admission after the event. However the operation typified their modus operandi with its callous disregard for human life. The giant was once again about to retaliate, and Afghanistan, under the leadership of despised sociopaths calling themselves the Taliban, had long been wilfully harbouring the al-Qaeda terrorists. On the seventh of October 2001, an attack on the Taliban regime was launched by the United States and the United Kingdom in response.

Life at Warminster continued. Days became weeks, and the weeks drifted into months. The winter came and went and spring once more returned. From October onwards WO2 Chris Spencer, and those both above and below him, waited for the movement notice for their deployment to Afghanistan. It never came. However eventually what did come was notice of redeployment to Northern Ireland, to Ballykelly in County Londonderry, and in April 2002 the residential tour began.

On the tenth of April 1998 the Northern Ireland peace deal was reached after peace talks ended with a historic agreement. After almost two years of talks and thirty years of conflict an accord was reached and was immediately dubbed the Good Friday Agreement. On the final day of talks negotiations continued to drag on more than seventeen hours after the deadline, but they were successful, and Prime Minister Tony Blair and the Republic of Ireland's leader, Bertie Ahern, finally succeeded where every predecessor failed.

It was thirteen years since Chris had last seen Northern Ireland, and the changes were incredible. Four years on from the signing of the Peace Accord and the peoples of the province had accomplished much. The atmosphere and very ethos of the place was changed, and there was a discernable difference in the apparent prosperity of the population, especially of the Catholic minority. The sheer naked aggression of the entire area was then replaced by a feeling of purpose, with commuters scurrying to and from work in the place of packs of massed rioters. There appeared to be an abundance of work and the opportunities which went with it. There were many more cars, the properties of the people were much improved with home owners once more taking a pride in their homes, and new houses and apartments had sprung up in areas which were once almost ghettos.

From an operational regard it was a remarkably quiet tour. The Royal Ulster Constabulary had taken over full control of all eight command areas, and the District Command Units were effectively wholly under their control. Uniformed troops were required to give support during the two marching seasons, on occasional search operations, and the police continued to call upon the available military support for the now rare bombing or shooting incidents, but for the most part it was an undisturbed and peaceful tour. For Chris Spencer the tour would really be remembered for no more than two things. In the early part of 2003 his original twenty-four year sign up period came to an end and, because of his service record and position he was allowed to sign for a further two years to assist with his pension. Towards the end of 2003 he was to receive what would prove to be his last promotion whilst in the British Army when he finally made WO1, a reward for service and experience which would certainly also help with his army pension.

For those like Jack, with an 'A' level in Russian, the language can be studied at Oxford on its own, although it is combined with linguistics for the first year. The course begins with a one year study of the language, translating and transliterating from and into Russian, improving grammar and vocabulary building, and an intensive study of literature from selected texts, which leads to the Preliminary Examination. It is a four year course which, in the third year, includes a compulsory year abroad in Russia or a Russian speaking country. Jack took the option of going to Russia's second city, St Petersburg, for that year.

St Petersburg, often called the 'Venice of the North' because of its myriad canals and waterways, can be a city of shocking contradictions, and was especially so to a particularly intelligent young language student as he approached the end of his twenty-first year.

To Jack the city appeared to be built on a grand scale, in part due to the vision of its founder, Peter the Great, one of the three great despots of Russian history, the others he knew were Ivan the Terrible, the first Tsar, and Iosif Vissarionovich Dzhugashvili – known to the world as Joseph Stalin – the man of steel, stalin being Russian for steel. Before leaving for the city Jack had researched its history, background and character. He found it facinating how the original city had come into being, learning that on the sixteenth of May (by the Julian calendar, the twenty-seventh of May by the later Gregorian calendars), 1703 Tsar Peter I, according to popular legend, after snatching a halberd from one of his soldiers cut two pieces of turf and, laying them across one another, declared "Here there shall be a town". Pushkin's later and more famous version of Peter's speech, which Jack had read as course work at Oxford, has it as "By nature we are fated here to cut a window through to Europe". Either way on a swampy area of marshland where the confluence of the Neva, Moyka and Fontanka Rivers empty their cold and murky waters into the Finnish Gulf of the Baltic Sea the city of Sankt Pieter Burkh, named then as it was in the Dutch fashion, first took root. Jack who had already known the city was named after Peter the Great's patron saint, the apostle Saint Peter, read with interest of the thousands of Swedish prisoners of war who had then been forced into service in dire conditions. Without even basic tools excavated earth had to be carried in workers' clothing, and thousands died during the building of exhaustion, disease, starvation and, of course, the biting bitter cold.

Three hundred years later he stood in a thriving, vibrant and lively city which lay in an area so far north the sun never properly sets in summer, and with winter days he would find that started to get light around ten in the morning and dark at four in the afternoon. For a short period after its initial creation capital status had yo-yoed backwards and forwards between St Petersburg and Moscow, with the title only returning to Moscow more that two hundred years later, after the Russian revolution in 1918. During those three centuries the citiy's name changed along the way from Saint Petersburg to Petrograd to Leningrad and in 1991 it returned to Saint Petersburg. Jack had read of the city's inhabitants who had withstood political intrigue, revolution and nine hundred days of Nazi siege. In the days of the siege the people suffered cruelly beneath the bombardment of artillery and endless bombing from the skies above. One point two million people were killed and tens of thousands maimed, some amongst the survivors forced to cannibalism. Now the greater city surrounding him had a growing population of more than six million who had shrugged off their past and were moving forward to embrace the promise of a brighter future with determination.

The city centre he would come to love lies along the southern bank of the Neva, with the curve of the four and a half mile long Fontanka forming its southern boundary. Built as it was to provide unimpeded access to the Baltic, with a mind to the trading and riches which lay beyond, it became a strategically important port, and one of the city planner's first main concerns was for that of the admiralty. The modern Admiralty Building has a great golden spire which was to provide him with a ready landmark throughout the duration of his stay, and wide roads appeared to fan out from it in many directions. Moskovsky Prospekt headed south, passing both internal and international airports, and on eventually to Moscow, eight hundred kilometres to the south east. Nevskiy Prospekt, which was to become Jack's favourite haunt, proved to be a wide avenue heading in a broadly easterly direction, and had provided the backbone of St Petersburg for at least the last two centuries.

The River Neva splits shortly before entering the Baltic Sea into the Little Neva (Malaya Neva) and the Big Neva (Bolshaya Neva), forming Vasilevskiy Island. Sitting majestically at the junction of the fork on the south bank of the Neva, overlooking a further small island on which stands the Peter & Paul Fortress, is the magnificent Winter Palace with the Hermitage, housing Europe's finest art collection, alongside. To the landward side is the extensive palace square called Dvortsovaya Ploshchad which surrounds the towering Alexander Column. Leaving Dvortsovaya Ploshchad beneath the triple arch of the General Staff Building, Jack, as a pedestrian, could pick up the northern end of Bolshaya Morskaya Ulitsa, designed by Carlo Rossi to fall along the Pulkovo meridian, which was the Tsarist equivalent of the Greenwich meridian, and follow it out onto Nevskiy Prospekt, along the course of which, he was to find, lay many of St Petersburg's greatest attractions.

Jack Bryant had studied the Russian language for ten years, had read a large number of Russian literary works in their original form and knew a great deal about Russian culture and historical background. Nothing he had read or studied quite prepared him for the full on reality that is St Petersburg which, despite the ravages brought about by more than seventy years of communism, remains a truly glorious city. For Jack the resplendent architecture of the city centre left him awestruck throughout the entire duration of his stay. For almost a year each and every day brought more sublime visions. A simple stroll along Nevskiy Prospekt, at any time of the year, rain or shine, warm or numbingly cold, never lost its thrill.

As an accomplished linguist he suffered no problems with communication in a culture which was in so many ways very different to his own, and with people far more direct in all that they did and all which they said. To Jack one of the resounding mysteries was the way in which the average Russian could instantly tell he was a westerner, long before he opened his mouth to speak. Taxis approaching from behind would pull over next to him and the driver would shout out "Taxi Mister?" in English, having passed thousands of other pedestrians. How did they know? Within the city there remained two pricing policies, one for Russian people, and another more expensive charging tier for all foreigners. Every riverboat, museum, church and attraction always charged him the foreign rate automatically, which he would then have to argue over and produce his student card in order to obtain the lower rate. He could dress up in locally purchased clothing, or dress down, wearing the ubiquitous black leather jacket, but he was still always seen as a westerner.

Before leaving for St Petersburg the University arranged accommodation for him through an agency, and he arrived to what the Russians call a one room apartment, as they do not count the bathroom or the kitchen, each of which are generally both small and cramped. He therefore had little more than a bed sitting room in a somewhat shabby apartment block which exhibited all the lack of beauty, subtlety and design innovation so typical of all that was wrong with sixties architecture. However it was well decorated and reasonably furnished and, with the double set of steel doors by which he gained entry, reasonably secure and safe from the ever present possibility of crime. Unfortunately it was badly positioned and at a distance from the centre, and it was the centre and all the life which went with it he enjoyed. A move was required.

Whereas the tenement blocks of sixties, seventies and eighties apartments, so loved by the Russian regime of the day, are eight to ten floors tall, the grand old buildings of the centre are usually a good two floors lower. This however is not the main point which differentiates the two. The older buildings towards the centre were built as a showcase to the world, with aesthetically pleasing lines and beautiful masonry and stone works. The rooms were large; some may well have been described as grand, with infinite attention given to detail.

Unfortunately communism had in part destroyed most of these old buildings, forcing many families into individual buildings, partitioning the large rooms to form several smaller rooms, and forcing many to share the same kitchens and bathrooms. Money was now flowing back into the economy and some of these beautiful old buildings had been purchased in their entirety and then gone through a phase of major reconstruction. This had most definitely not happened to all, and rooms or apartments could be rented in particularly desirable areas for what still remained a most modest fee, although decoration and furnishings were generally more than a little down at heel. In so many ways the properties of St Petersburg gave Jack the overwhelming impression of a grand old lady, still proud and resplendent in her finery, but forced by circumstances not of her choosing to wear tatty, stained and soiled undergarments.

After two weeks of searching for an apartment in a more favourable location he had a lucky break. Franz Muller was a German exchange student from Munich studying Russian in St Petersburg just as Jack was, and their paths crossed many times, leading to conversations in four shared languages. At just past twenty two years of age Muller was Jacks senior. He had arrived in St Petersburg ten weeks earlier, six weeks before Jack, and then been allocated a room in a communal apartment in one of the old buildings on Ulitsa Rubensteina. The rooms were small, poorly decorated and badly furnished, but the location was everything Jack would have wished for, and one room was vacant. He moved in that weekend.

One end of Ulitsa Rubensteina finishes at Nevskiy Prospekt, and the other runs to an area which is known locally as five corners for obvious reasons. A two minute walk beyond which is the Vladimirskaya station of the St Petersburg Metro. A major additional bonus Jack was to discover on Rubensteina was an Irish themed cellar bar called Molly's which sold draught Guinness and Murphy's, and provided an excellent Irish breakfast along with other good but uncomplicated food. It was a popular haunt for many ex-pats and showed popular sports from home on TV. It was also a very good meeting point in a central location where those from many different language and cultural backgrounds could congregate, associate, debate, and discuss.

Oxford had changed Jack, and St Petersburg continued the change. His home had been a pleasant place to live where all his physical needs were fully catered for. Unfortunately there was little to stimulate his towering intellect and he had found it almost impossible to make friends, mainly because there was nobody with which he could communicate. University entry opened the door to a very different world, a world in which instead of being a freak he was in fact quite normal. Here he was actively encouraged to join other highly intelligent individuals in discussions on all manner of subjects, and these subjects were debated for hours, with flaws constantly sought in well reasoned and eloquently voiced statements and opinions. Tested to the extreme in the white hot heat of intellectual debate opinions were sometimes swayed and changed, or amplified and reinforced. He thoroughly enjoyed pitting his wits against scholars of many diverse disciplines, arguing sometimes through the night in a number a different tongues to those from varying ethnic backgrounds and cultures.

He came to respect the Russian people for their sometimes simplistic view of the world and their ability to express exactly what they meant without layers of subterfuge and bullshit. His views hardened with constant testing, and many greys gave way to black or white. What happened to his mother had been very wrong, and he would never forget that, but the hell his father was then put through as a result was criminal, and that he could never forgive. Had the incident happened in Russia a far more simple solution may well have been available. Everything could be bought, from justice to retribution, and although he wholly disagreed with the corruption in the land, he did have more than a sneaking respect for a structure which seemed to shrug its shoulders when a deeply aggrieved individual sidestepped the system bypassing the judiciary to remove a problem forever.

Ekaterina Orlova came into Jack Bryant's life at the beginning of his third month in St Petersburg, and the relationship they struck up was to prove to be pivotal to his life. Katya was a tall slim green eyed blonde, with the looks, build and carriage so typical of the Nordic gene pool of the Baltic port nations. She was born to ethnic Russian parents who, at the time of her birth, lived on the banks of the Neris River in Kaunas, Lithuania's second city, as her father had previously been drafted in to Kaunas to manage a waterways and highway logistics operation based at the busy river port.

Vladimir Orlov, and his younger brother Yuri, were both born in the city of Perm, which is almost as far east as Europe gets, situated within sight of the foothills of the Urals. Yuri, six years Vladimir's junior, joined the army, but by then Vladimir had already been sent to St Petersburg to study, and there met his wife and Katya's mother, Ludmila. They finished their studies and married in a hurry as Ludmila became pregnant and gave birth to a son in 1978. Vladimir quickly proved his worth working in the shipping office in one of St Petersburg's many ports and he, Ludmila and baby Maxim were transferred to Kaunas, where they had a second child, Ekaterina, born in the early spring of 1982. By 1989 the winds of change had started to blow across the Russian Empire, and former satellite nations were far from happy with the number of ethnic Russians in their lands. To Vladimir it was obvious change was on the way, so he successfully and wisely applied for a posting back to St Petersburg, Ludmila's home city.

Much against his parents wishes young Maxim decided to follow his uncle's footsteps and joined the army at the age of eighteen. Four months later, in 1996, he was killed along with eight others following an ambush by terrorists in Groznyy, the capital city of Chechnya. Wounded in the ambush he was then captured by the terrorists and killed in a particularly gruesome manner. Yuri Orlov was also stationed in Groznyy at the time, but was no longer an ordinary soldier. At the age of thirty-three, and with fifteen years service, he had volunteered along the way for Special Forces – Spetznaz – and from there went on to join the anti terrorist elite, the very dangerous Alfa Group, and his detachment was tasked with apprehending and dispatching the terrorists involved. This was done at Yuri's direction 'Roman Style'.

Part of Jack's studies required his attendance at the St Petersburg State University. Ekaterina Orlova was also studying languages and, as with Franz Muller, Jack and her paths continued to cross. Katya lived in a three room apartment to the south of the city off Moskovsky, spoke English, German and of course Russia and Lithuanian fluently, and was studying Arabic. She was a strikingly handsome girl, which is always a pleasant thing for any male to behold, but for Jack it was her mind which really appealed to him.

Unlike good looking western women in general, and English speaking females in particular, Eastern Europeans do not worship their own good looks to the total exclusion of all else. It may well be because there are so many other highly attractive girls within their countries, possibly because they do not tend to be Daddy's spoilt little darlings, or it may be just a simple cultural thing, but even beautiful girls generally do not rely solely upon their appearance. Education and personal achievement remain highly valued and desired, and Katya was no exception to the rule. She possessed a quick, intelligent and sharp mind, was capable of following at least three conversations in different languages at a time, and supported no tolerance whatsoever for fools. She reintroduced Jack to chess and proved to be an adroit and proficient player, although she would never be his equal.

They took coffee together, enjoyed a beer together and sat down to eat together. Within days of their first coffee Katya spent the night with Jack and a relationship was born.

Katya enjoyed Jack's brain every bit as much as he did hers. Inside a month of their meeting she took him back to be introduced to her parents, and all went well. By this time Jack had stopped being amazed at just how much Russian people will give of what they have to their guests, to the extent they will part with their last crumb or drop of vodka. Jack reciprocated where he could by taking them out for a meal, but his finances were tight, so such events were rare. On one occasion when visiting Katya's parents her uncle Yuri was present. Katya had explained some of his background to Jack, who was at the time only mildly interested having been brought up in the knowledge that as special forces go Britain's were the world's elite, which of course by most recognised standards is true, but Jack was not particularly interested in those who had never properly grown up and still felt the need to play with guns.

Jack expected a bull of a man with a handshake like a vice and a booming voice, but Yuri proved to be nothing at all as Jack had imagined he would be. True Yuri was tallish at around six feet, and true he looked very fit with no evidence of any kind of fat, but the barrel chest was not there nor was the crushing handshake or loud voice. In a suit and tie he would have passed as any normal executive who spent a few hours a week in a gym and watched what he ate, certainly not a superman. He shook Jack's hand firmly and greeted him politely, kissing him on both cheeks. His face, as was normal for men of his age, was seemingly completely unlined, no wrinkled brow, no laughter lines around the eyes and no lines around the mouth from smiling or frowning, which was not at all unusual. To Jack most Russian male faces looked as if they had been recently ironed, as few use any form of facial expressions, almost always appearing deadpan, and Yuri was certainly no exception.

"So Englishman, you are sleeping with my beautiful niece!" Yuri made the statement, not phrased as a question, immediately formalities ended. He also said it in perfect, although accented, English.

"Not every night yet Sir, although I hope to." Jack replied in flawless Russian, looking him straight in the eye.

Yuri locked eyes with Jack and stared at him for a full five seconds, which for Jack seemed to stretch to eternity. He then reached out his right arm and, grasping Jack's left shoulder, shook him gently whilst turning to Katya and saying "I like him! Keep him!"

With that he turned back to Jack and squeezed the shoulder, and Jack then felt the jaws of a steel vice close on it.

"Now English, we eat, we drink, and then we tell our stories."

Food arrived and the small table soon piled up with it, and Jack was pleasantly surprised to see it was mostly Georgian, rather than the bland foodstuffs of northern Russia. Potato and onion soup was all well and good, as was borsch, but Jack felt he could only eat so much of it, whereas the spicy foods of the south were much more to his taste, as was the delicious sweet, fruity red Georgian wine. The food came, the food went, and then the drinks arrived. The hard drinking culture of Russian males has changed somewhat for the younger generation since Yeltsin's days, with a mass of the young enjoying a glass of one of Baltika brewery's numerous beers to a bottle of the various flavoured vodkas. Yuri and Vladimir were not the younger generation and Yuri had spent many years as a soldier, so vodka was what they drank, washed down every few glasses with small cups of strong sweet black coffee.

As was customary Katya and Ludmila left the men to their drinking and stories. Vladimir told of his work, his moves to and from Kaunas, his family, the loss of his son, his pleasure in his daughter's educational success. Drink flowed in the give all Russian manner and tongues loosened. Jack told of his homeland, his upbringing, his brother, the death of his mother and the devastating effect her death had on his father. Both men were obviously moved by Jack's tale of the death of Mary, but it was Yuri who asked the question.

"So is this Tvar dead?" Yuri used the harsh Russian word for a very low creature, something which is wholly unworthy, but has no suitable literal translation.

"No, he's in jail now, but he will be released in just over a year." Jack replied, looking down at the table.

"Could he not die in jail?" Yuri was obviously struggling to understand why Abdul Khaled still drew breath.

"No." Jack almost laughed. "Such things do not happen that way in England."

"Well it sounds to me that it is high time they did then!" Yuri stated emphatically.

"Yes." Vladimir joined in. "Perhaps you should employ someone to do the same as Yuri had done to those terrorist bastards in Chechnya who killed Maxim."

"Katya told me of your loss. I'm very sorry. It seems to me it was such a waste of a life." Jack said, and then went on, "What did happen to the terrorists? Did you ever catch them? Were they brought to justice? Katya will not speak of it, and it would be wrong of me to press her on something which is obviously still very painful."

Yuri and Vladimir exchanged glances. They said nothing, but the questions which hung so heavily in the air were obvious to all three – Can we trust him? – Should we say anything or keep quiet? Jack himself broke the silence.

"Please be assured I'll keep what is said to myself. I'll repeat nothing. If you wish to tell me nothing I respect your wishes and will pry no further, but if you do part with anything, such information will never go further!"

"We should trust him Yuri." Vladimir said. "Katya says he is very intelligent, but also that he has a good heart. He has lost a close one. He will understand."

Yuri inclined his head. "Knowledge can be very dangerous young English. Never forget that! Not as long as you live. Education improves the mind. Knowledge kills!"

"Firstly, to make sense of what I am to tell you, you must understand a little of the background. Alfa Group is a special operations detachment of OSNAZ, Independent Special-Purpose Motorised Brigade, attached to the KGB, now FSB, the Federal Security Service. It was created back in 1974 within the First Chief Directorate of the KGB on the orders of Yuri Andropov, who was at the time Chairman of the KGB. It was intended for secret foreign operations, although that changed quickly. I can tell you nothing of OSNAZ, except to say there are no headquarters, as groups are formed within the various directorates as and when needed, but you don't need to know more. Generally the primary function was and is to carry out missions of an urban counter terrorist nature, and these are usually sanctioned and controlled by the political leadership, which also supports the group well with funds, arms and equipment."

"Sorry to interrupt, but you said the secret foreign operations quickly changed. In what way?" Jack asked.

"Well the secrecy certainly disappeared back in 1985. Alfa Group was ordered out to Beirut when four diplomats were taken hostage by militant Sunni Muslims. By the time Alfa deployed, one of the hostages had already been executed. The terrorists and some of their relatives were identified by KGB operatives sent in as support. Our negotiation procedure is simple, there is no negotiation, and there are no negotiators. Those identified relatives were themselves taken hostage, and Alfa then removed some of their body parts. These were sent to the terrorists with a warning that more would follow if the hostages were not released immediately. The tactic succeeded and no other Russian national has since been taken hostage in the Middle East. However Alfa was no longer a secret force. The unit continued to exist after the breakdown of the Soviet Union and has been used in a variety of crisis situations since, such as the Moscow Theatre Siege in October, so not just foreign operations either."

"Thank you, I understand. Sorry to have interrupted. Please get back to what happened to those who killed Maxim." Jack asked.

"Chechnya is to us Russians very similar to what the Irish problem represented to you British. I know you have recently had peace break out - after what? Two hundred years? Your IRA would bomb, kill and maim indiscriminately, across your country, just as those of Chechnya do to us. You had a separatist movement theoretically based around culture, so do we. You tried keeping the peace by drafting in troops, as have we. Your troops were despised, attacked and sometimes killed, as ours have been, and your same troops sometimes retaliated, just as ours do. The two situations have far more similarities than differences, which is why even the most enlightened Russian will tell all other nations to keep their noses out of Chechnya, as it is our own domestic problem, just as you did to any who attempted to interfere over your Irish problem. Your original questions concerned the terrorists who killed Maxim, did we ever catch them and bring them to justice. Yes, we caught them, and yes, justice was duly meted out."

"So what do you do to those you capture in such situations? Do you intern them as we did with the IRA in special prisons, almost as prisoners of war, or do you simply jail them as common criminals?" Jack asked slightly intrigued by the story.

Vladimir and Yuri once again exchanged looks before Yuri went on.

"You must understand whilst there are many similarities there are also differences. The West values its people much more highly than most other cultures. With special forces there are probably only five nations which can put suitably equipped and trained personnel in the field. Our Spetznaz Alfa Group, your SAS and SBS, the German Kommando Spezialkräfte and GSG9, Israeli Sayeret MATKAL and S'13, and possibly America's Navy SEALs and their Delta Force. Australia tries, as do France, but neither have the will, human recourses or background. Now, America has its hands tied by all of its pathetic liberals, Germany does not want to offend anyone because of guilt over the holocaust – even sixty years on, and you British – well you don't mind getting your hands dirty if no one catches you, and you'll happily sacrifice, but those same liberals which trouble America are snapping at your heels. It is only Israel and ourselves who are happy to throw lives away on a good cause, and there are a lot more of us than them." Another look passed between the brothers. Yuri finished his glass of vodka and helped himself to another. He appeared to finally reach a decision and continued once again.

"You must understand I was immensely proud of Maxim. I have never married, and have no children. I believe in maintaining a strong army. We have a huge land which is very sparsely populated, yet potentially incredibly wealthy with the minerals which are beneath our soil. Whatever anyone thinks of our history and background we have developed our own culture which is rich, long and vibrant. All these things are worth protecting for the long term good of this land and its people. However few young people now see it that way. The army still drafts in idiots for boy soldiers, those who don't want to be there and who are willing to shoot off their own toes to avoid service. Rich parents will buy their sons out of service, or will send them to university or abroad in order to protect them from the chance of being hurt. To a degree it is understandable, but if everyone did the same there would be no army and there would be no defence, and everything which made them rich in the first place would be taken away at the point of another man's gun."

"Maxim was a volunteer, an increasingly rare thing these days. Vladimir and I argued over his joining up, which didn't matter anyway because Maxim was going to join up whatever was said. When he was killed I felt, at least in part, personally responsible. I was in Chechnya with a group at the time. My commander knew I had a personal interest, and knew how proud I had been of Maxim, so he gave me the duty, the privilege, of making amends. Technically I should not have been given the task because of my involvement, but my commander and I had served together for a long time and had washed our hands in the same blood."

"We thought we knew the group responsible so, like Beirut, we took our own hostages whom we 'interviewed'. Everyone cracks eventually, and these were no exception, except they cracked earlier than I had hoped they would. We rounded up the cell responsible, and then two more cells. Eventually we caught up with twenty-seven terrorists, all of whom had perpetrated acts against Russian soldiers and terrorist acts against Russian civilians." Yuri stopped and took another mouthful of vodka.

"So what became of them?" Jack asked curiously.

"We removed them!" Yuri answered.

"So where did you send them? Ordinary jail? Siberian prison camps? I know there are no gulags any more. What do you do with prisoners like that?" Jack could not contain himself.

"We dispatched them Roman Style. You do understand the term?" Yuri now asked.

"No, I don't believe I do." Jack replied.

"The Romans had a certain way of dealing with those who killed any of their troops. They spent time and recourses tracking the culprits down, made sure they had the right person or people, then executed them as an example to others. After which they executed their family, their friends, their neighbours, and anyone else who knew them. They killed their cattle, their dogs, burnt their crops and razed their homes. After they were finished those terrorists never existed. If you prosecute and eventually execute a terrorist you run the risk of creating a martyr. If you kill him and everyone who has ever known him – nothing! Nothing at all."

"So you mean you killed all twenty-seven terrorists?" Jack asked a little shakily.

"Yes, I did that personally with a bayonet." Yuri nodded. "Most of their families we then blew up in their homes. Some we spent weeks looking for, but we got them all in the end! Mothers, fathers, brothers, sisters, teachers, friends and neighbours, and their fucking dogs!"

"Oh my God," Jack whispered, "how many?"

"Four hundred and forty-two, not counting the terrorists themselves, or the twenty-one which committed suicide before we got to them." Yuri answered in a wholly matter-of-fact manner as if he were discussing a cricket score. "Interestingly things calmed down a bit after that, although they are back again now, attacking softer targets such as the theatre. I know all the terrorists died, but if I were still doing the job I would follow up. Smart people those Romans!"

Yuri had given Jack Bryant cause to re-evaluate many views. Manners Makyth Man. Several times after their first introduction they had sat late into the night discussing geopolitics in both historical and modern day contexts. Yuri liked the young Englishman, was fascinated as to how the young man's mind seemed to cut through matters to address the very heart of a subject, and enjoyed posing hypothetical questions. One he had advanced was unanswerable, but would continue to revolve in Jack's brain for a long time.

Whilst discussing the problem which was and continued to be Afghanistan, Yuri had asked, "What do you think the outcome would have been if America had left us alone in Afghanistan? I realise they were ideologically opposed to us at the time, so they could not and would not have stepped in to help us, but had they not continually supplied the Mujahideen with large quantities of highly sophisticated munitions do you think the Taliban would have come to power? If not, and al-Qaeda had not then been given free rein, would the attack on their twin towers ever have taken place? Do not forget we pulled out in 1989, and the imminent collapse of the Soviet Union was at the time obvious to everyone. It was said that Afghanistan was Russia's Vietnam. Does it not strike you as quite bizarre that twelve years later the situation within Afghanistan had deteriorated to such a degree that not only was an attack on the United States planned within a cave there, but that it was successfully carried out, leading to a full scale invasion of the country? The very thing we had been forced to do, yet were vilified for.

"So, would American and British lives, along with all the other nations involved, have been lost to the Taliban had the 'free world' allowed us to continue policing the area? It may well prove to be yet another Vietnam for the western forces, and at an economy collapsing cost. Frankly I am glad my country is out of it.

It proved costly to my people in both monetary terms and in young lives, but I have a distinct feeling the price you will be forced to pay shall be infinitely higher!"

Jack Bryant returned to Oxford after his year in St Petersburg with an advanced understanding of colloquial Russian, and a vastly different outlook on the workings of the world to the beliefs he held when he left. He had met Yuri Orlov several times after their first meeting and developed both a liking and a deep respect for the man. Yuri was single handedly responsible for fundamentally altering Jacks opinion of all things military. Jack came to understand all soldiers were not just stupid grunts as he had previously regarded them, but some really could think deeply and hold a well informed view of the big picture, and that was definitely something he had previously not thought possible.

Oxford at least had not changed during his absence. Jack found he had more time to himself in his final year, although much needed to be done to complete his degree and a very great deal had to be written up. He stayed in touch with Katya, but did not see her again throughout the year as money was in very short supply for him, and the degree work required his full attention without distractions, irrespective as to how appealing they may prove to be.

The exceptional linguistic abilities and ultra high IQ of Jack Bryant did not go unnoticed by interested parties, and those interested parties trod the deep pile carpets of the corridors of power. Jack's grasp of Russian and his ability to plan strategy was of particular interest to two very different organisations, and both approached him long before the end of his forth year, one quite openly, and one not so. Unsurprisingly the more delicate advance came from those whose headquarters are at Vauxhall Cross on the South Bank of the Thames, and who are the SIS (Secret Intelligence Service), more commonly known as MI6 (Military Intelligence, Section 6), The United Kingdom of Great Britain's external intelligence agency.

Their initial approach was of a casual nature, almost an 'accidental' meeting, where the operative concerned was supposed to sound Jack out on a number of issues in a subtle manner he was not supposed to see through. However Jack was not some bumbling buffoon who just happened to understand a few languages, he was a highly intelligent and somewhat intuitive young man who saw through the charade in minutes. Additionally he had already been forewarned by other students that he may at some stage be approached, as it had been common practice for MI6 to regard the Oxbridge institutions as ripe recruiting grounds for many decades. Jack politely rejected the approach, explaining the method adopted was unprofessional, the proposal unwanted, and the context wholly improper. He had no intention of being a spy.

The other approach was from a multinational banking corporation who indicated a wish to recruit an intelligent and informed graduate with a linguistic background to develop stratagems for a new department based in Moscow, which was being put in place to deal with the rapidly growing Russian gas and petrochemical industries. The job would mean working primarily out of Moscow, but would encompass much of the Russian Federation, and would include working out of the European financial centres of Frankfurt and London. The position required an individual who was capable of viewing the big picture, and possessing the ability to plan long term strategies to suit the ever changing needs of an exceedingly volatile industry. The package offered was impressive to say the least, and far more to Jack's liking. Terms and conditions were negotiated and eventually agreed. Jack finished his studies, picked up his degree and took a flight to St Petersburg to renew his relationship with Katya, before flying on to Moscow to start work at the beginning of July 2004.

Twenty Four

In February 2004 WO1 Chris Spencer's residential tour of County Londonderry came to an end, and he was deployed to Chepstow and 160 Brigade. Chepstow is a town in what is popularly believed to be South Wales as it is on the western side of the Severn Estuary. However, currently it is in England, as it is located at the extreme south western tip of the county of Gloucestershire. Down through the centuries the town and its castle have been much fought over due to its controlling position and strategic importance. The Severn Estuary has the second highest tidal rise and fall in the world with waters flowing more than forty miles upstream from Chepstow. The estuary widens below the town with tides and currents proving difficult for small craft. Consequently the town and its castle were seen as the gateway to South Wales for centuries.

Beachley Barracks at that time of the year seemed quite bleak even after the long period of wet weather which is always to be expected during the winter in Northern Ireland. Located where it was on a small headland sticking out into the waters of the Severn Estuary, virtually under the suspension bridge which provides one of the motorway crossing points to South Wales, it seemed a damp and misty place. He had seen pictures and heard stories that told of the beauty of the location in summer, but in the midst of winter it was dark, wet and miserable.

However, his deployment was to be a short one. In April of 2004, just seven weeks after arriving at Chepstow, less one weeks leave he had taken at Jimmy and his sister's village, Chris Spencer was once more redeployed. The long anticipated deployment to Afghanistan finally came about, and Chris, along with a battalion of Green Howards, was flown out to the country and to the task which was to prove truly unrewarding for those there, and deeply unappreciated by the vast majority of the British population, most of whom knew little and cared less of Operation Herrick.

Afghanistan was a country in turmoil. To Chris there was very little good to be seen in the country no matter how he viewed it, the one notable exception being the panoramic vistas which could be enjoyed from the tops of mountains or peaks of hills. The views aside, there was nothing. The people proved devious, double dealing and treacherous, could not be trusted in any way at any time, and would cut anyone's throat for a packet of cigarettes. Poverty was all around, perpetuated by discriminatory religious doctrine, the greed of bandit warlords, and unworkable governments. There was little education and no desire for it, certainly not for girls who were viewed in a lesser manner than an Englishman may regard his dog. The very land itself had been destroyed by over planting cash crops in previous times of greed, and then overgrazing. The animals which tried to live upon the land were fighting a losing battle. Nutrients had long since been sucked from the soil and nourishment was not to be found in anything growing from it. The cattle which survived were skin and bone, generally racked with disease and infested with parasites.

The winters were perishingly cold, and the summers intolerably hot. The water that was there from the winter snows was allowed to run off the land taking vital top soils with it. The development and formation of reservoirs and subsequent provision of land irrigation had never been considered. As a direct consequence rivers were impassable in winter and non existent in summer. Roads, the term used for mud tracks, could not be negotiated in winter or summer. In winter they were quagmires, and in the summer so congested with overheated and broken down vehicles any attempt to use them led to frustration at best, or death, from bad driving practices or the driver being used for target practice.

The only commodity the region produced which was capable of being marketed was the by-product of the poppy, Papaver somniferum, the opium poppy. Had it been grown for its seeds, which contain healthy oils, and fed to cattle, it would not have presented a problem. If the poppy were cultivated for ornamental purposes, which then provided a small income for the growers, the world may well have helped its farmers. This however had never been the case. It was the 'sleep-bringing-poppy', a narcotic, and was extensively farmed by extended families with children as young as three and four who were used to harvest the gum like secretion which provided the drug. This was then refined to be sold illegally around the world, with those who farmed it given a truly insignificant pittance when compared to its black market value.

Poppy fields could be easily destroyed as the crops burnt well, but the burning of crops succeeded in no more than driving those who were growers into the hands of warlords, the Taliban or even al-Qaeda. Whenever possible they were then armed and sent back to kill the foreign soldiers which had come to their land to destroy their crops. There were no quick fixes and no easy answers. The British Army, almost exclusively due to an ever more liberally minded and wishy-washy population of bleeding heart do-gooders at home, was also becoming progressively restricted operationally.

WO1 Chris Spencer, with the help of two corporals, was given the role of training and mentoring a platoon of the Afghan National Army. It was always going to be a difficult and a dangerous task. Chris Spencer had spent his entire working and adult life taking orders without question and was rewarded and had risen because of his ability to do so, and to do so both properly and efficiently. He had never been given illegal orders, and therefore never had cause to question the orders given.

What he was then instructed to do he also did without question, but did make his feelings known to his senior officer. Historically Afghanistan had long been a problem, with its people loyal to no one. The country existed in a state of feudalism as it had always done, with warring tribes, and warring factions within tribes. The countries people knew and respected no borders or authorities, and to bring them up to date with the modern world would take a dedicated educational system several decades to achieve. Those he was being asked to advise, coach, counsel, guide and instruct may claim to be the friends of Britain and the West today, but tomorrow they may well be mortal enemies, with no respect for any life, including their own, but with the tutored methodology of modern day warfare. That was an incredibly dangerous concept, and one Chris knew Britain would be well advised to stay clear of. His thoughts given and noted he continued with the training as he was ordered.

He did not like the Afghans under his command. He did not like the order he was given to train them, and he did not like the way Britain had to conduct itself on the battlefield. It went against the grain, and against everything he felt he was trained to do. He and his men were sent to Afghanistan to do a job, but were left under-equipped to do the job properly, and then had their hands tied. The enemy was trying to kill him and his men. They had taken up arms and were fighting men, and there were no rules of engagement on their part. To the south they would use roadside bombs, booby-trap their own dead and employ their own wounded to draw in medics to help them who they would then shoot. They happily used suicide bombers and infiltrate camps masquerading as recruits only to blow themselves and those around them to pieces, and these were the very people he was instructed to train to kill – more efficiently. This was not what he had joined up for.He had signed a two year extension which he would not again renew. In the middle of May, just five weeks after arriving in Afghanistan he gave the one year notice the army required to leave the service.

A somewhat disillusioned Chris Spencer served a six month tour in Afghanistan, initially in Kabul but was quickly moved north as part of the support for the provincial reconstruction team established in Mazari Sharif, the countries forth largest city, and Maymana, a town previously known for its wool and market for leather goods. Unusually for Afghanistan it boasted a river, and the climate in the region was less extreme. Whilst there Chris reflected as to how unfortunate it was that his senior NCO position actually disadvantaged him with regard the training duties, as a rapid reaction force had also been provided for the area, and he knew full well his talents could have been put to far more practical use with them.

For Jenny Andrews life in the village of Slyne, and marriage to Jimmy was everything she, as a younger woman, had ever dreamt it could be. Young Charlie was born without a problem of any kind, which was really only to be expected from a fit and healthy young woman of twenty-three. He had always eaten well and he grew well, putting on weight and growing in height almost before her eyes. Jimmy came home on leave whenever the opportunity presented itself and her big brother, the family hero, also made the journey to see them and to stay whenever he was in the country and could get away. Little Charlie's growth had always shocked Chris, who just could not believe how rapidly the young lad grew. Charlie possessed the same features as Chris, and it was plain to all the two undoubtedly shared the same genes. It was also abundantly obvious little Charlie remained the apple of his uncle's eye, and no mistake.

When Charlie first went to school the house seemed deserted to Jenny. It was early for Charlie as the county education authority took children in as rising fives at the September intake. Charlie's fourth birthday had only been two months earlier, but the young lad coped well with school despite his tender age. Surprisingly, given his father, uncle and genetic background generally, he developed a liking for academic learning, and consequently did very well with his education all the way through school.

Despite his size and background he was more interested in study than he was in sport and outdoor pursuits, except where it came to nature and wildlife. From the time he was a toddler Charlie showed an interest in birds and animals and, as he went through school, he avidly studied any books containing the description or habits of creatures of all kinds. There was an abundance of sea birds over Morecambe Bay, birds and squirrels in their garden, and the surrounding fields were filled with domesticated beasts. Charlie had never feared cattle the way some children do, terrified because of their size, or daunted by their numbers. He turned out to be a good all-rounder academically, but excelled in any biology or nature studies. It didn't come as a shock to anyone who knew him when, at the age of thirteen and when he was given his choices of subjects to study for GCSE, he took those which would help him move towards his chosen goal. One day he wanted to be a vet.

If he had grown well as a young lad, Charlie shot up through his early teens. At fifteen he was more than six feet tall, with shoulders almost as wide as his fathers and uncles. Had he trained in a sport requiring upper body strength at the time his performance would undoubtedly have proved outstanding. However, big though he was, he was gentle, placid and tender to a fault. At school he was admired by teachers, and approved of by other parents as a suitable friend for any who took him home. Older children liked him, younger ones viewed him as a role model, girls of his age felt they could approach and befriend him, and even smaller boys of his age sought him out. His two sisters always looked up to Charlie in much the same way as Jenny had in her day looked up to Chris, but in their case it was for his kindness and unbounded compassion.

It was some quirk of nature, some fork in the evolutionary path, which designed young Charlie to be so very similar to father and uncle physically, yet so very different to them in personality and outlook. It was not that Charlie was in any way disdainful about either man, or of what they did. In fact the complete opposite was true, in that he greatly admired the men they were, but the physical thing was not for him. Charlie deeply respected the way his father and his Uncle Chris were prepared to put their own lives on the line to protect their families, homes and country. He understood how deeply motivated both were, but he knew he would never have been able to contribute towards taking a life. He wanted to protect life, and life of all kinds, most especially those of the animals he saw around him.

NJF Industries continued to grow. The company's rise remained spectacular and the city had long wanted a piece of the action. Multinational financial institutions courted Susie, Jake and Nathan, and gentle pressure was applied. The pressure was resisted and NJF stayed wholly in private hands with large privately controlled resources, ongoing sales to a growing list of corporate entities, and a widening range of products. The design team had multiplied and was ably managed by the Hall McGregor partnership during Nathan's absences, and the company continued to turn out well constructed games, constantly moving forward to keep pace with technology, often instrumental in forcing change. The mobile telephone game section took off, following the explosion in the sales of the instruments, and evolved into an entirely separate section. The virtual malls continued to add millions to the coffers, with those top labels who failed to join when the project was originally floated clamouring to get on board.

By mid 2004 Nathan and Susie were spending an average of one week in six in the United States, and the house at Moss Beach proved its worth many times over. Chi Lu continued to build up the operation in China although never once in all her visits to the country had she let it slip she was fluent in the language, always speaking through an interpreter or interpreters. In doing so she learnt a lot, some mildly insulting on a personal level, some very devious on a business level, but all taken and absorbed without reaction, always to her advantage. The Chinese operation was growing into a thriving subsidiary which churned out mass produced goods at shockingly low costs when compared with the production costs in the US or Europe.

In late October of the same year Nathan and Susie flew once more to Silicone Valley for an in-depth examination of the Chinese operation with Chi Lu. She had done an incredible job, and employed excellent staff, all of whom were highly qualified, self motivated people who spoke English fluently. None suspected her ability to speak their language, but all appreciated her desire to sit down to eat with them, from the lowliest of the factory floor workers to the upper echelons of the management. She had never heard a single member of staff criticise the company, its aims, future ambitions, management or ownership. In fact the only thing she overheard of private conversations was something which quite amused her, which was how sorry the general workers felt for her, how she was so big and ugly, such a shame for so nice a boss.

The meetings regarding the general overview of the operation were most encouraging. China was now not only a worldwide supplier of NJF Industries goods but also a rapidly growing market in its own right. The first green shoots of consumerism had grown rapidly within the larger cities, and a marketing department was added to develop and increase both brand awareness and sales within the Chinese marketplace. The early figures indicated the success of the decision, which would in time swell the parent companies coffers still more.

Both Nathan and Susie deemed the visit a great success. A few short weeks later they were to find out the trip proved successful in more ways than one. Susie was pregnant.

In late October 2004, the tour of Afghanistan ended, happily without any loss of life, and troops were returned to Britain. Two weeks leave was to follow, which was once again divided between Chris's parents and his sister and her family. His entire family was surprised at his decision to leave the army as all thought he would remain in the service until his fifties.

He returned to Chepstow, and once again to Beachley Barracks and 160 Brigade. The setting was no better in November than it had been in February, and was still damp, dark and unappealing. Chris was already committed to leaving the army in May of 2005 when the news came through, in December 2004, which would have motivated him to leave had he not already formalised things.

As part of the re-organisation of the infantry the government announced, through the Ministry of Defence, a major amalgamation of regiments. The Duke of Wellington's Regiment was to be joined with the Prince of Wales's Own Regiment of Yorkshire and the Green Howards, and all Yorkshire based regiments in the King's Division, to form the Yorkshire Regiment. The re-badging parade was to take place on the sixth of June 2006 when everything which was historically unique about the regiment he had loved since a boy, and served for a quarter of a century, was to be swept away by penny pinching Whitehall mandarins. It was certainly time for him to go, and after five more months at Chepstow, with a nice little nest egg saved over twenty plus years and a reasonable pension, that is exactly what he did.

After twenty-four years in the army life outside was very different for Chris. Of course he had enjoyed periods of leave, but they were just short breaks, holidays, and there was always the reality, and in many ways security, of the army and his place within it to return to. He had risen to a senior NCO because of his abilities, a major one of which was the ability to plan ahead. He hadn't just left without a thought, and the period of one year's notice provided time to apply a great deal of consideration to what he would do. There were several things he could do, some of which he was eminently well qualified for, and some he would be completely fresh to. Unfortunately the ones for which he was well qualified were not the ones which now attracted him.

Word quite obviously spread and he received a number of offers months before his notice period ended, and some of the offers promised to be most lucrative. However without exception they related to 'security' work, which covered a multitude of sins, with emphasis on the sins, from mercenary work through hired assassin to minder, none of which interested him, and for some the legality of which was most questionable. He certainly did not wish to take up employment as a security guard at a factory, nor in moving money for banks. He toyed with, in fact deeply considered, the idea of taking on a freehouse country pub, preferably buying one outright using his substantial savings, and it was still something he was keeping in mind. However the truth of the matter was he really still didn't know what he wanted to do. It was much easier to work out the things he wouldn't consider than to try and figure out what he would like. He was remarkably well trained to fight, to kill, and to lead men in dangerous situations. Unfortunately there was not a great deal of call for those skills on Civvy Street.

Twenty Five

The following year passed rapidly for Jack Bryant as there was a dizzying amount to learn about the industry to which he had been recruited to help plan future strategy and policy. Even for an individual with a sharp, analytical and perceptive young mind there was an enormous quantity of information to accumulate. Before the collapse of communism, Russian oil production rivalled that of Saudi Arabia with an output of eleven million barrels a day. Following the break-up of the former Soviet Union production plummeted to eight million barrels a day by 1992, and to only six million by 1996, as both oil and gas industries underwent dramatic sweeping change.

Although the Soviet bureaucratic administrative structure had grown out of all proportion to effectiveness and efficiency both industries were left floundering with its demise. With state monopoly gone in the oil industry the door opened to a small number of companies to exploit the reserves, becoming extremely powerful as they did so. However the onshore fields exploited, although massive, had by then been producing for some time, and reserves were running down. Deposits in the Caspian Sea and the Artic were promising, and certainly the north western Russian Artic estimates made cheery reading, but all would first need huge investment.

Russia's proven natural gas reserves ran to around forty seven trillion cubic meters, very slightly over a quarter of the planets proven reserves, but were almost wholly controlled by Gazprom, a state-run near monopoly whose annual tax payments accounted for approximately a quarter of Russian federal tax. It did not help the economic situation that Gazprom had to supply the domestic markets heating and power requirements, by law, at government regulated rates which were below the market price, and insufficient export pipelines had long hindered the consistent sale of product outside the country.

Aside from government policies, which would have to change, potential growth in both gas and oil production was being hampered by the lack of modern technologies, western technologies, in the areas of exploration, development and even production itself. Unfortunately potential investors found Russia's investment climate inhospitable, even hostile, when considering myriad problems with tax laws and inefficient bureaucracy all the way through to corruption and extortion. As if this was not enough to consider, Russia had a tendency to use the power of its hydrocarbon industries as a bargaining chip on the international political table, allowing the lines between its energy policy and foreign policy to become somewhat blurred, especially when dealing with Africa, Asia, the Middle East and parts of Europe.

It made for a steep leaning curve, with a lot to take in, and Jack deeply welcomed the first holiday at home in Britain since taking the job. It was also to provide him with the opportunity to introduce Katya to his family, after the two of them first spent a few days in London. On Sunday the third of July Jack and Katya flew into London. They were due to meet his father and Sandy Cartwright for a late breakfast together, followed by a visit to the Tower of London, on the Thursday. Then all four were to return to Lymington, there to meet Danny, and Jack could hardly wait to see his brother again. They had stayed in touch throughout his time at Oxford, and since he took the job in Moscow, but unfortunately during Jack's holidays his and Danny's paths had rarely crossed as when he was at home Danny seemed to be away. Even when both were under the same roof at the same time, Danny tended to be tied up with his work, boats, diving and rugby.

Apart from his brother and father, Jack was also looking forward to meeting Sandy Cartwright again, a woman he deeply respected and greatly admired for all she had done for his father. To Jack's mind, his mother aside, Sandy was without a shadow of doubt the very best thing to have happened to his father. What she had done for him, the patience she exhibited, and the unstinting support she gave in his time of need was nothing short of saintly. She was a rock, in a very turbulent sea, which her father had managed to cling to, and who had in turn brought him back from the edge of madness to once again enjoy his life. There was very, very little in the world Jack would not do or give to Sandy Cartwright if ever he was asked.

Jack and Katya thoroughly enjoyed three and a half days of touring around London and seeing the sights. The good thing about having a well paid job was it enabled Jack to in part repay to Katya the kindness her family had shown him whilst he had stayed in St Petersburg, and he did so unstintingly. In the time available they were able to enjoy trips to Windsor Castle, view Buckingham Palace and amble around Hampton Court Gardens. They visited St Paul's, strolled along the Thames embankment and viewed the Houses of Parliament, Big Ben and the Palace of Westminster from Westminster Bridge, then taken a turn on the big wheel which is the London Eye. In the evenings they watched The Phantom of the Opera, The Mousetrap, and Mary Poppins, dining afterwards in Soho, Knightsbridge and Chelsea. They visited Harrods, the Natural History Museum and wandered around Oxford Street. Not a minute of their time was wasted, with everything planned to precision by Jack, and Katya had rejoiced, relished and revelled in everything they did.

Over many months, which stretched into a year and then two, Tom and Sandy's friendship gathered pace, albeit infinitely slowly. One evening, having finished a course of the meal they were eating, and whilst waiting for the next to arrive, Tom sat with a hand resting on the table and Sandy, in the midst of making a point, covered his hand with hers. For once he did not flinch or pull his hand away, but covered hers with his other and thanked her for all she had done. Finally the meaningful relationship Sandy had worked so hard at creating was born. A few weeks later Tom put his arm around her shoulders, and two weeks after that they exchanged their first kiss. It was to take another six months before they were to become lovers, and yet another eighteen months, and the start of a new year, before she once more changed her job and moved in to live with him, to the very great joy of both sons.

Mary had been dead for nearly six years by then, yet still Tom visited her grave every day, and still he vowed vengeance upon it. Despite all she had accomplished in bringing Tom back from the very verge of a complete nervous breakdown and possible madness she had done nothing to quell his hatred of all people and all things Muslim. In part it was because she realised in this she would fail as it was a part of his bond with Mary, and therefore a line she must never cross.

However, although she would never actually voice her thoughts, it also harkened back to where and when she had grown up. As a small girl she had lived in a large family house in Langley on the outskirts of Slough. It remained a wonderful setting until the immigrant population started to grow exponentially. Her school seemed to have been overrun, and standards both at school and the community generally started to drop, and then plummeted. Her father decided to move, and the family relocated to Virginia Water, eight miles to the south, never to look back. Slough was now history, completely overwhelmed with black and brown faces, with all the inherent drug and crime problems which go with a community out of control. No, privately she too had very little regard for the people Tom loathed.

Susie's pregnancy progressed without complication, and Nathan was thrilled with the situation far beyond his ability to express himself. He was in essence still a simple man. The almost incalculable amounts of money he, Jake and NJF Industries were worth meant very little to him. Whenever possible he still preferred to travel cattle class when flying, and much preferred staying in medium rated hotels. There was nothing at all flamboyant or ostentatious about his character. Certainly it was better to have money than not but for Nathan it mattered not at all. He just wanted to be comfortable and, above and well beyond all other considerations, he just wanted to be comfortable with a family to love, something he had been completely deprived of throughout the entirety of his childhood and early life.

At sixteen weeks, and again at twenty, Susie had an ultrasound scan. The second confirmed the first without doubt or equivocation, the baby was a girl, they were going to have a daughter. Nathan was almost delirious with happiness. It was all he could possibly have wanted. He would have been more than happy with a boy, but to have a little girl would be to have all of his hopes, dreams and desires come true. He firmly believed in the old adage – a son makes you a father, but a daughter makes you a daddy – and he wanted to be a daddy more than anything else in the world! A little girl. He and Susie had created a little baby girl.

As the weeks passed and Susie's belly swelled it became obvious she would not be able to carry on with her duties and heavy work schedule, nor would she be able to return to it after giving birth, as both she and Nathan agreed completely the baby's needs vastly outweighed the needs of the company. A short period of restructuring followed. The solid and dependable Mike Hall was promoted and put in overall charge of the mobile phone division. Iain McGregor had learnt discipline over the years, and he too was promoted, given the task of running the pc and video games section, but the biggest single change concerned Chi Lu.

For the years as head of the American operation she had never faltered, and was directly responsible for the success of the operation. In fact it was extremely doubtful the project would have thrived in the way it had without her enormous input. Additionally she had set up the business in China alone and without help or advice of any kind from the company's founders. They had extended a completely free hand due to her previously demonstrated abilities, and she had once again exceeded everyone else's expectations. Susie was clearly going to have to take more of a back seat role, and the only person to fill her shoes was Chi Lu.

The initial working relationship had over time developed into a genuine mutually respectful friendship between Susie and Chi Lu. So much so that as well as being maid of honour at the wedding she was a regular house guest during her visits to England, both at their own home, and on a few occasions at the Gatting family home at Foxton. When Susie offered the position of global head of the business to Chi Lu the proposal was snapped up immediately. Chi Lu had proved so successful in finding and placing good people the American end of the operation ran as smoothly without her continual presence as the British end did without Susie. Both parts of the company needed someone at the helm, but the business created had grown to a size, and was staffed and managed by such highly qualified and competent people, that it ran in a well ordered manner without constant minute tinkering from on high. Susie could have her baby, and Chi Lu could be relied upon to oversee all of NJF Industries corporate interests.

Towards the end of May 2005 a penthouse apartment overlooking the Thames was purchased as a residence for Chi Lu to use when she was in Britain. She flew across the Atlantic to instruct painters and decorators, and to enjoy a major shopping spree with Susie, ordering everything the two of them thought she might need in her new part time home. Susie was due to give birth on the twenty-first of July and it was decided Chi Lu should return to England two weeks beforehand. It was therefore mutually agreed she would fly back to England on Thursday the seventh of July, relax a little over the weekend whilst adjusting to the time change, and officially adopt the mantle of her new position on Monday the eleventh. She would remain a houseguest with the Jefferies during the weekend, moving into her newly decorated apartment on the Sunday evening.

Both Tammy Wild and Peter Parfitt clearly knew what it was they wanted, and both could see all they desired would eventually come to fruition. In the meanwhile they had to work out a reasonable compromise, and this they did. Tammy had little intention of returning to the world of modelling with all its mendacity, distortion and sham, and certainly did not need the money. Parfitt was a pilot, and was not the type who could ever be a kept man, so he would have to work to provide until they could work something out regarding money. Tammy had few friends in England, and none in South Africa. Parfitt had few friends in South Africa and much fewer in England. There was no reason why either place was more appropriate than the other for their relationship, except the weather was far better in South Africa, as was the lifestyle, the cost of living cheaper and the airport twenty five easy minutes away at worst.

After three weeks in the South African sun the return to England was doubly bad for Tammy. Firstly the man she wished to be with was six thousand miles to the south most of the time, and secondly returning to an English winter really was dreadful. Living two hours from Heathrow did not help the situation when Parfitt was in England, which was certainly something they would have to address. As it was she would have rushed to her man and lived in his garage if he were to let her, but she knew he would not, and she knew he would not out of respect for her. That respect, and his sense of duty, may well get it the way of their relationship, but without it Peter Parfitt would not be the man he was, and she wanted the whole man, not just a knocked about part of him.

The solution to the problem was not an instant one, or one to suddenly occur to either of them. More it came about slowly, over weeks, months and then years, and was driven by need and convenience instead of inspiration. Tammy had time and she had money, so she came and went from South Africa. To most the costs would have been prohibitive, but her money was working nicely for her and being properly and professionally managed. In reality she never even got around to spending the interest, and the odd modelling job to which she consented paid extremely well. Parfitt compromised a little and she partially moved in with him, spending weeks at his apartment at any one time. She also spent weeks in Britain, and it was on one of her visits the property at Cookham Dean came up for sale. The property was a highly desirable long term investment which could later be sold or rented if it no longer met her requirements. So she purchased it and decorated it, and it proved to be very useful for the two of them, as a base for short term visits, and for longer periods if Tammy was in England for any reason.

Five and a half years had passed since they met and both knew it was long enough. Their feelings had changed for one another since they met, but only to strengthen the bond between them. Physically each still excited the other as much as they had their first night together, but Tammy was now thirty-five, her biological clock was ticking, and if they were to have kids, which both wanted, now was the time. Parfitt was flying out of Cape Town on Monday the fourth of July, and they were to be married at a quiet little registry office in Brighton on Saturday the ninth. Peter was now in his forties and had amassed enough money to reasonably keep a wife. He had handed in his resignation, and was flying his last flight, although it was indicated he would be welcomed back if ever he wished to return. That though was unlikely. They were going to start their own business already having lined up just what they wanted, a Cape Town based concern organising tailor made tours of Southern Africa, and were going to make babies, hopefully three.

Six months after Sandy Cartwright moved in to live with Tom Bryant they decided to reward themselves with a little trip to London together, and they planned it to coincide with a homecoming visit by Jack, who they would meet there. Tom knew little of London. He was a man of the country, and had never felt the need to repeatedly leave the countryside he loved to visit a large, noisy and smelly city. Sandy was however raised on the very outskirts of London, and throughout her late teens and early twenties had been able to jump on an underground train and journey into the centre whenever she wished.

Although she had no wish to return to such a life she did want to take Tom and show him some of the landmarks. It didn't have to be much, and she certainly didn't want to rush all over town. It just had to be a short, relaxed and easy break of a few days. She decided to go up on a Monday lunchtime, and back on a Thursday evening in order to avoid traffic, and eventually found and booked a two star hotel situated a couple of minutes walk away from Baker Street underground station and overlooking Regents Park.

On Monday the forth of July Sandy drove Tom to London in her little Volkswagen Polo. Many years earlier Sandy had a friend who lived in Upper Halliford near Sunbury, whose tiny one bedroom house was built on a small estate where Windmill Road met Upper Halliford Road, and backed onto Upper Halliford station, part of the overland railway line. The station stood alongside the motorway, within a mile of the junction, and the area was safe and secure with plenty of parking where the car could be left without worry for the duration of their stay. A short trip on the train took them to Richmond where they changed to London Underground's District Line changing again onto Circle Line to take them to the Baker Street station, and a short walk with their overnight bags to the hotel.

Small though it was, the hotel was comfortable, clean and well sited. The Sherlock Holmes Museum, Madame Tussaud's and the Planetarium were almost on the doorstep, as was Regent's Park and its boating lake. Additionally Hyde Park, Marble Arch and Oxford Street were all no more than a short stroll, and the pair spent Tuesday and Wednesday happily wandering the streets. Tom found the racial mix and the number of different coloured faces a little disconcerting, but this was not the New Forest, and he was generally thoroughly enjoying the break.

Jack and Katya were already in town, but all four agreed to continue seeing the things they wanted to at their own pace, with the two couples finally coming together on the Thursday morning. They would then collectively visit the Tower of London before returning to Jack's hotel, picking up the young couple's bags, and all then getting a taxi across London to Sandy's car for the drive down to Lymington.

Jimmy Andrews loved his son without question, but sometimes struggled to understand him, possibly subconsciously asking himself why they were not more alike. As a father, although he would never voice such a thought, he had hoped for a chip off the old block, very much as many fathers the world over do. Well it had not happened, and it was not going to happen, so he just did all which he could to help with Charlie's education. For Chris there was no such conflict. Little Charlie – ha! not so little Charlie! – was his nephew, not his son, and as such there was no such paternal conflicts of any kind. He simply loved his young nephew well beyond anything else on the planet. He also loved his nieces, but Charlie was the first born and, sexist or not, Charlie was a boy and Chris could therefore identify with him. Most importantly Charlie was the son he would never have, so there was nothing he would not give or do for the lad, something Charlie instinctively knew. He had never and would never take advantage of it, but knew the bond existed, and it worked both ways. He had always felt very close to his Uncle Chris.

Charlie took his GCSEs and school broke up for the summer before his sixteenth birthday. He was expected to do very well with his exams, and was happy with what he had done. His uncle had left the army, a huge shock, and come to stay for a few weeks. The house was getting too small as the girls were growing, and there was much talk about converting the outbuilding into an extra bedroom with en-suite facilities for Charlie to move into. Chris stayed just down the road at the local pub and had time on his hands, something he was clearly not used to, so took it upon himself to help with the required building work.

The outhouse, which had stood for decades, was built on stone and of stone. A slate damp proof course was put in at the time of building, and there had never been any evidence of damp as a consequence. It possessed two windows, which were sanded, painted and retained, and a door which was replaced with a new thicker one. There was an existing water and power supply, and the roof had always remained dry, although Chris stripped it off and felted it before replacing the tiles. The old lathe and plaster ceiling was removed and replaced with plasterboard. A hatch was put in so as to use the loft space for storage, and fibreglass insulation now protected the building from upward heat loss. The old toilet was removed, the toilet doorway blocked up, and a hole cut through linking the toilet area to the new bedroom. A new toilet was purchased, and re-sited, along with a basin and shower. Chris then erected a studding wall with doorway across the end of the room and tiled the floor and walls of the new bathroom area. He arranged for plasterers to come in and skim out the walls and ceiling of the remains of the building, waited for the plaster to dry, then painted it. In three weeks he turned an old semi derelict store room into a well appointed and spacious separate guest bedroom with facilities. It was to be Charlie's, and Charlie was thrilled, as were both twins as they too would each then have a bedroom to themselves.

Charlie's sixteenth birthday came around and a small house party was held for family and friends, most of whom presented him with thoughtful and useful gifts. His parents furnished him with a microscope to help with his studies and there was a range of presents from theirs to the chocolates he received from his sisters, which was the first gift they had ever bought with their own pocket money and which meant a great deal to the lad. There was only one present not of a tangible hands-on nature, which was from his Uncle Chris, who was taking him to London on the train for a visit of three to four days duration.

Never having been to London before, Charlie really looked forward to the visit to his country's capital city. Living in Lancashire the opportunity had not previously arisen. He had travelled with his parents and seen much of the north of England, especially around the Lake District and up to the Lowlands of southern Scotland. On many occasions he had visited his grandparents, sometimes staying for extended periods during school summer holidays, and they took him to places such as Metroland at Gateshead, and up to Newcastle on Tyne, then back along the side of Hadrian's Wall. He travelled south to Alton Towers, and across country to Lincoln and down into Sherwood Forest, but had not yet visited London. Chris sat down with him for several hours working out an itinerary, and Charlie couldn't wait to see places he had only ever previously heard and seen pictures of.

Apart from the stay in London Chris arranged for them to travel there by train, and the train journey alone would have been an excellent present in itself to young Charlie. He knew a little of the recent background of the region's trains, mainly because the changes affected so many. Between his home and the view of

Morcambe Bay, a little to the north, was Hest Bank, a very small section of the West Coast Main Line. The WCML was the busiest mixed traffic railway route in Britain, and was essential to the provision of fast, long distance inter-city passenger services between the south of Scotland, including the North West of England, North Wales and the West Midlands, and London. It was also one of the busiest freight routes in Europe.

When he was nine years old Virgin placed the largest rolling stock order in British history, ordering a new class of train, the 390 Pendolino, for the West Coast Main Line network. The order was for one billion pounds. It had ever since stuck in his mind because it was the first time he had ever heard the figure used, and had asked his teacher to explain it to the class. The Pendolino was a high speed tilting train which ran at one hundred and twenty-five miles an hour, although it was capable of higher speeds, and Virgin had petitioned Network Rail to raise speed limits to take advantage of their new super train. Charlie had not yet been on one and was absolutely thrilled at the prospect of doing so.

Tammy drove in to collect her husband-to-be from Heathrow. She intentionally dressed a little like a tart because she knew how it made Parfitt's blood race. He was still an honest to goodness red blooded male, and she knew full well she still had a body to be justly proud of. As the old adage went – 'If you've got it – flaunt it!' – and Tammy didn't have a problem with flaunting it whilst she still had it. Her body was important to her, not in any vain or conceited way, but because she understood how others, especially Peter, appreciated it, and she thought it her duty to keep in as good a condition as she possibly could for him, and besides, it still helped with the odd pay cheque. It was nearly three weeks since they were last together because she had flown home to sort out all the wedding arrangements, and to buy the car which was to take them on the extended touring honeymoon around Europe they had planed. No, she thought to herself as she dressed, it never hurt to add a little spice to a relationship, especially if she was going to come back from the holiday pregnant as she intended.

She saw Parfitt coming, overnight bag in hand, and ran to him, throwing her arms around him and kissing him warmly, oblivious of the fact her skirt was far too short for that sort of thing, and giving a free view of her glorious naked bottom to several people who demonstrated very mixed reactions. As she turned she realised, giggled and pulled the skirt down, then grabbed Peter's free arm and led him off to the car. Parfitt thoroughly approved of the new car, and of the view he got as she slid into her seat. Tammy still drove really well he thought, very much like a man in her seating position and not constantly pressing her knees together. Her anticipation and spatial awareness were excellent, she had complete control of the car, and obviously knew where all the other vehicles were around her at all times.

"Well, what do you think of her?" Tammy asked, never once taking her eyes off the road.

"I think she is absolutely beautiful, and I can't wait to get her into bed." Parfitt replied.

"You can have that soon enough, and I can't wait either," she giggled, "but I did obviously mean the car!"

"It's beautiful, and I love the way you handle her. It's racy, refined and has beautiful curves. So what are you going to call her? Tammy?" Parfitt teased.

"You silly man!" Tammy laughed, and then continued more seriously. "I've got our schedule all worked out if it's okay with you. Today I thought sex, sleep, more sex, out to eat, back for sex and then sleep. Tomorrow get up late and then go and get your suit from the tailors, afterwards we have a lazy day and early to bed. Thursday we'll be up early and into the city. I have to drop the car off at Hendon for a service at eight a.m., then have an appointment with my broker and a couple of appointments after lunch with the estate agents for the house. Friday we'll get up late, have wild passionate sex in the house for the last time then drive down to Brighton. Saturday we get married then we spend the rest of our lives together, under the same roof and on the same continent. Anything wrong with any of that?"

"Most of it sounds alright, especially the last bit. I'm just not sure if there is enough sex though!" Parfitt replied.

"Well we'll just have to see what we can fit in then won't we." Tammy grinned.

The Wednesday suit fitting went perfectly. Parfitt had attended the tailors several weeks earlier for a measuring, and what was offered fitted like a glove the first time with no requirements for any alterations. Tammy's appointment with her broker was scheduled for nine-fifteen on Thursday morning at his office in Jewry Street, just off Aldgate and five minutes walk from Aldgate tube station, but first they had to drop the car off. It meant rising early, but it was important to ensure the car was one hundred percent as they would be relying on it for several thousand miles driving over the next few weeks. Tammy had purchased the vehicle from a specialist dealership in Hendon, and was going to return it for a service whilst seeing her broker. Peter was to accompany her because both knew it would be the last time they trod the streets of London for quite some time. After their tour of Europe it was their intention to return to Cape Town and set the wheels of the business in motion, and that would tie up their time for many months to come.

Twenty Six

Early on the Thursday morning, three days after Charlie's birthday, Chris gently roused his young nephew at five in the morning so they would be ready to leave the house by six, as he had arranged for a taxi to call to collect them for the journey to the station. Chris cooked a full English breakfast and with a bulging belly an excited Charlie left the rest of the house asleep as he climbed into the taxi with his uncle for the journey to Lancaster station. There Chris and Charlie made their way to platform four, the through platform for trains to the south, for the six-thirty three train to London's Euston Station where they were due to arrive at nine-fourteen, after calling at Preston, Wigan, Warrington and Stafford.

Charlie wanted to stay awake and enjoy the journey, but the lack of sleep due to excitement and the large heavy breakfast took their toll and he fell asleep shortly after their final en route stop at Stafford. Chris read the newspaper he had purchased at the station, occasionally looking out of the window as the countryside sped by. There were no delays to an uneventful journey, and they pulled into the station on time. As they were not in any hurry Chris took it easy getting off the train and leaving the platform. There was no point in trying to compete with hurrying commuters as they were on holiday with all the time in the world, whereas many of those around them needed to get to work. The station was busier than Chris would have expected after nine, but then many people now worked flexi-time he mused. The crowds were building up as he and Charlie approached the exit – but hey – it was London.

Leaving the house at quarter to seven Tammy and Peter made good time until getting caught up in the inevitable morning snarl up on the North Circular Road, and eventually arrived at the garage a couple of minutes after eight. The car was pre-booked and a youngish lad from the service bay took the keys leaving them with no more to do than cross the road to Hendon Central tube station, part of the Northern Line. As there were no seats available they decided to change onto the eastbound Circle Line at King's Cross St Pancras rather than changing at Moorgate. At eight-forty they stepped into the third carriage of the train only to see, not surprisingly at the height of rush hour, there were no available seats there either. However, graciously, a tall older man with greying hair offered up his seat to Tammy just as the train pulled away. She smiled warmly at the man appreciative of his courtesy, and Parfitt too nodded his thanks to the man, stepping back a little to give him room to stand more comfortably.

Thursday morning had seen Tom and Sandy up in reasonable time to pay for their accommodation and to then catch the tube across town to the prearranged breakfast rendezvous with Jack. They walked to Baker Street Station, purchased the required tickets, and at approximately eight-thirty climbed aboard the third carriage of the eastbound Circle Line train which would take them to Tower Hill, and to Jack and Katya. A tour party had just vacated many seats as they left the train heading for Madame Tussaud's and, considering the time, Tom and Sandy were extremely lucky to be able to find two empty seats together. The train filled up rapidly at the Euston Square stop, and again at King's Cross St Pancras.

In an act of chivalry so typical of his character in earlier years Tom offered up his seat to a particularly attractive younger woman who entered the carriage at King's Cross. She was accompanied by a fit looking and well tanned man of around forty. The woman smiled her thanks as Tom Bryant moved away a little to stand more comfortably by the doors, and the man who accompanied her also nodded his thanks as he stepped back to afford Tom slightly more room. Sandy was both pleased and touched by Tom's gesture. It was truly remarkable to see how much of the old Tom had returned during the past few months, and the trip to London had done him the power of good. In every way possible he was now almost completely back to the outgoing man she had originally met with his wife.

It was more than six years since Mary was killed and the journey had proved to be a long and arduous one, but the man she had always known was in there somewhere was back. They now had the rest of their lives together, and she would make absolutely sure they would both make the very best of the time they had together, ultimately banishing the demons from both their pasts. Sandy Cartwright could not have been happier. After all the pain, the loss and the sorrow, everything was going to work out perfectly, and there would be a happy ending. Deep in thought Sandy sat with a large smile on her face, just as Mary Bryant had as she walked to work on that fateful Spring morning.

Susie, although quite large from her near full term pregnancy, wanted to meet Chi Lu from her flight personally. The flight was due to arrive a little after nine-thirty, so she decided to ride the Piccadilly Line in with Nathan just as they had both done together so many times in the past, as it would be her last chance to do so before the baby was born. A car would be at Heathrow to collect her, Chi Lu, and Chi Lu's baggage as Nathan loathed London traffic and refused point blank to drive across the city. By any normal standard they had untold wealth and could employ a full time chauffeur, but such was far too ostentatious and to him riding the tube like everybody else was all the transport he needed.

Boarding the train at Cockfosters they found two seats together at the rear of the first carriage and there they sat together until King's Cross St Pancras where Nathan had to change. He kissed her before leaving and warned her not to lift anything, telling her for the umpteenth time he wouldn't know what to do with himself if anything were ever to happen to her or the baby. Susie stayed in her seat and continued on to Heathrow, thinking to herself how lucky she was to have found a man who cared so deeply about family. They would have more kids, at least another two, just as her parents had done, and what a life those kids would have.

The young black man standing in front of her stumbled a little and she instinctively put out a hand to help support him.

Part Two

One

At eight-fifty the three explosions occurred within fifty seconds of one another. The first to explode was aboard an eastbound Circle Line train as it travelled between the underground stations of Liverpool Street and Aldgate. The third carriage of the train, the one in which Tom, Sandy, Peter and Tammy sat or stood, was approximately one hundred yards into the tunnel when the bomb detonated.

Of the four Sandy Cartwright sat only two seats from the suicide bomber and she died instantly, the smile still on her face. Her body partially protected Tammy Wild, but the violence of the blast tore into Tammy. In an instant she lost her left leg at the knee and her left arm just below the elbow, her left breast was all but ripped from her chest and her right foot almost torn away at the ankle. Her jaw bone suffered multiple breaks and her lower lip was half wrenched from her face. Flying shards of glass pierced her left eye, and she was permanently deafened in her left ear which was also almost completely torn from her head along with half her scalp.

Tom Bryant's gracious surrendering of his seat had spared him from horrendous injury or death, but the force of the explosion lifted him from his feet and hurled him backwards into Peter Parfitt. Tom was steadying himself against the trains acceleration by holding the overhead bar with his left hand. The arm snapped in two places, he lost the little finger from his left hand, and three left ribs cracked instantly. Flying glass and debris lacerated the exposed skin of his hands and face, with glass driven through the cotton of his shirt to embed itself in the flesh of his chest. Peter Parfitt was perfectly protected from the blast, but Tom Bryant smashed into him sending him reeling backwards into another two men who stood behind him. The impact drove the wind from his lungs and the back of Tom Bryant's head impacted with his lower face, giving him a fat lip and loose teeth but, except for the temporary deafness all in the carriage suffered, those were the extent of his injuries.

Bomb number two exploded on the second carriage of a westbound Circle Line train. It had just left platform four at Edgware Road and was heading for Paddington. As with the eastbound train this one had also left King's Cross St. Pancras about eight minutes earlier.

The third bomb exploded on the southbound Piccadilly Line. This was aboard a deep-level underground train which was travelling between King's Cross St. Pancras and Russell Square when the explosion occurred. This tunnel, unlike the Circle Line tunnels, was a single track tube with only six inches of clearances. The bomb exploded roughly one minute after the train left King's Cross, by which time it had covered a distance of approximately five hundred yards. The explosion took place at the rear of the first carriage of the train, causing extreme damage to the rear of that carriage, as well as the front of the following one. The confinement of the tunnel concentrated the power of the explosion reflecting the force of the blast, causing much greater suffering to those people on board.

Susie Jefferies had attempted to help the young man who stood in front of her, putting up her hand to help support him as he stumbled. She didn't know the man was Germaine Lindsay, a Jamaican, known as Abdullah Shaheed Jamal after his conversion to Islam. He was a terrorist, and it would be the last move she would ever make. The explosion blew the entire top part of her body away. As with Sandy Cartwright she died instantly. However the foetus was already well developed and capable of sustained independent life. Protected as it was by a cushion of flesh and amniotic fluid her foetus survived the blast. Several of the survivors later claimed they were shocked to see her belly still moving as lights came back on a little after the detonation. Had an emergency caesarean been performed the baby girl should have survived. There was nobody to perform the operation. The baby died too, starved of the oxygen the mother's body usually produced she suffocated without ever knowing life. She had not been born. Consequently she was never fully featured in the death toll figures.

By the time the emergency services reached the scenes of the explosions half of London was in chaos. Within thirty minutes London underground had started shutting down, with trains pulling into the stations and stopping, leaving people to get to their destinations via the surface. It was at first thought and reported there had been six explosions, as survivors arrived on platforms to the front and rear of each of the incidents, and this took many hours to correct. The Piccadilly Line survivors were the most difficult for the emergency services to reach because of the confinement and clearance problems. With the Circle Line incidents access was possible alongside the wrecked trains, and they were relatively close to stations and therefore exits.

Despite which Tammy Wild should have died, and would have done so had it not been for the swift actions of Peter Parfitt. He realised instantly what had happened and, although all the lights had gone out causing complete disorientation, his long ago military training and more recent air crew training cut in. He first tested his own limbs and checked his neck movement. He could hear nothing apart from a loud ringing but understood it to be perfectly normal in the circumstances. He carefully stood, testing his weight on each leg as he did so. The man who had crashed into him was also trying to stand, but Peter could tell he had not come through it unscathed. He needed light. His mobile phone. He pressed a button and the face lit up. It gave off pitifully little light, but light nonetheless. The carriage was full of smoke but he could see the guy to his left who had crashed into him was cut and bleeding, his left arm shattered with the left hands little finger missing. He gestured to the man to relax and wrap something tightly around his left hand, the cuts he should be able to deal with later.

He knew Tammy was closer to the centre of the explosion and would have suffered much worse. He must reach her. There was a metallic smell of blood in the air mixed with the stench of burst, slashed and ruptured guts. From the phone's light he could see there was blood running everywhere. It was a slaughterhouse. He must help Tammy. He sensed rather than saw movement ahead of him. People were beginning to react, and reaction could bring blind, mindless panic, although it never did. He had to get to her. He eased himself past and over broken people and twisted limbs. She should be here on the left. He found her.

He could see at first glance she was dead. Half her body seemed to be missing. Training took over. Trauma had stopped her body from haemorrhaging. There was a slight but discernable movement to her chest and, unbelievably, she had a pulse. Terribly weak, but a pulse. He forced the stump of her left arm up into the air and wedged it there. He open what remained of her mouth and checked her airways, then pulled off his belt and looped it around the remains of the left leg just below the thigh muscle and above where the knee had been, tightening as much as he could. His tie came off and went around the lower part of Tammy's right leg below the calf muscle, pulling as tight as he could, and again he cut off the blood supply then tried to lash the foot in place. He returned to her left arm. Taking his handkerchief from his pocket he wrapped it twice around the arm above the elbow, tied it off tight, took a pen from his jacket pocket, placed it under the knot and twisted it, tightening the tourniquet still further. What remained of her scalp he pulled back into place. He removed his jacket and shirt, ripping the arms from the shirt then shredding the remains. With strips of shirt he bound her scalp back into place and roughly bandaged her hanging ear. His jacket he pressed into the place where her left breast hung from a strip of skin and muscle tissue, and he then bound it in place as firmly as he could. He again checked airways, pulled what remained of her lip back across her mouth, and used more shirt to support her lip and jaw, careful to keep the airways unblocked. When done he retightened the belt and tie around the remains of her legs, and further bound up what was left of her right foot.

She was still alive but she would not remain so for long. Although he had never seen action he had met a lot of people who had, and at one stage dated an RAF medic. He knew prompt action was crucial. He also knew the obvious was true, in that the very young, the elderly and the infirm usually died far more quickly than those who were fit and well. Tammy was thirty-five and one of the fittest women he had ever met, but her injuries were horrific. It was a miracle she had survived the blast, but she had, and he must keep her that way until help arrived and took over. The ringing in his ears was beginning to ease. Most of those who could walk had left, but the dead and badly wounded were left. His eyes could pick things up in the gloom now, and others who remained were using their phones as he had. He pulled a body out of the way so he could get to the floor of the carriage. The blood on it was beginning to congeal and coagulate. He needed to get Tammy onto the floor and get her limbs raised to reduce the blood flow. By getting gravity to work with him he should be able to gain a few more minutes life for her. He pulled what was probably once a jacket from the remains of a broken body and swept the floor clear of glass, debris and remains, then gently lifted her body down onto the floor and raised her legs onto the charred and tangled mess which had once been the carriages seats. He did the same with the stump of her left arm. There was nothing more he could do with her until help arrived, and if it didn't come very soon there would be nothing anyone could do.

Help did arrive. He saw the flashlights bobbing up and down as the first of the emergency service workers arrived. Others saw them too and all started to shout. Parfitt still could not hear properly but he was vaguely aware of a noise creeping past the ringing. He must get help, and get it now. He knew how these things worked but must not allow standard practice to prevail, or she would die. Generally those with basic first aid training are taught to quickly attempt to assess the situation, ignore superficial wounds and then concentrate on those they believe have a chance of survival so vital resources are not wasted. If this happened she would be left to die, but if she got help there was a chance, just a chance, she could survive. He must get her that help. He had to get them to give her that chance. He did.

Both Parfitt's previous positions require authority and control. He realised begging for help would prove pointless, it would fail, and Tammy would die. Again his training took over and he assumed at least partial charge of the scene. To the first emergency service worker he saw he shouted, "You! Do you have a radio?"

The emergency worker was slightly taken aback to have this half naked man covered in blood shouting at him in such an obviously authoritative manner, but he had a radio so he nodded his head. "Yes sir!" he answered.

"Does it function at this level?" Parfitt shouted. Again the man nodded.

"In that case we need Medics, stretchers, plasma and cutting gear down here now!" Parfitt continued. "I have an urgent category A case here. The victim has been stabilised but needs emergency evac now! Now get on that radio and get the help needed. I'll stay with the patient but keep in touch with me and find me immediately a stretcher appears. Once she's removed I'll help you. Now get to it!"

The man reacted as most human beings do when faced with a situation which is well outside their experience and where someone else has taken charge, he went along with what he had been told to do and did it.

Help then started to arrive rapidly as the gears in the big emergency machine began to mesh. Parfitt concentrated his efforts on Tammy's evacuation, literally grabbing the arm of the first stretcher carrier he saw and dragging him to Tammy's side. He then walked with her back to the platform, found out which hospital she was being taken to, collected a flashlight and then returned to help. There was nothing more he could do for Tammy. He had seen to it she was now in the hands of the best qualified people, would not be allowed into the operating theatre where she would have to go, and people here desperately needed help. Training and duty once more prevailed.

Training had taught him to put personal interests to one side in an emergency, so he spent a further ninety minutes doing everything he could for other wounded passengers. Three times he was ordered away but each time he refused to go, and nobody wished to argue with a man who had already proved his worth many times over. Finally he could see there was nothing left for him to do. The proper personnel and right equipment had arrived, and for him to stay longer would not help anyone.

As Parfitt climbed onto the platform someone threw a blanket around his shoulders. "We need to get you to a hospital sir." he was told.

"That's okay, I understand the procedure." Parfitt replied. "I'm not injured, so I'm not an urgent case. I'll ride along with someone with mild shock or trauma who needs to talk, and can help with a stretcher if it's any use to you. Your people obviously need as many hands on the ground as they can get."

Injured were still being stretchered away. Those worst cases who had not been trapped were already gone, as had most of the walking wounded. Less urgent cases were being treated by paramedics who were providing emergency on-scene treatment and stabilisation and the required pre-hospital medical and trauma care.

They had arrived at the scene quite rapidly and many lives were saved by their crisis intervention. Parfitt was ushered to a waiting ambulance, and a twist of fate which would one day bring about an unprecedented retaliation put him in the same ambulance as Tom Bryant, now lying bandaged on a stretcher.

Jack and Katya were due to meet Tom and Sandy at approximately nine o'clock outside the Towerhill tube station. This was planned to give Tom and Sandy time to get there, and Jack and Katya sufficient time to stretch their legs with a short saunter over Tower Bridge before meeting.

The young couple completed their walk and were at the appointed rendezvous with five minutes to spare. By ten past nine Jack could see there was something wrong with the tube service. At first it seemed far more people were coming out of the station than were going in. It was not until he noticed someone wearing more outlandish garb, shortly afterwards followed by a girl with noticeable pink hair, entering the station only to reappear within a couple of minutes that he understood station departures must have stopped.

He took Katya by the hand and walked into the station entrance, there to be met by a milling scene of confusion. Initially there was talk of an explosion caused by a power surge on one of the underground lines. Shortly afterwards a report came through of a problem involving a person under a train, to be followed moments later with talk concerning a derailment. At nine-nineteen, whilst Jack and Katya continued to try and get information as to what had happened a Code Amber Alert was declared and London Underground started shutting down its extensive network. Trains were brought into the stations and all services were suspended.

Emerging from Euston Station Chris Spencer and young Charlie knew nothing of the events which led to the pandemonium confronting them. The crowd of people in itself indicated something was wrong and Chris could hear talk of closed underground stations and explosions on the trains. He could see if it were true, and from the number of people present it would indicate it was, his plan to travel around London by bus so Charlie could see more of his capital city could become more than a little complicated.

Chris intended showing Charlie northern and eastern central London first. His basic plan was to travel east showing Charlie the Post Office Tower, then pass the recently finished Gherkin building, and drop down to see the Tower of London, Tower Bridge and H.M.S. Belfast. The following day they would cover the City, the Thames Embankment and the Houses of Parliament, then back up to Knightsbridge, Hyde Park and Oxford Street. However, to do any of that, they first had to get away from the chaos surrounding the stations, so they needed an east bound bus. As luck would have it Chris spotted a red double decker with 30 Hackney Wick on the destination screen. With Charlie following he lightly shouldered his way through the milling crowd and got to the bus where they clambered on board. Chris confirmed the direction of the bus with the driver, paid for the tickets and led the way upstairs. Although many passengers had boarded the bus it was still a long way from being full.

Just over half way down the upper floor of the bus, on the pavement side, Chris spotted two pairs of empty seats, one behind the other. He took the window seat of the front pair and, dropping his overnight bag on the seat beside him, indicated Charlie should take the seat behind which Charlie then did, throwing his bag in first and sitting in the aisle seat. They had just sat down when the bus started to pull away. In the circumstances they had done well getting through the crowds, as the train had only arrived at the station twenty minutes or so earlier.

The bus pulled out of the bus station and should have turned onto Euston Road, but instead was waved across it by a police officer and entered Upper Woburn Place.

"Looks like we'll be getting a magical mystery tour Charlie." Chris said whilst pulling a map and guide book from the pocket of his bag.

Charlie leaned forward with his arms resting on the back of Chris's seat so as he might look at the map which Chris unfolded on the top of his bag. As the bus moved forward in the traffic the guide book placed on top of the bag but under the map shook loose and fell to the floor beneath the seat in front of Chris. They were passing the British Medical Association building, and the bus was in Tavistock Square as Chris reached down to recover the fallen guide book. It was nine-forty-seven.

The violence of the explosion quite literally ripped the roof from the upper deck and utterly demolished the rear end of the bus. Witnesses were later reported to have seen half a bus flying through the air. Those passengers sitting at the front of both lower and upper decks survived, as did the driver. The explosion occurred towards the rear of the bus, behind where Chris and Charlie were sitting, and the brunt of the explosion was borne by those at the rear. Afterwards there was to be a lengthy delay in announcing the toll the bomb had taken in human life because of the extreme physical damage caused to the victim's bodies which were quite literally torn to pieces.

Had his guide book not fallen to the floor at the precise moment it did Chris would have died where he sat. As it was both his head and body were sheltered from the blast. Doubled over facing away with his head well down the series of seat backs protected him from the angle of the blast. Charlie was not so fortunate. Sitting up higher than most his head and both arms were fully exposed to the horrifyingly destructive effects of the explosion and were effortlessly plucked from his body and thrown to the front of the bus. The remains of his body then slumped back into the remnants of the seat before slowly toppling into the aisle.

Chris's professional experiences gained throughout the previous twenty plus years at first screamed out grenade detonation. Milliseconds later he understood it was a bomb, it was a terrorist, and Charlie would be down. Charlie was down. Years of training, of fighting violent deadly battles, of seeing friends and comrades injured, maimed and killed on many battlefronts had hardened him to the shock of savage bloody death and grim destruction. Nothing he had ever known or experienced prepared him for the sight he now saw of his happy, smiling, wonderfully friendly young nephew, the baby boy he had held a feeding bottle for and whose dirty nappies he had willingly changed, whose body now lay in front of him ripped apart and horrifically mutilated.

Battlefield training had taught him anger management, to never lose his temper in a crisis situation, and at all times to protect the innocent and engage only combatants. War is not personal and your enemy may not hate you, some may even respect you. Hatred blinds, and blindness kills. Soldiers of both sides, right or wrong, are only doing their job. The troops on the ground are following orders and, as long as those orders are legal, they should be followed irrespective of consequential loss or personal cost. But these were the streets of London. Charlie was a boy, not a soldier, not a combatant, not even a threat. These other victims were innocent peaceful civilians. There had been no declaration of war and no warning given. Even at the heights of IRA depravity warnings were given and most targets given some chance of being cleared. A semblance of respect for humanity was at least paid lip service. This now was a flagrant act of terrorism by a people with no respect for human life of any kind. This was not war. This was psychopathic butchering and the creatures responsible must be eliminated.

His mind raced through all of this in a fraction of a second. Had there been an available target he would have removed it as efficiently as those he had despatched in the past, streets of London or not. But there was no target. Chris Spencer, army trained and combat hardened, experienced, logical and level headed bringer of death, knew Charlie's savage demise was his fault. He had brought his nephew to this place and his nephew had been brutally and barbarically killed as a result, and it was wholly his responsibility. This was personal. This was as personal as life and death could ever get. This was much more than an attack on his unit, or even himself. This was an open attack on everything he had all of his adult life sworn to protect, defend and preserve, and this attack had cost him the one person in the world of whom he was most fond.

Chris Spencer had chosen profession over marriage and duty over family. To him the two did not mix. To him Charlie was his son by proxy, and he loved him every bit as much as any father possibly could. To him this boy was his only son and that son now lay dead, callously slain in front of him. That was unacceptable and those responsible would suffer.

A cold calm rage filled him. A fury he had never before known.

Tens of thousands from the Muslim world were to die before that fury was sated.

Two

The four bombs officially killed fifty-two commuters, tourists and workers, including the four suicide bombers, with a further seven hundred people injured as a direct result of the explosions. Some lives on the bus were saved because a number of doctors, in or near the British Medical Association building at the time, were on hand to provide immediate emergency medical assistance.

Despite the IRA's bombing campaign during the 'troubles' nothing on this scale had happened in London since the German bombings of WWII, which happened during a time when the British and German peoples were officially and publicly openly engaged at war.

Three

For Jack and Katya confusion reigned supreme. Rumour followed rumour, each overthrowing the last. Staff began to become impatient, constantly asked questions they would have dearly liked to have known the answers to themselves. Jack could see there was some form of major ongoing incident occurring, but at the time was not unduly concerned for his father, apart for the interruption the event would presumably cause to his journey. Attempts to raise his father by mobile phone continued to fail because the sheer number of calls was overloading the system. He and Katya assumed their best course of action was to remain where they had agreed to meet and in the meantime continue to try to make contact by mobile phone. Eventually facts began to slowly filter out, but nothing which helped shed light on their problem, except to now create cause for concern.

The life of Tammy Wild had been saved by the quick thinking, training and ministrations of Peter Parfitt. However he had merely put her life on hold. The real saving of life would only become a long term reality if it were possible to get her to a fully equipped hospital with a level one trauma unit within minutes of putting her on a stretcher. Fortunately The Royal London Hospital is approximately twelve hundred yards from Aldgate tube station and it was to there Tammy was taken.

The Royal London Hospital, part of The Barts and London National Health Service (NHS) Trust, can be found on Whitechapel Road. It operates a level one trauma centre whose department offers a twenty-four hour a day, seven days a week comprehensive emergency service. The service provides and includes senior accident and emergency staff, triage, nurse practitioners, trauma team, CT scanning, cardiac arrest team, decontamination facilities and specialist opinion from all major specialities.

From a helipad above Accident and Emergency (A&E) the Helicopter Medical Emergency Service carries a senior doctor and a paramedic to the scene of serious accidents. The helicopter operates seven days a week during daylight hours, and there is a fast response car for use when the helicopter is unavailable or cannot fly. St Bartholemew's Hospital (Barts) and The London have a major incident response plan which includes the provision of trained, mobile teams and a rota of trained medical incident officers. From Monday to Friday, nine in the morning to five in the afternoon, their Physicians Response Unit responds to medical emergencies in East London and the City, where senior A&E doctors are sent to category A emergencies along with paramedics.

The Aldgate bombing happened on The London's doorstep. The helicopter was not needed. A fleet of ambulances ferried the injured to the hospital where senior doctors and physicians had just come in to work for the day. Tammy Wild owed her life to the timing of the day and her proximity to that particular hospital. A full team worked on her throughout the day and through the night, then through much of the following morning. Her life then hung in the balance for seventy-two hours and she was in a coma for a further sixty. When eventually she came around Peter Parfitt was asleep in a chair at her side.

Not all the Aldgate victims went to The Royal London Hospital as its A&E filled rapidly. By the time Peter Parfitt surfaced The London was only taking emergencies, and he was not one of those. Casualties were being shipped all over London by then with the least urgent being sent the furthest. By his own admission he was uninjured, but he was told he had to go and be checked anyway. His main thought was to get to Tammy and see how she was, so he was quite happy to be put in an ambulance, along with Tom Bryant, which was going to St Barts, as that was where he thought she had already been taken. Along the way he listened to Tom who was more agitated at his loss than hurt by his injuries. Parfitt knew he must engage the man in conversation to stop him going into shock, and it helped to partially get his own mind off Tammy and her terrible injuries.

As Parfitt listened to Tom Bryant he could not help but feel sorry for the man's losses, despite his own agonising problems. Tom Bryant was in a state of mental torment and obviously felt a passionate hatred for those with a non European background which had not sprung from the day's events alone. On the way into hospital Bryant talked of his Mary, the life they had lived together, their home and kids, and the way it was all swept away in the hit and run accident which had taken her. He then told the story of how Sandy came into his life and slowly chased the demons from his mind. It had taken him a long time he explained, but he had come to deeply love her for her patience, kindness and the depth of her character.

Now Sandy was gone too, her life taken by the hand of a man with the same coloured skin as the one who killed his Mary and then tried to run away. Parfitt was concerned about Tom Bryant's ability to be able to deal with the events psychologically. Bryant seemed to be a genuinely decent and honest sort of individual, not very worldly, and certainly not the kind Parfitt would ever think to befriend, but definitely a decent dependable family man, despite his repeated desire for vengeance on a grand scale. He had clearly been deeply traumatised by his wife's death and left with a huge emotional scar – and now this. As Peter Parfitt listened he made a mental note to check up on Tom Bryant, after he caught up with Tammy, just to see how he made out.

Peter certainly had his own problems to deal with, and he knew they would haunt him for a long while to come, but he knew his sanity would hold up. He too would need to talk, but not to a civilian, even some well meaning counsellor. He needed to debrief, and that would mean sitting down with a military man who would listen and talk without some pathetic look of kindly sorrow written across their silly all-knowing know-nothing faces. He didn't need or want sorrow or sympathy; he needed to describe, examine and report, and would then need a mission.

Chris Spencer was a battle-seasoned front line solider that was used to taking control of situations and issuing commands coolly and calmly in the heat of a deadly fire fight. It would have done no good to those in his squad if he could not keep it together under pressure and in fact he would never have worked his way up to the position he had held if any report said he was anything but wholly dependable and completely unflappable under fire. His impassive relaxed courage was hugely inspirational to his troops who having followed him into battle once would have gladly marched with him through the gates of hell itself and taken on the devil in person if asked.

His country had called upon him to put himself in harms way on several occasions and he had always done so, standing fore square in the face of any and all enemy action. But those enemies of his country could usually be identified by the uniforms they wore, and the actions they took were generally mounted against those wearing uniforms like his. He had met those in battle who were both well equipped and well trained, and trodden the desert sands to take on a ragtag rabble army of poorly equipped but fiercely determined men fighting in their own homeland. Without question the IRA had carried out many terrible atrocities. They were terrorists and he had despised them for their tactics, but by comparison with this new breed of low life scum they could almost be looked back upon as gentlemen.

The people doing this, their parents and families, came to his country fleeing the problems of their homeland, the grinding poverty, lack of education, sanitation, medication and shortened life expectancies. Many came claiming political asylum, with tales of oppression, torture and death. They came with nothing, and could offer little to the land in which they chose to settle, save the problems they brought with them, the very problems they claimed to be running from. That land, his land, repeatedly took them in, protected them, nurtured them, offered comfort and gave them a sense of future and aspirations beyond their wildest dreams. In return they turned upon their host, and this death and destruction around him was how they repaid his country's help and goodwill. Well he knew the trade. He had done his apprenticeship, and he was now a master at the craft. He would take this back to them. If need be he would take them out one by one, more at a time if he could get help, and he was pretty sure he knew were he could get at least some.

At that moment he felt completely helpless. Charlie was dead and there was nothing he could do about it. The wounded on the bus were being treated where they were by highly qualified doctors who had rushed from the BMA building. No need for field dressings and nothing else he could do to help. The whole thing was a state of civilian chaos. The perpetrator died from the explosion of his bomb, classic suicide bomber tactic, so was presumably operating alone. The targeted bus was moving at the time of the explosion, probably chosen at random, and was diverted, so it would be reasonable to assume there were no back-up devices in close proximity, if at all. The police ordered him off the bus, and asked if he was travelling with anyone. He explained about Charlie, and the young police officer was a little taken aback at the calm manner in which the death was reported. His details were taken down and he was ordered to hospital. He needed to know where Charlie's body would be taken and was told he would be informed. The police wanted to clear the area so their various teams to come in to check, investigate and eventually remove everything.

He was taken to hospital along with everyone else who was either injured, travelling with injured passengers, or with a passenger who had died. Standard procedure. Check for shock, offer counselling then if all was well make a police statement. He wasn't in shock and he knew it, but he didn't really know where else to go or what to do. He was too fresh out of the military and was yet to get used to life where there were no procedures to follow. As they approached he could see St Barts was full of people from the various explosions. There was going to be a long wait, but life in the Army had taught him patience, and he may just learn something of his enemy.

Arriving twenty minutes earlier Parfitt had ridden to the hospital in the ambulance as asked. It was obvious St Barts had geared themselves up for the sudden influx of casualties they were receiving. He could only imagine the complete chaos which must have occurred as the first of the injured started to arrive in what presumably appeared to be by the coach load. However they now had a workable system in place, although the system naturally discriminated against the able bodied, such as himself. The hospital was inundated with casualties, and they were quite rightly getting priority. He endeavoured to obtain information about Tammy but was instructed to wait by the person he spoke to on reception, and again by one of the team of police officers who were slowly working their way through those who could and would talk to them. For the police it was going to be a long and highly labour intensive investigation.

There was little for Parfitt to do except that which was requested. All seats were taken, not that he had any inclination to sit, so he found himself a position near the door, reasoning if it was going to be a long drawn out frustrating time, and certainly it was going to be all of that, then at least he could spend the time people watching. It was the last thing he wanted to do with Tammy lying on a hospital operating table somewhere fighting for her life, but there were no other options given the circumstances. He was shocked at the sheer scale of the numbers of people still being brought into the hospital, and could see that system or no system the resources were being swamped by all manner of people, from emergency cases still arriving in ambulances as they were cut loose from the wrecked carriages, to those with no outward sign of any form of injury, much like himself.

A helpful passer-by gave him a clean white T-shirt and he put it on. It was at least a size too small for him but it was something to wear whilst he waited. The cleanliness of the shirt stood in stark contrast to his arms and face still covered in Tammy's and others dried blood. Air Force training had kept him fit at the time, and since leaving he had always maintained at least a reasonable level of fitness, running, swimming and working out with weights, so his body was still in better than fair shape. Standing at the door as he was, wearing a skin tight T-shirt, with arms and face covered in matted blood he gave the overwhelming impression of a deranged doorman, and it was small wonder no one approached him or attempted to make conversation.

Parfitt saw Chris Spencer as he arrived and immediately recognised him for the hardened warrior he was. Chris had already observed Peter standing by the door as he scanned the area whilst the ambulance he was in drew to a halt, and he too noticed the military bearing, instantly understanding Parfitt was a fly boy from sixty paces away. Spencer made his way to the information and reception area where he too was turned back and told to wait. He then made his way across to where Parfitt was standing and opened a conversation which was to eventually have dire consequences for the Muslim peoples of the world with two words.

"Air Force." It was delivered as a statement rather than a question.

Parfitt inclined his head and, raising an eyebrow replied, "Was. Army?"

"Until recently. Green Howards."

"You're a long way from home. How did you get caught up in this?" Parfitt asked, catching the unmistakable accent of the Yorkshireman.

"I brought my nephew down as a birthday treat and the bastards butchered him." Chris Spencer replied in a cold matter of fact voice which left Parfitt in no doubt as to both how much it meant to him, and how truly dangerous the man was. "And you?"

"My fiancée was blown to pieces. She's still alive I think, but only just. She lost a leg, an arm, the other foot, one of her breasts, an ear, an eye, half her jaw and part of her scalp." As he reeled off Tammy's injuries the enormity of what had happened suddenly hit home, and he literally staggered as if he had been violently struck.

Chris Spencer had seen it before and realised the fly boy needed to talk and keep talking to avoid shock setting in. That or sedation, and the hospital was busy enough as it was.

"Tell me what happened." Chris Spencer instructed. "Leave nothing out. You'll need to go through it again later with the police. We all will. So go through it with me now and get the thing in order in your head. Start from when you left home this morning and talk me through everything until you arrived at this hospital."

Nathan knew nothing of the explosions. He had left the tube which was carrying Susie and transferred onto the Hammersmith & City line, stepping aboard his train as the doors were closing. He was carried away from King's Cross St Pancras before the Circle Line train, thereby missing the explosion, which would have at least delayed his departure and indicated there were problems with the underground system. He arrived at his office still blissfully unaware and settled into his work, which was mainly of an administrative nature. The intention was for him to enjoy lunch in central London with Susie and Chi Lu, and he intended to get as much done as he could before then.

Shut away in his office he continued with the paperwork, having asked his personal assistant to field all his calls unless any were absolutely imperative in nature. This was done and he was not disturbed for more than an hour. The person who eventually managed to speak to him was Chi Lu, who called him from Heathrow on his private mobile phone. She was waiting for Susie to turn up, had tried to call her on her mobile several times, and wondered if Nathan had heard from her. Chi Lu assumed Susie was delayed by the tube bombings and was ringing through to Nathan to let him know she was taking a taxi whilst she had the chance, would come straight through to Nathan's office, and would keep trying Susie's phone on the way.

Knowing nothing of the bombings until Chi Lu's call Nathan was surprised to hear the news, even more so that it should come from Chi Lu. Unknown to Nathan Susie's body was still on the train. Rescue workers had quite properly first concentrated their efforts on the living, moving the walking wounded out, stretchering others out as best they could, and administering to those on site who needed help or were trapped. They were still to address the grisly problem of removing the dead and were a long way from identifying them. Nathan's reaction to Chi Lu's call was to immediately try to get hold of Susie, in which he failed, getting only an intercept telling him it was not possible to connect his call. He tried to put it out of his mind and returned to his work, but could not concentrate. As the minutes ticked by and half an hour became an hour frustration and mild concern was replaced with genuine worry. Several more attempts to contact Susie all failed and by the time Chi Lu eventually made it across London the first cold fingers of dread were creeping along his spine. He was not yet frantic with worry as such, but an inner sense was somehow triggered and he instinctively knew his life from that point on was never going to be the same again, and that his entire future and the life he had dreamt of from childhood had just been ripped from him and thoroughly destroyed.

Time was passing yet Jack and Katya were getting nowhere. News eventually filtered through indicating several bombs had exploded on the underground system, but details were anything but clear. By eleven o'clock Jack realised something was badly wrong. He could understand his father may have found himself caught up in things, but not for two hours without making some form of contact. Jack used a payphone and rang through to his brother to ask if Dan had heard from their father as he had repeatedly failed to make contact on his mobile phone, but Dan had not. Jack arranged he would continue to telephone Dan every hour to check, as mobile lines were still jammed virtually continually. Dan assumed, correctly, they would probably remain that way for some time, as people in a similar situation to Jack would constantly keep trying to get in touch with loved ones until they succeeded, all the time overloading the system.

There was something wrong, badly wrong, and Jack knew it. It wasn't so much he sensed something was wrong, but logic dictated to him, and that dictation screamed at him due to the circumstances his father would have called home, turned up in a taxi or made his way by bus or even foot if necessary. Somehow contact would have been made, if not with him then at least with Danny. Two hours late after a bomb blast meant his father was directly caught up in things, which meant he was probably in trouble, and Jack had already determined at least one of the explosions occurred on the Circle line, the line his father should have been using. There was a possibility his father was on a train on which an explosive devise detonated. If he and Sandy were, then either one or both may have been hurt, but statistically for such events to come together and affect his father was unlikely.

However it could not be ruled out completely so, given the lack of other viable options, perhaps the possibility should be investigated. But how?

There were long queues at bus stops and he had not seen one empty taxi. Ten minutes earlier the queues for the busses almost completely dispersed when a rumour spread about a bus also exploding in another part of the city, but they quickly reassembled. Inactivity was going to get him nowhere, and he would learn little more, if anything, from where he was currently stationed. In the two hours he and Katya had remained waiting they at least were able to establish where the Circle Line explosion took place. Aldgate was only one stop away from them, and Liverpool Street one more. At worst Liverpool Street was three quarters of a mile away, a fifteen minute walk, or a leisurely twenty, not that leisurely would be the order of the day.

He briefly explained his thoughts and reasoning to Katya, who fully agreed, and the pair set off to walk firstly to Aldgate. The roads approaching the station were cordoned off with the police on duty turning everyone away. Emergency workers could be seen scurrying back and forth, and several news crews had taken up the best visual positions resembling a flock of greedy vultures. A young police special stopped them as they drew near and began on what was obviously a well rehearsed speech. Jack immediately stopped him and explained his situation. The pimply faced special was so young that even to Jack he looked as if he should not be out without his mother. He could do nothing to help, but Jack was not interested in what he could not do, he wanted something done, and done then. Pushing past the baby faced special Jack headed in the direction of a more experienced looking police officer, who rounded on him angrily having seen him ignore his junior. Remaining calm Jack explained his position to the officer and gratefully found the man responded helpfully.

Two and a half hours had elapsed since the first of the explosions and the emergency services were starting to get on top of the situation. Years of coordinated planning, exercises and dry run rehearsals were obviously paying off, although it could also be seen the grim reality was much worse than any practice. The police officer felt the young couple in front of him were genuine and radioed through the two names Jack provided. Four minutes later the answer came back for one of the names. Jack now at least knew where his father was, and could make his way there.

Peter Parfitt told the background story which led to his arriving at the hospital to Chris Spencer, leaving out none of the gory details of what happened to Tammy. The talking helped, although it opened his eyes to the enormity and long term implications of the terrible situation. Chris Spencer was precisely the type of person he needed. He listened, he occasionally probed a little, and he clearly took things in. He stood throughout Peter's story with a neutral expression on his face, with no outward sign of the anger which was continuing to build within him

Parfitt finished his 'debrief' and felt he should attempt to reciprocate by asking Chris about his loss. Apart from a very slight narrowing of his eyes, Chris Spencer's face remained neutral and completed unfathomable. He would not be drawn into a conversation about the death of his young nephew, or anything leading up to it, but when he spoke his voice had a hard edge to it. Parfitt recognised Spencer for what he was, a man of action, not of words. If he said he had done something, then he had done it! If Spencer said he was going to do something, Parfitt absolutely knew the man would see it through. Throughout his entire life Peter Parfitt had lived around men of action, and had over time learnt how to read them. Nobody would have to tell him he was now in the company of, and talking to, probably the most dangerous man he had ever met, a man who could doubtless kill in at least a dozen ways with his bare hands alone, and probably a hundred ways given a knife, steel wire or length of rope. And the man was angry – very, very angry!

"We cannot just let this go." Chris Spencer said in a determined but quite voice. "We have to take this back to them! We know who they are and where they live. We have to teach them they cannot do this sort of thing to our people in our country. We have to make them pay such a heavy penalty this kind of mindless violence is no longer a viable option!"

"The trouble is the police and the courts have their hands tied." Parfitt reasoned. "If those who helped and planned this are caught their sentences will not even partially reflect what they have done!

"I'm not interested in police and courts!" Chris Spencer exclaimed. "This is something which we the people have to sort out. These animals must be flushed out and eradicated, as must all those which help and support them. For too long we have had a liberal pussy society. A line has to be drawn in the sand here today. We, the indigenous people of these islands, have been pushed too far. It is time to push back!"

"Interestingly you are not alone in those sentiments." Parfitt noted. "The chap I mentioned crashing into me on the train and who I rode here in the ambulance with said very much the same."

"Then let us go and speak to him. Let us speak to all who will listen. We have to change this. If our politicians feel this is acceptable our security forces cannot stop it, and believe me I've been there – they can't. The police and courts have their hands tied as you say, so it is the likes of us who will have to find a way. We can stop it!" As he spoke an idea was forming in Chris Spencer's head. He would not speak about it, would not rant or make threats, but he would do something about avenging Charlie no matter whether he had help or not. Help would be good, but if it was not forthcoming he would go in alone. He had not known what to do with his life before – but now he had a mission.

Neither man knew what to do with themselves. They both had to wait for the police. Peter wanted to find Tammy, and Chris Spencer could do nothing else until he found out where they were to take Charlie's body. The two men agreed they may as well stick together, but Peter had to first see how Tom Bryant was getting along, as he had promised he would. Chris Spencer decided to tag along; at least it would be a break from the monotony of just standing around waiting. They headed back to reception together and this time Parfitt managed to get the information he needed about Tammy. She was not in the same hospital, but was undergoing emergency surgery, and he would not be admitted. Tom Bryant however they could see, and both agreed to go up straight away.

As they left reception to do so a young woman stepped out of a telephone booth leaving it empty. Chris Spencer stepped straight in to make three of the hardest calls of his life, one each to his sister, his parents, and Jimmy Andrews.

It was apparent to Chi Lu Nathan was terribly overwrought. She was also aware she was unlikely to be able to perform at her usual peak performance because, although her flight had been uneventful, and as comfortable as transatlantic flights can ever be, she had not slept well and was nine hours out on her body clock time. However it was quite obvious she would have to take control of the situation as Nathan was on the verge of falling apart.

London was in chaos as she had journeyed across, although not as badly as she had anticipated in the centre as many of the streets were empty. It seemed most people had just given up and made their way home any way they could. Despite which it still took her nearly two hours to make her way from Heathrow where she had waited almost an hour for Susie before taking a taxi, and whom she had called repeatedly throughout the journey whenever her phone could get service, but to no effect.

Chi Lu could see the events in London overrode all other considerations. It was pointless trying to get any of the staff to continue with their usual work, so those who wished to leave were sent home. Those who stayed were put to work gathering information from any possible source. They as a company had multiple press contacts, and many reporters owed favours to NJF, some of which were called in. The police and hospitals were contacted, but all to no avail, Susie had disappeared, and disappearance in the circumstances was ominous. Chi Lu contacted Jake Ferris who put everything else on hold and drove over, suggesting they should personally visit those hospitals which had taken in bomb victims whilst the NJF staff kept up information gathering. He arranged for a second car and two drivers to be sent for their use and in a private aside suggested Chi Lu should stay with Nathan throughout until such time as Susie was located. So it was they set off in the two cars to scour the hospitals of London.

It was not Nathan, Chi Lu or Jake who eventually located Susie, but instead one of the telephone order girls who had stayed behind to help. She managed to get through to someone who broke established protocol and passed on the information all were dreading to hear. She reluctantly reported the news to Iain McGregor, who in turn, with a breaking voice and tears over spilling to run down his cheeks, telephoned the information through to Jake. Susie and the baby were dead. Their remains were in a hospital mortuary awaiting forensic examination and a post mortem, although cause of death was obvious. Jake instructed the driver to pull over, and for the first time since his childhood broke down and sobbed for the loss of the girl he regarded almost as a daughter, and for the baby he would never watch grow up or even get to hold or know.

It took Jake almost fifteen minutes before he felt he could manage to make the call to Chi Lu. Without telling her why he ordered her back to the office, to where he would return and break the news to Nathan personally. It was to be the worse duty he had ever been called upon to perform in his fifty-seven years of life, after which it was also necessary to inform the Gatting family.

Having stopped on the way to ring through to Danny, Jack Bryant and Katya arrived at St Barts Hospital, where they enquired at reception, were given his father's ward information, and proceeded through a very busy hospital to find him. They walked past his bed on the first pass, not recognising him as he sat talking to two large fit men; one covered in blood and wearing a very tight t-shirt and the other with a distinct military bearing, neither of which Jack knew. A nurse directed them back to Tom, who recognised Jack, a small smile crossing his lips for the first time since the bomb went off. His left arm was plastered and left hand bandaged, as was part of his chest which, along with his face, showed signs of several small cuts. From his actions and reactions he was obviously lightly sedated, but could still manage speech and was aware of his surroundings.

"Jack!" Tom Bryant almost shouted, breaking off from what Peter Parfitt was saying, then turned back to the men talking to him he said "This is Jack, my youngest son, the brains of the family. Jack this is Peter and Chris. They too have been caught up in this terrible business."

The two men reached out their hands and shook Jack's then Katya's.

"I guess we'd better go." Parfitt said to Chris Spencer.

"Please do not leave on our account unless you have somewhere special to go." Jack told them and then continued, "I would like to hear as much as I can of events if possible and, if you gentlemen know anything, I should be grateful if you would share it."

Chris Spencer looked impassively at the younger man. There was something about him he thought, he has a natural authority well beyond his years, and the bearing to go with it. His handshake was firm and his hand warm and dry. His eyes met unflinchingly, and Chris could appreciate the depths of the young man's character. Jack immediately reminded him of a young officer he once served under for whom he learnt to have enormous respect. The officer's tactical planning ability and intelligence had seemed boundless, and he was rapidly promoted. They are from the same mould Chris thought, while abstractedly wondering how Jack would perform as a military tactician.

Neither he nor Peter Parfitt had anywhere pressing to go, so Chris Spencer made the decision for both. The decision was to form another link in the chain, and was triggered by the simple words, "We have nowhere to go. We will stay and help where we can for a few minutes then leave you with your father. You will be able to find us in the reception area afterwards if you wish to talk any more."

Chris Spencer and Peter Parfitt stayed for fifteen minutes, during which time Jack learnt of Sandy Cartwright's death. He heard of the horrific injuries to Tammy, a woman he didn't know, but who had his genuine sympathies, and of the death of young Charlie. Both then left Jack and Katya alone with Tom Bryant and returned to reception, where they continued to wait and to talk. Three times they were interrupted. Once by a member of the hospital staff, checking up to see if they needed attention, as most cases had been or were being dealt with. They needed no help except information, on how Tammy was doing, and where Charlie's body had or would be taken. The young female orderly left them and returned a second time ten minutes later with information for both. The third interruption was from a police officer who asked after their details and connections, and enquired as to when it would be convenient for both to make statements.

The officer also informed Chris Spencer most of the bodies had by then been recovered and identified from what they were carrying. However a formal identification was still required, and could he make himself available the following morning, around mid morning, if he felt up to the task. As he was about to finish Jack Bryant joined the group. Jack explained his father was being kept in for observation in case of delayed shock. He was just popping out to buy pyjamas, fruit and drinks for his father but would be back to talk to Peter and Chris. The police officer enquired as to who he was, and then asked if he would be able, and available, to identify the body of Sandy Cartwright the following morning, to which he gave a positive answer.

The police officer left and Peter Parfitt asked, "Where are you both staying tonight?"

"Katya and I were supposed to have been going down to Hampshire for the night, but that has now changed completely." Jack explained. "In fact my brother is on his way up here to see Dad. We were in a hotel last night and our bags are still there. We may be able to check back in. Accommodation was one of the things I intended to sort out whilst I was out of the hospital. What about you chaps?"

"I have no idea at present." Chris Spencer said. "I had a room booked for Charlie and myself just south of the river for tonight, but I can't see the point in going down there now. I may as well get something closer for tonight. I don't have any change of clothes as I had to leave my bag on the bus, but the cop said I should get it back tomorrow after the identification process. So I don't know!"

"I haven't a clue either." Peter Parfitt admitted. "Tammy and I were staying out at her house at Cookham Dean, but tonight was to be the last night we were to spend in it. We were to see the estate agents this afternoon to run through the last details with them. Everything is packed up at the house and ready to ship. Her car is at Hendon currently being serviced. To be honest I don't want to go back there tonight, so I think I'll stick around locally as well." He looked at Spencer. "Maybe we could find a hotel with a couple of rooms together? Then at least we can have a pint or two and a chat."

"Sounds like a plan to me." Chris Spencer agreed.

"Well, I have to collect our bags and then find two rooms anyway. One for Katya and myself and a single room for my brother." Jack said. "Would you like me to see if I can book four? Then if you have no objections we could join you for that drink. We may be able to help one another with clothes etcetera and we have to do the identification bit in the morning. Danny is driving up as we speak, so we'll have a car available to us, and we could drop you back to your car in the morning Peter. I'm most grateful to you for what you did to help my father, in fact to both of you for taking the time to keep him company, so I feel it is the least I can do."

"I'd certainly go along with that if the hotel is local and not too plush." Parfitt replied. "Especially if you have a shirt and pair of jeans I could borrow. We seem to be about the same size. Above all I could use a shower."

"Cool!" Chris Spencer said. "Gets my vote. Guess I'd better find a place to buy a shirt!"

"Okay." Jack said. "I'll see what I can do. A shirt and jeans is no problem Peter, and don't worry Chris, I'm sure Danny will have spare shirts, although they may be a bit big on you."

Chris Spencer just nodded. Big on me, how big is this guy, he thought, but said nothing.

Jake Ferris did his duty. He loathed the thought of what he had to do, but accepted that ultimately it was probably better coming from him than it would have been from a stranger, especially from a stranger in police uniform. Chi Lu was sent to speak with Iain McGregor whilst Jake sat Nathan down to break the terrible news to him. In that way both would be informed at the same time, but it would be easier on Chi Lu not to have to be in the same room at the time with Nathan. Jake's sensitivity in the way he dealt with the situation greatly impressed Chi Lu, gaining him many points of respect, every single one of which he would gladly have thrown away if it meant changing any aspect of what had become the worst day of his life, and was infinitely more so for Nathan.

Nathan already knew before Jake told him. Somehow he had known and Jake was merely confirming what was already obvious. Maybe it was his background, his upbringing, or the bad luck which had dogged every minute of his early life. Whatever it was Jake realised somehow Nathan already knew, and the knowledge had quite literally crushed him. He appeared stooped, the skin of his face seemed to droop, and he had aged a good ten years since the morning. The younger man who sat before him, approaching his thirtieth birthday, was a multi billionaire, yet he had nothing. Everything which contributed to Nathan's world was gone, destroyed by an act of monstrous inhumanity the second the bomb on the train on which Susie was travelling detonated. Money meant nothing to him, yet his wife and daughter-to-be had meant everything. Jake knew Nathan was one of those incredibly rare super-successful people who would quite literally give everything for his family, yet nothing was asked, and still their lives were taken. Taken by creatures from a culture Nathan had always been careful to respect.

NJF Industries was very much an equal opportunity employer. Differentiation based on sex, colour or culture did not exist within the greater company, and had not from inception. People were employed purely on merit. Susie had been the head of an enlightened company which employed many hundreds of people directly, thousands indirectly, many of whom were Muslim. Yet Muslims struck her and many others down without care, thought or regard. Money generated by NJF did, through those Muslims employed, find its way back to their lands, to improve the lives of those which remained there and increase their life expectancies and chances. Jake knew it was not the fault of those employed by NJF, but he now despised them for the seeming utter contempt for human life demonstrated by those of their culture. A small voice inside his head screaming to be heard was saying, "It was nothing personal, she was just an unfortunate casualty of war." But a much louder voice boomed back "This was a friend, almost a daughter! It cannot get worse than that! This was a heavily pregnant innocent woman! If I had my way every single one of you disgusting cowardly fuckers would be exterminated!"

Jake knew in part this was a gut reaction. However he had no time to dwell upon his thoughts. Upset though he was, and he could not remember ever being more so, the young man in front of him needed his help and support, and no matter what he was going to get it. For the present that meant being there for him and helping him in just about every aspect of his life. Nathan's reason for living had been taken from him. If something could not be found to replace it, and replace it very soon, Nathan would also die. His heart was completely broken and his will to live already gone. Someone would have to stay with him for a while to come, and for the most part Jake could see it would have to be him. Tonight he would book them both into a hotel. Chi Lu and the staff would have to look after Nathan in the morning, because at ten o'clock he was meeting Phil Gatting at the hospital mortuary to formally identify Susie's body. Jake considered it was not a task Nathan should be expected to perform and, horrible and unappealing though it was, Jake felt he should be there, if only to support Phil Gatting who he could not forget had just lost his youngest daughter and unborn granddaughter.

Jack and Katya collected their bags and Jack booked the required rooms in a hotel belonging to a large multinational chain within half a mile of St Barts and near Liverpool Street tube station. The booking proved to be simplicity itself as the hotel had suffered a large number of cancellations, as presumably many others had in the area that night. Although uniform and characterless, the rooms were comfortable and not ridiculously priced. The hotel offered all the amenities the small group required and by early evening all were settled in, with the exception of Danny Bryant who was en route from The New Forest. Peter Parfitt managed to take the shower he so desperately needed, then changed into a clean shirt and fresh jeans provided by Jack.

Clean and far more comfortable once again Parfitt ordered a taxi which took him to The Royal London Hospital in an attempt to either see Tammy or to obtain information about her. It was explained to him there was no chance of seeing her as she was still undergoing emergency surgery. The receptionist suggested it was also pointless his waiting because there was nothing whatsoever he could do. Tammy was critical. She would be in the operating theatre throughout the night and in intensive care for some time afterwards – if she survived. It would not be possible for him to see her for at least forty-eight hours, but he should leave a contact number in case of emergencies. He left the Royal within ten minutes of entering and once more returned to the hotel by taxi.

Parfitt found Chris Spencer sitting in the hotel bar engaged in conversation with Jack as he re-entered the hotel. Both had pints of Guinness in front of them and as he joined them he ordered the same. Chris Spencer asked how Tammy was but Parfitt could only relay the lack of news he had just received.

"This is a bad business." Chris Spencer said. "I can't see there will be any payback from the authorities. When al-Qaeda took out the twin towers in New York it forced the Americans into action in Afghanistan, but the Madrid train bombings brought no retaliation from the Spanish, and the last penny of my money would be on the same happening here. Sure the authorities will wring their hands and wail, the press will be all self-righteous and indignant, and the police will rush around like headless chickens in order to be seen to be doing something, only to write some pointless report. I don't know about you two, but that's not going to be good enough for me. Not by a million fucking miles!"

"The difficulty is there is nothing much anyone can do." Parfitt said. "We can put Members of Parliament under a bit of pressure by writing fairly strongly worded letters, but they'll have little or no effect. We can petition for harsher penalties for those caught helping, funding or sheltering, but apart from a few new statutes little else will be done. I find what has happened utterly unacceptable but we are personally involved and have suffered loss. The society in which we live will be pissed off about the whole event for a few days, but then life will return to normal for them and they will soon forget all about it."

"And do you find that acceptable?" Chris Spencer asked slightly aggressively.

"No I don't! Not at all! But that is the reality of the situation, and we would be kidding ourselves to think otherwise." Parfitt replied rather shortly. "What on Earth can we possibly do about it?"

"We could take direct retaliatory action ourselves!" Spencer answered.

"Oh come on Chris, the law would then be against us. Anyway what would we do? Burn down a few Muslim businesses? Firebomb a mosque?" Parfitt asked scornfully.

"It would be a start, but nowhere near enough!" Chris Spencer answered him quietly. "I was thinking more of finding out who these people were, which will come out soon enough, and taking it back to them."

"I understand how you feel, but the bombers are all dead!" Parfitt reasoned.

"Of course the bombers are dead!" Spencer snorted, "But these people do not act in isolation, they work in cells, just like the IRA did. They also have families and will most definitely attend a mosque. They will have been trained somewhere and financed by someone. The key is to find the pattern, find who radicalised them, watch them and find another cell member, take them and break them."

Both Parfitt and Jack Bryant suddenly understood how very serious Chris Spencer was, and from the way he spoke neither doubted that not only did he know what he was talking about, but he had unquestionably carried out such operations in the past.

"Chris, I appreciate how you feel," Jack broke in. "My mother was killed by a hit and run driver, and my father nearly went mad. Sandy Cartwright, Dad's girlfriend, spent years getting him back on track, and now she too has been killed. The hit and run driver was an illegal immigrant and was a Muslim, doubtless as were the bombers. This could well send my father over the top into madness, and if such happens I shall have lost my mother, father and a very dear friend and stepmother-to-be to these bastards. Additionally my girlfriend lost her brother to them. She will not talk about it but her brother suffered a terrible drawn out death. I would happily see them all dead. However I should caution you the conversation we are now engaged in is in itself illegal on several levels, from incitement to racism. Please be careful with whom you discuss these things. You are entirely safe with both me and Katya and I can assure you, with my brother also. I assume the same goes for you too Peter?" Jack asked, raising one eyebrow to Parfitt.

"Oh, absolutely! Definitely! I feel very much the same way myself." Parfitt answered. "It's just I believe time and distance from this event will help, and in time scars will heal. That sounds a little bleeding heart liberal, I know, and I don't mean to, but right now we are reacting in the heat of the moment, and I'm not so sure it is either sensible, or the best time to talk about such things."

"That is indeed a very good point." Jack conceded. "However I must admit I am intrigued by what Chris has said, and would like to hear more. I would also like to add something. I've recently spent some time in Russia, which is where I met Katya. You're both military men so you'll have heard of Alpha Group. Katya's uncle was a member of Alpha Group, and has explained some of their thinking and operations to me. Some of what they did in the past, especially in Chechnya, would fit very nicely into what I would like to do to those close to these bombers."

"Does this uncle maintain contacts with those in Alpha Group?" Chris Spencer asked.

"Yes, I believe he does." Jack replied. "There is another point I would like to make. Chris you mentioned funding and training. Training would presumably require travel. Money and travel can both be traced. If you are looking for patterns they would emerge from such movements."

"Undoubtedly," Spencer retorted. "However you would need access to some fairly sophisticated computers inside either the better security services or the upper echelons of a very large multinational banking corporation, and we wouldn't have that."

"Maybe not the security services." Jack Bryant said. "But the computers of the banking industry are easy. That's part of my job, and I could check out a lot of things on different mainframes around Europe, although my bet is the information would best come out of Moscow. People there are used to investigations."

As he finished three people arrived at their table at once. Katya who had finished showering and freshening up in their room stepped out of the lift and walked across to join the three she knew at the table. Simultaneously to the lift doors opening a giant of a man came ducking through the front doors. Crossing the foyer towards the reception desk he changed his direction part way and headed for them. As he and Katya approached the waiter arrived as if he possessed a sixth sense.

The waiter was dealt with first, and disappeared with an order for five drinks, four of them Guinness and a dry white wine for Katya. With the waiter gone Jack set about introducing his big brother to everyone else there, finishing with Katya. Even Chris Spencer, who had worked around some big fit males in his time was impressed at the size of Danny Bryant, the guy, he thought, was simply huge. From birth Danny Bryant had always been big, but at twenty-five the last few years had seen his shoulders widen and his chest grow to the size of a not so small barrel. He had spent many long hours underwater whilst diving which, with eight years experience, was something he now taught to others. His rugby, diving, swimming and the water skiing all contributed to his extreme physical development. Danny was as strong as the proverbial ox, and looked it. Now I see why his spare shirt might be big on me, Chris thought with a wry smile, but again kept it to himself.

"Good to see you bro!" Dan said to Jack hugging his younger brother with one massive arm as he did. "I just wish it were under better circumstances! It's a shame we can't do something to badly hurt these bastards in return. Sorry Katya." He smiled apologetically in her direction, but she just smiled back and shook her head, still slightly overawed at the size of him.

"Interestingly we were discussing precisely that as you arrived." Jack told him.

"Really? Well we as a society should definitely take a tougher line with the animals. But, that aside for a minute, how's Dad?" Danny asked. "Will Sandy's death send him over the edge this time? First Mum and now this! Can he take her loss and hold it together? I can't believe Sandy's gone. She was such a brilliant person, and I was the one responsible for their meeting. God I wish I could get my hands on some of those little mothers, I would happily break them to pieces." His words tumbled out, and it was self-evident which subject had occupied his mind throughout the drive to London.

The conversation resumed very much where it had left off. Of the group Katya was the one exception in she had not had anyone close to her killed or maimed that day. However the events brought back to her the hate, anger and bitterness she felt at her brother's death, and the feelings of intense satisfaction whenever she heard another one of the creatures responsible was dispatched at the hand of her Uncle Yuri. She understood the mistrust and loathing of another race, but simply could not comprehend the British attitude of forgiveness and tolerance to those who wished to destroy their very society. To her Russian mind the British were a polite and courteous yet industrious people, and all those qualities required education and intelligence. So how could an educated and intelligent people be so stupid? Why did they let these lesser beings with their contemptible cultures and despicable values enter their once proud land? These 'New English' were the dregs of the world. Even their own countries did not want them. So why did the British, and of the British almost exclusively the English, let these creatures come to their beautiful and richly historic land? Surely when you have a cancer you cut it out? If your dog attacks your children do you not have the thing destroyed?

Katya became caught up in her own thoughts. She suddenly realised she hadn't been listening and Jack had asked her a question. "Sorry" she said in Russian, and continued in the same language, "I was daydreaming – remembering Maxim. What was it you asked me?"

Jack repeated his question in Russian. "You were asked if Yuri still has contacts within Alpha Force." Katya confirmed he did, and Jack passed it on.

"That was a neat switch of language." Peter Parfitt said, and then asked mostly for conversation. "How good is your Russia?"

Dan answered for him. "His languages are incredible, he is fluent in Russian, Spanish, French and German, and seems to have the ability to learn another language in a matter of weeks. A very useful guy to have with you if ever you are out of the country!" Dan was proud of his younger brother, and didn't mind who knew. "But then Katya is fluent in a whole bunch too. They're smart people!" he added proudly.

Attempting to bring the conversation back to the subject in hand Jack said. "Tomorrow we have to identify our dead. Shall we work out who wishes to go with whom, times and anything else we may need to discuss?" There were nods all around. "Following which, are we agreed we'd like to see something done about this dreadful situation?" More nods. "Do we think the authorities are going to do anything radical about it?" All heads were shaken. "Then if we are not satisfied with it should we at some date in the near future arrange to meet up again, after we've buried our loved ones, in order to discuss possible moves forward?"

"I feel quite strongly a pause to think would be most helpful," Peter said.

"I cannot let this go unpunished." Chris Spencer said. "I have to bury Charlie. After which I intend to do something about it. I'll wait until the funeral. Count me in."

"Hell Bro, you don't even have to ask me." Dan said. "I'm definitely in! Something has to be done to stop these creatures or England will never be England again."

Katya smiled at Jack and said, "I hope you don't feel you actually have to ask me!"

"So, we're all agreed. In which case we'd better exchange contact information. In case this gets nasty later I'd suggest no mention of this conversation ever takes place over the telephone." Jack warned the little group. "Not landlines, not mobiles, not faxes and certainly never by e-mail. If we wish to contact one another we can, but as little as possible. Meaningful conversations should only happen face to face, in randomly chosen locations with background noise to interfere with listening devices."

Chris Spencer nodded, as did Dan, but Peter Parfitt asked, "I do understand the reasons why obviously, but is that not being a little melodramatic?"

Jack looked at him for a moment thoughtfully, then answered. "Peter, the thing is none of us know what the future will bring. We are, as you so rightly said, talking in the heat of the moment but, after we have had a cooling off period we still feel the same way yet the authorities plainly wish to sit on their hands, what are we to do? Frankly I think it'll come to that. I truly feel we'll be back in the same situation in a week or two's time, having cooled down a little, but still extremely angry. Maybe we'll want to take some form of action or defer it still further. However one day we are going to wake up and have to make a decision. Do we forget our loved ones? Do we allow their lives to count for nothing? Do we sit on our hands and let this dross of the planet destroy our society? Or do we react? If we react, and I'm sure I'll feel the same way, and I pretty much think Chris will too, that reaction may well be – 'unfortunate' – for our enemies. That will put us – every one of us involved, or a party to any involvement – well the other side of the law. Can we be too careful? No! Melodramatic? If we take no further action – perhaps. But what will caution cost any one of us? Very little. Certainly think of today – but always have a plan for tomorrow!"

The group talked on for some time afterwards, but a meeting had already been agreed for fourteen days later, so nothing of consequence followed. They discussed what would have to be done the following day, and Danny agreed to take Peter out to the garage where Tammy had left her car that morning. Parfitt would then go back to The Royal London Hospital and try to see her. Danny was to return to the hotel to pick up Katya and Jack along with Chris Spencer who would travel with them to the hospital morgue. After the morgue Danny would drop him wherever he wished to go. Whilst Danny, Jack and Chris attended the morgue Katya would visit Tom and wait there for Jack, and eventually Danny.

Phil Gatting took Jake's call quite happily, he liked Jake, old rogue that he was. However he did not take the news Jake imparted well at all. He passed it on to Jane who crumpled in tears, and was inconsolable throughout the night. Eventually however she literally cried herself to sleep. Phil had not. He knew sleep would never come that night. He got up, dressed and went downstairs in order to avoid further disturbing his wife with his fidgeting. Bastards he thought. They had killed his beautiful daughter and, as if that was not enough, they killed the life she carried within her. The bastards! Someone should be made to pay heavily for this.

He arranged for a car to collect him in the morning, to take him down to London, as he knew he would be in no fit state to drive. Throughout the trip the thought of Susie's untimely death continued to eat away at him. He found it difficult to concentrate on anything else, in fact failing every time he tried. He struggled to believe his youngest daughter was dead. He knew as a father he should not have a favourite child, and he deeply loved all three of his children, but there had always been something very special about Susie. She was a character from the day she was born, kind, caring and loving in a completely selfless way, but with so much drive and energy. It was true to say he knew of nobody who had met her who didn't like her. His daughter or not, she was the nicest person he had ever known. Fucking bastards!

Jake Ferris also suffered a sleepless night. He asked if Nathan wished to return to his home for the night or, given the circumstances, would he prefer a room in a hotel. Nathan replied in a broken voice he would never again return to the home he had shared with Susie, and he never did. Jake booked a large twin room for the two of them for the night. He loathed sharing a room with anyone, even a willing woman, much preferring they went on their way once they had served their purpose, but someone had to spend the night with Nathan and Jake saw it as his duty. Almost a paternal duty. Nothing in his life had properly prepared him for Susie's death. He knew he loved her as he would have done a daughter, and as he did Nathan as a son, but Susie was Susie. She was irreplaceable. The lively vibrant confident girl who brightened up the lives of everyone she touched was gone. Dead! Killed by a brainwashed lunatic from a morally bankrupt culture.

Nathan hadn't slept either. Jake was aware of him breathing rapidly and then Nathan seemed to have shut down. Knowing little of medicine and medical disorders, and even less of psychological conditions, Jake was in no position to make any form of diagnosis, but even to someone with no qualifications in the medical world it was obvious something was wrong. Jake accurately guessed it must be a form of shock.

Nathan was actually suffering from acute stress reaction, a variation of post traumatic stress disorder, but Jake knew nothing of ASR and had only heard of PTSD in connection with war veterans, particularly from the Gulf. However he had heard of shock, guessed correctly Nathan was suffering from shock, whatever doctors now called it, and knew he had to get help so arranged for Chi Lu to come and collect Nathan whilst he went to meet Phil Gatting and identify Susie's body. When she arrived Jake asked her to get the best possible doctor to see Nathan as soon as she could and sent her off in a taxi, calling another for himself to transport him to his meeting.

Phil Gatting was already at the appointed meeting place. His normal straight backed stance was still in place, but he looked worn and haggard to Jake, who again correctly guessed Phil Gatting had not slept either. The man's penetrating steely grey eyes still bore through him, but there was something different about them, something Jake could not at first fathom. There was the obvious excruciating pain and suffering, which Jake expected, but there was something else, and it took a while for him to work out what it was. It was not until Phil Gatting spoke it finally fell into place.

Gatting approached with his hand outstretched and a forced wintry smile on his face. "Thank you for meeting me Jake. I truly appreciate it in the circumstances. I would not have liked to have done this alone, but would not have dreamt of asking Jane to accompany me. She has taken it very badly. Sheila has come down for a couple of days to look after her. Now let's go and see what these fucking animals have done to my little girl."

Jake was shocked. He had never heard Gatting swear before. Having lived in East London and made his living from the motor trade swearing had surrounded him throughout his life, and for him was a completely normal form of communication. It was not the fact Phil Gatting had sworn which shocked Jake, it was the venom with which he had used the word. Jake finally worked out what it was he had seen in Gatting's eyes. Hatred! He was completely consumed with a bitter, savage hatred for the people who had brought death to Susie and her unborn child.

If he felt like this now Jake was somewhat apprehensive as to just what Gatting's mood might be after he left the mortuary. At just turned ten in the morning they entered the building and spoke to an attending doctor, who pointed them in the right direction.

Danny dropped Parfitt off so he might collect Tammy's Porsche, then returned to the hotel in order to pick up his brother, Katya and Chris. They paid the hotel with Jack's credit card, loaded the suitcases into the back of the car and climbed in. The car was a Volkswagen Passat estate, normally a roomy vehicle, but Danny had had the driver's seat runners extended so he might have the leg room he required. This meant Katya was the only person who could sit behind him, but even then she had her knees swung over to the Jack's side restricting his legroom, whilst Chris Spencer sat happily in the front passenger seat, oblivious to Katya's contortions.

They stopped to let Katya out first then carried on with Chris and Jack until they reached the hospital morgue where the two passengers got out. Jack set about asking where they should go whilst Danny found a parking space. By the time he returned and joined them Chris and Jack knew which direction to take. They were led to the morgue by an orderly who, upon opening the door, saw there were two other older men already waiting there.

"I'm sorry, you'll have to wait here for the doctor. I'm sure you must understand we are not exactly geared up for such a terrible event. There may be a slight delay as the doctor will have to deal with these other two gentlemen first." He then turned and left the small group of men together.

The five stood around silently for a few minutes as the atmosphere was not conducive with flippant conversation. However Jake was a person with an outgoing personality, an extrovert in many ways, and was not used to silence when in company. He broke it by looking at the three new arrivals and asking. "I assume you gentlemen have also lost someone. Which train were they on? It's a terrible business."

Jack answered for all three. Nodding in the direction of Danny he said, "My brother here and I lost our stepmother-to-be at Aldgate, and Chris," he indicated Spencer, "lost his young nephew on the bus. What about yourselves?"

Phil Gatting answered. "The bastards butchered my little girl on the Piccadilly Line. She was due to give birth in the next few days. The evil bastards killed both of them. I hope they and their fucking families rot in hell. I would love to see them and their kind exterminated and wiped from the planet for good and for all time!"

"You and me both! The trouble is the authorities are going to do nothing about it. They will just let it go in a pathetic attempt to keep peace within our 'multicultural society'!" Chris Spencer almost spat out. "And that is a long way short of good enough for me!"

"Nor me, Sir!" Phil Gatting said angrily, and continued. "I would give millions to have their families and friends tracked down and exterminated, and frankly the way I feel about these creatures and their arsehole culture, that would just be for starters!"

Jake Ferris interrupted. "Steady Phil. We don't know these people. What you are saying could cause you future problems."

Chris Spencer continued as if Jake had said nothing. "If only someone did have that sort of money available, and were serious, something could be done."

"I'm sorry, but might I ask your name, and what it is you do? Phil Gatting asked.

"Spencer, Chris. I was a career soldier, WO1, recently came out of the army. I'm not doing anything at the moment. Well, I wasn't. Now I'm going to try to find who was behind this, then take them down. The biggest problem I'm going to face is funding." Chris Spencer answered.

"Mr. Spencer, my name is Phil Gatting." Gatting said. "I would very much like to continue this conversation with you, but here is not the place. If you are even part way serious we may be able to help one another. I am completely serious. If you are, you will have your funding!"

Their conversation was interrupted by the arrival of the doctor, who walked back with a couple in their fifties. The woman was openly weeping with red rimmed eyes, gasping for breath as she sobbed. The man with her was trying to support her whilst desperately trying to hold everything together, but failing as tears silently ran down his cheeks and dripped from his chin. They too had obviously lost a loved one, probably a child, Jack Bryant guessed. The doctor enquired who was next, then asked names and led Phil Gatting and Jake Ferris away.

"Well that was an interesting conversation," Jack said. "I wonder how serious he is. He certainly seemed pretty pissed off, just like we all are, but it is impossible to gauge how deeply he feels it, although I think you could take his promise to the bank. There's also something vaguely familiar about him, and I know that name. Did you notice his eyes?"

"I did," Spencer answered. "I've seen that look before on the battlefield when a corporal of mine lost two of his squad to a roadside mine and had a few more shot up while trying to collect the bodies. He wanted to kill everyone he saw who even resembled the enemy afterwards. Personal cost meant nothing. This guy now would happily kill every person in this country with so much as a fat lip or sun tan, let alone those that chant, wear stupid dresses or pray with their arses facing the sky."

"We'll see when they come out," Jack said. "If they just walk on by and don't make eye contact we'll never hear from them again. My money is they'll want to talk. Also there is something familiar about the guy who first spoke as well as the other one. I know his face from somewhere, but I can't place it"

"They'll stop," Spencer said in his customary short manner.

Phil Gatting, Jake Ferris and the doctor re-emerged, Gatting and Ferris looking even grimmer than a few minutes earlier. Gatting approached Chris Spencer and stopped directly in front of him with his cold grey eyes boring into Spencer's. Chris Spencer did not blink, flinch or look away, but just gazed straight back. An unspoken understanding was reached. Chris Spencer had a mission.

"Mr. Spencer," Phil Gatting said very quietly, "As I have said, I would very much like to continue our conversation. I will wait for you outside this place. Do not hurry. I will wait."

The doctor next led Chris in to see and identify young Charlie, and started to define the horrors of the injuries explaining to Chris how he should prepare himself, but Chris made clear his battlefield experience, telling the doctor to carry on and open the large sliding drawer cabinet. Charlie's identification was a formality and a pointless waste of time. Chris knew his nephew was dead, and had seen his butchered body after the explosion, or what remained of it. The police doctor present started to explain the victims were identified for the most part from their possessions and any identification they carried with them. He explained those further back on the bus could not be identified by sight at all, so extreme were their injuries the remains of some would never be formally identified as such. For the most part the relatives were not shown the bodies in their entirety, and the doctor cautioned Chris several times despite the repeated reassurances from the ex-soldier to the effect he had seen many such things before.

The morgue doctors had cleaned and reassembled the body as best they could in the circumstances and with the time constraints the emergency services, hospital and morgue were under, but as the sheet covering Charlie's body was drawn back there was no mistaking the severity of the blast which had taken his innocent young life. His body parts were in place, but horribly damaged. What remained of the face still shone with the freshness of youth, but it was a young face which would never know the joys or concerns of the ageing process. The doctor looked at Chris who nodded, identification was complete, but as the doctor started to draw the cover back over Charlie's dead body Chris stopped him.

"Just a moment doctor please." Chris said. "I want to see him one last time."

The doctor nodded and stepped back. Chris moved forward and put a hand on Charlie's naked chest and said in a voice chocked with emotion, "I'm so sorry Charlie. I should never have brought you to this place. Your death is my fault little lad. I'm the one responsible. I'll never forget the joy you brought to my life, and I'll never forgive those who have done this to you." He leaned forward and kissed the pulverised face, "You rest now little one. I have work to do." With that he stepped back, confirmed Charlie's identity, told the doctor he could cover the body, turned and left the room. As he walked out Danny and Jack could both sense the waves of barely controlled animosity and hostility emanating from the very depths of his being. It could not be seen in his bearing, or even his face, except the eyes. "Gentlemen, I'll be outside. I have to speak to Mr. Gatting and his friend."

Jack and Danny were ushered through to undergo an exactly similar process to the one Chris had just experienced. Whilst they were doing so Chris left the building and walked out into the sunshine of a bright and sunny London summer day. He didn't notice. The weather was a complete irrelevance. He had but one thing on his mind, a mind which was consumed with a burning hatred for those responsible for bringing about the death and mutilation of his nephew. He wanted vengeance. He needed to mete out retribution and to settle the score, and he had absolutely no desire to leave it at a simple life for a life. His intention was to take the violence back to the perpetrator's community, and he was going to exact a very high price, taking down as large a number as he could. Although he did not then know it his plan would have to change over time, and the change would bring about death on a truly epic scale.

Phil Gatting was waiting with Jake, as he had said he would. Despite the warmth of the day there was a bleak look about the pair, which turned from cold to a biting chill when looking into Phil Gatting's eyes. Gatting opened the conversation without preamble. "Mr. Spencer, I've just seen a part of what is left of my little girl and her baby, and I find this situation intolerable. I've lived my entire life abiding by the rule of law and respecting the law of the land. I've watched as my country and its culture have been polluted and overrun by the dross and scum of the planet, and my taxes have supported them. The rule of law, and the law itself, will do nothing to avenge the deaths of these people, and I find that completely unacceptable. I'm now prepared to step well over that legal line because I want these creatures hurt and I want them to be hurt much more than the pain they have inflicted here, and I wish their pain to go on for a long, long time to come. Now you said with funding something could be done."

Phil Gatting's bearing, directness, obvious intelligence and strength of character were all qualities Chris Spencer immediately responded to. As with Jack Bryant earlier Gatting reminded him of some of the better highly placed officers he had served under, and he instinctively accepted him in that role.

"Sir, I am in full agreement with all you have just said. I have no wife or children. My young nephew is lying dead in there, and his death will mean little to this country, a country I've spent all my adult life defending. His death will not go unpunished. I'll find these people, and I'll take them down. It may take me a month, it may take me ten years, but I'll find them, and I will kill them." Chris Spencer said in a way made all the more poignant because it was delivered in such a matter of fact manner. He went on, "It would be easier if I were funded, as I could use more elaborate methods to track them and their movements over time, and could bring in others I know who would then help. But with or without funding those responsible, and their organisation, will be hurt."

Danny and Jack joined the small group just as Chris finished speaking. Phil Gatting obviously wished to say something more to Chris but stopped as he did not want to say it in front of others. He knew he was safe with Jake, as they had got to know one another well since Nathan and Susie's marriage, and Chris appeared one hundred percent genuine, but he did not know him or these other two, and Jake's caution earlier had been prudent. Jack sensed the unease, and accurately guessed the reasoning behind it as all present had heard Jake's warning. Intuitively he was suddenly conscious of a possible future need for funding, and the part this man may then play. He knew he should not let this Phil Gatting go, or his friend, whose face kept nagging at his memory.

"Mr. Gatting, my name is Jack Bryant, and this is my brother Dan." Jack Bryant said, indicating his brother. "Six years ago an illegal immigrant killed our mother in a hit and run accident. Our father nearly went mad. The woman who spent years nursing him back to health, and whom he would shortly have married, is now laid out on a slab in there." He indicated the hospitals morgue with his thumb over his shoulder, he then continued, "Our father is lying in a hospital bed with broken bones, cuts and bruises. He will heal physically. Mentally is another story. We went through all this last night with Chris here, and another gentleman. At the moment the conversation we have had, although probably illegal technically in content, would be dismissed by any court due to the circumstances, and we would be regarded as doing little more than venting our anger, a perfectly normal human emotion. If however we take it further and we have a tacit agreement to do just that, then we are conspiring, and if we are doing that then we shall all have to be very careful. For the record Mr. Gatting, I intend to conspire. You and your friend may speak freely. You are amongst like minded people. We have just viewed some of the shocking remains of our stepmother-to-be. I would wish to see justice meted out, and I would rather we were responsible for delivering that justice, as I am certain the state will do nothing!"

There was a moments silence following Jack's explanation. Phil Gatting broke it with the words, "This is my friend, Jake Ferris –."

It was as if a powerful light had just been switched on in Jack's head, and Phil Gatting's words were cut short by Jack's sudden exclamation, "My God! Of course! Mr. Ferris, you are Nathan Jefferies partner." Then, as he said it, the whole picture opened up to him and he went on in an awed voice, "So – then these people killed your daughter Susie, Mr. Gatting. Oh Jesus, they don't know what they've done."

"No Mr. Bryant – they don't. One way or another they will be hunted down and hurt for what they have done," Phil Gatting replied coldly, continuing, "Jake and I were talking whilst you were still inside, and he is in full agreement with me, as I am sure my son-in law will be." He turned to Chris Spencer and said, "Mr. Spencer, you appear to be as passionate about this as I most definitely am. It would seem you have certain skills and contacts which I do not possess, but which will undoubtedly be required for what lies ahead. On the other hand we have something which may prove very useful to you, which is funding. I feel safe in saying we would be prepared to fund a private army if it is what is needed. You would have access to limitless funds, or at least limitless in everyday parlance."

Chris Spencer was more than a little taken aback and asked, "Do you mean – millions?"

"Mr. Spencer." Phil Gatting said. "I want these animals hunted down. I've had enough of what they have done to my country. Now they've attacked my family. That was a step much too far. Let me make myself absolutely clear. I would like to see them culled. I would be happy to see them exterminated, but I have to be realistic. I want them hurt, and I want them hurt a great deal. No – I do not mean millions. If required I mean billions. Am I right in saying that Jake?" Phil Gatting turned to Jake Ferris.

"Absolutely right in every respect Phil!" Jake replied. "Gentlemen you must understand, Susie was not my daughter, but I loved her as if she were. The child she was to have would have been the granddaughter I shall never have. The money I have available to me is now so vast as to be meaningless, and I absolutely know the same is true for Nathan! If you can Mr. Spencer, give the money some meaning! Destroy this growing social cancer forever if you can!"

Again a momentary silence descended over the small group. Billions Jack thought. Billions would take a lot of managing. Millions would be a problem, but billions! These men controlled sums greater than the gross domestic product of many nations. "Chris, Mr. Gatting," Jack said, in so doing acknowledging the establishment of a hierarchy, "funding on such a level would have to be very carefully managed. Money laundering legislation should make such things impossible, but outside of the United Kingdom there are ways around the problem of our legislation. If you are truly serious I can go through the complexities with you, but here really is not the place to be talking of such matters. Is it possible to go somewhere where we can all talk in complete privacy?"

"Indeed, quite right young man!" Jake responded, continuing, "NJF has a spacious boardroom we could use. It is regularly checked for electronic surveillance placed there by competitor's agents. We should be able to talk freely there. I would suggest we adjourn for a couple of hours and reconvene there at one o'clock. It will give me time to have the room electronically swept and provide some simple food, sandwiches and the like. Does that suit your requirements?" he asked Jack.

"Perfectly thank you." Jack replied. "It should give me plenty of time to visit my father, collect my girlfriend, and get out to you. Danny here is driving, but do you have a car or transport?"

"I have a car and driver." Phil Gatting answered for both of them. "However, if you are first to see your father perhaps we could help by taking Mr. Spencer with us. That way we can also get better acquainted before you arrive. How would that suit you Mr. Spencer."

"Suits me fine!" Chris Spencer replied in his usual no words wasted manner, and with that NJF's address was given and the car park meeting finished.

Danny and Jack made their way back to their father's hospital bedside. He was obviously sedated, drugged up to his eyeballs in order to keep him calm. Katya was sitting dutifully and patiently with him, calmly awaiting the return of Jack, although it was Danny she saw first because of his size. Tom was uncommunicative, unresponsive and in an obvious state of drug induced drowsiness. Jack spoke to the attending nurse and was advised to let his father sleep. It was suggested they should return in the late afternoon or early evening, but to try to give Tom Bryant at least five hour's sleep.

They left the hospital with Jack quite apparently deep in thought. Dan had grown up with his little brother and knew better than to interrupt him whilst thinking and Katya too had learnt it was pointless to try and talk with Jack when his mind was fully absorbed on problem solving. Both knew Jack could address a problem rapidly, objectively and logically, breaking it down into its component parts, minutely examine each, planning multiple moves and stratagems for dozens of scenarios, from the conventional to the ultra radical, with backup and get out strategies built into every move. In almost every way his brain was in complete contrast in its workings to that of Nathan Jefferies. Nathan's thought patterns of either 'open' or 'no' never properly allowed him to see the big picture. Jack's complex and convoluted pattern allowed him to see dozens of big pictures all emanating from any single event. Possible variances were theoretically limitless, but could be significantly reduced, narrowed and controlled if sufficient time and research was given to accurately ascertaining background facts, truths and realities. In this Jack excelled, testing and harrying every available argument and conclusion.

There was silence in the car for a quarter of an hour, which was broken when Jack looked up from the road in front of him, turned to his brother and asked, "What did you think of Gatting, Danny? You've always been good around people, and quite intuitive. Generally much better than me, but how do you read him? Well, how do you read the two of them?"

Danny then sat in thought for almost a minute before answering, "Gatting is the harder of the two because he's so controlled. Jake Ferris seems to be a friendly sociable kind of chap. He made me think of a wealthy man who has just had the only surviving relative killed and has no one to leave anything to. Gatting is difficult. His eyes are weird aren't they? He is obviously in a lot of pain over this and hurting, but there is something else there. I think he is probably a very well ordered, capable and organised man who cares passionately about his family and his people, whether they be friends, employees or even countrymen. That said I think if he had his finger on the button right now there would be no more North Africa, Middle East or any of the Stan's. Basically a bloody good bloke to have on your side, but a remorseless and relentless unforgiving enemy to those who deliberately offend him, as these bombers have. I'm of the opinion they started something here yesterday they will in time regret. How wealthy are these guys anyway? Billions is easy to say, but it's a lot of dosh. What are they worth, because Gatting will go the distance on this thing! He is not the type to stop or to back down due to economic considerations when it comes to his family. Now pardon my ignorance, but is Jake Ferris the games and telecommunications guy?"

"To that bit yes and no has to be the answer." Jack answered. "Jake Ferris is one of the two co-owners of NJF Industries, whose fortune is based around computer games, although they have branched out into many of the high tech industries over the past few years. The power behind NJF however is their genius designer, Nathan Jefferies, who is a bit of a geek, and in many ways Britain's answer to Bill Gates.

"They employ a staff of thousands, now worldwide, and have chains of their own retail outlets around the world, a huge manufacturing plant in China, US corporate headquarters and manufacturing plant in Silicon Valley, and their international headquarters here in the East End of London. As a company they are somewhat unconventional, mavericks in many ways, and have bucked just about every trend going. The City cannot make them out, mainly because they don't need money. They have an incredibly cash rich company, which is brilliantly managed by two women, Susie Jefferies, formerly Gatting, and a drop dead gorgeous looking Eurasian girl called Chi Lu Herepath. Jake Ferris has taken the back seat a bit in the last couple of years, leaving the running of the business to Susie."

"So Susie is the one who has just been killed?" Katya asked from the back seat.

"Apparently," Jack again answered. "Just what effect her death will have on the business we will have to wait and see, although I did read in the financial papers Chi Lu Herepath was due to take over global operations, and Susie was standing down to raise a family. That is the reason I know about them. There was a huge article about them in the Financial Times recently. According to the paper when Susie Gatting married Nathan Jefferies her father put on a colossal event which was spread over three days, and held the biggest private firework display in British history. I guess you can afford such things when you are already an independently wealthy multi millionaire and your daughter is marrying a billionaire. Phil Gatting himself is supposed to be worth well over two hundred million, and is reported to be a very astute yet highly principled man. An interesting character!"

"I would've thought the press will be all over this when they find out who she is," Dan mused.

"I'm surprised no one has tipped them off yet. They obviously haven't been informed or they would have been staking the morgue out. It's not as if they would let common human decency get in the way of a good story, so it can only be that so far they simply don't know. When they catch on they'll be all over NJF like a rash. Perhaps, in the circumstances, it would pay us to keep a very low profile when there, watch what we say and to whom, and take care as to whom we are seen with," Jack responded thoughtfully as Danny negotiated the London traffic.

With Jake Ferris and Phil Gatting sitting in the rear and Chris Spencer with the driver, all sat in comparative silence during the drive out to East Ham. Jake used his mobile phone to call ahead, giving instructions as to what he required with regard the boardroom and food, and to find out about Nathan who was still with the doctor. He managed to speak directly to Chi Lu who passed on the results. Despite the general lack of conversation in the car, mainly because all three were preoccupied, and there was the presence of the driver to consider, Jake's phone call prompted Phil Gatting to ask, "How is Nathan, Jake?"

"I know this is a terrible situation all round," Jake responded. "But Nathan has taken it very badly. I know you loved your daughter, Phil, and you know I did too. To both of us she is irreplaceable. However, to Nathan, she really was his world. You must remember I was there when they met, and knew him before. He had nothing in his life until he met Susie, and in every way possible she meant everything to him. He has no interest in money, business, even life itself. He just lived for Susie and the family they were to have. To say he is devastated doesn't even come close! Apparently he is traumatised and suffering from acute stress disorder, which I believe is the poncey name for shock. There is a specialist doctor with him, who has given him a sedative. It's thought he'll be alright eventually, but he's not taking it well. I just hope we can pull him around, and that he doesn't do anything stupid!"

"Poor little bugger." Phil Gatting said. "I liked the lad from the moment Susie first brought him home. I thought then one day he would do well for himself because of his skills, but never dreamt he would get involved in anything which would take off the way his games did. I would never originally have seen him as Susie's type, but there was definitely something which bound them together, and I could see he was totally devoted to her. What a terrible loss she is to all of us!"

With those words conversation dried up. There was little anyone could add, and nothing they could do. Susie was dead, and it was true to all who had known her that her passing was an incredible loss. The remainder of the journey continued in silence until arriving at the office and factory complex at East Ham. The security guard pressed the button to raise the barrier immediately he recognised Jake in the back seat with a polite "Good morning Mr. Ferris." However, as the barrier went up, Jake stepped out of the stationary car and had a quiet word with the guard, the entirety of which went unheard by all within the vehicle. Jake then opened the door, climbed back in, and directed the driver to the office block. On arrival he suggested Phil Gatting should dispense with the driver, and allow him to return to his base. They didn't know how much time the meeting would take up, and Jake would happily return Gatting to his home at the end of it. Gatting opened his mouth to protest, thought better of it and followed Jake's suggestion. The driver left with a tip in his pocket and a smile on his face. He would never know he had been a minor unwitting pawn in a game which would eventually change the future of many people, if not nations themselves.

The Bryant brothers, accompanied by Katya, pulled up at the security gate some half an hour later. The same security man stepped out of his small office to speak to them and, on ascertaining just who they were, directed them to the staff car park at the rear of the building instead of the visitor parking area to the front, as he had been instructed to do by Jake. They left the car and walked through the staff entrance where they were met by another security man, who then led the trio to the boardroom.

Whilst waiting for the Bryant's Phil Gatting and Jake quizzed Chris Spencer about his background, length of service, action seen, and about what he knew of the Bryant brothers. Chris was completely open and honest in every regard, and explained how little he knew of either, how they had met, and how impressed he was on a personal level with both men, especially the intelligence, grasp and leadership qualities of the younger one. His explanation had only just finished as there was a knock on the door and the individuals in question were ushered in. Immediately following their arrival two members of NJF staff appeared, each carrying a large tray, one contained assorted sandwiches, and the other mineral waters and fruit juices. When they left Jake closed and locked the door.

"We can freely discuss anything here." Jake explained to those present. "The room has been swept electronically, and the walls are lined with acoustic deadening panels. This was done for the obvious security problems surrounding NJF product secrecy, although I feel it is fair to say a discussion of the sensitivity we are about to hold was never envisaged! Anyway we are free to talk, and hopefully this room will prove a little more comfortable than a car park. I have no idea as to how to proceed with a meeting such as this, but feel it may be beneficial to all if we properly introduce ourselves, our backgrounds, and what has led us all to be here together. After that's been done, if we feel comfortable with one another, we can move on to what we feel should, could and will be done, firstly by the authorities, and then more importantly by a privately funded and independent group. Does anyone object to this sort of agenda?" Five heads shook.

"In which case, as I seem to have the floor I shall kick it off, unless anyone else wishes to?" He looked at the other five people, all of which once more shook their heads.

Jake started, gave his name, and launched on a brief résumé of his past. On finishing he handed over to Phil Gatting, who did the same. Moving clockwise around the table Chris Spencer then followed, leaving much of his past out, keeping strictly to the facts with a minimum of words. Dan Bryant told his tale and passed on to his brother. To avoid repetition Jack just outlined his qualifications, skills and occupation. Katya was the odd one out in the group in several ways. The three main ones being she was the only female present, was not British by birth, and had lost nobody directly related to her as a result of the bombings. Set against which she was with Jack Bryant who had lost someone due to the bombings, and his mother before. She had also lost her brother in terrible circumstances to terrorists in another land, and she passionately hated the Muslim world, for all that it was and all which it stood for. Odd one out or not, her skills and contacts were to prove most useful to the group over the years to follow.

The six around the table discussed the situation in generalities to begin with, each slowly building up trust and respect for the others present, then gradually they moved into areas which became more specific. They talked about others on the trains and bus who might feel the same way as they did, but completely ruled out expanding their group beyond the six present, with two possible exceptions. Both Jake and Phil Gatting believed Nathan would want to be a party to what was to follow, once he got over the effects of the shock, and his undisputed computer skills may well prove to be vital. Both Jack and Chris Spencer felt Peter Parfitt may bring something of value to their group. Chris felt Parfitt was a stand up sort of guy, and had got the impression he would be utterly trustworthy. Jack agreed, and spoke in Parfitt's favour, explaining how reasoned he had found Parfitt despite the fact his fiancée was lying in a hospital bed minus many of her body parts. Unbeknown to them at the time, Peter Parfitt's inclusion within their group would also later prove to be invaluable.

It was agreed by all present something had to be done which was not subject to the law of the land. Retaliatory moves must be made against those who were fanatical supporters of Islam. The British people, their European neighbours, and those from Western based cultures everywhere should be protected. If the required protection was not to be provided by the state or states concerned, then those peoples deserved a champion, and a champion they would have!

NJF and Gatting Group Holdings would fund and finance all aspects of any required outlays in relation to, or in conjunction with, the setting up of a strike force capable of taking terror back to the Muslim communities of Great Britain, mainland Europe, Australasia and North America. Chris Spencer was to be put on an immediate retainer as a security consultant to both companies, which would both give him a necessary income, and would help legitimise fund transfers to various places around the world as required – for corporate security. The banking and funding payments would be controlled through Jack Bryant, who would use his knowledge, position and contacts to move large scale funds around off-shore. On the face of it meetings between most of the key players would then be legitimised on a client / consultant basis, just in case at some future time any of the group should have fallen under the scrutiny of any official agency, British based or other.

The meeting finally broke up with an agreement, in essence the same as the one made the previous night, for all six to return two weeks later with a progress report, bringing in the other two interested parties, should they remain interested, and if available. Two weeks was considered a reasonable time period in which to test their own resolves and to make sure the details discussed and agreed upon were not just a knee jerk reaction to the bombing and subsequent deaths of their loved ones. The horrors of the day which had brought the six together were never far from any of their minds. Absolute secrecy about what they intended to do was not only agreed upon, but fully understood by those present, all of whom left with the distinct feeling what had started the previous morning would some day prove to be directly consequential in bringing about a state of change to many!

None even began to suspect the sheer scale of death and destruction their conversation would eventually bring about to those who followed the bomber's fanatical ideology.

Four

Peter Parfitt returned to the Royal London Hospital to hear Tammy's life was hanging in the balance, she was in a coma and there was nothing at all he could do until she stabilised, which included visits. With a very slight hint of annoyance in her voice the receptionist he spoke to pointed out the hospital had a number for him on record and assured him he would be called the moment there was any form of news. She could see from the patient's records the horrific extent of her injuries, and felt sympathy for the man before her, but it was her duty to also attempt to explain hospital procedures. If he could help, or things changed, they would contact him, but as things were he was not helping his fiancée, himself, or indeed the hospital by being there when there was not even the remotest chance of his seeing their patient. Reluctantly, and feeling somewhat chastised, he left.

Returning to Tammy's house at Cookham Dean Peter uncovered the bed which was almost ready for shipping, then telephoned her parents and spent twenty minutes in a very unhappy conversation with them, during which he promised faithfully to keep them updated as to any progress. He and Tammy's parents would have much work to do. The following day they were to have been married. Arrangements needed to be cancelled, and all friends and relatives attending informed as to the situation. Many already knew, and most of the hotels concerned gave full refunds to all guests due to the circumstances, not that any who were to attend had the slightest consideration for the money involved. The continental honeymoon reservations proved more difficult as Tammy had made many of the arrangements using the internet, and Parfitt almost felt he was invading her privacy as he trawled through her e-mails looking for booking references and confirmation mailings.

It was late evening by the time he finished and he suddenly realised he was hungry. He hadn't eaten all day, except for half a croissant for breakfast, but had been neither aware of the passage of time nor of his need for sustenance. There was no food in the house, not that he wished to cook anyway, and he had no preference as to what he ate, so it meant going out. He decided the first fast food place he found he would stop at and buy something, but knew there was nothing of the kind in Cookham Dean, heaven forbid, so took the car and headed for Maidenhead. In the growing darkness, and preoccupied as he was, he missed the turn, oblivious to it as he passed. With his brain on auto pilot, habit took over and he followed his usual route on to the M4, as if he were returning to Heathrow. Driving down the slip road he suddenly realised what he had done, but by then he was committed. The next junction was Slough West, but it was almost exclusively dedicated to the industrial estate. Just over a mile past was the junction for Slough central, Eton and Windsor. Slough was particularly unpleasant, but at least there would be plenty of instant food outlets, whereas Eton and Windsor were much less well supplied with what he needed, and would take him further away.

He left the motorway heading north, crossed a roundabout, the A4 Bath Road, and over a railway bridge, which put him at the extreme eastern end of Slough's huge industrial area, and west of the town centre. The first place he saw which suited his needs was a takeaway kebab outlet. In the circumstances, certainly not his first choice, but it would do. He drove past, turned left onto the industrial estate, left and left again, which brought him out just below the takeaway. He parked the Porsche in an open area in front of an office building and got out. There was a smell of chocolate in the air, coming from the big Mars distribution centre, but he wasn't interested in chocolate, just something to keep the hunger pangs at bay. He turned the corner, walked up to and entered the takeaway, then ordered a large mixed kebab with salad from one of three Turks serving, paying as he did so.

There were two tables and a collection of seats further down towards the back of the premises where a television was set on a bracket attached to the back wall. A group of six Asian lads in their late teens to early twenties sat together watching the news, which was still reporting heavily on the events of the day before. The two Turks who had not responded as Parfitt entered were leaning on their elbows also watching the television. As the pictures of the trains and bus wreckage started to play, followed by scenes of stretchers and ambulances, one of the lads jumped to his feet and shouted "The sword of Allah! Death to all infidels!"

Another then took up the cry raising his fist and shouting "Kill them all! Death to all non-believers!"

The one who had jumped to his feet turned and saw Parfitt at the counter. His eyes were gleaming with the passionate zeal of religious mania, and locked on Parfitt's, challenging, threatening. One by one his friends turned, all displaying the same maniacal gleam, and another stood, an act of open aggression. The chins of the others rose. A pack signal had been triggered and picked up. With his eyes still fixed on Parfitt's the first to have shouted again contemptuously repeated "Death to all infidels!"

In that moment, something very deep and profound changed about Parfitt's character. All he had ever lived for and believed in changed, and changed at such a basic and primary level it would, from that moment on, affect every day of the rest of his life. Suddenly, he understood his way forward. This Britain of today was no longer the stylised image of its once former splendour and glory, but instead what stood before him was the reality of the day, and tomorrow would be worse if nobody was prepared to stand against such things. He would join the others and he would kill. And he would kill. And he would kill again!

Eyes still locked, he smiled a cruel cold smile. "We will drive you bastards into the sea!" Parfitt said to the main aggressor, whose jaw muscles clenched as his face took on a yet more aggressive look.

The Turk who had taken Parfitt's order reacted first, holding out a bag containing his kebab and saying "You leave here. You go Mister!"

He came around the counter and stood between the two, breaking eye contact. "Go!" the Turk repeated pointing at the door, "Go out my shop! Go now!" He repeated in broken English. For Parfitt the spell was broken. He picked up the bag, turned and left the takeaway. Outside, even the heavy chocolate smelling air tasted better. He started to cross towards the car, but had second thoughts because he didn't want to get the smell of the kebab into the interior, so instead walked passed and carried on up the road, eating from the bag as he went, and thinking of what had just occurred. Adrenalin had surged around his system at the time producing a high, but as the levels fell away he started to shake a little. The kebab tasted like shit to him as his body's self made hormonal and chemically induced reaction subsided.

He heard nothing but some extra sense warned him of danger, that he was being hunted, and he knew the threat was coming from behind. There was street lighting, but also large areas of deep shadow. He chose to turn a dark corner, shaded from street light by a large warehouse and, as he did so, he turned and looked around the corner of the building back down the road he had just walked along. There were two of them, the two who had both stood up at the takeaway. As he watched they passed under a street light, increasing their pace in an attempt to keep him in sight, and the increase underlined the fact their intentions were indeed hostile. There was no traffic moving on the industrial estate and, apart from the traffic on the main road back from where he had come, no other sign of life. He was faced with the age-old dilemma, fight or flight. Until ten minutes earlier the answer would always have been an automatic flight. Not because of any form of cowardice on his part, for Parfitt was certainly no coward, but more because it was the sensible thing to do and avoided all sorts of potential problems.

Those ten minutes proved to be life changing. The past thirty-six hours had been traumatic in the extreme. If she survived the nature of Tammy's injuries were such she would never walk again, would never bear the children they had discussed having, and neither of them would come to enjoy the life they had both planned and so desperately wanted together. His life had already been turned upside down and his future destroyed. Now before he was even given a chance to come up for air he was being hunted on the streets of his own country by at least two individuals who he could now only regard as animals. Fight or flight? He had chosen flight all his life, but it would not be an option in future, and it certainly was not going to be an option here. Completely incongruously he thought to himself what would Chris Spencer do, and the answer brought back the slight cruel smile to his lips. Why Chris Spencer had no wings, and certainly no feathers! Well nor did he!

Unfortunately he was unfamiliar with the area, and there were at least two of them, possibly more. In his favour were his level of fitness and the self- defence courses which had formed part of his past training, much of which now flooded back to his memory. Additionally he knew they were there, removing their advantage of the element of surprise. He moved further along the side of the building keeping to the depths of the shadows, and in doing so stumbled and almost tripped over something. It turned out to be a length of hardwood, presumably discarded by a thoughtless truck driver after off-loading, but very welcome now. The timber was a piece of three by three rough cut, and was about three and a half feet long. Well it may well help to even up the odds Parfitt thought, but he must get rid of the kebab.

He couldn't know what lay ahead, but didn't want his hands cluttered. At the same time he didn't want the remains found later if things got messy. He had bitten into the meat and pita bread and doubtless traces of DNA could be retrieved from them. Also partial prints may have been left on the paper wrapping and plastic bag. He emptied the remains of the meat and salad down a drain. Rats would eat all of it by morning. The bread he threw Frisbee style onto a roof, knowing the early birds would devour it. He tucked the timber under his left arm and carefully wiped his fingers clean of grease on the paper wrapping and serviette, folded them and pushed them into his right hand trouser pocket, the bag he stuffed into his left pocket.

The end of the warehouse was reached without him being seen. He turned back to look and could see the two youths standing in the middle of the junction of the road behind him. They had lost him in the shadows and he had gained ground on them. Parfitt deliberately crossed the road so he could be seen. Another warehouse stood opposite, very similar to the one in whose shadows he had just been hiding. As he turned the corner which was formed by the end of the building he once more glanced back. The youths were jogging up the side of the road just out of the shadows. Parfitt sprinted along the back end of the building, on what was a larger and slightly better lit road. At the far end of the wall was another corner again in shadow with a small tree growing, further shading the area. No one was in sight. Parfitt leant the timber against the side of the building then ran back a dozen or so paces, once more turning about and casually walking back to the corner where the timber was propped. This time he heard them as they rounded the corner behind him, and turned towards them pretending it was the first time he had seen them. The 'Sword of Allah' was a good ten paces in front of his pack mate. Parfitt did as was expected of him and turned and ran. A shout went up and the two youths gave chase, the 'Sword' gaining more ground on his friend as Parfitt rounded the corner, grabbing the timber as he went, immediately stopping and hiding behind the trunk of the tree.

Peering around the trunk Parfitt watched as the 'Sword' approached. There was a glint of steel in his right hand as he passed under the final lamp post. He had a knife in his hand. Parfitt smiled. The younger man's intention was absolutely clear. Parfitt would feel no guilt now at what he was about to do. As the young man rounded the corner Parfitt stepped from the shadows with a grin on his face.

"Looking for me?" he asked. The look on the youth's face changed from a snarl to surprise to fear in three paces. His momentum kept him going despite his head telling him to retreat. It was too late. Decades spent playing cricket at air bases around the world going back as far as could possibly remember had taught Parfitt how to swing a bat to meet a high speed ball. He met the 'Swords' run with a perfect swing. The length of wood hit the youth full in the face at a combined speed of close to one hundred miles an hour. With a soft squelching thud, very unlike the satisfying knock of leather on willow, it made contact with his nose and forehead. His nose and skull broke instantly as his brain impacted with the front of his cranial cavity and he lost most of the front teeth from his upper jaw as the front of his face literally folded inward on itself.

Dying, with his head snapped back, his body continued forward out of control for two more paces as it started to collapse. It hit the ground with the head still back and no arms thrust forward to break the fall. The jaw bone shattered on impact, snapping the head forward and slamming the already broken nose hard onto the ground. The knife had fallen at Parfitt's feet. Crouching down he pulled the take-away bag from his pocket and picked the knife up using the bag as a glove. As he did, the second youth rounded the corner, again with knife in hand. Parfitt had no time to stand, let alone swing. The second youth took in the scene and instantly lunged forward at Parfitt, knife extended in his right hand.

Parfitt had to react from a crouch. He ducked to his right under the extended knife thrust and left handed drove the 'Sword's' knife straight into the centre of the chest of the oncoming youth. The body continued over Parfitt's shoulder snatching the knife from his hand and collapsed face down six feet from his friend forcing the knife even deeper into his own chest and speeding him on his journey to Allah. The whole incident had taken no more than ten seconds. No vehicles had passed or were in sight. There was nobody about who could have seen anything. Standing back in the shadows Parfitt surveyed the scene calmly, despite a racing heart and elevated levels of adrenalin. How would this appear to the police? Should he report it, or just walk away? Obviously he should report it, but did he want to? What linked him to this? How well would his face and features be remembered and reported from the takeaway? Would the other youths report that their friends had gone out knives in hand to search for him? Or would they try and distance themselves from the incident? Most importantly, were there any cameras along the route he and they had followed?

The ground on which he stood was firm and dry. There would be no heel marks in the ground around the tree, so no way the police could work out his height or weight. It was a fight between intentionally armed youths on the one hand and person or persons unknown. He was not marked, let alone cut. The police would be on the lookout for knife wounds at all local hospitals, but he had none. Apart from a few words in a local takeaway between an unknown white male travelling ostensibly on foot, nothing at all linked him to this. His was just another unknown face. Two of the Turks at the takeaway had gone out of their way to ignore him and demonstrate their supreme indifference. The other youths would almost definitely neither remember him nor want to get involved with the police. They would distance themselves as much as they possibly could. Parfitt stepped forward and checked both pulses. Neither body had one. There were only three possible areas of concern, cameras, the length of timber and the Turk who originally served him. The timber he could easily lose in one of the warehouse yards. He could do nothing about the Turk, but he could check for cameras. If there were any which appeared active he decided he would report the matter. If not, he would walk away and trust to luck.

There were no cameras.

Jake Ferris kept his word and drove Phil Gatting home after the meeting. He wanted to talk to Phil quietly and privately. Before leaving he checked up on Nathan, who had previously been given a sedative and appeared to be a little more relaxed, though his response was slow and his speech somewhat vague. Chi Lu had assumed full personal responsibility for all of Nathan's needs. She had taken the view the meeting may go on for some time and, although she knew nothing of what was being said, realised it was of a serious nature when she heard of Jake's request to have the room electronically swept and that unannounced guests were arriving via the back door. She knew Phil Gatting personally and, realising he had no connection with NJF Industries, correctly presumed the secret meeting was to do with the deaths of the day before. She therefore cancelled the hotel Nathan and Jake had stayed in the night before, telephoned a maid service and had them go around and make up the spare room in her penthouse apartment, instructing them to provide everything Nathan might need for a stay of up to a week.

Unbelievably the media had still not discovered Susie's death, or at least not connected the name. Jake would have dearly liked to believe that in fact they had learnt of her death but out of respect decided not to kick a man whilst on the ground. He almost snorted in disgust at his own thoughts. It could not last. By tomorrow they would be knee deep in reporters and cameramen. The last thing he did before leaving was to order in extra security for the following day, literally tripling the number of guards.

The drive to Foxton was uneventful. Neither man spoke during the first quarter of an hour of the journey whilst Jake negotiated the London traffic, and both had plenty on their minds. Phil Gatting was the first to speak, and the words which broke through Jake's thoughts were almost identical to what was going through his head at that precise moment.

"I liked those people." Phil Gatting said. "Meeting them in almost any other situation would be one hell of a bonus, and there wasn't one of them I wouldn't snap up and create a position for if ever they were looking for employment. What an incredible team they would have made along with Susie and Chi Lu! That young planner is incredibly sharp! I don't think I've ever met the likes of his intellect before. The speed with which he grasped concepts and issues, and then bounded back with solutions to problems was almost scary. His girlfriend didn't miss a single thing, and we were speaking of complex legal and financial issues in what, her third or fourth language? That mountain of a man, the brother, Dan, is no intellectual slouch either, and the soldier, Chris Spencer – well I've never before met a man like that who from straight off I felt was utterly loyal, dependable and with such an all encompassing sense of duty. I would have no hesitation in trusting him with my family's safety and every penny I've ever earned.

"I've been around some smart, strong, hard and dangerous people along the way in my time, but never anything like what we had around the table today, and never ever all put together like that. Interesting what fate throws up. I actually think we are going to slap these bastards back now, and I think we are going to slap them much harder than they can possibly be prepared for, and many more times than even the most unreasonable would consider judicious."

"Frankly there is little I can add to any of what you say. The funny thing is I was thinking along the same lines myself." Jake replied, continuing, "We'll have to be extremely cautious as to how we proceed. Young Jack Bryant is quite correct in that regard. We cannot be seen to be doing anything out of the ordinary. We have to keep it tight in order to maintain secrecy, and absolute secrecy is vital if we are to have any measure of success.

"Christ Phil, I can't believe we are having this conversation. Yesterday morning we were both successful business men, running our companies and thinking about future growth and profits. Today we are quite seriously planning mass murder with a bunch of people we have never previously met. The world has suddenly become a very scary place!"

"Susie's death may well yet prove to be the catalyst which heralds an era of change." Phil Gatting responded.

Jack, Katya and Danny, having left the meeting returned to the hospital to see Tom Bryant who was still asleep. They consulted the attending nurse who confirmed it would be fine to wake him. However the nurse also told them that before they did so there was a doctor who wished to speak with them about Tom's general condition and all three were shown to a small empty office. Two minutes later a somewhat rotund red faced man in his fifties entered. He wore a small round pair of glasses at the end of his nose and, had it not been for the clipboard in his hand, all would have thought the man had entered the wrong room. He more resembled a somewhat archetypical eccentric professor, so un-medical like was this appearance.

In a deep, almost booming voice the doctor introduced himself, shaking hands with each in turn. The office possessed a small desk with one chair behind and two facing it. On its surface was a computer terminal. The doctor sat and pointed to the seats opposite his. Katya sat and Danny indicated to Jack he should take the other, which left Danny towering over the room. The doctor, who's name was Peterson, tapped something on the keypad, obviously bringing up Tom Bryant's medical history.

Then, looking over the top of his glasses, he said, "I have both good news and bad news for you, and then several questions. The good news is, with the exception of the little finger on your father's left hand, he should make a full and rapid physical recovery. The finger is lost and there was nothing which could be done to save it. His left arm, although broken in two places, broke cleanly and has been reset. A few weeks in plaster and he should be able to start working it to rebuild the muscle tissue which will be lost whilst the cast is in place. He has three broken ribs, which will be painful for a while, but will heal as well. Within eight weeks, apart from the finger, he will be fully recovered – physically."

The doctor looked back at his computer screen, pursed his lips and, with his hands on the desk top, pressed his finger-tips together. After a moments silence he looked back up and continued. "I have to discuss things with you which may seem somewhat out of the ordinary in that in general health terms we communicate with the patient and not their relatives. However in this case I both need to inform you and obtain information from you. In most normal circumstances, if there is such a thing as a normal circumstance after a bomb explosion, we would have kept your father in for another night's observation then, given he should be on the road to physical recovery, we would send him home with you tomorrow. I'll be completely candid with you; my area of expertise is not in the physical area of recovery. I can see what happened to your father, what has been done to remedy the situation, and can report on the expected success of the physical part of the recovery process. However I specialise in matters to do with the mind, basically the workings of emotional responses and psychological trauma.

"Your father is currently sedated. This has nothing to do with the physical injuries he has suffered, but everything to do with the trauma of the event he witnessed, and his attachment to Mrs Cartwright. I can see from his medical history he has suffered a major psychological trauma before with the loss of your mother, something he received little or no counselling for at the time and the event left him with probable personality disorders which were never rectified. A traumatic event such as the loss of a loved one, especially someone who is extremely close, affects almost everyone, but we as individuals can deal with such events, with or without help, very differently.

"There are many ways the mind comes to terms with such things, from guilt to denial to full breakdown, but in many cases, once experienced, the mind is never the same again. With physical pain the mind tends to remove severity from memory, a classic example of which is childbirth. The memory of the nature of pain is stored, but the depths of the pain are automatically discarded as a part of the healing process.

"With psychological trauma this general rule cannot be applied in the same way as, as I have said, people respond in wholly different ways, sometimes predictably, but often not. Having experienced a deeply disturbing event some minds will become hardened to such things, as can be the case with front line troops, who tend to fall back on a sense of humour as a mental defence mechanism. However not all troops in the same place experiencing the same events react in the same manner. Some can become battle hardened – some can have their psyche damaged and suffer shell shock. Your father's ability to deal with a debilitating shock of this nature would appear to have been dramatically weakened by your mother's death. Everything which can be done will be done, but I feel it is important to inform you your father may never be the same person again. Now would you please help me by describing the events leading up to your mother's death, what followed, and any observations as to your father's reactions and mental stability afterwards? I appreciate you are not qualified in this field, but you probably know your father better than anyone else alive, and any observations may prove useful."

Danny and Jack Bryant gave the doctor as full a report on the circumstances surrounding the death of their mother as they could. Dr Peterson made several notes on his clipboard as they spoke. He was particularly interested in the ethnic background of Mary's killer, and of the lies and subterfuge which were offered during the court case, several times stopping whichever brother was talking to question a point or to ask for them to expand upon it. After twenty minutes of questioning and note taking he once more peered over his glasses at the Bryant brothers and thanked them for their help, which he claimed may well prove to be a most helpful insight into the workings of Tom's tortured brain.

"Tomorrow I'll have your father moved to a more comfortable ward." Dr Peterson explained. "He'll have his own room, and I shall endeavour to ensure he is nursed by those with a European background, as he has developed an obsessive behaviour response to peoples with a non-white skin. I believe it to be an anxiety disorder triggered by the bombing. I also believe it to have been in place for many years, and has either been dormant or he managed to control obvious outward signs. In his case it is a specific phobia akin to xenophobia. When confronted by anyone from a non European background the situation brings on either severe anxiety or a panic attack, depending on the proximity of the individual.

"As one of the most basic of human emotions, fear is programmed into the nervous system to work almost as an instinct. Something we depend upon for survival if we sense danger. Fear helps to protect us, acting as a warning, cautioning us to be careful and, as with other emotions, can run full spectrum from mild through medium to intense. Your father's fear may be irrational to others, but to him it is real, and the very essence of his being is flooded with fear at the most intense of levels. This has activated his nervous system and caused physical responses. You'll have noticed his rapid breathing, which has nothing to do with broken ribs, nor has the sweating, which is the bodies attempt to keep itself cool. His heart rate is increased, as is his blood pressure. These help pump blood into the large muscle groups in preparation for physical action – basically running or fighting.

"He is currently sedated in order to help reduce these physical manifestations of his fear. What has to be done now is to find a way to get an all clear message to his brain in order to turn off the response. A fear reaction is instantaneous, and the reaction occurs before the thinking part of the brain gets a chance to process and evaluate the information it receives. Fear in itself can be healthy if it cautions an individual to take precautions around anything which could prove dangerous, but overreaction can take over, causing more caution than a situation calls for. This can be counterproductive causing sufferers to avoid situations they fear, which does nothing to help overcome their fears, in fact quite the opposite, and can lead to a reinforcing of that fear. Given the opportunity rational adults can learn about their fears and gradually come to terms with it. Those with fears which are intense or long lasting often need help and support in overcoming them.

"However, in your father's case, I am concerned we may be dealing with a phobia, not a fear. Although in some ways affiliated, a phobia is more an intense fear reaction connected to a particular situation, experience, object or thing, and is out of all proportion to any potential source of danger, although to the individual the concept of danger feels very real. I believe that in your father's case the phobia probably developed with the death of your mother, but was neither recognised for what it was nor treated. With the passage of time your father slowly overcame it naturally, although he was probably inadvertently helped by Mrs. Cartwright.

"I'm sorry, but here it's a little technical. In complex vertebrates, including humans, a structure within the brain called an amygdale performs a primary role in the building and retention of memories coupled with emotional events, and can trigger strong fear reactions. Some people may be born with certain personality traits, or have inherited a genetic disposition, but in the case of your father I believe it to have been caused by the situations he has experienced, and his brain has learnt a response in order to protect the person.

"To overcome this phobia will take time, understanding, and a great degree of patience. As I have said I feel it was initially caused by your mother's death, an event which for him was traumatic in the extreme. It has now been reinforced by the horrific event he witnessed when the bomb exploded on his tube train, killing the woman in whom he had placed his trust and love, essentially his very being. You father is a man utterly devoted to those he loves. No personal sacrifice would be too great for him. Yet he has not been asked to make sacrifices of himself, but has had to endure the violent death of the two women he loved at the hands of those he sees as of the same background. His brain has built up a defence mechanism to protect him from those who threaten him. In this case those with brown and black skin. For him to overcome this will take willingness and bravery on his part, without doubt the extended help of a therapist, and time. Possibly a great deal of time!

"I believe it will be necessary to move him to a controlled environment, which I can do here, keep him mildly sedated initially, and under observation. It will not be a quick process, and there are no shortcuts. However the alternatives are far worse. Without treatment he may become violent to those he perceives to be his enemies, or be left with an inability to in any way fend for himself. In either case the authorities would take over and he would inevitably be incarcerated by one system or another. I would seriously suggest you pay heed to this matter and do not accede to any request on his part to sign himself out. If he leaves hospital at this stage it may lead to him being sectioned and institutionalised, the duration of which would then be open-ended."

Danny and Jack agreed to leave their father in the hospital, to then let him continue to sleep, and to visit whenever they could. With Katya they then left, and with heavy hearts drove back to the family home outside Lymington.

On the Sunday morning the three returned to the hospital and spent several hours with Tom before Danny delivered his brother and Katya to Heathrow Airport to return to Moscow, then Danny drove home alone. The conversation with Dr. Peterson had done nothing to soften their attitudes. Sandy was dead and their father was to be hospitalised for some considerable time. At least!

During the weekend which followed the bombing Nathan remained with Chi Lu who was unstinting in her help and overall caring. For a person whom the City and many around the world regarded as a single minded go-getting business woman her ability to deal with Nathan on the most human of levels was outstanding. Her warmth, kindness and devotion appeared to know no limits, and it was a testament to her seemingly limitless patience and understanding that within the period of a few days she nursed him from a near suicidal wreck to a person who could again at least function, even if normal action, reaction and interaction were not yet the order of the day.

She stayed in regular touch with Jake often updating him every few hours, which still was not enough for Jake who continually felt guilty about the fact it was not him looking after Nathan. On the Monday morning Chi Lu arrived at work with Nathan and again updated Jake, who had arrived earlier running the gauntlet of the press, and started to do the job she had crossed America and the Atlantic to take up. The change in Nathan over the weekend was immediately apparent. Although no one who saw him could possibly have described him as looking happy, none would have then considered him suicidal. Anyone not knowing him may well have thought of him as somewhat vexed, possibly angry. Those who knew him for the inoffensive, mild mannered, retiring person he normally was could see that just beneath the surface he was seething.

On the Friday evening a business journalist from one of the more up-market papers finally put two and two together after reading a list of the names of the dead. What started out for him as a possible coincidence as far as names were concerned had, with a little checking on his part, panned out, and the news hit the streets. Media frenzy followed with every news programme and newspaper seemingly trying to out speculate the one before. Reporters and camera crews had camped out at the gates of NJF ever since the news broke, and by the Monday morning some of them were a sorry looking lot. The bigger stations and papers rotated their reporters and crews, but by no means all.

Chi-Lu was a long term photographer's delight, a stunning looking woman who also happily happened to be most photogenic. She rarely shunned publicity, usually turning it to the advantage of NJF Industries, correctly claiming NJF just could not buy the advertising the press would give them for free. Nathan on the other hand was anything but photogenic and usually avoided the press as the antelope avoids the lion, but it was not something he was going to do that day. Stopping at the gate on the way in he got out of the car and spoke to the assembled reporters as cameras flashed and small electric motors whirled. His statement was simple.

"I know you people want to ask a number of questions, and understand you have a job to do. I am not; repeat not, going to answer questions here and now. At twelve noon I intend to call a press conference in the board room where a statement will be read and your questions will be answered. In the meantime I suggest you all get something to eat and, if you need to, get washed and changed. Give your names now to these gentlemen on security and you will be shown in on your return. Question me or press me now and you will be excluded from the conference!" With that said he got back into the car and was driven to the front of the building. Some questions were shouted, and security excluded those who had.

Some of the members of the press took the opportunity to shower and shave, and to grab a bite to eat on the run, but most did not, and the smell of some as they crushed into the boardroom told of how long they had waited for any form of interview or news. Five people represented NJF Industries with Nathan seated at the centre. To his right sat Jake, and to his left Chi Lu. Jake was flanked by the company media exec Naomi Parker, whilst Abe Cohen, the head of NJF's legal department, was seated to the left of Chi Lu. The press were somewhat crammed in, those which could sit sat, and those who could not stood. Cameras were set up where possible and an array of microphones faced those at the top table.

Nathan, despite always in the past trying to avoid the press, uncharacteristically led. He stood up and faced the assembled reporters.

"Most of you have been presented with a prepared statement, and there are copies available for those of you currently without them," he said. "The statement covers most things which can in any way be construed as relevant to the future of NJF. From a timing point of view most of you will know, and all certainly should know, Miss Chi Lu Herepath was to assume her new role of heading up the whole corporation as of today. That has in no way changed. Inevitably there will be some minor changes, but the big picture is business as usual. On a personal level my loss has been devastating and that is all I am prepared to say on the subject. I will not answer any questions of any sort with regard the loss of my wife and unborn child. Any of you who even attempt to form a question will be removed by security and will never again be allowed on any NJF property. I hope I make myself absolutely clear on that. We will now answer questions on NJF, and NJF only."

Nathan sat. There was a momentary hushed silence. It was quite obvious the reporters were there to poke, prod and pour salt into the open wounds. One, a somewhat dishevelled looking individual, decided to chance his luck.

"What were your first thoughts when you heard your wife had been blown to pieces?" the man asked. Microphones around the room were thrust forward. Nathan looked hard at the man, then glanced at the small security team at the back of the room and nodded. They shouldered their way through the crush, took hold of the man and literally dragged him from the room. When the hubbub subsided Nathan glanced around the room.

"Next?" he asked.

The next to speak was John Stenton, a respected and well dressed reporter from the business pages of a broadsheet.

"Mr. Jefferies, please let me start by saying you have my deepest and most sincere sympathies for your loss, and I'm sure those of every person in this room!" He glanced up and there were nods all around the room. He continued by asking, "I have read your release, and obviously knew of the changes scheduled to occur at the top of your business, but in reality what do you believe the terrible loss of your wife will mean to the long term fortunes of NJF Industries? After all she was a most dynamic and much respected young woman. I have great respect for Miss Herepath, but can Mrs. Jefferies be replaced in the boardroom?"

Completely unexpectedly, and totally unrehearsed Jake stepped straight into answering the question.

"No! She cannot! Chi Lu has the complete confidence of both Nathan and myself, and will be wholly and fully supported in her new role for which she has proven herself to be most capable time after time. But we'll never ever be able to replace Susie, and frankly I personally would never want to try! We've a brilliant and innovative design group, we'll continue to be very well managed, as you know we are extremely well funded and financed, and our global interests are not just expanding, but are expanding rapidly autonomously. We'll not be putting our feet up, and we'll all continue to take care of business – but we'll never be able to replace Susie!"

"How do you see your future role Miss Herepath? Have the events of last Thursday effected you?" someone shouted from the back of the room. Both the questions were expected and it would have been unreasonable for them not to have been asked. As Jake had, Chi Lu remained seated as she answered. Her smooth way of talking coupled to her North American drawl had their usual soothing effect. Even the yapping dogs of the world of the newshounds were usually silenced when Chi Lu spoke, and the press conference was no exception. Intelligent, educated and articulate individuals are usually listened to. When a person has all those attributes and a proven track record as a global achiever, can respond in a voice which sounded like honey running on silk, and whose words come from the lips of a face and body which would have left Aphrodite foaming with jealousy, it is not hard to understand why it was that a pin would have been heard dropping three floors away as she answered.

"My future role remains wholly unchanged," Chi Lu purred. "I will continue to build upon the successful blocks which have already been laid. We have wonderful global brand awareness and we do not just control, but own, every link in the chain from manufacturer to retailer. Every one of those links is either profitable, where we are selling, or extremely cost effective where we are supplying an in-house service. I intend to build upon the brands we have, and to further diversify into allied markets and acquire ever more of our core suppliers. The events of last Thursday have caused me to re-evaluate my view of the world and those who inhabit it. I have lost my closest and dearest friend, the one person in the world who not only could but did give me a chance at a proper career. I believe I will miss her terribly every day for the rest of my life, and I also believe that to be true of anyone who was in any way close to Susie. I feel if her untimely death does not change the world of its own accord, then something should be done to force change."

"What sort of change do you feel should be ushered in, and what do you think will be done?" The question was asked by a popular tabloid reporter, so it was obvious whoever answered the question, and whatever they said, would never be accurately reported. Nonetheless, as the question was aimed at her, Chi Lu took it and replied.

"I feel in fairness I should answer those two questions in reverse order. I would emphasise these are my personal opinions, that I am very angry, and my answers do not reflect the corporate ethos of NJF Industries." The gathered reporters sensed something important was about to be said, and there was a discernable move forward despite the crushed surroundings as Chi Lu continued. "I do not think the government of your country will do anything at all. It will sit on its hands and wail a little, perhaps pass some silly and bad laws as a knee jerk reaction, but will effectively do no more than further repress the common people of your land."

There was absolute silence in the room. None of the assembled reporters had in their entire careers ever expected to hear such a direct and politically contentious statement from any person in Chi Lu's position, but if they had found that controversial then much more was to follow.

"You ask what should happen. As all will see from my features I am of mixed race heritage, therefore what I say cannot be regarded as racist, something you British seem to have an obsession with.

"It strikes me that for years, consecutive British governments, irrespective of political persuasion, have continuously remained ridiculously lenient as to whom they let settle your land. Various cultures have been encouraged to establish themselves here, bringing with them their inherent problems which have in turn flourished. You have black crime out of control with no go areas for anyone with white skin, Asians who have taken over entire communities and industries, and illegal immigration at a level which will ultimately destroy your very society. Yet you allow it, and by you I mean all of you Brits, and you people of the press and media are as responsible as your government. What you should be doing is rounding up ALL illegals and deporting them. Those found to be supporting them should have their British passports removed and then also deported where possible, or incarcerated if not. Any alien committing a crime in your land should be deported along with their entire extended family. Non English speaking non Europeans should never be allowed residential entry permits, and you should immediately adopt an exit policy, with those who overstay their entry terms hunted down and deported with a lifetime ban on their return. Knife crime, gun crime, violent crime and muggings should be fairly reported, with the race of the individuals covered as well as their height, age and sex. If a certain group appears to dominate in a certain area of crime people from that ethnic background should expect to be targeted, in part at least passing the onus of responsibility back to the people of that community. I think the claims of some of these pathetic liberal do-gooders are ridiculous. How can someone complain they are fed up with being stopped and questioned when they haven't done anything wrong if, at the same time, their brother is out mugging a little old lady or stealing a child's phone at knife point? There has to be some form of collective ethnic responsibility. If they wish to stop being targeted do something about tidying up the act of their own community. After all, you white people have to, and it's your land!"

There was another momentary silence as the gathered reporters digested what they had just heard. Many could not believe their own ears. Did this vision of loveliness not realise what she had just said, and to reporters from national television crews and papers? Did she not understand some of what she had just said could not by law be reported in Britain? Freedom of speech had long since disappeared. They would love to report this as it was said, but they would have to run it past legal teams before they did so. Did she not understand the potential damage she had just done to NJF Industries? Yet all at the top table just sat there calmly waiting for the next question. Surely the lawyer at least should be trying to qualify what she had just said? But he too just sat there like the others with his fingers folded into one another.

John Stenton was the first to recover. He cleared his throat and started to form a question. As he did so just about every reporter present seemed to come to their senses, and all started to shout questions, none of which could be heard above the pandemonium which followed. Nathan held up his hand and the noise subsided, finally stopping.

"Mr. Stenton, you had a question? Nathan asked.

"Yes. Thank you." Stenton responded immediately. "Miss Herepath, frankly I don't believe any here expected you to be quite so candid! May I ask if there is anything NJF Industries intend to do either directly or indirectly in response to these attacks?"

"I'll answer that one myself if I may." Nathan said. "NJF Industries has lost one of its founders to an evil and insidious premeditated plot by a group of Muslim extremists. As you will know we have for the past several months been in talks regarding the building of a production plant in Indonesia. For round figures it is a two hundred million US dollar project. It was expected to create somewhere in the region of five thousand jobs in the region, which is an area badly in need of inward investment. NJF have never believed in exploitation of its workers, paying all of our employees well above what is regarded as the going rate. Our pay structure for those we planned to employ in the region was slightly above five times that which is considered the average. We believe those jobs would in turn create far more, as we always source locally where we can. The overall figure was likely to be around twelve thousand jobs, which would give housing, clothing, food and education to roughly one hundred thousand people. Indonesia is a Muslim country. As a direct result of the bombing I am cancelling the project, which we'll now move to Thailand, a non-Muslim country."

"But – surely that will cost you a fortune?" Stenton asked, somewhat aghast. All five people at the top table merely stared back at him, not a trace of emotion crossed their faces. Stenton chuckled.

"Your organisation has been accused of being somewhat unconventional in the past, and the term maverick has often been bandied about, but in all my years I have never seen a business take such a step based only on principle. Principles cost – but you really don't care do you? If you had shareholders they would go berserk. You will anger a lot of people in the Muslim world with the statements you have just made. How do you think it will affect your business around the world?"

This time Chi Lu answered his questions. "A fortune is a relative thing Mr. Stenton. We can easily take the loss and survive. As for unconventional and standing on principle, we believe we are right and others are wrong. Other businesses should follow our lead. If those we try to help slap us in the face that help should be withdrawn. Principles are worth paying for, and others should try to remember that. In answer to your question – yes – we do care. We care a very great deal! As for shareholders we have those too. The company was originally set up with one thousand one pound shares, only three of which were issued, one each to Nathan Jefferies, Jake Ferris and Susie Gatting. The two surviving shareholders are in full agreement with the course of action we are to follow and, as the Chief Executive Officer, so am I! As for angering Muslims, I will state for the record for every person who sits at this table, and for everyone else who was at any time connected with Susie, we will never, not ever, even come close to making them as angry as they have made us!

"Finally we are due to release two new games, both using the latest motion capture technology which we have helped pioneer, a range of related toys and other consumer goods, and an innovative, pay to play, on-line treasure hunt, which will be charged at a penny a minute per player, and will pay out a quarter of a million pounds to each and every winner. You are the first to hear of this. The announcement was due to be made in two weeks time when I was settled in the job, but I am making it now because of your questions. I believe the best way we can judge how the greater public feel about the statements we have made here today is to see how they take up our new products. If they sell well we will know what has been said has the general agreement, if not endorsement, of the British people, in which case the government should pay heed. If our products are boycotted, we will know we have overstepped the mark. Almost a referendum really! I suggest you all watch this space!"

There was a clamouring of inconsequential follow up questions, after which the short press conference was wound up with reporters literally running from the building, desperate to get back to their various offices and run the story none in their wildest dreams had expected to get.

Jake ordered another electronic sweep of the boardroom, had the three devices which were found removed intact, and had a long private word with Nathan. The anger in the younger man was plain to see, and would have been wholly unnatural had it not been present, but there was much more to it than anger. Nathan wanted vengeance, and he wanted it a lot. In reality it was he who approached Jake, almost as a son would his father, explaining how much he would like to hit back at any who were close to those who had killed Susie. Slowly, carefully, Jake dropped hints as to what had already taken place and been decided, until eventually the whole story was told. Nathan didn't care what it cost him, he wanted in!

Chi Lu's announcement forced NJF to bring the latest new games launch date forward by two weeks, which meant the desired levels of stock would not be ready if the usual demand pattern for new NJF releases held true, but such things were never an exact science, and the best which could ever be hoped for was a fairly accurate guesstimate. Motion capture had provided the games with the most lifelike characters the gaming world had yet seen. However what they had said on national television following Susie's death could well have turned public opinion, and the entire project could flop as a result. Public opinion should never be underrated by any in the retail business and NJF, through Chi Lu, had taken an enormous chance.

Over the years the game releases had become managed in a wholly professional manner, and the formula used was most successful with a well planned and executed lead in time. In this case it was almost back to basics. NJF were the trend setting international market leaders with a global brand following. Usually as new products were released they almost literally flew off the shelves of NJF's own and other retail outlets around the world. This time the pre-market advertising build up had not been fully in place, and NJF may have skewed their own market by the content of what was broadcast following the press conference on Monday the eleventh of July. They did not have long to wait to find out as the new release date was Saturday the sixteenth.

They did not have to wait until the Saturday to know the answer. By ten o'clock on the morning of Wednesday the thirteenth they already had it. Many gaming fans were bitterly disappointed. The presale orders had already swamped and massively exceeded the entire planned production run irrespective of the change of release dates. Before eleven o'clock on the Saturday morning retail outlets nationwide had run dry. By midday some lucky and enterprising purchasers were selling the games on eBay at five times the retail price, and they were selling instantly. It was the most successful product launch in more than a quarter of a century of gaming history, not just in the British Isles, but around the world. With the associated merchandise sales which followed NJF grossed over three billion pounds, netting nearly one and half billion before taxation.

In a manner of speaking the British people had voted. Their government ignored them.

Five

Peter Parfitt had left the scene, taken his shoes off at the car and placed them on the passenger foot well mat, then driven off in his socks. He pulled out of the side road and tucked in tight behind a passing truck which he followed to the motorway, from there he drove back to Tammy's home at a sensible speed, just under seventy miles an hour. He felt strangely elated. As he left the motorway, and with no vehicles following him, he lowered the passenger window and threw the paper wrapper, serviette and plastic bag he had used as a glove out into the night, to become just more pieces of wind blown litter.

Once at Tammy's house he picked up the passenger mat with his shoes placed on top and carried them to the porch where he opened the front door, but did not turn the light on. Making sure he was not being watched he stripped down to his under shorts, leaving everything on the floor of the porch. He returned with two large plastic bags, into one of which he placed his shoes. Everything else, including the mat, he placed in the second bag and then carried it through to the utility room, leaving the shoes on the porch. He emptied his trouser pocket of his wallet which he placed on a wipe down countertop, and put trousers, handkerchief, socks, shirt and mat into the washing machine, setting it for pre-wash, wash, and dry. He then showered, went to the bedroom and re-dressed from his suitcase. Leaving the house he picked up the bag with the shoes in and this time made sure he picked up the road he needed as he drove down into Marlow where he found just what he wanted, an overflowing builders skip, into which he pushed the bag containing the shoes, hiding it under builders' waste and rubble.

He returned to the house at Cookham Dean, suddenly beginning to shake uncontrollably. There was nothing left for him to do but go to bed, where despite the temperature and time of year he continued to shiver and shake. Sleep eluded him for many hours and, when eventually he did drop off he slept fitfully with troubling vivid dreams. Despite many years of serving his country he had never before taken another's life. Self defence or not, and with all which had happened to Tammy, it did not rest easy with him that first night.

By the morning the police had not arrived. His conscious mind pushed the subconscious to one side, rationalising what he had done, accepting it as a reality, almost pleased at having rid the world of the vermin. It had happened, it had been done, it could not be undone – move on. To interrupt his thoughts he telephoned the hospital asking after Tammy, but there was still no change, she was critical, unconscious, and he could not see her. On a whim he telephoned her parents and arranged to drive down to see them. He bagged up the clothes he had washed, left the mat on the garage floor to dry out fully, picked up the bag of clothes, and drove down to Brighton. Once south of the M27 and on the A27 he found a lay-by, tore the clothes, and put all the ripped up bits in a waste bin along with the bag. There would be no DNA residue, and nothing to link him with the events of the night before.

Tammy's parents were terribly distraught, and from the look of them they too had not slept. They had received some information as to how Tammy was, but nothing like enough whilst at the same time far too much, especially as they, like Parfitt, remained unable to see her. Their beautiful, caring, perfect daughter was in a hospital bed fighting for her life having lost several body parts, but in an unknown condition. If she survived she would never be the same. How would she even be able to move about? She had always been so beautiful. How would she cope without her limbs? She was an internationally known model for years – Oh, what on Earth was she going to do? If she lived!

Parfitt was there to share what information he could with them, and to open up a discussion regarding long term plans. It was blindingly obvious Tammy was going to need a lot of help, which he was more than happy to provide, but all their plans for the future disappeared forever the moment the bomb on their train detonated. They would eventually have to plan something entirely different, and those plans were likely to include her parents and the cottage in their grounds. He stayed with Tammy's parents through the rest of the day, phoned the hospital in the early evening to find there was still no change, and that night slept in the cottage, thinking about the future, and how very much was going to have to change.

He slept slightly better on the Saturday night. Perhaps the slight sea breeze wafting in from the English Channel helped, but whatever it was he awoke feeling much more refreshed, and with it went a feeling of optimism. He made breakfast for his hosts but failed to raise their spirits as their concern for their daughter remained all consuming. Not expecting to hear any better news he once again called the hospital, and the call sent his spirits soaring. Although still critical, and in a coma, Tammy had, in the early hours of the morning, been taken off the danger list and very slightly downgraded. She was now expected to live!

Promising faithfully he would call them with any changes Peter left Tammy's parents home and made his way back up to London to the hospital, arriving during Sunday lunch time. The receptionist this time asked him to wait as there was a note on Tammy's computer file from a member of her surgery team requesting a meeting with Parfitt should he turn up. That particular Sunday Peter's luck held out well. The surgeon in question was both on duty and had just finished his lunch when the message for him came through on his pager. Within fifteen minutes of entering the hospital Parfitt and the doctor were to be found sat in a small private room discussing Tammy's progress.

Jozef Bakowski was from Poland's second, but most visited city, Krakow, and had come to England fifteen months earlier in search of more rewarding employment. He was immediately snatched up by the NHS and had worked at The Royal London Hospital ever since. He was part of the team which worked on Tammy continuously for the first twenty-nine hours she was in the hospital, and he had some unbelievable news for Parfitt.

"Your fiancée was very badly injured when she was admitted." Bakowski told Parfitt. "At first it was by no means certain she would survive, and she would have had no chance of having done so if you had not taken the actions you did after the explosion. The damage to her was both extreme and severe, and at first we thought if she survived at all she would lose more than it would appear she has. She is obviously a very strong young woman, not just physically, but mentally as well. She has lost both her left leg and her left arm. That is the bad news."

"I saw that at the scene of the explosion." Parfitt said, adding, "I know she also lost her right foot, left ear, breast and eye, but I couldn't tell how bad her jaw was at the time, or if there was any damage to her skull under the scalp. It was pretty chaotic, the light was terrible, and I just did what I could."

"Well what you did in the circumstances was excellent, and without doubt not only did you save her life, but saved a lot more of her besides." the doctor told Parfitt. "You are wrong about what she lost. We do have some world class surgeons at this hospital, and not one of them who worked on your girlfriend were prepared to let her lose any more than she had before she came in here."

"So how bad is she?" Parfitt asked. Was the doctor trying to give him good news, or just seeking to reassure him?

"She is in a coma at the moment. That is in no way unusual, but I don't expect it to last for very long, maybe a few days, maybe a week. As I said she's lost her left leg and her left arm. In both cases she's been somewhat fortunate as both joints have been saved. The elbow stood a good chance from the beginning, but we expected to lose her knee. However we managed to save it."

Parfitt was shocked. He thought he knew the left leg had gone completely. He couldn't believe they had managed to keep her knee. "But that means she can be fitted with a prosthetic limb and should be able to walk in time!" he blurted out. "But what of the rest of the injuries? Did you manage to save anything else?" he asked hopefully, knowing the answer would undoubtedly be no because he had seen the extent of her injuries on the floor of the carriage.

"She has lost all hearing in her left ear. There was no skull damage. Her scalp has been sown back into place. Her left ear has been saved and also sown back into place. Any scarring should be hidden beneath her hair line in time. Again her lip has been sown back and there is little nerve damage. There will be slight scarring there also, but much should be able to be hidden with make-up. Her left eye was saved and she will have vision out of it, although it is unlikely it will ever again be one hundred percent. Her left breast we have managed to fully re-attach and it should not suffer long term damage. Any scars there would be fully covered by any top she is likely to wear, even swimsuit or bikini. Her right foot is by far the best news for you, in that we believe we have managed to fully save it. No infection seems to have set in, although it does remain a possibility. It has needed pins, and she will have to relearn how to walk on it, but given a little time she should get full use back with it." The doctor stopped and looked at Parfitt expectantly, but Parfitt just sat open mouthed staring at the doctor, completely dumbfounded, so the doctor continued. "You must understand she will have to spend a considerable amount of time in hospital, and then there will be extensive physiotherapy. She'll have to be fitted with prosthetics and they'll take time to become accustomed to but, in answer to your question, yes, she should walk again. In fact she should be able to do most of what she has done before. There will be limits, but as I said when I started, she is tough, and I get the impression she is probably a determined person. She will get over this and can still live a rich full life."

Parfitt couldn't speak. He had absolutely known Tammy had lost her right foot and left breast. He had seen her left ear virtually torn from her body, and couldn't imagine the damage which occurred in her left eye. Had these wonderful people managed to save any one of her injured parts it would have been an incredible bonus, but to have saved them all was nothing short of miraculous. Tears welled up in his eyes and spilled down his cheeks as he suddenly found himself pumping the surgeon's hand up and down in a wholly inadequate gesture of expressing his extreme gratitude.

It was late on the Tuesday night or very early Wednesday morning when Tammy finally came around. With the exceptions of finding some food and calling her parents Parfitt had remained there for every moment he was allowed from the time he had heard the news, at times just sleeping in the chair at her bedside.

Six

Chris Spencer headed north. He knew no one in London except those he met after the explosions. Arrangements would have to be made to get Charlie's body back to the family for burial, and he needed to speak to his kin, to look them in the eye and explain how he had so badly let them all down. He then wanted to contact some of the people he knew he could count on with his life, and would be there as and when he needed their help.

He had previously been offered mercenary work, but turned it down, and now realised he may soon be in a position to offer work of his own instead. Come hell or high water he would avenge Charlie's death. If the people he had met were serious, and there was absolutely no reason to think otherwise, he would shortly have access to an amount of funding well in excess of that available to many of the world's armies. He knew full well he would never need the sort of sums which they had discussed, but he also realised men with that sort of money and business organisations usually also possessed something else which may one day be needed. Power! A whole hell of a lot of power!

There was almost two weeks available to move things forward before reporting back to his new employers and he meant to use the time productively. Firstly he would cover his family duties, part of which meant having a very quite word with Jimmy Andrews, the only person he intended to share any of his plans with outside the group. Jimmy would understand, indeed he may well harbour the wish to get personally involved, but he couldn't. His was a responsible position within the British Army which he should not compromise and, despite the fact Charlie was his son, he had not been lost whilst with him. It was not the way things were done. Charlie died whilst under his care, control and command, and he was responsible. Never once in his life had he ducked his responsibilities, and he was certainly not going to now!

Although Chris had returned to his beloved Yorkshire on many occasions whilst a Green Howard it was always whilst on leave, a holiday. Generally whilst there he relaxed at his parent's home, strolled to the local pub with his father or old school friends for a pint or two, or walked the hills and vales where he had grown up, sometimes taking a whole day to explore the beautiful surroundings or following Staindale Beck into Dalby Forest, part of the North Riding Forest Park. He and Charlie once spent a week following the walks of the Cleveland Way and camping beside them. They had made their way from Scarborough north east along the side of the North Sea, past Whitby and up to Saltburn-by-the-Sea, then generally south until they finished at the village of Helmsley, effectively walking around and across more than three quarters of the North York Moors.

During almost all of his visits he ventured into Pickering and on several occasions travelled to Scarborough, watching the deep sea trawlers of the fishing fleet coming and going, plying their dangerous trade on the deep cold waters of their fishing grounds. He never lost the sense of enjoyment and the comfortable feeling familiarity with the area gave him. Little if anything had changed in the four decades covered by his personal memory, with many things remaining the same as they had always been for centuries, and there was something deeply reassuring about that.

Whilst deployed at Catterick Chris had stayed mainly on base, occasionally leaving with fellow NCOs for a visit to some of the local villages and small towns or, if he had a few days off, he generally returned to his parents' property, which he still regarded as home, or visited his sisters home and her growing family. What he had consistently failed to do on each and every trip and visit was to journey into the bigger towns and cities. At heart he remained a man of the country, happy and most comfortable there, amongst the open fields, country villages and small market towns, and a way of life – British life – Yorkshire life – which had survived and prospered there for centuries.

Having made his peace of sorts with his family on both sides of the country, and talked it over in great detail and at length with Jimmy Andrews, he set about his 'mission'. Information was trickling out about the bombers and, far more importantly, their background. He started to compile a form of coded dossier adding every fact he could as they became available. He also commenced regular reconnaissance missions into towns and cities he had previously avoided, and began to acquire at least a degree of familiarity with places he rapidly learned to loath for all they now represented. He struggled to believe his own eyes when faced with what he saw as the infestation of Asians in Blackburn, Darwen, Bradford, Manchester and the once beautiful market town of Dewsbury, now with an Asian population of more than one third, predominately Muslim.

Whilst deployed and put in harm's way to protect this his land, its people and their culture, another culture had been busy insidiously worming its way in, polluting and destroying as it did so, overwriting everything he had sworn to protect, and undermining all he held dear. His entire adult life he had spent fighting to ensure perpetuity of his country's rule of law, its overwhelming belief in man's freedoms and the established codes all Britons respected, even the criminal elements. Yet everything he and men like him were quite prepared to die to protect was being taken from his people and laid at the feet of the scum of the planet as a result of idiotic policy or failures on the part of the very politicians who had sent him to fight in other lands.

It seemed to Chris the hard working, honest, straight speaking, warm hearted people of the reformed counties of Yorkshire were being displaced and dispossessed, their livelihoods and the very nature of their cities changed beyond all recognition, even destroyed. Those taking their place exploited the benefit system, avoided taxes, defrauded insurance companies, lied, misled and thrived on subterfuge. They had no honour, could not look anyone in the eye and even demonstrated their disdain for the indigenous peoples with limp insulting handshakes. For Chris disgust rapidly gave way to abhorrence for all which was represented by this colonisation of social parasites.

He had returned to his home territory to deliver an act of vengeance to a community which collectively taught, fostered and encouraged an unacceptable act of pre-planned mass murder. The bomb which killed Charlie, and another twelve people, was detonated by Hasib Mir Hussain, an eighteen year old non-achiever born in Leeds General Infirmary and raised in Holbeck, a district to the south of Leeds. Prior to the bombing he resided with his brother Imran, and sister-in-law Shazia, at their home at 7 Colenso Mount in Holbeck. Chris had taken a drive around the run down and deprived area learning what he could of ways in and out as he fully intended to have a nice long private chat with brother Imran one day, but that would be after the police interest waned.

Whilst in the south of Leeds another area Chris wished to take a good look at was Beeston, home to another of the bombers. Shehzad Tanweer was born at St Luke's maternity hospital in Bradford and was twenty-two years old when he blew himself and seven other people to pieces, including Sandy Cartwright, on the eastbound Circle Line train. Tanweer's father, Mohammed Mumtaz Tanweer originally arrived in Britain from the Faisalabad region of Pakistan, and his son was said to have worked for him on occasions at his fish and chip shop. Mohammed was another person whose name appeared on Chris's list of people he wished to interview and have an extended 'chat' with, a chat several would never live to finish.

Beeston was also the home stamping ground of Mohammad Sidique Khan, at thirty the oldest of the four bombers, and the assumed leader, responsible for the westbound Circle Line train bomb. He too entered the world in Britain, at St James's University Hospital in Leeds. As with Tanweer's father, Khan's father, Tika Khan, was born in Pakistan.

Much was being made by the media of the fact these three bombers were British born. To Chris it was irrelevant bullshit. To his straightforward reasoning if a dog was born in a stable it did not make it a horse. That these creatures were born in the British Isles was just a geographical accident of birth. What was of far more importance was they had used the facilities of his country even, in the case of Tanweer and Khan, to gain a university education, and then turned on the country which had provided so well for them and attacked it.

Of great interest to Chris was the fact all three had attended the Stratford Street mosque in Beeston, with Tanweer and Khan also frequenting a drop-in centre for teens, the Harara Youth Access Point, which was assumed to have been used as a recruitment centre by Khan. A plan was forming in Chris's head as he drove around the south of Leeds. One day he would return, and the Harara centre and the Stratford Street mosque would be removed from the map, preferably whilst full. Semtex or C4 would sort the problem out, and he knew he could obtain more than enough without great difficulty; especially now he had more than sufficient funds.

He would have to work out a plan to plant or otherwise introduce the explosive into the buildings.

Seven

For Peter Parfitt, Nathan Jefferies, and those involved in the meeting of Friday the eighth of July the days passed rapidly. Peter Parfitt contacted Danny Bryant, ostensibly to ask after Tom, and they made an arrangement to meet in London on the evening of Sunday the seventeenth when Danny planned to drive up to see his father, whom Dr. Peterson was still most concerned about.

Both men discussed the tube bombings and what followed, although Parfitt did not mention the attack and subsequent deaths of the Muslims from Slough. Apparently the press had enjoyed a field day with the story, coming as it did a day after the bombings, but the police had no suspects and no leads. Firstly driving to Brighton, and then sitting in the hospital with Tammy, Parfitt missed all stories connected to it, but Danny had seen them and mentioned it. Parfitt could honestly say he had not seen any television or read about it in any papers, but then steered the conversation around to the meeting of the night of the bombings, assuring Danny he was most interested in becoming involved in pursuing some form of retaliation against the community responsible. As Peter's name had come up as an interested party at the Friday meeting Danny told Parfitt something of it, and mentioned the upcoming meeting of the following Friday. Parfitt assured Danny he was interested, and that he would certainly come along.

None of those who attended the Friday meeting had changed their minds about a single aspect of what they wished to do. If anything the days between the first meeting and the time the second was scheduled for actually hardened attitudes, but even if that had not been the case, then the events of Thursday the twenty-first of July would have convinced any who wavered they were doing the right thing by their country and their people.

At twelve-twenty-six on the twenty-first, a mere two weeks to the day after the bombings which killed and maimed their loved ones, a small explosion occurred on a train at Shepherd's Bush tube station on the Hammersmith and City Line in West London. At twelve-thirty another minor explosion occurred on a train at the Oval tube station on the Northern Line and, at twelve-forty-five, yet another explosion occurred on a Victoria Line train whilst at Warren Street tube station through which the Northern Line also runs. Forty-five minutes later, at one-thirty, a small explosion occurred on a number 26 bus in East London whilst travelling from Waterloo to Hackney Wick. There were no fatalities in any of the explosions all of which were of a petty nature, later to be reported as similar to that of a large firework. The only reported 'casualty' was of someone suffering an asthma attack.

In every case, only the detonator caps fired. Fortunately for those travelling on the London Underground that day the bombs did not go off. However, in direct response to the 'blasts', the stations were evacuated and a number of other stations cleared. Many parts of the system, including the Victoria, Northern, Hammersmith and City, Bakerloo, and Piccadilly Lines suspended services, further disrupting a large part of London's public transport system. The would-be bombers all fled the various scenes as their attempts to cause large scale loss of life failed.

Despite the disruption of the previous day the meeting in the boardroom of NJF went ahead as planned after a lengthy sweep of the room by state of the art electronic anti surveillance equipment, which Jake had upgraded specifically for such meetings. Apart from Nathan and Jake, Chris Spencer was the first to arrive and was dropped off by taxi at the front door, introducing himself to the receptionist using his real name and explaining it was to do with security consultancy. He was shown straight to Jake's office where he was introduced to Nathan.

Phil Gatting, the next to arrive, was known to the receptionists. He was joined in the reception by the three already present. Hands were shaken all around and the four men walked to the boardroom. Danny had passed along the message to Chris Spencer regarding Peter Parfitt's interest and, when he arrived, he too was shown straight to the boardroom where Chris introduced him to the other three men, none of whom he had previously met. Parfitt explained much of his background to those present whilst they waited for the Bryants and Katya. Jack and Katya had flown in the previous evening and were being picked up en route by Danny, who was given as much time off as he needed by a very understanding Mike Latham, still technically his boss. Whilst they waited Peter Parfitt asked for a quiet private word with Chris Spencer, who he then confided in regarding the attack in Slough. Chris's only reaction was to raise one eyebrow and say, "Fair play. Let's hope they're the first of many!"

Danny, Jack and Katya arrived, entering the building through the staff area, where Jake had someone from security waiting to immediately show them to the meeting. The eight were all then present, doors were closed and locked, and all mobiles were switched off, not that anybody could receive or send a signal from the room. Everyone present knew from that moment on they were about to conspire to commit mass murder, in fact it was to go beyond that. Eventually they were to plan destruction akin to genocide.

The meeting got under way with each of those present relaying what they had investigated or achieved in the preceding two weeks. The main focus was on Chris Spencer and Jack Bryant, although there was other input. The first order of business was to confirm whether or not those present were committed to the project, and would remain so for a protracted period of time. All were and would remain so. Although Jack and Katya were the youngest present Jack led after the general discussion had ended.

"Subsequent to our return to Moscow I looked into several aspects of what we discussed and have given the issue a great deal of thought." Jack started, continuing with what was to be quite a lengthy address. "The more I considered what we wish to do the greater the problem became and that is quite apart from the legalities of the project which, I am sure I don't have to remind anyone, would see every one of us incarcerated for the remainder of our lives. However despite the problems and the threat of spending life in jail I feel we have no option but to proceed if we wish to see our loved ones avenged and our country either purged or cleansed. Had I retained doubts they would have been removed forever following the events of yesterday.

"It is pretty clear to me our original conclusion regarding the reaction – that is the complete lack of action – of our government and its various authorities was absolutely correct. Government will do no more than use the opportunity to introduce terrorist legislation to further suppress the dwindling freedoms of the common man. Those we held dear will be forgotten and the whole matter will be brushed under the carpet as quickly as possible unless someone is prepared to make a stand. Nobody else is. So we either accept it as such, and let this filth continue on its current course, killing our people, contaminating our culture and destroying everything which has ever made our homeland special, or we can stand up and be counted. Fight. Take this war they have started back to them. It won't be easy, it won't be quick and it most certainly will not be safe. There is no guarantee we will succeed, even to a limited extent, it will be costly and it will be dangerous to the degree we too may not survive.

"As we have previously discussed, unqualified secrecy is an absolute given, and it must remain in place forever. We can never name our group as such, claim responsibility for any action we carry out, or even speak publicly or privately in favour of what we have done. We never make a single demand nor have any form of agenda apart from vengeance. We don't exist and can never do so. We must be content with the part we have played, and that must be the end unto itself. Wherever possible we must deflect blame and responsibility from ourselves and our country. I'm convinced there are a large number of ultra right wing, radical and white supremacist groups out there who'll be only too happy to claim credit for our actions, as will others. Arms, munitions, parts and equipment must be obtained from diverse global sources and acquired through or from parties who do not know us and who'll never come into contact with us as we are, no matter how indirectly. To that end it will be necessary at some stage in the future to create a number of false identities, but Katya will speak about those shortly.

"Money could be a major problem as it can usually be traced. I've been looking into ways to nullify the traceability and feel the laundering of it through the Russian banking system is probably the safest way to proceed, especially if we have false identities already in place. This is because their system is awash with dirty and questionable money already and I believe I can bury a substantial quantity without questions being raised. I'm also in a position to create fictitious accounts in several countries thereby keeping funds moving whilst at the same time ensuring they are easily accessible. It's absolutely imperative funds can never be traced back to the Gatting Group, Eastlond Properties, NJF Industries, or anything else we set up. Such an event could ultimately lead to the exposure of our little group. Funds suspected of being compromised will be instantly written off, although I'll endeavour to make sure no such thing ever happens.

"I earnestly believe the action we wish to take is possible and, if structured properly, will be successful. However there'll be no such thing as quick results. The setting up time for banking facilities we would need will take time to put in place, as will the covert gathering of desired equipment and munitions. The planning of any operation has to be meticulous and targets thoroughly researched. I feel it would be a mistake to retaliate in a knee jerk reaction here in this country, or to go after complete innocents, as the media backlash could be counterproductive.

"In my opinion it may well prove beneficial to first take out a target then targets in mainland Europe, create tensions in other communities, especially those with media which may be sympathetic to our cause, or those with less efficient police forces. We arrive on site; take out a target, then leave. A surgical strike in a land or lands where none of us live, work or are known. In the short term in our own community I believe we should concentrate on those who have entered the country illegally, are living under the national radar, and are preferably radical. We could take individuals such as those down and, if their bodies were found, I believe the press would be much less sympathetic. It could even be seen to be inter-factional fighting, which would play massively into our hands. If it is possible to mislead the press, perhaps with dropped hints and claims from an extreme Muslim group we invent, preferably from various sources around the world, so much the better.

"With such in mind I've been doing a little research. I've recently personally noticed a growing Muslim population in the Scandinavian countries, particularly the capital cities of Oslo, Stockholm and Copenhagen. All are societies with high standards of living and excellent social funding and welfare programmes. They are all attracting an ever increasing number of economic migrants, obviously calling themselves political refugees, who then bleed as much from the respective states as possible. This is beginning to anger the indigenous peoples, especially so in Denmark, where the taxes are the highest in the free world, but whose people have traditionally been the happiest in Europe. That happiness is slowly changing.

"Denmark would be a good place to start to involve other countries, and I feel a well placed press scandal could well ignite the tinder box. It is worth our looking at. Another nation on the verge of civil unrest with its Muslim community is Germany. For decades they relied on imported Turkish labour, but since the reunification with former East Germany Turkish labour takes second place to that of providing work for Germans to the east of the line. This has caused resentment on the part of the Turks who feel they should be given jobs for life, most of whom it should be remembered are Muslim, and on the part of the Germans who now have to pay to keep them whilst unemployed, as they refuse to return to Turkey. Resentment there runs full spectrum through all age groups, political persuasions, and social background, but is only starting to simmer. I've been trying to think of what can be done to bring it to the boil. Definitely a country to watch!

"The indigenous people of the Netherlands are also most unhappy with their Muslim community, and tensions have been growing since the murder of filmmaker Theo van Gogh last November. Since then there've been over twenty attacks on mosques and one, at Helden on the German border, was burnt down. There have been several calls from right of centre politicians to deport all radical Muslims, and those calls have huge popular support. Finally, of my top four, there is Spain. The Spanish people are still smarting, and rightly so, from the Madrid train bombings, where they lost one hundred and ninety-one people. There too, as with Britain, the authorities did and continue to do nothing. In fact if anything they are trying to cosy up to their Muslim communities with ridiculous offers of help, all to be financed by the Spanish taxpayer. Of Denmark, Germany, the Netherlands and Spain the best early target I believe would be Spain. The destruction of a mosque or mosques would, I truly feel, meet with across the board public approval, and a very slow police response.

"Attacks in other lands will have a destabilising effect within the countries concerned creating a knock-on to other nations which are either in the region, in any way affiliated, or are ideologically or politically aligned. For example an attack on a Muslim target in Copenhagen would definitely be seen by the Muslim community as a Scandinavian attack as well as a Danish attack, which could then attract Muslim reprisals against any Scandinavian nation, thereby drawing them into the fray. The more nations which become involved increase the tension and will lead to polarisation. If it ever spills over into armed national conflict the more of the world's nations which are involved the better. The Muslims may be fanatical and set a very low value on human life, but they are technologically highly inferior to the white skinned peoples of the world and, in comparison with either the Far East or the West, their manufacturing base is nothing short of pathetic.

"I would like to add a cautionary note at this stage. If we are successful in what we plan, there will undoubtedly be repercussions. We will upset a lot of people, and unfortunately it will not be restricted to the Muslim community. We will be constantly hunted by the likes of our own people, the police counter terrorist force, MI6, and the boys from Langley, who are very good at what they do and may prove to be very keen to stop us, although time will tell with that one. In any event we should remain constantly vigilant, never once dropping our guard. After this meeting the lives of every person in this room will be changed forever. By having this meeting, a meeting to plan the death and destruction of large numbers of Muslims, we've already crossed the line and are acting outside the law. We already, as of right now, are carrying out a criminal act with intent to commit murder. Some of what I've researched and outlined may well go beyond our original discussions, but as I've said I do see escalation and, most importantly, if we are to consider a payback it may just as well be on a grand scale. We will face no worst personal consequences for taking the lives of twenty thousand than we will for taking the lives of twenty. The law of our land, the law we've all previously respected, is now set completely against us. We are now also the public enemy.

"The real enemy will not be pleased with what we are about to do either. The day will come when we take out some of their 'soldiers', which may thwart one or more of their terrorist plots. They'll not take kindly to it and will themselves retaliate. This'll not be against us as they'll not be able to identify us. If anyone does, as I've already said, we'll be history. No, they'll retaliate against a bigger target, here in Britain, the US, mainland Europe or perhaps Australia. It's not possible to predict exactly where as our nations collectively have so many potential targets. I feel our attacks should be carried out in such a way as to confuse the enemy as much as possible, but such things can be worked into individual mission plans.

"It would also be advantageous for us to have a number of targets to hit in the

Muslim world which would be traumatic psychologically and cause huge loss of life. If there is to be any form of escalation, and there will be, then we have to be ahead of the game. To do so we must identify targets, thoroughly research them well in advance, and produce workable plans to take them down. I honestly feel a sensible pay back, and a way to remember everyone whose lives were lost, would be to take out a mosque for each of them! However to draft out and execute a plan of such magnitude will take a considerable amount of time, and a considerable amount of expert advice.

"Without a doubt every one of us around the table bring certain strengths with them and I'm sure with your collective blessing I could use the talents available to produce a working plan which would ultimately prove most effective. I think from here on formalities in any meetings we have are a nonsense, so I'd suggest first name terms all around. I've also considered how we can best meet. It strikes me we'll not always be able to do so effectively if we have to scurry around out of sight. Some of you guys are high profile individuals and it will eventually be noticed if we continue to have secret meetings. I would therefore suggest, with the relevant permission and agreements, we create formal positions within NJF Industries.

"I would also suggest an announcement of a working party set up as a joint venture between NJF, Eastlond Properties and the Gatting Group to assess the building, development and management of retail and entertainment complexes in emerging economies. I further suggest the appointment of a banker. You already now have a security consultant, but by following my suggestions our various comings together are legitimised. If I'm appointed your banker, Chris is security, and Phil, Nathan and Jake all board members five of us can meet without arousing suspicion. Katya can travel with me quite naturally, so the only two left are Peter and Danny, and I'll give some thought to that problem. The costs are negligible and the cover cannot be broken, especially if some work can be seen to be done at investigating markets. That I can do, doubtless with my employer's permission, particularly in present day Russia, if I appear to bring in a customer with the potential the new company could be seen to offer.

"In essence that's me done. It's been a busy two weeks. I think it would be interesting to hear from Chris, and Katya has some things to add, but I believe we all need to discuss a few matters generally, and work out an overall direction." Jack finished his address and leaned back in his chair, looking across the table at Chris Spencer. Nobody spoke. All were taking in the points raised by Jack. Suddenly the whole operation they were discussing undertaking became very real, and with the reality came the understanding of how far they were all going to stray from the path through life they had previously been following.

Jack and Chris already understood, and were prepared for the enormity which was to follow. Katya had been prepared to throw herself into a cause she deeply regarded as just since the day she heard of her brothers' horrific death. She had no other commitments and partially because of her cultural background saw it as her duty to support her man, admittedly not generally to the level they were discussing, but she held a deep seated utter loathing of anything Muslim because of her brother. Danny knew his brother well. To him if Jack said he had thought about it then it probably meant he had considered every move and possible counter move for the next ten years. Phil and Nathan just wanted to hurt, then deeply hurt, then hurt again the community which produced the bastards who had killed Susie and her baby, which pretty much summed it up for Jake too. For Peter, who had already killed two men, everything about his life changed that night. His fiancée had suffered horrendous mutilation, he was then attacked and, had neither of those been enough, although they most certainly were, this social cancer attempted to take many more lives in a repeat operation just the day before. It was his duty to help stop it!

Slowly every person present absorbed Jack's address. As they did so, one by one, their heads turned in the direction of Chris Spencer. All there realised they were about to embark upon an undertaking none would ever have contemplated possible, and would even have regarded the concept laughable sixteen days earlier. They were going to seriously consider, discuss and back a proposal to bring about the premeditated murder of people they had never met, with numbers unknown. Their attention turned to Chris because as each came to terms with what was being proposed, and they were agreeing to, each grasped the operation would turn on the ability of one man present to kill. Repeatedly. Over and over again!

In such an understanding they were two weeks behind Chris who clearly saw his path within minutes of the blast which ended Charlie's life. Having been in hot zones many times and gone through mission briefings beforehand, he could see what was happening, and could still remember his youth when suddenly all the fun of becoming a young soldier ended with the full on reality of that which had been Northern Ireland. Parfitt aside none of the others were either trained or blooded and Chris knew only too well how differently people responded to taking another beings life. All such things considered these people were responding to, and motivated by, a need for revenge, and vengeance was a very powerful driving emotion. They were incredibly lucky to have young Jack Bryant, he thought. The young man was gifted, and wasted in the banking world. People like him did not come along too often. He had read much of Bonaparte and of Rommel, and knew history would always remember them for the military geniuses they were. If he was not mistaken, and he was certain he was not, there was another one of their kind sat across the table from him. Chris knew Jack had no military training, but several of the things the younger man just said demonstrated his understanding not just of the big picture, but of consequential losses, escalation and fall back positions.

"If this young man is prepared to plan missions, I will follow them all the way through," Chris opened by saying. "I won't be making a speech here, and in all honesty there is no way I could follow Jack's report, but from what I've just heard this operation has my full and unqualified backing.

"Since our last meeting I've been to the north travelling around the areas the bombers came from. There are a few people I'd like to talk to up there, and a few targets I've picked out. I particularly like the idea of taking down mosques. They definitely provide asylum for those on the run, storage facilities for arms and bomb making equipment, help channel funds, and radicalise potential recruits before sending them to Pakistan for training. They are recruiting offices, not places of worship, and should therefore be regarded as legitimate targets.

"I have studied a number of these buildings, and am attempting to find a common fault whereby they can be taken down without an armed frontal attack. Rocket propelled grenades would work well, but they are far too obvious and much too noisy. C4 or Semtex would do the job nicely, but would have to be introduced into the buildings. It is something I shall have to work on, perhaps with Peter." Chris looked up enquiringly and got a nod from Parfitt. He then continued. "I also agree with Jack as to a time frame. There is no quick fix. If we're to do this we have to do it properly. No casualties and no one exposed to the possibility of capture, either by the police or the enemy. I think we would be helped if we can find a training ground. At the moment the terrorists have an advantage over us in that they can train in Pakistan with the support of local people. We have to find a similar training ground for our people.

"I've contacted a small number of people I trust completely, literally with my life, who I've worked with in the past. They are four members of my former unit, two ex Para's and a guy from the SBS who is a childhood friend and my first choice. Seven people in total, all of whom I know and have done so for years, and all have exceptional track records. I've revealed nothing to them of what we plan but have sounded them out as to whether they would be up for an independently funded operation. All said yes, as I knew they would. All think it is mercenary work, and none are concerned about domestic content.

"I do not recommend any of them to you. It's intended none of you will ever meet them, unless an as yet unforeseen circumstance creates a compelling reason to do so, and no names will go either way. Some have previously carried out 'private missions' and have contacts in the world of arms and armament. None would ever betray me, and consequently you, in the unfortunate event of capture by any authorities.

"I've also been considering munitions. Basically it depends on our plans as to what we need, which is fairly obvious. Despite anything the media tries to tell the general public about arms, and how efficient we are at stopping them coming into the county, all of that is nonsense. The country is pretty much awash with arms. Not in the way the US is, but if you need certain weapons here in Britain, and have the money, they can be obtained. Proper explosives are not quite the same, although home made bombs can be manufactured with off the shelf components relatively easily, as we all know to our cost.

"I've had explosive training courses, and used it in the field, but I'm not an explosives expert. Two of the men I've contacted most certainly are, especially the ex SBS chap who I'll refer to as 'Billy'. NATO forces tended to work with C4, mainly because of its US origin. Personally I've always preferred Semtex, as do my explosive chaps. If anyone is interested as to why I'll go into an explanation later. Semtex is available here in Britain, throughout much of Europe and Asia, the Middle East, North Africa and Russia.

"I would conclude by saying this is feasible. The targets I've identified are 'soft' targets, as were the tube's to the enemy. If you give me the go ahead those men I've mentioned and I will take them down. That's it from me, unless anyone wants to ask any questions," Chris finished, thinking to himself these people were committed.

Another silence followed, this time to be broken by Phil Gatting. There was no elected chair, but Gatting fell into the role quite naturally. Of all those present he was by far the most experienced with such matters and, as the meeting progressed, he filled the position ever more frequently until ipso facto he was the chair.

"Thank you Chris. I'm sure we'll have questions shortly. Thank you also Jack for a very interesting summation. I'll admit it would seem you've looked into and considered far more than the rest of us put together. I pretty much agree with Chris's viewpoint regarding planning if we can reach a consensus, of which I'm sure we will. However you said Katya had something for us regarding the setting up of alternative identities, which I can see will probably be very useful. Would you like to share it with us Katya?"

"It is a popular misconception in the western world anything can be bought in my country if you have the money," Katya started to explain. "This is not the precise situation. It's true much can be obtained through various black markets, but with regard to documentation much of it is fake, basically altered copies. Some are good copies, some not so, depending often on the price you pay. False documents can be obtained in Russia which will stand up to cursory inspection, but then the same can be said for false documents bought quite openly in Bangkok from any of the numerous outlets on the side of the road there. In Bangkok if you want fake University degrees or other institutional documentation, many of the worlds driving licenses or national identity cards they can be purchased for very little. Utility bills, bank statements and the like can be obtained these days quite easily over the internet, and all these things can help to set up a false identity – but that identity will remain false!

"To set up an identity which will stand up to in-depth scrutiny the documents obtained must be original. In other words - real. To do that money is certainly required, but far more importantly contacts are needed. With money and contacts a complete character can be established, and the character will to all intents and purposes be real. Birth certificates, school records, identity cards, qualifications, a trade, background, driving license, passport. An entire identity can be established. I say established as it is important to remember a thorough background search will include family, friends, schools attended, addresses, workmates and everything else which is involved in leading a double life, or in this case, being another person.

"All this can be done, but it requires someone on the inside to put everything in place. Deep cover operatives from various countries have been doing this for decades, and the cold war effectively turned the process into an industry. That industry still exists, and its areas of influence are far further reaching than many may suspect. We all accept Germany of today being Germany, a fully fledged founder member of the European Economic Community, now EU. Most tend to forget that just a few years ago it consisted of West Germany and the German Democratic Republic. The GDR was carefully watched over by the Ministerium für Staatssicherheit, The Ministry for State Security, better known around the world as the Stasi.

"The Stasi held records on everyone, and just about everything everyone did, not just in East Germany, but also very much so in West Germany, and the wider world too. It was widely regarded as one of the most effective and repressive intelligence and secret police agencies in the world. At the end of 1989, with the collapse of the communist regime in East Germany, officials of the MfS started shredding files. The general public heard of this and stormed the offices, halting the destruction, but not before five per cent of the files were already shredded. Within a year reunification occurred and the remaining files were publicly released allowing individuals to review their own records, and to see who was previously reporting them. The society which is the former GDR was deeply wounded by this and those wounds will probably never properly heel in our lifetimes.

"Those files which were shredded were bagged up for destruction – which never occurred. In 1995 reassembly of those shredded files began with a team of three dozen archivists working on the project. Ten years on some two hundred bags have been reassembled. Sixteen thousand bags remain. If you want a German identity – choose one! Almost anything you like. Having done so it is then a matter of having someone in the right position enter the required details. Checking is done, but it should be remembered this society wants to bury its past and put all of what occurred behind it. To 'unreasonably' question someone from the former GDR about their past is not considered the proper thing to do.

"In Russia it is a matter of who you know. With the connections my uncle has, creating an identity which would hold up is not a problem, and would never become so unless the individual with such an identity was captured carrying out activities within Russia which were regarded as an attack on the state. Another area where it is currently relatively simple to set up a 'real' identity is Serbia, or at least it is if using connections from Russia to the right people in Belgrade. Although Serbian nationality is not something many prize it may well be suitable for our needs, and their hatred of Muslims is not exactly a great secret, which may at some stage be useful to us or turned to our advantage. So without a great deal of trouble there are three national identities which could be set up as cover for any individuals who required them. In addition to those there are the false identities I mentioned at the beginning, which can be used to set up things such as bank accounts and are useful for moving money around the world. They should satisfy a traffic cop, but would not stand up to in depth scrutiny if the individual holding the identity were to be arrested, whereas the first three would because the individual actually is that person.

"One other thing which may be of interest, aside from the identity issue, is that of procuring munitions. Chris mentioned Semtex. I do not imagine there will be a huge requirement for arms as such, and where there is I presume western arms will be the first choice. By which I mean Armalites would be chosen over Kalashnikovs, but where there is a need for explosives, obtaining Semtex should not present a problem." Katya finished her delivery and glanced at Phil Gatting, acknowledging him as chair.

"Thanks Katya." Phil Gatting said. "I must admit there are two things I'm interested in from what's been said, one is to do with Semtex, but only because I am curious and it is something I know nothing about, the other though is something you mentioned Jack and I would like to come back to, concerning a large target. Firstly however I feel we should all see if anyone else has anything to say which may be constructive."

"Actually I would like to jump in there if I may?" Nathan said, before continuing quite forcefully. “Jack, you said we all had our strengths. I imagine you may look upon my strength as being a financial input, which of course it is in some way, but I’d like it to be more than just that! I’ve never had any military training such as Chris or Peter, nor am I as fit as Danny obviously is, but if you want any help with anything to do with computers or electronics I can be pretty useful with that kind of thing. I want to do more than just put in money if I can. I know Jake feels strongly about this whole matter and is prepared to put in a lot of capital, and I think we can all see how Phil feels. Although I’ve never been interested in money I’ve an enormous amount of it, quite literally billions. I’m quite content to spend every penny of my money removing the likes of the people who killed my wife and daughter from the planet, but I want to do more. I want to feel I’ve actively helped as well. So I would like you to call upon me for anything you may need of me. I understand my limitations. I cannot plan or even see the big picture as you can. But I can get inside computers. Probably anybody’s, anywhere. I can then obtain any information held on them and get out again without anyone knowing I’ve been there or, for those very few with systems so sophisticated they would detect my presence, make it appear to have come from somewhere else. If I can be of any use please call upon me!”

“Thanks Nathan. To be completely candid I’d intended to ask you something along those lines.” Jack Bryant responded. “Tell me, how difficult would it be to access the Home Office database? If it’s possible it may be a useful way of tracking down illegals, especially those who’ve committed offences here in the U.K., and not been removed as they should’ve been.

“The Home Office is about as secure as a paper bag, and as leak proof as a colander!” Nathan snorted contemptuously. “I’ve had a look around on it already, following something Jake told me about your mother’s death, and I found this, which I thought might be of interest to you.” As he spoke he reached into his inner pocket and withdrew an envelope which he then passed across the table to Jack.

Inside the envelope were three sheets of A4 paper. The Home Office letter heading appeared at the top, and a report clearly followed. From the hush which followed as Jack quickly read the report it was obvious nobody else present was aware of the contents. Jack finished reading. Without a word he passed the report to his brother and sat tight lipped whilst Dan read it.

“The bastard!” Danny exploded as he read. “He’s still here! And he’s been radicalised! The bastard! Jack, he has to die. Dad would never forgive us after all he’s been through if we let him live. I thought he’d been removed from the country, as we were promised, and was prepared to let it go, but if he’s still here, and wanted for terrorist involvement, we have to get to him first!”

Phil Gatting broke in. “I’m sorry to interrupt, but I assume this has something to do with your mother. Is it relevant to the task ahead of us?”

Instead of either of the Bryant brothers answering Nathan responded. “I had a little dig around in some Home Office files and came up with that information. It relates to a certain Abdul Ahmad Khaled, his convictions for Causing Death by Dangerous Diving and Attempting to Pervert the Course of Justice, his sentence and his release date in April this year. I know I’m correct in saying he’s the man who killed Mary Bryant, Jack and Dan’s mother. He was supposed to have been repatriated after serving his sentence but, due to one of those never-ending Home Office cock ups, he never was deported. He started his sentence at Wandsworth jail and was due for release last September, but after being involved in the killing of a fellow inmate last July, in a culture related incident, he was moved to Belmarsh High Security prison and lost part of his early remission allowance. During his internment at Belmarsh he shared a cell with a radical ranting imam, and after his release he joined a cell which was once attached to Finsbury Park mosque. The imam he shared the cell with was no less than Abu Hamza. There's an MI6 appendant on the bottom of the report regarding possible public safety issues. There's a current arrest warrant and deportation order in force. Known contacts are listed but so far the police have been unable to locate him. However I believe he is living at the address I have listed."

There was silence in the room. It was broken by the ever pragmatic Chris Spencer who said, "Well, unless I'm much mistaken, it looks like we have a starting place. How and when would you like him taken out?"

Again there was a pregnant pause, this time broken by Phil Gatting, who once more took control of the situation. "Well – that was a bit of an unexpected development. It certainly took me by surprise, and from the looks on others faces, I wasn't alone. I believe it will pay to return to that particular piece of information and give it due consideration shortly. Let's give it a chance to sink in. Whilst we do, shall we see if there is any other input? After which it may be beneficial to discuss where we wish to see this go. By which I mean – are we to pursue smaller targets? Are we going to target individuals? Would it pay to look into the practicalities of a major strike? These questions are relevant and something we should fully discuss and ideally reach a consensus. It's quite apparent we all wish to hit back, and I imagine hit hard. Frankly I'd like to see an immediate attack whereby we inflict considerable pain on these bastards, and then to follow up by hurting them a lot more. Basically in line with what they seem to be doing to us. However I also see the folly of such a course of action. Without a doubt our interests are best served by taking a longer term view and planning accordingly. Now has anyone got anything to include which may help with matters raised earlier, or shall we consider in which direction we wish to go, and what we should do about this Abdul Ahmad Khaled?"

Peter Parfitt cleared his throat and leaned forward to speak. "Before we go on I'd like to ask something with regard to a couple of points raised earlier. Firstly a training ground was mentioned by Chris. Can I ask what exactly is needed from a training ground? I imagine it is somewhat dependent on what target or targets we decide to take on, so we may have to decide in which direction we wish to go before looking for one. My second point really relates to something Chris asked me about, which is finding a way to introduce high explosives into a mosque. I've an idea which I'll discuss with him later, and work out the feasibility, but am I correct in thinking we don't have to be in any way conventional in our methodology? If we come up with some sort of conceptual plan, so long as it's workable, does it matter how bizarre it may initially appear?

Jack Bryant answered Parfitt's question immediately. "Peter, from my point of view, and I imagine the same applies to everyone here, it doesn't matter how seemingly outlandish any ideas are. I'm not a military expert but I imagine the more whacky and unusual an idea is, the less likely the enemy are to have a plan in place to combat it. I really don't think anyone will object to a thought through and reasoned idea even if it does seem a little off the wall the first time it's heard." Jack glanced around the table as he spoke and saw everyone was nodding their heads.

"I agree." Phil Gatting said. "Everything we're discussing doing here is somewhat unconventional, to say the least. I feel anyone who has any input should be heard and the matter considered. Nothing should be regarded as too silly if it could in any way further our aims. Back to your first question Peter. I agree there may well be a very real need for a training ground, but I also agree we should first consider the options available to us. Only from there should we then decide what we need, which I feel should pretty much apply to all we do. Consider options first, plan second, procure required equipment third – which would include personnel and training, and fourthly, finally, carry out the action.

"Now, we have covered a lot of ground today, and there is much for all of us to consider. I'd suggest we deal with the issue of Abdul Ahmad Khaled, then break up and reconvene in four weeks time if that suits everybody. I feel four weeks should be sufficient for what we have to consider and it should hopefully give Jack a chance to come up with some options regarding targets. In the meanwhile there will be plenty for all to do and go through following the matters which have been brought up. As for Khaled I feel his days on the planet should be ended. Does anyone object? If not, how should we proceed?"

There were no objections. Eight people committed themselves to murder. Chris Spencer spoke up. "Nobody needs to worry about how to proceed. That's my job, and the reason why I'm on the payroll. I'll question him first and follow up on anything he delivers."

"I'd like to be a party to that!" Danny stated.

"No." Chris replied.

"But it's personal!" Danny argued.

"Precisely! Still no. Ask your brother why if you need to. But it's a no!" Chris said emphatically.

Jack didn't wait to be asked. "Danny we would both like to be there. Which is precisely why we can't be, and for these reasons. When he dies or disappears, you, dad and I will be the first people in the frame which the police check out. Dad's in hospital so he's covered. I'll be in Russia, so I'll be covered. You'll be in the firing line. So make sure you keep a fairly public profile for a while. We cannot afford to have the police or security forces in any way interested in a single one of us. Additionally, and for the future, there'll be several things you'll not be able to be involved with because of your size. Look at yourself. You stick out like a sore thumb wherever you go. Everything about any of our operations has to remain low profile. Your size makes you high profile. There'll be plenty of opportunity for every one of us to contribute to what we are embarking upon, you included, but none of us can ever risk attracting attention at the wrong time, so forget it!"

The meeting ended after an agreement each would progress the allotted tasks as much as they could during the following four weeks. Jack had much to plan, Katya identities to process, Nathan computer records to scour, Chris had Abdul Khaled to dispatch and attack methods to plan with Peter Parfitt. Phil Gatting and Jake had to look into the setting up of a joint venture company, and consider how the news should be put to the media. The only person who had nothing to do was Danny who, as a result, felt he was not contributing. When he mentioned this to his brother, Jack reassured him. He would have, he was told. There was plenty of time ahead, and without doubt there would be much for him to do.

Eight

Abdul Ahmad Khaled was taken to a holding cell, following his conviction and sentence, and from there transferred to Wandsworth Prison. It was an unfortunate reality that for Khaled, brought up as he was in the hills and mountains of the Pashtun region in the great outdoors, prison was not a pleasant option for him. Even the work he had taken in Britain was of the outdoor type. Life for him had never been about being enclosed or, apart from the requirements of farm work in his youth, in any way regimented.

Subsequent to his arrest the time he spent as a remand prisoner at Winchester Jail, in a cell waiting for the case to go to court, agitated him greatly. However he was not confined to his cell all day, received regular exercise, and understood these white skins had their own peculiar way of doing things. He also knew throughout the period his incarceration was but of a temporary nature. He always knew he would be released after the trial and would be allowed to take his money and return to his homeland. It was suggested the Britain people may even pay for his airline ticket, which would leave him with more money for the land he so badly wanted. Once there he could then take a wife and raise a family, putting the dreadful experiences of the strange land in which he found himself well behind him. Whilst in jail he was fed, clothed and given shelter, all without cost, something never previously known. Although he loathed being shut away he realised it was for a short period only. It was something he could live with in the circumstances and he would somehow endure it.

To Khaled his release was an obvious and absolute given. Anyone listening to the facts would understand it was God's will. He was of the ideology, and he was a man. The one which had died was nothing but a godless woman. She was not of the ideology and had not even had her head covered. She was obviously nothing more than a shameless hussy, and it was God's hand which had steered his on the day, and it was obviously God who wished her dead, probably as an example to others of her kind, although it did not do to guess at God's reasoning.

His conviction and sentence were beyond his comprehension. Had these godless ones not understood? It had been God's will! How could he be held responsible for the will of God? What they had done was wrong, and their actions would anger Him!

His transfer to Britain's largest prison, within the small cell of a moving vehicle, was yet another reminder of the reality of his situation, and an altogether unpleasant experience, but nothing like as unpleasant as the one which awaited him.

Wandsworth was built in 1851. As an 'older' prison it lacks many of the creature comforts of more modern prisons. It was, and remains, unusual for the liberal society of Britain today, more punishing on its inmates. There prisoners have to share cells which have only one television and no en suite facilities. In an effort to make the Muslim inmates more comfortable they are usually 'banged up' together, provided with a mosque, and all religious requirements, such as the fasting at Ramadan, are respected, with cooks staying up to prepare food through the night for those refusing it by day. However, despite the attempts made to make life as pleasant and comfortable as possible for these unfortunate victims of British society, Wandsworth remains a prison and prison is still supposed to be a place of confinement and correction for convicted criminals.

As a convicted and confined criminal Abdul Khaled's life was thoroughly regimented with every hour of every day following a pattern. For some, a precious few, jail can turn them around, providing an education and an opportunity to obtain new skills so, when their debt to their society is deemed paid, they may re-enter that society and contribute to it in a worthwhile and productive manner. Abdul Khaled did not fall into such a category. In many ways, and for a far greater proportion than those who choose to better themselves, prison can be viewed simply as the University of Crime. Those convicted of car crime can hone the skills required for forced entry to property, and muggers can learn about armed robbery from their hardened peers and the old lags. Over time Abdul Khaled was drawn into the fringe of those involved with furnishing and controlling smuggled mobile phones, which in turn drew him inevitably closer to the drug trafficking within the prison, for which Wandsworth is notorious.

It was never his intention to get involved with anything, but his lack of intellect made him an easy target for those who wished to build both a power base and to profit from their fellow prisoners. The likes of Abdul Khaled could be used to move contraband or illegal substances around within the jail, and would be the fall guys if caught. In return they received protection and a sense of belonging, a need deeply etched on the psyche of some individuals, especially prevalent in those previously experiencing life in large family groups or institutions. Despite his hatred of his confinement Khaled initially determined to behave in jail for the duration of his sentence in the hope he would be released as early as possible, and to then depart the land which had brought him little but hardship and suffering. Unfortunately fate had chosen another path for him, over which, because of his lack of education, he was to have no control.

Had the series of incidents which led to the incarceration of Abdul Khaled happened ten years earlier he would doubtless have completed his time and left the country. However during those ten years many things changed within the British society, much of which was reflected inside the prisons and jails of the nation. Muslim crime and related convictions had increased. It would be an inaccuracy to describe it as exponential growth, but it was not far short. The knock on effect was such that the Muslim population within prisons increased four times faster than the average for other sectors of the community, and was continuing to do so. This in turn caused its own problems such as the hardening of views of white racist inmates, schisms appearing between Asian Muslims and those from North African and the West Indies, all the way through to the increasing difficulties of providing places of worship.

It was into the growing power base of the Asian Muslim prisoners that Abdul Khaled was inexorably drawn. Weeks dragged slowly into months and the Muslim population of the prison continued to grow. The original imam finished his term and left, to be replaced by a far more radical one. The time of prayer had long been recognised as a time when drugs, phones and other illegal products could easily be exchanged, and the prison mosque had throughout been regarded almost as a marketplace for such items. The new imam did nothing to change the practice, but did in fact in part encourage it, steadily gaining the trust and acceptance of those prisoners following a path directly forbidden in the pages of their holiest of books, the Koran, believed by Muslims to be the infallible word of God dictated to Mohammed.

Crime of any sort is specifically outlawed in the Koran, so there can never be such a thing as a criminal who remains a good Muslim. The fact that every one of the prisons inmates were convicted criminals, and therefore could not by virtue of the fact be good Muslims, has always been wasted on everyone from the prison authorities all the way through to the criminals themselves. However, rampant hypocrisy has never been a problem for those of the Muslim ideology, and it certainly was not going to stand in the way of the imam, who saw his mission on the planet Earth to be that of encouraging the destruction of the infidel. Not unlike Abdul Khaled, many of the Muslims who found themselves within prison walls serving terms at Her Majesty's pleasure were uneducated, illiterate and decidedly unworldly individuals, and consequently provided rich pickings for an imam bent on influencing and corrupting pliable minds. Indoctrination in the normal everyday world can present a very real problem for the establishment, even where there are many distractions and a huge number of external forces constantly at work. Within a prison, where the individual is unable to break free of the community around him, the intensity of the indoctrination can be magnified many fold.

Abdul Khaled needed the blessing of the imam if he was to continue to trade the wares of those within the prison whose bidding he mindlessly followed. Initially the imam appeared content to ignore the illegal trading Khaled carried out before his eyes, but eventually there was a price to pay. The price was insignificant, nothing more than a short conversation with the imam about his home, family and God. Khaled in fact welcomed the interest shown to him by the imam, and soon both came to talk to one another regularly. As they developed their relationship the imam explained why God had carried out the deeds which brought Abdul Khaled to Wandsworth, and further explained He would doubtless one day have a task for the young Pashtun. Obviously Abdul had been chosen by God for a mission, as he would not be there if God had willed otherwise.

This finally made perfect sense to Abdul Khaled. Previously he had never been able to understand his plight. Of course it made sense. He was special! God wanted him for something! Why had he not seen it before? Oh, how wise was the imam who could see such things! Suddenly prison was not so bad for Khaled. Especially as he now knew why he was there, and had a wise and friendly imam who could and would help him, because he was one of God's chosen ones. Khaled never once questioned the motives of the imam. To do so, quite apart from being inconceivable, would have been blasphemous in its very nature, and completely ridiculous.

Imperceptibly the months became years, yet still God had not called upon Khaled. The first cracks which were created by the schism within the jail continued to widen and, as they did so, the slight atmosphere became an underlying hostility. Over time the imam had developed several young Asian Muslims, radicalising them as he went, welding them into a loyal corps prepared to do his bidding without question. However the same could not be said for any of the Muslim prisoners from Africa or the Caribbean, who almost universally backed a militant black Caribbean extremist.

A prison can work like a pressure cooker, and so it was for those caught up in events inside the Muslim community of Wandsworth prison. Unfortunately, unlike pressure cookers, prisons are not designed or equipped with a safety valve. The build up of animosity between the two sections of the Muslim inmates reached critical, and something had to give. For the Afro-Caribbeans it was a particularly difficult situation. Their problem was with the imam, but they could not dispose of him because to do so would offend God, and then their chances of eating lamb in paradise surrounded by virgins would disappear the moment they ended his life. For the imam no such difficulty arose and he instructed his followers to take the life of his rival, explaining he had received a message from God, and their place at His right hand was assured if they carried out His bidding.

Eight of the imam's followers took part in the attack on the Jamaican extremist whilst the prison warden's collective attention was distracted by an orchestrated disruption. With three guarding the outside of the cell and stopping all entry, the other five quickly slipped inside, two of which were carrying freshly honed knives made in the prison workshop. The Jamaican was gagged, violently beaten and then strangled, after which he was beheaded. None were caught inside the cell, but CCTV coverage clearly showed who entered, the knives were found and those who had used them identified, both of whom were serving life sentences.

Abdul Khaled was one of those seen to enter the cell and it was quite obvious he took part. However he and the others without knives claimed they had entered the room after the killing and only stood inside the door. Those with the knives could do little but accept responsibility and were tried for murder. The other three inside the cell and the three outside faced various charges, but conspiracy to commit murder was never going to be proven. The decision was taken by the CPS, and approved by the DPP, that a lengthy trial which had little chance of success was not in the public interest, especially if the popular press played the religious or racist cards heightening public hysteria. It was considered beneficial for those due for deportation to have their remission reduced, extending their term of imprisonment, and to be deported forthwith at the end of their sentences. Those who were to remain in Britain faced charges, were convicted, and had their sentences increased accordingly. The group was broken up and transferred to separate prisons.

Wandsworth had rid itself of eight increasingly radical Muslims, but they still remained within the penal system. It was unreasonable to believe Khaled had not taken part in the murder of the Jamaican Muslim, even if it was not possible to prove it beyond all reasonable doubt in an open court. Proven or not he was party to a premeditated religiously motivated murder. That made him dangerous on various levels inside the penal system, and most certainly on the outside of it. Due to the serious nature of the incident with which he was involved, and his assumed and apparent radicalisation, it was deemed a necessary requirement to re-evaluate his status. The review panel considered options and recommended a re-classification. As a direct result Abdul Khaled was transferred to HM Prison Belmarsh at the beginning of June 2004, where he was to serve out his revised sentence, at the end of which his immediate deportation was required.

Ten days before Khaled's transfer another radical imam was arrested and detained on a US extradition order, and he too was imprisoned at Belmarsh. His arrest had been approved by the British people and celebrated by the popular press.

Mustafa Kamel Mustafa was born in Alexandria, Egypt in 1958, and entered Britain in 1979 on a student visa in order to study civil engineering at Brighton Polytechnic. In 1980 he married a Catholic convert to Islam who was a British citizen by birth and, after three years of marriage, he too acquired British citizenship. His wife's name was Valerie Traverso. However at the time of the marriage she was still married to her former husband and the subsequent marriage was therefore bigamous, rendering it invalid. Without the validity of the marriage, the obtaining of citizenship was called into question, and should have been striped away, although this can prove to be a long and drawn out process which costs the British taxpayer an inordinate amount of money.

Mustafa Kamel Mustafa was a Sunni Muslim and an ardent and vociferous support of al Qaeda, Osama Bin Laden and Sharia Law. He was to become the imam of Finsbury Park mosque and was better known in Britain as Abu Hamza al-Masr or, more simply, Abu Hamza.

In the early 1990's he had lived in Bosnia, using the identity of Adam Eaman, where he was fighting in the Arab Mujahidin against the Serbs. In 1993 he lost both hands and his left eye. He was later to claim the losses occurred from wounds received during a project to remove Soviet mines from Afghanistan, although other al Qaeda members have claimed them to have been from a nitro-glycerine accident at a training camp in Afghanistan. However, overwhelming evidence indicates the hands were lost in Saudi Arabia when they were cut off for theft, the penalty for such under the Sharia Law he supported.

HM Prison Belmarsh is a high security prison built in the south east of London. It became operational in 1991 and is a smaller prison than Wandsworth. It was built as a modern facility to hold nine hundred and fifteen prisoners, and it was into this prison and its wholly different regime that Abdul Ahmad Khaled was relocated. The prison was often used for detaining prisoners held for terrorist offences, and between 2001 and 2005 was used to detain a number of individuals 'indefinitely without charge or trial' under the provisions of Part 4 of the Anti-terrorism, Crime and Security Act of 2001, hastily drafted after the attack on New York's twin towers. This led to the prison being dubbed the British version of Guantanamo Bay until the Law Lords later ruled such imprisonment discriminatory and against the Human Rights Act

An unfortunate side effect to the internment of a number of like minded people with strongly held beliefs, which run contrary to those of the society imprisoning them, is that those ideas become reinforced. Abdul Khaled found himself at the centre of an increasingly militant and extreme Islamic culture developing within the boundaries of the prison. Although he was poorly educated the same was certainly not true of many others there, several of whom benefited from the educational resources of the country they were attacking, and taught how to use Britain's liberal laws to their own advantage. As a man of weak character and limited intellect Abdul Khaled found himself swept along an ever more radical and extreme path by those well accustomed to bending the minds and wills of their fellows.

By the time he left Belmarsh he loathed everything the infidel stood for, and knew it was his duty to fight them wherever he found them as God had decreed he should. Before the end of his sentence others within the confines of the jail started to help him fight his extradition order using the knowledge accumulated whilst in jail themselves, or from the education the evil state had provided them with. His opposition to the extradition order was duly lodged and was in progress when his release date became due. In such circumstances individuals are supposed to be detained after their formal release date, pending the outcome of their appeal against extradition. However, due to the Law Lords consideration of the 2001 and Human Rights Acts, he was released without further detention. It was immediately realised a processing error had occurred and a warrant for his re-arrest was issued, by which time he had gone to ground, hidden by a cell previously attached to Finsbury Park mosque and Abu Hamza.

Using Home Office records Nathan Jefferies accurately traced Khaled to an address known by the authorities which had previously been called upon by the police who held a current arrest warrant. Khaled never answered the door and, as the police could not show cause as to why a magistrate should issue a search warrant, the police had no power with which to enter the property so were forced to leave.

Chris Spencer, and two of the men he had recruited who were with him, were under no such legal constraints. Operating wholly outside of the law did have its advantages, as all three had learnt in Northern Ireland when operating as a snatch squad. Calling upon the training they received then the same tactics were put into operation. They hired a Ford Transit panel van using a false driving licence and credit card, and removed the number plates of an identical vehicle from the private yard of a courier company. Having driven to the address at dusk they exchanged the plates nearby and parked the vehicle to the rear of the address, one of the men remaining behind the wheel of the van. Chris and the second man then went to the front of the house where Chris knocked upon the door whilst his colleague remained in the shadows.

As expected nobody answered, so he patiently waited whilst counting to one hundred before knocking again. This time he was rewarded, not by an answer to the door, but by the quiet voice of his hidden partner saying, "Curtain moved, upstairs right."

So the property was occupied and those inside had checked to see if it was the police, Chris thought as he knocked again. This time a light went on, the door opened, and a reasonably large man wearing a T-shirt and track suit bottoms filled the frame. A man Chris instantly thought was an Afghani, but certainly not the target.

"What do you want?" the man asked contemptuously.

"I'm looking for someone." Chris answered in a normal tone.

"You're not the police! Fuck off!" The Afghani spat out as he made to close the door, which was exactly as it was supposed to go.

Chris kicked hard into the centre of the door sending it crashing back and catching the man behind it off guard, causing him to stumble backwards into his hallway. As Chris stepped over the threshold the man rushed at him, just as was expected. They always do it Chris thought as he sidestepped slightly shifting his weight. His left hand went out and grasped the back of the Afghani's head as he charged back up the hall, turning its direction and slamming it hard into the banister rail, instantly breaking the man's nose at the bridge. Chris pulled the back of the dazed man's head up and away from him then jerked it back towards him. As the head came forward Chris swung his right hand out and up, the lower part of his palm connecting with full force underneath the broken nose, driving the wedge of bone deep into the Afghani's brain. As the dead body slumped to the floor Chris's backup stepped through the door frame closing the door behind him, and Chris moved swiftly and silently forward checking rooms as he went. They were all empty, again as expected. There was no cellar, so whoever else remained in the house had to be upstairs. Nothing changes, Chris thought.

He dragged the body down the hallway to the rear of the house where the kitchen and back door were, switching off the light as he went. The backup flattened himself against the wall by the front door as Chris dumped the body face down, halfway through the kitchen door, then both waited. A couple of minutes passed before a voice could be heard calling out a name. There was a pause then the call was repeated. A minute later the upstairs light came on, and footsteps could be heard on the stairs. Chris tossed something into the sink which crashed and broke. The noise attracted the attention of the person on the stairs who then saw the legs leading into the kitchen. He shouted a name and ran to the aid of his fallen comrade, completely missing the man at the front, who silently followed him down the hall. The kitchen door was pushed open by the man, whose full attention remained on his comrade on the floor, bending forward to see what was wrong. Chris reached out to the stooped figure from behind the shelter of the darkened kitchen wall, grabbing the head with both hands as it came through the doorway. He forced it further down as he brought his right knee up with full force into the defenceless face. As the man sagged and fell forward Chris whipped the mans arms behind his back and secured them with a heavy duty nylon electrical tie, then rolled him over and taped his mouth with duct tape passed forward by his backup, who had then also entered the kitchen.

The second man was not Abdul Khaled. His eyes, ears, mouth and ankles were taped and he was left, still very groggy, face down on the floor of the kitchen. Carefully and silently Chris crept up the stairs whilst his backup took control opposite the base of them where he could watch the street outside and both doors without being seen, in case anyone unexpectedly entered the house. This, for Chris, was the most dangerous move so far, as he would be an easy target exposed as he was if caught on the stairs. He made the landing without a problem and faced four doorways. Clearly it was a three bedroom house with a bathroom upstairs. One door stood ajar and had a light on inside, too obvious a place to start. He switched off the upstairs light and let his eyes adjust to the darkened landing then, moving slowly in order to avoid creaking floorboards, he made his way forward, checking rooms as he went. The first, at the head of the stairs and back of the house, was the bathroom, and was empty. The next room, sited next to the bathroom at the rear of the property had the light on and he glanced in as he passed but could see nothing. He crept past and waited once more for his eyes to adjust to the lack of light as he made his way to the furthest door. Gently he eased it open. There was nobody inside, but there were several boxes stacked up and he decided he would return to those before he left. The last darkened room was the one from which the curtain had moved before they entered the property. There was a small body in the bed which looked to be a sleeping child. Chris knew he should neutralise them, but for the first time in any form of action since his days in the formed Yugoslavia he made another mistake.

Closing the door he let the child continue to sleep.

He had heard no noise or conversation from the bedroom to the rear of the house where the light was on, so he considered it reasonable to assume if anyone was in there they would now be alone. He eased the door open and once more looked inside. It was more than a bedroom. It seemed it doubled as a bed-sit which was also used as an office and store. There was a solitary individual sitting at a makeshift workbench inside the room with his back to the door. Around him was stacked similar boxes to those Chris had seen in the front bedroom, and several large sacks. On the bench was a set of scales. The man was weighing out the contents of the sacks and mixing them together. As Chris watched the man tipped the contents of a small box into the mix, swirled it around with a wooden spatula, then started tipping the contents into a cloth bag which appeared to be about nine inches long, four wide and two deep. The contents of the small box was nails. Chris was watching as the ingredients were being put together for a bomb. A suicide nail bomb.

Stepping into the room a floorboard creaked under Chris's weight. At the sound the man at the workbench started to turn, beginning to speak as he did so, "Hasib…" but he got no further. Abdul Ahmad Khaled looked just as he had in his Home Office picture. As the board started to creak Chris knew the element of surprise was lost, and rushed his target, swinging a hefty blow with some momentum behind it into the side of Abdul Khaled's face. Khaled sagged at the blow and, as he did, Chris rammed his face into the bench top and Khaled lost full consciousness. Again Chris quickly bound Khaled's hands behind his back, securing them with another nylon tie as he had done with the terrorist in the kitchen.

The room was a veritable treasure trove full of goodies any in the security forces would have each willingly given a full months pay to look at. Chris decided no matter what he did with the people there, it would be indefensible not to give those security forces a chance to do just that. He would have much preferred to take the terrorist in the kitchen with him to extract some information and a few names, but to do so would then leave those from the security forces with more questions than answers.

Full consciousness returned to Khaled who cowered away from Chris.

"Who are you? What do you want? You are not the police. You cannot do this to me, I have human rights!" he shouted out forcefully, pressing all the wrong buttons. Chris bunched his fist and hit the creature in front of him full in the mouth.

"Open your mouth to me again with anything but the correct answer to my questions and you will keep getting the same." Chris Spencer said quietly.

"You cannot do that!" Abdul Khaled shouted.

Chris Spencer hit him full force in the mouth again. "You see, you're wrong." Chris said mildly, "Now do you want to try it again?" he asked cocking one eyebrow, but Khaled shook his head.

"Get up, you're coming with me." Chris told him.

"Where are you taking me?" Khaled shouted out fearfully. This time Chris Spencer didn't bother to reply, but once more punched Khaled straight in the mouth, then grabbed him by the collar and thrust him in the direction of the doorway and out onto the landing.

Once more some form of sixth sense warned him. Once more it was a little late, but still he had time to thrust Khaled forward, which send him rushing down the stairs as Chris turned to face the danger. The child asleep in the bed had not been a child but a young woman, and that young woman now stood behind him with a pistol in her right hand levelled at his head. He looked from the gun, a cheap Chinese Norinco Type 213, into her eyes. There wasn't so much as a spark of humanity to be seen there. Chris started to smile as she squeezed the trigger. He had recognised the gun. The gun failed to fire.

"You have to take the safety off first." Chris said sweeping the gun and her right arm to one side with his left arm as his right closed around her head and neck. With her head trapped between the iron hard muscles of his upper and lower arm he pivoted and twisted, wrenching her off her feet, violently twisting her neck as he did so. It snapped like a dry twig and he dropped her lifeless body to the floor then followed Khaled down the stairs.

"Take him to the van. I have a call to make." Chris ordered, then watched the two men leave by the back door. When he was satisfied they were gone he opened the front door a crack and wedged it in place with the doormat, then went to the room at the front of the house where he had seen a telephone whilst looking into the ground floor rooms after entering the property. He lifted the telephone from its cradle and listened for a dial tone without putting the phone to his ear and, on hearing one, punched in 999 then left the property, climbing into the back of the van with Khaled and the man who was his backup. As the door closed the driver pulled gently away, slowly driving off, attracting no attention. When questioned later by police the van was never mentioned. It was never seen.

The van with all four men inside was driven out to North Acton. A plywood bulkhead separated the driver from the load area where a cheap blue nylon tarpaulin covered the floor and sides, and Chris Spencer, his backup man, and Abdul Khaled all sat on top of it. Apart from the men, the sheet and a long thin toolbox the van was empty.

At North Acton the driver followed Victoria Road around past the front of North Acton underground station then to the left as if heading for Harlesdon. He knew exactly where he was going as the three had walked around the area earlier in the day, invisible in their hi-vis jackets and hard hats, as they had searched for an appropriate location. Victoria Road was on the eastern fringe of a large industrial area which took in Alperton, Park Royal, North Acton and the southern areas of Stonebridge and Harlesden. To the west were the bigger factories such as the old Guinness Brewery in Park Royal and Heinz to the south of Stonebridge, but to the east were smaller units, and to the eastern side of Victoria Road many of the old factories had either been converted into smaller units or were in a state of semi dereliction, with many empty. They had found a small warehouse which stood empty and open to the environment, with no door, broken windows and part of the roof missing.

The van was backed onto the open doorway of the warehouse and Abdul Khaled dragged out. Earlier in the day a heavy duty cordless drill had made short work of drilling four holes in the old concrete floor, which were then plugged and had ring fixings screwed into place. Despite his struggling Khaled was quickly secured to these at wrist and ankle. The driver remained in the van, the backup positioned himself outside as guard and lookout, and Chris collected the toolbox from the van.

Removing a small but powerful torch from the box Chris switched it on. The beam was narrow, but more than enough to illuminate Khaled spread-eagled on the floor.

"What are you going to do?" Khaled asked in a voice which quivered with fear.

"I am going to ask you some questions, and you are going to give me full answers." Chris answered him levelly.

"What if I don't want to or if I don't know the answers?" Khaled asked somewhat more fearfully.

"It doesn't matter what you want, you will answer, and I'll know if you are lying, so I suggest you tell the truth. If you do not I'll gag you, and I'll hurt you." Chris answered in a completely matter of fact voice as he took a small ball pein hammer from the box.

"Why do you do this to me?" Abdul Khaled whined. "I do not even know you! I have never seen you before! Why?"

"Okay. That is your last question. From here on the questions get asked by me, but I will answer. A month ago I brought my young nephew to London to see the city. We were on the bus you Muslim bastards blew up. He was killed – blown to pieces. He was a child. I caught you making a bomb. You mean nothing to me, but you may have made the bomb which killed my nephew and a lot of other people. I want to find out all you know about the people you work with. Now – when you take too long to answer I'm going to hurt you – and when I do I'll be thinking of how I last saw my nephew. Eventually you will tell me all you know whether you want to or not. How much you suffer is up to you. Now I want you to tell me everything you know."

"But I don't know anything!" Khaled sobbed.

Chris roughly forced a large rag into and over Khaled's mouth and held it in place with his left hand. Picking up the small hammer with his right hand he hit Khaled with full force in his right knee cap. The small head of the hammer did not shatter the knee cap, but instead made a small hole in it, forcing the broken tissue between the knee joint. The pain for Khaled was excruciating and he convulsed in agony, writhing around despite his restraints.

Chris Spencer allowed a full two minutes for Khaled to calm down then removed the gag. Abdul Khaled was terrified beyond all reasoning. His nostrils were flared as he panted desperately and his eyes were wide with fright. Never in his worse nightmares had he ever imagined a situation like this. The imams had told him he was doing God's work. How could God treat him like this for doing His work? He started to sob uncontrollably as his bladder failed him. The last vestiges of defiance flowed from him as rapidly as his bladder emptied. He had met some people in his life who troubled and scared him. Some of those in jail suffered mental problems and enjoyed hurting people, but no-one he had ever previously come into contact with scared him on the level of the man who now sat over him. The man had not once shouted at him or even raised his voice, and had not threatened him, but just explained what he was going to do before he did it, almost in the same tone as an aunt had once used when showing him how to milk a goat as a child. This man alarmed and appalled him more than the devil himself and he would tell him anything and everything he wanted to know.

The change was immediately apparent to Chris, who had experienced such things before. Generally he disliked the cold blooded dispassionate violence which went with such tasks, but recognised the overriding need to extract information for the greater good. He understood the noises the bleeding hearts made about why such things should not be done, but was also amused as to how quickly they could change their minds if their own life or that of a loved one depended on such action. Principles are wonderful things to have whilst relaxing in a comfortable armchair, talking to reasonable people over a 'nice cup of tea' in a warm and cosy room, miles from any trouble spot. He was not in a warm and cosy room. There was no tea, and the creature on the floor in front of him had been directly involved in two killings and was picked up whilst making bombs. He could well have been involved in young Charlie's death, and he held information which could save many others a horrible death or life changing disfigurements.

"Tell me everything you know." Chris instructed his prisoner, switching on a small dictation recorder after removing it from the toolbox. "I know why you first went to jail. I want to know who contacted you in jail, both jails, who your contacts were when you came out, and all the information you have on anyone who visited the bomb factory, especially those who took anything away. I want to know how much has already been taken, by whom, and all the information you may have on targets and other cells. Do not hold back, and do not lie to me. I will know if you do either."

Abdul Khaled spoke without hesitation for over thirty minutes with very little need for any form of prompting from his interrogator. Had the circumstances been different Chris may even have felt sorry for the individual before him. In many ways Khaled was just a victim of the circumstances in which he had found himself. The more Khaled spoke the greater Chris's understanding of the power of the imams and Muslim religious leaders became.

Some of the information Khaled presented was of value, especially the names and physical descriptions. Although wholly expected it was unfortunate the simple man knew nothing of operational matters. It would have been crass folly on the part of the Muslim terror cell to have shared information with any but those who needed to know, and frankly Khaled was of insufficient value for any to have considered sharing anything with. He was nothing more than a tool being trained to carry out an eventual suicide mission, and was being used to pay for his keep in the meantime.

"What will you do now?" Khaled asked Chris at the end of his recital.

"I have to try to stop your people, so no other innocents will be needlessly killed as my young nephew was." Chris responded honestly.

"It will not be easy for you," Khaled told him, in a manner akin to friendship then asked. "What will you do with me now?"

"It is time for you to enter paradise, my friend," Chris answered him in the same manner.

Abdul Ahmad Khaled merely nodded, accepting his fate with a resignation Chris found hard not to admire.

"I thought so. As I told my story I understood God's use for me was finished. I cannot question His wisdom, but I wish He had chosen a different path for me." Khaled spoke his last words.

"I wish He had too, Abdul. Go in peace my friend," Chris Spencer told him as he took a machete from the toolbox, the reason for the toolboxes length. Regrets or not he had a job to do, and a part of the job was to sow the seeds of doubt and dissention in the ranks of the enemy. The schism in Wandsworth prison which led to the death of the Jamaican was to be exploited. Abdul's death had to look like a reprisal with a Caribbean twist, and his beheading may help with furthering such a view, a view which should be reinforced if the murder weapon was found in a black Muslim area, as it would be.

The life of the simple man which was Abdul Khaled ended on the floor of a derelict warehouse in an area of North West London, far from his home in the hills of Pashtun, with not a single one of his early dreams accomplished. A wasted life which had brought with it nothing but frustration and disappointment. A life manipulated and used with callous disregard by those who purported to be carrying out God's will, but in reality were doing no more than forcing their own deluded will upon those who could not defend themselves intellectually.

The body of Abdul Khaled was not found until late in the afternoon of the following day. It was discovered by a man walking his dog who entered the building to fetch his pet which had, unknown to the owner, been attracted by the smell of blood. He stumbled upon a sight which would keep him awake on many a night which followed. The body provided slim pickings by way of evidence as to who the killer or killers were for the police forensic team, but was the cause of much speculation; especially so following the body's identification.

Having left misleading evidence Chris and his men departed the scene quietly. They drove across London and disposed of the machete as intended and rid themselves of the other tools and toolbox along the way. Chris and the other man who entered the house eventually removed the tarpaulin from the back of the van and left it on a building site. The coveralls worn throughout the operation went into the River Thames, as did the ski masks worn at the interrogation site. The latex gloves which they had again worn from the start of the mission were disposed of in the waste bin of a meat packer, along with hundreds of similar ones. The 'borrowed' number plates were returned, and the van used was de-hired the following day after extensive pressure washing inside and out. There was nothing which would in any way connect them to the raid on the bomb factory, or the death of Abdul Khaled.

Khaled had been wanted by the police, and the address at which they previously called upon for him flagged up as the phone call from the 'bomb factory' came in. This diverted a nearby police patrol car. On finding the door slightly ajar the attending police officer pushed it fully open and then immediately entered the house after catching sight of the body on the hallway floor halfway into the kitchen. He called in support which rapidly arrived in the form of Special Branch, in turn also very rapidly followed by Bomb Disposal units and the Anti-Terrorist Squad, both of which had much to do at the property. Once the implications of the find were realised all attending officers were read the riot act. No news of any kind was to be allowed to seep out until officially released, and what was then issued would be carefully controlled and manipulated by the Metropolitan Police. The road was cordoned off, and neighbours moved out on grounds of safety and thoroughly questioned.

Although the find was incredibly useful to the Met politically, and undoubtedly saved many lives, it did raise a large number of questions, many of which would eventually be answered by the captured terrorist, but also many which would not. The two main questions were – Where was Abdul Khaled and, who on earth had attacked the bomb factory and then made the emergency number call? The answer to the mystery surrounding Abdul Khaled was to be found late the following afternoon, but in solving that question many more were raised. Those working both crime scenes reached some incontrovertible conclusions. Whoever carried out the hit on the bomb factory managed a slick and highly professional operation which was to be admired for its ruthless efficiency. The death of Khaled demonstrated all the hallmarks of a Muslim execution which, judging from the video cassette wrappers found at the scene, they presumably recorded, probably for use at some future training camp. The murder was also carried out in a very well planned way. If the same team carried out both raid and murder, they were good, very, very good. But why would they have alerted the police, why had they left one terrorist alive, and just who the hell were they? It seemed every answer provided infinitely more questions, perhaps some of which would never be suitably answered.

News slowly filtered out to a very hungry media, who seized upon every piece of information and speculated wildly over it, applauding the Met for their timely intervention in averting another horrific terror attack. The commissioner of London's Metropolitan Police lapped up the media praise, claiming as much personal credit as was humanly possible. A man of highly questionable honour, always keen to avoid accepting responsibility for any form of error, he gloried when basking in the limelight of success, and was most happy to claim credit for the actions of others, know or unknown. To the greater public the police had pulled off a magnificent coup, possibly, in the media view, with the help of unnamed Special Forces, and everyone knew that was code for the S.A.S.

In reality Chris Spencer's teams first operational hit was an unequivocal resounding success on every level imaginable, as were the follow up operations against the three names given by Abdul Khaled, all of whom met their deaths swiftly but without the use of weapons, allowing their deaths to be covered as accidents. Two of the three were known to be Muslin extremists by security forces, and the third an illegal wanted for terrorist activities by US Homeland Security. All were implicated by evidence found at the 'bomb factory', and all died before the police could question them. The Met secretly heaved a mighty sigh of relief, but also privately worried as to whether a power struggle was underway and, if so, who was involved. Unfortunately, aside from possible Afro-Caribbean Muslim overtones, they had not found a single piece of evidence to so much as help point them in a direction. Any direction!

Operation Mary had been wholly accomplished.

Nine

Over the years Jake Ferris's various business interests had grown quite independently of NJF Industries, and to him they were real, something NJF really never was. Had he not experienced the good fortune of meeting Nathan when he did his business ventures would have undoubtedly prospered, although without Nathan and Susie's help possibly not to quite the same degree. The businesses were essentially fairly diverse in their makeup varying from his many garages, most now with main dealer franchises, through manufacturing plants and printing establishments, to a medium sized construction company and a property management business which owned a myriad of commercial and retail properties.

Somehow he always managed to keep his finger on the pulse of all he owned, and maintained a policy of attempting to find good people, treat them well, train them up and, wherever possible, promote from within. Despite the size of his operation and its diversification he could still do most of the jobs any of his business interests called upon personally and, where he could not, he knew enough about the subject to take part in an in-depth informed conversation with any of his hand picked management personnel. He had many a time been known to pick up a broom and sweep a factory floor, frequently got his hands dirty under the bonnets of various cars, and even got on the shovel whilst on site. He was in every way still very much a practical hands-on guy and was never shy about rolling up his sleeves and getting dirty, which never failed to endear him with his employees.

He took an interest in his staff and, without exception, from labourer to director, one weeks service or thirty years, ever member of staff always got a birthday card with a ten pound note inside, so all could always have a drink on him on the day. It didn't cost a lot, but it paid off handsomely in respect earned. In addition every employee irrespective of job was encouraged to feel free to approach him, and to them all he was Jake, never Mr Ferris. Some of his staff filled more important roles than others within their respective companies but Jake treated everyone who worked for him equally. They were his people. To a man his staff liked and respected him, and were fiercely loyal well beyond that which was generally considered normal in any British company.

Despite the diversification there was one thing all his business interests had in common, and something which had fanned his entrepreneurial fire since his mid teens, the desire for property. Jake Ferris liked property and understood it the way some men do cars and others football clubs. The acquisition, ownership and control of property, whether green field sites or towering blocks, was his reason for being, and had always been that way for as long as he could remember. Aside from NJF Industries his personal fortune was vast and, although his business ventures turned in healthy annual profits, to Jake it was all based on property. He had a deep seated underlying mistrust of banks and banking institutions and, as a consequence, had always funded his projects 'in house', firmly believing the odd adage that a bank manager was a man who would happily lend an umbrella, but always asked for it back at the first sign of rain. As his interests grew he expanded that particular view to include those of the city, who he viewed as either circling sharks or chinless wonders who had never done a proper days work in their lives. This view was also firmly reinforced as the meteoric rise of NJF Industries attracted all sorts of interest and offers of 'help' from the arrogant, patronising, slimy handed pricks he had always despised.

Shortly after the turn of the millennium Jake finally did something he had intended doing for years, and brought all the various businesses and companies together under one corporate roof. Although there were a small number of far flung interests the vast majority of his companies, and the properties from which they operated, were in London, and most of those had their roots to the east of the city. From childhood East London had always been his stomping ground. He knew the area intimately and loved both it and its people wholly irrespective of their backgrounds, colours or creeds, although that in part altered forever with Susie's death. Eastlond Property Holdings was the vehicle by which he brought all his many interests together. Despite the now hundreds of millions involved he never once held any desire to float anything as a public company, which meant everything remained completely under his full personal control, to the annoyance of those with the cold wet hands and colder hearts of the city.

The announcement of the formation of a joint venture between the Gatting Group, Eastlond Property Holdings and NJF Industries shocked many in the world of business and high finance. Jake's interest in NJF was a matter of public record, but a tie in with Eastlond did not fit either companies past profile. The Gatting Group had a little in common with Eastlond, but again not a thing which appeared to dovetail with the long term interest or aims of NJF. There was much made by the popular press of the fact Nathan Jefferies had been married to Susie Gatting, who tragically lost her life in the underground bombings a little over a month earlier. However no known overlapping business relationship ever previously existed between the various companies, which raised a great deal of speculation as to just how long talks and planning had been going on behind the scenes, with most believing it must have gone back to Susie and Nathan's wedding.

The new collective enterprise, to be called Almeti International, was to be incorporated with the declared intention of building retail, entertainment and gaming complexes in emerging economies, primarily throughout the former Eastern Europe, but also very much in Western Europe, and were to also research African and Asian projects. Multiplex cinemas and sophisticated gaming halls were to be built with accompanying sports facilities, surrounded by medium to large sized retail shopping malls, where real malls would compete with the highly successful NJF virtual malls. Where possible, and with official community backing, these fully integrated commercial parks would be built on the outskirts of urban conurbations, and would include pleasure and amusement parks. NJF would underwrite such projects long term success by taking full control of the gaming halls and some of the retail units in each and every complex, including control of all amusement parks.

The announcement included details of bank and bankers, with a special mention for the young bank agent who had so successfully negotiated the deal between the three companies and his bank. Other appointments were set to follow. Eastlond and the Gatting Group both guaranteed a quarter of a billion pounds apiece to the new project, with NJF taking control contributing a one and a half billion pound stake. Jack Bryant's employers, who were mightily impressed with his abilities to land such a prestigious and cash rich account, added a one million pounds bonus to his pay check.

The details of the deal remained of great interest to the financial pages of the press, especially when Chi Lu Herepath added a footnote on behalf of NJF Industries, which resounded around the world. As a direct result of the London tube bombings NJF Industries had re-evaluated their interests and commitments on a nation by nation basis and made the decision to pull out of all Muslim and Muslim run nations. Additionally no future games would be released in any of the languages of those nations, and sales of games, telephones, software and all hardware stopped with all goods removed from the shelves. NJF had publicly closed the door on the Muslim peoples of the world and stated quite categorically the door would remain firmly closed until such time as the nations concerned took a strong proactive stance and swept all organisations, cells, terrorists and sympathisers from their respective lands.

Although they expected little from those concerned because of shareholder worries regarding returns, NJF encouraged other companies and nations to follow their lead. Predictably none did, with the sole exception of the newly formed Almeti International, whose Articles of Association specifically prohibited the group from conducting business affairs with any state, country, province or region which was controlled or partially controlled by any religious, fundamentalist or extremist governments or regimes. Loosely interpreted that meant no work, finance or aid would ever find its way from their corporation to any part of the Muslim world.

Some of Britain's bleeding heart brigade and parts of the domestic liberal press didn't like it, which was tough. Many of the former Eastern European papers hailed it as a major step forward by a far sighted enterprise who were seen as opening the door to the furtherance of full European integration. All in all Jack Bryant's plan proved to be highly successful. Private meetings could now be held quite openly under the spotlight of media attention without arousing suspicion or speculation as to what was being discussed. Those with high profiles could now be seen coming together. If any of the complexes did get built they should prove to be a financial bonus for those concerned.

Ten

Peter Parfitt and Chris Spencer agreed to meet up and discuss the ideas Peter had in mind regarding a way of introducing or delivering explosives to targets. There was no desire on either part to use the boardroom of NJF Industries. What they wished to discuss was by its very nature extremely sensitive and its content would remain committed to memory only, but both, especially with their military backgrounds, completely understood such things. They had in the past discussed many confidential matters quite openly in public places with others, and accordingly attracted much less outside attention. Should either man have been followed, which they were not and were unlikely to have been, those following would see nothing but two friends socialising. There was no specific venue chosen in advance, but they had agreed to meet at Canary Wharf and wander around until they found something suitable. Neither knew the area well, nor had either asked for recommendations, it was simply both local and accessible and featured a number of new bars. One would undoubtedly meet their needs, and one did, offering a broad balcony overlooking the water with an otherwise somewhat secluded table.

Having ordered and each collected a beer from the bar on the way through, both sat at the table overlooking the water, relaxing in the sun. Apart from the meeting a couple of weeks earlier, when they agreed a time and date for their discussion, they had not spent any time together away from others since the day of the bombings which first brought them together. Chris opened the discussion they were there for with a question about the events in Slough when Parfitt was forced into the fight he was neither looking for nor wanted.

"Did you ever hear any more about those ragheads in Slough?" Chris asked irreverently. "Any repercussions of any kind?"

"No. Not a thing." Parfitt answered then elaborated slightly. "Of course there was mention of it on the local television. The police were looking for a Caucasian male, and gave a height, approximate age, and brief description, but it was much generalised and would have fitted tens of thousands of guys. It will always be with me, but I haven't lost any sleep over it since, and I think the police will eventually have to put it down to yet another unsolved crime. There was an article in a local paper about it possibly being a reprisal attack for the tube bombings, but I don't believe the story was taken seriously or followed up. I did worry for a while that the police may look at the addresses of all those hurt and killed, and check up on next of kin and family living within the area. But then there were more than fifty killed, and seven hundred wounded, which probably makes for five thousand plus pissed off people almost directly involved, thousands more indirectly involved, and some others who just want an excuse to be violent. Then there are the gang wars and turf wars in the area, and the drug scene. The police will not have the resources to check everything out, and I'm not even registered as living in the country, so I guess they'll just wait hoping for a lucky break."

"Which they won't get unless you get careless. Don't visit or shop in Slough again just in case you are ever recognised." Chris stated.

"That I'll certainly not do!" Parfitt answered. "Tammy's house is on the market, and neither of us will ever be going back there. As far as officialdom is concerned everything is being taken care of by her father. When I'm not in London I stay at the cottage in her parents grounds, and am working on converting the place to accommodate her with her needs for when she eventually leaves hospital, whenever that may be."

"How's she doing?" Chris asked.

"She's alive Chris. Every day is hard. Hard for her especially, but also for her family and for me. But slowly she's improving. A month has gone by. Her right foot has started to reset properly and her jaw's been rebuilt, but lying in bed is all she can do at present, and with that goes muscle wastage. They think she'll be able to walk again eventually, with a prosthetic leg, but it will be months before they can even start any such treatment. She's lost the hearing in her left ear, but there is hope she may yet get some use from the left eye, although it will never see as it did again. The scarring is horrendous and she hasn't been allowed a mirror yet as it may prove too traumatic."

"Have you had a chance to see the Bryant lad's father at all?" Chris asked another question to change the subject slightly. In some ways death was easier to handle he thought. At least it gave a form of closure, unpleasant though it was. He certainly would not like to be in the fly boy's position, and realised he would not have a clue how to deal with it if he were.

"Yeah, I popped in a couple of days ago because I was nearby, gave another name and told them I was family. He hasn't improved at all. The reverse if anything! I think he's lost it forever. He should've been given help when his wife was killed, but didn't get it and just bottled it all up. It's coming out now, but it's just sheer rage. He cannot bear the sight of anyone who hasn't got white skin, and literally wants to kill them all." Peter answered.

"I kind of know where he's coming from, at least in part." Chris mused. "Shame about his mental state because there's some news which should cheer him up if only he could have it."

"Yeah, I gathered it was you!" Parfitt said with a small smile forming. "I read about it in the paper and did wonder. Apart from Abdul Khaled there were no names or proper address, but it seemed it was the right area from the address Nathan gave. Good for you!"

They sat in silence for a moment after that, watching as a small sailing boat crossed in front of them, the young couple aboard enjoying the sun and the slight breeze blowing across the open water as they tacked away again. Chris broke the silence. "I guess we had better get down to business. You wanted to talk about a couple of ideas you had with the mosque problem?"

"Yes, the mosque problem. I don't want to sound silly, but have you considered an airborne attack?" Peter asked.

Chris Spencer grinned. "Now wouldn't that be great. A converted 747 or old B52, and take out the whole of Towel Head Town while we are at it. Better still use stealth technology so we can make our getaway afterwards. Seriously, what are you thinking? Are we talking missiles? I've thought about them but there are inherent problems, not the least of which is transportation and targeting."

"No. Not missiles." Peter said, shaking his head. "I agree with you regarding the problems. I was thinking more along the lines of small aircraft. What size payload would have to be delivered in your opinion to cause a suitable amount of damage? I know a little about dropping bombs from training, although it wasn't my branch of the service, but have never had to calculate explosive forces or destructive capabilities. Generally there's someone else to do that sort of thing, and then there are the smart bombs which find their target so long as it is painted with a laser and the bombs are dropped close enough."

The weight question Parfitt raised was a serious one which Chris had already been mulling over for some time.

"The problem with answering that, Peter, is it comes back to the same thing, which is the question of a delivery system. Five kilos of Semtex detonating inside would probably do every bit as much damage as fifty kilos dropped on the building. A shaped charge fixed to the roof or walls would work, but we'll probably never be able to get to a roof and the walls can be seen. A small aircraft could drop something, but our munitions are not going to be very sophisticated, and the pilot would be collared by police the moment he landed."

"I understand all those things." Peter persisted. "Which is why I ask about payload. If the explosive produces sufficient yield from a five kilo charge then a remote controlled model could be flown in, as several designs are capable of carrying such weight and most are small enough to be flown through an open doorway! Or at least crashed through, because they would lose their wings, but at least they could be rigged to detonate inside."

Chris Spencer stared at Parfitt in amazement. Eventually he simply said, "Peter, let's get some food and another drink. I honestly think you may just have found a solution to the whole problem, but I really need to think things over for a minute."

They picked up menus, made their respective choices, and Peter went inside to order, leaving Chris deep in thought. When he re-emerged from ordering, carrying two pints, Chris looked up and asked, "Do you know much about these toy planes?"

"A fair bit," Parfitt answered. "But try to remember this one thing. Most of what I can tell you about are fully scaled models. They are anything but toys. They fly; some of them very fast, have some quite sophisticated power options, and can send and receive electronic signals and instructions."

"Okay, sorry, I take your point and didn't mean to belittle them." Chris said apologetically. "Do you mind if I ask some questions whilst we wait for the food?"

"Not at all." Peter assured him. "I can't say I will know the answer to everything, but I know all the basics. They've been a passing hobby of mine for years. I used to own and fly a couple of them before I went to live in South Africa, but never found the time after that, what with work and meeting Tammy. I'm rusty on the flying side, but I've kept up to date with what's available from magazines and things, and have to say they have come on a long way from the time when I was a kid."

"You know, to be honest Peter, I feel a bit stupid about the whole thing, and should have thought of the possibilities myself, but they never occurred to me." Chris admitted. "I've seen the idea of small pilotless model surveillance helicopters put forward for future battlefronts, and worked alongside the Americans in the Gulf when they were using their UAV's, but never even considered what you have just suggested. As I said earlier, I must be getting senile!"

Parfitt smiled. "It's more to do with thinking along the lines of personal expertise. From the differences in our training backgrounds and experiences to date you are bound to be more likely to think in terms of ground attacks, whilst I will undoubtedly go for the air option first. It's interesting you should mention UAV's. I did have some thoughts about them, but I think they can be reserved for other possible missions. Anyway, fire away with the questions, and I'll answer what I can."

"Well just expand upon the generalities to begin with." Chris suggested. "It's a subject I know dreadfully little about. Speed, size, weight, payload, range and communication distance, anything and everything you can tell me. Whatever you tell me will increase my knowledge."

"Umm." Parfitt mused. "It's a much bigger subject than that Chris. What you have just asked is a bit like me asking you to tell me all you can about guns."

"What sort of guns?" Chris asked grinning.

"Exactly. Point made!" Parfitt smiled in reply.

"Okay, serious stuff then. How fast can they fly?" Chris asked.

"Well obviously it depends a whole lot on make, model and engine size, but pylon racers usually compete at between one hundred and ten and over one hundred and fifty miles per hour. Some of the better jets will fly at over two hundred."

"Jets? You mean there are model jets? And they fly at that sort of speed" Chris asked incredulously.

"Oh yeah. But there are loads of down sides to them for our kind of application. They are mostly used in the US, are very expensive and, I would have thought, much more easily traced than the more popular propeller options, electric or internal combustion. Also if the pilot messes up trouble occurs incredibly quickly. In my considered opinion it would be foolish for us to so much as discuss the jet option. I do understand the advantages of mass and momentum, a classic example of which was the V-I and V-II of the Second World War. Both carried the same warhead, but the effect of the V-II was devastating because of the ballistic delivery system caused the blasts to be amplified by the released kinetic energy. No matter what we do we cannot compete with those concepts, so I believe it is desirable to work with the simplest possible system, which means we stay away from jets.

"With prop jobs there are three basic wing configurations and a bunch of build options, from ready to fly all the way through to building virtually everything from scratch. The wing options are high wing, low wing and mid-wing. Mid-wing are the most difficult to fly, and high wing, which is where the wing is above or on top of the planes fuselage, are the easiest. The reason for that is because these planes carry most of their weight, and any additional payload, below the canopy of the wing structure, giving the configuration an inherent stability, so the plane will act like a glider if necessary. Usually, with this design, if control is lost stability can usually be regained by returning controls to a neutral position, which allows the plane to quite naturally return to gliding, from where flight control can start again. The only real downside is in the fact their wing shape, its position, and the drag of the fuselage beneath the wing make them the slowest of all options. Despite their lack of speed they would still be my first choice and recommendation for such an operation."

"Okay. I can see that," Chris said. "Reliability is the single most important factor. We cannot, absolutely cannot, afford to make a mistake and drop one in the wrong place. Every one we launch, without exception, has to hit the target! So what do you recommend with build options?"

Before Peter could reply their food arrived, and both men waited patiently whilst plates, cutlery, serviettes and condiments were put in front of them by the waiter, who they both thanked before he left.

Peter then answered. "There's no real question about it in my mind. We certainly do not need to deal with time consuming kits. We could use 'Ready To Fly', which come complete as the term suggests, with just a matter of attaching wings to fuselage and off you go. However I feel the 'Almost Ready to Fly' would suit us better. These usually have an assembly time of around four hours, more if the owner wants to add detail, which we don't. The only thing we need to add is the explosive and a detonator. It will take time and some experimentation to work out how to shape, mould and insert the explosive into the main fuselage in order not to upset the trim and stability and therefore control of the plane, but once it is worked out in one I can see no reason why it would not work in many. Of course every gram which is added will affect the crafts flight, but I would suggest a detonator which detonates within one or two seconds of impact, but which we arm remotely only seconds beforehand. Although in the case of an accident such a system would leave evidence, it would also avoid any collateral damage."

"You've thought this through, haven't you?" Chris phrased the comment as a statement rather than a question. "Now, as to range, how far can they fly, and over what distance can they be controlled?"

"Two very good questions." Parfitt replied. "How far can they fly? Well, I know of two examples, 'Laima', although Laima is technically a UAV, and 'The Spirit of Butts Farm' also known as TAM 5, which have flown across the Atlantic."

"What!" Chris exclaimed eyes wide and jaw dropping open.

"Oh yeah, it's true." Parfitt assured him, "There's also a project called 'Vulture' currently being researched alongside NASA for a UAV which will be capable of staying aloft for about five years at a time. The two I mentioned made the crossing using less than half a gallon of fuel between them. Interestingly TAM 5 spent ninety-nine percent of its flight on autopilot, something which may be of use to us.

"Control is all about communication between the transmitter and a receiver, both of which obviously have to be on the same frequency. Most countries have a reserved frequency, and Europe has adopted thirty-five MHz throughout for model aircraft only. This helps to reduce the consequences of radio interference, which would otherwise be potentially catastrophic. I won't bore you with all the technical stuff about channels and sub-channels, crystals, phased-lock loops and spread spectrums as, if you don't already know about it, you don't need to know. I feel we would have to experiment with a few aspects of existing technology for control over greater distances, and I have a few ideas about that which I want to run past Nathan because he's done an amazing amount of research on communications, but I don't see any problems we cannot overcome!"

"What's Nathan done which could help with this then? I thought he was all about computer games?" Chris asked.

"No, not at all. In the early days, before he got into games, he did some outstanding experiments with communications. He started with line of sight stuff and worked his way up. A lot of his telecommunications division is still working with some of his early ideas. He is an incredibly gifted chap. Pretty narrow in his range of expertise, but within that range he's so far ahead of anyone else on the planet as to be unreal," Parfitt explained enthusiastically. "To be honest with you I can see he may be able to help with certain aspects of what we are doing, but at the moment I just can't see which. However I'm sure young Jack Bryant will come up with something."

"Now of that I too am sure!" Chris agreed. "Peter, this comes across as a relatively simple solution to what has proved to be quite a difficult problem. It would render the enemy powerless to adequately defend themselves and take them by complete surprise, yet all the while maintaining our anonymity. The last thing many of them would see would be a 'toy' aircraft flying at them out of control. So what's the size and weight of these things, and how much is it practical to plan on them carrying?"

Again Parfitt explained. "All of those things vary, and depend on personal preference or basic requirement, but suffice to say there are several which I feel would suit our purpose. As an informed guess, I think you will find we will end up with something weighing ten to fourteen kilos all up weight, including five kilos of explosive. The wingspan should be about six feet, with a similar or slightly longer fuselage length. It should be possible to transport in a small van or a people carrier, maybe even an estate car or tourer, and launch from most flat surfaces, although a downhill slope into the wind would help because of the extra weigh. Definitely one thing to look into is the possibility of remoulding the fuselage and actually using the explosive itself to form a part of it. If that could be done it could reduce the weight substantially. Either way I've been thinking about the power source. I usually prefer internal combustion, but then thought this is only ever going to be a one trip plane, and battery technology has improved enough so it may be able to carry the weight with an electric motor. However, to be safe, and we cannot risk failure caused by cost savings, I feel it is best to stick with internal combustion and use a bigger motor with proper bearings. We'll have to experiment with power to weight ratios, but I'm convinced it can be done!"

"Well as far as I'm concerned the whole venture sounds perfectly feasible." Chris concluded. "I guess we'll have to carry out a whole bunch of tests to check viability, but it certainly sounds as if you've done as much relevant research as can be done before testing. We have this next meeting coming up shortly and I'll certainly back the idea if you bring it up there. In the meanwhile I would suggest you very discreetly start looking into sourcing the various options you feel would fit the purpose. Whilst you do so I'll look into the explosive options, but I already know what I want to go with, and where to get it."

On that note their meeting ended. They walked together to the end of the quayside, shook hands and said their goodbyes. Just before both went their separate ways Chris turned to Peter with one last sentence.

"Peter, the very best of luck with Tammy mate!"

Perhaps not much of a sentence, or terribly profound, but heartfelt and meant. From a warrior with a great deal already on his mind, it touched Peter deeply. He thought the 'mate' part of it was probably a word not often used by the man who was Chris Spencer.

Eleven

Four weeks had passed since they all last met, six since the bombings, and during the intervening period much had happened. Ongoing events at NJF, the announcement of the new joint venture, and the continuing repercussions caused by Susie's death still made all those concerned interesting to certain members of the press on a bad news day, but things move on and for the most part the press had moved on with them. This made it easier for those attending the Friday meeting.

Jack once more flew over with Katya, this time flying in from Frankfurt where he was working, and both arrived quite openly. Following his apparent success at wooing the newly formed Almeti International he was to get a full time personal assistant. Several of those already employed within the organisation for which he worked had applied for the position. He had interviewed the three best and rejected them all. The position was then publicly advertised and Katya applied, passing her first interview. The bank knew little of Jack's relationship with her, which provided him with the opportunity to make absolutely certain the job would be hers, which would in turn make things easier for all involved in adequately explaining the reason she was with him and attending meetings to any of the media who might be interested.

Chris Spencer had taken his security cover very seriously, feeling it was morally incumbent upon him to do so as he was being paid to personally address the security situations of the Gatting Group, Eastlond Properties and NJF Industries, and would become the senior security consultant to Almeti. Throughout the previous month he had made his presence known on many of their various sites. At first it was resented by some, especially those who felt they were passed over and saw him as nothing more than a would be new broom attempting to sweep clean. However slowly but surely he won many over with his straight talking no nonsense character. He had never suffered fools throughout his time in the army, and was certainly not going to suffer them now. What started off as nothing more than a convenient cover just a few weeks earlier was in reality paying dividends for those who were technically his employers.

Chris endured a minor altercation with one of the existing guards, a tall shaven headed man with a large chest, an even larger belly, and an opinion of himself which more than matched his size. The man had been a bully all his life and wasn't about to be messed about and told what to do by some new boy just because he was an ex-squaddie. He was going to put this newbie in his place, told everyone he would, and set about doing so. After trying unsuccessfully to verbally push Chris into a fist fight he made the mistake of publicly throwing a punch at him. Grinning Chris had dodged the punch, used the big mans size and weight against him, and the momentum generated, to spin him around by the arm which threw the punch. Arm pinned behind his back and still moving Chris then walked him straight into a wall.

The big man collapsed with blood streaming from his nose and mouth where both had connected with the wall, and suffered a dislocated shoulder. Chris then drove the man to hospital himself, explaining along the way he would no longer be required. The news travelled like wildfire to all sites and shifts. His reputation was made and his authority thereafter fully accepted.

Phil Gatting was expected and immediately ushered through the now improved site security procedure, and it was Chris himself who checked Danny Bryant and Peter Parfitt onto the site before joining them at the meeting. When they were all assembled Phil Gatting once again quite naturally assumed the mantle of chair without question or resentment from any of those present. He first explained what had been achieved in the structuring of the new company before calling on Chris to report on progress. All knew something of the elimination of Abdul Ahmad Khaled and Chris brought them all up to date with what had happened since. He spoke briefly of the bomb factory and of the three individuals implicated by Khaled before he died who had also ceased to draw breath. His report was brief with no words wasted. As he finished he spoke equally briefly of the earlier meeting he and Peter Parfitt had, explaining he considered Peter to have come up with a viable option for taking down any of the British or European mosques they targeted. Parfitt then explained his ideas about radio controlled model aircraft to a very receptive audience.

"Have you looked into the practicalities of this option?" Phil Gatting asked Parfitt.

"Yes. Certainly as far as is possible at this stage," Peter answered before continuing.

"What are now needed are practical trials. I don't mean just buying and flying a model aircraft, as I've done so many times before. I've actually already bought one and played around with weight trials and engine configurations. So far I've been able to manage a downhill launch with a six kilo payload without any further alterations. I know I can improve upon performance and the payload may be increased, but once done the next thing are trials involving explosives. We'll have to find out what we require by way of detonators and will have to carry out experiments with live firing. Before we do so we'll need some explosives to work with, and that's probably a job for Chris. Additionally we'll need a place where we can carry out some of these experiments and for quite apparent and obvious reasons it cannot be anywhere near a populated area."

"So, Chris, what are the chances of obtaining some Semtex and detonators?" Gatting then asked Chris Spencer.

"In limited quantities I could lay my hands on some in the next few days, certainly within a week." Chris answered.

"What about the longer term, and enough to fully satisfy our requirements?" Jack Bryant asked.

Before he could answer Phil Gatting cut in again. "Chris before answering Jack's question could you fill us all in on what exactly Semtex is, its background and how easy it may be for us to obtain? There is no need to give us too much detail but it may later prove helpful if we all understand what it is we are discussing. I meant to ask you at the last meeting we had, but never got around to it. I think we probably all know it is a plastic explosive, but there most of our knowledge will probably end."

"Okay. I'll do my best." Chris answered. "I'll try to be concise and keep it relevant so as not to bore you.

"Semtex is a general-purpose plastic explosive originally invented in 1966 by the chemist Stanislav Brebera and manufactured by the Semtín East Bohemian Chemical Works which was then called VCHZ Synthesia, where Brebera worked, and is now named Explosia. The mixture was first made in a place called Semtín which is a suburb of Pardubice in the Czech Republic and, as the previous name suggests, is in eastern Bohemia, one hundred and thirty kilometres east of Prague and seventy from the Polish border. It comes in two basic forms and is used in demolition, commercial blasting and, of course, in certain military applications.

"Like other plastic explosives, especially C-4, it is easily malleable. C-4 is off white in colour Semtex is orange, although there is a white variant for industrial use, not that colour is of any importance to us. Back then the Czech Republic was a communist country and almost all its export policies were dictated by the Soviet Union. The product was widely exported with something like fourteen tonnes sent to North Vietnam during the Vietnamese War, but by far the biggest buyer was Libya, who imported a staggering seven hundred tonnes in a six year period between '75 and '81. From there it was used by the rag heads in the Middle East and by the likes of the Provisional IRA and the Irish National Liberation Army in Northern Ireland where, if you know where to look, there's still some to be found.

"Semtex became notoriously popular with terrorists because it was, until recently, extremely difficult to detect, as was made famous in the case of Pan Am Flight 103 back in '88, which was brought down using less than five hundred grams of the stuff. Because of its terrorist associations, and bowing to international pressure, current day production is detectable as it now has ethylene glycol dinitrate added which produces a distinctive vapour signature, and now all new production also has an identifying metallic code. However, although they are currently trying to shorten it to three years or less, Semtex has a shelf life of at least twenty years, so anything produced throughout the late '80's would suit our purpose, and there is literally tonnes of it still around from the period.

"I understand less than ten tonnes a year is currently manufactured but, as I've said, modern production would be useless to us. I've previously indicated I prefer to use Semtex to other explosives, one of the reasons for which is it's usable over a greater temperature range than the alternatives, which makes it incredibly stable. Interestingly there's an awful lot left in Libya, and some of what's left is available – to the right people. Now a few of those people still live in Northern Ireland and Eire and, although politics and policies have changed contacts still exist. A trip to Malta with the right person may well bring us all the product we would ever need."

"Pardon my ignorance, but why Malta?" Jake Ferris asked.

"By tradition Malta has tended to turn a blind eye to 'tourists' from Libya." Chris explained. "It is also a place where anyone from the British Isles is welcome, something which goes back to the days of the Crusades and The Knights Templar. It has been known for those from these islands to get involved in conversations in bars with people from other lands, and it has been known for those with Irish accents to end up in conversations with those from Gadaffi's homeland!"

"Do you have the necessary contacts?" Gatting inquired.

"Yes." Chris answered without qualification.

A thin satisfied smile appeared on Phil Gatting's lips. "Good," he said. "Excellent!"

"In that case, if I may?" Jack Bryant broke in, raising an eyebrow in the direction of Phil Gatting, who nodded as Jack continued. "I feel it is time for us to consider our long term objectives. At our last meeting I mentioned we all had our strengths and things we can each individually bring to the table. Collectively we've all moved on since then. Chris has certainly demonstrated his strengths and the ideas and information Peter has put forward have been excellent. Phil, Nathan and Jake have created a new company which can be used as an umbrella for many future operations. All of which give us a good start.

"However, we now need to seriously consider and discuss how we are going to use what we have, where we are going, what we are doing, and to then make decisions for the longer term. We've all accepted there is little we can do overnight so I feel we need to come up with workable ideas which can then be planned into missions. We all understand why we are here and what our overall objectives are, but I believe it is time to start planning for the long term and the bigger picture. The idea of the radio controlled model aircraft certainly works for me and I love the simplicity and anonymity of it. This too could work well but I do see the point raised by Peter concerning testing and, as was mentioned last time we met, ultimately we are going to have to find ourselves a testing ground and firing range. Doubtless the further down the road we take this the more complex the issues will prove to be.

"For now I feel we have to decide what we want to target, not in generalities as we have already done that, but narrow it down to specifics. I can completely understand we cannot today see all which the future will bring, and also understand as we advance additional targets may become available which we may have to prioritise but, that said, plans have to be made. We've all proved we're committed, our very presence is evidence of that, but if we are to successfully move the project along we need to agree upon targets and then plan accordingly, and there are a great deal of options and many alternatives. However, from my point of view I feel the whole issue hinges on just two main desires. Firstly to take terror back to the community from which the terrorists come and, secondly, to make them pay on an unprecedented scale. In other words to hurt them badly across the board – in terms of human life, economic costs and religious symbolism and associated edifices. There is one additional point. We must do what it is we do safely, without risk to ourselves, our country or our culture. With that in mind we may have to muddy the water as we go, deflecting responsibility along the way and, as I said earlier, where possible stirring up trouble and a growing distrust or hatred of all things Muslim by as many communities and societies as possible. They manage to do a damn fine job of that themselves, but I don't think it would harm our cause if we were to assist them.

"In terms of human life we can take out individuals or groups, and can attack en masse given the right circumstances and a viable plan. The work Nathan has done finding the creature who killed my mother proves what is possible. If we can find illegals who have transgressed, yet have either evaded capture or been wrongly released, and remove them from this world, they will probably get little press or public sympathy. However we would not be able to let any form of pattern develop and you, Nathan, will have to be very careful with your hacking, although I am sure you are, and equally sure you do not need me to tell you that." Jack looked up at Nathan who nodded.

"Taking them out in small numbers, ones and twos, will help us feel better, but it will not take fear to their communities." Jack continued. "In order to do so we have to hurt large numbers of them, which means we have to attack them in their homes, their places of work and preferably in their places of worship. We must never cloud the issue by seeing any as innocents or even as people, but merely as targets, as they do us, so nothing must ever be regarded as unacceptable. Whole areas of our country have now been taken over by these creatures. If bombs go off in busy Muslim shopping areas, cinemas or mosques so much the better. We must learn from their tactics – and adopt, adapt, improve as the old adage goes. The more that die the greater their fear will grow. It should not be forgotten cowardice is their cultural and social norm. If these creatures do not like this happening to them they can run away and leave our green and pleasant land, before they destroy it as they have their own, taking their troubles away with them.

"The loss of their lives is important, and many should die in order to underline the message we are not happy with them bombing us. It must be driven home. However of equal importance is to hurt them economically. It strikes me much as they hate us they do covet what we have in terms of goods, property and money. They seem to miss the point that we made it and they are incapable of doing so, so if they did rid themselves of us their new economy would collapse just as it has in their own screwed up lands. The point is they like and enjoy what they have here. So we should consider taking it from them. Burn their houses, their shops, their factories and their warehouses. Hit them financially, and keep hitting them.

"Finally religious symbolism and edifices. No matter their rampant hypocrisies, these Muslims purport to be a devout bunch. They do seem to love their mosques and their big religious buildings and complexes. Chris mentioned attacking mosques, and I think he is quite right. I really do like the idea of taking down a mosque for every person killed on those tubes and bus, but at the moment I am not sure of the practicalities involved. We would need to find a delivery system which worked, over which we had control, but one we could use without facing the possibility of being compromised or captured. There is of course the possibility indeed I believe probability, as I have already outlined, of escalation. However if we do this thing properly these creatures will not know who is hitting them. By which I mean they will not know from which country their nemesis comes, which should be relatively easy for us to accomplish as they have offended and hurt so many along the way. It must be confusing even for them when trying to remember who their enemies are, from Hindu to Christians and even different sects of their own culture, and warring countries within their own group.

"It would be advantageous to whip up press frenzy to fever pitch and create a furore around the world, but that too is something which will require some thought and will require subtle manipulation of the press. It would also be highly beneficial to help drive a wedge between their own sects, particularly the Sunni and Shiite Muslims where dissent already exists. With escalation in mind, or as a single long term objective, I believe we should be looking to hit something very big and very important to them. As I mentioned earlier there are three possible targets I have identified, the Petronas Towers, Medina, and my personal favourite, Bakkah." Jack finished and looked around the table to gauge a reaction to his words.

For the first time Jake Ferris spoke. "Now that is something I particularly like the sound of! I agree with all which has been said about hurting them here, and at various other locations around Europe, but the idea of attacking the very centre of their ideology does have a great appeal for me. Giving them a bloody nose is one thing, but to stab straight at the heart really should piss them off big time! But how on earth would we go about mounting such a mission? Chris, have you any ideas?"

"With regard to most of what was said I'm sure I could come up with some viable working plans, especially with Peter's help," Chris answered. "As for taking down Bakkah, that's more than a little outside of my field of expertise. It would take a very large air force with the backing of several nations' armies to do it, and even then I believe chances would be slim. It should be remembered Bakkah is a closed city. You have to be Muslim to go there. To get in and plant explosives with any chance of success is not going to happen. The best chance of success would be to attack in the same way they did the twin towers but, much as I wish to hurt them, suicide missions are a last ditch desperation measure and not really for those from our culture. The only remaining option would be to use cruise missiles, but firstly we would never be able to obtain those secretly, if at all, and secondly we would have to have a launch vehicle or vessel, and either would be picked up by satellites and or ground forces."

Chris finished, and again there was a short silence. Peter Parfitt broke it with a wholly unexpected comment, which would more than prove his worth. "Well with the recourses at our command we could build our own cruise missiles."

Chris Spencer smiled. "Year, nice idea Peter, but that would take an awful lot of money. I know there is a lot on the table, and I can see people are committed, but the development would take years and the costs would be prohibitive even for these gentlemen." Chris said nodding in the direction of Nathan, Jake and Phil Gatting.

"Well look, I'm sorry if this sounds silly to everyone here, but it has already been done," Parfitt retorted.

"What, someone built their own cruise missile?" Chris asked, sounding astounded.

"Yes, they have." Parfitt answered. "A New Zealander by the name of Bruce Simpson, also known as the Rocket Man. He developed a home made cruise missile in his garage for under five thousand US dollars. It was designed to carry a ten kilogram payload a distance of one hundred kilometres."

"Seriously?" Phil Gatting asked.

"Absolutely!" Parfitt answered. "The US government said it wasn't possible so he set about proving them wrong. He started to publish his work on the internet as a warning to governments they should be prepared for the possibility of that kind of sophisticated attack from within their own borders. When the Americans realised what was going on they tried to close him down by putting pressure on the New

Zealand government, who then claimed he was violating the International Missile Technology Control Regime. However he had already published it all on the net. He has even developed his own more efficient pulse jet engine which has made it more fuel efficient, effectively adding distance. He calls the engine the X-jet. Although it's not fast by some standards it's quick enough. It flies at something over three hundred and fifty miles an hour so, given its range, it is only in the air for about ten minutes. Too little time to scramble an aircraft with any hope of an intercept, and the missile itself is accurate to within ten meters. Basically, as with all cruise missiles, it is just a modern day version of the Second World War flying bomb, the V1, but far more accurate and sophisticated.

"It's all there, from design spec to power unit to payload, even down to GPS system and what servos are required. It works, and it flies. Interestingly he claims to be a man of principal and will not deal with terrorists or rogue states. Iran quite publicly tried to enlist his help but he refused. They still want it, and America has done its best to have the whole project hushed up, but the information is out there. I've got a complete download of the entire project which I've been looking at because I found it interesting. It is impressive. It really is a home made, ultra reliable, extremely inexpensive, accurate, explosive delivery system."

Every person around the table was looking at Peter Parfitt almost as if he had just demonstrated an impossible trick. Jack and Nathan were almost literally opened mouthed, although all rapidly came to terms with the implications of what he had said. Chris Spencer was the first with a question, practical as ever.

"What does he use as a launch platform?" he asked.

"Well the interesting thing there is he actually launches it from the back of a pickup truck. Obviously he needs the truck to take it away from any populated areas, but also uses the speed of the truck to help with the launch. I believe it can be launched from any platform, theoretically stationary or moving as, once launched, its on-board GPS takes over and corrects any variations in launch direction. Technically it could be launched from the back of a truck, the belly of an aircraft, the deck of a fast moving ship or any other platform." Parfitt answered.

"Could we make one?" Danny asked, possibly a little naïvely.

Parfitt chuckled and said, "I imagine we could make dozens of them, actually thousands if we wished. I think if we were to, with a bit of testing and upgrading, we could probably improve the range, payload and accuracy. It would probably cost a little more but ultimately we would have a pretty damn good, very deadly, easily portable weapon."

After yet another moment taken to let things sink in Phil Gatting said, "From the looks on peoples faces Peter it would seem you have presented us with a project well worthy of consideration. Does anyone disagree?" Without exception everyone shook their heads.

"Peter, would you mind if I had a look at the information you have? I don't want to look for it on-line because if what you say about this is correct, the site will certainly be monitored by the security boys." Jack Bryant asked.

"And a copy for me too, please!" Nathan added.

"Of course. I'll make copies for everyone if you wish." Parfitt replied to nods all around.

"Pardon my breaking in." Phil Gatting said. "But for the record I would like to say I like the idea of destroying a few mosques as much as everyone, but the idea of taking down Bakkah appeals to me beyond measure if it's at all doable!"

"Yeah, me too – big time." Jake Ferris added nodding thoughtfully. "Pretty much irrespective of cost too!"

"Then perhaps we should seriously look into the viability of such a project." Jack suggested. "But first let us all make sure we all fully understand what it is we are discussing and planning to do here. We are talking about embarking on a project, which will be of a long term nature, to build our own missiles, obtain explosives and launch those missiles against the Muslim world's holiest site! Would anyone be against such a venture if it proved possible?"

Those around the table merely shook their heads.

"Then I'll need time to consider the possibilities in order to come up with the relevant information to put a conceptual plan before you. Unfortunately I have a great deal to do regarding my current employment which I cannot reasonably shelve. It is unlikely I shall be able to get away in the next eleven weeks, possibly twelve, but that takes us to the start of November, which may seem a long time to some of you. I'm sorry, but to do a thorough job of research I shall need all of that time. Can you allow me those twelve weeks? Jack asked, looking around the table to those present, all of whom were nodding thoughtfully.

"I understand and agree completely." Phil Gatting said. "As we have already agreed it's pointless us arranging meetings for the sake of meeting alone, and they could in themselves lead to compromise if patterns develop. Twelve weeks should give us all time to advance certain aspects of what we wish to do. If we are to go for a big target, and if it is feasible it seems a much better option, then it is not going to be a quick fix, but then if we are going to do this well it is not going to happen overnight. I think it may pay to halt the minor domestic operations until Jack has a chance to study this and report back. Does anyone object to us following such a line?"

"From an operational point of view calling a brief halt may help." Chris Spencer said wholly unexpectedly.

"That's an interesting statement." Jake said. "Why so?"

"Confusion more than anything else," Chris replied. "The enemy, and the security forces, will be looking for patterns. If we take a break now any pattern we may have created will be broken. The recent deaths will look like the end of the campaign."

"The best part of three months will give me a chance to have a look at these pulsejet plans and see what I can put together too," Danny said, taking the opportunity to speak out. "I'll see if I stand any chance of making them myself."

"Could I have several photographs of each of you please, so I can get on with creating identities?" Katya asked.

"I'm sure we could all get passport photographs back to you this afternoon." Jake said helpfully.

"No! I'm sorry but that is precisely what I do not want." Katya told him. "It is a common mistake people make with false paperwork and identities. Pictures on various documents should not match. It would be highly unusual if your driving license picture was the same as your passport and, if you had a national identity card or tax identity card, to have all of them match would indicate they were false. No, they should all be taken at different times with a variety of clothing and preferably haircuts."

There was another short silence as those around the table all nodded.

"Gentlemen, Katya, I like this!" Phil Gatting said winding the meeting up. "I feel we are moving forward. Let us see where twelve weeks takes us!"

Twelve

During the weeks which followed there was much to be done by most of those concerned. Before splitting up completely Chris, Peter and Danny agreed to meet up and go over the plans Peter had for pulsejet engines. They chose to meet late on the Sunday morning, as the most convenient time for all, at a security office belonging to one of Eastlond's properties. The plans were examined and discussed, with copies given to both Chris and Danny. Peter then left for the Royal London to see Tammy, and Dan left also for the hospital, but for him it was to the psychiatric ward at St Barts, to once more see his father.

Jake had allocated Chris Spencer a small flat in which to stay in an area of East London which was due to be demolished to make way for the 2012 Olympics. Until such time Chris was allowed to use it for a peppercorn rent, all of which suited him admirably. With only two bedrooms, a small living room and kitchen diner it wasn't to be regarded as spacious, but it was well placed for the visits he had to make as part of his security duties, and gave him the option of putting up a guest when needed, as he did on occasions for Peter Parfitt.

"I looked at the info you provided on the missiles and thought it was brilliant. I'd never heard of such a thing and couldn't believe how much technical information was included. I really am deeply shocked not to have come up against such things. With the low cost and relative ease of manufacture I'm surprised every tin pot nation on the planet isn't launching them like champagne corks!" Chris said that evening to Peter, who was staying the night after visiting Tammy.

"Yes, I was impressed, and feel they should serve our purpose well," Peter replied.

Unbeknown to the pair, who were sitting enjoying a pint in the garden of a nearby pub overlooking the Thames, approximately one hundred miles to their south west Danny Bryant had just reached exactly the same conclusion. For several years, and to help further his interest in boats and the water, Dan had rented a workshop at the extreme south western end of Southampton Water, and it was to there he had driven with the plans and information regarding the pulsejets after spending some more deflating and depressing time with his father.

For him there was little point in rushing straight home. There was little for him there. The house he had loved, and the only one he had known since birth no longer truly felt like home to him. The very heart seemed to have been ripped from the property, leaving it as empty of atmosphere as it now always was of people. It proved to have been a magnificent home to grow up in, with a loving caring family atmosphere he knew would be difficult for many to equal and impossible to better. Much of which went when his mother was killed and more still disappeared when

Jack left so shortly afterwards for Oxford. The place then became more than somewhat depressing for a long time afterwards, with just his father moping about, but slowly warmth had crept back through the door with the friendship and joy Sandy provided for his father. All of which was now gone.

The conversation with the doctor about his father proved anything but uplifting. Not only was Tom still failing to respond, but had in fact withdrawn further into some dark place buried deep inside his psyche, and he would remain inside a 'protective' hospital for some considerable time to come. He may never get out. Their family home was now a house, the same building, but the home element was gone, flown away in the dark clutches of the angels of death who had taken first his mother and then Sandy. There was no warmth there now, even in the height of summer, and little reason for him to ever be there apart from it was where his bed remained and was therefore a place for him to sleep, but the homeliness, the very essence of the thing which returned with the smells of cooking, perfume and clean linen women at home had about them, was gone. It was his workshop and boat which were now his homes, and sometimes he never even made it back to his bed at night if he had something in the workshop to keep him busy, which he would work on until he finished and then sleep on the boat.

The pulsejet plans were laid out in front of him on the small table which was both his desk and dining table when at the workshop. In fact the small room the desk was in provided office, planning room and dining facilities for him, depending on the need. Over time Dan had taught himself a great deal to do with boats, mechanics and light engineering, and could carry out a multitude of tasks and repairs with the reasonably comprehensive tool collection he had managed to build up over time. As far as engines went he was shocked at the simplicity of the pulsejet. Surely, he thought, there had to be more to it than this! He would need a few more tools, and a simple press, but he could make these himself easily. Easily! He would have to talk to Jack and see if he would invest in the equipment needed, which he knew Jack would, but he could build something here in his workshop which would go a long way towards avenging his mother, Sandy, and his father. Now that really would give him a sense of involvement!

Phil Gatting drove home from the meeting with a distinct feeling things were moving forward. From the time he learnt of the death of his darling daughter and the baby she carried there was not a waking hour when he had not thought of them first, and then of the bastards who had killed them and the culture they came from. He knew himself well enough to know he could be very single minded, sometimes almost to the level of obsessive and, if he were a less disciplined person, he could give way to obsessions and let them swallow him. However he had developed a way to use them, to channel them, and to make them work for him, to turn them to exclude all else when business matters pressed, and he had profited greatly from his single mindedness in the world of business.

The death of his daughter was not business. The death, and far more importantly the manner and cause of her death, was the most traumatic occurrence and biggest single setback of his entire life. He had since been forced to watch his wife endure untold pain caused by the loss, and to observe the looks of devastating sadness on the faces of his son and eldest daughter, all the while unable to do anything about it, despite being head of the family and a man of huge personal financial resources. Not once since he picked up his first wage packet some forty-five years earlier had he ever felt so utterly helpless, but it was not something he was prepared to allow to continue, and the earlier meeting had helped. He was now in his sixties, so personal physical involvement was out of the question, something he regretted hugely when remembering how fit he had remained throughout his early years.

Less fit these days he may be, but he was not poor! In fact by most standards he was rich. Not rich as Nathan or Jake were rich as he could at least still count his hundreds of millions, and he was sure he would know, unlike Nathan, how many billions he had if he had them, but money made things possible, and that was going to be useful. He would use his money, every penny which was ever needed, to bring as much pain to those who were responsible for the death of his Susie, their families, communities, peoples and land, as he possibly could. He would now make it his life's crusade, a most appropriate term he felt, and he had the overwhelming feeling he was not alone, although not a word had been said on the subject. His feelings, whether they be intuition or empathy, had never let him down in life, and he could see Chris Spencer would also be in this for the long term.

The others could definitely be relied upon and they would see the job through. Nathan would not care how much he spent, nor for the most part would Jake, and both would probably remain that way for life, but Phil Gatting knew it would never come to spending countless billions on the project. It was time, not money, which would ultimately work against them. It would take time to do anything successfully if they were not to be caught, and time would see peoples resolve slowly diminish. It always did. He had seen it so many times before in all manner of enterprises, and it would eventually happen here for most, but whilst they were all on board they made an incredible team. Collectively, because of a string of wild coincidences, they had all lucked out in finding one another.

Young Jack Bryant's mind was the sharpest of anyone he had ever met, and he was ably assisted by Katya. Her smouldering hatred for all things Muslim would sustain her desire for retribution for years Gatting felt, but for Jack Bryant it would be the intellectual challenge which would keep him coming back. Both Danny and Peter also appeared to be very able and competent people, but he suspected that of the eight involved they would be the first two to fold once they considered the payback to have been sufficient. At heart they were decent people, and as such the scale of the blood letting he had in mind would eventually sicken them, although he knew the secret would remain safe with them throughout their lives as their personal honour would not allow otherwise, quite apart from any legal ramifications or physical reprisals.

Chris Spencer would remain, Gatting thought once more. The death of his nephew meant much more to Chris than just the loss of his young life, terrible though that alone would have been. He could see it represented an act of betrayal and treachery of such depth as to equate to treason in Chris's mind, and treason demanded the death sentence for all concerned, irrespective of numbers or reason. It was that simple. The fact the British Muslim community was responsible meant, to him, they were all guilty of treason, so all should face the death sentence.

He felt his and Chris Spencer's lives were now inextricably linked and were from the moment their eyes met at the morgue, and would probably remain so as long as both lived. Things were definitely moving forward!

As the days following the meeting became weeks, Jake, after consulting with Nathan and with the help of Phil Gatting and Jack Bryant, moved the newly formed Almeti forward. Funds were transferred into the new company and accounts were set in place. From Jake's point of view the idea of a joint venture operating along the lines Jack had suggested possessed more than a little merit in its own right, and he was convinced it would be a sound financial move wholly irrespective of any desire for revenge. Their virtual malls continued to bring home the bacon and he could see no reason why the concept could not transfer across into the real world.

After approaching several of the virtual mall customers and floating the idea past them he came away with the overwhelming belief that as a project it would work. Without exception every corporate entity he discussed the project with felt they too would support such a venture. He further discussed things with Nathan, who said he would be quite happy to go along with whatever Jake chose to do, and after a few weeks of examining all aspects Jake drove up to the Gatting family home to quietly discuss business.

The atmosphere within their home at Foxton was very different to that of any of his previous visits. Jane was putting on a brave face, but anyone who had known her before Susie's death could see she was struggling to maintain the façade, and it was not a battle she was winning. Phil Gatting was as difficult as ever to get the measure of, if not more so, as he tried not only to mask his feelings of rage and loathing from others but also from the wife, who had remained his dearest friend and confidant throughout his adult life, whilst simultaneously desperately trying to comfort and reassure her.

Business remained business, and the two men did what they could to push all other issues to one side in order to fully concentrate on the matters at hand, which Jake felt needed their attention.

"I had to talk this over with you personally Phil." Jake explained. "I've already spoken to Nathan and he is happy for us to discuss things in his absence, and will go along with what we decide."

"Well if it's business, his taking such a line doesn't shock me at all." Phil Gatting replied with a ghost of a smile on his lips. "He never was remotely interested in money!"

"No, and in some ways you have to envy him that." Jake retorted and Gatting inclined his head. "However let me get down to the reason I've driven up to see you."

Phil poured them each a reasonably sized tot of cognac into large balloon brandy glasses and swirled the drink around as he passed it to Jake, releasing the aroma.

"Now we are comfortable please continue." Gatting said.

"I've been looking into the ideas put forward by Jack Bryant regarding the Gaming Parks, Theme Parks and Malls, and have approached many of our virtual mall clients to gauge an interest." Jake started by explaining.

"Interesting you should bring up that particular subject, as it was something I planned to talk to you about in the very near future." Phil Gatting responded. "But do please continue. Was there any interest?"

"Very much so, and without exception all positive," Jake replied. "Now I actually think young Jack Bryant is on to something which could profit us all greatly, and it is something I would like to further pursue. I assume it is alright for us to speak openly here?"

"Oh, absolutely!" Gatting answered.

"Okay. Well the concept of the new company as a cover works well I believe, but I also believe it would work better if it were seen to be doing something tangible. That is all well and good, but we cannot be seen to be throwing millions around and constantly losing it all as questions would ultimately be raised. So what is to stop us actually doing it, either as the joint venture, or as NJF?" Jake asked, and then followed with another question. "What was it you were going to discuss with me about it out of interest?"

Phil Gatting once more swirled the brandy in his glass and savoured the fumes as they rose before answering. A small smile again appeared at the corners of his lips.

"I thought I would like doing business with you Jake." Phil Gatting replied. "We think along such similar lines, although in this case we have probably gone about the same thing from diametrically opposed directions. I too reached the conclusion the concept could and should work, but I have not followed the route of consulting potential customers. Instead I've been looking into the possibility of an initial site. One which would work well for us financially in the longer term, as well as provide 'cover' requirements in the shorter term for any operations, and I think I've come up with the ideal first site."

Jake chuckled then said. "The funny thing is I didn't want you to feel you were being steamrollered, or that I was attempting to use these tragic events to better my position. In reality I would like to better all of our positions, whilst at the same time helping to further our cause."

"Jake I feel I have to level with you, but what I tell you is said in absolute confidence. It cannot get back to even my family or Nathan," Gatting said.

"Phil I know you haven't asked for it, but if it helps you have my word," Jake replied.

"I don't mean to be melodramatic, but you will see why I need to keep things quiet as I continue. What I'm about to tell you now I've only previously discussed with lawyers, and even then I've not been able to discuss things as freely as I can with you. I've long held the view I do not wish to have my company, the one I built up from a jobbing builder, run by a bunch of soft handed directors who wouldn't know a shovel from a pick." Gatting explained.

"I know just what you mean. I truly do!" Jake told him. "But you must remember Phil, you have a huge advantage over me. You do at least have someone to leave it to. I was going to leave mine to Nathan and Susie's baby. Now I can only leave it to a dog's home or Nathan, but what good is a couple more billion to him? Billions, and he's not remotely interested!"

"Our problems are more similar than you would know Jake," Phil Gatting responded. "Neither Sheila nor Clive are capable of running my business, or in fact even interested. I have made suitable provision for both, but neither have the flair required. Susie did! She would have never allowed directors to walk rough shod over her, but the other two would, and if they're allowed to get away with it the directors will get greedy. Then they will eventually pull down the business and all the little men who have always supported it. I cannot allow that. I have to find an alternative.

"What I plan to do is slowly, so as not to rock the market, pull out of almost everything I own. I'll let the company continue, but massively reduce its size, scaling it back down to perhaps a mere ten million or so, removing directors as I go to leave a much smaller board, something Sheila and Clive should be able to manage, but won't hurt many people too much if they fail. The rest, which should come out to close to half a billion, I want to put into Almeti, and I want to do that for two reasons. Firstly I want it to be available for use for the private Almeti cause without questions asked, and secondly I want to see it used to continue building up an economic power base by capable and dedicated people, and for the first time in many years I truly feel we have found them."

"An interesting solution." Jake observed. "Something I'll have to look into for myself! But tell me, where is this area of interest for the first site?"

"Moravia, the region to the south and east of the Czech Republic, specifically where it borders both Austria and Slovakia." Phil Gatting answered. "Land there is cheap by almost any western standard, especially ours, and is at a far lower cost to what it would be if it were the other side of the Austrian border. The Austrian capital of Vienna and the Slovakian capital Bratislava are each only an hour away by car, and the airport of Czechs second city, Brno, is only half an hour away, with Prague a further two hours. It is surrounded by their wine growing region, there are rail connections, rivers and several lakes in the area and a motorway runs through the heart of it, so there would be no problems with logistics during the building phase. I haven't gone into it in depth yet, but the area currently has relatively low employment figures which would mean a plentiful supply of reasonably priced labour, but the thing which appeals to me the most is its location. Quite apart from what I've mentioned about the cities it stands at the geographical centre of the now unified Europe with good connections in all directions."

"It may well be worth taking a good look at then." Jake said. "One thing I thought we may be able to do if we follow such a course is bring Peter Parfitt on board with a legitimate job. Something with a title such as head of special projects, or senior project manager. Anything to keep the press happy. I get the impression he is quite a capable chap, and if we were to put him in harness with Chris Spencer, publicly sending the pair of them off to look into land purchase and acquisition on a semi regular basis a pattern would develop which we could use to our advantage if they have to cover the odd mission."

Phil Gatting briefly thought over Jakes suggestion then said. "I wouldn't have a problem with that. I agree he seems capable and is bright enough and articulate.

They would have to be supported by a properly trained staff, but then we already have such individuals within our respective organisations. Peter and Chris need be nothing more than the guys who knock on the door and establish contact. If something of interest comes up then we can draft in the troops to do the real work, but Peter and Chris would be seen by the press guys as the ones who opened negotiations, which in fact is exactly what whey would do. Funnily enough I wouldn't be at all surprised to see the two of them come up with some helpful and insightful background. We had better look into this, mention it to Jack Bryant to see if he has any input around it, find out if Peter Parfitt is interested, and move it along. It'll take time, so the faster we get the ball rolling the better!"

A further twelve weeks passed rapidly since their last meeting, and it was now four months since the lives of their loved ones were lost or irrevocably changed by the bombings on the London Underground. There was no weakening of will of those within what was to become the Almeti group. If anything their attitudes hardened as devastating losses gave way to resentment and an ever greater desire for retribution. The overwhelming need for vengeance was to prove a powerful driving force, especially so as each was reinforced by other like minded and focused individuals.

Phil Gatting started the meeting by briefly outlining what was discussed at the previous one. When finished he called upon Jake to explain what had been done on a corporate level, which he did.

"We have, as you'll already be aware, formed a company by amalgamating certain assets. Our individual businesses will continue to run independently, but the joint venture – Almeti International – will be funded by our collective business assets pretty much in line with what the press have reported. Outside of these meetings we have also had other discussions both amongst ourselves and with Jack to do with the financial way forward for Almeti. Now you may take the view the financial overview of the new company has nothing to do with you, which on the surface would be true. However we have come to the realisation the corporate side and our private interests will greatly overlap and both provide the cover we need for certain operations and, if carried out properly, may well prove to be self financing at the very least.

"With this in mind we would like to structure the new company in such a way as to move both it and our other project forward in a way which avoids any form of suspicion or press speculation. Chris, you are already covered and accepted as our security contractor, which should continue to work perfectly in the short and longer term. For obvious reasons, and as we have previously discussed, Phil, Nathan and I are all covered in what we do, as are Jack and Katya. Peter the new company needs a project manager so, if you do not have any other commitments, we would like to offer you the position, which will be a legitimate ongoing fully paid one, and one where you are technically answerable to us alone. You will be paid well for your work and will often find yourself teamed up with Chris to work on special projects. Dan, we are still working on something to suit your talents, but currently feel all interests are best served if you stay where you are maintaining a low profile.

"Now the interesting thing from our point of view is, having now had time to look into this a bit more deeply, we believe our financial interests, as well as our cover, will profit by our doing precisely what our press releases claim, which is to look into and follow up the development of the leisure complexes, retail outlets and theme parks in other lands. We have come up with a very distinct possibility for our first venture. If you take us up on the job offer Peter it will mean you and Chris taking a trip to the former Eastern Europe for a week to ten days to look into and report back on what you find. Now in a moment I'll hand over to Nathan, but first how do you feel about the offer?" Jake asked looking at Peter.

"Frankly, very interesting." Peter answered. "I won't be so crass as to discuss money with you as I can easily see how it would help provide mission cover, and give us a chance to experiment and test things outside of the United Kingdom at times, which may prove very useful. However I would point out I know nothing about land purchase on the scale you will undoubtedly be needing, and have never even considered filling in a detailed report on anything like it. That said I do not for one moment suppose you would be relying solely on Chris and me, so yes, I would be very interested."

"Good!" Jake Ferris said. "That's settled then, and you are of course correct in that you will have full backup in the form of agents, lawyers and a whole bunch of in-house staff. Your role will be to be the public face of Almeti International. None of us think we'll be able to do the things we need to do by sneaking about in the dark. Our plan is to be so high profile, so obvious, so much in the public eye that our other activities will never be attributed to us because the very concept would seem bizarre to the point of the ridiculous. To others we would have just too much to lose, and nobody seems to think in those kinds of terms as Jack has so rightly pointed out. The area we have picked out is in the very centre of Europe, in the extreme south eastern corner of the Czech Republic in close proximity to its borders with Austria and Slovakia. We would like the two of you to go out there, meet the local dignitaries, make some contacts and get a feel for the area. The important thing is everything you do should be of a high profile with maximum publicity." Jake finished his short address and handed back to Phil Gatting who then got down to what the meeting was originally called for, a report from Jack Bryant as to the possibilities facing them.

"Twelve weeks ago we were discussing what we could do to avenge those we have lost, and I was asked to look into the feasibility of an attack on Bakkah." Jack started. "I've obtained a reasonable amount of information and I think the best way for me to proceed is to provide you all with what I have learnt, discuss possibilities, and to then make a decision as to which road we wish to follow. If I start with the background first we can come back to specifics, then I'll put forward the suggestions I have. There were a couple of other targets I came up with, specifically the holy city of Medina, and the Petronas Towers in Kuala Lumpur, Malaysia, but both Phil and Jake liked the idea of going for Bakkah, and so do I, and – I think it's doable!

"The hajj is the annual pilgrimage to Bakkah, and occurs over a five day period between the eighth and twelfth days inclusive of the last lunar month of the Muslim year, Dhu al Hijjah – the month of the hajj. As a lifelong ambition for many, the hajj attracts Muslims from every corner of the globe and from all races, cultures, ages, and stations in life. It represents the culmination of the Muslim's spiritual life in which the pilgrim not only obeys the word of Muhammad, but also quite literally follows his footsteps. It is the world's largest religious gathering and the only thing many of these people have in common is – they're all Muslim.

"Over the years improvements in transportation and accommodations have led to dramatic increases in the number of visitors who enter the Saudi kingdom for the pilgrimage. Back in 1965 almost three hundred thousand Muslims came from abroad, primarily from other Arab and Asian countries, to perform the rites of pilgrimage. Within twenty years the number climbed to more than one million. Another ten years and this figure had doubled. These days it has again increased and in addition there are now three quarters of a million people living in the kingdom joining the rituals and swelling the numbers attending to well over three million. This influx obviously creates immense logistical and administrative problems which are addressed by the use of huge numbers of specialists, guides and assistants.

"The sites along the pilgrimage route are claimed to have been visited by Muhammad, and are said to have formed the most important events of his life. It is believed he received his first revelation at Jabal an Nur – the Mountain of Light – near Nima.

"The haram, the word itself means both forbidden and sacred, is the holy area of Bakkah, the Sacred Mosque, and is a sanctuary in which all violence is forbidden. Approaching the haram the male pilgrims change into the ihram, which consists of two pieces of white cloth, although some don this on entering Saudi, and then carry their luggage throughout. Women wear a white dress and head scarf. The Grand Mosque surrounds the Black obelisk, which is a cube-shaped sanctuary first built, according to Muslims, by Abraham and his son Ismail. The Black obelisk contains a black stone believed to have been given to Abraham by the angel Gabriel, but is probably a meteorite, and goes to the very centre of the Muslim's culture and beliefs.

"After their days of rituals the pilgrims go to Nima, a plain outside Bakkah, spending the night in prayer and meditation. In the morning they proceed to the Plain of Arafat where they perform the central ritual of the hajj, the wuquf – the standing. The congregation faces Bakkah and prays from noon to sunset when a cannon sounds and they all rush to Muzdalifah where they throw stones at one of three pillars which to them represent Satan. However the Saudis are in the process of changing and relaxing the timing rules on this in order to accommodate the now vast numbers attending. Finally the pilgrims return to the Grand Mosque in Bakkah and once inside they walk around the Black obelisk seven times and point to the stone or kiss it. Throughout the last day and night there can be more than one million people present and confined at each location.

"For many years the Iranians have challenged the Saudi right to be the custodians of the ideology, and have constantly criticised all the Saudis do. At one stage there was a ban on Iranians attending, which did nothing to improve relations between the two nations, and there is a great deal of resentment towards the Saudis from Iran, who would prefer to see some form of shared ownership and control of the religious sites. I am totally convinced we can exploit this bad feeling and use it to our advantage, adding to the confusion and deflecting responsibility. In time, and with the promotion of resentment and animosity, it may be possible to create a situation whereby Sunni and Shiite irritation with one another bubbles over into armed conflict. If we can be instrumental in its cause and can encourage Muslims to kill Muslims we shall have succeeded beyond our greatest hopes. However for the moment I feel we should concentrate our thoughts and resources on what we can achieve by ourselves!

"I would now caution everyone once more. If we do decide to go down this route it will be a few years before we put the plan into operation. Additionally it will be so big we will not be able to continue with any attempt to attack mosques here in Britain as it would attract attention to this part of the world, and that we would not be able to afford." Jack looked around the room as he finished attempting to gauge the reactions of others. They were not long in coming.

"At the start you said you thought this was doable." Phil Gatting said then asked. "Just how realistic is it as a project?"

"I believe with what we have previously discussed, and with the collective talent represented by the eight of us it is achievable, but it will come at a cost!" Jack answered.

"Before anything else is discussed here I would like to make a point and have it clearly understood." Nathan interrupted. "From this moment forth I don't want to ever hear the subject of cost mentioned again. I know Phil and Jake feel pretty strongly about this as well, but I'm prepared to cover any and every cost for every mission personally if need be, so please, irrespective of amount, just drop any consideration of finances. Understand this, these callous bastards have killed my wife and unborn baby. I don't know what measure anybody else in the world wishes to use, but to me there is nothing more innocent than a baby, and mine never even had a chance to draw breath. Mine was innocence personified, yet still she was slaughtered by creatures demonstrating supreme indifference, in fact quite literally less regard than I would at killing a fly. The money is there, and will continue to be there until we are all in agreement our retaliatory action has been sufficient, and for me the desire for vengeance runs deep, very, very deep! Now, pardon the interruption, and please answer Phil's question."

A brief silence followed Nathan's wholly uncharacteristic outburst, but the passion with which he had spoken left none in any doubt as to the strength of his feelings. Jake broke the somewhat awkward silence with a question so typical of his practical outlook.

"Assuming and accepting an attack on Bakkah is possible as you say, what do we need to do and what sort of time frame are we looking at?" he asked.

"I'm sorry to sound evasive, but I cannot answer either of those questions accurately at this time." Jack answered. "However, I can say this. We will need to acquire explosives, probably Semtex, and build a delivery system based around a simple but reliable engine, probably a pulsejet. In order to do so we have to build and experiment with engines and construct a missile. We have to test every single aspect of each and every piece of the equipment every step of the way, and for much of this we have to find a test site. Some testing we can do here in Britain, but for obvious reasons we cannot test fire missiles in Britain, or for that matter even in Europe."

"So we are not looking at weeks, or even months, so much as years?" Nathan questioned.

"Frankly I would think three years if we are to be realistic." Jack answered.

Again a short silence followed as those around the table absorbed what Jack had said and considered the implications.

"You've obviously thought this through Jack, and must have some sort of plan." Jake said, breaking the silence, then carried on to ask, "Would you share your thoughts to date with us? Just give a broad outline of what you have in mind so we can see what we make of it."

"Of course! I've considered many aspects of this from an operational point of view and this is what I believe we can do, and is what I propose. We continue to bring influence to bear on those who can increase anti Muslim feelings and resentment, as I have said before, expanding it into other countries, especially those, and there are many, who already foster such an outlook. There were some cartoons of Muhammad published in the Jyllands-Posten, a Danish paper, about five weeks ago which created a local stir. I've been talking to two friends of mine from my Oxford days that have the ears of a couple of other newspaper editors, and I think they can get them reprinted in the Netherlands, Germany and France. Basically freedom of the press stuff. I think if they get reprinted, and I'm sure they will be, it may cause a little controversy. If it spills over into violence – so much the better!

"We then further increase pressure with a successful attack on an important mosque in mainland Europe, using the model aircraft Peter spoke about at our last meeting. I would suggest Spain, and would time it to coincide with the Madrid train bombings in order to make it appear to be a Spanish attack. We then concentrate all our efforts on an attack on Bakkah.

"As to our needs. We will need pulsejets, which Dan is more than capable of building. Missiles into which the engines will fit, which I believe Dan and Peter can develop and produce. Nathan can devise and construct electronic brains for them, and explosives we require I have no doubt Chris can supply. We will need certain identities that Katya can provide, and planning which I can do. We need to find a testing range in an isolated part of the world. I suggest somewhere in Western Australia or, better still, Southern Africa, either South Africa itself or Namibia. This is something we have to look into and prioritise. There will definitely be a major need for cover, to be provided through Jake, Phil and Nathan in the guise of the newly formed Almeti. Incidentally, and I have taken on board all you have said Nathan, but I feel I should explain I would very much like to see this entire project run ultimately not just to be cost neutral, but actually return a sizable profit, and I think that too is achievable if we continue with the things we have recently discussed." Jack again finished and looked around the table for reactions.

Katya already knew much of what was on Jack's mind, in generalities, and during the time between meetings Jack had reviewed the progress in fabricating a pulsejet with Dan, who then discussed the building of both them and the missiles airframe with Peter. Chris had formed a close bond with Peter and the pair talked about deployment and missile possibilities together and with Danny, who had once more gone over things with his brother. Basically all which was needed was the approval of the money men for the project to begin.

"I'm definitely for it!" Nathan said breaking through Jack's thoughts. "I'm not remotely concerned about the time frame. Not in the least! They have hurt us and I want to hurt them back, and I want to hurt them a whole hell of a lot. I imagine the reason you talked us through the hajj and the numbers attending was because you believe that would be the best time to strike. Well I agree. If we can take out hundreds of them – wonderful! If we take out more – better still!"

"I'm certainly up for it as well." Jake Ferris confirmed. "I've already said I like the idea of an attack on Bakkah. It just seems right to me. They've had an indiscriminate swipe at our way of life and it's only right and proper we should have an indiscriminate swipe back! Simple eye for an eye and tooth for a tooth stuff to me."

"Count me in for sure!" Phil Gatting said. "I feel every bit the same as Nathan does. Susie was my little girl, and it was my granddaughter-to-be they killed. No matter how many we kill in return it will never be enough for me. The money is wholly immaterial to me too, but I do also like the look of, and fully back, this Czech project."

"Then the next item for discussion is that of the pulsejets. I know a little about progress but I'll hand over to Dan because it's his project and he can report far more thoroughly than I could. Danny, perhaps you should first explain what pulsejets are." Jack said bringing the conversation back to the more immediate problems.

"Sure. The plans Peter provided were reasonably comprehensive, and gave me at least a basic understanding of the construction of a pulsejet," Danny started to explain with confidence, having just read up on the subject and understanding the theory. "Now I've never worked on such a thing before and, except for newsreel stuff about Flying Bombs, had never heard about them or seen them. Basically a pulsejet is a very simple form of an internal combustion based jet engine where the combustion occurs in pulses. Typically a pulsejet will comprise of an air intake fitted with a one-way valve, generally referred to as a reed valve, a combustion chamber, and an acoustically resonant exhaust pipe, the length of which determines the pulse. Fuel is either mixed with the air in the intake or injected into the combustion chamber. Starting the engine usually requires forced air and an ignition method such as a spark plug for the fuel-air mix, but once running the engine only requires an input of fuel to maintain a self-sustaining combustion cycle. The extreme simplicity, low cost of construction, dreadful fuel economy and deafening noise levels characterise the engines.

"I was surprised as to just how simple they were both in concept and construction, but set about doing a little more research at the public library and found a couple of reports in magazines. From there I worked out what was needed and built a prototype."

"You mean you've already constructed a working engine?" Jake Ferris asked incredulously.

"Well yes, sort of," Danny replied. "As I said I built a prototype. It is not what we need and will not produce the power yet, but yes, I've built a simple working model."

"Incredible," Phil Gatting said to grins of approval and nodding heads around the table.

"What sort of time frame are we looking at to perfect them Dan?" Nathan asked.

"I'm sorry Nathan, that's impossible to answer at the moment," Danny replied. "It won't be something I can do overnight. As I said they are incredibly simple, but experimenting and tinkering will take time, and then there are other criteria Jack has asked me to meet, all of which will complicate the process. Objectively, and to be both serious and realistic, I would reckon on a couple of years. I could probably knock up a few in six months if I had to, but they wouldn't be the best I can do and, frankly, I don't want to produce second best or to cut corners. What I want to do is produce the very best I can after exhaustive testing. I want optimum performance, one hundred percent reliability, and the best power to weight ration possible. To get that will take time!"

"Take your time Danny!" Phil Gatting said. "I can assure you I'm more than suitably impressed with what you've done already, and I believe that holds true for all of us. At the risk of repeating what has already been said I will say this, there is no rush or urgency with this project. You have correctly prioritised things. Reliability will ultimately be everything and on that we can never compromise!"

"There is another very important factor." Jake broke in by saying. "Given the time we can build up the public face of Almeti. The longer we have the better known it will become, and therefore the greater operational cover it will give us. If we press ahead with this Czech venture that will take a similar amount of time to get operational, but if we do what I hope we can do with it, it will give us worldwide publicity."

"Then I feel we should proceed as rapidly as possible with both projects." Phil Gatting said. "We can move the public face of Almeti along loudly, courting publicity wherever we go and, at the same time, forward our private cause quietly, steadily but secretly."

"There is one last factor to keep in mind." Jack Bryant once again spoke out. "We have to consider the procurement of parts, equipment and basic materials. It is important they are sourced globally, as we agreed at an earlier meeting, but they must also be purchased wherever possible to cast suspicion on others. Finally I think this should be our last meeting as such. As was said last time there is no point in having meetings for meetings sake. It is counter productive. Yes we can meet when we need to, but only with the individuals concerned. It will be necessary for me to meet with Nathan, Phil and Jake. Peter and Chris will be working together from here and, at times, Peter will be working with Danny. If we keep it like that patterns will never appear because they won't exist. No one will have anything to follow. We all now know what we are about and what we are to do.

"Danny, get on building and experimenting with the pulsejets, then the missile airframe, then the launch platforms. Nathan, design and build an accurate guidance system. Katya works on identities and runs support for me. I work on a plan or, in reality, I work on many plans for each step of the way. Phil and Jake promote the public face of Almeti's financial side, and Chris and Peter take care of operations. Operations include flying the flag for Almeti, procuring all required materials, and carrying out any operations still deemed essential.

"Much as it would be good to continue with domestic operations they should be avoided unless we catch wind of a planned action on the part of the enemy. Nathan, keep a watch for movement with known targets, and Chris, take them out if they appear, but quietly and so it can be taken for accidents where you can. That aside suspend such operations where we can. We really do not want to attract attention. Now we all know what we are doing, and we all have plenty to be getting on with. I can get plans to you all as is required. Two years may sound a long way off, but I have the distinct impression the time will pass only too rapidly.

"Finally there is the matter of finance, profit and money. We cannot be seen to be exploiting the situation by profiting directly from what is to come. A successful attack will throw the world financial markets into complete disarray as it will be seen as an attack on Saudi Arabia and therefore as an attack on oil. I suspect the Saudi's will close their borders and there'll be a subsequent major increase in the price of oil. We cannot do anything which is monstrously out of the ordinary for any of the businesses beforehand as it may well be suspected we had prior knowledge, and then the whole thing could come crashing down. Certainly we can slowly build up gold reserves, but we couldn't buy oil on the futures markets the week before we launch our missiles!"

Jack grinned as a chuckle ran around the table, and paused before continuing. A moment of levity would do no harm considering the seriousness of the subject they were discussing.

"One way in which we can protect ourselves against financial fallout is to set Almeti up as a Euro account, not operate in pounds sterling." Jack continued. "I honestly believe the pounds days are numbered and I don't think it will be many years before we are forced to accept the Euro at terms which are a long way from preferable after the life is squeezed out of the pound between the dollar and the Euro. That's me done. If we never meet as a group again, although unfortunately I feel events will probably force it, then I feel by the time this is finished we shall have done what we can to avenge our loved ones!"

Thirteen

Three weeks later, at the beginning of December 2005, Peter and Chris flew into Brno-Turany airport in a private executive jet which had taken off from London's City Airport an hour and a half earlier. Carrying no more than a holdall and a laptop each they took the Docklands Light Railway to the airport in London and casually strolled to their private flight. They landed at Brno to what resembled a building site as the ongoing construction of Brno's new and futuristic terminal neared completion, and were met at the steps of the aircraft by a small limousine which instantly whisked them away to the new terminal where two interpreters waited with local dignitaries and a camera crew.

The new terminal, which was to be opened a few months later, in 2006, had already gained the accolade of one of the most important buildings of modern architecture in South Moravia, and much importance was given to the fact its designer, Petr Parolek, was a Czech architect. The dignitaries repeatedly stressed there were plans for a new train station, cargo terminal and logistic zone already in progress. The city of Brno wanted the Almeti investment for their region and none of those from the city were in any way shy in letting the two men know it.

"Not what I expected at all!" Chris Spencer remarked once they were finally taken to their hotel. They had deliberately avoided the Holiday Inn, the only five star hotel in town, and the Best Western, as both thought it would appear more politically correct to use an older and more traditional hotel whilst making first contact with the people of Southern Moravia. The hotel they had chosen was the one hundred and thirty year old Grandhotel Brno which was picked more for name and location than facilities, although it boasted a sauna, fitness centre and casino.

"In what way?" Peter asked as he grinned mischievously. Although he had not known what to expect either, he had found himself somewhat unprepared for the genuine warmth of their welcome. The mission brief Jack had prepared stated the region enjoyed the best weather, the most beautiful countryside, and the friendliest and most welcoming people of the Czech Republic. It was winter, it was cold, and they had seen little of the countryside, but if those too were as understated as they had found the people they would be in for a real treat. Although they were not to know it then, during the next two years of coming and going to the region they were never to be disappointed.

The two ex-servicemen made themselves comfortable, an easy thing to do in their fifty square meter deluxe business rooms. For Chris the rooms vastly exceeded all his preconceived expectations of Eastern Europe to such a degree he found it difficult to express himself. Both were single occupants in spacious corner rooms with large windows. Crystal chandeliers hung from original wooded coffered ceilings, and in addition the rooms contained large comfortable three piece suites and a work desk. There was the luxurious feel of times gone by about the rooms which was also reflected in other areas of the hotel. The only very minor downside was during the night there was the noise of church bells chiming every quarter of an hour and the slight sound of trains from the nearby station, although the station was another of the reasons they had chosen the hotel.

Brno, Southern Moravia, the Czech Republic, and its people were all to prove to be much more than either man expected. Over the following days they ventured out in their hire car, a Mercedes C class which was delivered to their hotel the morning following their arrival for their use throughout their time in and around the Czech Republic, and had first headed south towards Breclav. Here they left the motorway and headed west into Valtice, a town within sight of the Austrian border, then north east and over the river lake towards Lednice, effectively taking in the Lednice-Valtice Area. This two hundred square kilometre park, the largest landscaped area in Europe, clearly demonstrated the outstanding beauty of Mother Nature even in winter. The forested flood plain of the Dyje River had over time been transformed into a unique landscape by the skilful gardeners working for the aristocratic Liechtenstein family. The entire region with its wooded hills and meandering river valleys, beautiful castles and picturesque villages, was unlike anything either man had expected to see survive the dictatorial jackbooted regimes of first Nazism and then Communism.

They drove west through the pretty near border town of Znojmo with its inspiring views of the Dyje as it meandered down to the border proper of which it then formed a part. To the west of Znojmo the road dipped to the south as it followed the border. In places here the land was cold and misty, almost menacing, and devoid of any form of habitation. Concrete pill boxes stood in the near distance at regular intervals, each within sight of the next.

"Stop the car," Chris had said unexpectedly to Parfitt who was driving and, as the car pulled to a stop, he got out and walked back and across the road to a pill box built just two hundred metres away.

"Look at that," Chris said in a strangely hushed voice as Peter joined him.

"It's a pill box," Parfitt answered. "This is just inside the old border."

"But look at the machine gun slots," Chris said raising his eyes to the heavens.

"Overlapping fields of fire." Parfitt said with a shrug of the shoulders.

"You fly boys see nothing!" Chris responded scornfully. "Look at them again. Then work out the direction of fire. Then, if you can manage it, try and work out who the enemy might be and the direction from which they might be approaching."

"Well like I said, overlapping fields of fire, and then this one points this way." Parfitt said reaching up to touch the one he was speaking about. As he did so the enormity of Chris's observation hit him.

"Jesus Christ." Peter blurted out. "They're facing in Chris. Oh shit! They're not here to stop an invasion from the West. They're here to stop these poor buggers leaving!"

"Now you're getting there." Chris acknowledged. "Makes you wonder what these people were put through doesn't it?"

After several days of touring the area, something which left a very positive and long term impression, arrangements were made to discuss the possibilities of land purchase and development with interested bodies, and a meeting was called in Brno. Regional planners, town planners and road planners attended, as did the press. Jack Bryant had already suggested an area which proved to both how much research he did and just how incredibly accurate he was. The area of primary interest was to the south of Hustopece and between the villages of Zajeci and Sakvice, on the banks of the Nove Mlyny, a large lake formed by the river, and was an open green field site. It was slightly to the west of the E65 and a rail line ran through the area.

The meeting ran for three full days, with site meetings involving many interests. The area suffered from underemployment, despite the proximity of Brno, and would benefit greatly from the investment and the thousands of jobs it would create. Recreational facilities would be provided with all manner of non powered water sports available on the lake. There would be a spur to the Greenways, an existing system which provided a non road link from Krakow in Poland, through Ostrava and Brno in Czech to Vienna in Austria, for hikers, cyclists and riders. Stabling would be provided for horses and there would be a bicycle hire centre on site, and a fully equipped leisure and fitness centre would be built. However the main attractions would be the shopping mall, cinemas, gaming rooms and casino. These would be supported by bars, restaurants and several on-site hotels, all to be serviced by a service road to the motorway and a spur from the local railway. Three billion euros was earmarked by Almeti and fully backed by NJF for the start up of the project, but it was expected this figure would treble as more retailers came on board.

There was, as expected, a provisional agreement in place before Chris and Peter returned to England. At the beginning of 2006, with Christmas and New Year behind them, all manner of experts descended upon Brno armed with everything from calculators and slide rules to theodolites and tape measures. Lawyers, architects and public relations men tripped over one another as they spilled out of trains, taxis and planes, all attempting to prove their worth to the big spending Almeti people. For over a year both Chris and Peter were constantly called upon to revisit the site as work progressed at an incredible rate. By mid 2007 much of what was to be was taking shape and the two men were taken off the project, Peter to assist Danny who was making good progress with the pulsejet engine design and development, and Chris to continue procuring the parts and equipment needed from around the world. Both had thoroughly enjoyed the Czech Republic and were truly sorry to leave, but other things were moving forward, and their expertise was to be needed and used.

Nathan completed two more games during the period, at the same time working on missile guidance and still running checks on suspected terrorists entering the country. Chris and his men were called upon to despatch several unwanted individuals during the period of the ongoing Brno project, and this was done, interestingly mostly in and around Manchester and other northern cities. Despite a certain desire to step up these activities all reluctantly accepted they had to be kept to a minimum, and the number requiring Chris's unique form of attention could be counted on the fingers of two hands.

By Christmas of 2007 much had already been successfully accomplished, but much was still needed. Many of the parts and the vast majority of the equipment which would eventually be required had at least been sourced if not procured. Jack Bryant's plan was coming together as rapidly and successfully for the attack on Bakkah as was the building of the Brno complex, for which the demand by retailers had exceeded all expectations, bringing the project close to breaking even long before completion. Chris and Peter's input had also vastly exceeded expectations, bringing a wry smile to the face of Phil Gatting who had, following both his own instincts and Jack Bryant's advice, once again removed himself from the British property market, as he had told Jake Ferris he would two years earlier.

Phil Gatting liked success, and had always tended to encourage a successful team. To him the Parfitt Spencer partnership was paying dividends, and they were now as essential a part of the Almeti financial side as they were to its private side, earning both men his respect and appreciation, feelings which were shared by Jake and Nathan. Jake too had learnt to respect the two ex-warriors, along with Jack Bryant, and sometimes struggled to believe how successful and profitable the still reasonably new Almeti could be. Especially so when left almost wholly in the hands of three people whose first interest was not exactly business, and by two who had no background, training or grounding in the worlds of business or economics.

Fourteen

Chris made the arrangements and visited his sister, and friend and brother-in-law Jimmy Andrews, travelling north by train, which proved to be a somewhat poignant reminder of the last journey he had taken with Charlie. Well over two years on his sister had still not recovered from the death of her son, and Chris realised she never would. The loss had woven strands of grey into her hair and put permanent bags under her eyes. In short it had aged her, and the overwhelming sense of guilt he felt in her presence he knew would never leave him.

The twins, Michelle and Juliette, had grown and, resilient as children are, managed to put their brother's death behind them as they grew up. The sight of Charlie's pictures on the old fashioned mantelpiece over the fireplace in the families little cottage stirred up memories Chris had managed to suppress for many months. It was the first time since the little lad's funeral he had made the trip, and the passage of time had distanced him from all of them. Outside their group, and the few men whose services Chris had called upon and who were therefore partially involved, Jimmy Andrews was the only person who had any proper understanding of the events Chris was caught up in, and even his knowledge was extremely limited. Since Charlie's funeral Jimmy was the only member of the family Chris had seen, and then only when Chris had had reason to be operating in the North West.

It continued to be Chris's every intention to isolate his family completely from his actions, as he felt they had suffered greatly by his failing to properly protect Charlie and he had no intention of compromising them should he ever be caught. To this end he effectively estranged himself from all those whom he loved and cared for, so never again would any of his actions hurt them. It would be several more years before he discovered the excruciating pain this decision put his sister through, who effectively lost the brother she loved as well as the son she adored as a result of the tube bombings.

Jimmy had felt terribly awkward ever since. He was aware of a little of what Chris was doing and had known him better than any man alive before Charlie was killed. He thought he recognised his friend's style in some of the deaths which had occurred since, but never asked nor had it confirmed. He also realised just how much Charlie had meant to Chris, and knew Chris would never let the matter drop or rest until such time as he considered justice to have been meted out in full. With time he came to terms with the terrible loss of his son, but bitterly regretted the estrangement of his dearest friend and the pain Chris's self imposed exile continually created for his wife.

Although Chris had no intention of bringing his family into anything he did he needed a name, as a backup, and felt Jimmy Andrews should have one. Jimmy remained a career solider, accepting the end of the Green Howards as a regiment and their amalgamation into whatever new form they and others had taken, continuing along the promotion path to the position of WO2. Jimmy had never served under Chris and, Catterick apart, they were previously rarely deployed at the same place together at the same time. However whilst in the Green Howards they often followed one another and experienced very similar situations, and one of the places where they had repeatedly passed one another was Northern Ireland.

Owing to the lengthy duration of Operation Banner both men had been deployed to Northern Ireland on several occasions and, once there, both worked with the snatch squads. Over time, and working independently, sometimes without official sanction, some of those at work with the security forces built up a minor functioning network of contacts and informers, sometimes with those within PIRA who wished to keep the back door open, and often with those of the Protestant paramilitary groups. Neither Chris nor Jimmy Andrews were any different, and both worked their various small time contacts for the good of their units, regiment and countrymen.

Some time had passed since Chris last operated within the province, and this time he would be going it alone, without the backup of any lads in uniform, well after the 'troubles' had ceased and all arms and munitions ostensibly 'put beyond use'. Due to the nature of what he was doing all contact would have to be made in person, face to face. Above all, for the success of the task at hand, Chris wished to find his original contact and hoped to avoid being forced to take the risk of using Jimmy's, with all the inherent problems such an action would entail. Jimmy Andrews was aware of such and realised his low-life petty criminal contact could as easily inform on Chris as help him or refuse him, and was most reluctant to give his help. He explained as much but eventually relented as he knew Chris would continue either way. However the additional informants name was never used as, three days after his arrival in Belfast, Chris managed to make a form of contact with his own man or, more accurately, his contact reached out to Chris.

Liam O'Connell was lucky to be alive. In another era he may have been a swashbuckling buccaneer, mountain man or colonising pioneer or, if born in the future, would doubtless lead in the pillaging of far away planets. However he had not been born to another time, but was born in the spring of 1963 to a good Catholic girl from Bantry in County Cork, who had moved north with her husband in search of a more prosperous life, eventually settling in the border town of Middletown, midway between Armagh and Monaghan. Liam was in every way a living contradiction. He was tall with dirty blond hair and flashing blue eyes but with a Mediterranean skin tone.

His complexion came from his mother, whose own colouring could be traced back to one of the very few survivors of the catastrophic storm tossed Spanish Armada of 1588, but his height, hair and eyes were from his father, who in turn was the product of a union between a sailor from Cork and his wife from the old port of Bergen op Zoom in the southern Netherlands. His mother had borne seven children, six of whom survived and consisted of three boys and three girls, with Liam the second child and oldest boy. If his skin colour came from his Spanish genes then his height certainly came from his Dutch side. Where his animal cunning, guile and rakish disregard for custom, convention and all forms of authority came from only the devil could guess at. He was a warm and friendly, open and gregarious, charming and humorous cold blooded killer.

For years he profited by playing one of the most dangerous games on Earth, a role he was almost uniquely qualified for, the running of terrorists, guns, munitions and all things contraband into Eire and over the border into Northern Ireland. His mother may well have been a good Catholic girl but his father was a complete atheist and his grandmother about as firmly Protestant as is humanly possible. With mixed European blood, a lacklustre education and an ideology which could only be guessed at he had never properly fitted any mould, and his attitude to life left even the Irish with only one expression which accurately described him. 'Fuckin' mental!'

In 1987, shortly before his twenty-fourth birthday, Liam O'Connell was caught crossing the River Foyle from County Donegal and heading for Londonderry by a young corporal, just three months his senior, who was backed up by a mere four soldiers. In a move which could be described as nothing short of cocky, and easily bordering on the foolhardy, the young O'Connell had rowed the Foyle at the dead of night with two passengers in a small rowing boat. Unbeknown to him a small foot patrol somehow became alerted when their corporal, demonstrating a highly develop sixth sense, felt there was something not quite right with a part of the small area they were charged with patrolling. The corporal quietly sited his men in concealed positions from which they had a good view of the dark river and the land around it, and which afforded excellent lines of fire if needed.

The two passengers in the rowing boat proved to be wanted by the intelligence section of the security forces, and the papers they mistakenly carried earned them plenty of time in Her Majesty's Prison Maze, built in the former RAF station at Long Kesh near Lisburn, and better known colloquially as The H Blocks due to their shape and design. A fire-fight was avoided by the quick thinking of both the young corporal and the person who manned the oars, Liam O'Connell, who showed the good sense to know when he was out gunned and out thought. Corporal Chris Spencer used the opportunity and 'turned' him, or had to the extent it would ever be possible to turn a person such as Liam O'Connell.

Information passed on from O'Connell would later prove to be instrumental in stopping assorted events which may have proven costly in terms of lives, and a small number of those later interned within The Maze would find themselves there because of his tips, although none would ever know it. Lives were undoubtedly saved, and his protected status kept Liam from the same fate as those of whom he informed. However there was never a single big fish landed from Liam's tips, or a large cache of arms or explosives recovered. Everything passed on had a value, of sorts, but obsolete and abandoned weaponry and those of the criminal underclass with only tenuous connections to paramilitary groups were of little interest and no real benefit to the security forces. To the security services as a whole O'Connell was low level nonsense and probably not worthy of informer status, and his information was certainly not worth paying for.

Corporal Chris Spencer knew differently although he could not explain why, except to say it was an instinctive thing which came from the way the man reacted the night he was caught on the Foyle. The two passengers in the rowing boat were armed, which would normally have led to the encounter ending in a fire fight. It hadn't, because O'Connell had ordered the men not to draw their weapons, which was definitely not the action of a subordinate. Had he been nothing but the simple peasant lad he made himself out to be he should have carried a pistol which he would have drawn and started shooting whilst his passengers did their best to make their escape. To Chris it wasn't the fact there hadn't been a shot fired, it was about the way the passengers deferred to O'Connell. Whilst praising him for his actions and the resultant capture, the powers that be disagreed with the young corporals observations, concluding he had mistaken what he thought he had seen in the darkness. A career soldier did not argue with the big brass, he was mistaken. Only he knew full well he hadn't been.

The young Corporal Spencer had taken a particular interest in Liam O'Connell and his nefarious exploits, and over time a mutually respectful stand-off developed between them. They would never be friends, that went unsaid but was fully understood by both as they were ideologically diametrically opposed in every way imaginable, but both were young and bright and dedicated to following the path nature had dictated for them. The policies of politics had made them enemies of sorts but, at another time in another land – they still would never have been friends.

Whereas Chris Spencer was honest, loyal and devoted to his nation and its way of life, Liam O'Connell was solely self serving, valuing little and absolutely no one, loyal unto only himself. As such he succeeded in playing all sides off against the middle for years, and the middle had always been Liam O'Connell. Although perhaps not as smart as the owl, he had most definitely taught the fox all it had ever needed to know, successfully living by his wits for years. The young Corporal Spencer was the only man who had ever caught him, and the only one who even suspected his operation may be bigger than it appeared. On several occasions O'Connell considered having the Corporal killed, but to target him directly may have raised unwanted questions and he realised by drawing Corporal Spencer and his squad into a fire fight would give no guarantees, so he considered it better to let the soldier continue to live in ignorance.

Live Chris did, but not in ignorance, although there had never been enough tangible evidence to bring before his superiors, and certainly not enough to provide acceptable proof of anything to a court. An uneasy truce was eventually attained and an accommodation reached. Against all the odds politics eventually worked and policies changed accordingly. For Northern Ireland the pain of constant hostility evaporated, but the organisation Liam O'Connell had created and grown continued. The antagonism which fuelled his trade had proven highly lucrative, but he was quick to understand it was not the world's only conflict zone. Before the 'troubles' ended he started to expand into other markets, and Africa was always at war somewhere, profitably at war for his organisation. As world terrorism grew another rewarding market developed, a market in which he already had contacts, and a market which was to prove to be incredibly lucrative.

He could and did supply guns and armaments, explosives and munitions, mercenaries and assassins, and would accept payment for such in hard cash, gold, diamonds, oil or further armaments. The only thing he would not touch was drugs.

Not because of principles, because he regarded them to be an unnecessary encumbrance, but driven by practicalities, reasoning that drugs created a menace to all who touched them, eventually leading to sampling or theft, either of which could damage his organisation and his reputation. Additionally the world collectively appeared prepared to throw huge monetary and agency resources at combating what was perceived to be a horrendous threat, whereas most nations were prepared to turn a blind eye to the other services he offered. So he wisely stayed with what he knew, and watched his empire grow.

It had been years since he lived in Middletown, in fact years since he lived in Ireland, north or south, although he maintained multiple contacts there and occasionally drew upon the paramilitary trained resources of the island. It was through one of these many contacts he heard Chris Spencer was attempting to locate him. Curiosity got the better of him and he sent an agent to discover what it was his old adversary wanted, but was not at all surprised when the message came back to say the ex-soldier would speak to no one but himself, no matter what he was threatened with.

O'Connell arranged for Chris to be picked up and taken to Belfast International Airport, there to be flown by Aer Lingus, via Dublin, to Lisbon, travelling first class and accompanied by one of his agents. Chris insisted he should pay for his own flight and did so. At Lisbon they were collected from Portela airport and driven the forty kilometres to O'Connell's main residence, a large yet unpretentious property perched on top of the costal foothills of the Serra da Arrabida Mountains, set in its own small estate overlooking the fishing town of Sesimbra and the Bay of Setubal.

"Nice place you have here Liam. You've come a long way from Middletown. The gunrunning business must be good." Chris said after he was ushered into a very large, comfortable and open living area. The two men did not shake hands. They never had. O'Connell nodded his head in the direction of the minder who immediately left the room to stand outside, within easy view, but out of conversational earshot.

"I imagine it pays better than an army pension Corporal," O'Connell replied in an unhurried lilting Irish accent, causing a ghost of a smile to appear on Chris's lips. "But I'm pretty sure you didn't look me up to discuss property. I also think our little battle was put to bed years ago, so I have to admit to being intrigued, or quite obviously we would not be having this conversation."

"I need your help Liam or, if not your help, then your services," Chris replied honestly.

Liam O'Connell's features did not alter in any way, despite the shock he felt. He had not known what it was this old adversary might have wanted, and he was not the sort of man to make wild guesses, but what had just been said he certainly never expected to hear from the man before him.

"Will you be having a beer with me?" O'Connell asked. "I've the best draught Guinness outside of Dublin to be sure, and I'd be a poor host if I didn't offer."

"Yes to the Guinness, and I'll never fault you as a host," Chris answered.

"Sit down please, make yourself comfortable," O'Connell suggested waving his arm expansively as he stepped behind a small bar and poured two perfect pints of Guinness, carving a shamrock in the head of each with a flourish and without spilling a drop.

"I can suggest a couple of bars where you can look for work if ever your business dries up on you," Chris said as Liam O'Connell passed him his pint.

"Now don't you be worrying yourself about business drying up. The market is expanding nicely," the arms dealer replied with a wink. "Is that why you are here? Have you come looking for a job?"

Chris chuckled at the questions before answering. "Liam I'm sure we could go on sparing for hours, but if you don't mind I'd rather get down to business. As I've already said I'm in need of your services."

"Well I'm bloody shocked and that's no lie!" Liam O'Connell retorted. "I can't imagine what it is you want. It can't be men because you of all the people I know will have access to the very best there is. In fact I seriously considered approaching you when I heard you were coming out, but I knew you would turn me down. That honour of yours would get in the way. Pity really as you are one of the very few men I've met I know I can trust, and definitely one of only four I've ever respected. I don't know what it is you want, but there it is now, out in the open, if ever you want to earn some real money let me know and there'll be a place for you straight away."

"Thanks but no thanks to the offer, and thanks for the compliment but –" Chris started to say but was interrupted.

"Listen, it's not a bloody compliment. There were occasions when I considered having you killed. You were a bastard, a bloody great pain in the arse, and you fucked me about with what I did and the services I ran, but you were only doing your job, and you did it fairly and properly. You followed me like a shadow and knew some of the things I was up to, but you never set me up. Not once! If all the bastard bloody English were like you the world would be a better place, and there would be less room for the likes of me. I respected you because you earned it. You may have represented the enemy but you were cool, calm and collected at all times, never fired a shot in anger and never struck out at the defenceless or beat up your prisoners, and what's more stopped all of your men doing it too. No, you earned the respect and are the only man apart from my father and brothers who has ever had it! Now tell me what it is you are here for."

It was Chris's turn to be taken aback at what he had been told. He had never once suspected it, but it did suddenly account for many of the little things which had slipped by almost unnoticed during the times he had spent in Northern Ireland, but it was not the time to dwell on such.

"Men I can get and arms I can get. Given time I can get what I want to ask you about, but I don't want to wait, and I don't want to deal with people I don't know whether I can trust to either deliver or keep their mouths shut. Whatever our differences have been in the past, and no matter how much I despise your industry and your part in it, I believe I can trust you professionally to keep your end of the deal, and also to keep your mouth shut afterwards," Chris explained. "So, what do I want? I want two hundred and fifty kilos of Semtex, the clean stuff with no markers, preferably less than twenty years old, which probably means the Libyan stock I know you have access to, and I want it delivered, thirty kilos to the British mainland and two hundred and twenty kilos to a destination yet to be confirmed, but I expect to be South Africa. I need to know what it will cost and when it can be delivered."

Once again a short silence descended whilst Liam O'Connell took in and digested what he had just heard. None of it made sense to him. He knew he had not misjudged the man before him. He had never misjudged a man in his life, and what he had told Chris about respect was genuine. The request did not add up. From a lesser man it may have been the start of some sort of convoluted set up, but no such thing would come from this man. He had been provided with ample chances for such in the past yet had constantly proven he would never stoop to use such methods. His personal sense of honour would never allow it. No – it wasn't a trap. So what was it? It had to be mercenary work. Yet this man would not do the kind of work a paid private soldier could be called upon to undertake. He would object in principle, but if he had taken the money would feel obliged to carry out instructions he disapproved of, which would certainly compromise him, and that he would find unacceptable. So it wasn't mercenary work either.

It was personal. There was no other plausible explanation. Something had happened to this man. Something colossal had overtaken him which had hurt and angered him deeply, and it had nothing to do with the British Army. A friend, a girlfriend, a member of his family, someone he felt responsible for had been hurt. No – they had been killed, and in something other than an accident. But South Africa? It still did not make sense. O'Connell's instincts were finely tuned. He knew he was right, but he would have to find out exactly what it was. He would have it checked out.

"It would be pointless denying I have access to such commodities to you, but you must realise such things do not come cheaply." O'Connell eventually said.

"Money is not the greatest issue here," Chris retorted. "The two most important factors are those of guaranteed delivery and complete secrecy."

"What kind of time frame would I be working to?" Liam O'Connell asked.

"I think you'll find there is plenty of time, certainly for the bulk of it. For the South African delivery you would have at least six months if you wished. The British delivery depends somewhat on your stock availability. I will need about ten kilos of it in the next few months, with the rest at some time after the South African delivery has been completed." Chris replied.

"None of which would present a problem." the arms dealer mused. "Will you be wanting anything else?"

"Detonators. Twenty impact to go with the large consignment, and ten electronically armed three second delay for Britain to come with the first delivery, all of which must be the best available. Also with the main delivery I want two Milan ER's with MIRA thermal sights and ten missiles apiece. Two infantry type Browning five O's M2HB Flexibles with ten one hundred round cans each of armor-piercing incendiary tracer and M8 API rounds." Chris had worked out what he though would be required well in advance and committed everything to memory.

"Again not a problem. Will the missiles be used at moving or stationary targets?" O'Connell asked professionally.

"Slow moving or stationary." Chris answered.

"You're well covered with the Milan then. Now – payment. I've already told you this will not be cheap. It's certainly not a soldier's wages or pension money. How do you propose to pay? O'Connell questioned.

"I'll meet your terms," Chris told him.

"You don't even know what my bloody terms are yet," O'Connell scoffed.

Chris finished his beer by draining the glass. He looked at the empty glass in his hand before reaching out and placing it on a low glass topped table, then stared out of the open French doors at the land and the sea beyond. He did not want to betray his hand, yet fully understood he may in part already have done so in acting so very much out of his usual character. Off and on the two of them had played cat and mouse for many years, and it was not possible to do so without learning something of the others mindset. O'Connell sat and patiently waited whilst Chris continued to mull things over, until he eventually reached a decision.

"Liam, I'm involved in something, and it is something very personal," Chris stated confirming what the arms dealer had earlier deduced. "I did spend a lot of time years ago trying to unearth what you were about, but I was just trying to do my job which was to reduce the terrorist operations in order to ultimately save lives. It was never personal and I never made it so. What I am about now is not something I want anyone looking into. I just want to be left to get on with the job in hand. Before coming to you I thought things through as best I could. You are in the arms business, not publicity or the media. Your clients usually require discretion, which you have always provided. Had you not done so you would not have survived either physically or financially. Despite what may or may not have happened between us in the past I ask you to do no more than treat me like any other client. Now, I repeat, I will meet your terms!"

Their discussions continued for another hour. An agreement was negotiated and details worked out. O'Connell suggested Chris stay the night in one of his guest lodges, but Chris asked to be returned to the city centre with his overnight bag. Once dropped off he stopped a taxi and was driven to the NJF retail outlet where he carried out an unscheduled security check, much to the consternation of the manager and staff, who all visibly relaxed when he gave them a clean bill of health. From there he arranged an evening flight back to Heathrow and e-mailed Jake Ferris to assure him security at both Belfast and Lisbon was meeting the prescribed standards. Code for he had concluded negotiations regarding the required explosives and detonators.

Six days later, Liam O'Connell stepped off an Air Malta Airbus at Malta International Airport and made his way through passport control, collected his single small bag from the carousel and walked out of the terminal into brilliant sunshine in a clear blue sky and climbed into a taxi as it pulled to the front of the rank. He had flown from Lisbon to Rome where he transferred at Leonardo da Vinci Airport for the short flight to the Air Malta hub at the old RAF base at Luqa, eight kilometres from the capital Valletta.

The taxi took twenty minutes to take him down to his hotel, the Phoenicia, arguably the island's most prestigious, built facing the water at Floriana. The man who was once the boy from Middletown liked Malta, and he liked the Phoenicia.

Both felt comfortable. The island was never too hot or too cold and the hotel had never let him down, maintaining the levels of comfort it had taken him years to become accustomed to. Malta had also always been good to him financially from his very first visit.

Fate was a funny thing O'Connell thought as the taxi edged through the crowded streets. Here he now was procuring a clients needs as he had so many times before, but the client was Chris Spencer, the very same Chris Spencer who raised his rifle and called out the warning on the darkened banks of the Foyle twenty years earlier, a week after his first trip to Malta and his first purchase of Semtex. The purchase for which his two agents, who were with him on the fateful night, spent many long years at Her Majesty's pleasure locked up in the Maze. Their capture very nearly led to his undoing, and the financial consequences could have been unimaginable had he not been quick enough to divert the shipment and rearrange the delivery. But that was the past and many a shipment had since been delivered, and the funds they provided built up to more than he realised was in the entire world during the grinding poverty of his childhood.

By any accepted measure he was a wealthy man, and much of his wealth he owed to a lesson he had learnt from one man. Chris Spencer. In many ways he had seen the young corporal as a mirror image as himself, exact in every way but exactly opposite. If you faced your image to the north your reflection stared south. If you brushed your hair to the right your image brushed left. It did everything you did at exactly the same time using exactly the same motions, yet it was as opposite as anything ever could be. So it was with Chris Spencer. He was the same age, height, weight and build, with an obvious love for adventure and an ability to lead and command, in so many ways his double, yet his complete opposite. Good and evil, yin and yang. But the encounter that night had left him with two things, a grudging respect, and a lesson learnt.

The respect because it was deserved. He had never previously seen a person in so much control of a situation and all around him before. The troubles had brought out the best and worst in everybody, usually the worst. Most in Chris Spencer's position would have shot everyone first and asked questions afterwards, but he faced it down, and he had done so from point, putting himself up front, protecting his men, his sheer force of will alone keeping fingers off triggers. At least the three of them owed their lives to the young corporal's bravery that night, as did possibly some of his own force. Liam would never know what had alerted the soldiers but from the moment they had stepped over the rivers bank he had realised the situation was hopeless as the soldiers were all incredibly well positioned. The young corporal clearly knew his stuff and had bollocks, big bollocks.

The lesson came from understanding his enemy. To stand point, to protect what you had, but to use your troops skilfully. Never again did he put himself in a position of possible capture through an unnecessary act of meaningless bravado. His men could be paid, and paid well, to transport and convey the tools of warfare and, if captured due to an error or omission on his part, their families suitably compensated. His did not do the fighting, they merely conveyed. He was a wholesaler, a middleman, and profit was his aim, not ideology, nor even faith, just money. So take care of business and business alone, sending others to do the buying, the selling, the fetching and the carrying. The lesson had gone home and every move made from there on followed a thought through and calculated strategy.

His hotel with its majestic and imposing classical façade loomed up and the taxi stopped. O'Connell paid and tipped the driver, picked up his bag and strode under the middle of three arches and into the familiar building, which opened up into a V-shape as he entered. They were currently building a larger, grander hotel, to be called the Excelsior, but the Phoenicia had been good to him over the years, the rooms well furnished, bright, clean, and above all comfortable. The place had character and he liked it. Abu ibn Nafi on the other hand remained wholly devoid of any form of character from the very first day they met, and it had taken O'Connell a long time to work him out.

In February 1987, the year of his first visit to Malta, the world was a substantially different place. On the fifteenth of April 1986, following an order from President Reagan, the United States Air Force, Navy and Marine Corps launched a surprise bomb attack against Libya which was code named Operation El Dorado Canyon. Libya's Revolutionary Command Council, led by Colonel Muammar Abu Minyar al-Gaddafi, did not take kindly to the attack. They were already sponsors of terrorism, backing many types of terrorist groups operating throughout Europe, the reason why the US had attacked them, and were engaged in dealing with the IRA for years. The Libyan regime was intent on destabilisation and, as a direct result of the American raid ten months earlier, he was welcomed with open arms, figuratively if not literally, by their agent at Malta, Abu ibn Nafi.

However, by Abu ibn Nafi's demeanour it would have been difficult to know he was being made welcome, something which had never changed in the twenty years he had been doing business with the same man. Apart from explosives, and Semtex in particular, there was never any other common ground. Abu ibn Nafi appeared to have no interest in women, did not drink alcohol and would never be regarded as a conversationalist. It had taken O'Connell four years to find out his weakness, and when he finally discovered it he wished he hadn't, for the thing which got his contact's blood racing was pre-pubescent boys, who would come away from any liaison damaged, traumatised and physically scarred for life. Possibly due to his Irish upbringing child cruelty and sexual abuse was about the only thing in the world the young Liam O'Connell would happily kill someone for without thought of profit. The very concept utterly disgusted him. However money talked and he needed this contact if the profits were to continue to roll in, but from the moment he found out the man's secret he swore he would take Abu ibn Nafi's life the day he was no longer needed. Slowly and very, very painfully!

Were it possible O'Connell would have dispatched one of his agents with the buy order as he did for the majority of similar purchases, and would always do so for such an insignificant commission. Unfortunately from their first meeting forward Abu ibn Nafi refused to negotiate with anyone but himself.

This meant his continued personal involvement, something he had rarely troubled himself with for years outside of similar meetings on Malta, and something he would not now have bothered with for any but a miniscule number of regular customers – and Chris Spencer. Liam O'Connell's business had grown to such a size he generally only became involved in the negotiation stage with new bulk purchasers and with occasional visits to his various suppliers around the world.

There was no need for subterfuge on his part. He could travel the world quite openly and legitimately on his own passport as he plied his morally dubious trade, buying in Russia, China, South Africa, America, and for several years now, even Britain. All had huge arms industries, warfare was a growing business, and middlemen with a wide and diverse client base were always welcome. He was singularly disinterested in international politics and sold widely to Africa, Asia and South America, sometimes to nations and groups the armament manufacturers could not be seen selling to directly, but were happy to pass on profitable leads so an intermediary might make the sale. The numbers could be huge and the consequential profits vast.

His early attempts to distance himself from his Maltese connection failed due to Abu ibn Nafi's refusal to deal with any of O'Connell's subordinates. Had there ever been any hope of doing so such hope was dashed forever on Wednesday the twenty-first of December 1988, less than two years after his first successful purchase, when Pan Am flight 103 was blown from the sky whilst flying above the little town of Lockerbie in southern Scotland. Two hundred and forty-three passengers and sixteen crew members lost their lives in the Boeing 747-121 as it was ripped apart in the air, and eleven people in the houses below also died as the wreckage of the big bird, titled Maid of the Seas, crashed through the roofs of their properties in the middle of a cold winters night.

Libya was immediately suspected, and world condemnation followed swiftly. The country became regarded as a pariah state with all the associated sanctions, trade embargoes, and withdrawal of aid and diplomacy which go hand in hand with such labelling, as the world reacted with a 'measured' response to this oil producing nation's murderous act. Abu ibn Nafi reacted badly to the world collectively pointing the finger of blame at his nation, despite its guilt, and any chance O'Connell may have had to introduce a subordinate disappeared as his contact developed a persecution complex akin to paranoia.

The years passed and Liam O'Connell had flown to and from the tiny island on countless occasions in search of increased profits. Pragmatically he felt it helped greatly that he enjoyed the climate, the culture and the foodstuffs which, when added to the level of comfort he always enjoyed, made it a reasonably pleasant way to earn a living in a part of the world which was far more agreeable than most. Unfortunately the man he was to meet was far less agreeable than most.

Although he paid quite handsomely for it Liam thoroughly enjoyed the night he had just spent in his superior city view executive suite. Or, more accurately put he thought with a wry smile, he thoroughly enjoyed the girl he had bought for the night. She had been absolutely sublime, with a flawless body which she knew how to use to tease and to please to perfection. She also knew how to dress, and appeared as a picture of sophisticated elegance, tempered with just the slightest hint of the promise of an utter slut about her, and in that department she had certainly not disappointed, not at all!

She was dispatched in the early hours giving Liam a chance to rest and relax, lying in till gone eight o'clock, well past his usual six o'clock start. He showered and ate a leisurely breakfast, wandered around the hotels seven acre sub-tropical gardens, then strolled down past Valletta's medieval city walls to eventually ramble along the long since familiar pavements of the Triq Pinto. Here he gazed above the craft, bobbing gently on the light swell of the water, at the two forts of St Angelo and St Michael standing at the extended ends of their two tiny peninsulas. Time passed and eventually he retraced his footsteps along the Triq Pinto as he headed for the Valletta Waterfront and the Pintonino Restaurant where he was to meet his contact.

Abu ibn Nafi was already there, which was unusual as the man was traditionally late, showing his disdain and contempt for those he was to meet by keeping them waiting. Liam had long since given up expecting a response as he offered his hand to the puffy fleshed individual who always refused to either stand or to take it. There really was nothing about the man Liam liked. Abu ibn Nafi was by far the most disgusting, repugnant and odious creatures he had ever been called upon to do business with. As the years had passed, contrary to mellowing with age, the man's sickening and vile ways had multiplied as his sense of invulnerability grew, and this had grown because of his status and wealth. Wealth Liam knew he had greatly contributed to.

Although he had never enjoyed full diplomatic cover, and was attached to no embassy or consulate, Abu ibn Nafi was recognised by the authorities very much as his country's representative and, due to the special relationship Malta enjoyed with Libya, concessions bordering on diplomatic immunity were extended. Additionally since he started operating from Malta some twenty plus years earlier his wealth had grown, and with it his 'influence' with the authorities, which in most nation's terminology meant the bribing and corrupting of highly placed officials. As a result he was never so much as questioned, let alone charged, with any of the multitudinous offences he committed against young boys, most of whom were runaways, and which on at least two occasions to O'Connell's knowledge had resulted in their deaths.

O'Connell had made it a habit over the years to have his contacts thoroughly checked out and researched, and this applied to both buyers and sellers alike, as information in the arms trade always possessed a value. Abu ibn Nafi was an ethnic Arab born to a people known for their wandering tented lifestyles. He was a Sunni Muslim by ideology whose family, despite their wanderings, were reasonably wealthy in a traditionally poor country, and therefore influential. At the age of twenty-one he started to attend Al Fateh University, Libya's most important institute of higher education, located in the nation's capital, Tripoli, where he was enrolled to study medicine. Before completing his course he hurriedly left the university and the country following an 'accident' with a much younger male fellow student who also came from a somewhat influential family.

At twenty-four years of age he was bundled off to Malta with a large allowance and a semi official government paid job. He had effectively been held at arms length by his nation and told to make contacts which could later be used to either spy upon or destabilise their own nations, and in this he had done well. Unfortunately he was unable to hold his highly perverted predatory carnal predilections in check, which led, over the years, to a string of similar accidents of an ever increasing and worsening nature to the one which had first seen him cast out of his own land. With his growing power his depravity increased, and the knowledge gained from his medical training added to ever more invasive acts to his beaten, battered and often drugged, pre-teen sexual victims.

It proved to be the most disturbing report of its kind O'Connell ever commissioned, and left him with a feeling of utter loathing for the man who was its subject. It did not help to read his competitors were often wont to provide young victims for the sick and twisted pervert as part payment or a pot sweetener for the goods he in turn had access to and could provide. With a Catholic upbringing, and from a land which loves its children, the international arms dealer who would happily sell cluster bombs and land mines to rebel groups, and explosives to terrorists, recoiled in horror at the suffering and misery Abu ibn Nafi inflicted on young male runaways, orphans and those trafficked.

Once again however, with a fixed smile of greeting on his face, Liam held out his hand as he approached the table at which the loathsome predator sat. Once again his gesture was ignored by the man he had come to meet, who chose instead to wipe a spot of grease from his chubby and permanently pursed down turned lips, caressing them with the index finger of his right hand as he did so. With his left hand, a hand whose fingers contained a large gold ring on each, but where flesh oozed out around them, he imperiously waved Liam to a seat whilst never once looking in his direction. O'Connell, whose smile faded, seated himself in the proffered chair and waited. He knew better than to speak first.

"You are late!" ibn Nafi stated. Their lunch appointment was set for twelve-thirty. The time was twelve twenty-eight. Liam O'Connell had not been late for an appointment in over twenty years. He said nothing as the minutes ticked by.

"What is it you want of me this time?" the Arab finally asked, tilting his head back and looking down his nose whilst the sweat dried in the folds of his multiple chins.

"I wish to purchase some more of your product," Liam responded.

"You will have to pay more this time. The price has gone up. It has doubled." Still the man did not deign to look at Liam as he spoke, choosing instead to run the tip of his index finger once again over his liver coloured lips.

"That's a substantial increase," Liam replied. "Why so?"

Finally ibn Nafi slowly turned his head and looked at Liam in a manner which could only be described as wholly disdainful.

"Since when did you feel you had the right to question me?" ibn Nafi asked arrogantly.

Liam said nothing. Something had changed. Never before had the Arab been the first to arrive at one of their meetings. Not once in twenty years. Now the price had doubled. There had been price increases before, price increases Liam always suspected went into his contacts pockets, but never anything on this scale. So what the hell was going on? He was not going to have to wait long to find out.

"I have been recalled to Tripoli. My country is in a state of change and I am needed back there. Within two months I shall be back in my home country. This will be your last chance to purchase from me or from my land. Stocks have run low over time, so you will have to pay more. Do not waste my valuable time in attempting to negotiate. You know the new price. Pay it or leave me," ibn Nafi said haughtily.

It had long been a matter of international public record that Libya was changing and opening up to the world. Things had changed greatly since the overthrow of Saddam Hussein. As a direct result Libya had suddenly become willing to allow international inspectors into the country to observe the dismantling of its weapons of mass destruction program. Tourism was becoming actively encouraged, and Colonel Gaddafi's son, Saif al-Islam al-Gaddafi, was finding himself in an increasingly prominent role. So change was afoot, and Liam was quick to recognise it would be a change which should bring with it major alterations to the structure to one arm of his business. It was also change which would render this creature before him redundant, and redundancy would seal his fate, not that the pompous arrogant prick could see it Liam thought.

"No I will not negotiate in the circumstances. But, instead of the quantity I came for, I will take everything you have in one single purchase," Liam O'Connell responded thoughtfully, a plan slowly developing as he sat calmly looking at the creature that so utterly disgusted him, without the slightest trace of what he was thinking showing on his face. A hovering waiter, quite professionally watching body language, noted the sudden relaxation and approached the table. Both men ordered, then continued with arrangements whilst they waited for their food to arrive, and successfully concluded business before the waiter returned with their order. In a final gesture of contempt Abu ibn Nafi rose and walked away without a word of explanation, leaving his food uneaten and the bill to be paid by his customer.

The following morning one third of the agreed figure was transferred to the private Swiss bank account of Abu ibn Nafi. Ten days later a further third was transferred upon the confirmation of shipment, and the remainder on inspection and transhipment at sea. Liam O'Connell sent Chris Spencer a postcard from Lisbon. On it he had written 'Weather here wonderful, but seriously considering taking our next holiday in South Africa. Hopefully in about six month's time'. The message was clear, the explosives they would need were available. Chris would have to confirm the destination was to be South Africa, but Liam wished to deliver six months from the date given at the top of the card, which was nine days later than the postmark. Funds were immediately transferred to O'Connell from an account set up by Jack Bryant, and drawn on a bank in Belgrade. Twelve days later another message arrived, and this required Chris Spencer and Peter Parfitt to take a drive to a prearranged collection point in Norfolk. They returned with the goods they had ordered.

Six weeks after the meeting between Liam O'Connell and Abu ibn Nafi the people of Malta were shocked at the news of a violent murder which had taken place on their sunny island. The media reported on a man's body which was found horribly mutilated after the victim was tortured to death, although many of the details were withheld from the press. Those police officers who first discovered the body, following an anonymous tip off, received extensive counselling, but still suffered from what they had seen for years afterwards. It had taken Abu ibn Nafi more than three days to die, and every second proved agonising beyond even his wildest imaginings. The two butchers who worked on his body were each paid ten thousand dollars an hour bonus for every extra hour they kept him alive, whilst at the same time removing or opening up as many areas of his body as possible, the bleeding cauterised with boiling tar and blow lamps.

They had demonstrated a great desire to earn as large a bonus as they possibly could, and had done well, due in part to an admirable working knowledge of stimulants as well as butchery. Abu ibn Nafi had apologised profusely for his past actions over the years and easily parted with the clearance codes for his Swiss account in the first hour, which was most fortunate, as within four hours he had bitten off and swallowed his tongue. Despite which he still managed to scream almost without stopping for the first forty hours, and continued long after his genitalia, eyes and then face were removed. Fortunately, for what remained of him, total insanity had long since taken him before his belly was opened and his entrails draw. The autopsy which followed had difficulty determining the precise cause of death but concluded he finally died of multiple organ failure. What remained of his body was by far the most gruesome and horrific sight any would ever see.

Abu ibn Nafi would never again prey on young boys Liam thought when he heard the perverted predator had finally died. He also felt the eight hundred and eighty million dollars which was successfully transferred from Switzerland into one of his accounts adequately compensated him for the trouble he had taken whilst making the arrangements for ibn Nafi's demise.

Fifteen

As the days since the tube bombings had slowly but relentlessly turned to months profound changes occurred within Peter Parfitt's life. Previously, and virtually since birth, he had led a somewhat trouble free existence. A life he thoroughly enjoyed was greatly enhanced by his devil may care attitude and the necessary funds which allowed him to be comfortable. Apart from his deeply ingrained senses of loyalty and duty his days could only best be described as carefree and untroubled. Meeting Tammy Wild had done nothing but bring more happiness into his world, and never once had the clouds of doom and despair been seen on so much as the horizon of their relationship, as they do with so many over time.

A chance meeting had brought together two people who just so happened to be perfectly suited for one another. Both offered exactly what the other needed, and a great deal more than either would have looked for in a partner had they been looking, which at the time of their meeting neither were. Parfitt was strong, enjoyed participating in various sports, and was fit, passionate and good looking in a very masculine way. He had an easy going relaxed manner about him, was open minded and generous of spirit. Additionally he was intelligent, non judgmental, travelled, was articulate and could converse freely with king and pauper alike. There wasn't a single thing Tammy had not liked about him, and from the moment their relationship commenced there was never anything about him she ever sought to change.

Although Peter was not looking for a relationship at the time of their meeting, by the time Tammy returned to England he had wanted nothing more. She was easily the most beautiful girl he had ever met, and there was infinitely more depth to her beauty than just her captivating appearance. He had never previously met a woman who enjoyed the delights of the great outdoors as much as she did. She seemed to love everything about the water and, although reasonably good and confident on it himself, could literally leave him floundering in her wake when it came to sailing and windsurfing. She was without doubt the best female swimmer he had encountered above or below the surface and enjoyed cycling, tennis and just about anything which kept her out in the air. She had grown up with many friends who kept horses, and had been around them most of her life.

The South African veltland proved a source of unending pleasure for her, and upon them she had successfully introduced Parfitt to the joys of riding. She was very much a physical girl in every way, and had the sexual appetite to match. Parfitt found her to be an incredible lover, considerate yet adventurous, caring but abandoned, and utterly faithful. He had never experienced anyone like her and knew, having met her, he would never look for another woman as long as he lived. She was lively, bright, witty, and an interesting conversationalist who was worldly and experienced well beyond her years. Parfitt loved her almost to the point of idolisation which, in return, was fully reciprocated.

The bomb blast changed everything for which they, as a couple, had ever hoped and planned. Such appalling and horrific injuries would have been devastating and life changing for anyone, but for Tammy, who had throughout her life always craved outdoor physical pursuits, they were of such an overwhelming nature as to come close to threatening her sanity. Many privately thought throughout the period of her painful healing it may have been kinder had she died, although none ever voiced such thoughts. Tammy herself considered suicide, but her injuries were of such a debilitating nature as to make putting such thoughts into practice impossible. By the time enough of her strength returned to make such an attempt possible the thoughts were pushed out of her head by her indomitable nature, strength of character and humour.

The months of her confinement within the walls of the hospital dragged for Parfitt. He visited her and stayed at her bedside whenever he could, but the continued operations and the toll they had taken on the body of the woman he loved had also taken their toll on him, constantly reminding him of the events which led up to her injuries, ceaselessly hardening his attitude towards the perpetrators and all who supported them. Of all those which made up their little group he was originally by far the most tolerant, accepting and forgiving. However day by day he watched as his mate in life was cut apart, wasted away and aged before his eyes. The very spark of life seemed to flicker and slowly die in Tammy as she realised the full extent of her injuries and the repercussions they were bound to have on both her and their relationship.

Humour was one of the qualities Peter and Tammy had always shared. Greek mythology would have it that when Pandora opened the jar, which became known as her box, in defiance of the Zeus's instructions, she unleashed all the evils of the world upon mankind, with Hope alone remaining. For Peter and Tammy that hope was kept alive by their humour. Infinitely slowly, almost imperceptibly to Peter, Tammy turned the corner and started to improve. Gram by gram what remained of her body started to flesh out and as it did so colour crept back into her waxen features. The doctors stopped their cutting and sewing, the sedation eased, and slowly but steadily bandages were removed from her tortured body, revealing angry red scars beneath. The girl who had once been one of the world's premier swimwear models now resembled a hastily sewn patchwork quilt. Miraculously her right ankle healed perfectly, and all the skin grafts took. After what seemed like an eternity of constantly laying in the same position her bed could be raised and lowered, so she may sit up and lie flat without increasing pressure on her left eye or ear. However her once beautiful face and body would at the time have frightened small children, and resembled the exaggerated accomplishment of a Hollywood special effects artist.

After months of being confined to her bed she could stand it no longer and, much earlier that even the most optimistic doctor had predicted, pushed herself over the side of her bed so she might stand on her remaining leg. The first attempt produced extreme pain and nearly led to her collapse, but Tammy was nothing if not determined and, against instructions, constantly pushed herself until she could stand on the one leg, and then hop. Physiotherapy followed rapidly with constant warnings about overdoing things, all of which were totally ignored. She was going to show one and all that she could do it, and she did. The scarring faded and scar tissue softened with the ridges of the tears, cuts and patches slowly reducing until they flattened out. With a diet aimed at putting protein and fat back into her body her muscle tissue grew and her body continued to fill out. Discussions were held about her teeth and it was decided she would eventually have new ones screwed into her jawbone, but first that too had to complete its own healing process, so a plate was made for her.

As she so clearly demonstrated her determination to return to at least a semi active life doctors, in open admiration, helped her in every way possible, exceeding what was expected of them so they might help speed her recovery whenever humanly possible. The physiotherapy, diet and general help from doctors all aided the recovery of a most determined and previously extremely healthy young woman. Thoughts of suicide were long gone, to be replaced with the desire for the fitting of artificial limbs to the stumps of her left forearm and lower left leg. After months of constant hospitalisation she was eventually released to return to the little cottage in the grounds of her parent's home at Brighton. The cottage had been subtly altered with thoughts of her accommodation needs in mind. Peter Parfitt had overseen all the work personally and missed nothing. A position was created for him as a senior projects manager for the recently formed Almeti, and it was a position which allowed untold flexibility, with trips out of the country rarely exceeding two or three days. As the building alterations progressed he dropped in to inspect at least once a week, fitting it in around visits to Tammy and working on the project. A project he could not wait to see being put into effect as his hatred for those who had maimed his treasured Tammy grew.

Whilst Tammy slowly but surely healed Peter Parfitt and Chris Spencer worked together many times, as their projects increasingly overlapped. As they did so mutual respect between the two men grew and with it a friendship germinated and developed. Because of the nature of what they wished to collectively accomplish, and due to their respective backgrounds, the two found themselves thrown together, occasionally joining Danny Bryant for the use of his workshop facilities, which had been impressively equipped by Jack Bryant at the expense of the bonus he had received. Danny was concentrating on the pulsejet development, and from what Peter and Chris could see his part of the project appeared to be moving steadily forward, with two heavily modified prototypes already finished. Both Chris and Peter liked the giant Danny, who gave the impression of being an extremely capable and dependable young man, so much so Chris felt he would happily have given five years off the back end of his life for every soldier like Danny he could have had in his squad.

Despite the reason behind the trip, it was with a degree of pleasure Peter and Chris found themselves once more heading to the New Forest on a mid Thursday afternoon of early March. They were joining Danny for what was going to be the final testing done in Britain before going operational with the planes, and to look over progress made with the pulsejets. Chris was behind the wheel of the dark blue five series BMW Tourer which went with his new job and, with the back seats folded down, just so happened to be the perfect size for carrying two of the model aircraft Peter had specified, two of which nestled together behind them, hidden from view beneath a travel blanket and behind tinted windows. Beneath the flattened seats lay the Semtex which would provide their cargo, and under the driver's seat, covered in cling film were a pair of number plates. German number plates, registered to an exactly similar car from Dresden, stolen from the car whilst at the Central Station's car park in Amsterdam.

The press had long since given up interest in the victims of the tube bombings. As the months passed it became old news, and victims and their families had already been forgotten, as predicted. Ironically a young Brazilian worker by the name of Jean Charles de Menezes had been wrongly shot by non uniformed members of the Metropolitan Police in what could only be described as a killing frenzy. This had occurred at Stockwell tube station on Friday the twenty-second of July, three weeks and a day after the tube bombings. The cover up which followed was deeply embarrassing to the Met, but not so embarrassing as to cause their head, Sir Ian Blair, to properly do the honourable thing and resign. The story was set to run for a very long time, probably years. It was apparent to all the tarnished reputation of the Met was far more important to the British establishment and press than the inconvenience caused by the butchering of a few of its citizens. However the ongoing lack of interest and concern exhibited by the press worked to the group's advantage, in that its members could associate far more freely.

In most cases connections were never made by the press between passengers killed and injured in the tube and bus blasts and their relationships and overall relative employment positions. It may have been because of the large number killed and injured that the job would have been monumental, or looked at cynically it could be the story wasn't considered newsworthy, and therefore not profitable. Susie's death indicated the latter were true in that her loss may have had a detrimental effect on NJF, which would then have been newsworthy because the story would concern big money. As it was Chi Lu was performing brilliantly, and the company was continuing to grow. Either way interest in those killed and injured had waned then disappeared.

Although Chris was with Charlie when he died, and reported such to the police, his nephew's loss was never linked to his coincidentally newly created position at NJF, a company who had lost their CEO to the same atrocity. Living in South Africa Parfitt was not at any time linked with Tammy Wild, who had throughout her career retained her maiden name professionally for the fashion world and press. The Bryant brothers were not publicly associated with Sandy Cartwright. Interestingly even the Oxford educated bright young wiz kid working for a multinational banking corporation out of Moscow had never had a personal in-depth background search, despite his position and the press interest in the family at the time of his mother's death. It spoke volumes as to the anonymity of the banking world, and yet more still about the lack of professionalism demonstrated by the modern day sensationalistic British press.

Whilst all still maintained a high degree of security this lack of interest allowed members of the group to meet one another far more freely, and so Chris and Peter were to meet Danny at the Bryant's family home in Lymington. With Tom still in the hospital psychiatric ward, and Jack in Moscow, bedrooms were going begging, which the two visitors filled. Danny, having arranged with Mike Latham to take the Friday off work whilst the two were down, booked a table at a quaint local pub where he was known, and where all three ate hearty meals, drank several superb pints of cask conditioned real ale and talked. Whilst not mentioning the mission directly they were able to publicly discuss the likes of engine configurations, power to weight ratios and servos. As far as other locals were concerned Danny's friends were there to visit the National Motor Museum at Beaulieu, and any of the somewhat dull conversation overheard was quite obviously related to the visit.

The following morning the three left Lymington reasonably early in the morning and headed first for Beaulieu then on to Fawley, with Chris in the BMW following Danny in his Passat. They by-passed the still quiet towns and travelled south east towards Calshot where Dan's workshop was located, just to the north of the town and at the far end of the quay road, where it was the last building on a track which was an extension of the road running alongside the quay. Directly in front of it there was a concrete slipway running into the water. There boats of various sizes could be winched up or lowered into the end of Southampton Water, almost at the point where it joined the Solent. The workshop was solidly build, more so to protect it against winter gales than with thoughts of break-ins, with a large wide steel shutter door reaching up to fractionally below the roof. It was quite apparent it was originally purpose built to accommodate vessels of various widths, heights and configurations and, although not large at around three thousand square feet, felt spacious inside when there were no boats present.

Both Peter and Chris had visited the workshop before, but were still impressed at the array of tools and equipment inside. Outside Danny deliberately kept the place looking a little down at heel so it might remain in keeping with all the other working quayside buildings. Inside it was as clean as an operating theatre, pristine in every way possible.

"See you're still keeping the place tidy," Chris noted in a droll manner which made Peter chuckle. With services training both men were themselves quite fastidious, but Danny was obviously very professional in what he did and the way he went about it, and his workshop was a credit to him. The years spent working on, in and under all manner of craft had taught him well. His welding abilities were absolutely first rate on both stainless steel and aluminium, the two metals he was most called upon to use where salt water was concerned. Over the years what had started as a passing interest developed into a reasonably lucrative sideline which supplied more than enough income to pay for the rent and outgoings of the premises, as well as for a personal motor cruiser which was regularly changed, always trading upwards.

He then owned a Birchwood Commodore 31 built in 1986, which he had personally shot blasted before epoxy coating and anti fouling. He had partially broken down both of the one hundred and thirty horse power TMD30A turbocharged diesel engines and fully serviced them. It was loaded with navigation equipment, could comfortably accommodate six, with an aft galley which was reasonably spacious and would not disgrace a larger craft. Danny had owned her for over a year, in which time he had used her mainly for offshore diving, and a little for entertaining various girlfriends. He had just accepted an offer of eight thousand pounds more than he had paid for her and was looking forward to once more trading up until he managed to get to his all time favourite, which would be one of the Sunseeker range.

The time and energy he could devote to boats and the water had become somewhat limited however since his brother charged him with providing a solution to the pulsejet problem. The simplicity of the engine construction greatly impressed him, and the early working model he had first built two years earlier was long gone, improved upon time after time as Dan progressed along his own learning curve. Increasing the size had proved straightforward, as had fabricating one from stainless steel, the chosen material. However construction, adding the required improvements, and the all important testing took time, a lot of time.

The two prototypes already finished were ready to go. They were fashioned from normal sheet steel and to Chris they resembled little more than two six inch rainwater down-pipes which swelled a bit at one end before tapering off and flared slightly at the other. They certainly did not resemble any form of engine he was familiar with. He knew there was more to it than that, but it really was much more to do with Peter's area of expertise. Peter understood the principles, and could appreciate what Danny had managed to accomplish. He could also see from the discolouration to the metalwork of one of them it had already been successfully tested. The three men were there to test both engines, and to tweak anything extra they possibly could from the two planes lying in the back of the BMW.

"So what exactly have you got planned for us?" Chris asked Danny as the giant lifted the discoloured engine and carried it to a huge workbench.

"Basically I want you both to see these things working as they are and see what you think. I'll fix this one in place here and run it up a bit then we'll let it cool before the next test." Danny answered as he clamped the engine into place and fitted up the fuel supply.

"What I'd like from you guys is suggestions, thoughts and advice," Danny added. "I've altered a small two man sailing boat, which got smashed up and lost its mast in a storm, to take an engine, and want to go out onto a quite section of The Solent with you two and test the thrust on the water. It's not a job I can practically do alone, but let's see what you both think of this first."

Conversation ended as Danny attempted to start the engine. It coughed, caught and died two or three times before it ignited properly. When it finally started the noise was deafening. A jet of flame shot out the larger bottom end and heat rapidly built up until the metalwork glowed first an angry red, then passed through to orange and eventually almost white. The bench on which it was clamped had begun to shake and shudder causing both Chris and Peter to step back instinctively. Danny grinned broadly as he shut off the fuel supply letting the engine die.

"Frightened you then did it?" Dan asked still grinning.

"Noisy little bugger isn't it!" Chris growled in reply.

Peter Parfitt looked at it thoughtfully, and his response was somewhat more objective.

"I think there are a few questions which immediately spring to mind Danny. In fact from my point of view three important ones, which are about the start up, noise production and heat build up. Frankly once it goes beyond the testing stage here we can forget about noise. The heat build up goes with the territory I know, but it will mean we have to be somewhat discerning in our choice of build materials and equipment used. The obvious concern is to do with the starting up. Have you given the subject much thought or attention yet?" Parfitt asked, holding a hand out as he did so towards the rapidly cooling engine which ticked loudly as it contracted.

"To be honest the start up is my biggest area of concern at the moment too. I haven't given it a great deal of consideration yet though as I've been concentrating on power to weight ratios as we discussed last night." Danny answered, then continued. "I took the view the best way for me to start was to study the power to weight grafts and thrust calculations I was given and use those as a base from which to start experimenting. We roughly know the weight of the required equipment, know the payload, can work out the weight of the body of the missile itself, but we don't yet know the weight of the engine or its fuel requirements. There is also air density to be factored in and the fuel type, which will of course affect the weight. Because the entire concept is reasonably new to me I felt the best way to proceed was to familiarise myself with the mechanics, which are incredibly basic, and see how I could adapt it as a propulsion system. Hence the experiment out on The Solent later."

Whilst Danny was speaking Peter moved over to glance at the second and so far unused engine.

"I see this one is slightly different. You've modified the fuel supply to give it two inlets. Was this your own modification?" Peter asked.

"Well as you can see I've not run the engine up at all yet." Danny answered before explaining, "As you noted with the model on the bench, starting is a problem. It's not one I'm going to fully address yet as I just explained, but each engine I've produced I've altered slightly, subtly, nothing major, but enough to slightly alter performance readings which I then study and which should eventually let me optimise performance."

"What do you find are the main problems you are up against with starting?" Parfitt asked with genuine interest.

"Basically they are threefold. There is air intake and temperature, fuel delivery and type used, and ignition. Now obviously the ignition will vary according to the fuel used. For example it would be pointless to inject diesel in and try and ignite it with a spark plug. Combustible or not all I would end up with is foul smelling half burnt vapour, although technically they will run on it. In fact they will run on sawdust, coal dust and just about any combustible fuel" Danny told them.

"Have you tried adding ether to the mix?" Peter questioned.

"No I haven't. I did think about it but felt by adding even a small canister to the missile it would include unnecessary additional weight. It would only be needed for start up, but the canister and pipeline would have to be carried by the missile throughout its flight, adding weight and reducing overall effectiveness," Dan answered.

"Not if it wasn't contained within the missile, but left on the launch platform," Peter argued. "As I understand it the problem with these engines is starting them. Is that not so?" Danny nodded and Peter continued. "Now once they're started and run up to temperature they'll run until the fuel is switched off, runs out, or they are smashed to pieces. Once in the air the vagaries of wind and air density may take their effect causing the missiles to drop slightly off target as happened with the V-1's despite their gyros, but the engines should continue to run throughout despite wind or air density. Surely it's just a question of getting them to start and then getting them hot, which is all about the fuel mix and the volume of the air blown through at the right temperature, is it not?" Peter asked, cocking one eyebrow in the direction of the younger man.

"In essence – yes," Dan replied, "But I don't see how that helps with the problems of start up. Actually there is something you said I must correct you on, and that's to do with the effects of wind and air density on targeting. In our case they will have no effect as ours will have their own on-board guidance systems. Not only should we be able to hit a large object with what we have, but we should be able to accurately target specific parts of it."

Peter stood and looked at Danny thoughtfully for a moment. He could see Danny had taken what he had said as criticism, which it most certainly was not. He liked the younger man and could see how much progress he had made, and done so in an area in which he possessed a very limited working knowledge and absolutely no previous experience. What Dan had already accomplished was exceptional. What was being asked of him was to produce a miracle. Interestingly Peter also thought Danny would be able to deliver that miracle, as it could be seen the younger man's grasp of the engineering complexities involved were already way beyond his own, but Peter had grown up around jets and was conversant with the concepts and of many of the problems.

"Danny, please don't think I'm criticising what you have done." Parfitt tried to explain. "Personally I think you have already performed brilliantly. However the thing is, as I know from experience, anybody working alone has only one input, one way of looking at or addressing a subject, yet many problems can have more than one solution. In this case not only will you be working with these missiles, but you will be working on their launch platforms.

"When you watch a Saturn V take off you probably realise it is a hugely complicated piece of equipment which has to put the astronauts of the Apollo programme into space in such good order they may live to tell the tale when they return. Sophisticated though the rocket undoubtedly is, it still remains tethered to and serviced from a launch platform until the last possible second. Now the point I was trying to make is systems which may prove useful to the missiles flight, but not needed on the journey, could be built into the platform to be sacrificed on take off. Simply put, when an aircraft takes off from a carrier on a mission it doesn't need to take the carrier along with it.

"In the case of these missiles they have to be fire and forget, which means they have to respond remotely, and for that they have to be ultra reliable. This you know. So, if I might suggest, why do you not look to put hot air blowers and an ether pump on the platform? When you were starting the engine just now it fired up straight away when you introduced the flame from the welding torch. I'm not suggesting you should fit welding torches to each missile, but I'm sure the three of us can come up with a solution as to how to introduce the required amount of heated air, or improved fuel mix."

"Peter, I'm sorry." Dan grinned back. "I didn't mean to sound tetchy, and I have to admit you're right. Putting systems like that in place on the platform wasn't considered, and they could well work. I'll take on board what you've said. It does make sense!"

"Yeah, he does that at times. Not too bad for a fly-boy. Now if you two have kissed and made up I think you'll find we have work to do." Chris broke in, the NCO training once more coming to the fore.

The three men went outside leaving the pulsejet to further cool whilst they scurried about at Dan's direction making everything ready for the sea trial he planned. He had repaired the small sailing dinghy's hull with fibreglass resin. Where the mast was previously mounted there was now a reasonably substantial mounting plate securely fitted to the hull, bracketed where possible to the various ribs of the small craft, spreading any loading. Protruding from the top of the plate were what could only be adjustable engine mountings, rubber mounted to reduce vibrations and fatigue. On top of the bow was a small rubber aerial with a cable running back to a waterproofed electronic box from which ran control wires to two fairly hefty servos. From each of those a stainless steel rod ran back to control the rudder. The boat was radio controlled with build in redundancies as both servos could push and pull, and an allowance made for varying engine configurations. A small fuel tank was located near to the front of the craft on the left side with a twelve volt car battery on the right, and each was fixed behind heat resistant bulkheads. The fuel pipe had both manual and electrically controlled shut off valves, and the only loose equipment was a small bottle of compressed air. Both Peter and Chris were impressed. Danny Bryant obviously knew what he was about and was clearly capable of planning and building around problems.

The now cooled pulse jet was eventually brought out, bolted in place, and hooked up to the fuel tank. A plastic backed canvas cover with a purpose cut hole for the engine was put over the craft to help reduce it shipping water, and another canvas sheet was wrapped around the pulsejet itself. Finally after Dan went through a series of checks to his own vessel the Birchwood put to sea with the little test boat in tow.

Danny's boat may well have been comfortable, very much so for a dive boat, but it certainly wasn't fast. Travelling at only six nautical miles per hour it took nearly an hour to get down to Needs Ore Point, the destination Danny had in mind to start the trial. The water of The Solent was flat, a light breeze blowing in from the south east leaving the waters in the lee of the Isle of Wight. Passing Cowes on their port side Dan cruised down the coast south westerly in the direction of Lymington. Having cleared Cowes the majority of the small craft disappeared leaving only open water along the coast of the mainland. The coast itself was also deserted as it normally was along this section, especially at that time of year, where the southern edge of the New Forest grew down to the edge of a narrow beach and the nearest road was well over a mile inland.

Peter Parfitt always enjoyed being on the water and the day was no exception. The weather was mediocre with high thin cloud which, although it left everything below slightly overcast, brought no threat of rain with it, and kept the warmer air arriving from the continent beneath it which fortunately raised the otherwise chilly temperature by a few degrees. Chris had received a certain amount of training on the water, but it had always conjured up bad associations for him. In the past he had generally found himself cramped, wet and cold whenever he was afloat, and usually dreadfully poorly quartered. He elected to stay below, where he did what soldiers of the British army the world over did whenever they were given the opportunity – he found the galley and got a brew going. Without a thought of asking the others what they would like, or how they would like it, he produced three mugs of steaming sweet black tea and stumbled up to join them.

Dan cleared Needs Ore Point and turned slightly to a west south westerly heading, then closed marginally with the coast where he anchored, just a little shy of directly opposite the Isle of Wight's Newtown Bay. He untied the test boat and pulled it around on the starboard side until it was alongside the bow, where he then loosened and removed the two covers. With the ease of a man who has done such a thing many times he casually jumped over the side of his boat landing almost cat like in the dinghy below. He passed a line through a U-bolt at the stern of the dinghy and tossed one end up to Peter Parfitt, asking him to make it off. When Parfitt finished Danny threw the other end up to Chris and instructed him to hold it in order to keep the test boat alongside. He then turned his attention to the engine, first turning on the fuel manually then shouting up to Peter asking him to fully open the electric control valve until the engine fired up, then to reduce the flow but keep the motor running.

Holding the pipe from the compressed air cylinder and a hand held flare in one huge hand Dan pulled the tab on the flare and turned the valve for the air. Blowing compressed air into the engine's air intake along with the heat from the flare Dan turned on the engines fuel supply and it started up, instantly roared into life, died down, and then stabilised as Peter struggled with the remote control to the fuel. As Danny climbed back aboard his motor cruiser the dinghy was straining slightly at the rope Chris held as it attempted to pull away from the Birchwood. Danny took the end of the line from Chris and slowly let it play out almost to the end when he then tossed it overboard and reeled in the slack from where the other end was tied off. The line slipped through the U-bolt and the dinghy was free. When done Danny took the controls from Peter, opened the throttle a little and tested the steerage controls. Satisfied he remotely opened the fuel valve. A bright orange candle roared out from the back of the pulsejet and the dinghy instantly responded by surging forward. Danny eased off on the control so as not to swamp the dinghy then slowly and steadily increased the power. The dinghy moved across the water noticeably gaining speed, roaring like a single cylinder motorcycle with no exhaust pipe.

Playing with the controls Danny carved an S through the water, then turned the dinghy and brought it back towards his cruiser, causing it to pass on the port side. He had it complete two anticlockwise turns around his boat then once more straightened it on a bearing for Lymington. Keeping it in line of sight and conscious of the Lymington to Yarmouth ferry, and other craft, Dan once more turned it back towards the cruiser. With nothing else between him and the dinghy, and nothing likely to cross its path, Danny slowly opened the fuel supply effectively giving the craft full throttle. Its pace increased across the flat water as it approached, its bow rising and riding the water well as the speed built up. As it passed his cruiser he guestimated the speed to be something over forty knots. The engine as it passed could be seen to be glowing, but functioning perfectly, steaming slightly as droplets of sea water splashed up from the bow, landed on it, and instantly vaporised.

Dan cut the power, completed a final turn and brought it back in the direction of the cruiser, turning the fuel off completely as it came alongside. The engine coughed twice and died. As the dinghy bumped into the side of the cruiser Danny reached down and secured the bow with a line before dragging it to the rear of the cruiser and making the line off on the stern rail. Weighing anchor he turned the cruiser and, with the little dinghy dancing in the wake, slowly made his way back through the quiet waters to his workshop. After slightly over half an hour Dan judged the engine should have cooled sufficiently to cover once again, so heaved to and put the tarpaulins back in place before closing on Calshot Castle, one of Henry VIII's device forts, built at the end of Calshot Spit to guard the entrance to Southampton Water, and a place where passing tourists could well have binoculars and cameras. All knew it didn't hurt to be careful, for security was crucial.

They returned to Danny's workshop and whilst Dan moored and tied his cruiser off alongside the quay Chris and Peter unbolted the now cold pulsejet and carried it into the workshop. There was one last test to perform, which may lead to its destruction, but first the reed valve had to be changed. Jack Bryant had asked for the engine to be tested at maximum throttle for a full hour, which greatly exceeded reed valve life, or to destruction, whichever occurred first. Danny had constructed a cage in which to test it, and this was then covered with inert insulation material to reduce the noise the engine would produce.

The engine was once more mounted on the test bench and bolted in place. All but one section of the insulated cage was placed around it and a long pipe with baffles in the end was placed over the exhaust so the hot gasses may be ducted to the rear of the building and out through a vent. Danny carried out final checks and once more started the engine. With the fuel and control valve on the outside the final piece of protective cage was lifted into place and secured. Dan felt there was little justification in treating the engine gently at this stage so turned the fuel fully on, instantly opening the engine up to maximum power. It didn't go bang.

Confining the engine within an insulated enclosure would not allow the heat to dissipate as it would naturally in almost any application in which it could be used. By comparison with more conventional engines the pulsejet works at incredibly high temperatures, usually heating its own metalwork to a glowing orange white, so the trial should lead to overheating and failure. Danny had set up a small microphone under the test bench and two camera lenses were built into the cage along with various thermometers so the test could be fully monitored and recorded for the duration of the trial. This way when the engine exploded, as was expected, it would be possible to determine where, when and how it failed. To Danny's surprise the barking roar from the engine did not change in note throughout the trial, so he decided to increase the tests duration by thirty minutes, hoping for catastrophic failure. It didn't occur. Eventually the fuel was shut off and the engine stopped. Despite the insulation the entire workshop had warmed considerably and attempts to remove the cage were postponed as the metalwork was too hot to safely remove even with protective gloves.

"Well Danny if the thing runs that well for that long in those temperatures it should do us proud." Chris was the first to observe after the test was complete.

"Yes indeed!" Peter agreed. "The longest one will have to run in action should be less than fifteen minutes and, although it could well be as much as fifty degrees where they will be going, it will seem cool after being in that cage. You could easily have boiled a kettle in there!"

"Yeah, easily." Danny confirmed. "One hundred and thirty degrees C beneath the bench, and just under two hundred and ten above. I can't believe it didn't destroy itself. The reed valve at least should have failed. They should only be good for about twenty minutes, which is plenty for our demands, but I haven't had any fail yet and they should. It's a shame really because had it failed we would have had more to analyse."

"I don't think you can complain at a resounding success like this." Peter chuckled.

"Too right!" Chris laughed. "The sea trial was brilliant as well. I actually enjoyed myself out there today, which was a whole new experience for me as far as being on the water is concerned. So how do you go about working out the thrust from that Danny?"

"I don't have the first idea. I can work out the displacement of the dinghy, and a little of the drag coefficients, but basically I turn over all the information to Jack, who goes into a huddle with Peter. They get out their slide rules, graphs, books and perhaps an abacus and work out things which are beyond me." Danny answered laughing, much happier with the trials than he wished to let on.

Five and a half hours had passed since they entered the workshop at around seven-thirty that morning, and hunger pangs were setting in.

"What do you want to do about lunch?" Dan asked.

"Well we're not here for a dining experience." Chris replied gruffly. "Anything will do for me."

"Yes, I agree." Peter responded. "Some ready made sandwiches would be good. I'm not fussy about the filling."

"Yeah! Make mine brown bread, would you?" Chris added.

Danny left to fill the order whilst Peter and Chris reversed the BMW into the workshop and off-loaded the aircraft from under the rug in the rear of the car. Both aircraft were almost fully assembled, lacking only the securing of wings, which the two accomplished in less than two minutes. Having stripped them of every gram of unnecessary weight the two aircraft had already been extensively tested by the two men working together. Plasticine modelling clay was used in place of the explosive because of its similar density and inherent pliability. This was shaped, moved and altered with various sculpturing tools until the planes flew perfectly. They had discovered the optimum payload was very slightly less than six kilos which, if delivered properly, should cause considerable damage, especially if detonated within a confined space.

The distance from launch site to target was another major consideration, as most targets were nowhere near possible take-off strips. Almost all mosques were in the centre of towns and cities with few flat green areas nearby, and certainly not unobserved green areas. For accuracy the person controlling the plane had to be reasonably close to the target, but for security surrounding the launching the planes would generally be required to take to the skies at some distance, usually miles from the targets, which was well beyond the range of the remote control units. The problem this posed was addressed and eventually resolved. With Nathan's help the hand held units transmission range was increased and although illegal this was considered wholly unimportant when considered alongside the scale of illegality of what they were generally about. The signal boosting helped, but did not resolve the problem, which was finally conquered by continued experimentation.

Chris had taken Peter north to his beloved Yorkshire where, amongst the moors he had so loved as a child and young man, he and Peter tried all manner of experiments. Peter taught Chris how to fly the models until he became quite proficient. Eventually Chris proved to be a reasonably accomplished pilot of the tiny craft, although he would never reach Peter's standard, flying as he did by instinct, with the slightest deft touch to the controls making the process appear simplicity itself. Using two remote control units, transmitting on the same frequency, they managed to take it in turn to control an aircraft whilst in the air. They found by moving ever further apart control could be passed back and forth between the units, which covered a far longer area, although still not as great as they would have liked.

The controllers range proved to be roughly equal to the distance they could see plus a little, not that the little extra distance matter because it was impossible to accurately control the planes once they were out of sight. Both possessed good eyesight and found if they put a distance between themselves as one of them lost sight of the plane and the other picked it up full control could be maintained throughout the flight. Eventually it was discovered the little planes would continue on their own in straight level flight if they lost the signal from the remote control unit, presumably until they ran out of fuel, although such had never been allowed to occur. With this discovery the two placed themselves ten miles apart and found the aircraft could leave one section of controlled airspace and continue to the next, alone and without problems, so long as there were no strong gusts or a prevailing cross wind in between. The problem of distance was solved.

With weight, power and distance problems behind them they had but to remove the Plasticine and replace it with the shaped and moulded Semtex. Their delivery devices would then be ready for a mission. However it was first necessary to double check and retest the planes with their changed payloads, in case the trim of either required further adjustment. It was far too dangerous to test them openly whilst loaded with explosive, in case of an accident, despite the fact there would be no explosion until the detonator was armed. To avoid the risk of any possible exposure, and for the sake of security, Danny had purchased two industrial extractor fans and fashioned a small wind tunnel from them. With one at either end the tunnel was set across the back of the building, sucking air in from one side and blowing it out at the other. The fan speeds were altered and increased until they could suck and blow to create a simulated wind speed of seventy miles per hour, and it was into this wind tunnel the planes were to go.

Danny returned with a carrier bag of sandwiches, pies, pasties and fruit, and the three took twenty minutes from their labours to eat much of the contents and drink a cup of tea which Chris brewed whilst waiting. With Danny's return the conversation about the pulse jet continued in generalities.

"So where exactly do you wish to go from here Dan?" Peter asked.

"Well I've broken this whole missile project down into various categories, the input which is needed, and by whom. I will certainly need help, and there are some things I cannot do at all. I definitely need your help with the airframe design as you presumably understand the loading dynamics. I can take care of the construction of both airframes and pulsejets, and the engine testing, but will again need your help with the launch platform design. Nathan will have to take care of the design and installation of the flight control system, and again he may need your help with advice regarding servos etcetera. Once we get the design for the launch platform sorted out I can get on with the construction side, but I'll need the help of both of you with its testing. Then everything we do will be all about testing. Guidance testing, full system checks, flight testing, explosive testing and even detonator testing, and that will need the three of us and Nathan." Danny explained.

"Sounds like I can relax and take it easy." Chris Spencer muttered, which caused both Danny and Peter to laugh.

"Don't tell Jack that!" Danny told him. "I said I felt left out of things after the first meeting and he told me not to worry, there would be plenty for me to do. Then it just poured in! Believe me, I know my brother, he's working to a plan. He'll have worked out all of our various strengths and weaknesses and will have woven some wonderful plot around them using each of us to best advantage. I guarantee you he'll continue to surprise you with what he comes up with. He still does me and I've known him all my life. I also think he will yet surprise Jake and Phil. He won't be content to do this at their expense. I'd wager a sensibly sized bet he'll be working out how we can all profit substantially from what we do, but without compromising us in any way!"

Returning to their work all three donned latex gloves and food manufacturer's hats with hairnets before moving on to the next step of the operation. Dan then set up and tested the wind tunnel whilst Chris and Peter stripped back the bellies of both aircraft, removed the Plasticine, inserted the Semtex and wired in the detonators before once more sealing up the undersides. Nobody within the group ever touched either plane except Chris and Peter, and neither of them ever worked on the assembly or interiors without gloves and hair protection. The plane's exteriors would be washed down with alcohol before their final flight, when they would crash and explode leaving little evidence, but even a little evidence remained evidence, and nobody involved underestimated the abilities of many nations law enforcement agencies. Nothing which could be traced back was ever to be left at the site of any operation. Not a fingerprint, not a hair, no saliva or tissue, or anything at all from which a DNA sample could be taken which even future technology could analyse. It was considered better to cancel any mission, no matter how important, than to ever, in any way, compromise security. Therefore nothing was to be left on or in the remote controlled aircraft, even though they were to explode.

The first aircraft was placed in the wind tunnel on the far side of a Perspex screen. Dan had built what amounted to three small pylons inside, consisting of nothing more than oval tubes, on which the aircraft could be mounted by its wheels. Through the centre of the tubes ran thin braided stainless steel cables which could be attached to the aircrafts undercarriage and wound up and down by three small wheels on the outside of the tunnel. In this way the aircraft could be tethered in place with it's engine running at tick-over as the tunnel was switched on and, as wind speed increased, engine speed could also be increased whilst the tethers loosened until the aircraft was safely flying under its own power, and where its attitude could be checked and monitored. At the end of the test the aircraft could be slowly winched back down onto the pylons as the wind speed dropped. It was hardly a state of the art device, but it had proved simple to construct with off-the-shelf materials from large stores where anonymity was guaranteed. Most importantly – it worked.

Despite every care being taken to fit and balance the explosive in precisely the same way as the Plasticine the first aircraft tested badly. The weight was too far forward and had to be moved back, and it took four attempts before it flew as Parfitt wanted. With the second plane they over compensated for the mistake made with the first one, with the plane flying tail down and heavy to its port side. It took over two hours and seven attempts to put things right before Peter finally passed this one too. Both planes were then permanently sealed and once more wind tested. This time both passed. As Chris removed the wings and thoroughly cleaned the surfaces of the two planes Peter and Danny partially stripped and cleaned the tiny engines, before reassembling them and giving both a final test. It was long since dark by the time they finished, but both aircraft were now fully operational. Their next flight would be their last.

Throughout the Saturday they helped Danny with a variety of ideas and concepts, although for obvious reasons the bulk of these came from Peter Parfitt. In the early evening they took their leave of Dan and drove down to Portsmouth, stopping en route at Fareham for a large leisurely meal at a small restaurant on the A27, just outside the town, where they could park the car directly in front of the window in which they sat. At twenty to ten in the evening they pulled into a numbered lane on the characterless Portsmouth dockside and waited to board the Normandie, a one time flagship of Brittany Ferries, which sailed at twenty-two-thirty to the tidal port of Ouistreham, twelve kilometres or so north north east of beautiful but often missed Caen, capital of the Basse-Normandie region.

The vessel, so typical of the Brittany Ferries fleet, was just about as comfortable as it is possible for a ferry to get, and the Commodore Class cabin they booked gave Chris reason to reconsider all he had ever believed of life afloat. There was no opulence or outlandish luxury, it was a ferry, but it was comfortable and dry with cabins far more spacious than he would previously have dreamt possible. Heading straight for the shared cabin as soon as they boarded they took to their beds, ignoring the changing view of the passing coastline as they tried to sleep, mindful of the long drive before them and the lack of time in bed.

The ferry docked at six o'clock Central European Time, which was an hour ahead of Britain, and they were woken by the crew an hour before docking. Their sleep was short and the drive would be long, but fortunately not rushed. If border guards or customs officials were on duty neither man saw them as they entered France with their deadly cargo. They by-passed Caen then picked up the Autoroute de Normandie, for Rouen, then Paris. Once clear of the ferry the early Sunday morning traffic was light, and the BMW simply ate up the kilometres to Paris. In less than two hours the two found themselves cruising around Paris's notorious Boulevard Peripherique, incredibly quiet in comparison to its normal manic traffic. Clearing Paris to the south they joined the Autoroute du Soleil for the five hundred kilometre drive to Lyon, their destination for the night, and the site of an early morning meeting the following day with those who were to start the window dressing as to the official reason for the trip. They were ostensibly on a visit for Peter, as senior projects manager, to check out various possibilities of sites for another new retail and gaming complex, and for Chris to take a view on the regional security issues surrounding such a venture.

Apart from Peage booths, where they halted momentarily to pay the road tolls, the four hour drive south from Paris was interrupted only once at a service station outside Chalon-sur-Saone, south of Dijon, where they stopped for fuel. At shortly after one o'clock in the afternoon they arrived at their hotel, the towering circular Radisson SAS Lyon, Europe's tallest hotel, set in the business district and close to the historic town centre, and where the car could be parked beneath the hotel in a secure area under cameras. In contrast to the previous night they each had superior panoramic double rooms, and there they left their bags and headed for the hotel's Bistro de la Tour, with its informal French brasserie where they enjoyed the offered dish of the day. After lunch, simply for exercise and something to do, they strolled into and around the city centre, returning in the evening to shower and change before once more eating. This time they were to have their taste buds delighted with exquisite regional cuisine served at the hotel's gastronomic restaurant, the Arc en Ciel, before turning in for an early night.

The following morning's gathering was held in the hotel's meeting room. Jack Bryant planned the business aspects of their trip to once again be high profile, attracting media attention wherever possible. Of the ten people at the meeting two were from the local press and one from a trade magazine. In addition there was the NJF Industries regional manager, accompanied by a company lawyer, an architect, and a representative from each of the local and regional governments. All had been informed these were to be nothing more than initial exploratory talks, yet the air was charged with expectancy. As window dressing went it couldn't get much better.

Although both Peter and Chris were fully aware all here was part of their cover, both had also been reminded by Jack Bryant that something tangible on the investment front may follow from it, as it had in Brno, so they had to proceed accordingly. The two officials were both keen to attract development of a potential new complex to the local region, mindful of the employment it would create and wealth it would ultimately generate. They regarded it as southern competition to Euro Disney, and wanted a slice of the pie if they could possibly get it, so much so that subsidies and tax breaks were discussed at a very early stage, all lapped up by the ever hungry press. An area to the south west of Lyon was discussed, virtually in the centre of the triangle formed by Lyon, Vienne and St Etienne, an area easily accessible from all three, and a potential future draw to the area if global warming continued to shrink the ski season so many in the region depended upon. The meeting broke up by midday allowing Chris and Peter to continue their journey south.

Once more the BMW purred south, gobbling up the kilometres as it passed Valence, Nimes, Montpellier, Narbonne and Perpignan. At Avignon the E15 had become the Autoroute La Languedocienne as it reached out for the Spanish border, but as the border was crossed it found itself with another name, the Autopista del Mediterrano. The border itself, built at the top of a long rise, had virtually ceased to be, with European Union registered cars streaming through unchecked in the left hand lanes. In the right lane heavy trucks laboured up to the border crossing point, generally to be waved through, but occasionally stopped if they looked to be overweight, with punitive fines then handed out and drivers forced to offload goods if they proved to be too heavy. The BMW with its British plates didn't attract the slightest attention. They had entered Spain.

Five hours and six hundred kilometres south of Lyon brought them to Barcelona, where they stretched their legs and changed drivers. Another three hundred kilometres passed before they stopped to eat at a restaurant a little to the south of Valencia at around seven-thirty in the evening. To both the half an hour break from driving was every bit as welcome as the food they consumed, which they washed down with strong black coffee. Then it was back to the car and another one hundred and fifty kilometres to Murcia, where the motorway ended, before continuing on the final slower four hundred kilometre leg to Malaga.

They reached Malaga at one o'clock on the Tuesday morning, gritty eyed and fatigued from the drive which, had they taken it over two days would have proved to have been scenically particularly beautiful and even, in places, almost inspiring. However, two days was not available if they were to work to the schedule, and scenery, beautiful though it undoubtedly was, did not feature anywhere on their list of essentials, so slipped by very much unnoticed. Their high quality four star hotel was newly built and re-built, and consisted of two completely refurbished buildings which retained their original façade dating back to the nineteenth century, and included an additional new build. Standing in front of the cathedral at the very heart of Malaga's cultural and commercial centre the location was perfect. The deluxe double rooms were spacious, comfortable and tastefully furnished and decorated, with great attention given to every detail. Neither man noticed or cared, and Chris, who had finished the driving, merely kicked his shoes off and fell asleep across his bed fully dressed. Peter Parfitt, who managed to sleep in the car for the last hour and a half of the journey, felt somewhat better and enjoyed a shower before also hitting his pillow.

The arranged meeting for those in Malaga was organised in a very different way to the one at Lyon. It was due to start at noon with the intention of using the usual Spanish siesta as an extended working lunch, continuing through the afternoon. Again the cover was real, in that there was a legitimate NJF interest already in Malaga, and the idea of constructing a high tech leisure complex and retail centre was authentic. Year on year Malaga's population had grown and the city's urban sprawl continued to both expand and develop. Additionally the Costa del Sol sucked in millions of visitors each year, all there to spend and enjoy. Before their departure Chris and Peter were well briefed on the business side of their trip by Phil Gatting, Jake Ferris and Jack Bryant, each of whom stressed different angles and features.

Over breakfast, and recovered from their long drive, the two men discussed the meeting ahead. Chris started the conversation by asking Peter how he thought they should proceed.

"I believe the best bit of advice we received came from Jake to be honest with you," Peter said, adding. "I think I quote him accurately when I say – 'Gain what you can, give nothing away.' He's a wily old bugger and sharp as a tack. I know at times he sits there and appears to do nothing, but he takes in every word said and asks some bloody good questions at times. The funny thing is I think young Jack Bryant is working the business side of things as well as he is the other matter, and I can see this really taking off, which will be worth billions if it goes properly."

"Yeah, I believe you're right." Chris said before continuing thoughtfully. "Never in my life did I ever think I would so much as sit in at a meeting like those in Brno and the one yesterday yet, having done so, I kind of enjoy it in a funny sort of way. It's an almost unreal experience, surreal even. There's me, a parade basher, Chris Spencer, sitting down with guys who have spent years in universities, talking about figures I don't even understand. Seriously, how much is two and a quarter billion Euros? And I am serious!"

"For the likes of us Chris, six noughts is a million, seven noughts sets you up for life. After that it's just an abstract." Peter laughed.

Held in the small conference room of the hotels business centre the meeting got off to a good natured start which remained throughout. This time there were four more people present, two representing the media, a local councillor and an accountant. Apart from them the breakdown was much the same as those who attended in Lyon. The councillor went to great pains to explain to the two Englishmen why Malaga was dubbed the Capital of the Costa del Sol. He stressed the lager lout era was dead and buried, and since the 2003 opening of the Picasso Museum cultural tourists had flocked to the city, to the museum and the beautifully refurbished artists birthplace. Although once the poor cousin, Malaga was now competing with Andalusia's capital, Seville, and Malaga's Pablo Ruiz Picasso Malaga International Airport was one of the busiest in Spain, with up to sixteen million passengers using it each year. The city council had petitioned the European Union in a bid for the 2016 European City of Culture, and improvements to the city would continue throughout the next decade with the achieving of that goal in mind. Finally the city intended to start construction of a Metro system linking such key areas as the International Congress Centre, to the west of the city, and Malaga's large university campus. Their project, should they choose to build at Malaga, would definitely be included with its own Metro stop, possibly two.

"Bloody hell mate, I could get used to this fat cat world! Do you think they would have agreed to call the Metro stations the Parfitt and Spencer Stops if we'd pushed them?" Chris had questioned, laughing out loud after a most successful meeting concluded and broke up.

"So you got the impression they were interested in us did you?" Parfitt retorted.

"Interested? I think they just might have been, and then some! I loved their suggestion that they would lay on a couple of hookers or so at their expense if we wanted them." Chris answered laughing again. "But seriously, it just goes to prove how much homework Jack Bryant does. He predicted they would play it like that, almost line by line. He also said they wouldn't mention the water problem, and they didn't. That young lad impresses me more with every move we make. Not only does he have a brain like Einstein, but he understands complex business concepts at the most fundamental of levels!"

"I can't fault you there," Peter agreed. "However I'm not surprised Spain in general and the Costa del Sol in particular is trying to draw in more attractions which use less water. They told us about global warming affecting the winter tourist trade in France. Here it is much worse. For decades now the answer to expansion and job creation here was to put in another golf course, but each one uses about the same amount of water as a town of fourteen thousand people. Soon they will have to choose between their precious golf courses or their population, but that'll probably be after tourists have stopped coming because there is not enough water to wash in. I saw a report which claims Spain will see its first desert forming within the next twenty-five years."

"Well I'm deeply shocked the good councillor neglected to mention the point," Chris said, still smiling. "We may have serious work to do tomorrow, but I've enjoyed today!"

Having dined well both Chris and Peter once again enjoyed an early night. On the Wednesday morning both rose at seven, showered, ate a light continental breakfast and checked out slightly before eight o'clock. This time they headed north from Malaga, over the hills which protected the city from the cold in winter, following the 331 towards Cordoba, one hundred and fifty kilometres away. The journey took almost two hours, negotiating the twisting hilly roads, but became easier after they picked up the E05, the main road for Madrid, which was a dual carriageway. They were to stay in Madrid that night, and this time with nothing but a minor meeting with the staff of NJF's Madrid office scheduled for the early morning of the following day. However, before they got to Madrid they had another task to attend to.

They passed through to the south of Cordoba without stopping, but pulled over a few kilometres out to the east of town behind a drab, derelict and uninhabitable building which screened them from the road. There Chris pulled on a pair of latex gloves whilst Peter, who had already done so, ripped off the British number plates and stuck double sided tape to the bodywork of the car where the plates had previously been. Chris, with gloved hands, retrieved the German plates from beneath the seat, unwrapped them, and stuck them to the car as Peter peeled off the GB country index sticker from the cars tailgate. The British number plates went back beneath the driver's seat, and the tape backing, sticker and gloves were placed in a paper bag which already contained solid paraffin barbeque lighters. The plates were for roadside cameras, if any, or casual observers. There was nothing they could do about the steering wheel, but it was unlikely anyone would look that closely. If they did, and it was later reported, it would either be dismissed or add to the confusion. As they started off again Peter removed the British tax disc from the windscreen and placed it in the glove box with the new GB sticker, ready for later replacement. Every move had been rehearsed many times, and the tasks were completed in silence.

They drove on for another twenty kilometres until they approached the town of Pedro Abad, lying on a fertile plain of patchwork fields which rose very slightly in front of them. Their conversation once the number plates were changed was in German, mostly with Chris speaking and Peter answering in simple phrases. It was a pretence they intended to keep up for the next two and a half hours just in case they were overheard at any stage, after which, if all went well, they would revert to their genuine identity. If they failed they would have a chance to learn Spanish as they spent the rest of their lives incarcerated within a high security Spanish jail.

With a population of around three thousand, Pedro Abad was not a big place, and both ex-servicemen felt they knew the place almost intimately which, after studying the intel one of Chris Spencer's men had provided, they should. Every road had been photographed, gradients roughly noted, distances calculated and every major building reported on and mapped. It was a remarkably thorough job, just as Chris had expected, and gave them a complete working knowledge of the town and its surroundings. Every detail had been worked out, every move prepared, practiced and drilled until both knew exactly what they had to do, and knew Pedro Abad as if they were born there. The town ran from an industrial estate at the north-east as an oval to the south-west. The E05 snaked in a gentle S around the town with the top of the S enclosing it as it ran north then west around the outskirts. Access was provided by slip roads at either end of the town which were linked by an additional service road running along the north-west side of the main highway.

They pulled off the E05 and onto the down ramp of the first slip road keeping to the left hand side as they approached the T junction, from which they could turn either right to the town or left to the service road. On the left at the bottom were some bushes and small trees, and on the right stood a white painted oblong single story building with a red tiled roof. Along the side facing the slip road sixteen arches could be counted, with a further four across its southerly end. At the northern end was what appeared to be an office or administration area, although it was not, over which there was a small dome. Adjacent to the northern part of the building was a tarmac area which would be used for parking, with grass, small shrubs and a palm tree between the tarmac and the slip road. The rest of the ground around the building was simply stony red soil. The building stood at the extreme western edge of the town, and separated from it both by a short distance and by style and design.

No vehicles followed them down the ramp or could be seen on the other roads. Chris stopped a little short of the junction and Peter quickly stepped from the car. He rapidly made his way around to the rear of the vehicle and, as Chris slowly drove away, stepped behind the bushes where he was instantly swallowed from sight, completely screened by them. Chris turned left at the junction, following the road beneath the E05, where he once more stopped and waited momentarily for Peter to rejoin him. As he did so Chris again pulled away, this time turning right, following alongside the E05 for almost two and a half kilometres until they came to another junction by a large transport motel with a restaurant and heavy vehicle parking area. Here they again turned right, then almost immediately left onto the industrial estate, driving through it to the western end which boasted several well laid out roads but no buildings, obviously planned and waiting for future development. In the far right corner, just as described and photographed, was a track a car could follow but which was too narrow for a large truck.

The area was naturally deserted, with no need for anyone to go near it. Along the track and to the right there was a large flat raised area of short grass from which anyone approaching could be heard from a distance and clearly seen, unlikely though such an event may be. Chris turned the car and reversed up the track before stopping. Once more they put on latex gloves and hairnets, unloaded the two aircraft and again washed down all their surfaces with solvent before final assembly. Fuel was added and the engines started and run up to working temperature as all servos were checked for the final time. When finished the planes were placed one behind the other on the ground. Two harmless looking toys. Bringers of death and destruction.

At eleven-forty-five, leaving the planes in place but under a camouflage cover, Chris drove Peter back around the service road skirting Pedro Abad and dropped him at the deserted spot behind the bushes he had visited and approved a little earlier. Neither man spoke, but just nodded at one another as Chris drove off. Traffic was very light, with even the main road almost deserted, and Chris was back in position by eleven-fifty-five. There was no evidence of anyone having been anywhere within the vicinity. Leaving the planes unattended for ten minutes had been a calculated risk, but an incredibly minimal one which they could have talked their way out of and aborted the mission had it happened. With the gloves still on he started the first engine, which burst into life immediately. He ran the revs up, holding the tail of the little plane against the strain, then released it. The ground sloped slightly down towards the town and the little planes speed increased over the grass of the hard packed ground until it lifted into the light oncoming breeze. It flew away from Chris and out of range as he turned to start the next one, which in turn followed the first. With a final check around him Chris bundled up the camouflage sheet and climbed back into the car to once again head back for Peter Parfitt. The few people he passed at a distance on the industrial estate failed to notice him. Effectively he had never been there.

More than thirty-five thousand years ago those who are now accepted as modern humans entered the Iberian Peninsula. They were the first of many waves of would be invaders and those who wished to colonise. Celts, Phoenicians, Carthaginians and Greeks all preceded the mighty Romans. For five centuries, from 218 BC, the region was ruled by the Romans. Eventually they left and control passed to the Visigoths – until 711.

By the eighth century Islam dominated northern Africa, with Arabs and Berbers converted to the new culture. In 711, with Visigoth kingdoms warring with one another, a raiding party crossed the Strait of Gibraltar and won a decisive victory, defeating and killing a Visigoth king, Roderic. After being substantially reinforced the advance continued and, by 718, most of the peninsular was dominated. Further advance into Europe was stopped in 732 by the Franks, under the command of Charles Martel, at the Battle of Tours, but for the Iberian Peninsular the Moors had arrived.

In Roman times modern day Morocco and Algeria was known to the Romans as Mauretania, and the Berber people of the area by the Latin name Mauri, from which the word Moor is derived, although the term was applied to all Muslims conquering Iberia. Fanatical about their new culture they successfully warred with the indigenous peoples, but also experienced divisions between themselves, broadly explaining their failure to conquer the entire peninsular. Should they have done so a Muslim state may well have remained until today.

Except for an enclave in the extreme north-west, from where the Christian re-conquest would eventually begin, the new Moorish land was known as Al-Andalus. Hispania had become part of the caliph of Damascus, the capital of the Muslim world, and its history would be shaped differently to that of the rest of Europe as it was forced to accept and adapt to a new language, culture and theology. This wave of invaders had brought no women with them, which led to the next generation being half Hispanic and, along with converted Christians, these came to dominate the land.

Independent Muslim states became firmly established during the next seven hundred and fifty years, whilst to the north the small Christian kingdoms slowly began to recover the land in what came to be known as the Reconquista. Almost constant warfare between Christians and Muslims followed throughout the Middle Ages until, by the mid thirteenth century, the Emirate of Granada remained the only Muslim realm. After the King of Aragon, Ferdinand, and the Queen of Castile, Isabella, united the two most powerful Iberian kingdoms by their marriage in 1492 their forces toppled Granada and saw the formation of the Kingdom of Spain. The creation of the Inquisition followed, and those who refused to convert to Christian Catholicism were exterminated or expelled.

Muslim culture had rapidly established itself, particularly in the south, with Cordoba and Granada becoming the centre of Arabic learning and culture. In Cordoba, under the rule of Islam, the Mezquita de Cordoba, or Great Mosque of Cordoba, was built as the world's second largest mosque. The Reconquista transformed it into a church, replacing Islamic columns and arches by basilica in the early Baroque style. It currently stands as a Roman Catholic cathedral, the main church of the diocese of Cordoba, typifying the Christian Reconquista's view of Islam. Other mosques were similarly treated, destroyed or converted to Christian places of worship, until a mere handful remained, and for seven hundred and fifty years there was no further construction of purpose built mosques.

In the early 1990's Spain's Muslim population stood at around fifty thousand. By the time the Madrid train bombings occurred in 2004 the figure hovered around one million and Islam had become the second culture of Spain, with a desperate shortage of places of worship. The majority of the Muslims, predominately Moroccans, lived in the south of the country. 1982 had seen the inauguration of the first purpose built mosque since the Middle Ages but, by the time of the bombings, two more had followed, in 1992 the Mezquita de Madrid and in 2003 the Mezquita de Granada.

The construction of the mosque opened in 1982 had in many ways been pivotal, if possible providing a rallying call to the faithful. Islam was seen to be once more on the march in a land from which it had previously been banished. As such the mosque was almost revered. Venerated for what it had achieved. The focus of Islamic passion. The Mezquita Basharat, the name means 'Good News', had been built in the small town of Pedro Abad which lies about twenty-five kilometres to the east of Cordoba.

As the town started shutting down for the midday siesta the wail of the voice calling the faithful to noon Namaz, prayer time, could just be heard by Peter Parfitt, standing in his secluded spot two hundred and forty meters from the mosque. He stood above and to the left of the front entrance and could view those entering, as they had been for several minutes. He could not see inside, but could visualise what was happening to those who entered the open doors. Inside the entrance would be a foyer with Islamic scripts on the walls, and quotes from their holy book painted straight onto the surface of the plaster. Shoe racks would be bulging with shoes as each newcomer added theirs to those already there. Afterwards they would continue to the ablution room for ritualised cleansing, before continuing to the prayer room.

His thoughts were cut short by a movement in the clear blue sky still some way off to his far left. He looked around carefully, but could see nobody who was likely to move in his direction, or who could see him. He carefully withdrew the remote control from a tiny blue backpack he had slung over his left shoulder, and extended the telescopic aerial. The small device which would send a signal to arm the detonator was fixed to the back of the remote and wired into it. He had only to press a button on the top when he was satisfied to cause it to go live. What seconds before was a small spec in the distance was growing in size and defining shape as it closed with him. He switched on his remote and once more glanced around before gently moving the small levers. He had control.

The little plane was high but he left it there as he brought it on, banking in a slight turn, before once more straightening up. The noise of the tiny engine still could not be heard from where he stood, and certainly wouldn't be within the mosque. He continued to bring the plane on and once again banked it in a turn, this time losing height as he did so, purposely side slipping. As it dropped there was a slight but discernable increase in speed as the engine struggled less to drag the weight through the air. With an experienced eye he lined the little craft up with the open door when it was some four hundred meters away. Travelling at over thirty meters a second it covered the distance in roughly thirteen seconds. At just over one hundred meters out, or four seconds, he armed the detonator.

Parfitt had flown model aircraft for years, recently constantly practicing until he was completely familiar with the little planes handling dynamics. The front doors of the mosque were wider than the wingspan of the model aircraft, the light breeze was constant and the weather conditions ideal. He judged it perfectly. The model actually passed through the first doorway. Inside was another matter as it caught its starboard wing on racks of shoes, ripping it from the fuselage and causing the plane to skew violently to the right. Spinning and flipping over, losing body parts as it went, its momentum kept it going. Startled worshippers cried out in alarm as the remains of the toy most boys would have been rightly proud of skidded on to the edge of the prayer room.

One. Two. Boom. Parfitt counted silently from his place of concealment. The boom hadn't quite cleared his thoughts when a flash of orange burst from of the doors he was watching. It was instantly followed by the real boom and the front of the mosque appeared to change shape as glass blew out of the windows set around the building and behind the arches, and screams of pain and terror could be heard. It was a mark of the mettle of the man that he remained totally impassive, turning his attention back to the sky, searching for the second plane. He stood unmoving for over a minute whilst he scoured the sky in the direction from which the first tiny movement had appeared. Not once did he fidget or take so much as a quick glance back at the mosque, despite the sounds coming from its direction. As he picked up the little speck close to were the first had appeared he once more glanced around him. Some men were staggering bleeding from the damaged front of the mosque, and in some cases others were helping them. He turned his attention back to the sky, totally devoid of emotion.

As with the first aircraft the second one was high. He took a last glance around and could plainly see there was not a soul who might be interested in him. He brought the second aircraft down a little lower as he banked it around on a similar course to the first. This time, as he started to line it up he decided on a different approach. Instantly he lifted the model and had it circle out to his right whilst he worked out the best line of attack. Once more the little plane lined up, then came in from the opposite direction to the first. Blindsided by the building Peter slightly misjudged trajectory as he armed the detonator. From where he stood he didn't see the very tip of the port wing clip an archway as it went through, but it was gone.

This time the drag on the wing did not break it off but turned the small aircraft as it powered its way into the building, causing it to fly straight into the back wall of the foyer area, the area through which sobbing men were attempting to drag screaming wounded. It exploded there, instantly killing twelve people and blowing out the internal support walls and the wall around the entrance. Slowly one of the mosque's two minarets collapsed onto the roof which in turn then also collapsed into the building, and onto those below. Many more were crushed to death immediately, and injuries were caused from which several continued to die for three days afterwards. Peter wasn't remotely interested in effects or figures. He had done his duty and completed his mission. Calmly he removed a baseball cap and sunglasses from the mini backpack, put the glasses on and pulled the baseball cap low over the top of them. He then packed the remote control back into the backpack, slung it over his shoulder and strolled along behind the bushes to the junction, from where he saw Chris approaching. Again nobody noticed the German BMW as it quietly made its way out of town. It was Wednesday the eleventh of March and four years since the Madrid train bombing.

For the third and final time Chris drove along the service road away from Pedro Abad. Neither man spoke until they were clear of the junction where they had originally turned onto the industrial estate. They now spoke in English as the car climbed and dropped whilst they made their way over the mountains. Twenty-five kilometres closer to Madrid two ambulances passed going in the opposite direction at high speed, obviously heading for Pedro Abad, and were presumably from the larger town of Andujar. They passed a few cars and several articulated trucks before the main road north from Granada joined theirs at Bailen, and where the road also split off to Albacete, but apart from them the road was very quiet, almost deserted.

After one hundred kilometres, and having past La Carolina, they climbed the mountains to a height of thirteen hundred meters at Estrella. Here they pulled off the road into a rest area, which doubled as a picnic and viewing area. Save for one heavy truck the site was empty, as expected so early in the year. The cab of the truck had its curtains pulled around, the driver obviously asleep in his bunk. Even so Chris drove back around and pulled up close behind it in the blind spot for the truck's mirrors. Rapidly they changed the plates and stickers back again, putting any backing tape into the paper bag along with the latex gloves. Chris took the bag and walked back to a ring of stones where many a barbeque had previously been held and set fire to the bag whilst Peter put the back seats in order, removed the plastic sheet from the floor area on which the aircraft had rested, replaced the tax disc and changed out of his casual outerwear and trainers into a business suit and shoes. His clothing and trainers went into a small empty suitcase, as did those of Chris after he returned from the small fire.

The final two hundred kilometres to Madrid they covered easily despite stopping twice, the first time to smash the remote controls to pieces with a hammer brought along for the purpose which, after the parts were scattered, also went into the suitcase with the discarded clothes. The German number plates were buried separately, one on either side of the deserted stretch of highway. The second stop was simply for fuel, but where the hammer was left at the pump with petrol splashed over the head and shaft. The small camouflage sheet, plastic load area cover and clothes they had worn would disappear in Madrid after which there would be nothing so much as a tyre mark to link them to the blasts at Pedro Abad.

Their Madrid hotel was comfortable and the meeting, which was little more than a courtesy visit, straightforward. There was much mention of the explosions at Pedro Abad on the televisions in their rooms with both CNN and the BBC World Service speculating wildly. Security services said little except to confirm an investigation was already under way. However, in the bars and restaurants where conversations could be overheard most Spaniards appeared to be enthusing about the death and destruction brought to the Muslims four years to the day since the Madrid train bombings which had taken one hundred and ninety one lives.

Despite the comfort of the hotel and the obvious pleasure with which the Spanish NJF staff greeted them, neither man enjoyed Madrid, both finding it boring, uninspiring and hugely overrated. The E05 north was much more to their liking as the BMW virtually flew along the dual carriageway on their first two hundred kilometre leg to Burgos. There they picked up the motorway which would take them, via Bilbao, to the border at Irun, where they returned to the E05, now the Autoroute de la Cote Basque, and passed Biarritz and Bayonne as they made their way north to Bordeaux. Here the road skirted the city anticlockwise before it crossed the Garonne and Dordogne, becoming the Autoroute L'Aquitaine, which then ran parallel with the mighty Gironde estuary as it flowed back and forth along its sixty kilometre course to meet the Atlantic at Royan.

By now both men were fatigued, and weary of the driving involved, wanting nothing more than to get home and relax. However cover was everything, and they had one last meeting at what was arguably the most beautiful of all of France's seaside towns and cities, La Rochelle. For Peter the visit was always going to be a little painful, a reminder of the life he might have had if only they had taken a different train on the day of the tube bombings, as La Rochelle was to have been the first major stop planned on the honeymoon he and Tammy never started. Before the explosions it had long been a place they both wanted to visit but, much as he enjoyed the company of the hard man from Yorkshire, he knew he would have regrets and it would bring back the memories of that dreadful event. The up-side was at least they should hear how many of the bastards they had taken out at Pedro Abad, although it could never be enough. The news reports the previous evening, so soon after the attack, proved to be quite naturally contradictory and confusing. An extra day should have provided journalists with far more information.

The operation against the mosque was carefully considered, practiced and executed. They had chosen to carry out a daylight operation because it was unavoidable, despite adding to the risk factor. However, well planned as the attack was, there remained a tiny element of doubt and a small nagging voice asking if they had overlooked any minor detail which may later provide the slightest lead. They had not.

They spent two nights in La Rochelle, which lived up to all Peter had expected of it. Their hotel was well appointed in the old town just off the old harbour, and was comfortable in the extreme. The exploratory meeting went well, and very much along the lines of Lyon. Set on the coast, half way between Bordeaux and Nantes, the ancient vibrant city had a buoyant economy, based very much on tourism, providing a playground for the wealthy with the old port constantly filled with expensive yachts and huge motor cruisers. However the wealth was somewhat localised, mostly to be found within the area behind the city walls. The picturesque Vieux Port was the beating heart of the city, lined with seafood restaurants, packed in summer with the wealthy and the beautiful. The surrounding area, full of history, was very rural and, to the north, covered with small canals laid out almost on a grid pattern and very popular for inland boating over a large marshy area known as the Venise Verte.

Jack Bryant had scheduled the La Rochelle meeting to take place after the Pedro Abad mosque attack because, as he had pointed out, it would not do to be seen running away from Spain with their tails between their legs following such a high profile start and after the bombing. Unlikely though it was an investigative journalist may just speculate as to the speed of their withdrawal. To hold another high profile pre-scheduled meeting two days after such an event really did not fit the profile of those engaged in a covert operation. Once again it was his every intention to hide Peter and Chris under the full glare of media interest and, if they were to build the complexes under discussion La Rochelle would be another outstanding location.

Saturday saw the two military men finally heading for home. Travelling via Nantes and Rennes they made it to the port of St Malo by the early evening and, after parking the BMW in one of the dockside boarding lanes, wandered into the old walled town for a decent meal and several much needed beers before boarding Brittany Ferries Mont St Michel ready for its twenty-two hundred hour sailing.

On return the car was professionally cleaned before going to auction. It was replaced by another which exactly resembled the first. Operation Sandy had in every way been successfully completed without loss or detection. A short break followed for both men. Chris was then once more despatched to lands afar with a list of required items and suppliers. Peter was also then to jet away to another land in the hope of obtaining an essential need.

Sixteen

For a professional pilot it can be as difficult to be flown by another pilot as it is for a professional driver to be driven by someone else. Especially if the person behind the controls is deemed to be less deft with those controls than they should be by the passenger, even if the thoughts are not conscious or intended. So it was for Peter Parfitt as the British Airways Boeing 747, known around the world as the Jumbo Jet, hit the runway at Johannesburg just a little harder than it should have done, triggering a stream of semi-conscious thoughts about angles of decent, speed and power. It was unusual for Peter to be sitting in the passenger section for the trip down from London, although he had done it before, and almost unheard of for him to be travelling anything but South Africa Airways.

There was no need for any form of subterfuge on his part. Any of the agencies of various governments who may later look for either patterns or something out of the ordinary would find nothing unusual about his movements by air to and from South Africa. After all, he owned a property there and had long term interests in the country. The only thing in any way slightly out of the ordinary was his choice of carrier. It would never be questioned, but if it were he could tell the truth, or his version of it. Had he flown SAA he would have known all the crew. Many would have previously crewed for him. He didn't want to be asked many painful questions about what had happened to him, or what had happened to Tammy.

His passport and visa were in order, which enabled him to clear passport control with all the ease of a returning resident. He collected his two bags from the busy carousel and walked out of the baggage hall, through customs control and into the teeming ranks of the arrivals hall. Having negotiated the customary wall of overly keen representatives and generally stupid relatives he made his way to car hire where he had pre-booked exactly the car he wanted based on his knowledge of the country and the terrain he would be crossing. Paperwork was duly signed and Peter was given the numbered location of the car, which he found and carried out the customary bodywork checks before driving off.

He had ordered a white five door Volkswagen Golf with a diesel engine and air conditioning. The white was to reflect the heat of the African sun. Experience had taught him for his style of driving front wheel drive cars handled much better over the gravelled surfaces and dirt tracks he knew he would have to use on many occasions throughout the trip. The diesel engine helped with the torque it produced, especially at low revs on loose surfaces, but was mainly wanted for the extra range the fuel gave, because there were to be many long drives without conveniently spaced filling stations with the tasks ahead. The car was relatively new with less than ten thousand kilometres on the clock, the tyres showed no damage, neither did the bodywork and the windscreen was free of chips, quite remarkable for an African car. Finally he had wanted a European car, preferably German engineered or designed. The Golf suited him admirably.

He headed north from the airport, avoiding Johannesburg, the largest settlement of man in sub-Saharan Africa and the murder capital of the world, but didn't join the motorway, which enabled him to stop in Kempton Park where he found a telephone kiosk and made a local call. After returning to his car he headed north to Pretoria where he had a room booked for the night at the Holiday Inn Crowne Plaza. Parfitt could have stayed in Johannesburg, but he hated the place, whereas fifty kilometres away lay Pretoria, and the two cities were as different as chalk and cheese. Johannesburg was big, loud, uncouth, aggressive and dangerous, a most uncomfortable city. Pretoria was noted for its stately, historic homes, its parks and gardens with their splendid wealth of indigenous flora, was a centre of research and learning, and was home to the largest correspondence university in the world, Unisa. It was a city of lofty buildings and tall jacaranda trees, and was the administrative centre of the country, comfortable and welcoming.

His room was also comfortable though lacking in character, not that character was in any way a requirement. The position was perfect for him, in the centre of the south of town, near to the Union Buildings of the country's government, and only two blocks away from the State Theatre and Opera House where he planned to go that night, as it would probably be his last chance at a bit of culture for some time. He left his larger bag just inside the door to the room and placed the smaller on the room's built-in chest of drawers, opening it as he did so but taking nothing from it. He kicked off his shoes and lay fully dressed on the bed. He was moderately surprised to discover he had found the flight more tiring as a passenger than he had when sat up front in the driving seat. He dozed off but the telephone woke him with a jolt, and he came around feeling somewhat disorientated for a moment. He collected his thoughts, realised where he was, and picked up the handset. It was reception ringing to inform him there was a gentleman in the lobby waiting to see him who claimed to have an appointment. Peter put on his shoes and headed for reception.

Ruan van Heerden was a tall, wide-shouldered, fit and rugged looking man, with a thick crop of strawberry blond hair and eyebrows to match. He looked every inch exactly what he was, a Boer of Dutch extraction, and he was every bit as fit as he looked. As a Boer, he and Parfitt should have hated one another instinctively, as their ideological backgrounds were simply poles apart. Completely contrary to that, and to all the unwritten rules, they had found themselves each liking the other from the first moment they met. Only two years younger than Peter, their first encounter had occurred when van Heerden was assigned as Parfitt's co-pilot, on what was van Heerden's first flight into London. Although they were introduced beforehand the flight sealed an excellent working relationship which lasted for years, ending only with van Heerden's promotion, although the personal friendship continued unabated.

Raised to a traditional Boer family with values predating the Boer Wars and going back to the days of the Great Trek, van Heerden was brought up on the family farm to the south west of the town of Magaliesburg near Krugersdorp which had, during his childhood, been in the Transvaal state, but was now in the new province of Gauteng, and was west of Johannesburg. Traditional in his case meant long hours of hard work toiling in the fields alongside black workers, taking his schooling seriously and attending church, the Dutch Reformed Church, every Sunday, where the Boers used only the 1933-53 translation of the Afrikaans Bible, never the "New Living Translation", and to bow his head before the Voortrekker Monument. Farm life had never been the life he wanted and to avoid the loss of choice which went with compulsory military service he had joined the South African Air Force and eventually flown. After what he had regarded as the destruction of his country in the early nineties he joined SAA, later to fly the big busses with Parfitt.

To the British the Boers often appear a difficult, stubborn and deeply conservative people, rooted in the past, diametrically opposed to any form of change, and full of brooding hatred for the world around them which has treated them so unfairly, especially the British, and of the British the English in particular. To the Boers the British (English) were, indeed are, greedy, underhanded and devious with no care or understanding of the lands and people they conqueror and subjugate in an ever increasing lust and desire for power, rewards and profit, all of which were the worse attributes of the tyrannies of empire. To most there is no middle ground, but to those few who find it, the rewards gained in the understanding of each others cultures are rich indeed.

So it was for a very English Peter Parfitt and an equally Boer Ruan van Heerden, thrown together by a similar love of flying and by major political and cultural changes in their respective countries. Parfitt's love of the country which was South Africa was obvious and, to a Boer, unusual in an Englishman. Once on British soil van Heerden warmed to the ancient history, culture, pageantry, pomp and ceremony he was shown, and came to a much deeper understanding of the roots of the people his history had constantly encouraged him to despise. A friendship which originally started from a mere two commonalities grew as the men continued to find subjects and activities they both enjoyed. Although Parfitt would never be Boer and van Heerden would never be English both cast off the differences of their cultural backgrounds and through the many hours they sat next to one another forged a deep and meaningful relationship. Into that forging went another of the more important of all human qualities – trust. An undeclared but implicit all encompassing trust which is only ever found between males, and of those males usually only warriors. A trust on which their lives and the lives of all they hold dear can so easily depend.

During their many flights through the night Ruan had on occasions discussed the history, future, and plight of the Boer and Afrikaner peoples, whom previously Parfitt had not even realised were different. The Boers sought their own homeland in which they could be independent and follow an ongoing policy of self determination. They had participated in the Great Trek and fought in the Anglo-Boer Wars. They saw the Covenant made with God by the Voortrekkers before the Battle of Blood River as binding and to be celebrated. The Day of the Vow, the sixteenth of December, they wished to keep as a holy day. They fully embraced capitalism as their general policy of economics and utterly opposed any form of communism.

The Boers felt the empty lands their forefathers settled and farmed generations before had been taken from them, not as some form of restitution, but to assuage the black peoples of the world for the slavery which took place between the north western and central parts of Africa and Europe and the fledgling America. A trade in which they took no part, and in many cases was further removed from them geographically than it was from America. Apartheid, in nature if not in name, had then been introduced to Southern Africa by the British Empire in order to encourage the separate development of the white and non-white peoples who existed in the country, but who later withdrew their support of the system without doing anything to put an alternative in place. The Boers and Afrikaners were by then the long established white tribe of Africa who had developed their own language and culture. They strongly believed they had a right to remain on the land they had irrigated and cultivated, and had done so long before the arrival of migrating black tribes from their north and east. They, the white African people, belonged to this land and if they could not have all they had settled and farmed, then at least they should be allowed a part of it.

To that end in the late 1980s Professor Carel Boshoff had formed the Afrikaner-Vryheidstigting, generally known as Avstig (Afrikaner Freedom Foundation). Avstig proposed a Volkstaat – People's state – in what had become the Northern Cape Province in a region which was largely rural and minimally developed. In 1991 Avstig bought the town of Orania and turned it into a model Volkstaat, unique among South African towns in being the only all-Afrikaner enclave in Africa. Orania is situated along the Orange River where the three provinces of Northern Cape, Eastern Cape, and Free State all but intersect in the arid Karoo region of the Northern Cape Province, and became the first existing realisation of the Volkstaat concept. According to Ruan the purpose of Orania was to create a town where the preservation of Afrikanerdom's cultural heritage was strictly observed and Afrikaner self reliance was an actual practice, not just an idea. All jobs, from management to manual labour, were to be filled by Afrikaners only. Non-Afrikaner workers are not permitted. In time it was hoped it would grow and eventually secede from South Africa.

Peter thought it may be necessary to meet some of the influential Boers if his initial plan did not work out, but it was not to Orania he first wished to go. His intention, if he could get the introduction and be received, was first to stop near Ventersdorp, and there to meet the man they called 'The Leader', Eugène Ney Terre'Blanche, one of the founders and the leader of the AWB, Afrikaner Weerstandsbeweging, or Afrikaner Resistance Movement.

For Parfitt it was in many ways a difficult situation to be placed in as his entire life was built around opposing any regime which stood for principles and policies in any way similar to those of the AWB. He had much more than a grudging respect for the hard men and women of the farming communities who had tamed such a wild and savage land, and deeply felt the condemnation heaped upon them by the outside world, who knew nothing of the salient facts, to be a fundamental wrong in itself. However he could not approve of some of the tactics and rhetoric of the AWB in general or Terre'Blanche in particular. He understood if the Boer and Afrikaner people were to be heard then they needed someone who was both a firebrand and a good orator, lest they be crushed under foot by well intentioned but appallingly badly informed international do-gooders. That aside some of the previous actions, policies and statements were plainly wrong at the most elementary level, and would never gain his endorsement, no matter how much their help was needed.

Ruan van Heerden's family were Boers, strongly agreed with much the AWB stood for, and the family were generally, by tradition, long term supporters of Terre'Blanche, who was known to them on a personal level. The AWB had managed to motivate thousands of Boers and Afrikaners and had brought them together in the seeking of a common goal despite their differences, or their Swastika styled flag with its three sevens which had rightly attracted the contempt and condemnation of the outside world. Peter hoped Ruan could affect an introduction because the help he needed was not from the Boers, but from the Afrikaners and, unlike many of the Boers, Terre'Blanche had much influence with the Afrikaners to the west.

Ruan had once told Peter the background and differences between Boer and Afrikaner, and had explained, "Since the Anglo-Boer war the term 'Boervolk' has rarely been used because of an attempt to assimilate the Boervolk with the Afrikaners. The reason why some Boers still referred to themselves as 'Afrikaners' is because both ethnic groups speak the same language – Afrikaans. However many 'Boers' view the term 'Afrikaner' as an artificial label which undermines our history and culture, thereby turning 'Boer' accomplishments into 'Afrikaner' accomplishments. Many believe the Western-Cape based Afrikaners, whose ancestors trekked neither eastwards nor northwards, took advantage of the republican Boers' abject poverty following the Anglo-Boer War, later attempting to assimilate the Boers under a then new politically based cultural banner as Afrikaners. Over time it became increasingly clear to many Boers the differences between our two ethnic groups were unbridgeable, certainly for the foreseeable future, and that the Boervolk remain a distinct cultural group."

The conversation came rushing back to Peter as he crossed the lobby towards the grinning Boer. The two friends shook hands warmly. It was almost three years since they had last met and, quite apart from what Peter had to ask, there was a lot of catching up to do, but the lobby was not the place to do it.

"Have you had lunch yet?" Peter asked.

"Sus man. Fat chance you gave me for that with your order to get up here! Anyone would think you were still in the driving seat," Ruan joked with his friend. "I don't know what you would like to eat, but if you are happy with a huge choice there is a great roadhouse a couple of blocks over, and they do the best Surf 'n' Turf burger you'll ever eat."

"That sounds good to me," Peter responded. "It's been a while since I ate proper food under a cloudless sky. Your car or mine?"

Ruan drove them to the roadhouse and parked under the hanging stretched out canvases with his car windows down, maximising on the cool air the shade would provide for the car. They picked up menus, glancing both at them and the specials written on the wall, all one hundred and fifty plus of them.

"You know, Ruan, I've missed this kind of thing. This is what this land is all about, abundant food of ridiculously good quality, wonderful surroundings and a climate that puts Greece and Spain to shame. Moreover we will both eat huge portions for less than it would cost me for a burger and fries at Heathrow. God I miss this land," Peter repeated himself as they seated themselves at a table whose cloth was gently flapping in the light breeze. The hovering waiter arrived as soon as they comfortably seated themselves, took their order and promptly returned with two glasses of bubbling yellow Castle Lager, in glasses already dripping condensation.

They made small talk until the plate size burgers arrived and a large bowl of fries was placed between them, along with a bowl of salad. The waiter then left them and walked back to a shaded area out of earshot where he was instantly laughing and joking with a dozen or so others, but could keep his eye on his charges throughout. Africa – thought Parfitt – perfect!

Small talk over Parfitt's voice took on a serious note as he started to speak. "Ruan, I asked you to come up because I need to ask you a favour. I checked your schedules and waited until I knew you would be home before flying over, so I am deeply appreciative of your coming out with no notice and without any questions asked."

"This has to be something important man. And something very confidential if you have flown down here to talk rather than telephoning. Peter, you have to know I'll do anything I possibly can to help you, just as I know you would for me. I heard about Tammy, and I can't tell you how sorry I am. I have to assume this visit is in some way related." Ruan responded, demonstrating an instinctive intelligence.

"Thanks. I see you haven't become stupid in your old age," Peter joked, before continuing far more seriously, "Look Ruan, this is a bit difficult. I would love to be totally open with you, especially in view of what I have to ask, but there are certain considerations, certain lines I cannot cross. Please do not view this as a trust issue. I do not mean this in any way disrespectfully, but it is very much a need to know matter. We've both had military training, so I know you'll understand security issues. The problem I have is not so much with you but with what I have to ask of you without giving you any information to go on. Suffice to say I certainly see what I am asking for as extremely serious.

"Well you've got full marks for melodrama, man," Ruan said with the ghost of a smile.

"Yeah, I guess it does come across as a bit cloak and dagger – so let me try to explain. It is extremely cloak and dagger! No one who isn't directly involved can ever know of this conversation, let alone the content, and I will not inform you of any more than I have to for your own security. The less you know the better for you, from all sorts of standpoints. I thought long and hard before I approached you as I didn't want to draw you in, and I still refuse to – but I need your help. However by speaking to you on the subject I make you another link in a chain, and that chain has to be as short as possible," Parfitt attempted to explain.

"Peter. You and I have sat next to one another for endless hours discussing all the problems of the world. You know me, and you know my background just as I know yours. The lady I know you loved above all else in this world has been badly hurt by people I think of as less than human. I can only assume that has some bearing! If you want something of me you only have to ask it, which you already know. You do not have to protect me or try to cushion me. Ask of me what it is you want and I will do all I can to make it so for you. If you cannot explain why, so be it, I will still do all I can. You must know this because I know you would do the same for me, but also because if you did not feel so you would not have flown down here and we would not be discussing this now. Tell me what it is you want." Ruan was becoming a little frustrated. He liked this man and understood him, but this silly English thing about not coming to the point was alien to his culture. Parfitt obviously had something which was troubling him deeply, but the Boer in Ruan could not understand the British bullshit and or English reserve. If he had something to say or to ask, then say it or ask it.

Peter gathered himself. "Ruan, you once told me your family has a bond with Terre'Blanche. I need to talk with him. I need to ask something of him. I, more precisely, some friends of mine and I, need something which flies in the face of all I have previously held dear. We need a piece of land on which to test something, and the something is not the sort of thing which can be tested or seen by anyone else. We need an area of the Western Cape were we can test munitions, a large tract of land where we can experiment, adapt and improve a small warhead without fear of what we are doing ever reaching the outside world. We are not a terrorist cell in the accepted sense or in everyday terminology, but we are a small group of people who wish to strike back against those who wish to undermine and destroy our culture. You Boers, more than anyone else in the world, should understand that, which is why we are now having this conversation, most of which can never be revealed or repeated. Yes, you are right! This has got something to do with Tammy. I cannot live with what has been done to her without feeling the need for retribution and that retribution must both punish them and satisfy us. Again I know you will understand that."

There was a short pause, which seemed to drag out because of the enormity of what Parfitt had just said and asked. It was some twenty seconds before Ruan spoke, but it seemed much longer. "Peter, as a Boer I understand all you have just said. As a man I completely understand and I am sure would wish to react in the same way. As your friend I will help you with all I can do without any need for explanation, but also as your friend I would question this – Peter, what have you got yourself into? In all the time I've known you I've had nothing but respect for you. You've always been the most broad minded man I've ever met, so accepting and understanding of others, no matter who they are, what they are, or where they are from. You, and you alone, taught me to open my eyes and see the world in a very different light, almost, and I know it is a cliché, but almost to embrace the brotherhood that is man. Yet now you ask me to help you with a project which can only lead to you making war on man. Of course I will help you, and help you as fully as I can, but I question is this the real you?"

"Ruan, what I am about to tell you I have never before discussed with anyone. Not to the counsellors, not to friends and not even to the people I'm now associated with, save one, a soldier, and even to him only in part. I was with Tammy on the train when the bomb went off. It was fucking carnage in there. It was like a madman had got loose in a slaughterhouse with a chain saw. I was completely unhurt, but Tammy was ripped to pieces. Now you met Tammy. I loved her Ruan, and still do. She was the most beautiful woman I've ever known. She had the body of an angel, but it didn't end there. She had, and still has, an inner beauty and strength of spirit. I loved her and respected her, and the respect has grown since the bomb. But I can never forget her as she was. And I will never forget picking up her severed body parts or trying to bind parts back on her. She should have died Ruan! But she didn't. She fought it. She survived. But every day I see her and see the scars on her body, that once beautiful body, every time she has to put her teeth in, every time I help her strap her false arm on, and her leg, and watch her try to walk, I hate them. I fucking hate every one of them. And I want to see them die! Not just one or two, but tens of thousands! And every time I see her fall and try to pull herself back to her broken foot and plastic leg with her only remaining arm I want to kill more! I want to see their entire civilization utterly destroyed for all time so no other Tammy will ever have to endure the living hell mine goes through every minute of every day! I am not the broad minded person I used to be, and I never will be again! It doesn't go away, it doesn't dissipate. Every day, every time she fails to hear me because I am on her deaf side, every time I watch her try to brush her hair with her remaining hand, to cover the scars on her face and neck, I hate them afresh, and each and every time I do, I hate them more! Every time I have to dress the blistered and bloodied stump of what was once a beautiful leg I want to see Muslims die! Every night when she takes her prosthetic limbs off, and every morning when she straps them back on I want to take the lives of an entire community! My beautiful, kind, passionate, caring woman has been mutilated beyond description without reason. I cannot live with that without requital. It is a question of honour and a matter of duty. It will be repaid, and it will be repaid with interest, a lot of interest!"

Ruan van Heerden stopped eating whilst Peter spoke. His appetite for food had completely evaporated. Like most others he had never once thought about the aftermath to such events as the explosion which had devastated his friend's life. He was of course terribly sorry for both Parfitt and Tammy when he heard the news, and happy for both when he later heard of Tammy's survival, but had never considered the consequences for the once beautiful woman, or for his friend. What Peter described and the passion with which he had spoken touched a part of Ruan's soul and from that moment on neither the man nor the Boer in him would have let him walk away. Had Parfitt then asked Ruan van Heerden would have happily gone to war in support of his friend, but that was not what he was being asked to do. "What is it you want of me Peter?" van Heerden asked gently. "I will gladly do all that is asked and more besides, anything I possibly can!"

"I know the AWB was recently re-activated, and I know there is a strong Afrikaner following from across the country." Peter said. "The reason I wish to contact Terre'Blanche is because of his possible contacts within a community which knows how to keep its mouth shut, and has done so for generations. I cannot approach him directly because I would never get to see him, or even if I did I would not be listened to. As I said we need a large tract of land in a deserted area of the Western Cape. The area we have in mind is around a very small town called Granaatboskolk, which is north east of Brandvlei and east of Springbok. Basically we need somewhere flat where we can practice certain skills, train, test some equipment, and carry out a few experiments. I don't want to tell you more as I don't want to compromise you, but I realise that'll make it difficult for you as you'll have to ask on my behalf without even being able to use some of the things we have already discussed. Now - what we need is a building, a barn, which is covered from any form of surveillance and would sleep up to ten men, although I do not envisage there ever being more than six there, if that. It has to be in a deserted area, which of course Granaatboskolk is, but where those, in the unlikely event they ever did see anything, would keep the information to themselves for life. Now it could well be

Terre'Blanche is being watched by some security force or other, so I could never be seen with him but, given your background and ties, it may not seem in any way unnatural for him to visit your farm, and if your family did not object, I could be there. I cannot visit Ventersdorp or at any time be seen with him. One wrong photograph in the hands of decent security forces and questions could be raised which may lead to all I am doing collapsing, and we cannot afford such a thing.

"In addition to all of that we also need something else, which may be slightly more difficult. Eventually we will need to ship something out of the country. It will not be a great deal and we'll have a vessel, but we'll need to load the equipment without a lot of questions being asked. The equipment will seem quite innocent to the casual observer, but we would still rather load it somewhere where bills of lading do not exist and where any dockworkers know not to pry. It would help if some form of cover story could be circulated which was both plausible and innocuous. We would prefer to use Port Nolloth to the west north west of Springbok, and to load directly off the jetty there.

"Finally we realise there may be no desire to help us, after all we are British, and I do understand your people have long memories, but we would be prepared to help you in return. I know how badly both Boers and Afrikaners have been hurt economically by the changes which have taken place in this land, how unemployment for your peoples has risen by the greatest percentage of all groups in South Africa, and that much money will be needed to purchase more land if a proper working Volkstaat is ever to exist. We can help provide such money and, when our operation is over and the dust has settled, we would put in place an enterprise which would generate its own wealth within your community. I may be British and my nation's forefathers treated yours appallingly, but I am not them, and those I speak for will fully honour every word of what we agree, and on that Ruan I give you my own personal word."

"You know my people well Peter. It is true we will never forgive you for Kitchener's scorched earth policy or the concentration camps and the unnecessary suffering and death of our womenfolk and children. But in this case those memories may work in your favour." Ruan replied, then fell silent for over a minute whilst he thought things over. "There is an additional small problem you have not mentioned, which may seem silly, but to the man in question it is important. Terre'Blanche speaks English but he views it as the language of the oppressors of our people, distrusts it, and avoids its use at all times. The things you ask are possible, and I'm sure a meeting can be arranged along the lines you suggest, but although you may prefer otherwise I think you'll find he insists on my presence, as your friend, as mediator, and as interpreter if there are any points he 'struggles' to understand. Peter, in view of the circumstances and the depth of the subject this will sound crass, but I will be asked, how much money are you talking about?"

"Money is not really a consideration." Peter responded somewhat absently.

"Peter, money is always a consideration!" Ruan chuckled despite the seriousness of the topic. "If you give me the figure I'll put it forward. It could well help. At one stage the AWB was reasonably well supported and funded, but time and court cases have taken their toll. Funding at the moment would be both useful and appreciated I'm sure, but again I need some sort of figure to put before them."

"Well as I said, money isn't really a consideration." Peter repeated. "But I do see your point. I was thinking something in the region of fifty million rand."

"My God man! Where on earth are you going to find money like that? Are you sure you don't mean five million? Even that's a huge amount here" Ruan was shocked.

"Ruan, let me explain one thing to you. At the danger of sounding like a stuck record I will repeat, money is not a consideration. That's not to say I'll countenance it being thrown around like confetti, but we're serious. We need the use of the land and feel we should help those who are prepared to help us." Peter explained.

"Well just out of interest, and strictly between us, what sort of funding do you have available to you?" Ruan was truly intrigued.

"In normal terminology it is almost limitless." Peter answered.

"What are we talking – millions?" Ruan asked in a somewhat hushed voice.

"Billions." Peter again answered in a wholly matter of fact manner.

"Rand?"

"Pounds."

As the figures slowly registered with Ruan the implications followed. They were talking figures greater than several nations GDP.

"Oh my God Peter – what have you got yourself into man? I'll see what I can do to arrange a meeting. Frankly I'm sure he'll go for it, but I certainly will not mention several things, especially your funding, because he would run a mile. Peter, you buy entire African nations for that sort of money, not just rent strips of land!"

Their conversation and meeting eventually ended and van Heerden drove back to his family's farm after returning Parfitt to his hotel, where he added an extra night to his room booking. They had made arrangements for Peter to call from a public phone late the following afternoon. Nothing would be known much before then, but by the middle part of the afternoon an answer should have been forthcoming and, with luck, the answer would be positive. Peter followed his earlier plan for the night, enjoyed an early evening meal and went to the State Theatre and Opera House where he thoroughly enjoyed the production of a play by a young and upcoming Afrikaans playwright, before once more making his way back to his hotel, phoning to check on Tammy, and retiring relatively early.

The next morning, with time to kill, he set about revisiting a city he had not spent quality time in for several years, and he wanted to do something about that as Pretoria was a city he was very fond of. Mainly due to its significance he drove out to view the Voortrekker Monument on Monument Hill, about four miles from the centre, which commemorates the pioneers of the Great Trek of 1830. Designed by the architect Gerard Moerdijk the huge granite structure stands on a base forty meters square and is built to a height of forty meters. It was designed as a 'monument that would stand a thousand years to describe the history and meaning of the Great Trek to its descendants'.

Peter entered the monument through a black gate fashioned from wrought iron and found himself inside a large circle of wagons drawn by oxen and carved from granite. There were sixty-four laagered wagons, one for each of those which took part in the Battle of Blood River, one of the most defining moments of the history of Southern Africa, and in essence the moment when a people came of age. Lost in reverie Parfitt was struck by the parallels of the struggle the Boers had endured with the Zulu and the campaign in which he was now engaged.

He felt that as with the Boers his people too had extended the hand of friendship to those of another creed and culture and, just as the Zulus had done, the Muslims had destroyed all trust by turning on the unprotected in a despicable act of barbarism and betrayal. Not unlike the Boers their small force would take the fight back to the land of those who backed the perpetrators and, like the Zulu, the Muslims would be punished and would die in great numbers. His people would not go on to forge a nation, as his nation had already stood for centuries, but their actions could well help to start to cleanse the nation of the various nests of vipers which misguided acts of kindness and naïve generosity had encouraged to grow and fester.

Ruan van Heerden himself answered the telephone on the third ring. Peter spoke without introducing himself. Jack Bryant had relentlessly impressed upon all of them the need for awareness relating to security issues when using any form of communication. Avoid anything but face to face wherever possible, always use public phones, always keep it short, never give specifics. "Hi Ruan, I just wondered if the offer of a bed for the night still stood?" Peter asked.

"Ja, man, of course it does. If you could make it to us by late morning we could all have lunch together. I understand you are then going on to the Cape. It will be good to see you. We can catch up, talk and make plans." Van Heerden answered somewhat cryptically, as Parfitt had explained the need to keep all conversations low key. In this particular case if any of the world's security forces were monitoring the conversation between two old friends about a bed for the night and did check up for any reason, identifying Parfitt, they would find no more than two old friends who had flown together for years. Terre' Blanche's presence would of course complicate that innocent scenario but, innocent or not, communication security was a good habit to get into, and to keep to.

The interesting point was the news had been positive. It would seem Ruan had actually progressed things further than Parfitt had envisaged. So Terre'Blanche had agreed to meet as quickly as lunchtime the following day – and he was going on to the Cape. Hopefully that could only mean there was a contact in the area around Granaatboskolk, but it was pointless guessing. Late morning for lunch meant he had to get there beforehand as he must be the first to arrive. He could not afford to be seen in the company of the man so many around the world despised and reviled, and who could often be followed by a media circus as well as the security forces. Peter realised it would pay him to take the drive down to Magaliesburg to check out van Heerden's farm, as he had never been there before despite the years he had flown with Ruan. It would be foolish to arrive the following morning and have to drive around looking for it, so he would use the time productively and check it out straight away.

From where he was in Pretoria there were two reasonable options, so he decided to go by one and return by the other in order to ascertain which to take the following morning. He drove west out past Hartbeespoort Dam, then followed the valley road between Magaliesberg and the Witwatersberg mountains, eventually dropping into the town of Magaliesberg from where the farm was clearly signposted. The region was beautiful with the backdrop of mountains, valleys, rivers and native woodland.

The van Heerden family had lived in the area for nearly a hundred and fifty years. Janni van Heerden had settled in the valley, in which three of their now five large family homes still stood, eight generations earlier. Over time the family's fortunes had yo-yoed, but despite the changing fortunes of history additional land had constantly been acquired along with supporting barns and outbuildings. Parfitt knew the family now owned two large working farms, with ground totalling something over a thousand hectares. Despite the acquisition of the second farm the family continued to live in the main house of the original.

The five hundred and sixty hectare farm with its three large family homes was situated twelve minutes drive outside the town and was set back about four hundred yards from the road. The property consisted of three homes; the main one of which was a large house and looked to have about six bedrooms. The other two were smaller, each with three bedrooms, all had large front and rear "stoepes" or porches, and all three homes enjoyed lawned gardens and tall shady trees. The numerous outbuildings appeared to include an implement and tractor shed, carports and what appeared to be a laundry. There were workshops, single and family labourer's quarters, about fifty calf-rearing pens, good cattle handling facilities, kraals and sheep sheds, plus an old dairy building. The farm ran mixed dry crops alongside mainly livestock farming. There looked to be something in the region of three hundred beef cattle and over a hundred sheep on the farm, which was divided into several grazing camps and a large kraal, and there were also plantings of maize and sunflower on the land. All in all it had the appearance of a well run and well managed lucrative operation which, had it been sited in south of England, would have been worth a fortune.

He had found it and seen it, and would be able to park the hire car out of sight in the implement shed and cross to the main house without being seen from the road. Secrecy was all, and in this case it would be relatively easy to maintain. He considered the drive there to have been well worth the effort as he drove back to Pretoria via the N14 and past the south of the Sterkfontein Caves, where the remains of the earliest species of primitive man known today were once discovered. With all the region's turbulent and violent recent history it seemed strange to think of the earliest proto-hominids freely roaming those ancient lands whilst living in total harmony with nature, two million years earlier. Especially so when considered alongside the reason he was now on that land, and how out of harmony with nature his objectives were!

Having enjoyed a very good nights sleep Peter checked out of his hotel without taking breakfast as he knew from experience it was best to turn up to a Boer's table hungry. He took the far more interesting northern route to the van Heerden property, parked his car out of sight as he had intended, and was inside the main residence before eleven in the morning. Ruan met him at the door personally, and walked him through to the very large but comfortable family room with huge sliding windows leading onto the stoep which in turn overlooked the sizeable shaded garden with the farmland behind. In the middle distance stood the mountains, providing a magnificent backdrop to a setting which was an incredible mixture of seemingly timeless European cultivation set against the typically harsh and unforgiving African landscape.

Terre'Blanche arrived with a small convoy of three vehicles just minutes after midday. The first car pulled away from the others as it arrived and followed the access road around and between the buildings, obviously a small reconnaissance task. Satisfied the driver parked it and the others pulled up alongside. Three black clad individuals emerged from each car and spread out, whilst the drivers remained within their vehicles. The so called Iron Guard, the inner circle. Again satisfied one returned and opened a rear door of the second car, and Eugene Terre'Blanche clambered awkwardly from its interior.

Conventionally Terre'Blanche warmly greeted his host first who, with Parfitt, had strode out to meet him.

"And you must be the man I have come to meet." Terre'Blanche said offering his hand to Parfitt and speaking in heavily accented English.

"Peter Parfitt. It is very good of you to see me, especially having done so at such short notice," Peter replied taking the hard dry hand.

"I would suggest we seat ourselves on the stoep," Ruan suggested. "Lunch will not be served for an hour, but I have drinks available and we can discuss things in general terms before we eat."

The three men arranged themselves around a substantially built table on the wide stoep. The Iron Guard were waved away and remained out of earshot but within sight as they flanked the property. Ruan explained he would have to serve them himself as he had ordered his family and servants from the house, but neither of his guests asked for anything more complicated than iced water.

None were there for small talk and all knew the issues. Terre'Blanche came to the point directly, speaking in English despite Ruan's explanation of his normal reluctance to do so.

"I understand you need a certain piece of land in the Cape. I would like you to tell me as much as you can about your requirements. Ruan has explained you cannot or will not tell me all that you need it for, but I want to know what damage will be done, how long you will be there, how many men you will wish to have accommodated and what services you require. I also need to know something of this vessel you wish to load at Port Nolloth, and I wish Ruan to be present as he can explain anything your language does not adequately cover. Afterwards we will discuss the cost."

Parfitt struggled not to smile at the reference to language. Terre'Blanche was obviously baiting him. It was a test. A minor one to be sure, but a test nonetheless! He ignored the bait and answered without preamble.

"As I'm sure Ruan explained we need a piece of land in a deserted area of the Western Cape. I'm also sure you already know the area we have in mind is around the town of Granaatboskolk. We wish to test something. As I told Ruan there is an outside possibility of ten men, although I cannot see how there would ever be more than six at any one time, and usually not more than four. We'll need somewhere undercover for them to sleep but it doesn't need to be of any quality. An electricity supply for power tools where we can work on our project would be useful but not essential as we can bring a generator or generators. However a large private outbuilding where we can park two vehicles and carry out the work we need to do is absolutely essential.

"In addition we need a weapon testing and firing range. The weapons we are using are 'clean'. Apart from a small number of minor holes, which we will fill in, there will be no real damage and certainly no lasting damage. We are definitely not using any form of biological or fissionable weapon. In fact the largest explosive we intend to test will not amount to anything bigger than a mortar shell. We would like to be there for some time, possibly as much as two months, and some of those there may have to leave and return whilst what we are doing progresses. We are prepared to generously compensate all those who help, especially those whose property we use. Above all else we wish to avoid any form of surveillance." Peter explained.

Terre'Blanche had seemed amused at the beginning and now said something in Afrikaans to Ruan who also smiled and then explained to Peter, who had understood nothing but the word Granaatboskolk.

"Peter, you refer to Granaatboskolk as a town. I've been told to explain to you it is not exactly a town. English doesn't have a word for it. If you called it a village you would be exaggerating the size as it is not big enough to be classed as a hamlet. It is apparently a collection of, we think, four dwellings along with some barns and workshops. It has no electricity, certainly no such thing as gas, and any water comes from bore holes. There is no shop or garage, and its nearest neighbour, Halfweg, a railway stop, is an even smaller place over twenty-five kilometres away. The nearest town is Loeriesfontein, some one hundred and twenty kilometres to the south, and even that isn't big enough to be considered a town by most standards. It is more than a little isolated and, if there is an agreement, you and your people would have to take in everything you needed, and take away everything, rubbish included, when you were finished. It was thought you had better understand the point before we proceed. Does it still suit your requirements?" Ruan asked him.

"It sounds even better than I already thought," Peter answered.

Terre'Blanche who had listened to this exchange grunted at Peter's answer, then again spoke, but this time far more clearly. He was known as a great orator and Peter knew the man was toying with him, probably checking for inconsistencies, faults and failings in his story.

"What exactly is it you wish to test, and whom will it be used against?" The AWB leader asked.

Although the question was anticipated he knew anything he said would be less than acceptable. "I'm afraid I am not permitted to answer that," Peter replied.

"You cannot or you will not?" Terre'Blanche probed.

"Simply put – both! I'm aware of the eventual target, but the entire project is secret, known only to those of us involved. We've no desire to expand upon that as to do so may ultimately compromise what we wish to do and we cannot allow that. I know you'll tell me you'll reveal nothing and realise it would be pointless to argue with you. However if you simply do not know you can never reveal anything, and frankly we wish to keep it that way. However I will say we're all of the opinion you would not disapprove of our mission." Peter vainly attempted to explain his position.

"Can you at least tell me who your target is not? Is it a Christian or European nation?" Terre'Blanche again pressed.

"I've already said we feel you would approve. From which you must draw your own conclusions, but I will not confirm or deny anything. I'll be a little more honest with you and hope it helps. We would like and appreciate your help. I'm here because I know Ruan, and was aware of the fact that he knew you. I've convinced the others I'm involved with to try this option first, but this isn't the only option. We simply couldn't afford not to have backups.

"We have two alternative sites, one in Western Australia and one in Utah. However this is our preferred location. It may well have proved possible to carry out what we wish to do without contacting you, but we considered that course of action short-sighted, as we may well need to call upon you for help, supplies or something similar in the future. To have bypassed you would have alienated you, and we do not wish to do that. I'll admit we don't share all of your ideals, but we're prepared to help you in the future and, I'll repeat, we're quite prepared to pay for what we now need, and pay well." Peter knew he was asking a lot without giving more information. He was also lying about the Utah option. That was ruled out at conception as being far too risky. Australia was a real possibility, but far less safe if anything was ever seen by so much as one single individual. No, the location they were really holding in reserve, their real second choice, was Namibia, but such information could not be revealed to Terre'Blanche as he was bound to have numerous contacts there.

There was silence whilst what was said was given due consideration. The silence was briefly broken as Ruan and Peter ripped the ring-pulls from the top of two cans of Castle Lager which Ruan had passed over. Terre'Blanche poured himself another glass of water before asking another question. "Would you consider one of my men going with you to oversee your operation, and make sure you only operate strictly within the terms of our agreement, if we were to agree?"

"Absolutely not!" Peter answered. "In fact we would want those living in the area to agree never to pry into our affairs and, if by chance they did see anything, never to reveal it to another living soul. On top of which we wish you to agree if ever you work out, after the event, what it is we've been involved with, and the operation we've carried out, you also will never reveal it to anyone. I had no intention of explaining any of this to Ruan, or speaking in front of him. Outside of those of us who are personally involved the two of you now have more information concerning the operation than anyone else on the planet. That fact alone scares each and every one of us involved, and scares us so much that without your acceptance and word that you will adhere to those conditions regarding what I have just asked, I am unable to proceed further."

Again there was silence whilst Peter's words were digested. Terre'Blanche eventually retorted, "You put me in a very difficult position. You want me to trust you implicitly yet come perilously close to insulting me by showing you do not trust me in return. If Ruan had not vouched for you in advance, and were we both not guests at his home, I would have had you thrown out of wherever we were physically. However you have been vouched for by a family whose integrity I will never question. I will think about what you have said whilst we eat and will give you an answer after that."

Parfitt would push it no further. Logic itself indicated Terre'Blanche to be keen to reach some form of agreement. Had it not been the case he would not have driven for over an hour with his entourage in tow the very day after he received the call. Money talked. It was as simple as that. Ruan signalled across to one of the other properties and two people arrived minutes later laden with hampers which they placed on the stoep before disappearing into the house, only to reappear and bustle around the table placing crockery and cutlery. When the places were suitably set the hampers were opened and a huge array of food was unloaded onto the table. There were perfectly cooked cold cuts of various meats, some of which Parfitt knew well, but some he did not recognise at all. Aside from the home grown beef there was ostrich, kudu, springbok and something Parfitt later discovered was crocodile. Bowls of tomatoes, cut lettuce and radishes abounded, as did homemade avocado dips and bowls of corn on the cob, along with all manner of speciality South African dishes and fruits, all of which surrounded the bottles of Cape wine from Franschhoek, Stellenbosch and Paarl, placed in the centre of the table.

As they ate they talked. Not about the subject of the meeting, but about matters of state, the ongoing problems with Zimbabwe and how it was beginning to affect South Africa to its detriment, and the overwhelming desire for an Afrikaner homeland. Terre'Blanche was a totally different character when seen sitting at the table of a fellow white man of Africa to the one portrayed by the western media. He came across as a true patriot, a man who cared deeply for his people and the land which they populated, and he was nothing like the gibbering idiot vested interests had the world believe. He explained to Parfitt how many Boers and Afrikaners could trace their ancestry back to a time before the first Europeans had ventured as far as the America's, yet Americans, a nation of people who had wantonly butchered their own aboriginal population, now wanted whites out of Africa. Would they even discuss giving America back to the North America Indians and leaving the country for good? Don't be ridiculous. Australia had also objected to the South African system, but they could afford to since they had systematically purged their land of their aborigines, denying education, medical care and property rights to those few who survived. He fundamentally disagreed with the unfairness of a system which vilified him and the whites of Africa, yet had supported Mugabe and worshipped Mandela, a convicted self confessed terrorist incarcerated in his day for planting bombs in shopping malls targeting women and children.

Parfitt found Terre'Blanche an interesting character and a man clearly well informed with regard his subject, and an ability to reiterate retained facts and information in a manner which the listener found fascinating. However there was the other side to the man which Peter knew about and was not comfortable with, mainly the seeming emulation of Germany's Nazi party. He could easily see Terre'Blanche's black clad Iron Guard strutting around in jackboots and, as for their flag and its resemblance of the swastika it typified all which Peter abhorred. Good lunch companion or not, and much as Parfitt strongly agreed with the acceptance of a white homeland in Southern Africa, there were things about the man's history which troubled him. However the reality of the situation was they needed him and, if they could enlist his help, his backing could prove to be hugely beneficial.

They finished eating despite the small mountain of food which was left on the table, and resumed their discussion. Terre'Blanche opened with a question which was in reality a statement, and caught Parfitt well off guard.

"You do not agree with some of my policies, ideals or politics, do you Peter?" he had asked, using Parfitt's given name for the first time. Parfitt was taken aback by both the question itself, and the familiar use of his name, but instinctively understood a decision of some sort had already been reached by the AWB leader. Somewhat to his consternation he did not have the first idea what the decision was.

"Frankly, no I don't," Parfitt replied truthfully. "I absolutely agree with a Boer Afrikaner homeland, but I believe the way you are going about trying to get it is self defeating. I'm sorry but I cannot agree with all you do."

For the first time since his arrival Terre'Blanche laughed. "Spoken like a true Boer. Ruan was right about you. You are an honest man. Most would have lied to me in the attempt to enlist my help. They would not have received it! You shall! I like to deal with honest men, those who will say what they mean despite the possible consequences. You will have my help, and I will ask no further questions as to your intentions. Now I will tell you what is possible, we will discuss the requirements for your vessel, and we will talk money."

Relief flooded Peter's system. Obtaining the land and help they needed in South Africa solved the single biggest problem of the entire project. For the next ninety minutes Parfitt and Terre'Blanche discussed the matter alone. Ruan understood he had done his part and his presence was no longer needed, so he personally tidied the table, took food to the AWB men then left them alone in discussion with no more than a supply of drinks. Terre'Blanche explained how although he personally had no contacts in Granaatboskolk the AWB stretched out a long way and those who lived in the tiny hamlet were Afrikaners. There would be no trouble enlisting their help. Nor would there be any problems at Port Nolloth where he did have contacts, and help there would be assured. Terre'Blanche had not been told by Ruan how much Peter was prepared to spend and, as a consequence, asked for substantially less than Peter had budgeted for. It was agreed the communities of both Granaatboskolk and Port Nolloth should benefit by a sum of five million rand each, approximately a third of a million pounds apiece. For the AWB as part of its funding, and for the help it would contribute Terre'Blanche wanted twenty-five million rand, and interestingly he wanted it paid into a numbered account in Euros as he had no trust of the rand, pound or US dollar. All in the deal cost a little under thirty-five million rand, two thirds of what he expected to pay, and much less than he would have been prepared to go to, had he been pushed.

Slightly before midday, three days, later saw Peter entering Granaatboskolk from the east. The trip from Magliesberg had turned out to be more than a little frustrating. Had Tammy accompanied him the two of them would have enjoyed it immensely, but the journey on his own had, at times, been boring in the extreme despite the magnificence of the changing scenery. Following the meeting with Terre'Blanche Peter stayed the night as a guest of the van Heerden's in their family home. The following morning shortly after breakfast the two men shook hands and Peter took his leave. He dropped down to the N12 and made his way south west across the country. It was approximately five hundred kilometres of easy driving down to Kimberley where he stayed the night. With time on his hands he visited the 'Big Hole' which was the site of the old diamond mine. Interesting, but it would have proved so much more so if he had someone to share the experience with.

An early night and a late start followed before he took the seemingly arrow straight R357 across to Prieska, a distance of a mere two hundred and forty kilometres, where he spent another early night in a comfortable lodge overlooking the Orange River. The drive passed by in well under three hours, but it was as far as he could go. No matter how much he had tried he was unable to find any other accommodation between there and his destination when checking on the internet from the hotel the previous evening. Well, he thought, the project relied on isolation, and isolation was certainly what appeared to be in front of him.

It most certainly was!

Peter arose and ate breakfast early on the day of the final leg to Granaatboskolk. He again followed the R357, but it was no longer arrow straight. After sixty kilometres the tar road ended after the turn off to Copperton. A winding gravel and dirt road now lay in front of him for over two hundred and sixty kilometres, and the little Golf left a cloud of dust billowing in its wake as it sped across a land virtually devoid of any human presence. After a hundred kilometres he passed through the small settlement of Van Wykslei, where there was a crossroad, minor dried up river and small lake. Another one hundred and fifty kilometres of dirt road took him to the tiny town of Brandvlei.

He had travelled the Karoo before, but never this far north, and the difference between a mid English spring to a mid African autumn could not have been greater. It was hot. Very hot. The gauge in the car was showing an outside temperature of thirty-nine degrees centigrade as he approached Brandvlei and it seemed to get worse as he dropped down to the side of the salt pans, rising to forty-two. The area was only remarkable in its utter lack of remarkability. There was nothing there, apart from a store and a small garage, where he took the opportunity to refill his tank. Whilst filling up he learnt the town's only claim to fame, although it was hardly a town, was that in 1929 Donald Campbell raced his Napier-Arrol-Astor Bluebird on the salt flats trying, and failing, to beat the three hundred miles per hour barrier.

Fascinating Peter thought, yawning as he picked up the road for Granaatboskolk, although road was not quite the correct term either for the hard packed earth trail he then had to follow for another eighty kilometres. He drove for twenty-five minutes before he saw anything but the packed earth road and small coarse growths hugging the surface of a savage land. The large salt truck passed him going in the opposite direction, its second trailer semi-superimposed on the first, swaying back and forth across the road and kicking up a dust cloud he had seen approaching from five kilometres away. Something he would have to remember, as dust clouds may later give away their location and attract unwanted attention.

He was not aware of his approach to Granaatboskolk. There were no signs of any kind. The first thing he absently noticed was a reflected glint ahead, something which would not normally be noticed if there was anything else to look at, but here there was nothing else. Parfitt was struck by the sheer desolation of the place. He hadn't even passed a windmill for at least seventy kilometres. The passing truck was the only thing he had seen to break the monotony. The glint grew as he approached, eventually showing itself to be a new corrugated iron roof to an outbuilding, behind which was a home, with another outbuilding further away to his left. From the description he knew this was the place he was there to see, although he really didn't now need to see it as he already knew it was perfect. The land around was flat in almost every direction except for a small outcrop of rocks to be seen in the far distance to the south. It was flat, it was hot, it was deserted, and it was thoroughly unwelcoming in every way imaginable. It was perfect!

Even had he not been expected, any car pulling up at such a place would doubtless have attracted attention. Pieter Skinstad came out to meet Parfitt as he stepped out of the car into the brutal baking heat. Skinstad was a hard looking man without any sign of fat about his being, constantly burnt off as it was by the harsh conditions of the life he had chosen to live. He was under six feet tall, but wide shouldered with a mass of black body hair over skin which had turned to the colour of mahogany by the unrelenting sun. Somehow he managed to make a modest living and support a wife in a place Peter thought no sane person would normally wish to step foot upon. Skinstad was an Afrikaner, and was instinctively suspicious of this pink skinned Britisher before him. Xenophobia ran rampant in the tiny and isolated communities of the area, and Skinstad was no exception. Quite apart from which he had no use for the English language, the tongue of the oppressors, and had not used it in years. However 'The Leader' had sent a messenger who had called upon him, Pieter Skinstad, to help this man and his companions, as it would help with the cause and, if 'The Leader' asked he, Pieter Skinstad, would never refuse. It didn't hurt that this Britisher was paying each of the other three homes one million rand to look the other way, and two million rand to him for the same thing plus the use of his barn. Two million rand was more money than he could earn in twelve years, and he, Pieter Skinstad, was doing 'The Leader' a personal favour, as well as helping the cause. Even a Britisher could have his barn for that – so long as he cleaned up his own shit after himself.

Skinstad drove Peter around the area where he took pictures and drew diagrams and maps of the other properties in the area. There were three other permanent dwellings and several outbuildings, but not a soul was seen. Skinstad then drove his old and beaten Toyota jeep out across the scrubland so as to show part of the land around the area, and finally took Peter back to look at the barns, both of which he was making available. The larger would be used as a garage and workshop and the smaller to be set aside for a sleeping and eating area. There were absolutely no creature comforts. No bath, shower, sink or even toilet, nor bedding, beds, cooker or fridge. Everything would have to be brought in, and everything would have to be taken out afterwards. So be it Peter thought, the place was ideal, exactly what they were looking for if not better. Young Jack Bryant had done his homework properly again. The young man was incredible Peter thought as he thanked Skinstad and held out his hand which Skinstad reluctantly took. The site inspection was done, the site approved, and then some.

It was a further two hundred kilometres across deserted dirt roads to Springbok, with only the one village of Gamoep along the way, nearly one hundred and thirty kilometres further on. There was nothing in-between except for two crossroads. Between Granaatboskolk and Gamoep he neither passed nor was passed by a single vehicle travelling in either direction, nor had he seen dust clouds approaching the crossroads. For all he knew the entire human race had left the planet and he was the sole remaining being. The vastness was staggering and the sheer nothingness mind numbing. Never in his life had he felt so isolated, or so vulnerable, or so completely and utterly reliant on a single small diesel engine.

After passing Gamoep the road improved and other vehicles occasionally materialised as he started the uphill climb to Namaqualand. Giant granite boulder stacks known as koppies started dotting the landscape, between which stretched savannah land where occasional goats and sheep came into sight. Gradually, and almost unnoticed, colour crept back into his world as the scrub land disappeared behind him and the wild beauty which attracted visitors from around the world took over from the drabness and monotony of the northern section of the Great Karoo.

Ten kilometres out of Springbok he found himself back on tarmac once more, and the road climbed then fell as it dropped into the town. Springbok lay in a deep low plain between rugged mountains. It gave the impression of prosperity and, with its population of fifteen thousand inhabitants, seemed an enormous conurbation after the bleakness and desolation of the Great Karoo.

The hotel he had arranged to stay at was one he had long wished to visit with Tammy, having been recommended by all he had known to have stayed there. Set at the end of King Street, in the very heart of Springbok, Annie's Cottage was the old manor house and had been sympathetically restored to former colonial glory with as much love as money. He was booked in for two nights with the reservation made and held on someone else's card, although he would pay in cash. It was probably an unnecessary precaution, but if followed up electronically he would never have been there. For the same reason he could not phone Tammy, or anyone else, from any landline or his own mobile, which had had the battery and SIM card removed before he left Kimberley.

His en-suite room was luxurious, and enjoyed a private entrance to the garden where, had he been there with Tammy, they would have been able to sit and relax with a cool drink in hand under the shade of the Jacaranda trees. The thought of which, and all other things their lives would now miss, angered him and he was in a bleak mood as he made his way on foot around the town to find a restaurant where he was to once more dine alone. Neither the quality of the food nor the luxury and style of his room lifted his spirits as he again turned in for an early night.

A restful night's sleep in a comfortable bed, after the previous day's hard drive, lifted his spirits by the morning and he ate a hearty breakfast, served by a most helpful and friendly staff, before setting off on what in real terms was his second site inspection. Heading north from Springbok he drove the forty-five kilometres to Steinkopf, where he turned east towards his destination of Port Nolloth. The little Golf climbed up through the Aninaus Pass the other side of which the land fell away rapidly as it dropped towards the coast, still some seventy kilometres away. As he descended from the mountains the temperature rose dramatically, and surrounding vegetation fell away to resemble the scrubland of the Great Karoo.

It was a tarmac road all the way so he made good time, well under the two hours he had allowed, and arrived well ahead of his scheduled appointment, so took the opportunity to drive around the town and get a feel for it. It was a town which showed all the obvious outward signs of terminal decay. Jack Bryant had chosen the port specifically. In part because of its proximity to the testing range at Granaatboskolk, partially because of the isolated nature of the area and in some measure because the whites working the area were Afrikaners, but mainly because lack of hope for the future should easily allow their silence to be bought.

Jack's research had thrown up Port Nolloth which seemed in every way ideal for their needs. It was built in the mid 1850's to service the copper mine at Okiep, a hundred and sixty kilometers inland from the bay. The copper produced in those days had then been transported by horse drawn carts, which were replaced in the 1870's when a narrow gauge railway line was put in and the port was lengthened to two hundred and twenty feet. Bolstered by fishing activities the port grew, but unfortunately it had an Achilles heel in that it only enjoyed a shallow draught, and within forty years ships had become too big to enter. Ore shipping then naturally declined, but in 1925 alluvial diamonds were discovered along the coast and this led to a major influx of prospectors. The respite this offered was to be short lived. Eventually large scale shipping was reduced to the fortnightly visit of one vessel which made the journey from Cape Town to exchange supplies for fish and diamonds.

The dependant population of thirteen thousand was also in decline, all still relying on fishing and diamonds to prop up their crumbling economy. In 2006 the costs of running the vessel from Cape Town proved no longer worthwhile and the service was duly terminated. Shops and bars closed, warehouses and wharfs emptied, but still people hung on in hope, although their situation was hopeless by any kind of measure. The harbour became silted up to less than four clear meters and the reef and wrecks just offshore prohibited entry to most vessels. The town was probably no longer viable as a community, but the quay still functioned and a small working crane remained.

Parfitt had left his hotel at nine-thirty for the midday meeting in case he encountered problems along the way, which he had not. With three quarters of an hour to waste he saw all there was to see of Port Nolloth, and then some. He drove back to the quayside, parked his car and stepped out, braving the forty plus degrees and hoping for a sea breeze which would help to cool him. It didn't. He had not the first idea as to what the two men he was there to meet looked like and they knew nothing of him. However it had been pointed out there was unlikely to be another white Volkswagen Golf with Johannesburg registration plates within two hundred kilometres, and certainly not pulling up to the quayside of Port Nolloth at midday containing a pink skinned Englishman.

Following the reception he received at Granaatboskolk he was expecting little from those he met at the quayside, but he took the view he was on a mission, and the mission was not about making friends. It was all to do with putting the pieces in place which would allow their little group to carry out their reprisal raid against those who had attacked his people. That simple!

Given Parfitt was expecting another frosty reception at best, if not outright hostility, it made an unexpectedly pleasant change to be so widely welcomed by the two men who approached him, both with wide smiles and outstretched hands. Both were Afrikaners and were the same large size and build. Each had blond hair with just the slightest tinge of red to it, with eyes as clear and blue as the African sky above their heads, colouring almost identical to Ruan van Heerden's, and could directly trace their family lineage back to a time before Andries Pretorius. They were unmistakably father and son, so similar in every way did they look, the only marginal difference between them was one's face appeared a little more worn and leathery. Family fortunes had changed over time, but for the two of them those fortunes looked set to change again, for the better, and because of this Britisher before them.

Willem was the first to speak. He introduced himself in an accent which would leave nobody in any doubt as to his ancestry as he warmly took Parfitt's hand. "My name is Willem Pretorius and this is my son Vurnon. You will be the Englishman we're here to meet. We've been instructed to provide you with all the help and assistance you may require and it will be our pleasure to do so! Please tell us what it is you would like to see and feel free to ask any questions you wish of us."

"It's good to meet you gentlemen." Peter replied as he turned and shook hands with the son. "I don't know what you've so far been told, but I would rather go through things with you directly in order to avoid any misunderstandings."

Vurnon spoke this time, and in a voice identical to his fathers said, "That is good. We know only that you wish to bring a boat in here, refuel it and load provisions. We know nothing of size, dates or cargo. Perhaps if you tell us what you wish for we can ensure it is provided." He indicated the jetty and all three men strolled in its direction, Peter walking in the middle so both would clearly hear all he had to say.

Parfitt liked this. Both father and son appeared positive, and both were friendly and outgoing. Pieter Skinstad had slightly irritated him with his surly hostile nature and Parfitt had never enjoyed working with men like him. On the other hand men such as the two now with him were a pleasure to work with, and much more like those he was used to. Although Peter knew little of the vessel they required Jack Bryant had given him some details, based on what he had planned for them to use.

"Our vessel is roughly thirty-five meters long, six meters wide and has a draught of two meters. We'll require something around twelve thousand litres of diesel and the crane there to help load our provisions, which will be packed in five or six wooden crates. At the moment we are not sure about dates. We are hoping to make a start in about six months, but it does rely on matters over which I have no control." Parfitt explained to the men, indicating the single crane on the quayside as he spoke.

"We understand it is something very secret." Willem Pretorius said then asked, "Is it anything of a dangerous nature?"

Parfitt was prepared for the question, and had a cover story ready. He laughed at the question, and any tension evaporated as he answered. "No it's not dangerous, and it's not so much secret as highly confidential, although in this case the two amount to the same. We'll be loading delicate and fragile marine instruments, with which we wish to carry out sensitive experiments to do with tidal drift.

"Living here you will be familiar with the Benguela current. It's cold and flows north along this coast and up past Namibia and Angola, where it eventually joins the southern equatorial current. The Benguela currents sources include South Atlantic subtropical thermocline water which mixes with the warm south flowing Agulhas current of the Indian Ocean off the Cape of Good Hope. Further north, as the Benguela current passes the Kalahari, the southern trade winds blow from east to west displacing the top waters and moving them west, then to the north west because of the coriolis effect. This means the deep cold waters move upwards replacing the costal waters.

"It's thought this movement of current could produce literally limitless hydroelectric power, which could be generated fairly close to the surface, and therefore relatively inexpensively. Elsewhere on the planet it would have to be under the thermocline, making repairs and servicing impossible and the project economically unworkable. If this power source is workable and adopted it would bring untold wealth to the developers and the region. In theory it could eclipse worldwide oil production, would be safe, and sustainable to the level of tens of thousands of years.

"If controlled through a Boer and Afrikaner homeland your people would make the Saudi royal family look like paupers by comparison. For obvious reasons many interested parties would like to get their hands on this information, whether they be petrochemical corporations who would like to take control themselves, government agencies who also wish to have control, or simply pressure groups who do not wish to see Africa prosper. Any which way we cannot afford to let anything of what we do get out. Simply put we do not exist."

It was a lie. But it was a plausible lie, especially for those who lived with nothing but hope. As he had spoken the two men at first appeared confused, not fully understanding all he was saying, which was the intention – bullshit baffles brains as they say – but by the time he finished they would have done anything to help without the money or the coercion of 'The Leader'. Their own future with the full five million rand coming their way, less a few minor payoffs, was assured. They would buy themselves the family farm they had always dreamt of but never thought they would see. Now there was a chance, just a chance, they could do something which would not only benefit themselves, but be of enormous help to their people and their land. No matter what happened from that moment on they would remain utterly discreet and fiercely loyal, helping with anything and everything which was asked of them. Parfitt envisaged no problems whatsoever at Port Nolloth. Site two was checked and thoroughly approved.

Parfitt drove back from Port Nolloth a happy man, spent a very comfortable night in his hotel after walking around the streets of Springbok, where he eventually found another suitable restaurant, dined and retired for the night. The following morning he set out for Cape Town and arrived five and a half hours later. He had but one task remaining, and it was a simple one, the purchase of two vehicles. This was the city he loved, a place he truly regarded as home and where he had friends. His days of solitude should be over, and he was once more free to telephone Tammy and her parents whenever he wished, which was the first thing he did after walking through the door of his old apartment. She was fine, which meant she was as good as could be hoped for in the circumstances. His mail had been forwarded and the apartment maintained in his absence, leaving little for him to do there.

When planning the journey it proved impossible to gauge the effectiveness of the visit or the likely duration. He had two vehicles to purchase but with that done it would be an end to his need to be there, which meant he was well ahead of schedule. He allowed himself two further days in case of problems and then successfully moved his departure flight forward. Having rearranged his flight he took the Golf to a car wash, bought some papers and car advertising magazines, and headed for the Victoria and Alfred Waterfront to relax over a beer, reading the magazines amid the comforting hustle and bustle of the cosmopolitan setting. In total there were ten vehicles which suited his requirements, four of one type and six of the other. Having explained to the black waiter who served his beer his desire to purchase a vehicle he enquired if he might use the telephone to make some local calls. The one hundred rand note which changed hands instantly provided a telephone. Telephone numbers were called and appointments made, two of which were easily possible for him to call upon on his way back to his apartment.

The first visit was a pointless waste of time, but the second was the complete opposite. The diesel hi-top long wheelbase Mercedes Sprinter was a combi van, with five seats and twin opening sliding side doors, both with black one way glass, and full height rear doors. At just under two years old it had never been worked hard and had obviously been lovingly looked after. Parfitt previously considered the van to be the hardest of the two vehicles to find and instantly realised he would not beat the vehicle before him, so left a healthy deposit and assured the owner he would return the following morning with the balance in cash, which he did.

After paying for the van and collecting keys and paperwork he went in search of the second vehicle. King-cab pickups were in plentiful supply and could be seen on the roads and streets everywhere throughout Southern Africa, precisely the reason why he wished to purchase one, although the model he needed had to be four wheel drive. He wanted nothing ostentatious but instead something which would quietly blend in so as to be hidden in full view. A new one might attract attention, whereas an old one may prove unreliable, something they could not possibly afford. He had chosen to buy one between eighteen months to three years old, depending on the service it had seen and condition.

Unlike the Mercedes he needed to visit all six sellers contacted the day before, and was fast running out of both hope and patience by the time he reached the final one. All those he visited had grossly misrepresented what they were selling in both the advertisements and on the telephone. Every one without exception was badly beaten about and damaged or had seen excessive service and been repeatedly grossly overloaded, damaging everything from bodywork to suspension to drive train. The owners had lied and, as a consequence, wasted his time, which left him fuming.

He very nearly gave up on the last one without looking at it, but having worked a route out he was due to pass within a few hundred meters so made the effort believing it to be a forlorn endeavour. Fortunately it was not, and the vehicle he was presented with was in every way what he wanted, right down to the slightly bowed tailgate and minor scratches to the bodywork. At two and a half years old and forty-eight thousand kilometres on the clock the diesel Toyota should do all which was required of it. Parfitt haggled slightly and bought it, again paying in cash.

Having purchased both vehicles all which remained was to find a garage which would fully service each and store them safely until they were required. He was familiar with two garages who had maintained his car in the past so approached them to see who they might recommend for a large van. Separately they suggested the same place; a family run franchise out near the airport, which could not have suited him better. With the help of an obliging taxi driver he shuttled both vehicles out to them, returned to his apartment and packed his bags. The next day saw him driving his previously familiar route out to Cape Town International Airport, where he returned the Golf and caught his British Airways flight to Heathrow, well ahead of schedule and way under budget. A successful mission.

Seventeen

It had taken time. A lot of time. The weeks had become months, seasons changed, and the years slipped by, but now an end was slowly coming into focus. It was still a way off, and much remained to be done, but a great deal had already been achieved and gradually the end of the project was drawing ever nearer. His mother had been dead for years and it would soon be a decade, yet still he thought of her virtually every day, and without exception every time he visited his father, contained and confined within a secure wing of a hospital, ostensibly still for his own protection, although all concerned knew it was to stop him giving vent to his suppressed homicidal rage.

Tom Bryant had now been hospitalised for more than two and a half years, ever since Sandy's death, and with every day which slipped by any chance of him ever leaving diminished. His father! The gentle, caring, loving man who had steadfastly helped raise him and his brother, whose patience with two young boys had proved boundless, and for whom nothing was ever too much trouble. The man who picked him up whenever he fell, encouraged him and Jack in their every endeavour and praising both at even their most minor successes. The loyal, reliable, faithful man who taught him and Jack about fairness, kindness and morality, and who had passed on to both of them values, standards and principles, unwavering throughout in his love for his wife and children.

They had succeeded in meting out justice for his mother and Sandy, and then some, but his father continued to endure a living hell from which he would never be released unless he learnt of how his womenfolk had been avenged, something which could never happen. More than anything it was his father's fate which continued to drive Danny. That and his sense of duty, which so closely reflected exactly similar traits to those of Peter Parfitt, who in so many ways found himself in an almost identical position due to Tammy. Peter and Chris Spencer, two men thrown up by fate that he had come to respect and admire like no others he had ever known. Friendship had grown during those two and a half years and something much deeper and more profound had formed between them. For obvious reasons they had a very real sense of shared purpose, but a form of interdependence had evolved and an alliance shaped which would remain in place for life. The bond of brotherhood.

Starting in America the world slowly slipped into the recession his brother Jack had warned everyone about. The world was about to enter a period of financial turmoil never previously experienced, and their actions would do nothing to help the situation. In fact it would probably greatly exacerbate the situation. His position, so long as he was protected by Mike Latham and wanted the job, should remain safe as long as oil continued to flow. All connected to NJF would remain fireproofed due to the astronomical cash balances available to them and their one hundred percent ownership of their company. Phil Gatting's decision to follow Jack's advice and liquidate much of his groups assets should once again stand him in good stead and Jake Ferris's ownership of vast amounts of property in and around the area of the 2012 Olympics could only lead to increasing his overall wealth, despite falling property prices. The official Almeti project in Brno was nearing completion and was already finance neutral, and would go on to created further huge financial reserves.

Recession, even the coming economic depression, irrespective as to how bad it got, would neither slow nor deter them from reaching their objective.

In early March his two friends had carried out an attack which had in part avenged Sandy, a most effective attack which sent shockwaves rippling around the world, horrifying and frightening many, comforting and encouraging others, especially those like themselves who had lost loved ones to the lunacy which was the current Islam. The attack was far more successful than they had hoped for, and had caused them to change their plans, sending Peter Parfitt alone on a mission to find a testing ground, a mission in which he once more succeeded spectacularly. He had returned and all three settled into perfecting the pulsejets and launch platform. Danny now had eight finished pulsejet engines, varying slightly in size, output and configuration, although all were built with quad spark system, which had proved the most efficient and reliable in their trials of remote ignition. With the tools he had available fabrication of such a simple device had become progressively easier as he became more accustomed to what he was doing, and he was now completely confident he could build the pulsejets on site with ease.

Building from scratch had however proved a steep learning curve, but he had conquered the subject in all areas but one, the one he had worried about when testing on the Solent prior to the Spanish mosque attack, reed valves, the age old problem of pulsejet reliability. He had learnt reed valves operate in a similar manner to heart valves, opening and closing upon changing pressures across opposite sides of the valve and do this in order to restrict the flow of gasses to one direction. In an engine of incredible simplicity they consist of nothing more than thin flexible strips of material, usually metal but sometimes fibreglass, fixed at one end. They are pulled open by a partial vacuum created by an over expansion of combustion gasses. This opening then allows a charge of fuel and air into the engine, which explodes, increasing the internal pressure and snapping shut the valves. The cycle then repeats, but the valves have a tendency to burn out quickly. The valve-less version which resembles a U bend tube Danny had rejected at conception due to weight and aerodynamic issues.

After much thought and some discussion he and Peter had opted to base the design on the Second World War Fieseler Fi 103, better known as the V-1. This they did for several reasons, but mainly because they knew the V-1 had worked, and if it had worked in the 1940's, then with the technological advancements made in the sixty years since they knew they could improve upon it. Besides Nazi Germany found itself very short of resources towards the end of the war, which was not a problem they would have to face. Another major plus point was in the amount of design and construction information available surrounding the V-1, something which was impossible to come by for the modern cruise missiles even with Nathan's hacking skills, and the use of which alleviated the need for huge amounts of research and development time.

Jointly he and Peter had continued to work on the missile design, whilst Nathan developed several variations of on-board guidance systems, all based on GPS systems which were purchased over the counter one at a time from retailers in various countries. These were always paid for in cash, purchased from retailers with no CCTV, and by Chris's operatives usually wearing somewhat dishevelled dress, unshaven faces and glasses. It was not intended as a disguise, but just enough so they would not be remembered. They had plenty of time as it was known in advance there would to be some time between purchase and use, but once again too much care could not be taken if no trail was ever to be left. None was.

The plans of the V-1 were a joy to work from. Although the V-1 was in reality the world's first cruise missile, and technologically advanced for its day, sixty years on it seemed incredibly crude, and Danny knew he could put something vastly more sophisticated together in his workshop, even working alone. It was quite scary to think what might have been if advanced electronics and composite materials had then been available to the Nazis – but they hadn't been. For Danny they now were! The V-1 had weighed two thousand one hundred and fifty kilos, of which eight hundred and fifty kilos was the warhead weight. It was mostly constructed of mild steel, had a range of two hundred and fifty kilometres, one hundred and fifty miles, and a speed of six hundred and forty kilometres per hour, four hundred miles per hour. It also carried heavy and cumbersome guidance equipment.

The missiles he and Peter were developing and building were to be built of Kevlar and use electronics attached to servos in order to control guidance, pitch, roll and yaw, and their overall length would be only slightly over two meters. With a maximum warhead weight of twenty kilos, and they were expecting less, the hope was the missile they were developing would weigh in at around one hundred kilos all up, but pack a punch comparable to the old V-1. Everything had gone far better than any had expected. They had no timetable as such to work to and no concerns about finance which, as Peter pointed out, would have put them in a truly enviable position had they been running a business, but they were not. Despite the lack of timetable all concerned wanted to proceed with the Bakkah attack as rapidly as possible.

There were to be no code or operational names as such, but Danny had become aware, working alongside the two ex-military men, that Chris and Peter developed names for the missions between themselves. The hunt for Abdul Ahmad Khaled, his execution, and the tracking down and despatch of others who were connected to him had become Operation Mary, and the destruction of the mosque at Pedro Abad they openly discussed as Operation Sandy. Now they were referring to the big one, the strikes on Bakkah and Nima, as Operations Susie and Charlie, and this was what all concerned had been working towards for the last two and a half years.

It was Peter, before leaving for 'Operation Sandy', but after the trials on The Solent, who cast doubts on the potential viability of the missile they had spend much time and resources developing for over two years

"Now I've seen one in action and had a bit of time to think Danny, I've come to the overwhelming conclusion we have a problem with the design of the missile." Peter had said with a note of genuine concern in his voice.

"Really? I thought it was coming on well." Danny replied. "What's the problem?"

"Well, we've based the design on the old V-1. I know we've altered it dramatically, and I'm pretty sure all we've done is good and we have improved it, but there's one thing about the V-1 we've never addressed, which is their take off." Peter responded.

"But that's what we're building the platforms for!" Danny retorted.

"I know that, but we're building them with the wrong set of criteria in mind. The Germans had trouble with the things themselves. They either air launched them from a specially converted Heinkel He-111's or, when launched from the ground, used chemical or steam catapults which accelerated them to about three hundred kilometres per hour. Those two solutions overcame the problem of the low static thrust of the engine coupled with the stall speed of the small wings. As they are I don't think our missiles will take off under their own power," Peter Parfitt explained to a crestfallen Danny.

"Oh shit!" Danny said, sitting down with a look of utter desolation on his face. "But there must be an answer Peter. We've come too far to give up on what we've already done. It's two and a half years work. We can't abandon that, and no one will want to give up on the project. There must be an answer. If you've had time to think about it you must have some ideas, especially with your background!"

"Well I have given it quite a bit of thought." Peter told him. "However, all the conventional solutions are unavailable to us. There's no chance of an air launch, catapult or even a runway. The only thing I've managed to come up with, although it may seem a little far fetched, is booster rockets. With many spacecraft, particularly the Shuttle, booster rockets are an intrinsic part of the design. If we could mount a rocket either side of the fuselage, behind the wings, it may provide the answer. If they butted into the wing they should not affect the aerodynamics whilst producing thrust and, once the required speed or height was reached, could be jettisoned by the use of a simple servo to avoid altering the flight dynamics. Both they and the servo will add to the take off weight, but the thrust provided will massively offset any weight issue. By the time the missiles get up to speed and the boosters are dropped the fuel weight will have decreased compensating for the minor weight increase of the remaining servo, although I suspect it won't prove anything like as critical by then!"

"What about the booster rockets though? We can't start designing and building them as well." It could be seen Danny liked the idea, but the new problem had hugely disappointed him.

"We don't have to worry about any of that!" Peter assured him. "There are dozens of shops selling the kind of things we need. There is quite a thriving model rocket industry out there, somewhat akin to the model aircraft industry, and there will be all the motors and propellants we need, although I would suggest buying in the US and shipping directly to South Africa if tests prove them to be effective. Nathan could probably get everything we need on line without leaving a trace. If model rockets prove impractical I'm sure Chris will be able to conjure up some rocket propelled grenades from which we can use the rockets. I think it's quite feasible, but we will have to make allowances for them on the platform, size, weight, etc., but the greater the thrust the greater the possible angle of take off and therefore the smaller the platform, but probably a corresponding increase in the flotation requirement to counteract downward pressure."

Chris was given the task of procuring the bulk of the components considered essential for the eventual construction of the missiles, with the sourcing of all electronic equipment left to Nathan. Under his own name and travelling quite openly whilst using his legitimate passport Chris made his way around the world buying and collecting the required elements whilst carrying out security duties for the various companies he now served. The purchases he would make using assumed names and identities and have the goods and materials shipped to a myriad of destinations where they would once more be shipped to further destinations. Where possible, and for the more minor items, he would delegate the jobs to his small squad, but where something was of critical importance to the overall program he made a point of completing the acquisition in person, although always using a front man to accompany him and finalise any purchase. They were about to construct the weapons which were at the very centre of all they had planned to do from the time their tiny group first came together. Nothing could be allowed to hamper or destroy their plans if their goals were to be met and their loved ones properly avenged.

The various designs Danny produced for the pulsejets all worked, and would probably all be capable of delivering the required sustained flight for their missiles, but would need to be thoroughly tested to make sure they put the best possible design forward for the building of twelve or more similar ones. The construction of the missile body proved substantially easier than the building of the pulsejet engine, but had never been tested, as it was something which could not be safely done in Britain. All realised the pressure would be on them in South Africa. No matter how remote the area was, or how well the local people could keep their secret, the longer trials went on the greater the chance of their project being discovered.

Raw materials, parts and tools were shipped to Cape Town, where a clearance and handling agent was contacted and payment for services rendered transferred from an account in the Cayman Isles. A number of consignments were beginning to build up ready for collection from a secure warehouse. Almost all the equipment arriving at Cape Town had already made a journey to another destination, where deliveries were completed, paid for and signed off before reshipping occurred. Every trail was cold and a later in-depth investigation would be further confounded by the extended time frame. For every one of the group concerned, vengeance was indeed a dish best served cold!

At a very early stage Danny completed a comprehensive list of the tools he would require at any test site, and almost all were eventually purchased from Snap-on Africa (Pty) Ltd in Durban by a contact of Peter Parfitt, after the deal for the test site was agreed, ostensibly for his own use when he returned to the country and started a business. There was nothing suspicious or out of the ordinary about them, except the commission cheque for the very happy salesman, and the tools were then transported to a winery outside Paarl where they awaited collection at Peter's convenience from the home of an old friend.

The model rockets Peter suggested as boosters proved impractical. Despite finding three alternatives which provided sufficient thrust all were prone to propellant problems when in contact with water. After less than a week of trials the model rockets were scrapped and a somewhat dejected Danny and Peter called upon Chris for consultation and advice. The conversation with Chris started reasonably downbeat, but both Danny and Peter had their spirits lifted by the end. Peter had some knowledge of rockets, but in an area of use which offered limited help to the project. Chris however showed an excellent working knowledge of exactly what was needed and, as was so typical of him, wasted few words discussing anything but the task.

"The problem we face, Chris, is in having the missiles produce enough thrust to leave the platform," Peter explained. "We now believe it can be overcome by using booster rockets as an aid to take off, but the rockets we've tried so far had problems with water contact. What we though may help is to use RPG rockets which could be dropped after take off once they've boosted the missile either up to a sufficient height or to a suitable speed."

"Unfortunately we know too little about the subject, in fact I know virtually nothing." Dan admitted. "If you can explain any of it I'd be grateful! At least a little to give me a basic background and working knowledge would help."

"Okay, but I'll spare you the history lesson on mortars and rockets, although I'll correct you on one point straight away, although it's probably not relevant." Chris replied, then explained, "Most people in the West believe the abbreviation RPG originates from rocket propelled grenade. It doesn't exactly. Now I know your brother and Katya would pronounce this correctly, and I won't, but it actually originates from the Russian phrase Ruchnoi Protivotankovye Granatamyot, which means hand held anti tank grenade launcher. This really made it a LAW, a light anti-tank weapon, like the American M-72 LAW."

"Er, thanks Chris." Danny said with a look of complete confusion on his face. "I now understand I know substantially less than I thought I did when I thought I knew very little."

"Yeah, and I'm bloody glad you spared us the history lesson!" Peter said laughing. "Now can you tell us something of the rockets themselves, how they work, the distance they are good for, what they weigh and anything you can about thrust?"

"Sorry, I guess that was a bit of an information overload." Chris said grinning, paused, then went on to explain more about the weapons propulsion systems. "At the moment there are several systems which would suit your needs, the best two of which are the M-72 LAW I mentioned and the Russian designed RPG-7. For our use I would suggest the Russian system, mainly because it is so common and therefore pretty much impossible to trace. There are hordes of them everywhere, in every hot-spot in the world, and every place there's ever been one. They've been around since the sixties, sixty-one I believe, are used by over forty different countries and by terrorist organisations from Latin America to the Middle East. Every man and his dog seem to have the things these days.

"As with larger missiles these weapons have a built in rocket propulsion system. Because of their background all measurements and weights I give you will be in metric. Each rocket weighs one point eight kilos, they are four hundred and sixty millimetres in length and have a calibre of eighty-four mil. For general combat use they have an effective range of about three hundred meters, although that can be trebled in the hands of a skilled operator, and a muzzle velocity of two hundred and ninety meters per second, which equates to about six hundred and fifty miles per hour.

“The whole assembly is made up of the warhead, of which there can be several types, none of which you’ll need, which is then screwed onto the sustainer motor and the booster. The booster contains a stabilising pipe with four fins folded around one end and two at the other which spread out as it leaves the launcher and causes the warhead to rotate in flight. This keeps it stable, very much like a spinning rugby ball, although you won’t need that either. The back end of this pipe is encased by a cardboard container, and inside it is a squib of nitroglycerin powder which is wrapped around the pipe, with a gunpowder charge used as a primer pressed into the pipe end.

“To fire the whole thing the operator pulls the trigger, causing the hammer to hit the percussion cap which ignites the primer. Gasses then build inside the chamber of the launcher and this build up breaks the cardboard container apart, forcing the assembly along the barrel of the launcher. The force behind these built up gasses fires the grenade out of the launcher at about one hundred and fifteen meters per second, and the abrupt acceleration in itself triggers a piezoelectric fuse which ignites the primer, which consists of a pyro retarding gunpowder mixture. The ignition of the primer fires off the nitro squib which in turn activates the sustainer motor’s rocket propulsion system. Bingo!”

“Can you get hold of any of these?” Danny asked.

“By the boat load!” Chris replied. “How many do you need?”

“It would be good to have a few here to play around with, say ten, but if they work out we’ll need maybe about a hundred and fifty more in South Africa. Would that present a problem for you in any way?” Danny again asked.

“Absolutely not! I’ll get ten to you within the next few days. Have a look at them and see if they are any good to you. If they are I’ll have the rest delivered to S.A. I’ll try and come and help, but do be bloody careful with the things. Even without the warhead they can be pretty dangerous, and the back blast from the gasses alone would ruin the rest of your life!” Chris cautioned the other two.

Chris was as good as his word and personally delivered ten of the rockets four days later, then set about helping disassemble two of them, which they did with ease and without accident. Peter and Danny had produced twenty-two tubular fuselages and twenty-two perfectly matched nose cones from their supply of Kevlar, twenty each of which had already been crated and dispatched to Cape Town along with a multitude of winglets. They kept the remaining two missiles at Danny’s workshop with which to continue experiments. Twelve would eventually be used in the attack they planned, which left them with eight to test to destruction in South Africa, and two to use in England with which to perfect as much as they could before heading for the testing ground.

Danny constructed a test frame with which to measure the thrust capabilities of the various rockets he and Peter continued to experiment with, and the test figures sent off to Jack and Nathan to analyse. The results indicated a rocket either side would not generate enough thrust, certainly not for anything approaching a vertical take off. However it appeared four would be more than sufficient in combination with the pulsejet, so Danny re-engineered the clamp mechanisms he had designed to take two either side, slightly altering the housing behind the winglets to accommodate the extra bulk. A prototype was soon completed and, as far as was possible without electronics, was smoke tested inside Danny's wind tunnel to check aerodynamics and drag coefficients. All were pleased to see the missile performed remarkably well, especially at higher speeds, which allowed Danny to turn his attention to the launch platforms.

As they had progressed with the project Danny gradually turned more attention to the launch platforms, and the more work he did on them the greater the number of problems which manifested themselves. Peter had proved to be most adept with the moulds whilst working on the various nose cone and fuselage sections, and after completing the third one successfully Danny left him to it so he could turn his full concentration to the platforms. He decided very early on single launch platforms were pointless, as were twins, and triple ones could prove inherently unstable whilst launching. However large ones also offered inherent problems. Eventually he chose three platforms with four bases for wholly practical reasons. They would be lighter to handle, more manageable in the water, easier to crate, pack, disassemble and reassemble and, in the highly unlikely event one might be discovered there would remain a chance the other two might not be.

At slightly over two meters in length, depending on the eventual overall length of the engine, Danny's version of the flying bomb was considerably smaller than the original. It had a width from the tip of one winglet to the other of a mere ninety-five centimeters and an external diameter of the fuselage of just thirty-five. This meant his launch platforms could be restricted to two meters square whilst allowing sufficient room for all the equipment the launches would require, as long as the missiles proved to be capable of taking flight at an angle in excess of forty degrees and a chosen maximum of seventy. Each missile was to be mounted on a corner at ninety degrees to one another with their exhausts and rockets back blast all centered on the water in the middle of the platforms. The missile mounting clamps were most complicated as they had to steady and secure the missiles in place, yet not hinder their launch. All four rockets on each missile would have to fire at the same time but after the pulsejets had stabilised, and the front and rear of the pulsejets would have to be plugged to avoid water penetration, yet the plugs would have to be removed as the platforms surfaced.

The solution to the problems associated with mounting clamps and plugs proved to be simplicity itself when the idea occurred to him that, although the engineering was somewhat more complicated, everything could be done using the flotation of the pontoons on which the platform would sit, very much as a ball valve works in a toilet cistern. Even limited experimentation proved one hundred per cent successful every time.

On their arrival, two of the rockets motors were thoroughly greased before being tied to a line and dropped into the sea to remain suspended beneath Danny's boat for three weeks. When they were eventually removed they were clamped into a test frame. Despite their immersion both fired the instant the hammer hit the percussion cap, proving in every way perfect for their plan.

Eighteen

As time slipped by NJF Industries continued to prosper at the hands of Chi Lu. With its diversification into allied industries growth had followed growth. However the first year following Susie's and the baby's death were very difficult for Nathan. His ability to concentrate on work and to successfully design new products was stifled by his one all consuming passion, the death of as many of those who had so callously taken the life of his beautiful Susie and their unborn baby as possible, and the overwhelming desire to damage the structure of their despicable culture. In many ways in this, although far less vocal about it, he was remarkably similar to Tom Bryant, only much better supported by people who understood there could be a problem and wished to help.

Chi Lu's interest in Nathan had never waned and continued unabated despite the fact Nathan took no notice of her or, as Chi Lu came to realise, had not yet noticed her. She was both genuinely fond of him and concerned for him. She was a very perceptive and intuitive young woman, but above all she was highly intelligent, and her intelligence had benefited from a world class education. She knew Nathan was a genius in his own field, something he had clearly demonstrated on many previous occasions, but also understood his genius ran along a fairly narrow band. He had no real grasp of business and few of the concepts surrounding it, so was incredibly lucky to have crossed the path of Jake Ferris, a man she had originally grossly underrated, something she had never previously done, and who had since grown in her estimation phenomenally.

All, including herself, fully realised she had done well picking up the reigns of NJF at a time of absolute crisis as she had. However, although she would miss Susie for the rest of her life, having taken on the business when she did allowed her to firmly put her own stamp on it very quickly. In the first few months her biggest single worry was whether genius could become madness, but as time progressed she slowly began to appreciate Nathan's somewhat obsessive and secretive nature was not driven by any form of madness, but by distraction, and it was a distraction she knew nothing of. Such things intrigued her. She felt it was better not to pry or to in any way investigate, but she certainly was not going to forget or ignore it either. She was sure something would eventually come out, and when it did she would be waiting to react accordingly.

Although Chi Lu brought about several beneficial changes to NJF when she took over she was more than a little surprised at the rate of change of other matters going on around her during those early days. Matters she believed she should have been informed about in advance but had remained totally unaware of. Within the first three months of her starting it was announced NJF would be the major partner in a new joint venture. A venture she had previously not so much as heard discussed, and with the figures involved she felt she should have been fully informed before she agreed to take the job as it could have a major impact on NJF. However, despite her concerns, it appeared the new venture was getting good advice from their whiz kid banker, although he was another area of minor concern for her, as she had no idea at all as to where he had suddenly appeared from.

For Chi Lu a further matter of petty disquiet was overall corporate security. Certainly not with any security issues as such because the company's relatively new head of security was, without a doubt, well on top of his job and obviously prepared to travel anywhere in the world for the company at the drop of a hat. There was no questioning the man's abilities, or dedication. Although short on words he appeared long on talent, and had actually succeeded in improving on site security whilst reducing costs, which spoke volumes as to his ability. The problem to her mind was where had he come from, why at that particular time, why did he have to fly off and inspect so many minor areas and, most importantly, why was he a consultant answerable to Jake and Nathan and not employed directly by NJF and therefore answerable to her? She understood security issues, and could appreciate the benefits for a person of the security adviser's ability spreading his interests across NJF, the Gatting Group and Eastlond Properties, but why was he, with a lowlier position, within the inner circle when she was not?

So much seemed to have happened about the time she started. If she had not already known the company and the vast bulk of its management before she took the job some of the things would have gone unnoticed. But she had known the company and its structure. It was something much bigger than a matter of them not trusting her, but it was more than enough to give a lesser girl a complex. So what the hell was going on and what were all these secret meetings about to which she was not invited? Why had NJF, for which she was responsible, agreed to help float a joint venture and underwritten their part to a value of one and a half billion pounds? Whilst on the subject what sort of name was Almeti? She had Googled it and run it through other search engines but found nothing, yet the initials did not correspond with either the individuals or businesses concerned. Another enigma.

With the passage of time Nathan slowly became accustomed to his losses, although he would never accept them and continued to loathe those responsible. He eventually returned to his comfort zone, which was another small one bedroom flat in East London, and from where he could walk to work, the place where he spent the majority of his time. Occasionally in bad weather he would make his way to work by taxi although he still owned a car, a small Volkswagen Golf, but he very rarely drove and hated doing so. Nothing, since Susie's death, could ever make him take the tube. For a multi billionaire he led a ridiculously quiet life. Chi Lu thought were it not so tragic it could almost be comical, as Nathan still had no real concept, and worse still no interest, in what either he or his business interests were worth. If his personal assets were banked, even at normal deposit rates, the interest alone would amount to very nearly half a million pounds a day, yet he led the life of a part time shop assistant.

As the first year progressed, and the terrible shock wore off, Nathan slowly returned to being productive and his concentration appeared to return. During the second year he managed to complete another game based on submarine warfare which was named GIUK Gap, and sold as rapidly as his previous games, causing money to once more flow into the coffers of NJF's gaming arm. This increased liquidity was helped by the release of two games from the McGregor/Hall partnership for the younger market, Char Wars, for the under ten's, a comical fight between tea ladies, and Convoy USA, for the teenage market, a game involving cops chasing and attempting to stop robbers escaping in an articulated truck on a busy interstate. The trade press had absolutely lapped up all three. Jefferies was back!

From Chi Lu's perspective Nathan appeared to be well on the mend, but then suddenly, about two and a half years after Susie's death, he unaccountably became withdrawn again, working secretly through the night or locking himself in his office/workshop and taking no calls. His sudden withdrawal occurred around the time of the dreadful bombing in Spain, where a mosque was attacked and blown up whilst full of worshipers. More people had died there than did with the London tube bombings, with the attack happening exactly four years to the day after Madrid train bombings. Despite the fact those who died were Muslims she felt it must have reminded Nathan of Susie's death, setting his recovery back to who knew when. She could do little to help and could only wonder how long the set back would last.

Nathan, Jake Ferris and Phil Gatting, whilst not exactly revelling in the accomplishments of Peter Parfitt and Chris Spencer and what they had managed with the Spanish mosque bombing, finally saw, quite graphically displayed on their televisions and on the front pages of the newspapers, exactly what their group was capable of. Retribution. Pay back time! To many around the world the pictures of the carnage which occurred at Pedro Abad was shocking, and the idea of another secret Spanish group, willing, trained and capable of carrying out such an operation, was quite disturbing.

Founded in 1959 a group advocating traditional cultural ways had evolved and taken up arms, demanding independence for the Basque people. Euskadi Ta Askatasuna in the Basque language translates to Basque Homeland and Freedom. It is far better known by its initials ETA, and is the armed separatist organisation of Basque nationalists responsible, since 1968, for the killing of more than eight hundred people, maiming several hundred more and for a multitude of kidnappings. It was well known ETA, generally due to security reasons following infiltration by Spanish and French law enforcement agencies, had on several occasions changed its internal structure.

It was also known the original three substructures of the organisation representing political, military and logistical interests had recently split into eleven sections following the captures and detention of members. According to security forces the changes were significant but ETA's reasons and intentions remained unknown. There was much press speculation as to whether the mosque attack was the responsibility of ETA, or perhaps a breakaway or splinter group of former ETA members who had either become disaffected or enraged at their losses at Madrid. If so it indicated a major change of direction and or a dangerous escalation to a far more aggressive stance, if such were possible.

Another possibility which had received a lot of press speculation was, if anything, even more disturbing. Could the attack have been officially sanctioned and carried out under a special operations mandate. Spain had no lack of military and police units with such capability, and had a long history of combating violence with violence at the hands of specially trained warfare and intervention units. If this were the case it was considered probable such an attack would have been carried out by the Spanish Navy's Unidad de Operaciones Especiales, Special Operations Unit, UOE.

Comprising of approximately one hundred and thirty men, plus command and support personnel, the UOE is garrisoned in the Tercio de Armada at San Fernando on the Costa de la Luz, at the major port city of Cadiz. It is under the direct control of the Spanish Admiralty through its Naval Special Warfare Command and is the Spanish Navy and Marines elite special operations force, tasked with special operations in maritime and coastal environments, usually within fifty kilometres of the sea. However the UOE is not distance restricted and its teams have been known to operate deep inland. Pedro Abad is two hundred and fifty kilometres from Cadiz and less than half that distance from the sea.

One thing was certain, the media assured viewers and readers for days after the attack, whoever carried out the operation was well trained, equipped and funded, and most assuredly Spanish. To Nathan, Jake and Phil Gatting other things were certain. The operation was an outstanding success and proved their capabilities to themselves. It also proved beyond any shadow of doubt the incredible planning abilities of Jack Bryant, and it didn't hurt any that the commercial cover behind the operation also looked very likely to bring in the Lyon adventure park, cinemas and shopping complex.

Although Nathan continued to work on the problems created by the complexities of building their own missiles his efforts were split between that and his work. When he saw the effect their minor operation accomplished in Spain it galvanised him into further action, effectively pushing him back into prioritising the project and putting it before work. He didn't know it but Chi Lu's thoughts were both right and wrong about him. Despite not fully understanding his wealth he was aware he didn't have to worry about money, and could also see the business ran itself, not that he would have been able to contribute much to its overall running as management really was not his thing. She had also been correct in assuming the mosque bombing reminded him of Susie's death, but was very wrong in her diagnosis of a set back.

In the two and a half years since Susie's death there was not a day which passed when Nathan had not mourned her, the baby girl they should have welcomed to the world, the other possible children they would probably have had, and the wonderful life they should all have enjoyed as a complete loving family. Such words as loathe and hate came nowhere close to his feelings for the people and their culture who had so indifferently and uncaringly taken all such things from him. He would never again properly rest or relax until he felt satisfied with what he had done to bring about their end. Fate was indeed a fickle mistress he realised whenever he took a very rare moment to consider life from a philosophical point of view. Life provided him with nothing as a child, then everything, only to have it all violently removed again, whilst at the very moment of removal giving the tools with which to cause untold pain to those who had so badly wronged him. The tools given were those with whom he had formed Almeti International.

The Erinyes of Greek mythology, known as the Furies to the Romans, were cruel earth goddesses who symbolised divine vengeance. They were created from the blood of the Titan Uranus when his son Cronus castrated him, taking revenge for the loss of his siblings, and sprang from his blood as underworld goddesses of vengeance or supernatural personifications of the anger of the dead. The Erinyes were terrible looking creatures with appalling features, burning breath, poisonous blood dripping from their eyes and heads wreathed with serpents. They prosecuted crimes such as disrespect, injustice, perjury or arrogance and, above all, murder, especially within the family. It was believed in early epochs human beings might not have the right to punish such crimes, instead leaving the matter of retribution to the Erinyes.

The Erinyes were three sisters who stood for the rightness of things within the standard order. Predominantly, they were understood as the persecutors of mortal men and women who broke natural laws and, without mercy, would punish all crime including the breaking of rules throughout all aspects and strata's of society. They would strike the offenders with madness and never stopped following criminals. They would also be the guardians of the law when the state had not yet intervened or did not exist, or when the crime was a crime of ethics and not actual law. The Erinyes were connected with Nemesis as enforcers of a just balance in human affairs, but their lust of punishment knew no bounds, and they kept punishing a sinner even after his death, until he finally showed remorse. They were called Alecto, she of unceasing anger, Megaera, the grudging, and Tisiphone, the avenger.

Alecto, Megaera, Tisiphone – AlMeTi. The name meant nothing to others. It was meaningless and led nowhere, but to their group it was to be an inexorable and relentless divine retribution well beyond that of Nemesis, and it was truly international. They had the required wealth, the power and certainly the will, and they would hunt down, kill and destroy their enemy wherever they were to be found, using any means available to bring about their end. Socially accepted standards of modern warfare and national or international laws meant nothing to them, for they had learnt from their enemy. Only one rule or law applied. Vengeance! Ceaseless unremitting vengeance!

The fate of the mosque at Pedro Abad reinvigorated Nathan. Despite his early request for direct personal involvement it had never happened. He had done what he could by scouring computer records from various sources, eventually whittling those down to three, the Home Office, what he still thought of as the Department of Health and Social Security, and roughly twelve airlines. The information held on government departments computers was so easy to hack into or otherwise obtain they might as well have kept their secrets as headlines on the front pages of the Times. The airlines computers proved somewhat more arduous with varying levels of complexity built in to confound hackers, but he had found nothing he could not break through.

He devised a program to run with the information obtained from his three main sources and had initially been surprised, actually he was absolutely amazed, at the almost unimaginable stupidity of those charged with the security of his nation. Not only was there no exit policy in place, but the system actually allowed illegal aliens to make claims against the state and to obtain grants from it. He was horrified to find the government, using his taxes, had in part funded those carrying out the acts of terrorism on the tube, which had destroyed his life, through a variety of councils and government sponsored bodies. He discussed the point with Chris Spencer one day, when handing over a list of names and addresses, and the ex-soldier was most forthright in his views.

"Makes you wonder if these Muslim terrorist fuckers just apply to the 'New English' politicians and get a direct grant for murder, which is delivered with the proviso they are only allowed to kill indigenous whites. Perhaps we should seriously consider taking out all Muslim politicians too!" Chris mused when shown the facts and figures.

Nathan liked Chris Spencer. The man came across as a hardened, grizzled professional, and he was every bit of that and more, but there was a sense of balance and utter fairness about him. Even Nathan could see Chris tended to view the world in terms of black and white, which was interesting to see in a person of his age, and he also tended to be a man of few words, but his words were almost always worth listening to. Despite not being able to get personally involved at the dispatch end Nathan was able to furnish Chris with nearly two hundred names of those suspected as being involved or on the fringe of socially unwelcome activities, namely aiding and supporting terrorism, most of whom were illegals. Well over half the names had shortly afterwards left the screens of the government departments. Not all were connected with terrorism. Most of those who were not were told to leave the country and of those the majority complied. Those who did not were paid a second visit, and they then entered paradise.

"We can all make silly mistakes, but they shouldn't take the piss." Chris once said.

His illegal alien program was a relatively simple one to Nathan. It did no more than check incoming aliens from Muslim states against issued visas then ran a check to see if they left by any of the airlines on his list within the deadline of their visas. The majority did, but many did not. He would have been the first to admit his records were not foolproof. Illegals could come in from other countries or by other far less popular airlines. They could also leave by these airlines, sea or road unnoticed, or return to third countries, but this was most definitely not the general pattern, and patterns were the easy bits to follow. He was convinced the state could put a much improved and infinitely more secure system in place, and it would certainly pay to do so. Identity cards were a smokescreen devised to deflect attention. Biometric passports and photocard driving licences already existed, so it seemed both ludicrous and potentially confusing to add a further tier of bureaucratic bullshit to the mix, although it would provide an enormous source of income for organised crime. He firmly believed if he were able to get hold of the national computers and tweak their programming he would save the nation billions – and remove a lot of very nasty people. But he would never be called upon to do such a thing.

'What if' was a pointless road to follow, and one from which he would never achieve a sense of satisfaction, let alone vengeance. Far better for him to follow this road to Bakkah, to take this war back to those bastards who had brought it to the shores of his beautiful homeland, and to drive the barren hillside and desert dwelling scum back to the hovels of their far away lands. He, and the other members of Almeti, had not wanted this war, had sought no part in it, but it had been brought to them and, although innocents, they were forced to suffer unbelievable pain as a result. So he returned to the missile project with renewed vigour and threw himself into it, working every spare hour he had available.

Drawing upon Peter Parfitt's knowledge, and obtaining all the information he could from available downloads he quickly accumulated a working knowledge of flight control systems and the difficulties he may encounter. Many months earlier he had given the matter his attention and drawn up a short list of items he felt he would require for the project, allowing time for their procurement, and this was long since done. Danny had passed on plans for the V-1, but Nathan instantly discounted and rejected them. There were far more versatile systems on the market which would be superior in many ways to the ancient and long since obsolete 1940's technology, almost all of which he knew he already possessed.

His first main aim was to design, build and program a guidance and flight attitude control system, which proved far easier to do than he had suspected it might. He could see each missile would require only three items, apart from relevant servos, all of which were off the shelf parts. They consisted of a GPS system with computer interface and software, a simple single board computer he would put together himself for what would become the onboard computer needed for flight control, and an infra-red stability system. The last item was suggested by Peter Parfitt at one of their progress meetings and was commonly available for model aircraft. Its inclusion would keep the missiles flying on a straight and level line between the course corrections initiated by the GPS controlled on board computer system.

The servos presented a minor dilemma for him. Danny had a belt and braces philosophy and as a consequence designed everything with built in redundancies. Nathan heartily approved of such a pragmatic approach for general applications but felt that for the loads imposed by high speed flight it was essential any servos used on flight surfaces could cope, which led to large units capable of providing much greater strength and torque but which weighed significantly more. This would mean only one could be used per function as everything was a trade off against weight. He chose the one servo option but went for units designed for the particularly large one quarter scale models, and these proved to be perfect for the application.

During the testing stage only the later trial missiles would be given target information, and should therefore be fire and forget. The early ones would help form their learning curve, and would have to be controlled from the ground in order to flight test the engines and airframe. This part of the testing was crucial, and would have to be done before fitting any onboard guidance system. He toyed with the idea of fitting an onboard camera for the initial testing but decided against it. He didn't want any more radio signals flying around than were absolutely essential, and to hope to recover anything from a recording device fitted within a missile was unrealistic after crashing it, so he decided he would set up a string of cameras in the line of flight to record every movement of each flight from the ground at the testing area.

Again Peter advised Nathan in the needs of radio controlled transmitters, and the work he and Chris had so successfully carried out with overlapping signals which had proved to be so effective when targeting the mosque at Pedro Abad certainly helped. The work Nathan had himself carried out on line of sight transmissions using satellite dishes for transmitting computer signals several years earlier, and the working knowledge then gained, also helped. For the flight testing of the missiles Nathan felt they would need to have an advanced radio control system capable of transmitting to a relatively fast moving object over a range well outside normal amateur radio controlled capabilities, yet still of a short range signal type which remained impossible for overhead satellites to pick up.

The problem was solved with a reversal of his earlier experiments. His eventual solution would include a twenty-five kilometre command wire with transmitters evenly placed along it at regular one kilometre distances and cameras monitoring the flights. Once the flight control system was installed it would all become superfluous as the GPS would supply the critical latitude, longitude and altitude information to the computer in order to make flight corrections. However everything had to be perfected before the introduction of the GPS as they wished to keep the project secret, and secrecy could well be lost as soon as the missiles GPS equipment started hunting for information, as the very information they needed came from satellites – and satellites told tales! The final addition to Nathan's design preparations was a miniature timing chip to be used in the attack missiles. The missiles were expected to fly for approximately fifteen minutes. If they failed to take off or encountered problems they would self destruct thirty minutes after engines were instructed to start up. He was finished with all which could be done on the bench. His flight control system was ready to be trialled and he did not envisage having any problems with it.

Danny had built a small quarter size platform with which to experiment. The missiles themselves were finished, and a selection of engines with various configurations completed. The booster rockets had been tested and trialled in every possible simulated condition and never given even the slightest cause for concern. The fact they were designed with battlefield conditions in mind, with the excesses of heat and cold, wet and dry, snow and dust, and all which follows armed conflict made them robust and serviceable in a myriad of climatic conditions, superb for the task ahead.

To build the first small experimental platform Danny worked with a cut down rear end of a missile, first considering every aspect of the missiles needs, then working forward from there, building support equipment as required with simplicity of design and operation as the only criteria. He benefited from a practical, hands-on upbringing and had always demonstrated a natural aptitude towards mechanical engineering, which he used to his advantage from the moment he discovered boats.

Despite the fact he had never received the slightest degree of formal training on the subject he remained highly competent. The lack of training may in some ways have assisted as it enabled him to take a unique view of the subject without being constrained by accepted norms.

Dan had sat down to an interesting and informative discussion with Peter and jointly drawn up a list of what would be needed on the platform. Danny had never left his day job at Fawley, and had nothing to do with Almeti, NJF, the Gatting Group or Eastlond Properties and, as a security precaution, rarely if ever visited any of the other members of the group. Generally he was left to get on with his part of the project, occasionally helped by Chris, but far more frequently assisted by Peter, who generally drove along from Brighton and stayed for a couple of days at a time. Peter carried news of progress in both directions, sometimes advising and then discussing Danny's advances with Nathan, and then also bringing news of the work Nathan completed back to Danny on a regular weekly basis.

"Peter, I have my own ideas of what this platform will require, but I would love to hear you run through things at this stage to double check I've not missed anything." Danny said as the latter stages of the work progressed.

"Well given we now pretty much know the weight, dimension and thrust capabilities of the missiles themselves, we first have to work out the preferred angle for take off. We should avoid the vertical as their missiles paths may cross on take off and the last thing we would want is a mid air collision. At the same time I feel with the thrust available we should set them above forty-five degrees as, if there is a stall problem or booster failure, a height advantage may give the engine and GPS time to recover." Peter mused thoughtfully.

"Yeah, we covered some of that before. The basic platform, as it is, has four missiles on it with one missile in each corner facing out. I realise that although the missiles on each platform will all start at about the same time they certainly won't all start or lift off together at exactly the same moment, which means as each takes off the platforms will be bucking about a lot even on a flat sea. The idea is they start by going off in four totally different directions and alter course as the GPS comes on-line. The problem is with the platforms twisting, turning and maybe even spinning in addition to the bobbing motion it is impossible to predict where they will go." Danny said expressing concern.

"Forget it Dan." Peter replied. "There is absolutely no way you can predict such things, so in my opinion it's pointless trying. To be honest it's much more difficult to hit something flying through the air than most people think. Even with purpose built hi-tec surface to air missiles with heat seeking capabilities it's possible to miss. Remember in the Iraq war when Saddam was trying to strike at Tel Aviv to bring the Israelis in and escalate things? Well the Scud missiles he was using were nothing more than old WWII V-2's, really old technology, but even America's most modern Patriot SAM's couldn't hit them every time. Once you've removed the vertical aspect the risk of your missiles hitting one another in the air is, I truly feel, negligible in the extreme. Forget it!"

"I'd never thought of it like that. It makes sense. I guess there comes a point when anyone can become too focussed on something. Thanks! I'll take that advice."

Danny said with a note of obvious relief in his voice.

"To answer your original question," Peter continued, "the missiles obviously have to be clamped to their platforms, which is simple, but they have to be freed of those clamps before firing. The pulsejets will need a quantity of air forced through them to aid their primary ignition, plus a little ether if possible, and all booster rockets will have to fire pretty much simultaneously on each missile if a successful take off is to be achieved. Those will be your primary problems.

"The secondary problems will come from the submerging of the platforms, if the plan is to be followed. They have to sit on the bed of the sea until activation, yet the pulsejets and the boosters have to remain dry for a better chance of firing, as do all onboard electrics and electronics. Above all else the systems have to be reliable, absolutely one hundred per cent reliable. It will be a challenging task, but then you're not the type to back down from a challenge are you?" A grin had spread across Peter's face as he finished speaking.

The problem with the clamps, which Danny had originally thought may be the cause of sleepless nights, disappeared in an instant. With the missiles set at an angle of sixty-five degrees from the horizontal the underside of the clamps he designed doubled as a support and had several small rollers built in to reduce friction on take off. Dan decided to use nylon rollers from the rear shutters of commercial trucks as they were sealed against road film so should, he reasoned, offer sufficient resistance to sand and water. The upper part of the clamp was lightly sprung and designed to swing away as the platform surfaced, forced back as the float which had held it snugly in position fell free as its buoyancy ended. A compressed air cylinder could be used to both inflate the necessary floats when beneath the surface then blow air through the pulsejets until they stabilised, the valve switched by the same float, and ether was introduced in exactly the same way. The rockets were already sealed and the sealing was augmented with a simple layer of grease. Both ends of the pulsejet engines were plugged, again waterproofed with grease, all to be held in place by water pressure, with the plugs pulled clear by the clamping arms as they released.

Semi simultaneous firing of the booster rockets could be accomplished mechanically or electronically. Danny did not like the mix of electronics and water no matter how well sealed systems were supposed to be, taking the view the foolproof mechanical route was always the safest one to follow. Wet or dry the percussion cap would fire and it was an easy matter to design a simple sprung loaded hammer for each rocket. These he set in pairs, each pair tied off and held in tension against its opposite pair. The ties were designed to be burnt through by tail flames as the pulsejets stabalised. He experimented with various man made materials until he found what he desired, something impervious to water which would burn through, breaking in less than fifteen seconds of applied flame, allowing all four hammers to hit their relevant percussion caps within milliseconds of one another. The material he eventually chose was nothing more complicated than simple nylon cable ties, and worked two hundred times out of the two hundred tests he applied.

At less than a meter square the experimental platform performed perfectly on land so he then went about designing the pontoon floats which would carry it. Several months earlier he tried various materials but had soon chosen Valmex, the material of choice of the manufactures of various makers of white water rafts. The surface conditioning offered the exact airtight and watertight seams required and was sufficiently elastic, yet seemingly unsusceptible to minor mechanical damage. The material had done all which was asked of it, and after two weeks of sitting on the bed of The Solent it resurfaced the instant it was re-inflated. Valmex was produced by a German company which sold their product widely from several locations around the world. One of Chris Spencer's operatives was despatched to purchase a quantity from their outlet in Istanbul, Turkey, where sellers were told it was going to Iran. It was in fact repackaged, crated and shipped to Southampton and then Cape Town, effectively ending the trail in Turkey.

The missiles, launch platforms and pontoons were now all designed. Danny was finished and ready to have the missiles tested. He had worked hard and tirelessly for many months, and this was recognised by all. By any standards he really was due a break, but there were still things to be done, and his brother had another mission in mind for him.

Nineteen

Despite the magnitude of the expenditure the mission would require Danny Bryant was finding it extremely difficult to keep even a relatively normal expression on his face. He was finally on a mission, and it was an important mission. Actually it was a vital mission and much would hinge on how well he performed. He must remember that, concentrate, think of the dead and what lay ahead, despite the job he now had to do. God bless America he though, and laughed out loud, startling the elderly lady sitting next to him.

"Sorry." Dan said gesturing at the in-flight magazine on his lap. "It's a funny article." The old lady looked away raising her eyebrows. She hadn't found anything funny in the entire magazine let alone the article about the property market crisis in Spain the idiot next to her was reading, and reading it in cursed English. She now wished she had been allocated a seat somewhere else on the plane, yet had thought herself lucky at the check-in desk when given an exit row seat. Pity they had to seat an imbecile next to her, especially a giant imbecile!

In some ways Dan had told her the truth. It was the article which triggered his thoughts. The crash of the Spanish holiday home market came as a direct result of the credit crunch, in turn brought about by the US property market and its horrific failure. Had it not been so he would never have been on this flight he reasoned as he laughed again.

Danny was on his way to America, flying out of Charles de Gaulle Paris, and bound for Miami Florida. He was flying on Air France flight 90 which had left bang on time at five minutes to eleven in the morning and would be landing at quarter past two in the afternoon, both times being local, and neither his home time zone. Not that he cared. Not that he cared for one single solitary second, because he was on a mission of a lifetime, one which he would willingly have given at least ten years of his life for, and one which he was uniquely qualified to carry out. God bless America, he thought again as he laughed once more. Sod the little old lady – he was going to have the time of his life – and then some, and it did not hurt his enjoyment of the trip to be flying Air France, eating some of the best food served in the air, and served by air hostesses who not only looked wonderful but had the sexiest voices on the entire planet. He would have to get a French girlfriend when this was all over he promised himself. Much better to buy off-shore he felt, chuckling once more at his thoughts.

Despite his high spirits he tried to sleep. Not because he was tired, but due to the time difference which he wanted to adjust to as rapidly as possible. France was an hour in front, Florida was five hours behind – whatever difference either made, because he knew he couldn't change it. He couldn't sleep, but then he had known he wouldn't be able to, excited or not. Dan knew aircraft seats around the world are designed for undernourished Japanese juniors and he had no chance of being comfortable in cattle class. He also had no chance of travelling at the front end of the bus where the rich folk live because he may have attracted more consideration and therefore attention, and at his size he already got much more than enough of that. Although he was trying to avoid unnecessary attention he was not flying under one of the available alternative identities but was using his own passport, and was already recorded on airline computers around the world, all of which noted his height, as they do for anyone six foot five and over. This was why he had the extra leg room the exit seats afforded, and the reason he had those rows whenever he flew. So the length allowed for his legs was fine, but it was a pity about the lack of room for his upper thighs and chest. Hell – That's flying! – he thought.

The flight into Miami International Airport was without incident. Even the little old lady eventually got tired of scowling at him and went to sleep, or into a coma, or whatever it is little old ladies do when they have managed to piss even themselves off. The pilot put the bird down smoothly and taxied to the appropriate jet way, where the rich people were allowed to exit the plane in their own good time. Cattle class then fought their way off and Danny found himself in concourse H, which he would do if he flew from Charles de Gaulle, something he would have to remember on the way home.

He had visited the US three times in the past and the stamps were there in his passport to show the immigration official he was a good boy who always went home on time.

"You are flying out of France on a British passport, sir," the immigration man stated.

"I most certainly am!" Danny answered somewhat flippantly.

"And why might that be, sir?" the man asked.

"Well, it's about one hundred pounds more return," Danny answered, "But the food is a zillion times better, and – man – the ass is the best in the world. What more can I say?"

A small smile appeared fleetingly on the official's lips. "Are you here for work or pleasure Sir?" he asked.

"Well I'm here to do a week's diving or so," Danny answered, "Can I answer the question on the way out?"

This time the official did smile. "Do you have sufficient funds to support yourself whilst in the United States, sir?" the guy asked, just doing his job by the numbers. He already knew he was going to stamp this big friendly giant's passport.

"I sincerely hope so!" Danny again answered. "But I know how you people like to party, so I brought my AmEx card just in case!"

At that the immigration man chuckled. He wished they were all like this. "You enjoy your stay, sir, and have a nice day now, y'hear?" he said as he stamped the passport, and Danny walked through into the mighty US of A.

He found the carousel, waited what seemed like forever – nothing much changes there he thought – collected his one somewhat modest bag, and headed for car hire, where he managed to take advantage of the 'Deal of the Day' and shortly afterwards drove off in a mid sized Dodge something-or-another with wall to wall plastic. Well, he thought, a decent BMW would probably stick out like a sore thumb here. He made his way across to Interstate 95 where he then headed north, past

Hollywood, and on up to Fort Lauderdale, which he knew from a previous visit boasted more than three hundred miles of navigable waterways and the largest boat show in the world, not to mention seemingly endless boating competitions and annual regattas.

Just north of Fort Lauderdale, known as the 'Venice of America', he left the interstate turning right onto East Oakland Park Boulevard where he headed east. He crossed the intracostal waterway and continued towards the ocean where he once more turned north on North Ocean Drive, continuing with the beach and sea over to his right. He knew he could have stayed on the interstate for a few more miles, as it ran parallel with the beach, but he was a creature of the water and loved the sea. Four miles further north he spotted his destination.

The Atlantic Sands Resort and Spa stood some ten floors high at an angle to the beach, allowing the majority of its eighty-five rooms to enjoy a splendid sea view. It claimed to be one of Pompano Beach's finest oceanfront resorts, purporting to offer a unique mix of opulence and warmth, which Danny fully intended to put to the test. He pulled off the road onto the hotel's driveway and found himself a parking place. After parking he swung himself out of the driving seat and pulled open the door behind him where he had tossed his bag at the airport. He rummaged around in his pockets, removed all pound and euro notes and coins along with his passport, opened his bag and put everything into a zipped pocked inside. Danny Bryant's trip to America had temporarily been put on hold. He had a fake US driving license in case the hotel asked for ID, but which he hoped not to show, and a legitimate Master Card. As Steve Turner he collected his bag, locked the car and headed for reception.

The reception area was reasonably busy with people coming and going, and big Steve wandered up to reception with a mobile phone to his ear, although it had remained switched off since Paris and would stay that way for days, 'uhuhing' as he did. He placed the paperwork from the internet reservation made from a cyber café on the countertop along with the Master Card and driving license, whilst he continued with his 'conversation' of sure's, yup's and umhum's. The receptionist could see her guest was busy so continued to process his registration whilst he spoke requiring only his credit card, after all the guest was paying more than five hundred bucks a night to stay in the studio suite he had booked. She finished and smiled up sweetly holding out a paper for him to sign, which he silently did as she passed across his plastic perforated key. He smiled and winked at her, raising his eyes and indicating the phone. Just another harassed employee or henpecked husband. She again smiled at him, pointing to the room number on the paperwork and raising all ten fingers before pointing to the lift. Tenth floor. He was there and he was signed in. From that moment on it would not matter who heard his English accent as it was highly unlikely his identity would be questioned during the three nights he spent at the hotel, and even if it were noted he was doing absolutely nothing illegal in using a professional pseudonym.

Danny's plane had landed on time, but the trek through the airport and then the drive which followed had cost another two hours, so it was now after four in the afternoon local time, or nine in the evening for his body clock. The food on the plane had proved to be good, but it was still food on a plane, and he certainly felt the need for something more substantial. However he also felt the need to exercise. Although he was based in an office he did usually get a chance to get involved in physical pursuits of one kind or another every day so he thought he had better come up with a plan. The hotel boasted a fitness centre, Jacuzzi and, despite being positioned on the beach, its own swimming pools. He chose not to run along the beach as it would probably draw the wrong sort of attention, settling instead for the weights in the fitness room, which was well kitted out but completely devoid of people as he entered it.

He spent thirty minutes working out on a skilfully engineered and comprehensive weight machine, pushing himself well beyond the comfort zone, feeling the burn in each of the muscle groups as the reps built up and sweat ran down his back and chest, soaking into his cotton vest. He had neither seen nor heard the young woman enter, so engrossed was he in his workout. With muscles still pumped he roughly towelled the sweat from his chest and face as he stood, catching sight of her in a large mirror as he did so. She was facing away from him, standing on a workout mat and bent double at the waist with her straight legs apart. Her right arm was stretched out to touch her left ankle and her left arm stretched upwards into the air. As he watched she rolled her upper body so that her left arm then touched her right ankle. She had long golden hair pulled back into a tight pony-tail, which bobbed from side to side as she exercised, cascading across the shiny skin tight white lycra leotard she wore, with a golden thong over the top for modesty – or accentuation. His view of her rear end was perfect, possibly by accident, but probably by design. He understood the leotard look had gone out with the early nineties – God bless America he thought once more, grinning again as he did.

She sensed his gaze and turned, still bent double, to look back at him. He didn't glance away guiltily, but continued to stare. She smiled slightly then literally wiggled her bum as she straightened up and turned to face him.

"Hi," he said as he ran his eyes over the perfection which was her body in a manner which was obvious in the extreme.

"Hi," she responded, the tip of a perfect pink tongue pushed between two perfect pink lips which were slowly licked as she ran her eyes down as far as his crotch.

"I didn't mean to put you off your exercise." Danny said grinning at her actions before continuing. "Please don't stop on my account. Always good to watch someone else working out, and you seemed to be doing so well!"

"Always a pleasure to have an appreciative audience. You weren't doing so badly yourself when I came in. Is that a British accent I detect?" she asked in a soft North American accent he really couldn't place.

"Yes, I'm from England. My name is Danny," Dan answered as he stepped forward with his hand outstretched. There was no need to lie about his identity to this honey he reasoned.

"Sabine Moliere. I'm from Laval near Montreal," she responded taking his hand firmly.

Danny knew he should be going, but hell, no single man of his age with a red blood cell in his body was going to pass up on a girl like this. He had to keep talking to her. She was obviously interested, and he certainly was.

"I see, that accounts for your accent. I couldn't place it. Have you been down here long? Are you here on work or play? Are you with a husband? Boyfriend?" Dan asked one question after the other.

"Okay," Sabine answered smiling as she did so. "I arrived yesterday. I'm here on vacation and have twelve nights left. I'm twenty-six years old. My best friend married my cousin nearly two years ago, and this is really their summer vacation. I split up from my long term boyfriend four weeks back when I found out he had something going on with his secretary at work. My friend and cousin suggested I come with them to give me a break from it all and I kind of tagged along. I've never been married and don't have a current boyfriend. I know that answers more questions than you asked, but if you have any more you will have to buy me a drink so my throat doesn't run dry!"

"You must have read my mind," the big man replied. "I assume there is a bar at the pool. I was intending to have a bit of a swim. Then of course I have to eat later, and I do so loathe eating alone. I'm happy to skip the swim, but perhaps we could enjoy a drink at the poolside bar after I've had a shower if you can give me fifteen minutes, and then maybe I can persuade you to join me for a meal?"

"Oh, you really won't have to persuade me," Sabine said in a somewhat suggestive manner. "I already know my cousin and friend won't miss me, or if they do it will be in a positive way! Fifteen minutes it is then," she said as she wrapped a towel around her narrow waist and draped another over her shoulders. They walked to the lift then travelled up together. She exited two floors below his and, as the doors opened, she touched his chest just below the neck and ran her finger down to his sweat sodden vest. "Now don't start without me!" she said, touching the end of her finger to the tip of her tongue as she turned away and the doors closed.

Back in his room Danny stripped off his gym gear and stepped into the shower, grinning at his luck, but at the same time wondering if this girl, beautiful though she was, might just create an additional complication. Complication or not she was a perfectly formed female of the species and he knew he was a pretty good representation of the male side. It would be a crime against nature to walk away Danny thought, grinning some more, besides it was only a drink and dinner – wasn't it!

The drinks went well, the conversation flowed, the meal they shared was perfectly prepared and presented, and the sex afterwards was a deeply satisfying end to an excellent evening for both of them. Danny had thoroughly enjoyed the sight, sound, smell, touch and taste of her. She was one of those unusual lucky women who look even better out of their clothes, and Danny was anything but disappointed as her slinky little number slid from her body revealing she wore nothing beneath.

"Ah – I was looking forward to seeing how naturally blonde you were," Danny said, "but you've removed the evidence!"

Sabine laughed and, as his mouth closed on hers, said. "Don't worry, I'm one hundred per cent natural." They were both fit young people with trained and toned bodies. The sex they enjoyed three times during the night was exciting and energetic, with both doing their best to stimulate and please the other. In between both slept comfortably with Sabine snuggling up under one of Danny's huge muscular arms.

At half past six in the morning Sabine rose, showered, pulled her dress on and gave Dan a long deep kiss, then left. Dan himself then rose and showered. The previous day had been a long one and he had not slept as much as he might have done, but his body clock told him it was late morning and he was excited about what lay in store for him later in the day. He had an appointment at eleven-thirty that morning, but couldn't wait until then. He pulled on clothes, left his room and then the hotel. Taking his car he crossed the intracostal waterway heading directly towards the North Federal Highway, the road he wanted. There he drove for two miles directly south until Lettuce Lake appeared on his left. As he approached the lake he swung the car across to the centre of the road and followed a slip road beside a large showroom which led down to a small island where he parked the car.

He stepped out of the car and strolled down a wide alleyway when suddenly he spotted her. The sun had already been up for well over two hours and she looked unbelievably beautiful in the warm rays of the new day. The sight of her literally took his breath away. He really could not remember seeing anything as exquisite in all his life and felt an almost overpowering desire to rush forward and run his hands lovingly over the gorgeous curves of her body, caressing her and breathing in the intoxicating smell of her. She was lithe and lovely, everything he had known she would be, but there was so much more. Resting as she was she gave the appearance of being conceived for those with only blue blood, but even relaxed as she was he could tell there was something very spirited, even naughty about her, and she had a style about her which was almost aggressive and which he knew would leave all others trailing in her wake. He would bet his last penny in the world she would be a simply wonderful performer – she just oozed and exuded sensuality.

"God," Danny groaned out loud. "I just can't wait to play with you, you beautiful creature."

The Sunseeker Predator 108 almost seemed to hear him. A small swell caught her and lifted her slightly as Danny spoke, giving him the impression she had curtsied in response. Danny's heart went out to her. He had been around boats and boating all of his adult life, and under Mike Latham had learnt to expertly handle large power cruisers and motor yachts, but he had never even moored one like this before. Certainly he had seen them, and Sunseeker's headquarters at Poole was less than half an hour from his home. He had viewed them in awe at the Southampton Boat Show and had even visited their stand at the new London Boat Show held at the Royal Victoria Dock, but he had never so much as stood on the deck of one at sea. She was perfect, and within a few days, if she lived up to expectations, which he already knew she would, funds would be transferred from an untraceable source and he would take her to sea on the start of a journey which would eventually take her to the other side of the world.

For now he had seen her, by midday he expected to be on her decks, afterwards taking her out for a sea trial. He drove the few miles back to the hotel and was back in his room before eight o'clock, his curiosity temporarily satisfied. His body clock was still out of zone. If he was to perform at peak efficiency later in the day he ought to take the opportunity to get a couple of hours' sleep. He set the alarm to go off at ten o'clock and immediately went to sleep enjoying two hours of blissful slumber. At ten he arose again, dressed smart casual ready for the meeting, then went down for breakfast stopping at reception on the way to order a taxi for eleven-fifteen. Breakfast finished at ten-thirty so he rapidly ordered ham and eggs over rye, coffee and two glasses of orange juice. His food arrived swiftly and he started to tuck in but, as he did so, three people who had finished their breakfast and were leaving walked past his table, one of whom was Sabine. She told the others she would catch up with them, asked Dan if he minded her joining him, sat down and ordered a coffee to keep him company. He had explained the night before he would be working but she asked if he was free that night, which he was, so they made hasty plans and she departed.

The taxi dropped him at his destination, Sunseeker Yachts on the South Federal Highway, five minutes before his appointment and, as Steve Turner, he was politely ushered straight into the plush offices whilst asked if he would like coffee. Belinda Harrison-Smythe joined him and they exchanged the usual pleasantries then discussed the Sunseeker brand and product in generalities. Unbeknown to BHS, as she was known, Danny could well have been the most knowledgeable potential customer she had ever spoken to. Since Jack had tasked him with the mission and given him the required specifications Danny had worked tirelessly to find the best tool possible for the task ahead. He started with an open mind, trying to determine what vessel would most suit their needs, had a proven track record and was available. He added an additional requirement of his own. As it was not his money he was spending he had to make sure every penny spent was used wisely, with residual values always a major consideration.

Although there were a huge number and variety of vessels in existence very few made it to his short list, and the front runner from the beginning was never bettered. The Predator 108 was not Sunseeker's largest offering, that place went to their thirty-seven meter Trideck Yacht, the veritable jewel in their crown, a vessel which could comfortably accommodate ten guests and quarter eight crew in unsurpassed floating luxury. However the Trideck was not as sleek as the Predator, and the 108, at one hundred and eight feet in length, was the largest performance motor yacht Sunseeker built, truly one of the greatest super yachts of all time, and absolutely perfect for what was needed, in fact without exception surpassing every single one of Jack's criteria.

BHS spoke briefly of the last owner, the problems with the American property market, and how little service the 108 he was there to view had actually seen, all of which Danny already knew as he had spent time researching the background to this vessel once he discovered her. He felt a little sorry for the guy who was losing this beautiful lady, a guy who had made and lost seemingly countless millions playing the property market, but chancers can fail, and this one had big time. Ho hum, there's a silver lining to every cloud thought Danny, and in this case it meant the lady was coming his way. They discussed the configuration of the vessel in question, this one had the master stateroom version rather than the master suite with adjoining lobby, and BHS managed to slide an option into the conversation almost without it being seen as a sales pitch. Of course Danny understood if he wanted any alteration done they would be more than happy to customise the vessel in line with his tastes. Well the vessel was certainly going to be customised, but if he explained how to BHS she would have first been shocked, then horrified, and would then most certainly have called the police and FBI. No, Danny was going to trial her and then take her away almost exactly as she was.

They left the office, passed through the showroom, and walked out into the bright Florida sunshine, and there she was again, this time from the other side, every bit as beautiful close up and in brighter light as she was early that morning. As he stepped on board Danny was impressed, to the level of simply thrilled, with everything he saw. He knew the technicalities and specifications, and understood the construction and engine capabilities, but those were just dry statistics, and important though they were statistics alone could not explain this living, breathing, dancing beauty. Once aboard and cast off the skipper and crew proved their worth and sheer professionalism to Danny from the moment they extracted the vessel from its tight, cramped berth. The bow and stern thrusters were balanced perfectly and the motion almost indiscernible as they moved off sideways from the berth and showroom. They crossed the pond which was Lettuce Lake and headed north on the Intracostal Waterway for the Hillsborough Inlet, about three miles away, and the ocean which lay beyond. Traffic along it was light, and they seemed to quickly pass the old Hillsborough Lighthouse as the blue green waters of the Atlantic beckoned. They eased off shore gently before the skipper started to open up the engines and the Predator threw off her ladylike persona and became the snarling minx that the tens of thousands of successful design hours had made her.

Danny was used to bow lift as power was applied in the craft he usually handled, but that just did not happen with this unleashed beast. Stern lift was provided by surface piercing props, one of which counter rotated, giving a wonderfully steady running attitude. The three two thousand horsepower Arneson ASD 16 engines were perfectly synchronized and the combined six thousand horsepower power-plant was capable of pushing the Predator through waters at an extremely impressive forty-three knots, almost fifty miles per hour. She could go from dead-idle to top speed in under a minute despite weighing eighty-four tons at half load, and she was one of the biggest, fastest and fastest accelerating vessels of her class in the world. When the three were combined there was nothing on the planet to touch her. As a performance motor yacht she quite literally was in a class all of her own.

Once in open sea Danny was invited to take the controls himself and he jumped at the opportunity. He sat comfortably in the large centre right Besenzoni helm chair, a huge left hand holding the small carbon fibre wheel between his legs and the right resting on the set of electronic engine controls. The helm station, in empire blue, was easy on the eye and boasted charts, navigation and radar on separate screens. Apart from the main engine controls full information regarding the ships systems was fed to the station through a comprehensive array of onboard instrumentation.

Seas were short, cresting at four to six feet, and to Danny that would usually mean slightly choppy, but not so in this dream-boat. She just took to the seas and cut through green water like a hot knife does through butter as he carved simple turns across the oceans surface whilst all the time running at an attitude which allowed him to constantly see over the bows. Nothing he ever controlled before had quite prepared him for the incredible thrill it gave him, and it was a long way from ending there. The skipper sitting in an identical seat on his right pushed a button and the roof slid back out of sight, salty smelling fresh air then flooding the spacious control area.

He drove the boat down as far as Miami then spun her around for the journey back, returning control of the vessel to her skipper whilst BHS took him on a guided tour of the guest quarters, crew quarters and entertaining areas. The tour started where they were as the helm with its row of four identical Besenzoni chairs was forward of the saloon, which in turn connected to the galley below by a dumb waiter. When Danny first walked in he had been impressed with the height. At his height he was used to wandering around most vessels bent double. With the Predator there was no need to do so as there were lofty ceilings everywhere, a comfortable nine feet of headroom throughout the saloon area.

The saloon boasted an eight place dining table, a top of the range Linn home entertainment system complete with hard disc music library, and a retractable forty two inch LCD television. To the rear of the table there was a sophisticated living area / drawing room, with large L shaped leather couches facing one another across cocktail tables sited on wide teak flooring. The adjacent cherry wood bar with icemaker, fridge, and hot and cold sink could be comprehensively stocked, and there was a sliding door which then gave access to a barbeque in the cockpit, which could be enjoyed day and night in the open air.

Below decks the accommodation space was wonderfully comprehensive with full attention given to every detail. A full galley adjoined the crew quarters and connected with the dining and saloon area above via a separate dedicated staircase in addition to the dumb waiter. There was a very well fitted out owner's office with walls and furniture in light cherry wood, a second saloon, a large stateroom and three guest cabins for two. All sleeping accommodation was luxurious, with quiet subtle tones of English leather and light cherry over floors of polished teak. Linn entertainment equipment had not been spared and all en-suite heads contained granite floors and countertops. Satin cherry abounded throughout, and the overall impression was that of unashamed opulence on a grand scale.

The crew quarters proved to be equally impressive if not so opulent. Having crewed on several vessels in his past Dan could appreciate the quarters provided for the crew, and the level of comfort they too obviously experienced, a world away from hot bedding in a cabin not big enough to either stand in or to sleep whilst stretched out. The crew quarters here actually put the master's quarters to shame in most of the small yachts he had previously sailed in, when he would have given his eye teeth for a night of the quality comfort provided on the Predator.

To Danny's mind all he had seen was off the scale as far as impressive was concerned. However to him generally, and certainly for what would be required in the not too distant future, the most important room on any powered boat was the engine room. He had long felt far too many people put to sea in a vessel which relied wholly on power to propel it without even rudimentary mechanical knowledge. This was not only bordering on insanity, but could prove costly in terms of lives, unfortunately not only their own, which might otherwise be considered just if applying Darwinian terms. Initially Danny had taught himself the way around engines, starting with simple outboards then moving on to inboards. Interested with all things to do with the water he had taken a fairly detailed maintenance course at night school and worked in a shipyard at times during holiday periods. He could not break down an engine and forge weld a crankshaft, but he could rebuild one without a workshop manual if he had the parts and, most importantly, he had both a good mechanical ear and could problem solve.

They accessed the engine room via the large swim deck, lower aft, on which the tender currently sat. The big diesels looked and sounded perfect. There was not a knock, rattle or tap anywhere, and the room had all the appearance of a freshly scrubbed operating theatre without a trace of oil or grease to be seen. The only downside was it was pretty tight inside with the three enormous mills squeezed in. He would later take his time and get to know each and every component part intimately, though he could see it would not be a fast process with so much within the room, from the water maker to the hydraulic power equipment, and the emergency shutdown equipment all the way through to the tool box.

Leaving the engine room they went back on deck and enjoyed the pollution free air and rays of an offshore Florida afternoon. He finally wandered up to the sharp end grinning at the hot tub built into the deck and the fixed loungers surrounding it, and paced out the distance from the moon roof opening at the rear of the helm seats to just short of the bows. With a wide smile of satisfaction he returned to the large teak deck behind the main superstructure which provided the general outside seating and dining area, where he gratefully accepted a large glass of a darker Samuel Adams beer, infinitely preferable to his tastes to international yellow fizz.

How to strike a deal? He certainly did not want to lose her, but he wanted her to come for the right amount. A cost at which they could easily sell her on again – after the operation! The market was currently somewhat deflated, but she was for sale for eight million dollars, which was the upper end of the current market price-wise, and certainly more than he wished to pay even though he was previously told he could give full asking price. In the past he had bought and sold his own cars and boats along the way, always striving to cut a good deal for himself both ways, but the most expensive boat he had ever purchased was slightly less than eighteen thousand pounds. That one had been up for sale for twenty-one thousand, all but a fiver, and he had haggled the reluctant seller down over three grand. However these people were professionals – very professional – and they would not be so easy to drive down in price. Still the same rules applied despite the sum involved, or the experience of the sales staff. Go in low. You can always go up, but rarely down. You won't insult them, it's just business he told himself, and as far as they were concerned he was just an agent.

He sat on a wide comfortable seat facing aft, watching the rainbow which formed and disappeared in the plume of spray above their wake which sped out into the distance behind them. He sat in silent thought, contemplating and calculating, occasionally gulping down a mouthful or two of his beer. Another glass appeared in front of him as if by magic. Very slick. Very professional. BHS sat close to his left side, relaxed, silently leaning back into her seat, her hair tied back but with several strands which had escaped blowing in the wind. To a casual observed or passer-by, and at a steady thirty-five knots there would not be many of those, they could have been taken for a couple who had known one another for years sitting in companionable silence. It was broken.

"It's a shame," Danny said. "I had hoped I wouldn't like her."

BHS said nothing. She just sat and looked at him with an almost sympathetic expression on her face, forcing him to break the silence again. Very professional.

"Basically I know what my principal is prepared to spend, which includes purchase price, transportation costs, fuel and service." Danny continued. "I also know the asking price and what I've been instructed to offer. I'll be honest with you in telling you it is the only vessel I've viewed and know it will suit his purposes perfectly. I can also see it's just been serviced which removes one of the items from my list. The big question is what will she come for, because at the moment we are a little apart?"

They haggled whilst on the ocean, continued as they passed the Hillsborough light house, and as they gently cruised down the Waterway. They haggled across Lettuce Lake, and even continued after they tied up. During negotiations more beer arrived for him, but he had played those games before. He was a big lad, had played rugby for years and sunk many a pint in various clubhouses, and could handle quite a large quantity. Both had seen a potential advantage, but in learning of that advantage each knew the other had seen their own weakness. Danny's weakness was that he wanted this boat, and his continued interest underlined just how interested he was. BHS's weakness was in that she had a genuinely interested customer who had money to spend, albeit of an undisclosed amount, and moneyed customers were in very short supply thanks to the credit crunch and the state of the international money market.

It was for sale for eight million, although she could comfortably take half a million less, but this cheeky bugger had offered her six and a half million, and that was subject to a service update and full tank of fuel, the tank of which held nearly three thousand gallons. She had come down her five hundred thousand, but he had only gone up two and that most grudgingly. She was forced down another two, but that really was as low as she could go, whilst he had only come up another fifty thousand. They were still over half a million dollars apart and she didn't have the discretion to sanction writing it back anything like as much as that. Unfortunately for her she made a tiny mistake when Danny suggested she ring his offer through – she blinked. She blinked and he sensed he had the upper hand. As he suspected, this sale was being forced by the bank. They had given her latitude, but not that much. She had blinked and he was given the smallest of glimpses at her cards, but the smallest glimpse was all he needed.

It was past six in the evening when they berthed and tied up alongside the Sunseeker showrooms, which was far too late to put the offer to the bankers. A taxi was called and Danny left with the gut knowledge the boat was his. The final sale offer price was dropped to seven and a quarter million, a price he could and would happily pay, but one he also knew he would not have to. He made it clear to BHS he would be leaving early in the morning of the day after next. That effectively left the bank with the option of accepting or rejecting the offer by close of play the following day, an offer of real money in a world currently starved of it. The banks were bankers, not boat salespeople. They would want to mitigate their losses. They would take the offer, but they would probably come back first with an alternative offer for him, probably seven million – which he would reject – if they managed to contact him. They would then leave it to the last moment to let him sweat or to see if he would blink – which he wouldn't do.

He wondered what Sabine was doing the following day and did not have long to wait to find out.

He walked into the hotel a happy man. The Predator would be theirs. He had then been on the ocean and water for most of the day, but hadn't had the chance to even dip his toes in the water, let alone swim. Swimming was one thing he really wanted to do to unwind; besides, the pool area was where he and Sabine had hastily agreed to meet. He went to his room, changed into a pair of swimming shorts and then headed back for it. At the poolside he threw his shirt and a couple of towels onto a lounger and dived into the water, which was substantially warmer than he expected. The two pools were only small, certainly nowhere near Olympic size, but they were wet, and at seven in the evening almost deserted. He swam several lengths fast, then several more at an easier place. Finally he dived under the water and swam below the surface, turning underwater and pushing off for the next length, eventually coming up for air at the end of the fifth. As his head broke the surface he realised he had emerged between the legs of a young woman. She had sat on the side of the pool with her legs over the side and her back to the sun. Rubbing water from his eyes and squinting into the sun he started to stammer out an apology.

"Well if you are going to be such a pervert in a public pool you could at least have the decency to grope me," Sabine laughed down at him, before continuing seriously, "I don't know how you do that. I thought you were never going to come up. I do a bit of diving, but not free diving, and there's no way I could hold my breath like that! Anyway, what are you doing tonight? I need a couple of drinks, something to eat, and someone big and strong to take me to bed. Do you know anyone who could help?"

"Umm. Well I've had a bit of a busy day," Danny answered, and Sabine's expression changed to one of disappointment. "In all honesty I'm also a bit tired after a long day and night yesterday." The disappointment on her face increased. "But I too could do with a drink or two, and I need to eat. Afterwards I could help you look for someone big and strong to take you to bed if you wish."

She laughed out loud, a lovely sexy sound, then reached out, caught hold of the back of his head and pulled it towards hers kissing him full on the lips and forcing her perfect pink tongue between his lips and into his mouth. Danny couldn't resist the urge. He grabbed the back of her shoulders and launched himself backwards into the pool hearing her squeal just before his head again disappeared beneath the surface. This time as his head broke the water there were no legs, just streaming golden hair and a laughing face.

"You silly man, I've got my clothes on." Sabine said still giggling.

"Then take them off and dry them out." Danny suggested helpfully.

Sabine cocked her head on one side then shook it. "Mad." she said with a look of pity, "Stark, staring mad!"

"Mad I may be, but you are the one standing in the middle of a swimming pool with your clothes on holding a conversation. Who do you think all those people watching you think is mad?" Danny asked reasonably. "I think we'd better go up and change before that drink, don't you?"

They went to the lift and Dan pressed the button for the tenth floor.

"Mine's the eighth." Sabine reminded him, but Danny made no move to press anything else and Sabine smiled, reaching down to squeeze something at the front of his swimming shorts which seemed to be growing.

Sabine had not returned to her room but stayed with Danny for the night and the couple took breakfast together early the following morning. She rang her friends from the lobby to let them know what she was doing then left with Dan for the day. He had weighed up the risks of taking her with him and come to the conclusion she should not compromise his mission, besides she was good company and he was getting to like her. The more he talked to her, the greater the depth he found to her character, and he soon realised his first impression of her was a long way off the reality.

Sabine was a beautiful woman who had experienced one long term relationship, which recently turned sour when she caught her former boyfriend having an affair at work. When she confronted him and questioned as to why she was told she was boring, unexciting and dowdy. The words stung her and hurt her far more than the fact she had caught her man cheating, something she knew she would have come to terms with in time. Her job she knew was uninspiring, but that did not make her boring and dowdy. She was previously consistently encouraged to dress down because her former boyfriend did not like the attention her natural beauty attracted, feeling somewhat threatened by it. Boring and dowdy had made her seethe. The relationship ceased immediately. She had gone out and replaced the vast majority of her wardrobe and when the opportunity to join her friend and cousin cropped up she jumped at it. She piled the bulk of her new far more outgoing and sexy clothing into her suitcase, added a couple of items such as her old leotard which Danny had first seen her in, and which she had not worn since a teenager, then headed south. She had seen Danny entering the hotel's fitness centre, taken an immediate shine to him and rushed upstairs to change into something which she hoped would get her noticed. According to her she had never done anything like that in her life before but found the entire experience absolutely thrilling.

"Sabine, I have work to do for an hour or so in Fort Lauderdale. Are you likely to be free when I get back?" Danny asked.

"Well I'm free all day, so why don't I go with you? I wouldn't have to join you in whatever work it is you have to do. I could easily go shopping for an hour if you drop me off nearby. Then you could collect me when you finish, we could have lunch together somewhere and maybe hit Miami Beach in the afternoon." Sabine suggested.

"Sounds good to me! Give me your mobile number and I'll ring you when I've finished the business," Danny suggested, and a little later dropped her off at a huge mall before going on to his destination, an international yacht shipping company which he and Jack had discovered during research done before he left England.

Global Yacht Shipping, was a division of International Relocation Inc., and licensed with the Federal Maritime Commission as a Non Vessel Operator Common

Carrier or NVOCC. Global had well over a quarter of a century of experience in shipping yachts, boats and all manner of vessels via land, air or, most importantly, by sea. They were a successful company whose success sprang from their provision of a personalised service carried out in a thoroughly professional manner, which often exceeded the expectations of their clients, and was handled by a highly experienced and diligent staff. They claimed to be able to move a vessel from and to anywhere in the world irrespective of size, but this was never going be put to the ultimate challenge by Danny. With their worldwide headquarters based in Fort Lauderdale and subsidiary offices in Durban, South Africa, as well as several in Europe and other lands, they would have been a natural choice anyway, but their credentials spoke for themselves. Danny had rung for an appointment as Steve Turner and arrangements were made for ten o'clock.

Danny, once again as Steve Turner, was shown into the comfortable offices of Sidney Glendive III, a big man at six four, although he didn't feel it as he stood to shake hands with the huge Brit who walked into his office. Over the ever present coffee Glendive outlined the company's background, specialities and services. He promised the utmost efficiency and security, something which was of paramount importance, and explained how Global specialised in the movement of vessels of all sizes by way of their various services, of which only the lift on lift off or possibly float on float off were of any interest. Danny already knew Global worked with some high profile clients around the world, including yacht racing teams, and were well capable of doing all which was required as far as delivery of the Predator was concerned.

For forty minutes they thrashed things out, from delivery of the Predator to Global, through shipping cradles, document preparation, custom validation, insurance cover, voyage preparation, marina services and crane and special lifting services at the delivery point. Re-configuring the vessel for cheaper shipping was briefly touched upon but declined, as was shrink wrapping the yacht. Danny was somewhat concerned with cradle design and manufacture, and wanted reassurance the loading and lashing was handled by experienced professionals who completely understood loading points and weight distribution. It was his intention to ask and pay for one of Sunseeker's staff to be present when the Predator was lifted or floated on board.

Finally, having agreed a deal, Glendive sought to assure Danny all would be safe and well if left in his hands. Just before parting he launched into a well rehearsed and practiced speech.

"Now don't worry!" Glendive said, "You can be absolutely confident your motor yacht will arrive at its destination in the same condition in which it is handed over to us. Our safety record for cargo shipments has exceeded all industry standards. The Customs Regulations 19 CFR we discussed only applies to motorised vehicles designed to be used on land, so boats don't require title clearance. Not that it's your concern anyway, as we will take care of all documentation and export formalities. You can ship through us with complete confidence!"

Danny phoned ahead from a public phone after leaving Global's offices and Sabine was waiting for him where he had dropped her off. Full marks to her Danny thought. She had only two small bags, was waiting as arranged, and made no attempt to drag him around the shops, in fact she didn't even mentioned the idea. In keeping with most males Dan had no overwhelming desire to see the inside of any shop, let alone spend time being dragged around from one girlie boutique to another, and the desire of any woman to so emasculate him always led to him saying goodbye.

His meeting with Global had gone well and he spent less than an hour with them, which meant they were running ahead of schedule. They drove the fifteen miles down to North Miami Beach, eventually stopping to the south at Surfside. There they enjoyed an early but extended and leisurely lunch before taking a lengthy walk along the sea shore at the waters edge whilst discussing all manner of things. Although nowhere near as advanced as Danny Sabine had previously taken diving lessons and it was a sport she enjoyed despite her limited experience. One of her long term dreams she explained, was to make the journey down to Key West and dive the reefs there, something Danny had wanted to do whilst on this trip. The sun, sea and sand had their effect, and before they left the beach they both agreed to take a week out to go and do just that.

Leaving Surfside before three-thirty in the afternoon the couple followed the coast road north to Hollywood where they cut inland to pick up the interstate in order to by-pass Fort Lauderdale. They reached the hotel a little after four and, whilst collecting his keys after Sabine had walked away from reception, the receptionist explained to Danny there had been several phone calls for him, the last two of which left messages. As expected they were both to do with the Predator, the hotel's number being the only way of contacting him. Danny explained to Sabine it was work, he would have to make some phone calls, and he would probably have to go out again for an hour or so. They made arrangements to meet early evening and Danny headed for his room.

BHS sounded a little put out as she came on the line when Danny was put through to her. Her voice betrayed the slightest traces of both frustration and relief, causing Danny to grin widely. She explained that at lunchtime the bank had agreed to a reduction in the price to seven million dollars, but that she had told them she was sure her client would not go above the six and three quarter million he had offered. By three-thirty they had come back with a revised figure of six million eight hundred and fifty thousand, which was how things still stood. She had to get back to them urgently with his answer and needed to know if he would be prepared to go up the extra hundred thousand to make the deal work for everyone. He had told her to wait ten minutes whilst he phoned his principal, after which he would get back to her. He then stepped into the shower, once more grinning widely.

Mainly motivated by devilment he kept her waiting for more than fifteen minutes. When he did again telephone through he first apologised for the delay explaining to her his principal had discovered another Predator for sale lying in Dubai, and if he had not closed the deal at six and three quarter million then he should first view the Dubai vessel. There was no vessel in Dubai, but it should take at least a day of phone calls, e-mails and faxes to establish that, and neither BHS nor the banks thought they had the time. In the circumstances his answer had to be no. He would honour his offer, but would not go up. It was a buyers market and everyone understood that. BHS asked him to stay on the line whilst she made her call and he had to sit through nearly three minutes of classical music whilst waiting for the answer he was positive he would get. When BHS once again came on line there was a much more relaxed sound to her voice. The pressure was off and Danny knew he had the deal long before she confirmed it. The Predator was his for six and three quarter million. They had the boat they needed and Danny had saved one and a quarter million dollars on the purchase price, which meant they would be able to dispose of it after the mission without huge losses.

He called a taxi and headed for the showroom and offices. Once there he had the taxi wait whilst he went inside to sort out the money transfer. Account numbers were exchanged and paperwork was duly signed. BHS had used Global Yacht Shipping many times in the past and would be most happy to both deliver the boat to them when funds had cleared and to supply someone to oversee loading when the time came. This time Danny made no attempt to haggle, he had enjoyed doing business with them and knew he would be able to leave matters safely in their hands.

As he was taking his leave BHS asked him. "Is there really another boat in Dubai Mr. Turner?"

Danny grinned as he answered. "No of course not, but do please call me Steve."

BHS smiled. "I thought not. You certainly know how to play the game. If ever you wish to have a change of employment you know where we are. It has been a pleasure Steve." With that she stuck out her hand and shook his firmly. From her point of view the commission on six and three quarter million dollars, whilst not as good as on eight million, was infinitely preferable to a lost sale.

Sabine had told her cousin and friend how her plans had changed, explaining she would be gone for a week, would be back before it was time to return to Montreal, and would stay in touch whilst she was gone. Both were most happy for her and for themselves because of the extra freedom it would give them. Danny was due to check out anyway, which he did separately and privately to avoid letting Sabine know he was registered under a false name with all the questions and possible mistrust that could raise. Sabine checked out but reserved the room for her return, which would give her the last two nights of her holiday back where she had started.

This time they picked up Florida's Turnpike south, veering east then south onto the Homestead Extension around Hialeah, in order to avoid Miami. At Homestead, and the end of the Turnpike, they followed on to Highway 1 to cross the mangrove swamps of the southern Everglades. Shortly afterwards the roadway became raised above the level of the land before becoming a bridge as they crossed the sea to Key Largo. From there the road ran as a four lane divided highway for some fifteen miles down as far as Tavernier where it reduced in size and became a principle highway. After about one hundred and fifty miles and a little under three hours driving they stopped at Marathon where they purchased some provisions. Continuing then for another ten miles they stopped at No Name Key and pulled over to a picnic spot in a truly beautiful natural setting where they stretched their legs then hungrily devoured the food they had bought at Marathon. An hour later found them in the centre of Key West, and looking for accommodation in Duval at the heart of the Old Town.

Location, location, location. The same rule applies to a shop, store, garage or hotel. The Crowne Plaza Hotel La Concha is a historic hotel located directly on Duval Street, which is at the centre of Old Town Key West, and is part of the up-market Duval Square Shopping Plaza which boasts, among other things, many fine restaurants. Built in 1926, the La Concha is somewhat unique, possibly even inspirational, and has in its time been home to the likes of Harry S. Truman and Ernest Hemingway, and Tennessee Williams is said to have written A Streetcar Named Desire whilst there. It provides one hundred and sixty rooms over seven floors, has a fitness room, swimming pools, parking and, on the seventh floor, a lounge and deck from which a spectacular three hundred and sixty degree panoramic view is provided of all Key West including the nightly sunset celebrations.

It was perfect for them, it was available, and they were fortunate to secure a larger room on the opposite side of the hotel to Duval. Both were suitably impressed with the size of the bed and room, the cleanliness and character of the building and of the friendly helpful nature of the staff. A Starbuck's coffee shop was at the lobby level and all major attractions, shopping, entertainment, and nightlife appeared to be within walking distance. The only thing left for them to find was a decent diving operation and they were pointed in the direction of Garrison Bight Marina by a very helpful bell hop / doorman.

They followed the directions given and found a diving business which also seemed to suit their needs admirably. They had already decided to split their time at Key West so, after showing their dive certificates, booked three days diving to start two days later, giving them a full day to explore and find their way around beforehand. The evening took them to the legendary Sloppy Joe's and next door to the less well known Lazy Gecko, a tropical island themed bar offering mouth watering frozen daiquiris, fully loaded deli-style sandwiches and mouth-watering fresh pizza. The next day they took a leisurely tour of the home and gardens of the late Ernest Hemingway, visited the pirate museum and the Southernmost Point of the continental USA. In the afternoon they saw Key West from an open-cockpit biplane, riding up front as an experienced pilot flew them above shipwrecks, sharks, dolphins, and some of the coral reefs they hoped to be diving.

The high-speed catamaran dive boat was set up for just six divers and departed at eight in the morning. The cat was brand new, roomy and comfortable, and the outfit operating it claimed to reach the best dive sites long before their competitors. Danny wanted to try some underwater photography so rented a Nikonos 5 which he used extensively whilst on a guided tour around the wrecks and reefs the area is famous for, improving his technique and later providing irreplaceable holiday memories. After their first dive the crew changed their tanks whilst the divers relaxed, enjoyed the complimentary beverages, and talked about the dive they had just experienced which had vastly exceeded Sabine's wildest dreams. She was so excited and enthused to such a degree Danny laughingly suggested she may be suffering from nitrogen narcosis, to which she stuck out her tongue, giggling at her own loquacity.

The first dive of the day they had taken over wrecks, the second was reef diving. The crystal clear waters of the Gulf of Mexico yielded up the beautiful hidden bounty of its underwater world. A myriad of colours flashed before their eyes as they gently propelled themselves along the course of the reef with the help of their long flexible flippers. The entire experience appeared almost surreal as the quality of the light, far from being dulled by its passage through the water seemed almost to have been magnified, effectively spotlighting the wonderfully coloured corals and reflecting back off the multi coloured shining scales of schools of incredibly diverse and abundant tropical fish. Here was a world even Dan with his years of diving experience had never before seen, and he was left awe struck by its mesmerising and indescribable beauty.

Over the three days the couple found they had unlimited bottom time on their second dives, and the longer they stayed down the more the reefs gave the impression of consenting to the revealing of ever more secrets. However their most memorable moment came as they were once again diving a wreck and were joined by a small pod of dolphins. For them, as for most, the dolphin encounter was an almost spiritual experience as they were suddenly surrounded by a family of friendly, playful and intelligent warm blooded creatures. The evolutionary miracle which dolphins usually represent to the human psyche was not missed by either Dan or Sabine, as individuals swam past displaying characteristics which were deeply human in nature, despite the fact they were animals perfectly adapted to their aquatic world.

The diving was over all too soon for both of them, but they wanted to see as much as they could whilst in the area, so the following day booked places on a high speed catamaran for the seventy mile trip to the islands and waters of the Dry Tortugas National Park and Fort Jefferson to the west of Key West. On their last full day they hired bicycles and cycled around the full extent of the island, soaking up the sun, sights and sounds of an island which for them had become truly magical. As a final treat Dan booked them on a romantic sunset sail and, with his arms wrapped around her, they watched as the sun gently sank into the sea on which they were floating, in the most spectacular sunset either could ever remember. Still locked together they continued to view the heavens as stars slowly started to appear in an ever darkening night sky. As a shooting star flashed overhead they both secretly wished for the same thing, that the week could go on forever. Unbeknown to Danny as Sabine made her wish tears caused by emotions ranging from blissful happiness to deep sorrow at the thought of their parting silently ran down her cheeks, dripping from her face and blowing away on the breeze, adding just a few more drops of wind blown spray to the warm night air.

The morning they were to leave Key West neither was in a hurry to depart. Each had deeply enjoyed their time on the island, but mostly both rejoiced in the company of the other. Their days had been filled with energetic outdoor adventure, their evenings loaded with novel eating and drinking experiences, and their nights full of sated sexual passion. For the entire week they remained completely out of contact with anyone they knew, save for one call each, Sabine to confirm all was well with her, and from a call box Dan checked to see if the funds had transferred successfully for the Predator, which they had. Apart from the requirements of ordering food and drink, and receiving instructions from boat and dive crews, neither so much as conversed with anyone else. Danny had never experienced anything like it with a female before. In the past he had usually found them quite boring after a very short period, usually between two minutes and two days, but Sabine was totally different. For Sabine she had never before met a man firstly of his size, but mainly anyone as considerate, thoughtful, amusing and downright masculine. She would then have quite happily curled up in his suitcase to be taken anywhere in the world by him, but knew it was not to be.

Instead Danny took her back to the Atlantic Sands Resort and Spa at Pompano Beach which, although she was resigned to it, was not quite all she dreamt of. This time Dan did not check in, but spent the night with Sabine in her room, a night of extraordinary tenderness interspersed with consummate passion. As the rays of the early morning sun crept around the edges of the thick curtains Sabine knew the day had arrived when he would be gone, and she didn't have a clue as to whether they would ever again meet, something she discovered she wanted above all else in the world. She clung to him and this time wept quite openly in front of him, never once asking him to stay or to take her with him, but just thanking him for giving her the best few days she had ever known.

Danny knew not where the path in life he was currently destined to follow would eventually take him. In a normal life he would have moved heaven and earth to be with this girl, but knew his was not going to be a normal life, at least not for some time to come, possibly some considerable time, and there were far greater things at stake than personal happiness. Things he could not and would not shrug off. He considered parting with his address, or at least a phone number, but decided against it. Nothing must compromise the mission. Instead he wrote her a note and told her she was the most interesting, sexy, fashionable and exciting female he had ever met, that he would have loved to have spent more time with her, and profoundly wished his life would allow him to do just such a thing, but unfortunately at that particular time it would not.

Regrets and wishes flooded his mind as he drove away from the hotel. He left in plenty of time to make his flight, diverting through Fort Lauderdale to check the Predator was now sitting in a new berth, waiting to be loaded for her transatlantic journey. She was, and he was once more thrilled to see her magnificent lines, but regretted he would not see her again before November. Unhurriedly he drove back to Miami International Airport where he returned the hire car before heading for check in. Just before checking in he opened the top of his bag to remove any and all paperwork and documentation zipped inside. On top of his clothes was an envelope, on the front of which was written 'Please do not open until after departure'. He folded it around the credit card and fake driving license for Steve Turner and zipped them into an inside pocket of his light jacket, checked himself and his bag in for the flight and strolled through passport control.

Air France once more took off on time. On this flight the little old lady was gone, to be replaced by a couple of a similar age to himself. He imagined conversation with them would have been easy but he was not interested in conversation, nor did his interest lie with the in-flight magazine or even the food when it came around. He relaxed as best he could in the still cramped seat and closed his eyes. He was tired, the night before had not allowed for much sleep, but he was more inclined to think than sleep. He thought of his mother and her untimely death, his father and his torments, of the mission ahead, and of the Predator in all her resplendent glory. And he thought of Sabine! He thought of Sabine a lot, every time trying to push the thoughts away and to replace them with others, every time failing.

He fought the urge to open the envelope for over two hours, but eventually took it from his pocket, unwrapped it from the cards, zipped them away, then sat with it in his hand for another twenty minutes before reluctantly succumbing. He had enjoyed himself with Sabine, and enjoyed himself a great deal. In fact the time spent with her had proved to be by far the happiest he had enjoyed since before his mother was killed. But he could not allow it to get in the way of the mission. Quite apart from his feelings and desire for retribution others too were relying on him - his team - and one of the many things rugby had instilled into him from an early age was you never let your team down. Jack was lucky in a certain respect in that Katya, rightly or wrongly, was involved from the beginning, a veritable member of the inner circle. Sabine could never be involved, or ever know. Compromise would follow, and compromise would kill.

Slowly, almost tenderly, he opened the envelope and removed the single sheet of paper. Upon it in her strong bold style she had written – 'Danny, my time with you has been more pleasurable than any other of my life. I wish with every fibre of my being we could have continued it forever. Neither of us has anyone else, and I now know I will not have the desire to so much as look for a long time to come. I had intended to have a fling, a holiday romance, something I had never done before. Something shallow, selfish and self indulgent. Perhaps such things are not in me.

I cannot say I will wait for you forever as things in life change. I will not say I will wait at all. I will say if you call, and I am free, I will come, and I will come anywhere, at any time, and will give you all that I am without reservation. But if you call and I come I shall never again be able to leave you. Sabine.'

Below she had written her address and work address, mobile number which he already had, home and work telephone numbers, along with two private and one work e-address. She was obviously very serious, yet had made no attempt to pry into his life or search for skeletons. During the time they spent together not only had there never been a cross word, but not even a misunderstanding, and never once had she attempted to apply any pressure, ask for a single thing or try to change him in any way at all.

The French trolley dollies still looked wonderful, and their voices were still sexy. Unfortunately they were not quite as wonderful or as sexy as they had seemed to be on the way out.

He hoped he could find himself a French Canadian girlfriend when this was all over. One from Laval outside Montreal.

He thought of his mother. He thought of Sandy. He thought of his father, languishing in what was to all intents and purposes a padded cell. Duty came first. Sacrifices had to be made. Regrettably!

Twenty

Mike Latham was understanding and exceptionally helpful to Danny, showing a great deal of latitude as far as his subordinate was concerned. Having no knowledge of Danny's involvement in the group behind and which was Almeti he believed the time he was making available covered the extra required for visits to Tom, which was only true in part. Dan had no desire to compromise the man who was not only his boss but also a true friend, and realised the time the project would demand in its final stages would be significant. It would be impossible for Mike Latham to cover his absence for the amount of time the testing itself should entail, let alone all which would follow, so decided he would have to explain certain things to Latham, but stop a long way short of being one hundred percent open, something which left him feeling somewhat awkward.

Danny had walked into Latham's spacious office and said, "Mike I need to talk to you. Can I make an appointment for a time which suits you?"

"Heavens Dan, that sounds a bit formal. Grab a seat. Is it not something we can discuss now?" Latham responded.

"Well it's a bit difficult for me because I'm going to have to tell you something you probably don't want to hear, and I feel I'm going to be letting you down a bit." Danny started to explain, sitting as he did so.

Latham was curious. He had a great deal of time for the younger man and much more so than ever Danny realised. Latham had never married and knew he never would. Although it was his choice, and despite the great deal of fun the freedom had allowed along the way, he understood it came at a price and, in his case, the cost to him was the lack of a family. Should he ever have had one he would have loved a son just like this bright, friendly, giant of a man before him. In many ways Danny was his surrogate son, a giant of a man in every way who, despite his horrific losses, continued to meet each new day with a smile on his face and a spring to his step. Latham was convinced Dan, with his resolute nature, relaxed friendly character and general intelligence, should one day go far, and he would do all which he could to improve the young man's chances. Could this, Latham wondered, have anything to do with the girl Danny had met in the States? Why he had not followed up on her was completely baffling.

"Mike I'm afraid I'm going to have to give you my resignation." Danny explained. It was not what Mike Latham expected, not by a long way, and it left him confused.

"What on Earth is the problem Dan? Have you been offered something else? A better position? Better prospects? More money? If it's any of those things I'll see what can be done to more than match it. I'll really rather not lose you!" Latham told him.

"Mike it's got nothing to do with money, prospects or position. You've always been good to me, better than good. I've not been approached and honestly wouldn't be interested anyway!" Danny replied.

"So what is it? What's the problem? Is it your father or the girl you met?" Latham asked.

"No, well in some ways neither, in some ways both. The fact is I need some time. I want to travel a bit, see a few things, take some time out and think about where I want to go in life. It's true meeting Sabine has made me think. Dad's never coming out of hospital, so I'll never be able to leave for good, but it leaves me feeling a little trapped. I enjoy my job, and I like working with you. Frankly it would be impossible to ever find a better boss than you, but I just feel I need some space, a chance to do something a bit different for a while. I know it won't be for ever, but I need some time, maybe as much as a year or so, maybe less, but just time to view my life from another perspective," Danny explained.

"So where do you want to go, and why do you want to resign?" Latham questioned.

"Well first off I don't really want to resign, but I can't see an alternative. If I wanted a week or even a month I would ask for a little extra holiday or compassionate leave because of Dad, but it's not for that and I don't want to mess you around, because after all you have done for me it would not be either right or fair. As for where I want to go I'm not completely sure, but I can tell you this and I'm sure you'll appreciate it. Jack has asked me if I'll skipper a boat for one of his clients. It's to be picked up from somewhere in South Africa and delivered to the South of France. It could be shipped but the owner wants it sailed around, via the Horn of Africa. He and a party will be on board for part of the trip and rejoining for some diving in the Red Sea. They need a captain with good dive experience. Jack mentioned me and they lapped it up. I went for a meeting – and – well I've got the job if I want it, and I would just love to do it! Can you understand any of that? Does it make sense?" Danny asked.

Mike Latham chuckled. "Make sense? I'd say it does! I'd love to join you myself on a trip like that. It might be a bit dangerous off the coast of Somalia, pirates and all that, but what a trip! I don't want to lose you, but at your age you'd be completely deranged to turn something like that down. What's the boat?"

"It's a Sunseeker Predator 108." Danny replied.

Latham just laughed out loud. "A Predator? You lucky, lucky bugger! Danny get out there and do it. I won't accept your resignation. Instead I'll give you an extended leave of absence. Shall we say anything up to two years? Go and have the time of your life. I envy you all you will be up to. My only suggestion is this, when you have finished, and if she is still free, give the girl in Canada a call. If you can, fly her over to the Med for a few days on board with you and take it from there. Now go on, get out of here and enjoy yourself, but send me a card or two along the way you lucky sod!"

It was a far better reaction than Danny could possibly have hoped for, and much more than he would have considered asking. His job would be kept open, but he was free to complete the project. Hell, he may even take Mike's advice and give Sabine a call afterwards, if he survived and was still free.

For Chris Spencer there were no problems with family or employers to consider. His employers were the project. He could and would give it his full and undivided attention.

Peter Parfitt also had no considerations to make with regard to employer, but Tammy and her needs were another matter. She had come a long way in the three years since the explosions. She would never be able to hear in her left ear and reading was difficult for her left eye, but her new teeth were now screwed in place and her lip had recovered as much as it ever would. It enabled her to drink, eat and talk as before, although she would never again properly purse her lips, or at least her lower lip. Her right foot had made a complete recovery as had her left breast. The scarring to her lip and breast had all but disappeared, and many of her other scars had faded. She had taken readily enough to her prosthetic arm and was slowly learning to use what remained of the muscles and tendons to slightly manipulate the fingers, although she would never be able to so much as tie a bow with them.

Her left leg proved to be her single biggest problem, and she spent months having it adjusted and altered. In the early stages, partly because she pushed herself too hard, the stump was left swollen, red and sore, occasionally even bleeding. Progress with it had continued at a frustratingly slow pace, but since Peter returned from Spain that progress had increased substantially, to the degree whereby she could take short walks with her parent's dog, an elderly Jack Russell, and stroll around the Lanes with Peter at weekends. Sex also returned to their lives, fully initiated by Tammy who finally straddled him one night after weeks of listening to Peter's excuses, understanding he didn't want to hurt her, but still needing to have her physical desires fulfilled. Unsure of himself initially Peter had responded and, as the weeks progressed, lost all thoughts that he might be taking advantage of her or, far worse, that the sexual activity might be regarded as morally suspect, even perverted.

Tammy could once again manage steps and stairs, walk and do most of the things an ordinary able bodied person could. The Cayman Coupe had long since been sold and she would never again slip behind the wheel of a sports car, or anything with a particularly low centre of gravity, as access was just too difficult, but she was determined to drive again, and she was going to drive something she liked, even if she did have to compromise a little. Compromise for Tammy meant another Porsche. The Cayenne S was not low to the ground but it didn't need steps, so she could easily slide in and out, and slide in and out she did. It was nothing like the Cayman, but with a 4.5 litre V8 it had all the grunt she could want, and with the Tiptronic S transmission in automatic mode she could choose from multiple gearshift patterns, which helped her to deliver the power smoothly, even in Sport setting. Within a short space of time she found she was able to influence gear changes using the throttle alone. Tammy was back to driving and, quite apart from the increased independent personal mobility it afforded her it was something she enjoyed, especially so in a car she liked which came fully loaded with gadgets and goodies.

Although blissfully unaware of the details of the secret Almeti project Tammy knew Peter was employed as a senior project manager. She was pleased he had managed to find gainful employment which allowed him to spend the amount of time he did with her, as long haul flying would not have done so, and short haul may well have proved most disruptive. Having endured the pain caused by her injuries and the discomfort of countless seemingly unending operations she was not about to let a silly little thing like the loss of two limbs destroy her life. She had a man she loved who had quite literally saved her life and then stood by her throughout, enough money to enjoy a reasonably comfortable life, had thoroughly enjoyed her life before the bombing, and accepted she was young enough to adapt to that which life had thrown at her. With the help of her prosthetic leg she could walk and with her new teeth she could once again enjoy a full range of foods. She could smell the sea, still marvel at a beautiful sunset and hear the birds calling from the trees. Not as well as before admittedly, but much better than the doctors had expected and all she had hoped for. She was alive – and life tasted good. Peter had explained to her about a large project he had coming up which would mean his being out of the country for at least one extended period, possibly two, during which he would mostly be completely out of contact.

If not yet quite fully recovered Tammy was not far short of it, and could now fend for herself easily. However, although neither then knew it, the rollercoaster which is life had not yet finished with her, but Peter was free to continue with his part in the project.

For Nathan Jefferies there were no complications with family – the bombers had made sure of that. He was a partner in his own companies and needed no permission from anyone if he wanted to work, rest or play. His interests were of a sufficient size and so structured as to be able to survive without him for extended periods. Money continued to flow into the global coffers of NJF Industries with Asian and South American markets growing rapidly. The public face of Almeti was also doing well, with the project outside Brno in the Czech Republic approaching an opening date, and the agreement for the Lyon Virtual World almost ready for signing at state level.

Nathan was needed in South Africa, and for his own peace of mind, to feel he had properly contributed, he needed to be there. However it would be impossible to leave his companies and fly off to South Africa for many weeks without any form of explanation. Press speculation would run rife and could lead to the undoing of the entire project. Fortunately in 2010, for the first time ever on African soil, South Africa was hosting the football World Cup, where it was intended to use ten stadia, five already built but to be refurbished, and five to be newly constructed. Here the interests of NJF, Almeti International and the secret Almeti project all neatly coincided, synchronising completely with the desires of the South African authorities and developers.

Peter Parfitt had worked alongside Jack Bryant and they narrowed the ten sites down to three with which they felt Almeti International would like to be financially associated. Two were the new ones to be built at Port Elizabeth and Cape Town and, of the five facing refurbishment, the stadium requiring the least work, Rustenburg.

The South African Football Association was determined from the outset the new stadia should be built to both meet the requirements of hosting a FIFA World Cup and to serve local people in a practical, relevant manner thereafter. As far as Port Elizabeth was concerned extensive discussions concluded the Eastern Province rugby stadium was not suitable for upgrading. Investment had therefore been channelled into designing and building a new fifty thousand seat three tier stadium, the Nelson Mandela Stadium, set on the shores of North End Lake on the outskirts of the city and near the Coega industrial port development. The futuristic stadium, incorporated within a multi-purpose facility, was designed specifically to serve the community well for many years after the football event ended. Its location, two kilometres from the coast and on open land, was ideal for the kind of further development Almeti was ostensibly set up to progress, expand and advance, and appeared perfect in every way for their commercial plans.

Cape Town's new Green Point Stadium, built in the suburb of Green Point, after which it was obviously named, was to have the fantastic backdrop of ocean and mountains, scenery as stunningly beautiful and picturesque as any on the planet. With a seating capacity of sixty-eight thousand the retractable roofed stadium was to be built on ten and a half hectares of land previously occupied by a golf course and the old stadium which was demolished to make way for the new. Built adjacent to the M6 Western Boulevard and some six hundred meters from the V & A Waterfront, its central location offered all the city had to give along with enviable access. With the attractions Cape Town already had to offer and given the city's three and a half million population it presented Almeti with an investment opportunity the region was highly unlikely to ever see come again.

Their third area of interest, Rustenburg, was different in every way imaginable to the other two stadia. Sited several hundred kilometres from the ocean the Royal Bafokeng Sports Palace is twelve kilometres from the Rustenburg city centre. However it is also only a twenty-five minute drive from the gambling and luxurious opulence of Sun City, or thirty minutes from Pilanesberg National Park. The stadium was originally built as a venue for the 1995 Rugby World Cup and was already a very well equipped multi-purpose venue which included an athletics track. Its thirty-eight thousand seat capacity was to be altered to seat forty-two thousand, apart from which refurbishments were merely cosmetic. However in this case it was not the stadium development which attracted the interest of Jack Bryant, and therefore Almeti, so much as Rustenburg and the local region.

Rustenburg was the fasted growing city in South Africa, and had a major claim to fame. Platinum. The city was home to the two largest platinum mines in the world and boasted the world's greatest platinum refinery, Precious Metal Refiners, processors of approximately seventy per cent of the planet's supply. The Royal Bafokeng Stadium is named after the Bafokeng people who live in the area and who, in 1999, won a legal battle entitling them to twenty per cent of the platinum mined from their historic or cultural land, effectively giving the Bafokeng shares in platinum mining. Affluence was being extracted from the very ground and there were other local attractions. The potential for vast disposable wealth to be retained within the area long after world cup madness died was very real. Jack Bryant, Jake

Ferris and Phil Gatting liked that. It might prove to be fertile ground indeed for Almeti International, and land was cheap, very, very cheap by almost any European standard. All that was needed was agreements in place with tribes, as well as government to protect against future land grabbing and the suicidal land rights insanity which had so heavily contributed to the economic destruction of Zimbabwe.

For Nathan a visit to the venues of interest might well attract press speculation, healthy speculation. Hints were dropped in the right ears. Nathan was available to continue work on the project in South Africa.

Nathan Jefferies, accompanied by Almeti International's senior projects manager, Peter Parfitt, and the group's leading security advisor, Chris Spencer, boarded a British Airways 747 on Saturday evening for a flight through the night. Nathan had long since given up booking his own flights and had consequently been booked to travel first class, a far cry in price from the cattle class he would have booked if doing so himself. Chris Spencer, who took the time to look at his ticket, was shocked to see each one way ticket was priced at almost six thousand pounds, ten times as much as an economy return. After flying in troop transports he felt he would rather have a little less comfort if it saved him nearly five hundred pounds an hour, an observation which made Peter Parfitt laugh.

Seated in first class comfort the journey was uninteresting and uneventful. The British Airways stewardesses were attentive and helpful, chosen by the airline for their competence rather than their looks, part of the reason Danny Bryant rarely flew BA. However a flight through the night remained a flight through the night, something best done by others. Time passed slowly, as generally tends to be the case when suspended seven and a half miles above sea level in an aluminium tube. Alcohol helped to deaden the pain and eventually the three men endured what passes for airborne sleep, complete with dehydration and headaches, neither of which were helped by the alcohol.

Mainly driven by curiosity, as they lined up for landing, Chris asked about the airport.

"Peter I know you've flown in and out of here many times, so pardon my sounding stupid but I've never been here before. What is the name of this airport? It seems to have various references."

"That's a very good question." Peter answered with a chuckle. "Africa's busiest airport. We've got the time so I'll give you the full version."

"Is he going to regret asking?" Nathan broke in, with a flash of humour which was rare for him around the two warriors of whom he was in total awe. Both men laughed before Peter answered, first asking a question of his own.

"What have you heard it called?" he asked.

"Well I've always just thought of it as Johannesburg, but I remember hearing it called Jan Smuts. When we were boarding I heard someone refer to it as Tambo." Chris replied.

"In which case all three are correct, and there's a forth one, Palmietfontein." Parfitt explained. "Palmietfontein International Airport handled European flights from 1945. It was renamed Jan Smuts in 1952, two years after Smuts' death. Interestingly it had the distinction of ushering in the jet age in the same year, as the first commercial flight of the ill fated de Havilland Comet landed here after taking off from Heathrow. In 1994, with the government dominated by the African National Congress, it was announced they were changing the name to Johannesburg International Airport. South African airports should not be named after political figures the world was informed. At the tail end of 2005 it was once more renamed by the same ANC politicians to Tambo International Airport after the anti-apartheid politician Oliver Tambo."

"But..." Chris started.

"Hypocrisy?" Peter asked raising one eyebrow. Chris nodded.

"Have you ever seen the film Blood Diamond?" Peter asked another question. Chris shook his head but Nathan who was also listening nodded. "There is a line in there where DiCaprio is talking at a bar and explains D.I.A. 'Dis Iz Afrika'. Remember that whilst you are here. I love this land and its people with a passion but – Dis Iz Afrika!"

Nathan and Chris thought about the possible implications as they finished their approach and the aircraft slammed into the runway with another hard landing.

"Ouch!" Chris exclaimed. "I think we need more air in the tyres!"

"We're 'hot and high' here. Must be a new or unfamiliar pilot," Peter laughed.

"What does that mean?" Nathan asked seriously.

"Well it's probably a bit boring, but the airport is built at almost seventeen hundred meters, about five and a half thousand feet, over a mile above sea level, and the air temperature can be high. Consequently the air is thin," Peter answered as the aircraft started its taxi to the jetway.

"What implications does that have?" Nathan was interested to know.

"I guess I can best explain by way of example. As you know I used to work for SAA, mostly out of Cape Town, but also out of Jo'burg because it's their hub. Flying the Airbus from Jo'burg to Washington D.C. it has to stop at Dakar in Senegal to refuel. Owing to decreased take-off performance at Jo'burg the 'bus cannot take off fully laden with passengers, cargo and fuel. Also it's necessary to use a longer stretch of runway to gather take-off speed. Flying back is a non-stop fifteen hour flight, but Dulles lies at a fraction under one hundred meters above sea level. I use Washington as an example as Dulles-Jo'burg is one of the longest non-stop commercial flights in the world," Peter once more explained.

"I didn't have the faintest idea about any of that." Chris spoke out honestly whilst Nathan merely sat looking thoughtful.

Leaving one week later there was no need for any form of subterfuge on Dan's part. He booked a flight to Cape Town and paid for it with his personal credit card. He was going to South Africa to skipper a boat, and to deliver such boat to its owners at a port in the south of France. There was nothing he had to hide. He had once been Christmas shopping to New York and flew there with Virgin Atlantic. The pre-Christmas atmosphere onboard had proved almost magical and he had never forgotten it. On the strength of the New York trip he once more booked Virgin. Flight VS603 non-stop to Cape Town International took off at its scheduled time of twenty-thirty-five for the twelve hour flight, arriving at ten-thirty the following morning. There was nothing magical about the flight. The passengers were of a very different type, noisy, rude, sweaty and wearing loud and ridiculous clothing, and for the first time in a long time he regretted not booking with BA, where he would have expected at least a little decorum, cattle class or not.

It was the beginning of September and, as a group, they had slightly less than three months to get everything working just as they wanted it, or they would be forced to wait an additional forty-eight weeks, and waiting was not something anyone wished for as it would substantially increase security issues and detection possibilities. Danny knew that like him the other three would work day and night if need be to meet the deadline, and he was sure all could be achieved within the time period. Apart from any difficulties which may arise from the project itself, the only problem they had to address was taking care of Nathan's public appearances, and Danny was particularly pleased to be no part of that.

At twenty-one degrees Cape Town was just two degrees cooler than London but, unlike London which was set to get colder, Cape Town and South Africa generally would be warming up as summer approached. Dan had never previously been to any part of Africa, and his first sight of Cape Town as the aircraft came in to land blew every preconceived idea he held regarding the continent straight out of his head. The taxi ride to Peter's apartment, where he was to stay and to be joined by Peter the following day, was interesting almost to the degree of sensory overload. What he could see of Cape Town as they passed through looked fascinating and he intended heading for the V & A Waterfront Peter had enthused about so often, but first there was work to do.

As the taxi made its way down Victoria Road towards Camps Bay Danny understood completely why Peter had chosen the area to set up home. Although intelligent and articulate he realised he had nothing like the vocabulary needed to decently do justice to the beauty of the sight, or the sounds and smells which assailed him. He asked the taxi to wait whilst he carried his medium sized suitcase and flight bag up to the apartment and let himself in. He merely left the two items of baggage in the hallway then turned around and hurried down to the taxi, asking the driver to take him to the garage where the two vehicles Peter had purchased earlier in the year were kept. He had taken the taxi to the apartment first so he may know the way when he returned; worried he might not have found it alone. He could see such worries were unfounded as everywhere appeared to be well signposted, something else he had not expected. The taxi eventually dropped him at the garage and the driver left with a huge bright smile of perfectly even white teeth and a two hundred rand tip.

Peter Parfitt had contacted the garage after arriving in South Africa and asked them to prepare both vehicles for driving, and to have the pick-up ready for collection by a friend of his, whom he named and described. The owner, who was used to large South African males, had assumed Peter was exaggerating Danny's size, but simply held the keys to the truck out to him as he walked through the door, wondering how a person of his size managed to get a car seat back far enough to drive.

Peter, Chris and Nathan collected their hire car from the airport, a silver BMW 320 automatic, and with Peter behind the wheel vacated the city as fast as he possibly could. Jo'burg was not Peter's scene. He considered stopping off at Ellis Park, renowned for its world class rugby then in the process of being downgraded to a multi function stadium for the football, but decided against it.

Parfitt wanted to finish the project, and to hit back hard at those who had turned the lives of so many upside down. Then he wanted to get home and marry the woman he loved. However his one overwhelming desire whilst in South Africa with those who had become his friends was to make sure they had an enjoyable time whenever they could. He knew the days and weeks spent at Granaatboskolk may well prove gruelling in the extreme, and doubted if Nathan, or even Danny, were adequately prepared for what lay ahead despite all he had done to explain it.

Faced with a visit and meeting at Rustenburg he had sought Ruan's advice regarding accommodation, and taken it. Thaba Phuti Safari Lodge is situated just south of the Magaliesburg Mountain Range and the town of Rustenburg, was widely known in the region for its premier five star accommodation, and was less that an hour and a half drive from Jo'burg. He was told the Lodge's somewhat exclusive seven en-suite guest rooms gave extended panoramic views of the surrounding African bushveld, and each had their own private deck which overlooked cliffs and waterhole below, providing guests with a unique view of the Magalies Meander and a place where game could be viewed from a position of privacy at their leisure.

Ruan had explained that apart from the guest rooms the Thaba Phuti consisted of a restaurant, two bar areas, a very good wine cellar, swimming pool and conference centre, and assured Peter the friendly and helpful staff made visits to the lodge a pleasure, providing guests with an enjoyable and usually particularly unforgettable stay. Additionally a number of activities could be provided which included clay pigeon shooting, elephant rides, freshwater fishing, bush picnics, wine tasting, game viewing and camera safari's. However what really sold it to Peter was the information that on request the lodge could make arrangements for its guests to go on off-site hot air ballooning trips, and from these the African bush could be seen and experience from a wholly different perspective, presenting game viewing opportunities of a lifetime. It was something Parfitt had booked in advance for the three of them, and which immersed all in the magnificent and mysterious world which is Africa.

Meetings followed during the following two days and exploratory talks took place with tribal leaders and various officials at both provincial and national level. Almeti's financial strengths were by then well known, and its international experience in the building and construction industries well documented. The South African authorities had not missed the size of the construction project taken on to the south of Brno, or what was rumoured to be starting outside Lyon, and would greatly welcome inward investment of the size discussed and the large number of jobs it would bring with it. Offers of cooperation and promises of consents and streamlined paperwork followed in quick succession. Even the press agreed, an entertainment village with supporting network of accommodation and retail outlets would be of great benefit to the area well after the football had passed, would contribute to a greater buoyancy in the area's economy, and make it far more attractive to those wishing to hold future events. Doubtless one day South Africa would put in a bid to host the Olympics, and how much stronger such a bid would be if a working viable infrastructure was already in place. Almeti would be welcomed with open arms.

Precisely the same response followed at Port Elisabeth. The sea, and access to it, added an additional dimension to the concept of a theme park, as did the lake, and once again land was priced at ridiculously low levels by any British standard, as were unit labour costs. Cape Town was less simple. Labour was plentiful and as a consequence the cost was low, but the price of land was significantly higher. However a deal could be made and once again they would be more than welcome.

Throughout the week the press had followed with interest, but all were aware that nothing was likely to happen for some time, if at all, and after the first few days interest waned as the world moved on. Jack Bryant had suspected as much and planned around it. The story had also been leaked during the early days of the trip that Nathan was to spend a few weeks in the country taking a much needed break. As the discussions and negotiations at Cape Town finished he effectively dropped off the press radar, left free to mingle with others who were relatively well heeled relaxing at the world's most attractive and well presented waterfront.

Peter Parfitt rejoined Danny, picked up the Mercedes Sprinter and collected the shipment of tools ordered by Danny, then organised transport to collect the various consignments from the docks and clearance warehouses. These were delivered into another store, from which they were shipped once more to various addresses where the transport drivers were duly stopped and the goods transhipped into either the van or the pickup truck. In the unlikely event any trail previously existed it had just gone cold. A small secure workshop was rented for an extortionate amount for a one month period, although they would only use it for a few days. There everything was removed from the delivery crates and packaging, checked off and thoroughly inspected.

What was not going to be needed on site was re-crated and returned to another dockside warehouse. Most of the crates which remained were burnt along with much of the polystyrene and cardboard which originally wrapped and protected the items they contained. One large crate of cable drums and stainless steel sheets was despatched through a trucking company to a warehouse at Springbok in order to reduce the size of the load to be carried in the van and pickup. If any cable or steel was pilfered it could be replaced, inconvenient though it may be. Much of the other equipment would prove difficult to replace, certainly in a hurry.

All the items needed for an extended stay away from civilisation were purchased, from foodstuffs to drinking water, camp beds to generators and fuel to toiletries. There would be precious little water for washing and they would need facilities before they re-emerged into civilisation proper as they would be pretty dishevelled and stink, not the sort of thing which would be expected from a person of Nathan's position, and therefore something which could well lead to unwanted questions being asked. The remaining stores, parts, equipment and tools were carefully loaded into the two vehicles, again with every piece painstakingly checked off. Five days after Danny arrived in Cape Town they were finally fully loaded and ready to depart. The store was cleaned and scrubbed down, all evidence and indication of their having been there removed with caustic soda. It was time to leave the city and head north for the very different environment of the Northern Cape and the Great Karoo.

They left early on the Friday morning, Peter driving the Mercedes as the lead vehicle with Dan as his passenger and Chris following in the pickup with Nathan. It was to be a reasonably long drive for the two ex-forces men, with little chance of changing drivers. Nathan had no confidence in his abilities on the roads ahead, and although Dan could fit in the van and easily drive it if needed there was little possibility of his taking the wheel of the pickup for any reasonable distance, designed as it was for considerably shorter and smaller people. They travelled north on the N7 for four hundred kilometres until they reached the town of Bitterfontein, where they stopped to stretch their legs, refill their fuel tanks and take lunch, after which they left the town turning right onto the R358. Seventy kilometres further on they passed through Kliprand, and after one hundred and forty more they reached Granaatboskolk.

Pieter Skinstad did not come out to meet them and there was no sign of his beaten about Toyota. Parfitt had informed Ruan of his arrival in South Africa in order the information could be passed on, so they were expected, but Skinstad's absence was unsurprising. Both vehicles were reversed into the large barn where the tools and equipment were unloaded, then the Mercedes pulled across to the smaller barn and stores were offloaded. Chris went about setting up home, Spartan in the extreme though it was, whilst Danny, Peter and Nathan set to putting the equipment in order, dividing it up into various categories. Having unfolded camp beds, two small folding tables, and four chairs Chris was all but finished with 'home making'. On one table the cooking equipment was placed, which consisted of little more than a plate, bowl, mug and cutlery for each of them along with a two ring camping gas cooker and three saucepans. He then stacked their provisions, consisting almost exclusively of tinned goods, pasta and dried meat, the spiced biltong so common in South Africa, to one side and carefully piled up their most precious resource, water, so it would not fall or create an obstruction.

Outside, to the rear of the large barn or workshop, a hole was dug to be used as a toilet, and at the rear of the workshop a shower was hung, although it was little more than a piece of plastic garden pipe with a shower rose on one end and a foot operated pump on the other, which the person showering pumped away at as they went. The shower would not be able to be used however until they acquired a quantity of water in three top sealing two hundred and five litre drums used to transport much of their more delicate supplies and equipment. By the time the equipment was sorted and categorised dusk had fallen, and Chris brewed up and started a meal under the light of a single twelve volt bulb on the end of a small cable running from the pickups battery. Five star luxury and the delights of a cuisine of choice were gone, and a very early and somewhat uncomfortable night's sleep followed for all.

"Hell, this is an unwelcoming and desolate place, Peter!" Danny commented the following morning.

"Wait a few months before you comment on hell," Parfitt advised, chuckling as he did so. "At the moment it's cool. What is it? Twenty-five or six degrees, and quite comfortable at night. This is the very best time of year! If we are here as long as I expect us to be the temperature will rise to about forty, possibly slightly more, and with still air we will all feel it."

"Great – I can't wait," the big man muttered, grinning as he went off to bolt a pulsejet into the missile assembly at six in the morning, a pattern they were all to follow over the weeks to come.

For the next three days Peter and Chris carried out Nathan's instructions putting a line of cameras and transmitter aerials in place at one kilometre intervals, and running fifteen kilometres to the south south west of where the two men had picked out what they both considered their ideal firing range. The start of the test area was itself nearly five kilometres to the south of the barns and behind the only natural feature to be seen in any direction, an outcrop of rocks. The missile crash site was in a small salt pan six kilometres long and four across, ten kilometres away from a dirt road to Loeriesfontein to the west and fifteen from the railway to the south east, and most certainly not the sort of place where there were ever likely to be any casual observers. On the second day Chris was sent to Springbok in the Mercedes to collect the crate containing the cable and steel, and to fill the drums with water so all may shower. By the end of the third day all cabling and cameras were in place and wired up, needing only Nathan's deft touches to connect the recorder, monitor and radio controlled transmitter.

Whilst Chris and Peter were out in the field working, Danny and Nathan concentrated on the needs of the missiles. Dan completed the assembly process of two and Nathan finished the required wiring. The GPS systems, although not to be used until everything else worked perfectly, computers, flight attitude control systems and radio control packs were all successfully installed, as were dummy payloads. Danny selected the two engines he had put together which he believed provided the greatest chance of success, and mounted one on each of the missiles. Both Nathan and Danny were clear to proceed with flight testing.

The next morning saw all four men out on the 'firing range', on land which was flat in every direction, seemingly devoid of any form of life except for short stubby sparse areas of grass struggling to survive against all nature hurled at it. Telephones were connected at either end of the multi core control wire Chris had collected and laid with Peter, and the whole system was powered by a generator with a transformer supplying the few milliamps needed. The hard wired telephones allowed Nathan and Danny at the firing end to communicate, without fear of eavesdropping, with Chris and Peter who were to remain sited at the crash zone.

Nathan took control of the operation for the first time. In awe of the warriors or not, this was what he was uniquely qualified to do. All realised the entire project now hinged on his ability to not so much make the missiles fly as, with Peter's help, Danny had already made sure of that, but to fly under control along a predetermined course and to end their flight as and when dictated.

"This is not going to be a trial and error exercise," Nathan explained. "What I intend is to have a successful and controlled flight from the first. A lot of time and research has gone into this on the test bench. We know all the component parts work, and should all work in unison. What we are here to learn about and perfect is launching, flight dynamics and in-flight computer control."

"Tell us what you want from us and we'll do our best to deliver," Danny told him, speaking for the three of them.

"Tell us what you want of us and we will deliver!" Chris corrected him.

Nathan smiled a thin smile then told them, "I want Danny at this end monitoring take off, and would like the two of you down on the salt pan. From the moment each lifts off they'll be under control and monitored down the line from here. I want to learn as much as I can from the two flights we'll be making today. There is a small flight recorder in each missile which should provide me with plenty of information, but I want to retain both fuselages if possible for additional flights. So, with that in mind, what I need is for you, Chris, to man the telephone at the far end, and for Peter to take over control of the missile as it approaches you with his own remote. I've gone over this with Peter and he knows what to do, but I need you to let me know when he is ready to take over control so I can shut down the system from this end as it passes to Peter.

"Peter, I know we have already gone through this, but once you have control bring each one down as best you can. They will be coming in fast so it won't be easy. The one thing we cannot afford is to lose one. If you have any doubts about control – bring it straight down. I'd much rather see a fuselage destroyed than lose secrecy.

"That's it! We all know what we are doing so if you guys want to get on down to the salt pan check the remote control and ring through when you're ready."

Whilst Peter and Chris made their way across the scraggy grassland in the pickup truck Nathan and Danny readied things at their end. Danny had built a small adjustable launch platform which was fixed to the ground by stakes driven down through the hard soil to prevent movement. Whilst the configuration of both missiles to be tested was the same the engines were not. One was slightly larger and more powerful than the other, but as a result required more fuel with all the weight implications and reduced payload which went with it. It was thought the smaller one would be capable of sustained flight, but there was a concern about boost power required at take off. Both would need booster rockets for the take off, which would be dropped as the missiles reached a preset height, but if the smaller engine performed at or above the level which was considered desirable, allowing a reasonable power safety margin, then the warheads could be increased by two kilos, and the bigger the warhead the greater the potential destruction.

"We're in position," Chris said over the landline telephone, and Nathan relayed the message to Danny by simply holding out his right fist with his thumb up.

"Thanks Chris." Nathan said as Danny nodded. "Stay on the line and I'll let you know as soon as the first missile is loose."

The dining table from the barn had been brought along. On top of it Nathan had set up his computer, which acted as a firing and control centre, two monitors, which were connected to the cameras, and a further monitor giving readout information from the computer. The set up was simplicity itself but had proved most effective during exhaustive testing and experimentation on various test benches in England. The flight pattern was already pre-programmed into the computer, and flight information was to be relayed via the short range transmitter and its various aerials along the line of cable. The launch platform was wired directly to the computer, and all which was left to do was for Nathan to press the enter button.

Once pressed a message was transmitted to the on-board computer which would then instruct the miniature pump to start pumping fuel whilst at the same time directing the quad spark assembly to begin firing. A further message was relayed from the on-board computer to the launch platform to blow compressed air through the engine and continue doing so until the exhaust from the stabilised pulsejet engine reached a certain force, blasting down on a plate which would lever the airline out of the way of the engine. As this occurred the exhaust flame would burn through the nylon tie, a sensor on the launch platform would inform the on-board computer, the hammers would fall and fire all booster rockets, and within milliseconds the missile should launch.

In total the man hours spent on the project before coming to South Africa collectively added up to many years' work. Although none of those who had given so much of their time were specialists in anything like the fields of rocketry or missiles they were intelligent and adaptable people. They were also highly motivated and dedicated to their cause. Nothing was ever too much trouble for any as the project had progressed. However all their hopes were contingent upon a successful firing and flight. As Nathan pressed the enter button he did so with confidence, and rightly so. Every single part responded and acted exactly as it was designed and supposed to do, and within twelve seconds the missile was streaking aloft almost as fast as Nathan and Danny could watch.

"It's away," Nathan said over the telephone to Chris in a voice bordering on wonder.

"Roger," was the only reply from the unflappable and stalwart ex-soldier.

As the missile lifted clear of the launch platform the small plug in its tail section pulled free severing control through the platform. Flight control passed automatically to the on-board computer and servos started to move as the flight stabilisation system relayed information and flight control surfaces moved in accordance. After dropping slightly the missile levelled as it found its course and streaked away leaving Nathan struggling to follow it with high powered binoculars as it disappeared into the rapidly warming air. The signals passing back and forth between missile and ground control aerials alerted each of the bank of cameras as the missile approached, and gave a seamless record of the missiles passing performance. As it approached the salt pan Chris informed Nathan who cut his ground control transmissions as Peter attempted to take control.

The transfer of control succeeded, but the controlled crash landing which was supposed to follow failed dismally. Peter took charge of the rapidly oncoming missile and managed to reduce altitude without mishap, but it was travelling so fast full control failed and he had no choice but to bring it down hard. The launch and flight proved a resounding success, the attempted landing a total failure.

"It's down." Chris reported by telephone. "But I'm pretty sure it's not going to be in one piece."

He then started the pick-up, collected Peter and they drove out across the saltpan to the crash site. The remains of the experimental missile were spread over a distance of nearly four hundred meters. Despite its Kevlar construction the fuselage was completely destroyed and the engine ripped clear. Everything was photographed where and as it had landed before being collected and placed in the back of the pick-up. Some of the electronic equipment appeared on the face of it to have survived the crash, as did the engine although it would need attention, but their stock of airframes had definitely been reduced by one. With the various parts photographed, the places they had come to rest catalogued, and all removed from the saltpan, Chris and Peter returned to join Nathan and Danny.

Dan remained elated by the resounding success of the take off and flight, which even the crash and destruction of the airframe could not dampen, and his enthusiasm was infectious. So much so that at ten thirty on an already very warm South African morning the four men opened a cool box and celebrated their first proper flight with a can of Castle Lager apiece. Sitting on the rocks, laughing and joking as they drank their beers, the reasons behind their experiments were temporarily forgotten as they soaked up the success of the moment.

The second flight proved a carbon copy of the first, despite the use of the smaller engine, which proved to have all the power needed for the flight but flew very slightly slower. The landing with the second test was as catastrophic as it was with the first. However three of their greatest challenges and issues were completed and solved on their first day of flights, which provided all four men with a positive mindset with regard to the project generally and their mission ahead. With pulsejet size and payload determined Danny started to churn out the simple engines as the others continued with various tests and experiments. Four airframes were destroyed before one was landed in a way which made it possible to reuse, and from that moment on Peter Parfitt managed to bring them all down in a manner which allowed more than a single flight from each.

Twelve fuselages were completed, fitted with winglets and filled with electronics. When fabrication of twelve of the smaller pulsejets was finished, all were carefully packed and crated, loaded into the Mercedes and despatched to Port Nolloth. Peter took Chris along on the trip to both split the driving and to give Peter a chance to introduce Chris to Willem and Vurnon Pretorius, who once again projected a genuinely warm and friendly attitude towards the two friends. Chris commented on the contrast between the two of them and their so called host, Pieter Skinstad, whom they had seen but three times in their weeks as ‘guests’ on his property, and who had struggled to greet them cordially on any of those occasions. The trip to Port Nolloth also gave them a chance to re-equip themselves with provisions, especially water, which they had all but run out of for their primitive shower. Whilst on their return trip they stopped briefly at Springbok and used a public internet provider to send a very brief message to a friend in Germany telling of the joys of their trip.

As the weeks at Granaatboskolk passed the temperature increased as Peter had told Danny it would. They steadily acclimatised and became hardened to the lack of creature comforts the land provided, but the relentless heat was unendurable much after midday driving all under cover of shade in the afternoons. It was fortunate all had gone as well as it did with the early tests as the project may well have been badly delayed had it not been so. As it was systems could be improved and perfected under cover and tested in the early mornings before the heat built up to a degree all felt as if they were being beaten upon an anvil. A thin polypropylene sheet was brought back from Port Nolloth and stretched from the roof of the barn so work might continue outside, shaded from the sun and shielded from anything which might just pass overhead. All four felt sure the project remained wholly unknown to the outside world as their isolation was almost complete, and they were aware of an average of only three vehicles a day passing their workshop and living quarters. Of those almost all were salt trucks passing at night and none of the vehicles drivers would have known anything of their presence.

Danny built a launch platform and then set about refining every part of it. After ten days of doing so he was finally satisfied with the overall design and improvements. He then set about breaking it down into manageable sized pieces which could be prefabricated ready for later assembly. This he rapidly accomplished and, with the afternoon assistance of both Peter and Chris the aluminium was cut and drilled by them as he prescribed and welded where required by him. With the additional help all three platforms were soon finished, test fitted, all snags resolved, and all pieces marked up ready for quick assembly when on station.

Nathan too was kept busy. Every test without exception provided him with an ever increasing wealth of information, and with the information came a deepening understanding of everything to do with the flight of his missiles. He now understood drag coefficients, speed and range abilities, construction techniques and flight stability. Dan had slightly altered the winglets early on, following tests and Nathan's recommendations. The alterations helped minimise the work done by the servos when correcting control surfaces and the demand on the tiny sealed lead-acid motorcycle batteries used to power everything on board.

The alterations also reduced drag and added to the missiles stability, a long running concern of Nathan's. Stability was something which could be produced by the missiles aerodynamics and by automated systems. With this, Nathan had adopted Danny's belt and braces philosophy and went for both in the belief that aerodynamics was the key to success hence the alterations to the winglets, but an automated onboard stabilisation system should be able to deal with turbulence and any other external forces.

From the time of their first test they had not experienced any problems with the missiles staying on course, but that was always with straight line firing, and when they were ultimately deployed the conditions would be very different. At first Nathan and Danny experimented with altering the launch platform by degrees from the vertical and with changing compass direction, eventually facing the opposite direction to the intended flight path. Every time the electronic messages from the control line had taken over and corrected the flight path perfectly. The tests moved on until the missiles could perform reasonably complicated predetermined aerial manoeuvres whilst in flight, circling out to either east or west to ultimately attack from the south. Again the thousands of man hours spent perfecting the design on the test benches in England paid off in dividends. The remote control was removed from the test missiles and the control line taken up. The GPS's in each of the remaining test missiles went live.

A hand held GPS gave an exact longitudinal and latitudinal reading for the centre of the saltpan, and this was pre-programmed into the missiles electronic brains. Their own on-board GPS systems interfacing with the missiles computer through the supplied software instantly began feeding information back allowing flight control to be processed and control commands given. Their last five launches all destroyed the airframes, the last two utterly so, as both had active warheads. All five missiles hit the centre of the target area, all with a spread of less than three meters, well within tolerance levels, especially so as they approached the target from varying directions. Dan had fabricated a tank from the remains of the sheets of stainless steel, and the final two missiles were stored in it, covered in water brought back in the barrels from Port Nolloth. These were launched wet without the slightest problem. The missiles were ready to go.

The site was cleared of unnecessary equipment and all rubbish. This along with the crated launch platforms was loaded into the Mercedes and Peter was despatched to Cape Town along with Danny. The rubbish was disposed of at a municipal site and the crate of aluminium parts offloaded at the dockside warehouse which already held their other items. Both then returned to Peter's apartment for the night for the first decent meal, shower and comfortable nights sleep either had enjoyed in many weeks.

There had been one minor change to the plan as it was discussed after the bombings over three years earlier, and the change involved contact between those of the inner circle and the contacts of Chris Spencer. It was originally agreed none of Chris's 'workforce' should ever come into contact with the others, and this was followed rigidly over the entire period with just one exception, Chris's right hand man, the ex SBS man, Billy Sutcliffe, and had come about not so much by design as much as expedience. Apart from Chris the only person he had previously met was Peter Parfitt, but that was about to change.

'Billy' Sutcliffe was originally christened Peter Sutcliffe, but picked up his lifelong nickname whilst training under what is arguably the world's hardest training regime, that for entry into the British SBS, which is also one of the world's most secretive Special Forces organisations. Later, after the notorious exploits of the Yorkshire Ripper who just happened to share his name and county background, he was only too pleased to widely accept the name 'Billy'.

Billy had been a childhood friend of Chris Spencer's but had always liked the water. When Chris went off to Catterick Billy joined the Royal Marines, the Royal Navy's amphibious infantry, a force kept at a state of permanent readiness to be deployed around the world. Just as the majority of the SAS find their way there via the Para's, the SBS arrive through the Royal Marine Commando's and, after a little over two year's service this had been Billy's path. He had passed through Special Forces Selection with the SAS and later qualified as a Swimmer Canoeist, and ultimately a Sergeant, SC1. Of all the forces, special or otherwise, if there is water involved the SBS are invariably the first into action, a point greatly underlined, and just as greatly overlooked, in the Falklands 'war'. Although without question the first choice for water they are also highly skilled on dry land, and have been known to operate in the deserts of Iraq and landlocked Afghanistan, the only theatre of operations where Chris Spencer and Billy Sutcliffe were ever in the same land at the same time, although neither knew it whilst there.

When Peter and Chris stopped at Springbok and sent the e-mail to a friend in Germany it was 'opened' by Katya a day and a half later at a cyber café at Amsterdam Airport Schiphol, where she had driven whilst Jack completed a work related visit to Brussels. From there she sent other e-mails before discarding wig and glasses and returning to collect Jack and spend the night in the beautiful Belgium city of Brugge. The various e-mails Katya sent created a minor flurry of activity. In England Billy readied himself for a trip, and in Fort Lauderdale Sidney Glendive III of Global Yacht Shipping finally shipped the Predator to Cape Town.

The morning after they returned to Cape Town Peter, accompanied by Dan, drove the Mercedes around to the Park Inn on Greenmarket Square and collected Billy, who had then been staying for nine days of a pre-booked fourteen. After introducing Danny the three men drove down to the docks in search of the Predator, which was not hard to find.

"Bloody hell, she's beautiful." Peter said as they drew up next to her.

"Ah-ha, a bonus." Billy Sutcliffe said. "Nobody told me it was going to be a Sunseeker, and a Predator at that."

"Are you familiar with them then?" Danny asked. He had remained somewhat apprehensive of meeting Billy because of the stories he had heard. Although Danny didn't know him he was still more than a little in awe of the man's abilities, and the fact he was built like a brick out-house didn't help. Although he was short next to Danny, at slightly less than six foot, he seemed about as wide with a neck like horse and a chest and arms like a silverback, and about as hairy, although there wasn't a hair on his shaven head.

"A bit I guess," Billy replied with what all would eventually learn was his customary understatement. "They're based in Poole, and so was I obviously. I was attached to M squadron. Sunseeker were sometimes helpful with training."

"What sort of training was that?" Danny asked attempting to make friendly conversation.

"It's difficult to remember now. It was a while ago." Billy replied evasively, causing the conversation to dry up.

The relevant paperwork showing proof of ownership was produced to the harbour authorities and the Predator was cleared. The vessel was inspected, engines were run-up to temperature and the three men took it out on a short sea trial. Billy then carefully inspected the engines and running gear whilst Peter arranged for the delivery of their crates and Dan saw to organising the ships stores. The morning rapidly became the afternoon as all three went about completing their various tasks. Finally the vessel was pulled onto a bunkering facility and its tanks were topped off. The boat was prepped and ready for sea with a lot of their equipment already loaded so Dan and Billy were required to spend the night on board. Peter ate on board with them then left for another night at his apartment before returning to Granaatboskolk the following day alone, although he would have a great deal on his mind throughout the drive.

After leaving the other two, and before going to bed, Peter rang through to Brighton for the first time in weeks and spoke to Tammy. To his surprise even her voice seemed stronger if such a thing was possible. However it was not her voice which shocked him to the quick, but her words, and it was almost enough to cause him to abandon the entire project so he might rush back to be at her side. Apart from the doctor who examined her nobody knew, not even her parents, as she had wanted to speak to Peter first. Against all the odds and with all her body had had to endure throughout the past three and a half years it would now have to endure more for another six months. Tammy was three months pregnant.

The Predator had been renamed 'Karma', and was registered at Gibraltar, which allowed for the flying of the Red Ensign, a flag known around the world and still respected in much of it. Karma put to sea shortly after first light for the relaxed run up South Africa's west coast to Port Nolloth. There was no hurry for the two men on board as they were not due until the afternoon of the following day. It was a journey of around four hundred miles, which would have been getting towards the top end of standard fuel tank capacity, but which the vessel could easily accomplish in ten hours. They had thirty-five, and by the time they reached their destination both men were determined to know all there was to know about what would become their floating home and weapons base for the next few weeks of their lives.

Peter Parfitt also left early that morning for the long lonely drive to their test site. He made reasonably good time, although he was completely oblivious to its passage as his mind was overflowing with other matters.

Chris and Nathan used the three days most productively, Chris spending the first two scouring the surrounding land in the pickup truck, removing all sign of their having been there. Every single scrap and shred of evidence was removed and carted back to the barns. On the third day, whilst Peter drove back from Cape Town and Karma motored up the coast, he bagged up all waste and finished crating the remaining equipment. Nathan had spent the time tinkering and improving whatever he could, but mainly working on his computers, planning courses, approaches and trajectories for the forthcoming missile attacks. Two sites were picked and the missiles had to launch and attack both of them approaching their targets from varying angles. Although it was originally planned to do all such work once on board Karma everything had gone so well they were ahead of their previously hoped for schedule, and in three days Nathan could get a lot of work completed on a computer. Finally even his work was packed away and both barns were cleared, the polypropylene cover was taken down and the latrine filled in. When Parfitt arrived they were ready to leave.

Between them they loaded all rubbish, waste and debris into the pickup. When finished all their crated parts, computers, explosives and general equipment went into the Mercedes van. The three men then left the place which had provided their home for eight weeks in the two vehicles and made their way across to Springbok where they stayed for the night, Parfitt booking and paying for the rooms in cash using false names. At last both Chris and Nathan could wash, eat and sleep in comfort. The following morning they again parted company, Chris and Nathan heading south for Cape Town and Peter on to Port Nolloth alone.

Once at Port Nolloth, where he had deliberately planned to arrive during early lunchtime, Parfitt contacted the Pretorius father and son and arranged their final meeting. They arrived once more happy and cheerful, extending their hands as they approached Peter where he waited at the dockside.

"So today is the day!" Vurnon stated with a broad smile.

"Your equipment has been well looked after." Willem said. "It can be brought up here in minutes as soon as your boat arrives. Have you any idea when it will be here?"

"The plan is for them to arrive this afternoon. They'll try to make the most of both daylight and high water because the last thing any of us needs is to hit the reef." Peter answered.

"What time would you like to start loading?" Vurnon asked.

"Well we can work around you a little with that." Peter told him.

"Good God man!" Willem exclaimed. "No! We will work around you completely! Anything you want, and any assistance you need you just say and you will have it! The money you are paying us will change my family's lives forever! Don't you understand that? So you tell us what you want. You don't even have to ask, just tell us!"

"Well thank you." Peter said. He liked these people a great deal. If only there were more in the world like them. He had already thought it over and knew no one would object to them having a minor bonus for their help.

"There is just one more thing I would like to ask of you if I may," Peter said to them.

"You ask. You are helping us more than you can imagine. You are helping our people, The Leader has told us that, and you are helping the cause. What can we do for you?" Willem asked.

"I would like you to clean this vehicle thoroughly inside and out," Parfitt said indicating the Mercedes. "I want all evidence of our ever having been in it removed completely."

"Of course we can do that," Willem said smiling. "I thought you were going to ask for something difficult. Is there anything else?"

"Just one thing. When it is clean, and I do mean really clean, I want you to keep it. Here are the vehicles documents. It's yours if you want it." Peter told them as he held out the paperwork.

"That we can certainly do." Vurnon said whilst laughing out loud, and then became serious. "Listen man, I know you told us what it is you are doing, and that is the story everyone here will be told, but it is obviously just a cover. We do not need to know what it is you are doing and will never pry. We have spoken of this. Your secret, whatever it is, is safe with us and always will be. You were never here, we have never met, and nothing will ever make either of us speak of it again. There is however one other thing we would like you to know. If ever at any time in the future you need our help you will have it. We will be leaving Port Nolloth soon, but you will always be able to contact us through The Leader. It is our pleasure to have met you or, officially in this case, never to have met you. I can assure you there will be no trace of you or what you have been carrying left in the vehicle, and deeply thank you for the gesture!"

Karma made her way gingerly into the port. Danny Bryant and Billy Sutcliffe picked their way through the fishing vessels and diamond prospector's boats on the afternoon tide successfully avoiding the costal reef which extended across the channel, and slowly came alongside the jetty. Lines were thrown and the vessel was secured beneath the only crane.

“Good trip up?” Peter called out to them.

“Bloody good skipper and an outstanding boat.” Billy answered him. He had got on well with the friendly giant and respected Danny’s skill with the boat.

“What’s the plan for loading Peter?” Danny called out.

“They’re ready here whenever we are.” Peter answered and then asked. “When would you like to load?”

“Well, so long as there are no cameras around I guess there is no time like the present.” Danny responded. “We’ve got light on our side at the moment, and it’ll give us extra time.”

Peter relayed the request to the Pretorius’ and within minutes those obviously used to handling goods and boats swung into efficient action. As the cases were craned aboard and lowered through the moon roof just behind the Besenzoni chairs of the helm the loose equipment was carried into the saloon and carefully deposited so as to cause no damage to the boat, its furniture or furnishings. Whilst loading continued fuel was pumped aboard and the tanks topped off. The entire operation, which Danny and Peter had allowed three hours to accomplish, was carried out in under an hour.

“It has been our very great pleasure to have done business with you,” Willem Pretorius said as he shook hands with Peter when the loading was completed.

“We wish you well with your task, whatever it may be,” Vurnon added as he in turn shook hands.

“And I hope you find the home and land you seek,” Peter replied earnestly as he climbed aboard the Karma.

Once more Danny cautiously negotiated the channel as Karma again put to sea. It was originally thought it may have proved necessary to stay tied up alongside the jetty at Port Nolloth overnight, not something any desired, and now not something any had to consider as they cruised steadily south with the sun sinking gently into the sea off their starboard rail. Billy spelled Danny at the controls, guiding the boat through the night as they headed back to Cape Town. The sun was on the rise again, this time over land to their port side, as they passed Robben Island and entered Table Bay with the awesome majesty which is Table Mountain standing stark in front of them, growing in size as they approached their berth within Duncan Dock.

Nathan and Chris had returned to Cape Town, offloaded all rubbish just as Peter and Danny had earlier, and returned the pickup to the garage from where Danny first collected it, as arranged by Peter. Nathan then went high profile with a press release to the effect he had enjoyed his time touring South Africa viewing potential sites whilst waiting for his boat to arrive. He intended to take a break aboard his luxury yacht whilst cruising along the South African coastline. The boat had recently arrived and was currently being sea trialled by his crew in readiness for the voyage. It was due to return the following day when he and his Chief of Security would go aboard. All being well they would sail the same day.

Karma berthed and refuelled. Minor provisions were taken on board before Mr Jefferies arrived with his security man. The Karma’s crew of three lined the rail, neatly turned out in their ships uniforms as their boss stepped aboard. The small contingent of press who turned up had little of interest to report. Nathan Jefferies was old news. The crew neatly and professionally left their berth, once more putting to sea. A rich man playing with his toy, the lucky devil!

The crates loaded at Port Nolloth were stripped down and their contents moved below along with those previously loaded at Cape Town, which had included the all important fuel bladders essential for increasing their range. All the component parts of the missiles were on board Karma, as were launch platforms and arms, to be fully assembled whilst at sea. Had the press even suspected such things a media scrum would have followed as all on board were arrested. However the group's long held desire for subterfuge and secrecy continued to pay off. Ahead of them lay the deployment of the missiles, something they should be able to do overnight once on station, but first they had to get there, through some of the most dangerous waters and shipping lanes on the planet.

Jack Bryant had a plan for that, and the contacts to see it through.

Twenty One

Karma cruised eastwards along the South African coast at a comfortable and steady thirty-five knots. With Billy Sutcliffe now on board they could travel virtually non-stop as he and Danny carried out back to back six hour watches, although Peter soon picked up a mastery of the controls and rapidly learnt to spell one or the other of them. The Predator seemed palatial after the rigours of the Karoo, and the sea air ambrosia itself when compared to the baking dry heat they had endured for weeks. The space, comfort and general facilities aboard, despite the quantity of their equipment, provided Nathan with all the conditions he needed for continued work on the various flight paths for the missiles. Meanwhile Chris inspected, oiled and serviced the armaments he had ordered from Liam O'Connell in what seemed like half a lifetime before.

They refuelled the same evening at Knysna, afterwards cruising unhurriedly through the night, a pattern they would continue to follow. Dawn of the following day saw them making their way into the port of East London having travelled some six hundred miles from Cape Town. The next leg was north east to Durban then once more through the night to Maputo at the southern tip of Mozambique. Here they rested for a few hours whilst refuelling and finally had to fill two of the fuel bladders as their next fuel stop was to be Beira, which was a little beyond their standard tank range. For the most part they kept the coast of Africa beyond vision over their port rail as they continued north east along the Mozambique Channel, never once catching sight of Madagascar well off to starboard.

The refuelling sites were as time consuming, and generally tedious, as they were necessary, and their final site in Mozambique, Pemba, was no exception. Beira to Pemba was the longest leg of their journey so far, well beyond tank range. The additional fuel bladders Danny had organised and shipped out from England were standing up well to what was required of them, but he was aware their life expectancy was limited and they would not survive too many refills, so would only be used when absolutely necessary. Having topped off their standard tank at Pemba on the morning of the fifth day at sea, they sailed north to Dar Es Salaam, the main costal port and largest city of Tanzania, refuelled once more, then continued north through the night to the port and island city of Mombasa, Kenya's second city.

Karma moored just outside Kilindini Harbour after refuelling, and waited through the remains of the day and the night which followed. Chris and Billy checked and rechecked their munitions, grunting in satisfaction with everything they lay their hands on. With over thirty tonnes of fuel on board the Predator sat lower in the water than usual and would be slightly more sluggish in response at sea, but every single drop of fuel would be needed for the next perilous leg of their journey.

Jack Bryant, along with Katya, had boarded Lufthansa flight LH3720 at

Frankfurt slightly before its 07.35 departure time and flown Business Class in order to sleep as they headed south. They landed at a little before 19.10 in the evening at the particularly ugly Jomo Kenyatta International Airport and took a taxi to the Intercontinental Hotel. Both were travelling on German passports obtained by Katya, and continued to speak only in German at the hotel, which they had chosen because the language was catered for there. The hotel was pre-booked and paid for with a wholly legitimate German credit card registered to the passport holder and drawn on an existing account. Everything was wholly legitimate – except it was false.

The following morning they took the eight-thirty Kenya Airways flight to Mombasa which duly landed an hour later. Carrying nothing more than carry-on bags they cleared the airport within twenty minutes of landing and were on board Karma before ten-thirty, when she immediately put to sea.

Danny was overjoyed to see his brother, and both Jack and Katya were more than suitably impressed with their first sight of the Predator and, at the grand old age of twenty-six, Jack finally came to understand his older brother's interest in boats and fascination with the sea.

"Good trip down, Bro?" Danny asked as they headed into deeper waters.

"A flight is a flight, but it's good to be here, and great to see you!" Jack replied as Danny kissed Katya on the cheek.

"What have you been doing to yourself Dan?" Katya asked in flawless English as she ran her eyes over the man whose size she had never quite got used to. "You didn't have any fat in the first place, but you all look so fit and tanned I have to say I've never in my life seen a better looking and fitter collection of males!"

Danny laughed out loud. "Nice of you to say so Katya, and you don't look so bad yourself, but all I can put it down to is the African sun and the joys of the Karoo. It certainly burns off what you don't need!"

Billy Sutcliffe approached, and Danny turned to him and said, "Billy. This is my brother Jack, who I may just have mentioned, and this is Katya. Guys this is Billy Sutcliffe, arguably the best man I've ever sailed with."

The three shook hands and Billy responded by saying, "Your brother's not a bad skipper either Jack. Now would you like me to spell you behind the wheel Dan, whilst you show them around and sort out accommodation?"

"Yeah, thanks Billy. I'll do that. Then I want to call everyone on board together so we can go through everything we may have to do over the next couple of days. I'll give those below a call whilst I'm down there so we can start in about twenty minutes." Danny said.

Leading his brother and Katya Danny first went below and showed them to the stateroom.

"Before you say anything we decided you should have this room because there're two of you," Danny explained.

"What an incredible room. It's hard to believe what it is we are doing once you step aboard this boat." Jack replied looking around the cabin.

"We should not have this one, this should be Nathan's," Katya said

"Ah hell, he didn't want it, nor did any of the rest of us, so it's yours. That was decided way back. Now drop your gear and let me show you around. Karma's an incredible lady. Pretty, comfortable, and can be very, very lively, although not with the weight of fuel we currently have on board," Danny told them, with more than a note of passion in his voice for the vessel he had come to love.

Jack and Katya were shown around, the others were called, and all assembled in the saloon. Seven very dedicated people. Six dedicated by conviction, because of the pain, suffering and loss of loved ones, and one because of the three million US dollars he was to receive for his part. The Karma was halted and a sea anchor put out. They were out of the sea lane but still Dan and Billy kept looking around, casting wary eye's over the ocean, ever on the lookout for approaching problems.

"Okay everyone, the reason I've called us all together now is because, as we all know, we are about to enter some pretty dangerous waters," Danny said, glancing around at everyone as he did so in an attempt to gauge their attentiveness. Happy with what he saw he continued, "We are currently approximately two hundred miles south west of Somali waters. That's about six hours away, so we'll reach it before dark. At around one thousand nine hundred miles Somalia has mainland Africa's longest coastline and it is impossible for us to get around it without refuelling, even with the long range bladders. We cannot refuel in Somalia, it's just too dangerous, and so we have to refuel at sea, something Jack has arranged. If we miss the refuelling boat our entire mission is over. It really is that critical.

"Now the real problem we are faced with in these waters is the ever present danger of pirates. These guys are not colourful characters as romanticised and sanitised by Hollywood. We will not find any Johnny Depps complete with eyeliner posing as Captain Jack Sparrow, but what we could come up against is the very scourge of the sea.

Given a chance these people will attack without warning in an attempt to seize the boat and ransom both it and us, and I need not remind you we have a billionaire with us. If we are taken we are absolutely finished! There is no nicer way of putting it. The ransom will be huge, we will miss our target, and doubtless everything we are about will come out. The end of the story for us.

"Therefore if we come up against pirates, and it is most likely we will as we are nice ripe pickings for them, we may well have to fight our way out. Doubtless our passage up the coast will have been noted, and a call has probably already been made from Mombasa informing those concerned that we have left. Also it will not have been missed that we have one critical weakness, which is the fuel I have already mentioned. I imagine they will be waiting for us, which means we will have to fight. That is not my area of expertise and I cannot answer any questions on it, so I'll hand over to Billy who will be able to." Danny finished and turned his attention to the waters around the boat. They were comparatively quiet with only one costal steamer and a very large crude carrier on the horizon. He could relax a little and listen.

"I think the easiest thing to do is for me to give you the basic background as to what we are up against." Billy began. "There is a lot to it but I shall skip bits in order to keep it as brief as I can. Afterwards I'll try and answer any questions you may have.

"To start I guess I had better explain what is and what is not piracy. To qualify as piracy the act has to be committed in international waters, which makes it an international crime, and consists of acts which can include violence, detention or depredation, all of which are illegal. Depredation is the act of pillage, plunder or robbery. These acts are committed for private ends by the crew, or passengers, of a private ship against another ship or the people and or property on board. This is similar with aircraft but that does not concern us.

"As I said, these acts have to take place beyond any nation's territorial jurisdiction. The same acts committed within territorial waters do not constitute piracy, but are instead usually referred to as sea robbery, which is usually armed robbery. International law permits any nation's warships to intervene and repress such attacks in international waters, but only international waters. Therefore this type of criminal tends to operate in waters where a government is weak or lacks the political will to deal with them effectively. The Somali waters are a classic example of this, and pirates working from the country are now operating at an ever further reach, rapidly returning to Somali waters where they cannot be touched.

"The Royal Navy has been joined by warships from the US, France, Denmark, Russia and Japan in patrolling these waters. Recently India added their presence and even Pakistan threatened to rattle its sabre, but wanted too much in return. Despite all the warships, attacks have recently been on the increase, probably because it can be hugely profitable, but mainly because nobody is paying any attention to the root of the problem. Interestingly there has been one recent exception you may have heard about. When a French yacht was attacked the French shot up the pirates and pursued them into territorial waters then, when the pirates landed, chased them inland with helicopter gun ships, shot them up some more, snatched the survivors and they are now on trial in Paris for piracy."

A mutter of approval for the French tactics rippled around the table as Billy continued. "What all this means to us is that we are on our own. We have a plan to change the name and colour of the boat, for security and confusion, but if we come up against the pirates, and we will because we are just too ripe and rich a target for them to pass up, then our only option will be to fight our way out, or use Karma's speed to outrun them. Outrunning them would be my first choice, and this old girl is very fast. However they may well have several light inflatables, with which they try to surround us, as well as their mother craft if they follow their usual M.O.

"We are equipped for a fight, in fact we are well equipped, but I also want us to be well prepared. It could be they try and take us at night, and they have become fairly good at doing so recently, so we must be vigilant during darkness and put on an extra lookout. However if they come it could be at any time, and we will be in dangerous waters for the next forty-eight hours. What anyone on lookout must report instantly is anything at all out of the ordinary. Some vessels have been taken because their crews were slow to react or were lured into dropping defences thinking they were going to another seafarer's aid. If anyone spots an inflatable adrift fifty miles out to sea it's a pirate, not someone in trouble! We just shoot them up and get the hell out of it as quickly as we can. If we find ourselves surrounded, which is the normal tactic, we shoot everything which moves. We do not play Mr Nice Guy. That will lead to our capture or death. We will be much better armed than them, something they will not expect, and if we are surrounded we take everything down. We don't have to kill everyone as long as we sink their boats. With that done the sharks will do the work for us. If we are attacked and surrounded, stopping us from outrunning them, a fire fight will follow. If such happens the mother ship will try and make a run for it as soon as it looks like we have the upper hand. We will then have to go after it and sink that too. No survivors. Any questions?"

Peter Parfitt broke the thoughtful silence with a question. "How far along the coast do these guys operate, how far from land, and how many gangs are there?"

"They can operate virtually anywhere along the coast and have been known to attack targets over four hundred miles from land, which is why we cannot go around them." Billy answered. "They are well equipped. Keep in mind over twenty million pounds have been paid in ransoms so far this year alone. I guess the most dangerous area is off the Nugaal region. The port town of Eyl is off limits to anyone from the world outside and it could well be argued it is the very epicentre of piracy.

"Currently there are four known organised pirate groups operating along the coast. Starting in the south, the first we'll face is a group calling itself the National Volunteer Coast Guard. They are based in Kismaayo, but shouldn't be too much of a problem for us as they tend to be best at intercepting small vessels and fishing boats, although this would make a wonderful prize for them. Further up the coast, and based around the town of Marka, you have the originally named Marka Group. The Puntland group are made up of traditional Somali fishermen working off the coast of the Nugaal region I mentioned, and finally, working from the same area, there are the Somali Marines. This one is the group I most fear we will come up against in a fire fight. They are the most powerful and sophisticated of the groups and have a military structure. They tend to treat their captured 'guests' well, but we really don't want to sun ourselves on a Somali beach no matter how nice the treatment is. So if we have to – we fight!"

"You said we are well equipped for a fight. What are we equipped with?" Danny asked.

Billy smiled slightly and asked, "Do you remember helping me carry a number of cases down below whilst we were at Cape Town?"

"The chunky ones which arrived mysteriously in the dead of night?" Dan responded.

"That'll be the ones. Well they contain our deterrent. Chris and I have been all over them checking and cleaning everything. When this conversation is over we can fetch them back up to this saloon and keep everything up here from now on. We have two leg mounted MILAN launchers and ten extra range missiles for each. MILAN's were developed by the French and are 'Missile d'infanterie léger antichar' or, in English, Anti-Tank Light Infantry Missile and are wire guided, which means the sight of the launcher has to be aimed at the target in order to guide the missile. Ours have come with MIRA thermal sights, so we shouldn't have any problems if we are attacked at night.

"We also have two Browning five-O's, probably better known as fifty-cals. These have one thousand rounds each of armour piercing incendiary tracers and armour piercing incendiaries. Again we can take them on day or night, and our guns are much bigger! Our ammunition can perforate nineteen millimetre steel plate from five hundred meters and anyone it hits is toast. So if the bad guys want to take us on with their grenade launchers and AK-47's they will have to do it when we're not looking because our missiles are much bigger with a far longer range, and our machine guns can knock them down at three to four times the range of their guns with ease!" Billy reassured the non combatants.

No further questions followed so Danny once more pointed Karma to the north east and gently ran her up to their thirty-five knot cruising speed as Chris and Billy slowly brought their 'toys' up to the saloon assisted by Peter and Jack. Heavy with fuel Karma still ploughed through the waves as the ex military men went about setting up their weaponry whilst keeping it out of sight. A MILAN was positioned inside the hot tub at the front of the boat, which gave it nearly three hundred degrees of cover, and the second was stationed at the rear of the saloon from where it could cover one hundred and twenty degrees, and could easily be moved onto the deck if more manoeuvrability were needed. The two infantry versions of the fifty cal could be carried into position in moments if and when required. All hoped the weapons would not be needed. All suspected they would be.

Running through the gentle swell Karma slowly shed weight as she burned up fuel. Darkness closed around her rapidly as the sun lowered itself and finally plunged into the sea. Partly due to the actions of the pirates the shipping lanes were ill defined but, despite never running too close to any other vessel, nobody had wanted to start changing Karma's appearance whilst it was light. As the sun started to dip the work began and Karma started to disappear as the classic Sunseeker navy blue base under white was altered. A broad red band one meter wide was laid down the entire length of the vessel. Around both sides a broad white band was laid over the blue and the same red which ran down the centre appeared as vertical lines over the top of the white, small bands at the front to wide at the rear. Time had been spent on the computer working on various pictures and overlays to see what worked best to change the boats appearance without altering the vessel itself. It now looked taller and broader, but shorted. It was an optical illusion, a trick of the eye, but it provided a consummate transformation.

The final touch to the vessel itself was another change of name. Karma had appeared tastefully on the stern panel and occupied a position in the centre slightly under a meter wide, with Gibraltar stencilled beneath it in smaller letters sized to fill the same width giving an impression of implied good taste and refinement. The red band completely covered both. In red on the remaining white, and white across the top of the red band, the new name almost filled the entire panel from one side to the other. Novaya Russkaya was written large in Cyrillic script, with Sankt Peterburg beneath. On either side of the stern, in small Latin letters it was repeated in English, subtly exhibiting Jack Bryant's somewhat deep sense of humour. Novaya Russkaya, New Russian, was the name given by the ordinary Russian people to the Nouveau Riche, a deprecating, mocking term for those who often had vastly more wealth than taste or style.

The Red Ensign which had fluttered proudly in the breeze over the stern for the previous three thousand miles was hauled down, and the white, blue and red lateral tricolour of the Russian Federation was run up. The changes would mean absolutely nothing in the dark, but in the daylight or under searchlights it might just cause a few minutes confusion, and in a few minutes they could be miles away. The changes also made refuelling possible if Jack's plan was to work.

Yuri Orlov had spent the vast majority of his adult life in the service of the Russian military machine. Whilst on an extended mission to, and working from, Vladivostok, in the extreme south east of Russia, he became involved in a romantic entanglement with an attractive young lady called Oksana Petrova. The relationship went nowhere, but it did provide him with an introduction to her father, Dmitry Petrov, who featured in his mission profile and was a major part of the reason the relationship with Oksana had started.

Vladivostok is Russia's biggest port city on the Pacific, the end of the Trans Siberian railway, is close to the borders of China and North Korea and, most importantly, is home to the Russian Pacific Fleet. Originally part of China it, and the entire maritime province on which it stands, including the island of Sakhalin, became part of Russia in 1858 by the Treaty of Aigun. China had just lost the Opium War with Britain and was unable to act. The following year Russia founded a naval outpost, and the first child was born there in 1863. Between the 1870's and 1890's fortifications were erected and a telegraph line opened in 1871. By 1903 the Trans-Siberian Railway was completed connecting Vladivostok with Moscow and therefore Europe. Its military importance continued to grow and it became a closed city to foreigners between 1958 and 1991, with even Soviet citizens required to obtain official permission before entering.

In one hundred and fifty years the small port has grown into a city of some six hundred thousand people, but throughout that time its very reason for being has remained unchanged. Vladivostok is a port. Its main industries are shipping, commercial fishing and the naval base. The city exports fish and timber, but imports virtually everything else. Dmitry Petrov was an ethnic Russian and member of the communist party, which he had to be to maintain his managerial position within Sovcomflot, one of the countries state shipping companies, and was the director – the Russian term which usually refers to the general manager – of a coastal steamer company. Dmitry Petrov was not an ideologically natural communist. Had he been born in what was euphemistically called 'The Free World' he would have been a profiteering capitalist and, with his natural talent and flair for business, he would undoubtedly have prospered greatly. However he lived under a system which did not tolerate free enterprise.

This had presented both Dmitry Petrov and the state with a problem. Petrov was undeniably gifted at his job and someone the state understood they had lucked out with. A person born to follow a certain trade was actually following it, which was certainly not always the Russian way. However it was recognised Petrov was flawed in that he had the desire to run things not only efficiently, which was just tolerable, but profitably, which most definitely was not. Petrov was a capitalist working in a communist closed city. In most cases the solution to such a problem was simple, removal or internment, but Petrov was good at what he did for the state as could be seen by his promotions and advancement. Petrov was also well connected to the party machine.

Partly due to his brothers shipping and transport background Yuri Orlov was sent to Vladivostok to carry out an examination of Petrov and his affairs and, if deemed necessary, to see to it Petrov met with an unfortunate and fatal accident. Yuri Orlov was utterly loyal to his country and a dedicated and motivated individual who could be trusted by his superiors and country to get the job done no matter how messy or bloody it became. Even in the late 1980's, when the fall of the Russian communist system was already suspected by some, Petrov remained a loose cannon within the system. Had Yuri Orlov considered his mission wholly pragmatically and objectively, as he was usually wont to do, Petrov would have died. However Yuri found himself liking the man, for the first time in his life taken in by natural charm and magnetism. Petrov was without doubt a character, and a very likeable outgoing one at that.

Instead of accidentally drowning in a dock or being crushed by a truck or crane Petrov lived. Yuri Orlov had visited him, explained the situation in no uncertain terms, and told Petrov to change his ways and keep his head down whilst the wind of change blew. Change did come, and it was to be change on a hitherto unprecedented scale. Virtually everything which was previously state owned was privatised, mostly with no lead in time at all, and sometimes literally overnight. Management and workers were given the companies they served with vouchers allocated by the state, as there was no such thing as a Stock Exchange at the time and shares did not exist. Generally the higher the position of manager the more vouchers, with far fewer to the workers. The state just walked away, strolling off into the sunset in most cases, with the exception of the tax police, never to be seen again.

Removing himself from Sovcomflot Dmitry Petrov received his vouchers, in fact he received a great deal of vouchers then, as many other managers did in so many of the suddenly privatised industries, he set about buying up the vouchers of the workers. He was lucky to avoid the blood letting which often followed such a move, and shortly controlled and owned his offices, and the coastal steamers. Privatisation suited Dmitry Petrov and over the years which followed he grew his business. Since the early 1990's the Russian merchant marine, once unrivalled in the world, had continued to shrink. In fifteen years it had shrunk from some one thousand eight hundred vessels to one hundred and seventy-two. The reason for this was due to re-registration and the flying of flags of convenience, and it was to Liberia that Petrov had decided to have his fleet re-registered. The privileged terms offered, bottom-low taxes, no demands in respect of crewmembers rights and a simplified procedure of registering documents made it too attractive to pass up, so his fourteen vessels were amongst those which left the Russian merchant marine.

Petrov prospered, and prospered immensely. He now ran a much bigger operation trading between Japan, China and South Korea with his container vessels, had two Large Crude Carriers sailing between The Gulf and India, Thailand and Japan, and a small fleet of bunkering and ship supply vessels most of which were under contract to the Russian Pacific Fleet, but not all. His vessels were all named after the bay from which they sailed and big cats. From his offices overlooking the Golden Horn Bay Petrov still ruled his empire with the flair which had once angered his communist overseers but now brought in the Roubles, Yen, Yuan, Rupee, Baht and myriad Dollars by the container load. Yuri Orlov's visit had not just saved his life but set him on a course which had given him more money and power than he would once have dreamt possible, and it was something he had never forgotten.

Despite offers of employment, property, land, girls and cars, Yuri had not once accepted anything from Dmitry Petrov. What he had done had not been done with profit in mind, or of being bribed, and he would take nothing. It was a matter of honour. Despite that Petrov never forgot, and never would do. As long as Yuri Orlov lived, even if he outlived Petrov, Petrov, and his corporation, would be in his debt, a debt which could be called upon and would be paid in full. Anytime! Anywhere!

Running without lights Novaya Russkaya maintained her course throughout the night, and remained at a steady thirty-five knots as she powered through the silent waters of the Indian Ocean. Despite a steady and rotating lookout only two sets of lights were seen during the hours of darkness. They crossed the equator, and daylight saw them well to the north of Kismaayo, presumably beyond the usual chosen waters of the National Volunteer Coast Guard, but deep into the waters of the Marka Group.

The early morning light spotlighted two small craft some way off to their port side, sandwiched between them and the land, but they were too far away to make out distinctly. Despite concerns over fuel conservation speed was increased to forty knots for an hour increasing the distance between them and effectively ending any chase if they were pirates. By midday they had passed to the east of Mogadishu and were gradually making their way out of Marka waters, still without yet seeing a single warship or a confirmed sighting of a pirate.

"How far until we bunker?" Peter, who was sharing lookout duty with Chris, asked Danny as he sat behind the wheel also watching, but with one eye on the charts.

"About two hundred and fifty miles," Danny answered casually.

"So about seven o'clock this evening?" Peter enquired.

"If all continues to go according to plan," Danny said before asking, "Why do you ask?"

"Just confirmation really. I thought it was the time Jack said, but didn't consider the implications then. We'll be back on watch then, and I was just thinking about it. That'll definitely be the time when we are at our most vulnerable. If we are attacked then it will compromise our ability to defend ourselves. A couple of tracers through the hull of the bunkering ship and we could all have problems." Peter said.

"Don't be such a pessimist!" Danny laughed. "Just think about it positively, we'll have a load of extra lookouts!"

"Actually it's not being attacked there which worries me," Peter said. Then continued seriously, "The possible problem I've just thought about is this. If the pirates are interested in us, and have worked out our fuel weakness, it won't take a person of your brother's intellect to work out we have to bunker at sea, and we'll probably do so when our tanks are at their lowest in order to get full benefit from the bunkering. If they understand that they may well be on the lookout for a tanker and, if they find it and board it, then all they have to do is wait for us to turn up knowing we won't have the fuel to run away."

"I thought I told you not to be a pessimist?" Danny inquired. "Anyway, don't worry, I'm sure we'd hear their distress call!"

"Fat lot of good that would do us!" Peter responded obviously genuinely concerned. As he was speaking Jack had climbed the steps from the galley below.

"Proper timing." Danny said grinning. "There's the man to ask. Put it to him."

Peter repeated his thoughts to Jack, who merely answered, "Don't worry, it's protected."

Once more a huge red glowing tropical sun suddenly plunged into the sea as they approached the coordinates of their rendezvous. Just before it disappeared a glint of red reflected from the distance, in fact, worryingly, two glints of red reflected and the radar picked up two contacts dead ahead. Undaunted Danny, now once more behind the wheel, continued towards the contacts at the same steady thirty-five knots. When they were still half a mile off the boat ahead was suddenly flooded with light as the tankers crew attempted to afford an easier approach for the Novaya Russkaya.

Danny rounded the stern of the Liberian registered Zolotoi Tigr – Golden Tiger – and eased alongside using only the thrusters as it was important the graphics they had stuck along the sides the previous night were not disturbed. Nathan remained below throughout the two hours they nestled under the lee of the Zolotoi Tigr, and the four crew of the Novaya Russkaya, Danny Bryant, Peter Parfitt, Chris Spencer and Billy Sutcliffe busied themselves about the vessel in their red polo shirts. From above it could be seen the powerful, wealthy and well connected owner and his beautiful girlfriend watched on, occasionally instructing the well drilled crew, but generally leaving them to do their job. The young man, obviously the son of an oligarch, stayed in control and aboard his own vessel, even after the ladder was lowered, though his girlfriend ventured up and greeted the man who had earlier been lowered to their vessel at sea by helicopter. The crew of the Zolotoi Tigr kept well clear. The odd word in Russian floated across to them from the beautiful girl, but this was not their business and none had spoken a word to the man, who was so obviously Special Forces, from the moment he came aboard. When things like this happened at sea, they stayed at sea, never to be spoken of again. The Russian warship which had shadowed them down the coast of Africa, and was to escort them eight hundred kilometres out to sea afterwards, kept station at a one kilometre distance.

Yuri Orlov raised his hand to Jack after the Novaya Russkaya's tanks and fuel bladders had once more been fully filled and his niece had returned to her decks. Jack inclined his head by way of reply as his brother eased away from the bunkering vessel. They were heavy in the water once more, but Novaya Russkaya was soon accelerating away through the buoyant water. The Zolotoi Tigr extinguished her floodlights and the Russian warship started to get underway. Their job was done. Dmitry Petrov had paid his marker.

"My God," breathed Peter to Danny as the two vessels riding lights disappeared over their stern. "Not only did he organise a mid ocean bunkering facility, but he got it protected by a bloody great cruiser. Does your brother ever miss a single thing?"

"Not since his third birthday," Danny chuckled.

“He’s unbelievable! If ever I question any part of a plan again just tell me to shut the hell up!” Peter told him.

“Peter, seriously, it never hurts to question things. Keep it up! We cannot forget or overlook a thing. Not once. Not ever. Voice every concern you have, just in case – you never know, even the very best can make mistakes,” Danny replied earnestly.

Their good fortune held as their passage across the darkened tropical waters under a changing collection of flickering stars continued. Radar contacts increased as the distance to the Horn reduced and the vessels coming from and heading to the Gulf of Aden from all points south became more densely packed. These waters were better patrolled by warships of the many nations, but the area of sea was vast, and their deterrent effect consequently somewhat reduced. Holding to their north east course at a steady thirty-five knots their wake sped out behind them as their journey progressed, mildly phosphorescing as legions of miniature creatures caught up in its turbulence blinked on and off.

Some of the contacts picked up by the radar could be reasonably accurately guessed at. Due to the size of the signal bounced back from such craft as the VLCC’s, as they trudged across the ocean plying their trade carrying the crude lifeblood of industry around the world, or the huge slab sides of container vessels, these could be easily noted and little detour was required. Smaller contacts were met with slightly more trepidation, and a clear route was picked through them in order to provide plenty of sea room if sudden flight was considered necessary. The hours passed and the watch changed two hours later than usual so those who had been off watch but helped with the refuelling should benefit from some quality sleep.

Danny, Peter and Chris trudged below to their cabins to get their own much needed rest as Billy, Jack and Katya came up fresh from below. Tensions had been running high since leaving Mombasa, and certainly so since they entered the waters off Somalia, but at the refuelling point they had covered more than half the danger area. The sun would once more rise before six in the morning, with nautical dawn around five. By daybreak they should be close to ten degrees north, and four hours later, all being well, they would have reached the Gulf of Aden, rapidly leaving their pirate problems behind them. By nightfall they should be well outside the danger area.

Just before four o’clock Billy picked up a contact behaving strangely ahead, just as they passed eighty miles offshore of the town of Ely, which won its name from the river which empties into the sea there when its waters flow. Three times he slightly altered course as he approached, zigzagging across the ocean in order to avoid contact. Three times the vessel ahead seemingly responded, it too altering course. It could be coincidence and have a perfectly innocent explanation, but Billy did not like coincidences, and hated them in pirate waters.

“Can either of you see anything out of the ordinary?” he called out to Jack and Katya.

“Nothing,” Jack shouted back from the port side.

“No, not really,” Katya shouted from starboard watch.

“What does ‘not really’ mean?” Billy asked, raising his voice above the noise of their passage.

"Well, it's just as you shouted the question I noticed a short line of phosphoruse in the water, but I couldn't see what caused it and it's disappeared now," she answered.

"Get below and get everyone up here. Start with Chris. I want him here now and I want Danny pronto!" Billy snapped out.

Chris, Danny and Peter all arrived in the same order less than half a minute apart with Chris on deck within a minute of being woken. Danny came shaking a head obviously woolly with sleep and even Nathan appeared a minute later.

"Danny, take the helm!" Billy instructed then added. "And whatever you do keep an eye on this contact and keep me informed as to what it does! Chris take a five-O and get up front in the hot tub. Take some night glasses and open up on anything if I do. Peter, just keep him supplied as we have discussed. Jack – Katya, keep the information coming in no matter how seemingly trivial. Nathan, you keep me supplied. Now someone give me some glasses and point in the direction of the phosphoruse trail Katya."

"It was out there between two and three o'clock," Katya replied pointing as Billy studied the direction she indicated.

"Contact!" Billy shouted. "Three o'clock. Small inflatable about a mile out. It's vectoring in. Danny, hit the throttle, and take us ten degrees to port! Let's see if we can outrun them."

"Forward contact is altering course," Danny shouted out above the increase in engine noise as the Novaya Russkaya responded to the demand for more power.

"Port contact at eleven o'clock!" Jack shouted out.

"We've also got one on our six." Billy called back.

"They're bloody quick." Danny remarked. "I don't think we'll outrun the inflatables easily, they must have some meaty engines, and the forward contact has increased speed to intercept."

"They've done it before and had quite a lot of practice. They're beginning to get quite good at it." Billy replied to Danny matter of factly. He then raised his voice and bellowed out. "We are going to have to fight our way through! Peter, tracer rounds to Chris!"

A strange calm broke out aboard. There was no eerie silence, the sound of the water on the hull and noise of the engines saw to that, but there was no nervous conversation, just a calm acceptance that they would have to put up a fight.

"Drop the speed back to where we were and swing back to our original course Danny," Billy instructed as the Novaya Russkaya rapidly closed on the still unseen contact ahead.

"Contact changing course." Danny reported back in a voice demonstrating a complete lack of concern.

"Let them close on us people." Billy said. "They are clearly hostile and obviously want us. They're attempting to box us in. Let them continue to do so. We want to know how many there are because we want to take them all down!"

Half a minute ticked by, which seemed as if it was half an hour to those who had never trained or faced combat. It infinitely slowly became a minute, which in turn became two.

"All right everybody, there are four inflatables arranged around us, and the mother-ship ahead. They are well within our firing distance, but still outside their own. We'll let them all close a bit more. Danny, on my mark slow down to five knots. I want those behind to catch up quick and confuse those ahead. Nathan, get ready to supply me with more tracer rounds. Peter, let Chris know we are about to reduce speed. The inflatables will turn back into him. Take the furthest one out first and pile it into them. The nearest one will turn as soon as we open up. Take it out on the turn if possible. He's to wait until I open up on the two behind. We'll bag them all." Billy issued the instructions in an orderly flow. He had total control of the situation. The pirates may well have been experienced, but he was way more so and had received the finest training of its kind in the world, and knew the odds, whereas the pirates didn't have a clue about what they were up against. All of that was about to change for them.

Peter had gone forward to inform Chris as instructed. Another twenty seconds elapsed as Billy peered over the stern through the night glasses.

"Kill the speed!" he roared at Danny, and the forward motion began to fall away instantly. If those in the fast light inflatables behind were shocked at the sudden loss of speed of their quarry they showed no sign of it as they rapidly closed on their prey.

"Port forward contact turning in to us." Jack shouted out.

"Starboard contact turning too!" Katya yelled.

"Okay people, this is it. Danny keep an eye on the mother-ship. She'll run. We want her to!" Billy shouted his last order. As he did so he dragged the cover from the M2HB already set up on its tripod, and squatted behind it. The pirates were getting close behind the stern. The leading inflatable was now just within AK47 range, but only just, and in a small unstable pitching vessel with the weapon in poorly trained hands the chances of hitting anything was negligible. Dawn would break soon, but Billy wanted to take the rubber boats down whilst he still had the benefit of the bright starlight. He could see the two vessels closing on them from behind now. Not clearly, not even as a proper silhouette, but he could see two shadows moving on the water and the slight shimmering of their wake.

Nathan jumped like a startled gazelle as the fifty cal opened up next to him. He had expected noise but was totally unprepared for the sheer volume. His first instinct was to dive for cover, but a split second later his senses cut back in and told him this was outgoing fire, which was good, not incoming, which would be bad. Instead of hanging on to the trigger for dear life, as Nathan would have done, Billy was firing in short bursts. Looking over the stern Nathan watched as a line of what looked like high speed fireflies sped across the ocean and disappeared into – what – a shadow. As he continued to watch the barrel next to him swung slightly and another line flew into a further area of darkness. From the other end of their boat the same chattering bursts could also be heard as Billy's gun stopped its work. From one of the two boats to their rear there had been a momentary series of yellow orange flashes, but that was it. Nathan sat there rigid, partly in fascination, partly fear. Why didn't Billy shoot some more? When would he need more bullets? Shoot! Shoot! Shoot! He thought. Was Billy hurt? Shit, had Billy been hurt? Fear clutched at him as he turned to see how badly hurt Billy was, but Billy was standing up.

"Billy!" Nathan shouted. "Shoot them! Shoot them!"

"It's alright Nathan, they're all dead," Billy reassured him sympathetically before turning towards the helm and shouting, "Danny, what's the contact doing?"

"He's turning away from us and heading for land." Danny yelled in reply.

"Follow him. Twenty knots. I'm going forward to have a word with Chris. Close on him, but maintain a thousand meter gap," Billy ordered.

Billy walked forward and joined Chris and Peter. Had he known neither he would have instantly recognised them as men of action, as both were casually sitting on the lip of the hot tub chatting amiably. The contrast between them and Nathan could not have been more stark.

"Obviously clear then!" Billy stated.

"No resistance. Both down. They're history. What about the mother-boat?" Chris asked.

"We'll take her too. Is your MILAN ready?" Billy asked.

"Billy! How long have we known one another?" Chris responded grinning.

"Okay. Well no pleasantries with the next one. We chew her up big time with the five-O's as we approach, then slam a couple of missiles apiece into her around her water line. Take down anyone who moves, armed or not. If anyone goes over the side chew them up too. No prisoners, no survivors. They attacked us. We were never here and don't want any witnesses. Any problems?" Billy asked in the full knowledge all he had just said was wasted on Chris, who would have done exactly that without instructions.

"Only one. Have you checked your own MILAN?" Chris asked with a large grin.

"Fuck off!" Billy responded and all three men burst out laughing.

For the others, now gathered around Danny at the helm, it was their first fire fight, not that it had proved much of a fight, and their first glimpse of any action. The burst of laughter from the sharp end mystified them. All had come through it well, and pretty much as predicted, Nathan possibly suffering a little through to Danny who was utterly unperturbed and obviously so, lifting him further in Billy's opinion as he walked in to study the charts and radar. They were rapidly closing on the runaway mother-ship.

"Danny, I'd like to overhaul them fast now. Bring us alongside her at one thousand meters whilst we study her, then we'll close to six hundred meters and take her down. Mirror her every move, but if she starts to return effective fire, which I think is extremely unlikely, move away to fifteen hundred meters. I'll leave all that to you now because I'm going to finish off on deck. Does anyone want to volunteer to help me in case I need it? Billy asked, having finished his instructions.

"I will!" came the most unexpected reply from Nathan.

"Okay, thank you! Jack – Katya, keep you eyes peeled. It'll be getting light before we finish. I want to know the instant you see anything, or if Danny picks any contacts up on radar coming our way." Billy told them.

"Will do – okay," the pair muttered.

At nearly three times the speed of the fleeing mother-ship the Novaya Russkaya rapidly overhauled her. Dawn arrived although the sun was yet to make an appearance, hiding as it was beyond the horizon, but its first rays highlighted the upper superstructure of their target as the distance between them once again rapidly bled away. Closing to one thousand meters her crew could be seen through the clean air, crowding the rails of what had once been a fishing trawler, as the rising sun crept down her hull. A few aboard were bearing arms, but most just moved about the vessel pointing and gesticulating, which increased as the Novaya Russkaya moved in closer.

Both fifty-cals opened up within a second of one another, so close was the timing it would have been impossible to state which gun broke the relative silence first. Still in partial shadow the armour piercing incendiary tracers could be watched flying into the other boats hull. With bursts of fire moving up her sides a ragged white flag rose and many of those on board seemed to try to grasp the disappearing stars, so high did their hands go. The boat under attack cut her engines, and Danny followed her action, bringing Novaya Russkaya to an almost dead stop.

A burst of gunfire cut through the pirate crew, and those who survived ran from the rail. Slowly Danny inched forward and gradually circled the old trawler as half inch incendiary fire raked her other side, and those trying to lower a boat. Wisps of smoke appeared and flames could just be seen above her engine room as, with a woosh followed by a bang, the first missile slammed into her perforated side. She started to list almost immediately and the speed increased as another two missiles thumped into her bow and stern almost simultaneously. She began to roll away from them, displaying a filth encrusted hull as yet another missile smashed its way between the barnacles, and she went down fast. Within fifteen seconds she was beneath the waves with nothing but a torrent of rising bubbles and a small amount of oily debris to mark her passing. A large shark perhaps three meters long broke the surface, a human arm trailed from its mouth.

Danny completed two slow circuits of the site. As more debris sank the field reduced. There was nothing left to shoot at except a slight oil slick, so he opened the throttles and sped away, once more to the north east. The fifty-cals and the MILAN's had once more been hidden and covered in case of further trouble, but they expected none, and in this they were proved correct. Other vessels were sighted but none approached, and by two-thirty in the afternoon they cleared the Horn, cutting the corner between the headland at Tooxin and 'Abd al-Kuri' island. They had reached the Gulf of Aden unscathed.

Novaya Russkaya then sped north west across the Gulf of Aden in the direction of the Yemen town of Al-Hawrah, turning west towards Aden shortly before entering Yemeni territorial waters. The run in with the pirates had cost them a small amount of extra fuel, and for the leg of the journey they had then completed they had no margin at all, so were forced to reduce speed in order to conserve what they could. As a consequence they arrived at Aden shortly after dawn, instead of the early hours of the morning as was previously planned, which was unfortunate but, in the circumstances, unavoidable. Despite the enormity of their mission those who were on watch were somewhat awed by the sight before them, as well as being relieved at making landfall where they could refuel, even if it had to be carried out whilst light.

Aden's natural harbour is ancient, first used at least fifteen centuries ago, and lies in the crater of a volcano long since extinct, but which now forms a peninsular joined to the mainland by a low and narrow strip of land. The old town and original port city, Ma'alla, is situated within the crater, with Aden proper located on the isthmus, as are the city's main offices, diplomatic missions, university and Aden International Airport, the former RAF base of Khormaksar. Bypassing the ancient port they headed for bunkering facilities in the modern port of Tawahi, better known in British colonial days as Steamer Point, built in the huge natural harbour enclosed on the eastern side by the peninsular, and on the western side by an almost mirror image called Little Aden, the site of an oil refinery and tanker port.

Running in with the strengthening light many of the city's eight hundred thousand population could be seen scurrying about their business as another day proper started. Taking advantage of the confusion this created, Novaya Russkaya slipped into an available berth, met with the agent taking care of the fuel transaction on the quayside, refuelled the standard tanks within the hour, and rapidly returned to the open sea. Billy, the only one seen on deck, was wearing a baseball cap, large sunglasses and sporting a ten day beard, and communicating in a mix of broken languages, it would be unlikely he would ever be recognised again. In any case all Russians looked the same to the agent – but their payment in US dollars was always welcome!

Four hours later, with the Yemen close to their starboard side, and the coastline of Djibouti and then Eritrea within easy sight over the port rail, they entered the Red Sea to an almost discernable increase in buoyancy caused by the rising salt levels held in solution within its waters. Following the Yemen coast on a north north easterly heading, and passing between the mainland and the Hanish Islands, they made for the port of Al Hudaydah, the forth largest city in the Yemen, and also known as Hodeida. Here the Russian boat was again expected, but this time met with a warmer welcome, despite arriving after midnight. With the smell of coffee and leather hanging on the air, two of the major exports of the port, they once more refuelled the standard tanks.

After a disastrous fire destroyed the port facilities and much of the city in 1961 it was rebuilt with Soviet aid and became a Soviet naval base into the 1980's. As a result a mixture of Russian and Katya's superb Arabic was all the crew needed for communication, the reason the port was chosen for refuelling by Jack Bryant many months before. They left Al Hudaydah before dawn and headed north east across the Red Sea in the direction of the Eritrean Dahlak Archipelago, the site of another former Soviet naval base during the Cold War. En route they destroyed the fuel bladders, cutting them to pieces and consigning them to the sea as they would not be needed again as standard tanks should suffice throughout the remainder of their journey.

The Dahlak island group consists of one hundred and twenty-four small islands, almost all of which are uninhabited, and two large ones. Here they once more topped off the fuel tanks before finding a safe and secluded anchorage in a protected bay off one of the northernmost uninhabited Islands. There Novaya Russkaya disappeared forever. As the sun started to dip over the horizon the red vinyl of the stripes along the sides was carefully removed. With the constantly prowling satellites in the heavens above all such work was done by night, when even then thermal imaging could be used, but detail lost. After darkness was finally firmly established the vessel's name was removed, as was the crude broad stripe which ran down her length, but Karma was not yet to make a return.

When Danny had first been tasked with finding the best boat for the job his brother had presented him with a certain set of criteria which had to be met, and this he had done, in reality actually exceeding most demands. Apart from the size and speed issues, and meeting a design specification a billionaire would be comfortable with, the vessel Jack had instructed Danny to look for had to fit in as an exclusive up-market live-aboard dive-boat, many of which could be found along Egypt's and Saudi Arabia's Red Sea coasts.

Egypt had long exploited the diving possibilities along its coastline, and with the huge expansion in both popularity and the size of Sharm El Sheikh, at the southern tip of the Sinai Peninsular, the industry had undergone unprecedented growth, attracting many tens of thousands of visitors in its own right. This influx of wealthy visitors continued to contribute to the ever swelling coffers of the regions rulers, financially allowing and encouraging further expansion of an already growing market. The live-aboard dive-boats, some of which continue to take comfort levels to the palatial, have been increasingly encouraged, as dollars and euros can be gathered without the necessity for building the expensive support infrastructures hotels require.

The longest coastline on the Red Sea is that of the Kingdom of Saudi Arabia, a country which remains very conservative and exceedingly cautious about opening its doors to visitors, but offers a wealth of diving possibilities. Despite the difficult formalities of obtaining visitors visas, these possibilities and the associated attracted wealth have not been lost on the Saudis, and in recent years the live-aboard dive-boat industry has also taken off there too, with a plethora of boats and companies based at the port of Jeddah, with the boats more usually to be seen at sea, working from their busy bases at the huge port.

Live-aboard dive-boats working from Egypt, Saudi Arabia and the Sudan are becoming an ever increasing sight on the Red Sea and, apart from navigating around them, are generally overlooked by the authorities unless flagrantly breaking the laws of the individual states within their territorial waters. The Saudis require visitors to adhere to their standards of legal morality in dress, demeanour and public behaviour. If visitors, especially seaborne visitors, can work within the rules they are largely ignored. Both they, and the vessels on which they take their short holidays, have effectively become invisible.

The all-white motor yacht Sea Sphinx cruised north north west from the Dahlak Peninsular on a line for Port Sudan. Flying an Egyptian flag her beautifully simple lines were marred only by the advertising along her sides. The big blue vinyl lettered sign boasting Red Sea Diving was superfluous. It was obvious to all who saw her she was a live-aboard dive-boat, and the sign did nothing but detract from the beauty of the vessel as she cruised along at a steady thirty knots, doubtless proceeding towards the next dive site where those wealthy individuals on board would once again don their equipment and disappear off the rear end swim platform.

She reached Port Sudan in the late afternoon, refuelled and exited the port as she once more put to sea on an east north easterly heading, presumably to take in the underwater beauties said to be present along the Saudi coastline. One hundred and twenty-five miles later, having crossed the deepest section of the Red Sea, Danny Bryant used the depth finder to locate an area less than one hundred meters beneath the hull. Slowly moving northwards this was eventually detected, and the vessel came to a halt. She lit up above and below the waterline with lights pointing in all directions except the stern. The flashing lights on her communication mast let those who could see her know there were divers in the water engaging in a night dive and thereby warning all to steer clear.

Billy Sutcliffe, having taken the helm, constantly checked the position of the Predator, ready to correct the instant she shifted off station. Meanwhile Danny, Chris and Peter carried one of the preassembled launch platforms from the saloon to the stern, and painstakingly set the missiles and launch equipment gently in place as Nathan checked the devices wiring. Whilst Nathan carried out a computer simulation the others attached the flotation sacks and anchor, double checked all grease points and seals then winched the entire assembly over the side with the much improved tender winch. The cable, attached to the platforms anchor, played out until the platform settled on the sea floor. A float was attached to the surface end of the cable and a signal sent to the platform below. The sealed, battery driven, twelve volt winch attached to the platform drew the thin cable and float beneath the slight waves and down to a depth of ninety meters. Those involved had worked throughout the operation in silence, every person involved knowing exactly what was expected of them.

With work finished on the first platform the boat was slowly moved a further half mile to the north until a second suitable site was found. There the process was repeated and by the time the third site was found the last rig was ready to swing straight into place. Once the final platform had gently settled itself down to the sea bed the Sea Sphinx extinguished all lights and headed for the coast. As the last platform was cast loose a small inflatable was pumped up on the Sea Sphinx's swim platform, and a powerful electric motor attached to its rear before sliding it off the stern. Chris and Billy jumped in and a small solar powered transmitter was handed down to them in a waterproof case.

As the case was handed aboard the inflatable cast off and Danny gently pulled away leaving the inflatable free to make its way to the coast. There Chris took charge of the inflatable whilst Billy went further ashore and found a suitable location where the miniature transmitter could be left without any likelihood of discovery. As expected the two men were undisturbed, rapidly completed the work, returned to the dingy and left the deserted Saudi coast. Slightly ahead of the estimated ten minutes in, ten minutes on shore and ten minutes out, they had to wait a few minutes for Danny to return. When he did the two men were quickly pulled aboard and, as the Predator's engines started to growl, the little inflatable was dragged over the stern and secured

Three and a half years of meetings, talks and planning. Seven day working weeks and seemingly endless experiments. Procuring goods and parts from around the world, testing and re-testing, and the abductions and killings all were a party to had led to this – the placing of all their hopes on the bed of the sea and cruising away in the dead of night through unknown waters. There was a discernable and tangible feeling of anticlimax amongst all on board, and silence prevailed for many miles as they cruised steadily away. Each had their thoughts, and for the most part they were very different. For Billy there was a degree of elation. Three million dollars worth of elation. He had sacrificed a few weeks of his life for a job which presented very little real danger, yet would be rewarded at an unprecedented level. Not a bad month's work! He rolled over in his bunk and went to sleep with a satisfied smile on his face.

Sitting in the saloon Jack was interested as to how it would all work out in an almost abstract and academic way. Of all aboard he was the most detached as he attempted to estimate possible death tolls, the resulting reactions, and the effects their attack would have on the world's already broken economy. As far as he could reasonably believe they had left no trace of who they were, where they were from or, far more importantly, what they wanted. They would not as a group claim responsibility or make any demands, and without such things any investigation would be greatly hampered.

"What will they have to investigate Jack?" Nathan, who was working on his laptop asked, almost reading Jack's mind, and whose own mind had also been running along a very similar course.

"Hopefully very little." Jack replied. "There will be engine and missile fragments, and parts of the launch platforms. Then there's the explosive, but that's about it. They'll look for terrorist groups, threats, claims, previous patterns, but there is nothing there. I think they'll eventually come down on the side that it was carried out by the Iranians, and that's the general hope behind the false leads, but there will be insufficient proof for them to act, although we may well see an unattributable disaster in Iran in the next couple of years.

"How did Winston Churchill once describe Russia? – as a riddle wrapped in a mystery inside an enigma. Basically I believe that is all anyone investigating will be left with! But we are putting the cart before the horse, the missiles have yet to fly."

"They'll fly!" Nathan assured him.

In the otherwise empty galley Chris and Peter, whilst making a brew, were also engaged in conversation, discussing the future and their general wants and desires. Both understood that effectively the mission was over for them despite the fact they still had to get home and, as a result, both felt somewhat deflated, Chris much more so than Peter, who couldn't wait to get back to the woman he loved and to help her through her pregnancy, something he hadn't mentioned to anyone.

"What do you plan to do next?" Chris asked him.

"To be honest I really don't know long term. Now we have completed our part in the mission I'll tell you this, when we were in Cape Town I spoke to Tammy on the phone and she's pregnant. So beyond anything else I want to get back to her. I guess I'll take it from there afterwards," Peter told him in reply.

"Good God man, why didn't you tell anyone?" Chris asked, somewhat shocked Peter had kept the news to himself.

"Because I didn't in any way want to change the emphasis of the mission or create any sort of unnecessary distraction. It was a matter of duty to you all," Peter explained, then changed the subject. "But what are your plans now?"

“I’m not at all sure. I kind of feel as I did when I was about to leave the army. I know you’ve been asked to stay on with Almeti, and so have I. Jake and Phil have asked me to stay with the building project security, and to continue with security for Eastlond and NJF. It was just the sort of job I would have loved to have had when my army career finished, but after all we’ve been through I’m not sure it will be exciting enough for me, and I don’t want to feel anyone is just being charitable with the job,” Chris replied.

“I don’t think it will be done out of charity, Chris,” Parfitt told him. “As I said I don’t know what my long term plans will be, but I’ll certainly take up their offer for a while whilst I mull things over. Since the bombings I’ve been kind of focussed on the project, but now it’s virtually over I don’t intend to overreact. My suggestion to you is to give it time and see how things go. One thing is for certain I cannot see that I’ll ever again get a chance to work alongside such like minded people, and I’d miss every one of them if I chose another direction.”

Chris just sat and nodded. That was certainly something he had thought about a lot.

Danny sat at the helm, steering the Sea Sphinx through the dying night as dawn approached, heading north east for Egyptian waters and away from where they had deposited their deadly cargo. They had one more refuel to complete before striking out for Sharm El Sheikh, then it was a simple passage through the Suez Canal to the waters of the Mediterranean. Sitting in companionable silence with Katya he too was considering his future.

“You look deep in thought,” Katya said breaking the silence.

“Sorry, I didn’t realise it showed,” Dan replied.

“You were thinking about her weren’t you?” Katya asked, although it really wasn’t a question.

“Who?” Danny asked, in what he hoped sounded an innocent response, instantly realising it wasn’t as he saw Katya raise her eyes to the moon roof above. “Well yes, I was actually. The problem is, Katya, I don’t know what to do about it.” he answered honestly.

“Men. You’re the same around the world. Danny you’re a nice, interesting, easy going and intelligent man. How can you be so very stupid at the same time?” Katya asked.

“What do you mean?” Danny asked in reply, totally mystified as to what she meant.

“Ring her!” Katya told him.

“But I don’t know what I can offer her,” Danny replied.

“You stupid man! Did she ever ask you for anything? No! Ring her!” she repeated.

“It’s difficult Katya. There’s all we are doing. She knows nothing of it, and never could, but she could so easily get caught up in things and hurt if we’ve made any form of mistake, and I couldn’t live with that!” Danny told her.

“You really do care about her don’t you?” Katya said. Again it was a statement rather than a question.

“To be honest – yes I do. A lot!” Danny replied, looking down at the chart

“Ring her. And when you do tell her that,” Katya once more told him, and then again, looking him in the eye as he turned to look at her. "Ring her!"

They once again refuelled successfully at the live-aboard diving holiday centre port of Ras Honkorab situated at the south eastern end of Egypt's Eastern Dessert. Here another dive-boat looked perfectly natural and raised no interest or attention at all. Billy had taken over the helm as those who wished to, or needed to, slept through the day and evening, but all were woken and came on deck an hour before entering Sharm El Sheikh. The fifty-cals and MILAN's, with all their associated ammunition was cast over the side, as was anything and everything which could in any way link them with being anywhere to the south. Sea Sphinx gently came alongside an affluent looking quayside, at a fraction after midnight, and tied up amongst other vessels similar to her class.

They had only been on board, mostly at sea, for a mere twelve days on the trip up from Cape Town, and seven for Jack and Katya from Mombasa, but for all of them the anxiety, pressure and excitement had given the impression of much greater time, even to the ex-military men. For the first time since leaving Cape Town all could rest comparatively easily in their beds for the night. The following morning arrangements were made to ship Sea Sphinx through the Suez Canal and before lunchtime they entered the Gulf of Suez, cruising the length of it in under six hours and were at Suez ready to enter the system below station nine long before dusk. The single lane canal with four passing places ran north for over one hundred and ninety kilometres, exiting into the Mediterranean at Port Said, and was to take the Sea Sphinx fifteen hours to transit. Traffic moving along the canals course was monitored by nine stations, and the pace to those on board seemed quite pedestrian after an almost constant thirty-five knots for the journey from Cape Town, although all appreciated it would have been a lot slower if the canal were not at sea level where they had to negotiate locks as would have been the case at Panama.

The slow pace gave way to boredom, and those who could sleep did, but the following morning saw them still chugging along at a man's running pace, waiting in the passing places for the line of vessels heading south to clear so they might proceed.

Sea Sphinx and all on board cleared the canal at Port Said before mid afternoon and cruised west along the north Egyptian coast crossing the Nile Delta as they headed for Alexandria, their final fuelling point on the continent of Africa, which they reached just as the sun was setting. Immediately after refuelling they once more put to sea, this time on a north easterly setting, and reduced speed to twenty five knots through the night. They were in the Med, the pressure had lifted completely and the air of relief was palpable. They had only slightly over three hundred miles to go to their next port of call, and this one they could stay in and relax if they chose to without any concerns in the world. Sea Sphinx disappeared as Karma returned, the white vinyl consigned to the deep and every last area of adhesive polished clean with solvents. There was no longer any need to rush as they planned to enter port after the sun had risen and to breakfast together for the last time before entering.

By the time all were assembled in the saloon the following morning the sun was well up and the island could be clearly seen over the port rail. They cruised along at just twenty knots, savouring the feeling of being back in European waters, breathing deeply of the fresh clean air of the sea subtly mixed with a trace of cultivation blowing on a slight breeze off the island. For Danny in particular nothing in his life had ever smelt so sweet – they were nearly home – Europeans travelling in European water. It may be Europe's most southerly point, but it was Europe, and with every turn of the props they were getting deeper into Europe. The island of Crete, home of Zeus, the ancient Minoan civilisation, and arguably home of European civilisation itself, could not only be clearly seen, but could be smelt as well, and it smelt beautiful.

Long before they approached the port they could wave out to the passengers on the low flying aircraft as they followed the coast in to the airport, dipping and dropping some twenty miles out as they followed their flight path, at the same time giving travel weary passengers a glimpse of the island on which they were about to set foot. Karma rounded the breakwater and glided into the harbour of Heraklion, dominated by a magnificent Venetian fortress, and tied up overlooking a sea of working fishing boats. There was no need to hurry to bunker, in fact for most there was no longer any need to hurry to do anything – except relax. Nathan and Peter were the exceptions, both of whom were to return to England.

Jack and Katya didn't even need to properly show their false German passports as they left the dockside. They stepped up to the first taxi in the rank and asked to be taken into town, to a car hire office, and there they hired a people carrier using their false identity. Returning to the dock they picked up Peter and Nathan and drove them to the airport in the hope they could find a flight to London. December is a long way from the height of the tourist season and they managed to find seats on an Olympic fight departing at four-fifty in the afternoon, changing at Athens and arriving at nine-fifteen in the evening at Heathrow. Nathan booked the flights then both men phoned England.

Peter spoke to Tammy who assured him she was perfectly capable of driving up to Heathrow, pregnant or not. She added the line, "I'm not a cripple you know!" which caused him to smile – he had so missed her over the months. Nathan spoke to Chi Lu, who was very happy to hear from him and purred how pleased she would be to pick him up in person. After booking the flights and making the calls the two returned with Jack and Katya to the docks and once more boarded Karma to pack their bags and say their farewells. They all left Karma and walked into the old town for lunch through occasional swirls of windblown dust caused by on-going road works.

Even in early December there was still a mixture of European languages to be heard in the restaurants and narrow market streets. From Cape Town they had cooked and taken their food on board, using the wonderful built in facilities their vessel offered, but there nobody had demonstrated interest in food, and it was then nothing more than fuel for the body, sustenance. Now they could let themselves go, and had the huge spread of a proper Mez layed out on a large table set up on the pavement of the town's central pedestrian precinct. There was sliced artichokes with lemon, cubes of Feta cheese, fried squid, chunks of freshly baked bread, sliced tomatoes, butterbeans, olives, Cretan sausages, sweet almond bread, souvlaki and tiropitta, the savoury pastries. All to be washed down by copious quantities of local red wine, and for those who could, raki, the same spirit as ouzo, without the aniseed but with more power, drunk neat from tiny glasses. A wonderfully self indulgent treat after two weeks at sea, consumed in a relaxed manner in a beautiful setting and served by those exhibiting all the friendly qualities so typical of Greece.

Eventually they finished the meal and made their way back to Karma, where Peter and Nathan collected their bags so they could catch their flight. Jack was once more going to take Katya with him for the short journey, but she had other plans.

"No, I'll stay here. Take Danny with you. He has a phone call to make!" she told him.

"No I haven't. Well – it will wait!" Danny responded, obviously more than a little taken aback.

"Take Danny with you Jack, and make sure he makes a phone call!" Katya insisted.

Nathan and Peter made their flight, and Danny made his call. Nearly eight months had passed since they had last spoken and there had been no other form of communication between them.

"Hi, Sabine," Danny had started, catching her at home before she left for work as she was six time zones behind him. He got no further as she had immediately recognised his voice and he heard the first sob before he got any further and the sound of it closed his own throat choking him. There was silence between them as the monumental personal implications rushed through both their heads. Sabine broke the silence.

"Where and when do you want me?" she finally managed to ask.

"Nice, in the south of France as soon as you can." Danny replied.

"I will come, but – Danny, it will be a one way trip. I will never leave you again," Sabine told him.

"That's the general idea," Danny assured her with the ring of absolute sincerity to his voice.

"I'll need time to make all the arrangements this end," she warned him.

"How long?" Danny asked a note of disappointment creeping in.

"I'll leave in four days," Sabine answered, and Danny laughed out loud.

"I'll ring you back when I can and sort out the details with you. Sabine, I never want you to leave again!" Danny reassured her, ringing off as her heard her sob again.

There was silence in the car as Jack drove him back to Karma.

Nathan and Peter landed at Heathrow right on time, cleared the aircraft, picked up their frugal bags and headed out through customs to flight arrivals. They had arrived from Europe and were both carrying British passports. The only entry stamp they had received whilst out of the country was that of South Africa. For some reason the officials there had not marked either with an exit stamp, but it was not unusual, and it would have taken a lot of work finding the relevant South African stamp in Peter's passport as there were just so many.

Tammy and Chi Lu were both waiting, but separately because neither knew the other as they had never met. Peter was simply overjoyed to be reunited with Tammy, rapidly introduced her to both Nathan and Chi Lu, then whisked her away as quickly as he politely could and drove her back to Brighton for the happiest night he had had in months. However things worked out he felt he had done his bit. He had loathed the Muslims for what they had done to his beautiful Tammy, but there had been payback and retribution and time had passed. During that time Tammy had improved enormously and now they were to have a child. He wanted to marry her and settle into a normal life as quickly as possible. He was most satisfied in the work he was doing for the public face of Almeti, but for him there would be no more killing because of the tube bombings. It was time to move on and to enjoy the future he could share with the person he loved beyond life itself.

Chi Lu hailed a cab, opened the rear door and stepped in with Nathan following her complete with his bag. What the hell had been going on she wondered without asking. No captain of industry just left his corporation for months at a time, without any form of suitable explanation, and disappeared the way he had. She understood the interest Almeti had in South Africa and could see where interests overlapped, but there were so many questions. Brno was about to open, and the Lyon project was already signed and looked ever more promising. South Africa showed great potential, but she was still not a party to anything to do with Almeti. Why not? Why had Nathan rushed off to a country he had never before been to, and stay for months? Where had he stayed? She knew Peter Parfitt had an apartment there, but would Nathan wish to stay with his project manager for months without contact? If so – why?

They just weren't that close, and he had also taken his security man with him. Why? Where was he? And what on Earth was this thing she had heard about a super yacht? Question after question rushed through her head.

"Did you have a good trip?" she asked smiling sweetly, completely masking the turmoil in her head.

"Yes, certainly for the most part. We'll just have to see how things turn out," Nathan replied.

Now what the hell does that mean she thought, but said, "I wasn't sure what your immediate plans might be, so I haven't booked any room for you, but I have had my guest room made up ready. I trust that will be suitable? We can sort out any other needs you have from there." Chi Lu spoke with authority, her question not really a question. She wanted to take charge of the situation straight away because she was working to a plan, and for her plan to work the way she desired it things would have to happen in the order she had planned. A led to B, and B to C.

"That's fine Chi Lu, and thank you, but I have to be up early tomorrow because I will have lots to do, and I'm sure there are things I need to catch up with," Nathan replied.

"I don't see how that could be a problem," Chi Lu responded patting him on the leg in a familiar manner most unusual for her. Nathan didn't flinch. What the hell has happened, Chi Lu thought. There was something very different about him. He had a confidence, a self-assurance that most certainly was never there before. What the hell was going on?

The taxi drove them in relative silence through the cold bleak English winter weather into the city, passing along the way drab leafless trees and the odd person bent and heavily clothed against the cold wind. The Karoo seemed a long way away to Nathan as he looked out the cab window on a land which was obviously suffering from the bite of the recession Jack Bryant had warned them was coming well over a year previously, but now seemed like centuries earlier. Eventually they reached their destination and Chi Lu paid the driver whilst Nathan held the door for her. He hadn't considered money for months he had suddenly realised whilst in the cab, and was carrying none. Mainly Peter, but also Danny and Chris, had taken care of anything to do with money for so long he had forgotten the need for it.

Chi Lu was a minimalist as far as her apartment was concerned and certainly followed the 'less is more' philosophy. Beautifully furnished, good taste and refinement was subtly understated everywhere, it was a world away from squalor, grime and clutter he had grown up with, and untold luxury after the Karoo. For the centre of London the size was indeed remarkably spacious, and the guest room she had made up for him boasted intricately hand carved furniture everywhere, including the super king sized bed.

"Would you like anything to drink?" Chi Lu asked.

"No, not for me thank you. All I really need is a shower and a good night's sleep!" Nathan answered her.

"There's an en suite behind there." she told him pointing at what he thought was a second wardrobe. "There is everything you need in there."

Chi Lu withdrew and left Nathan to make himself comfortable. So far so good she thought, as her plan progressed smoothly. She had endured enough of this nonsense over the years. It had gone on far too long. Susie had been dead for nearly three and a half years, yet even now she missed her, and was sure Nathan did, but three and a half years was three and a half years, and she had to move on with her life one way or another. Chi Lu was quite objective about herself. She knew she looked remarkably good, had the brights needed, and the ability to use them. She could have any man in the world she chose, except the one she had chosen over ten years before.

He had had someone else then, and that someone became her own closest friend in the world, a friend she would never have attempted to betray in any way. So she had worked tirelessly for the company then corporation they owned, and she had dragged it forward a long way. In ten years it had grown into the biggest corporation of its kind in the world, hugely profitable, and a recognised brand worldwide, yet was still privately owned. She had many a time been approached with fantastic offers, the press seemed to be in constant awe of her if business page headlines were anything to go by, and she had long since given up counting the highly eligible suitors she continually turned aside over the years. She had remained there for him and done his bidding without question, dropping all standards to cook, clean and provide secretarial services, but she had never even been noticed.

Well, one way or the other that was certainly going to change. She wasn't getting any younger and was no longer going to just throw her life away, fantastic career in other people's eyes or not! If things did not change, and change without delay, she would be forced to take up one of the many offers before her, even if it was not what she had always really wanted or was a forced compromise. Once, during one of their girly talks, Susie had explained how she and Nathan had got together for the first time in the shower, because Nathan would never have been the one to make the first move. She had never forgotten the story, but it was not something she planned to repeat – a girl has to be original, she thought. Without intentionally eavesdropping she was aware of the shower running in his room, and also when it stopped. Guys don't pamper themselves like us girls do she reasoned and gave him five minutes to get into bed.

Before picking Nathan up she had showered, and shaved all her important little places. Whilst he was in the shower she had prepared herself, although it was difficult because she had no idea what worked for him. She decided it would be best to emphasise her assets, to literally show everything off to best effect, and for that she needed but two props. She brushed her hair out so it shined with even more than its usual raven lustre, and applied a miniscule amount of makeup to her eyes before anointing herself with oil. The oil brought out her skin tone and smelt exquisite, even to her discerning tastes, and the makeup highlighted her slightly almond eyes. A black satin ribbon tied at the back of her neck exactly matched the colour and sheen of her hair, and accentuated how beautifully slender her neck was. The thin gold chain worn around her waist stressed its leanness, at the same time showing off the slight swell of her hips and small but beautifully formed breasts. Wearing nothing more she moved to his door and knocked lightly upon it.

"Hello," Nathan called from within.

"May I come in?" Chi Lu asked somewhat huskily from the other side of the door, but without waiting for an answer opened it a fraction and switched on the rooms main light, which she had adjusted earlier so more light would fall on and around the doorway. Virtually naked she pinched her nipples and glided into the room.

Nathan would have been somewhat less shocked if the Pope had ridden naked into the room on a six legged unicorn. His eyes flew wide open and his jaw literally fell to his chest, yet no sound came out of his mouth as Chi Lu moved towards him with all the feline grace of a prowling panther. Still open mouthed he watched as she pulled the covers back revealing his own nakedness beneath. He made one minor attempt to hold on to the cover before his manhood was revealed, but Chi Lu just jerked it out of his grasp and tossed it to the foot of the bed. Slowly, very slowly, she ran the tips of the nails on her right hand up his inner thigh and grasped his scrotum, then squeezed gently and, as he started to swell, covered him with her mouth. When he reached full size she climbed onto the bed and mounted him, riding him as she would a horse at slow canter. Finally Nathan spoke.

"Jesus, Chi Lu you're beautiful. I, well, umm, what I mean is – you are beautiful," he stammered out, still shocked beyond believe and not yet fully registering what this vision of loveliness was doing to him.

Afterwards she pulled the covers back up and curled around him and over him as she gently ran a finger tip up and down his chest, teasing slightly. All thoughts Nathan had of an early night disappeared completely.

"Do I still keep my job?" Chi Lu purred to his chest.

"Chi Lu, I don't know what to say. I thought all this time you didn't like me very much. I've always been really wary around you. It wasn't so bad when Susie was alive, but I knew you both liked one another a lot, although even then I always felt uncomfortable," Nathan lamely tried to explain, realising he was beginning to babble because he didn't know what to say.

"Why on Earth would you think I didn't like you?" Chi Lu asked, genuinely intrigued.

"Well, from the first time I ever met you I was very conscious of you looking at me, and you were just so smart and so beautiful, even sounded and smelt great – well I just felt inadequate. You had a good family background and a wonderful education whereas mine was absolute rubbish. I suppose I felt you were looking down on me," Nathan said in an attempt to answer her question.

Chi Lu was flabbergasted, almost as shocked as Nathan had been at her first approach. "Look down on you? It was in every way possible directly the reverse. I admired you beyond explanation. You were my hero. I studied you at Harvard and wrote a paper on you. From the moment I first heard about you I wanted to meet you and, when the opportunity came, I wanted to work for you! I knew about your past, your education – or lack of it, and your upbringing, yet against all that adversity, and working with really basic tools you reshaped an entire industry and yours became the marque all others wished to emulate. Even now I don't believe you fully appreciate exactly what it is you have achieved. At first I respected you from afar and that has never changed, even though you have ignored me for ten years!"

"I don't think that will ever again be possible, do you?" Nathan asked by way of reply.

Karma had once more put to sea, this time far less hurriedly, with the intention of sailing only by day and mooring in safe harbours with pleasant surroundings by night. The same evening they moored in the port of Zakynthos on the island of the same name, but better known to the British as Zante, the third largest of the Ionian Islands, and home to wild alcohol fuelled summer night parties and loggerhead turtles. Unfortunately usually spoilt by the tourists it attracts, it remains a warmly welcoming island, and proved to be so to the crew of a rich mans super yacht in early December. Moored between ferries connecting the island with the port of Kyllini on the mainland, Karma rode easily on the almost indiscernible swell whilst all who had remained aboard, now wearing jerseys against the dropping temperature, ate at one of the nearby tavernas where the owner, demonstrating centuries old Greek hospitality, provided another magnificent spread.

In the morning they refuelled and started west, crossing the Ionian Sea. With Sicily dead ahead they steered a course to the north, cruising between Sicily and mainland Italy through the Straits of Messina, with the city of Messina lying off their port side on the banks of Sicily opposite Reggio di Calabria to which it is linked by ferry. The Straits formed a funnel as they headed north, slowly shrinking to a mere three kilometres across at its northernmost extreme. Here it appeared to be joined to the mainland as a small headland above Messina projected towards the toe of the Italian boot, almost wrapping around it. Clearing the headland they once more resumed their westerly course, along the Sicilian coast to the islands capital, Palermo, founded by the Phoenicians two thousand seven hundred years before. The temperature had dropped to a chilly fifteen degrees, brought down at least in part by something those from the Karoo had not seen in over three months, rain.

The Red Sea salt was washed away by the rain whilst Billy and Chris went about refuelling Karma. It had taken a little more than twelve hours to cross from Zakynthos to Palermo, but they had gained an hour as they proceeded ever westwards, and now only five time zones separated Danny from Sabine. It was after seven on Friday evening in Palermo, but just after lunch in Laval outside Montreal, so Danny entered a hotel in order to use a telephone and rang through to her office. The young North American voice which answered was sorry but the party he was calling no longer worked there and he could give no further information. Danny then tried her home, and the call connected on the forth ring.

"Hi, I just tried your work number and they told me you no longer worked there. You hadn't mentioned it. I thought today would be your last. When did that happen?" Danny enquired.

"Ummm. Hi Danny, and how are you too?" Sabine giggled down the line, then added more seriously. "I gave in my notice yesterday, and was given one hour to clear all my effects from the office."

"Why, what on Earth happened?" Danny asked in a somewhat shocked voice.

"Oh Danny, don't worry. You know I said I could leave in four days? Well that is why. It's standard procedure. If you give notice but cannot or will not give a full or acceptable reason, or if they suspect you may be going to a rival, you clear your desk and drawers and leave straight away. They still pay your month's salary, but they see it as a security issue, and I knew they would," Sabine told him, much to his obvious relief.

"Are you still okay with it all then?" he asked, understanding how stupid the words sounded as they left his lips.

"Of course I am, silly!" she answered confirming how dumb the question had been. "In fact I'm ahead of schedule. I've already finished packing. I'm only bringing two suitcases. I've given notice on my apartment and paid for it, given away loads of stuff to my cousin and best friend, and have two crates of all which remains of my worldly goods in their garage, which they will ship to me if and when I give them an address. I'm ready!"

"That's wonderful news, Sabine. I promise I will always do all I can to make sure you never once regret the move," Danny told her, humbled by what he could see she was giving up.

"Danny, I know that or I wouldn't be doing it! Now stop being so slushy and write down these flight details," she told him. Danny paid the exorbitant telephone bill in cash without a thought about the amount he was being charged. It didn't matter, nothing mattered, Sabine was coming.

They moored just off shore for the night and ate on board, turning in for an early night and generally sleeping soundly despite aircraft noise from Palermo's airport. The following day they awoke to sun and clear blue skies once more, and sailed early on a north westerly heading across the Tyrrhenian Sea which brought them to the eastern coast of northern Sardinia. This they followed north until they cleared the Maddalena Isles, where they turned west into the Strait of Bonifacio, passing the white cliffs and clearing the southern tip of Corsica to enter Bonifacio's compact harbour shortly after mid afternoon. They were finally in French territorial waters, to all intents and purposes in many ways home, or at least what was to be home for Karma for many months and years to come. Most importantly they could reassemble their mobile telephones at last and use them without fear of compromise.

That evening all from Karma dined on traditional Corsican cuisine in a family run restaurant in the Old Town, which is situated at the top of a hill overlooking the port on the western side and winding cliffs to the east. The mix of traditional French and Italian architecture was wasted on all. To travel the Mediterranean on a luxury yacht as they were would normally have remained an unobtainable dream for them, but for a mixture of reasons all aboard by then wanted to see the end to a journey that had become more than a little wearisome. Consequently, despite no need for any form of urgency they once more left port early on their last short leg following the rugged but stunningly attractive west Corsican coastline north, before leaving it for the three hour journey across the extreme western edge of the Ligurian Sea to Nice, and the Bassin Lympia.

Nice. One of the gems of the Cote d' Azur. St Tropez, Cannes, Nice, Monaco, Monte-Carlo. The playground of the rich and wealthy. My boat's bigger than your boat. Stunning scenery, gorgeous year round weather, oozing history and culture in every little shaded alleyway and Old Town wall. Overrated and horrendously overpriced, full of the greedy, rude, posturing and pretentious. A place where badly cooked, poorly presented undersized portions of what laughingly passes as food is delivered by arrogant and condescending waiters who feel they are worthy of large tips for their obnoxious service. Full of likes and dislikes, highs and lows, natural splendour and the tragedy that is greed and avarice, the twin gods of Nice.

The port was relaxed, friendly, well positioned and clean, and head clearing walks on the Quai des Etats Unis and the Promenade des Anglais with cyclists and joggers was quite reviving after time at sea. Ultra modern trams bustled through a prosperous litter free centre. A great city to stop at, for the visitor who is going somewhere else, but otherwise generally forgettable and one night in the city of the superficial was more than enough for both Chris and Billy. Their flight departed at midday, landing at Gatwick two hours later at thirteen hundred, gaining an hour from Central European Time. This dovetailed nicely with Danny's plan to collect Sabine, whose flight was due at ten-twenty.

Danny hired a car to go to the airport, as it was substantially cheaper than taking a taxi both ways, despite a distance of only eight kilometres. Chris and Billy left in the car were moved twice by parking attendants whilst Danny waited for and met Sabine, then carried her two suitcases to the car.

"Jesus Christ!" Billy exclaimed as he saw the two of them approaching.

"Looks like the lad has done well for himself!" Chris chuckled looking at the beauty holding on to Danny's arm. "Bloody good luck to them!"

"No one told me she was such a babe!" Billy responded then joked, "I might have stayed on for a day or two just to ogle."

Chris laughed. "The lad's done his work, and done it very, very well! Now he can relax and have fun. He deserves it! I just wish I'd had a few like him in my squad years ago!"

"Too bloody right mate! A damn fine bloke and an excellent skipper," the ex-SBS man said, uttering the highest words of praise imaginable.

Silence fell as Danny and Sabine reached the car. Introductions over goodbyes followed as the two ex-military men strode off with their bags to make their flight.

Danny returned to the boat with Sabine and introduced her to Jack and Katya, both of whom were very, and obviously, pleased to meet her. The four young people enjoyed lunch together and spent the early part of the afternoon talking and forming bonds which would allow them to be comfortable in one another's company for decades. All too soon Danny had to take his brother and Katya to the train station, where they were to catch a train to Frankfurt, and then a plane to Moscow. Their two week European vacation was over. Technically they had spent all their time on mainland Europe, mostly Germany, but with a short trip to France, and their passports confirmed they had not left the continent. It was Sunday the seventh of December.

The annual hajj had started two days before, on the fifth, and would run to the ninth.

Twenty Two

A small buoy attached to one of the launch platforms time released and slowly floated up to the surface through almost three hundred feet of water. As it broke free the antenna wrapped around it, and pointing up six inches above, allowed a half second short range signal to be sent from the battery powered chip inside. The signal was instantly recognised and relayed by a far more powerful solar powered transmitter hidden on the shore. From a small perfectly aligned dish the signal was beamed up through the troposphere to the exosphere far beyond, there to be gathered by a satellite in geosynchronous orbit twenty-two thousand three hundred miles above the equator. The satellite in turn immediately beamed it back to the Iridium system, to be taken up by one of the sixty-six active satellites which make up the constellation in low Earth orbit, at a height of four hundred and eighty-five miles. Communicating with its neighbouring satellite via Ka band inter-satellite link the signal bounced back to Earth and was delivered to a satellite phone which had never existed. Nathan had made absolutely sure of that. Within seconds two more identical messages came in. The messages were simple. The platforms were ready to rise.

Nathan pressed the hash button on the keypad and the signal returned via the same route. The buoy transmitted the go signal to the platforms and slowly compressed air was released into the flotation chambers of the pontoons. The platforms crept up through the silent salty waters until they broke the surface, where they bobbed gently on water devoid of waves. As they surfaced the plugs Jack had previously made sure formed a watertight fit to the air intake and exhaust of each of the engines, and the back of the rockets, were pulled out by the weight of the float mechanisms which had until then kept them tightly in place. Once again electronic signals passed back and forth. Valves opened and the compressed air then started to blow through the intakes of the pulse jets. Automatic ignition was signalled and the multiple spark plugs initiated a burn. The forced air from the compressed supply stabilised the engines until they heated up. As thrust reached critical, and with the pontoons bucking against their still anchored tethers, the boosters ignited and, one by one, the clamps fell away and the missiles broke loose of the platforms, starting flight in varying directions to be immediately corrected by their on-board global positioning systems. Every missile launched perfectly. The time spent working and experimenting under the rigours of the African sun paid off in full.

As the last of the missiles broke loose the buoys sent their final signals. With the signals transmitted, explosive bolts broke the pontoons tethers and small charges destroyed each of the buoys. On shore the hidden transmitter melted down. Spent booster rockets rained down into the sea as the pontoons carrying their now redundant launch platforms floated free, drifting for a few minutes driven by the off shore wind whilst their clocks counted down. Before the missiles had climbed the hills on their approach to Bakkah the explosives on the platforms detonated. The pontoons and the framework of the platforms were obliterated, with broken pieces forever consigned to a large area of the sea floor. In London Nathan had already left the presumed site of the new Southern super mosque, from where the signal had been transmitted, and within minutes the satellite phone was in a furnace.

The Royal Saudi Air Force operates five Boeing E-3 Sentry rotodome aircraft, which can be used for both defensive and offensive air operations. Designed and built by Boeing's Defence and Space Group using Westinghouse radar the rotating dome is mounted on the converted Boeing 707. Flying at high altitudes the radar operators of these AWAC's can identify friendly or hostile aircraft at a distance of some two hundred and fifty miles.

A little over two hundred miles to the north east, an E-3 Sentry picked up the movement whilst flying a standard pattern, which covered airspace from the Iraq and Kuwaiti borders and The Gulf to Qatar, across to Jeddah on the Red Sea, Medina and Bakkah. Riyadh and the all important Saudi Royal Family were well protected. The radar operators watched as twelve small and unidentified blips suddenly entered Saudi airspace coming from the direction of Port Sudan in the Sudan. For two vital minutes they were confused with the readings they were getting as they appeared too small and too slow to be threatening. They were moving much too slowly for either missiles or fighter aircraft. From their signature they could be microlites, except they were too fast and there had never previously been microlite activity in the area before, and certainly none had see anything like twelve holding the same course.

The operators simultaneously contacted King Abdul Aziz International Airport, King Fahd Naval Base, the Royal Saudi Air Force and the Royal Saudi Air Defence Force, all based in Jeddah. None had anything unusual to report and there were no ongoing exercises. The missiles travelling at something over three hundred and thirty miles an hour were covering more than five and a half miles a minute. The furthest any had to travel was eighty-one miles, a flight of less than fifteen minutes. Small and hugging the land they were invisible to the airport and armed forces bases, but with their downward looking radar the AWACs could see them steadily making their way towards Bakkah, whatever they were.

Developed from the F-15 Eagle, the McDonnell Douglas / Boeing IDS F-15E Strike Eagle is a modern strike fighter with all weather capabilities. Having proved its worth in Operation Desert Storm seventy-two F-15 S's, a variant of the F-15E whose only major difference is radar performance, were purchased by the Royal Saudi Air Force to run alongside and ultimately replace the earlier F-15 Eagle air superiority fighter. Returning to Jeddah from a coastal patrol along the northern stretches of the Red Sea two Strike Eagles were tasked with a visual intercept and report on whatever it was that was approaching the area of Bakkah. The two young pilots slammed the pedals down on their Pratt & Whitney F100-229 afterburn turbofans as they changed course and climbed away from the area. The missiles had by this time been flying for slightly over nine minutes and had started to separate as they sought their individual targets. The pilots of the Strike Eagles, flying aircraft which are arguably amongst the very best in the world, with some of the most sophisticated technology mankind has so far developed, didn't stand a chance against engine technology which had been around for well over a hundred years, because they still could not be in two places at the same time.

Strike Eagles can hit two point five Mach, around one thousand six hundred and fifty miles per hour, well over two thousand five hundred kph. With three external and a conformal fuel tank they have a range of two thousand four hundred miles. Approaching the area from the north the patrol, still with plenty of fuel on board, was retasked whilst on approach ninety miles out. The intercept range was approximately one hundred and fifty miles, or ten minutes flying time. Had the pilots been able to intercept they could in theory have taken even multiple targets down with their array of missiles or M61 Vulcan Gatling guns. However over a packed city they would have been faced with a dilemma, to shoot them down and kill hundreds below or see if they flew by. They were never to be faced with the problem. By the time they arrived on station all the four men in the two planes could do was gaze upon the damage and destruction below in utter horror.

Dropping over the far side of the foothills they had climbed the missiles quickly crossed the sandy, barren, and destitute valley beneath them. Loud though their pulsejet engines were few heard their approach above the hubbub of the hajj, and the general cacophony of noise produced by a busy city.

Without any form of warning the first missile slammed into the north western side of the Black Cube detonating on impact. Fragments of granite exploding from the destroyed face scythed through the crowd killing and maiming as if the rock were shrapnel from a grenade, and was followed by super heated engine parts. Two seconds later, long before any had time to react, the second missile struck the south western face with exactly similar results. Fear immediately took over those of the vast crowd who could move and blind mindless panic set in as the crowd started to surge. Within four seconds of the second impact a stampede occurred with people fighting and clawing at those in front in order to get past. As the third missile exploded on the south eastern wall those within the mosque went berserk. Already many had fallen. Those who had were crushed to death by others trying to flee over the top of them. Many of those also fell and were in turn themselves crushed. In what was a lucky strike the forth missile flew straight through the door in the north eastern wall of the Black Cube and detonated inside. The explosion within brought the already destroyed structure crashing down, crushing the Black Stone into sand and gravel. Pandemonium broke out.

Many tripped, stumbled and fell, to be crushed beneath the panicked flying feet of those thinking of nothing more than saving their own skins at any cost. The walls served only to contain the surging mass of frenzied humanity. As the bodies beneath their feet started to break the metallic odour of blood permeated the air, further fuelling the terror stricken horde. Guts ruptured as broken bones were driven through punctured and pounded flesh, and the stench of the slaughterhouse filled the air. Hysteria took over as the fifth missile struck one of the seven towering minarets which ringed the 'Haram' The Sacred Mosque. Although the minaret stood the effects of the blast, masonry and debris rained down on those crushed together below further inflaming the situation. Missiles six and seven, the last two aimed at Bakkah, slammed into a further minaret and one of the mosques sixty four gates almost simultaneously, bringing marble columns crashing down on the unfortunates beneath. By then it was impossible to further frighten the already terrified crowd as they were mindlessly herded backwards and forwards trampling all below as they each attempted to avoid the volley of deadly blasts.

An estimated seven hundred and eighty thousand worshipers were contained within the walls of the greater structure of the huge Mosque as the first missile struck the Black Cube. Within two minutes the attack on Bakkah was over. Hundreds had perished as a direct result of missile blasts and flying stonework, but that figure was totally insignificant when considered alongside those who died as a result of the universal panic within the Mosque. The hysterical crowd could not be subdued and the terror fuelled panic continued for nearly twenty minutes after the last impact. Thousands died by the minute as they continued to stumble and trip over the injured, maimed, dead and dying. The horror was refreshed as two war planes sped overhead, circling for what all below wrongly assumed was to be another attack.

In many ways the effects could not have been more devastating with tens of thousands dead, dying or horrifically injured, mutilated in cases beyond recognition as even human, but much worse was to occur at Nima, five kilometres to the east, on the road from Bakkah to the Hill of Mercy.

Nima is located in the desert and, throughout the year, is generally a somewhat inconsequential and insignificant place. However all of that changes for the duration of the Hajj when it turns into a vast tented city, which becomes home for five days to teeming millions of worshipers and pilgrims. In the valley of Nima stands the Bridge of Pillars, and it is from this that Muslims carry out a symbolic ritual called the Stoning of the Devil. Over a million people can at any one time be either on or in close proximity to the bridge, which has in the past been the cause of many fatal accidents. In the hope of reducing the number of fatalities the original single tier bridge, which had stood since its construction in 1963, was demolished and replaced in 2006 with a multi-tier bridge.

The Bridge of Pillars is a pedestrian bridge the purpose of which is to enable pilgrims to throw stones, these days seven pebbles, at the three jamrah pillars which have now been extended to lengthy walls, from either the ground level or from the bridge, and these pillars extend up through three apertures in the bridges mighty structure. After the January 2006 Hajj ended, the old bridge was demolished and construction by the Bin Laden Group began on a new multi-level bridge. The ground and first levels were completed in time for the 2006/7 Hajj, which in that year passed without incident, with construction of the remaining two levels completed in time for the 1428 AH Hajj, which for those in the real world using the Gregorian calendar meant December 2007.

The new greatly enlarged bridge was wider than the original, containing an interior space free of columns and with the jamrah pillars now many times longer than their predecessors. New ramps and tunnels were added to the building facilitating easier access with bottlenecks planned and engineered out. In the event of an emergency, and in order to help with rapid evacuation, additional ramps were put in place alongside the jamrah pillars, and in order to spread the footfall and general congestion a fatwa was decreed by the Saudi authorities to the effect that stoning may take place throughout daylight hours, quite literally from sunrise to sunset. The relaxing of the time constraints allowed the vast numbers of Muslim pilgrims greater access to the jamrah pillars than the after sunset stoning which tradition had previously dictated. It also provided the Saudi authorities a more staggered end to the hajj and therefore slightly more control.

The missiles tore along the valley of the Al-Sarawat mountain range as they travelled across from Bakkah, covering the distance to Nima in less than forty seconds. This time, with their distinctive engine sound, their passage was noted by those below as all five missiles roared pass in their irregular flight pattern. It was just past noon on the last day of the Hajj and the Bridge of Pillars was packed with worshipers performing their final act of Ramy al-Jamarat, throwing their stones to register their defiance at the wrongs of the Devil. Unknown to all, the Devil had endured enough and was about to lash out in reply, and when the Devil struck back his blow was to cause untold pain.

The first missile flew in low on the approach to its target, dropping so low those on its path ducked as they felt its wash as it passed overhead. The on-board guidance system responded perfectly throughout its short flight and continued to do so as it sought out the middle of a support column of the bridge. The explosion in the tightly packed mass of humanity was devastating. The massive structure shook but shrugged off the blow. Those caught within the confines of the building had no chance of shrugging it off and died instantly as the explosive force rebounded between the supports, floor and ceiling, literally ripping the victims bodies apart.

Following just one second behind, missile number two struck a support pillar alongside one of the emergency ramps, driving survivors away and further into the central sections. Again the mighty structure shrugged aside the blow. On the various levels of the bridge herd mentality kicked in just as it had at Bakkah as frenzied masses endeavoured to fight their way free of those around them. There was a gap of no more than five seconds before missile three detonated on another support pier just in front of that struck by the second missile. As it did so a crack appeared in the structure which rapidly spread laterally and the huge building this time groaned as the vast number of people surged as one away from the impact area, once again crushing anything or anyone who fell beneath the tens of thousands of terrified sandaled feet.

Missile four smashed straight into the same area of the already damaged support blasted by the first missile, and on the other side of the structure to missiles two and three. Again those on the bridge surged away en masse, dramatically transferring their combined weight from one side of the structure to the other. As they did the lateral cracks below them widened as concrete cracked beneath the swaying motion set up by more than a quarter of a million pairs of feet, all responding to the same stimuli. The bridge was designed to support the heavy downward force created by a huge number of people uniformly spread across its various surfaces. Tolerances were designed in to cope with surges, but surges of this kind had not been foreseen and the side to side motion of those on the bridge were contributing greatly to Jack Bryant's masterful plan.

The bridge was on the point of failure as missile five struck home into yet another pillar so far untouched but nevertheless already cracked. As it did so once again the crowd above surged and this time the structure groaned loudly in protest. Those at ground level looked on in abject terror as two of the main supports started to crumble. Slabs of concrete began to break loose and rain down on those crouching below. The now exposed steel reinforcing which was revealed below began to twist and, as it did so, a much louder groaning was given off by the collapsing structure. Those above, stumbling and falling over others, were momentarily oblivious to their fate as they were completely disorientated and in a state of high panic. To them the groaning of the rebar could not be heard, nor could the crashing of the fracturing concrete, as the cries and screaming of those on the levels above the damage drowned out all other sound.

The first any knew of the imminent failure of the structure on which they stood or lay was as it started to tilt, slowly moving at an angle as one of the main support legs broke apart. With ever increasing speed a part of the bridge started to sag along one section, then to droop, then fall. As the bridge began to collapse the vast majority of those on and under the structure suddenly realised the enormity of what was happening. With a rumble, and with ever increasing speed, the entire structure collapsed into a cloud of its own dust. As it did so many near the edges jumped in a last ditch attempt to throw themselves clear. Most failed and leapt to their death. As the support legs failed the uppermost horizontal levels fell upon the levels below crushing everything beneath them. However, as was to be expected they did not fall evenly, but at an angle. The mighty slabs, collectively weighing thousands of tons started to slide one upon the other, their movement eased and greased by the crushed bodies trapped between them. Blood ran from their lower edges as orange juice does from a squeezer.

Thousands managed to escape, the highest number running from ground level, although many of those died as they fell and were trampled. Despite the fall a surprisingly large proportion of pilgrims on the uppermost level were amongst those who lived, although of those who did many suffered horrific injuries. For anyone who had stood on the other levels, including any which failed to escape from the ground floor, death was almost a certainty, with not a single survivor found from the first level. Some may have in fact survived the collapse, but none were brought out of the rubble alive. For those who were buried alive few made it through the night, and there were no further survivors found after the late afternoon of the second day. Lack of water and the desert heat took those who were not crushed by the fall, and those trapped in the tunnels died by the thousand of suffocation.

It was later calculated there had been approximately two hundred and sixty five thousand people on or under the Bridge of Pilars as the attack started. Over twenty thousand ran clear or escaped unharmed, with a further twelve and a half thousand initially surviving the collapse but sustaining varying levels of injuries. However, of the injured survivors almost a thousand were still to die of their injuries, or lack of hospital facilities which were utterly swamped and were forced to leave many to die so they may concentrate their resources on those with a greater chance of survival.

The Saudi authority's response to the attack was swift. They immediately closed their borders and put a large number of their available aircraft into the skies. All four French built Royal Saudi Navy Al Medinah class frigates and four US built Al Sadiq class corvettes put to sea in the Red Sea along with two British built Sandown class minesweepers. Every aircraft in the skies of theirs and others airspace, and every vessel on the sea, irrespective of size, was logged and thoroughly investigated. Many of the vessels, and all which in any way appeared suspicious, were boarded, a move which in turn led to several more deaths. To cover their backs their four US build Badr class corvettes were also ordered to sea in The Gulf to augment and assist those vessels already there protecting vital oil interests.

According to Intel from the AWAC's crew the incursion had come from the direction of Port Sudan, and entry into Saudi airspace from that direction was confirmed by the records of their on-board computers. Five of the Royal Saudi Navy vessels were tasked with monitoring and identifying all shipping entering and leaving the port of Port Sudan, and shipping moored within the port at the time of the attack was also to be checked when possible. A blatant act of war had been carried out against the Kingdom, but surely, in reality, it was inconceivable the attack could have been performed by the Sudanese? However it was possible the attack was mounted from the Nubian Desert or the heights of Jabal Kaiai in the Red Sea Hills behind and above Port Sudan by people unknown.

It was well known the Sudanese regime's leaders had direct ties with al-Qaeda, and a network of international jihad camps were run within the country with al-Qaeda instructors. That went back to 1992 when Usamah bin Muhammad bin Awad bin Ladin, better known to the English speaking word as Osama bin Laden, moved to Sudan establishing a new base of operations for the Mujahideen at Khartoum. It was also well documented that, unlike his father, Osama bin Laden was certainly no friend of the Saudi royal family, due mainly to his ceaseless verbal attack on King Fahd which, in 1994, had led to the confiscation of his passport and the ending of his seven million dollar a year allowance. After pressure from Saudi Arabia, Egypt and the US he was driven from Sudan in 1996. Although al-Qaeda still remained within the Sudan, an attack by them would surely have been carried out against the palaces of Riyadh, and not the holiest of holies within the Islamic world?

Friction had also long existed with the government which currently ran Iran. Although also Muslims their minority Shiite Muslim background had long been incompatible with the teachings of the worlds vastly greater Sunni majority. However since the Shah was deposed, and the frightening shrieking of Ayatollah Ruhollah Khomeini was first heard, the incompatibility had grown. The much hoped for slight softening after his demise had not lasted and many a concerned Royal Prince turned a worried eye upon their troublesome neighbour to the east, especially since their leader, Mahmoud Ahmadinejad, had taken such a hard line with the West. Could an element of their bizarre regime be responsible for the atrocity, and if so why?

If it were still the 1970's or 80's the hand of Libya's Muammar al Gaddifi would have been strongly suspected but, although still so recently removed from America's list of state sponsored terrorists, Libya had remained quiet for many years. However an attack of this magnitude had to come from a state or, if a terrorist organisation, al-Qaeda! There was simply no other plausible explanation as the funding and planning for such an attack would have been colossal, and there were no other independent groups with either the finances or abilities required for such a devastating operation.

The investigation was to run for many years. Minute parts recovered from the sites of the various explosions would eventually confirm the global positioning systems used were manufactured in Korea under an American licence, but sold around the world, and proved to have been sourced in more than one country. The servos used were of German origin, and the material and resins of the missiles bodies were later proved by chemical and spectrographic analysis to have originated from a batch from France. The residue proved the explosives used to be Semtex, old stock with no metallic markers, which instantly reignited thoughts and speculation as to Libya's possible involvement. Remains of the platforms were discovered as was the on shore radio. The radio gave up little information except that it was of Japanese manufacture and was part of a consignment shipped to Australia. The aluminium framework of the platforms was of Canadian origin and the flotation devices were made of material from a stock sold in Turkey as part of a consignment destined for Iran. Of the greatest interest of all recovered fragments were those of the pulsejet engines. The stainless steel proved to be German in origin and the overall rocket design found to be that of a New Zealander, published on-line. However no amount of investigation would ever help trace the engines back to Danny Bryant, Peter Parfitt or Chris Spencer, or Danny's small workshop in the corner of a boatyard on the edge of the Solent.

Slowly a vast amount of debris was recovered, from twisted and tangled metalwork to the Indonesian battery parts and from plastics to residues. Every part recovered, no matter how microscopic, and every bit of information uncovered was painstakingly sifted through and investigated. Hundreds of thousands of man hours were put into chasing down each and every lead, no matter how small or seemingly inconsequential. Unfortunately for those concerned it was a thankless task consistently leading nowhere. Every lead was followed, yet every one came up blank. Whoever the perpetrators were they had covered their tracks completely, to such a degree that even those involved in the investigation came to grudgingly respect them, whoever they might be, despite the horrors of their actions.

Although never ended eventually the investigation was wound down. Not a single thing had ever come to light which was either conclusive or could accurately point the finger of blame in any direction with even the slightest degree of certainty. The Iranians remained the most likely suspects in the eyes of the world, mainly due to computer records which showed their long term interest in the pulsejet project and wish to purchase or construct their own ultra low cost cruise missile.

One fact alone remained. Whoever was responsible had brought untold pain, suffering and dreadful remorse to a simply vast number of Muslim families. The buildings of their culture, damaged and destroyed, could be repaired and replaced, but the lives of those taken could not be. Very much like those of the lives of the Christians and the Hindus, and the educated non believing white skinned peoples of the world, whose lives continue to be lost to the manic extremes of religious fervour.

Twenty Three

For those who were Almeti their mission was over, with this particular chapter of their lives behind them. For all a future lay ahead of them with the happiness and joy, sadness and gloom which is a part of normal life to all humans.

They had dared to confront those who would oppress them and undermine their way of life. They had defied the laws of man and looked the gods square in the eye in an open challenge of opposition, and had carried the day.

But Fate is a fickle mistress, and her testing and trials of those who had formed Almeti International was not over. She would circle back on them and stalk her prey, waiting for a moment of weakness or a dropped guard, when she would pounce in an attempt to cruelly and pitilessly maul those who had dared to throw down the gauntlet, and the blood of man would freely pour once more.